George
MacDonald Fraser

George MacDonald Fraser

Flashman
at the Charge

Flashman
in the Great Game

CHANCELLOR
PRESS

Flashman at the Charge first published in Great Britain
in 1973 by Barrie & Jenkins Ltd.,
reissued in 1982 by William Collins Sons & Co. Ltd.
Flashman in the Great Game first published in Great Britain
in 1975 by Barrie & Jenkins Ltd.,
reissued in 1981 by William Collins Sons & Co. Ltd.

This edition first published in Great Britain in 1983 by
Chancellor Press
59 Grosvenor Street
London, W.1.

ISBN: 0 907486 37 1

Printed in Great Britain at The Pitman Press, Bath

George MacDonald Fraser

Contents

George MacDonald Fraser

Flashman at the Charge

From The Flashman Papers 1854-1855
Edited and Arranged by
George MacDonald Fraser

For "Ekaterin",
rummy champion of Samarkand

Explanatory Note

When the Flashman Papers, that vast personal memoir describing the adult career of the notorious bully of *Tom Brown's Schooldays*, came to light some years ago, it was at once evident that new and remarkable material was going to be added to Victorian history. In the first three packets of the memoirs, already published by permission of their owner, Mr Paget Morrison, Flashman described his early military career, his participation in the ill-fated First Afghan War, his involvement (with Bismarck and Lola Montez) in the Schleswig-Holstein Question, and his fugitive adventures as a slaver in West Africa, an abolitionist agent in the United States, and an erstwhile associate of Congressman Abraham Lincoln, Mr Disraeli, and others.

It will be seen from this that the great soldier's recollections were not all of a purely military nature, and those who regretted that these earlier papers contained no account of his major campaigns (Indian Mutiny, U.S. Civil War, etc.) will doubtless take satisfaction that in the present volume he deals with his experiences in the Crimea, as well as in other even more colourful —and possibly more important—theatres of conflict. That he adds much to the record of social and military history, illumines many curious byways, and confirms modern opinions of his own deplorable character, goes without saying, but his general accuracy where he deals with well-known events and personages, and his transparent honesty, at least as a memorialist, are evidence that the present volume is as trustworthy as those which preceded it.

As editor, I have only corrected his spelling and added the usual footnotes and appendices. The rest is Flashman.

G.M.F.

The moment after Lew Nolan wheeled[1] his horse away and disappeared over the edge of the escarpment with Raglan's message tucked in his gauntlet, I knew I was for it. Raglan was still dithering away to himself, as usual, and I heard him cry: "No, Airey, stay a moment—send after him!" and Airey beckoned me from where I was trying to hide myself nonchalantly behind the other gallopers of the staff. I had had my bellyful that day, my luck had been stretched as long as a Jew's memory, and I knew for certain that another trip across the Balaclava plain would be disaster for old Flashy. I was right, too.

And I remember thinking, as I waited trembling for the order that would launch me after Lew towards the Light Brigade, where they sat at rest on the turf eight hundred feet below—this, I reflected bitterly, is what comes of hanging about pool halls and toad-eating Prince Albert. Both of which, you'll agree, are perfectly natural things for a fellow to do, if he likes playing billiards and has a knack of grovelling gracefully to royalty. But when you see what came of these apparently harmless diversions, you'll allow that there's just no security anywhere, however hard one tries. I should know, with my twenty-odd campaigns and wounds to match—not one of 'em did I go looking for, and the Crimea least of all. Yet there I was again, the reluctant Flashy, sabre on hip, bowels rumbling and whiskers bristling with pure terror, on the brink of the greatest cavalry carnage in the history of war. It's enough to make you weep.

You will wonder, if you've read my earlier memoirs (which I suppose are as fine a record of knavery, cowardice and fleeing for cover as you'll find outside the covers of Hansard), what fearful run of ill fortune got me to Balaclava at all. So I had better get things in their proper order, like a good memorialist, and before describing the events of that lunatic engagement, tell you of the confoundedly unlucky chain of trivial events that took me there.

It should convince you of the necessity of staying out of pool-rooms and shunning the society of royalty.

It was early in '54, and I had been at home some time, sniffing about, taking things very easy, and considering how I might lie low and enjoy a quiet life in England while my military colleagues braved shot and shell in Russia on behalf of the innocent defence-less Turk—not that there's any such thing, in my experience, which is limited to my encounter with a big fat Constantinople houri who tried to stab me in bed for my money-belt, and then had the effrontery to call the police when I thrashed her. I've never had a high opinion of Turks, and when I saw the war-clouds gathering on my return to England that year, the last thing I was prepared to do was offer my services against the Russian tyrant.

One of the difficulties of being a popular hero, though, is that it's difficult to wriggle out of sight when the bugle blows. I hadn't taken the field on England's behalf for about eight years, but neither had anyone else, much, and when the press starts to beat the drum and the public are clamouring for the foreigners' blood to be spilled—by someone other than themselves—they have a habit of looking round for their old champions. The laurels I had won so undeservedly in the Afghan business were still bright enough to catch attention, I decided, and it would be damned embarrassing if people in Town started saying: "Hollo, here's old Flash, just the chap to set upon Tsar Nicholas. Going back to the Cherrypickers, Flashy, are you? By Jove, pity the poor Rooskis when the Hero of Gandamack sets about 'em, eh, what?" As one of the former bright particular stars of the cavalry, who had covered himself with glory from Kabul to the Khyber, and been about the only man to charge in the right direction at Chillianwallah (a mistake, mind you), I wouldn't be able to say, "No, thank'ee, I think I'll sit out this time." Not and keep any credit, anyway. And credit's the thing, if you're as big a coward as I am, and want to enjoy life with an easy mind.

So I looked about for a way out, and found a deuced clever one —I rejoined the Army. That is to say, I went round to the Horse Guards, where my Uncle Bindley was still holding on in pursuit of his pension, and took up my colours again, which isn't difficult when you know the right people. But the smart thing was, I didn't ask for a cavalry posting, or a staff mount, or anything risky of that nature; instead I applied for the Board of Ordnance, for which I knew I was better qualified than most of its members, inasmuch as I knew which end of a gun the ball came out of. Let me once be installed there, in a comfortable office off Horse Guards, which I might well visit as often as once a fortnight, and Mars could go whistle for me.

And if anyone said, "What, Flash, you old blood-drinker, ain't you off to Turkey to carve up the Cossacks?", I'd look solemn and talk about the importance of administration and supply, and the need for having at home headquarters some experienced field men—the cleverer ones, of course—who would see what was required for the front. With my record for gallantry (totally false though it was) no one could doubt my sincerity.

Bindley naturally asked me what the deuce I knew about fire-arms, being a cavalryman, and I pointed out that that mattered a good deal less than the fact that I was related, on my mother's side, to Lord Paget, of the God's Anointed Pagets, who happened to be a member of the small arms select committee. He'd be ready enough, I thought, to give a billet as personal secretary, confidential civilian aide, and general tale-bearer, to a well-seasoned campaigner who was also a kinsman.

"Well-seasoned Haymarket Hussar," sniffs Bindley, who was from the common or Flashman side of our family, and hated being reminded of my highly-placed relatives. "I fancy rather more than that will be required."

"India and Afghanistan ain't in the Haymarket, uncle," says I, looking humble-offended, "and if it comes to fire-arms, well, I've handled enough of 'em, Brown Bess, Dreyse needles, Colts, Lancasters, Brunswicks, and so forth"—I'd handled them with considerable reluctance, but he didn't know that.

"H'm," says he, pretty sour. "This is a curiously humble ambition for one who was once the pride of the plungers. However, since you can hardly be less useful to the ordnance board than you would be if you returned to the wastrel existence you led in the 11th—before they removed you—I shall speak to his lordship."

I could see he was puzzled, and he sniffed some more about the mighty being fallen, but he didn't begin to guess at my real motive. For one thing, the war was still some time off, and the official talk was that it would probably be avoided, but I was taking no risks of being caught unprepared. When there's been a bad harvest, and workers are striking, and young chaps have developed a craze for growing moustaches and whiskers, just watch out.[1] The country was full of discontent and mischief, largely because England hadn't had a real war for forty years, and only a few of us knew what fighting was like. The rest were full of rage and stupidity, and all because some Papists and Turkish niggers had quarrelled about the nailing of a star to a door in Palestine. Mind you, nothing surprises me.

When I got home and announced my intention of joining the Board of Ordnance, my darling wife Elspeth was mortified beyond belief.

"Why, oh why, Harry, could you not have sought an appointment in the Hussars, or some other fashionable regiment? You looked so beautiful and dashing in those wonderful pink pantaloons! Sometimes I think they were what won my heart in the first place, the day you came to father's house. I suppose that in the Ordnance they wear some horrid drab overalls, and how can you take me riding in the Row dressed like ... like a common commissary person, or something?"

"Shan't wear uniform," says I. "Just civilian toggings, my dear. And you'll own my tailor's a good one, since you chose him yourself."

"That will be quite as bad," says she, "with all the other husbands in their fine uniforms—and you looked so well and dashing. Could you not be a Hussar again, my love—just for me?"

When Elspeth pouted those red lips, and heaved her remarkable bosom in a sigh, my thoughts always galloped bedwards, and she knew it. But I couldn't be weakened that way, as I explained.

"Can't be done. Cardigan won't have me back in the 11th, you may be sure; why, he kicked me out in '40."

"Because I was a ... a tradesman's daughter, he said. I know." For a moment I thought she would weep. "Well, I am not so now. Father ..."

"... bought a peerage just in time before he died, so you are a baron's daughter. Yes, my love, but that won't serve for Jim the Bear. I doubt if he fancies bought nobility much above no rank at all."

"Oh, how horridly you put it. Anyway, I am sure that is not so, because he danced twice with me last season, while you were away, at Lady Brown's assembly—yes, and at the cavalry ball. I distinctly remember, because I wore my gold ruffled dress and my hair à l'impératrice, and he said I looked like an Empress indeed. Was that not gallant? And he bows to me in the Park, and we have spoken several times. He seems a very kind old gentleman, and not at all gruff, as they say."

"Is he now?" says I. I didn't care for the sound of this; I knew Cardigan for as lecherous an old goat as ever tore off breeches. "Well, kind or not as he may seem, he's one to beware of, for your reputation's sake, and mine. Anyway, he won't have me back—and I don't fancy him much either, so that settles it."

She made a mouth at this. "Then I think you are both very stubborn and foolish. Oh, Harry, I am quite miserable about it; and poor little Havvy, too, would be so proud to have his father in one of the fine regiments, with a grand uniform. He will be so downcast."

Poor little Havvy, by the way, was our son and heir, a boisterous malcontent five-year-old who made the house hideous with his noise and was forever hitting his shuttlecocks about the place. I wasn't by any means sure that I was his father, for as I have explained before, my Elspeth hid a monstrously passionate nature under her beautifully innocent roses-and-cream exterior, and I suspected that she had been bounced about by half London during the fourteen years of our marriage. I'd been away a good deal, of course. But I'd never caught her out—mind you, that meant nothing, for she'd never caught *me*, and I had had more than would make a hand-rail round Hyde Park. But whatever we both suspected we kept to ourselves, and dealt very well. I loved her, you see, in a way which was not entirely carnal, and I think, I believe, I hope, that she worshipped me, although I've never made up my mind about that.

But I had my doubts about the paternity of little Havvy—so called because his names were Harry Albert Victor, and he couldn't say "Harry" properly, generally because his mouth was full. My chum Speedicut, I remember, who is a coarse brute, claimed to see a conclusive resemblance to me: when Havvy was a few weeks old, and Speed came to the nursery to see him getting

his rations, he said the way the infant went after the nurse's tits
proved beyond doubt whose son he was.

"Little Havvy," I told Elspeth, "is much too young to care a
feather what uniform his father wears. But my present work is
important, my love, and you would not have me shirk my duty.
Perhaps, later, I may transfer"—I would, too, as soon as it looked
safe—"and you will be able to lead your cavalryman to drums
and balls and in the Row to your heart's content."

It cheered her up, like a sweet to a child; she was an astonish-
ingly shallow creature in that way. More like a lovely flaxen-
haired doll come to life than a woman with a human brain,
I often thought. Still, that has its conveniences, too.

In any event, Bindley spoke for me to Lord Paget, who took
me in tow, and so I joined the Board of Ordnance. And it was
the greatest bore, for his lordship proved to be one of those
meddling fools who insist on taking an interest in the work of
committees to which they are appointed—as if a lord is ever
expected to do anything but lend the light of his countenance and
his title. He actually put me to work, and not being an engineer,
or knowing more of stresses and moments than sufficed to get me
in and out of bed, I was assigned to musketry testing at the
Woolwich laboratory, which meant standing on firing-points
while the marksmen of the Royal Small Arms Factory blazed
away at the "eunuchs".[2] The fellows there were a very common
lot, engineers and the like, full of nonsense about the virtues of
the Minié as compared with the Long Enfield .577, and the
Pritchard bullet, and the Aston backsight—there was tremendous
work going on just then, of course, to find a new rifle for the
army, and Molesworth's committee was being set up to make the
choice. It was all one to me if they decided on arquebuses; after a
month spent listening to them prosing about jamming ramrods,
and getting oil on my trousers, I found myself sharing the view
of old General Scarlett, who once told me:

"Splendid chaps the ordnance, but dammem, a powder monkey's a powder monkey, ain't he? Let 'em fill the cartridges and
bore the guns, but don't expect *me* to know a .577 from a mortar!
What concern is that of a gentleman—or a soldier, either? Hey?
Hey?"

Indeed, I began to wonder how long I could stand it, and settled for spending as little time as I could on my duties, and devoting myself to the social life. Elspeth at thirty seemed to be developing an even greater appetite, if that were possible, for parties and dances and the opera and assemblies, and when I wasn't squiring her I was busy about the clubs and the Haymarket, getting back into my favourite swing of devilled bones, mulled port and low company, riding round Albert Gate by day and St John's Wood by night, racing, playing pool, carousing with Speed and the lads, and keeping the Cyprians busy. London is always lively, but there was a wild mood about in those days, and growing wilder as the weeks passed. It was all: when will the war break out? For soon it was seen that it must come, the press and the street-corner orators were baying for Russian blood, the Government talked interminably and did nothing, the Russian ambassador was sent packing, the Guards marched away to embark for the Mediterranean at an unconscionably early hour of the morning—Elspeth, full of bogus loyalty and snob curiosity, infuriated me by creeping out of bed at four to go and watch this charade, and came back at eight twittering about how splendid the Queen had looked in a dress of dark green merino as she cried farewell to her gallant fellows—and a few days later Palmerston and Graham got roaring tight at the Reform Club and made furious speeches in which they announced that we were going to set about the villain Nicholas and drum him through Siberia.[3]

I listened to a mob in Piccadilly singing about how British arms would "tame the frantic autocrat and smite the Russian slave," and consoled myself with the thought that I would be snug and safe down at Woolwich, doing less than my share to see that they got the right guns to do it with. And so I might, if I hadn't loafed out one evening to play pool with Speed in the Haymarket.

As I recall, I only went because Elspeth's entertainment for the evening was to consist of going to the theatre with a gaggle of her female friends to see some play by a Frenchman—it was patriotic to go to anything French just then, and besides the play was said to be risqué, so my charmer was bound to see it in order to be virtuously shocked.[4] I doubted whether it would ruffle *my* tender sensibilities, though—not enough to be interesting, anyway—so I went along with Speed.

We played a few games of sausage in the Piccadilly Rooms, and
it was a dead bore, and then a chap named Cutts, a Dragoon
whom I knew slightly, came by and offered us a match at billiards
for a quid a hundred. I'd played with him before, and beat him,
so we agreed, and set to.

I'm no pool-shark, but not a bad player, either, and unless
there's a goodish sum riding, I don't much care whether I win or
lose as a rule. But there are some smart-alecs at the table that
I can't abide to be beat by, and Cutts was one of them. You know
the sort—they roll their cues on the tables, and tell the bystanders
that they play their best game off list cushions instead of rubber,
and say "Mmph?" if you miss a shot they couldn't have got
themselves in a hundred years. What made it worse, my eye was
out, and Cutts' luck was dead in—he brought off middle-pocket
jennies that Joe Bennet wouldn't have looked at, missed easy
hazards and had his ball roll all round the table for a cannon, and
when he tried long pots as often as not he got a pair of breeches.
By the time he had taken a fiver apiece from us, I was sick of it.

"What, had enough?" cries he, cock-a-hoop. "Come on,
Flash, where's your spirit? I'll play you any cramp game you like
—shell-out, skittle pool, pyramids, caroline, doublet or go-back.[5]
What d'ye say? Come on, Speed, you're game, I see."

So Speed, the ass, played him again, while I mooched about in
no good humour, waiting for them to finish. And it chanced
that my eye fell on a game that was going on at a corner table,
and I stopped to watch.

It was a flat-catching affair, one of the regular sharks fleecing
a novice, and I settled down to see what fun there would be when
the sheep realized he was being sheared. I had noticed him while
we were playing with Cutts—a proper-looking mamma's boy with
a pale, delicate face and white hands, who looked as though he'd
be more at home handing cucumber sandwiches to Aunt Jane
than pushing a cue. He couldn't have been more than eighteen,
but I'd noticed his clothes were beautifully cut, although hardly
what you'd call pool-room fashion; more like Sunday in the
country. But there was money about him, and all told he was the
living answer to a billiard-rook's prayer.

They were playing pyramids, and the shark, a grinning specimen with ginger whiskers, was fattening his lamb for the kill.

You may not know the game, but there are fifteen colours, and you try to pocket them one after the other, like pool, usually for a stake of a bob a time. The lamb had put down eight of them, and the shark three, exclaiming loudly at his ill luck, and you could see the little chap was pretty pleased with himself.

"Only four balls left!" cries the shark. "Well, I'm done for; my luck's dead out, I can see. Tell you what, though; it's bound to change; I'll wager a sovereign on each of the last four."

You or I would know that this was the time to put up your cue and say good evening, before he started making the balls advance in column of route dressed from the front, and even the little greenhorn thought hard about it; but hang it, you could see him thinking, I've potted eight out of eleven—surely I'll get at least two of those remaining.

So he said very well, and I waited to see the shark slam the four balls away in as many shots. But he had weighed up his man's purse, and decided on a really good plucking, and after pocketing the first ball with a long double that made the green-horn's jaw drop, the shark made a miscue on his next stroke. Now when you foul at pyramids, one of the potted balls is put back on the table, so there were four still to go at. So it went on, the shark potting a ball and collecting a quid, and then fouling—damning his own clumsiness, of course—so that the ball was re-spotted again. It could go on all night, and the look of horror on the little greenhorn's face was a sight to see. He tried desperately to pot the balls himself, but somehow he always found himself making his shots from a stiff position against the cushion, or with the four colours all lying badly; he could make nothing of it. The shark took fifteen pounds off him before dropping the last ball—off three cushions, just for swank—and then dusted his fancy weskit, thanked the flat with a leer, and sauntered off whistling and calling the waiter for champagne.

The little gudgeon was standing woebegone, holding his limp purse. I thought of speeding him on his way with a taunt or two, and then I had a sudden bright idea.

"Cleaned out, Snooks?" says I. He started, eyed me suspiciously, and then stuck his purse in his pocket and turned to the door.

"Hold on," says I. "I'm not a Captain Sharp; you needn't run away. He rooked you properly, didn't he?"

He stopped, flushing. "I suppose he did. What is it to you?"

"Oh, nothing at all. I just thought you might care for a drink to drown your sorrows."

He gave me a wary look; you could see him thinking, here's another of them.

"I thank you, no," says he, and added: "I have no money left whatever."

"I'd be surprised if you had," says I, "but fortunately I have. Hey, waiter."

The boy was looking nonplussed, as though he wanted to go out into the street and weep over his lost fifteen quid, but at the same time not averse to some manly comfort from this cheery chap. Even Tom Hughes allowed I could charm when I wanted to, and in two minutes I had him looking into a brandy glass, and soon after that we were chatting away like old companions.

He was a foreigner, doing the tour, I gathered, in the care of some tutor from whom he had managed to slip away to have a peep at the flesh-pots of London. The depths of depravity for him, it seemed, was a billiard-room, so he had made for this one and been quickly inveigled and fleeced.

"At least it has been a lesson to me," says he, with that queer formal gravity which a man so often uses in speaking a language not his own. "But how am I to explain my empty purse to Dr Winter? What will he think?"

"Depends how coarse an imagination he's got," says I. "You needn't fret about him; he'll be so glad to get you back safe and sound, I doubt if he'll ask too many questions."

"That is true," says my lad, thoughtfully. "He will fear for his own position. Why, he has been a negligent guardian, has he not?"

"Dam' slack," says I. "The devil with him. Drink up, boy, and confusion to Dr Winter."

You may wonder why I was buying drink and being pleasant to this flat; it was just a whim I had dreamed up to be even with Cutts. I poured a little more into my new acquaintance, and got him quite merry, and then, with an eye on the table where Cutts was trimming up Speed, and gloating over it, I says to the youth:

"I tell you what, though, my son, it won't do for the sporting name of Old England if you creep back home without some credit. I can't put the fifteen sovs back in your pocket, but I'll tell you what—just do as I tell you, and I'll see that you win a game before you walk out of this hall."

"Ah, no—that, no," says he. "I have played enough; once is sufficient—besides, I tell you, I have no more money."

"Gammon," says I. "Who's talking about money? You'd-like to win a match, wouldn't you?"

"Yes, but . . ." says he, and the wary look was back in his eye. I slapped him on the knee, jolly old Flash.

"Leave it to me," says I. "What, man, it's just in fun. I'll get you a game with a pal of mine, and you'll trim him up, see if you don't."

"But I am the sorriest player," cries he "How can I beat your friend?"

"You ain't as bad as you think you are," says I. "Depend on it. Now just sit there a moment."

I slipped over to one of the markers whom I knew well. "Joe," says I, "give me a shaved ball, will you?"

"What's that, cap'n?" says he. "There's no such thing in this 'ouse."

"Don't fudge me, Joe. I know better. Come on, man, it's just for a lark, I tell you. No money, no rooking."

He looked doubtful, but after a moment he went behind his counter and came back with a set of billiard pills. "Spot's the boy," says he. "But mind, Cap'n Flashman, no nonsense, on your honour."

"Trust me," says I, and went back to our table. "Now, Sam Snooks, just you pop those about for a moment." He was looking quite perky, I noticed, what with the booze and, I suspect, a fairly bouncy little spirit under his mama's boy exterior. He seemed to have forgotten his fleecing at any rate, and was staring about him at the fellows playing at nearby tables, some in flowery weskits and tall hats and enormous whiskers, others in the new fantastic coloured shirts that were coming in just then, with death's heads and frogs and serpents all over them; our little novice was drinking it all in, listening to the chatter and laughter, and watching the waiters weave in and out with their trays, and the markers calling off the breaks. I suppose it's something to see, if you're a bumpkin.

I went over to where Cutts was just demolishing Speed, and as the pink ball went away, I says:

"There's no holding you tonight, Cutts, old fellow. Just my luck, when my eye's out, to meet first you and then that little terror in the corner yonder."

"What, have you been browned again?" says he, looking round. "Oh, my stars, never by *that*, though, surely? Why, he's not out of leading-strings, by the looks of him."

"Think so?" says I. "He'll give you twenty in the hundred, any day."

Well, of course, that settled it, with a conceited pup like Cutts; nothing would do but he must come over, with his toadies in his wake, making great uproar and guffawing, and offer to make a game with my little greenhorn.

"Just for love, mind," says I, in case Joe the marker was watching, but Cutts wouldn't have it; insisted on a bob a point, and I had to promise to stand good for my man, who shied away as soon as cash was mentioned. He was pretty tipsy by now, or I doubt if I'd have got him to stay at the table, for he was a timid squirt, even in drink, and the bustling and cat-calling of the fellows made him nervous. I rolled him the plain ball, and away they went, Cutts chalking his cue with a flourish and winking to his pals.

You've probably never seen a shaved ball used—but then, you wouldn't know it if you had. The trick is simple; your sharp takes an ordinary ball beforehand, and gets a craftsman to peel away just the most delicate shaving of ivory from one side of it; some clumsy cheats try to do it by rubbing it with fine sand-paper, but that shows up like a whore in church. Then, in the game, he makes certain his opponent gets the shaved ball, and plays away. The flat never suspects a thing, for a carefully shaved ball can't be detected except with the very slowest of slow shots, when it will waver ever so slightly just before it stops. But of course, even with fast shots it goes off the true just a trifle, and in as fine a game as billiards or pool, where precision is everything, a trifle is enough.

It was for Cutts, anyhow. He missed cannons by a whisker, his winning hazards rattled in the jaws of the pocket and stayed out, his losers just wouldn't drop, and when he tried a jenny he often missed the red altogether. He swore blind and fumed, and I said, "My, my, damme, that was close, what?" and my little greenhorn plugged away—he was a truly shocking player, too—and slowly piled up the score. Cutts couldn't fathom it, for he knew he was hitting his shots well, but nothing would go right.

I helped him along by suggesting he was watching the wrong ball—a notion which is sure death, once it has been put in a player's mind—and he got wild and battered away recklessly, and my youngster finally ran out an easy winner, by thirty points.

I was interested to notice he got precious cocky at this. "Billiards is not a difficult game, after all," says he, and Cutts ground his teeth and began to count out his change. His fine chums, of course, were bantering him unmercifully—which was all I'd wanted in the first place.

"Better keep your cash to pay for lessons, Cutts, my boy," says I. "Here, Speed, take our young champion for a drink." And when they had gone off to the bar I grinned at Cutts. "I'd never have guessed it—with whiskers like yours."

"Guessed what, damn you, you funny flash man?" says he, and I held up the spot ball between finger and thumb.

"Never have guessed you'd had such a close *shave*," says I. "'Pon my soul, you ain't fit to play with rooks like our little friend. You'd better take up hoppity, with old ladies."

With a sudden oath he snatched the ball from me, set it on the cloth, and played it away. He leaned over, eyes goggling, as it came to rest, cursed foully, and then dashed it on to the floor.

"Shaved, by God! Curse you, Flashman—you've sharped me, you and that damned little diddler! Where is the little toad—I'll have him thrashed and flung out for this?"

"Hold your wind," says I, while his pals fell against each other and laughed till they cried. "He didn't know anything about it. And you ain't sharped—I've told you to keep your money, haven't I?" I gave him a mocking leer. "'Any cramp game you like,' eh? Skittle pool, go-back—but not billiards with little flats from the nursery." And I left him thoroughly taken down, and went off to find Speed.

You'll think this a very trivial revenge, no doubt, but then I'm a trivial chap—and I know the way under the skin of muffins like Cutts, I hope. What was it Hughes said—Flashman had a knack of knowing what hurt, and by a cutting word or look could bring tears to the eyes of people who would have laughed at a blow? Something like that; anyway, I'd taken the starch out of friend Cutts, and spoiled his evening, which was just nuts to me.

I took up with Speed and the greenhorn, who was now waxing voluble in the grip of booze, and off we went. I thought it would be capital sport to take him along to one of the accommodation houses in Haymarket, and get him paired off with a whore in a galloping wheelbarrow race, for it was certain he'd never been astride a female in his life, and it would have been splendid to see them bumping across the floor together on hands and knees towards the winning post. But we stopped off for punch on the way, and the little snirp got so fuddled he couldn't even walk. We helped him along, but he was maudlin, so we took off his trousers in an alley off Regent Street, painted his arse with blacking which we bought for a penny on the way, and then shouted, "Come on, peelers! Here's the scourge of A Division waiting to set about you! Come on and be damned to you!" And as soon as the bobbies hove in sight we cut, and left them to find our little friend, nose down in the gutter with his black bum sticking up in the air.

I went home well pleased that night, only wishing I could have been present when Dr Winter came face to face again with his erring pupil.

And that night's work changed my life, and preserved India for the British Crown—what do you think of that? It's true enough, though, as you'll see.

However, the fruits didn't appear for a few days after that, and in the meantime another thing happened which also has a place in my story. I renewed an old acquaintance, who was to play a considerable part in my affairs over the next few months—and that was full of consequence, too, for him, and me, and history.

I had spent the day keeping out of Paget's way at the Horse Guards, and chatting part of the time, I remember, with Colonel Colt, the American gun expert, who was there to give evidence before the select committee on firearms.[6] (I ought to remember our conversation, but I don't, so it was probably damned dull and

technical.) Afterwards, however, I went up to Town to meet
Elspeth in the Ride, and take her on to tea with one of her Mayfair women.

She was side-saddling it up the Ride, wearing her best mul-
berry rig and a plumed hat, and looking ten times as fetching as
any female in view. But as I trotted up alongside, I near as not
fell out of my saddle with surprise, for she had a companion with
her, and who should it be but my Lord Haw-Haw himself, the
Earl of Cardigan.

I don't suppose I had exchanged a word with him—indeed, I
had hardly seen him, and then only at a distance—since he had
packed me off to India fourteen years before. I had loathed the
brute then, and time hadn't softened the sentiment; he was the
swine who had kicked me out of the Cherrypickers for (irony of
ironies) marrying Elspeth, and committed me to the horrors of
the Afghan campaign.* And here he was, getting spoony round
my wife, whom he had affected to despise once on a day for her
lowly origins. And spooning to some tune, too, by the way he was
leaning confidentially across from his saddle, his rangy old boozy
face close to her blonde and beautiful one, and the little slut was
laughing and looking radiant at his attentions.

She caught my eye and waved, and his lordship looked me
over in his high-nosed damn-you way which I remembered so
well. He would be in his mid-fifties by now, and it showed; the
whiskers were greying, the gooseberry eyes were watery, and the
legions of bottles he had consumed had cracked the veins in that
fine nose of his. But he still rode straight as a lance, and if his
voice was wheezy it had lost nothing of its plunger drawl.

"Haw-haw," says he, "it is Fwashman, I see. Where have you
been, sir? Hiding away these many years, I dare say, with this
lovely lady. Haw-haw. How-de-do, Fwashman? Do you know, my
dear"—this to Elspeth, damn his impudence—"I decware that
this fine fellow, your husband, has put on fwesh alarmingly since
last I saw him. Haw-haw. Always was too heavy for a wight
dwagoon, but now—pwepostewous! You feed him too well, my
dear! Haw-haw!"

It was a damned lie, of course, no doubt designed to draw a
comparison with his own fine figure—scrawny, some might have

* See Flashman.

thought it. I could have kicked his lordly backside, and given him a piece of my mind.

"Good day, milord," says I, with my best toady smile. "May I say how well your lordship is looking? In good health, I trust."

"Thank'ee," says he, and turning to Elspeth: "As I was saying, we have the vewy finest hunting at Deene. Spwendid sport, don't ye know, and specially wecommended for young wadies wike yourself. You must come to visit—you too, Fwashman. You wode pwetty well, as I wecollect. Haw-haw."

"You honour me with the recollection, milord," says I, wondering what would happen if I smashed him between the eyes. "But I—"

"Yaas," says he, turning languidly back to Elspeth. "No doubt your husband has many duties—in the ordnance, is it not, or some such thing? Haw-haw. But you must come down, my dear, with one of your fwiends, for a good wong stay, what? The faiwest bwossoms bwoom best in countwy air, don't ye know? Haw-haw." And the old scoundrel had the gall to lean over and pat her hand.

She, the little ninny, was all for it, giving him a dazzling smile and protesting he was too, too kind—this aged satyr who was old enough to be her father and had vice leering out of every wrinkle in his face. Of course, where climbing little snobs like Elspeth are concerned, there ain't such a thing as an ugly peer of the realm, but even she could surely have seen how grotesque his advances were. Of course, women love it.

"How splendid to see you two old friends together again, after such a long time, is it not, Lord Cardigan? Why, I declare I have never seen you in his lordship's company, Harry! Such a dreadfully long time it must have been!" Babbling, you see, like the idiot she was. I'm not sure she didn't say something about "comrades in arms". "You must call upon us, Lord Cardigan, now that you and Harry have met again. It will be so fine, will it not, Harry?"

"Yaas," says he. "I may call," with a look at me that said he would never dream of setting foot in any hovel of mine. "In the meantime, my dear, I shall wook to see you widing hereabouts. Haw-haw. I dewight to see a female who wides so gwacefully. Decidedwy you must come to Deene. Haw-haw." He took off his hat to her, bowing from the waist—and a Polish hussar couldn't have done it better, damn him. "Good day to you, Mrs Fwashman." He gave me the merest nod, and cantered off up the Ride, cool as you please.

"Is he not wonderfully condescending, Harry? Such elegant manners—but of course, it is natural in one of such noble breeding. I am sure if you spoke to him, my dear, he would be ready to give the most earnest consideration to finding a place for you —he is so kind, despite his high station. Why, he has promised me almost any favour I care to ask—Harry, whatever is the matter? Why are you swearing—oh, my love, no, people will hear! Oh!"

Of course, swearing and prosing were both lost on Elspeth; when I had vented my bile against Cardigan I tried to point out to her the folly of accepting the attentions of such a notorious roué, but she took this as mere jealousy on my part—not jealousy of a sexual kind, mark you, but supposedly rooted in the fact that here she was climbing in the social world, spooned over by peers, while I was labouring humbly in an office like any Cratchit, and could not abide to see her ascending so far above me. She even reminded me that she was a baron's daughter, at which I ground my teeth and hurled a boot through our bedroom window, she burst into tears, and ran from the room to take refuge in a broom cupboard, whence she refused to budge while I hammered on the panels. She was terrified of my brutal ways, she said, and feared for her life, so I had to go through the charade of forcing open the door and rogering her in the cupboard before peace was restored. (This was what she had wanted since the quarrel began, you see; very curious and wearing our domestic situation was, but strangely enjoyable, too, as I look back on it. I remember how I carried her to the bedroom afterwards, she nibbling at my ear with her arms round my neck, and at the sight of the broken window we collapsed giggling and kissing on the floor. Aye, married bliss. And like the fool I was I clean forgot to forbid her to talk to Cardigan again.)

But in the next few days I had other things to distract me from Elspeth's nonsense; my jape in the pool-room with the little greenhorn came home to roost, and in the most unexpected way. I received a summons from my Lord Raglan, of all people.

You will know all about him, no doubt. He was the ass who presided over the mess we made in the Crimea, and won deathless fame as the man who murdered the Light Brigade. He should have been a parson, or an Oxford don, or a waiter, for he was the kindliest, softest-voiced old stick who ever spared a fellow-creature's feelings—that was what was wrong with him, that he couldn't for the life of him say an unkind word, or set anyone down. And this was the man who was the heir to Wellington—as I sat in his office, looking across at his kindly old face, with its rumpled white hair and long nose, and found my eyes straying to the empty right sleeve tucked into his breast, he looked so pathetic and frail, I shuddered inwardly. Thank God, thinks I, that I won't be in *this* chap's campaign.

They had just made him Commander-in-Chief, after years spent bumbling about on the Board of Ordnance, and he was supposed to be taking matters in hand for the coming conflict. So you may guess that the matter on which he had sent for me was one of the gravest national import—Prince Albert, our saintly Bertie the Beauty, wanted a new aide-de-camp, or equerry, or toad-eater-extraordinary, and nothing would do but our new Commander must set all else aside to see the thing was done properly.

Mark you, I'd no time to waste marvelling over the fatuousness of this kind of mismanagement; it was nothing new in our army, anyway, and still isn't, from all I can see. Ask any commander to choose between toiling over the ammunition returns for a division fighting for its life, and taking the King's dog for a walk, and he'll be out there in a trice, bawling "Heel, Fido!" No, I was too much knocked aback to learn that I, Captain Harry Flashman, former Cherrypicker and erstwhile hero of the country, of no great social consequence and no enormous means or influence, should even be considered to breathe the lordly air of the court. Oh, I had my fighting reputation, but what's that, when London is bursting with pink-cheeked viscounts with cleft palates and long pedigrees? My great-great-great-grandpapa wasn't even a duke's bastard, so far as I know.

Raglan approached the thing in his usual roundabout way, by going through a personal history which his minions must have put together for him.

"I see you are thirty-one years old, Flashman," says he. "Well, well, I had thought you older—why, you must have been only—yes, nineteen, when you won your spurs at Kabul. Dear me! So young. And since then you have served in India, against the Sikhs, but have been on half-pay these six years, more or less. In that time, I believe, you have travelled widely?"

Usually at high speed, thinks I, and not in circumstances I'd care to tell your lordship about. Aloud I confessed to acquaintance with France, Germany, the United States, Madagascar, West Africa, and the East Indies.

"And I see you have languages—excellent French, German, Hindoostanee, Persian—bless my soul!—and Pushtu. Thanks of Parliament in '42, Queen's Medal—well, well, these are quite singular accomplishments, you know." And he laughed in his easy way. "And apart from Company service, you were formerly, as I apprehend, of the 11th Hussars. Under Lord Cardigan. A-ha. Well, now, Flashman, tell me, what took you to the Board of Ordnance?"

I was ready for that one, and spun him a tale about improving my military education, because no field officer could know too much, and so on, and so on. . . .

"Yes, that is very true, and I commend it in you. But you know, Flashman, while I never dissuade a young man from studying all aspects of his profession—which indeed, my own mentor, the Great Duke, impressed on us, his young men, as most necessary—still, I wonder if the Ordnance Board is *really* for you." And he looked knowing and quizzical, like someone smiling with a mouthful of salts. His voice took on a deprecatory whisper. "Oh, it is very well, but come, my boy, it cannot but seem—well, *beneath*, a little beneath, I think, a man whose career has been as, yes, brilliant as your own. I say nothing against the Ordnance—why, I was Master-General for many years—but for a young blade, well-connected, highly regarded . . . ?" He wrinkled his nose at me. "Is it not like a charger pulling a cart? Of course it is. Manufacturers and clerks may be admirably suited to dealing with barrels and locks and rivets and, oh, *dimensions*, and what not, but it is all so *mechanical*, don't you agree?"

Why couldn't the old fool mind his own business? I could see where this was leading—back to active service and being blown to bits in Turkey, devil a doubt. But who contradicts a Commander-in-Chief?

"I think it a most happy chance," he went on, "that only yesterday his Royal Highness Prince Albert"—he said it with reverence—"confided to me the task of finding a young officer for a post of considerable delicacy and importance. He must, of course, be well-born—your mother was Lady Alicia Paget, was she not? I remember the great pleasure I had in dancing with her, oh, how many years ago? Well, well, it is no matter. A quadrille, I fancy. However, station alone is not sufficient in this case, or I confess I should have looked to the Guards." Well, that was candid, damn him. "The officer selected must also have shown himself resourceful, valiant, and experienced in camp and battle. That is essential. He must be young, of equable disposition and good education, unblemished, I need not say, in personal reputation"—God knows how he'd come to pick on me, thinks I, but he went on: "— and yet a man who knows his world. But above all—what our good old Duke would call 'a man of his hands'." He beamed at me. "I believe your name must have occurred to me at once, had His Highness not mentioned it first. It seems our gracious Queen had recollected you to him." Well, well, thinks I, little Vicky remembers my whiskers after all these years. I recalled how she had mooned tearfully at me when she pinned my medal on, back in '42—they're all alike you know, can't resist a dashing boy with big shoulders and a trot-along look in his eye.

"So I may now confide in you," he went on, "what this most important duty consists in. You have not heard, I dare say, of Prince William of Celle? He is one of Her Majesty's European cousins, who has been visiting here some time, incognito, studying our English ways preparatory to pursuing a military career in the British Army. It is his family's wish that when our forces go overseas—as soon they must, I believe—he shall accompany us, as a member of my staff. But while he will be under my personal eye, as it were, it is most necessary that he should be in the immediate care of the kind of officer I have mentioned—one who will guide his youthful footsteps, guard his person, shield him from temptation, further his military education, and supervise his physical and spiritual welfare in every way." Raglan smiled.

"He is very young, and a most amiable prince in every way; he will require a firm and friendly hand from one who can win the trust and respect of an ardent and developing nature. Well, Flashman, I have no doubt that between us we can make something of him. Do you not agree?"

By God, you've come to the right shop, thinks I. Flashy and Co., wholesale moralists, ardent and developing natures supervised, spiritual instruction guaranteed, prayers and laundry two bob extra. How the deuce had they picked on me? The Queen, of course, but did Raglan know what kind of a fellow they had alighted on? Granted I was a hero, but I'd thought my randying about and boozing and general loose living were well known—by George, he must know! Maybe, secretly, he thought that was a qualification—I'm not sure he wasn't right. But the main point was, all my splendid schemes for avoiding shot and shell were out of court again; it was me for the staff, playing nursemaid to some little German pimp in the wilds of Turkey. Of all the hellish bad luck.

But of course I sat there jerking like a puppet, grinning foolishly —what else was there to do?

"I think we may congratulate ourselves," the old idiot went on, "and tomorrow I shall take you to the Palace to meet your new charge. I congratulate you, Captain, and"—he shook my hand with a noble smile—"I know you will be worthy of the trust imposed on you now, as you have been in the past. Good day to you, my dear sir. And now," I heard him say to his secretary as I bowed myself out, "there is this wretched war business. I suppose there is no word yet whether it has begun? Well, I do wish they would make up their minds."

You have already guessed, no doubt, the shock that was in store for me at the Palace next day. Raglan took me along, we went through the rigmarole of flunkeys with brushes that I remembered from my previous visit with Wellington, and we were ushered into a study where Prince Albert was waiting for us. There was a reverend creature and a couple of the usual court clowns in morning dress looking austere in the background—and there, at Albert's right hand, stood my little greenhorn of the billiard hall. The sight hit me like a ball in the leg—for a moment I stood stock still while I gaped at the lad and he gaped at me, but then he recovered, and so did I, and as I made my deep bow at Raglan's side I found myself wondering: have they got that blacking off his arse yet?

I was aware that Albert was speaking, in that heavy, German voice; he was still the cold, well-washed exquisite I had first met twelve years ago, with those frightful whiskers that looked as though someone had tried to pluck them and left off half-way through. He was addressing me, and indicating a side-table on which a shapeless black object was lying.

"'hat do you 'hink of the new hett for the Guards, Captain Flash-mann?" says he.

I knew it, of course; the funny papers had been full of it, and mocking H.R.H., who had invented it. He was always inflicting monstrosities of his own creation on the troops, which Horse Guards had to tell him tactfully were not quite what was needed. I looked at this latest device, a hideous forage cap with long flaps,[7] and said I was sure it must prove admirably serviceable, and have a very smart appearance, too. Capital, first-rate, couldn't be better, God knows how someone hadn't thought of it before.

He nodded smugly, and then says: "I un-erstend you were at Rugby School, Captain? Ah, but wait—a captain? That will hardly do, I think. A colonel, no?" And he looked at Raglan, who said the same notion had occurred to him. Well, thinks I, if that's how promotion goes, I'm all for it.

"At Rugby School," repeated Albert. "That is a great English school, Willy," says he to the greenhorn, "of the kind which turns younk boys like yourself into menn like Colonel Flash-mann here." Well, true enough, I'd found it a fair mixture of jail and knocking-shop; I stood there trying to look like a chap who says his prayers in a cold bath every day.

"Colonel Flash-mann is a famous soldier in England, Willy; although he is quite younk, he has vun—won—laurelss for brafery in India. You see? Well, he will be your friend and teacher, Willy; you are to mind all that he says, and obey him punctually and willingly, ass a soldier should. O-bedience is the first rule of an army, Willy, you understand?"

The lad spoke for the first time, darting a nervous look at me. "Yes, uncle Albert."

"Ver-ry good, then. You may shake hands with Colonel Flash-mann."

The lad came forward hesitantly, and held out his hand. "How do you do?" says he, and you could tell he had only lately learned the phrase.

"You address Colonel Flash-mann, as 'sir', Willy," says Albert. "He is your superior officer."

The kid blushed, and for the life of me I can't think how I had the nerve to say it, with a stiff-neck like Albert, but the favour I won with this boy was going to be important, after all—you can't have too many princely friends—and I thought a Flashy touch was in order. So I said:

"With your highness's permission, I think 'Harry' will do when we're off parade. Hullo, youngster."

The boy looked startled, and then smiled, the court clowns started to look outraged, Albert looked puzzled, but then he smiled, too, and Raglan hum-hummed approvingly. Albert said:

"There, now, Willy, you have an English comrade. You see? Very goot. You will find there are none better. And now, you will go with—with 'Harry'"—he gave a puffy smile, and the court clowns purred toadily,—"and he will instruct you in your duties."

I've been about courts a good deal in my misspent career, and by and large I bar royalty pretty strong. They may be harmless enough folk in themselves, but they attract a desperate gang of placemen and hangers-on, and in my experience, the closer you get to the throne, the nearer you may finish up to the firing-line. Why, I've been a Prince Consort myself, and had half the cutthroats of Europe trying to assassinate me,* and in my humbler capacities—as chief of staff to a White Rajah, military adviser and chief stud to that black she-devil Ranavalona, and irregular emissary to the court of King Gezo of Dahomey, long may he rot—I've usually been lucky to come away with a well-scarred skin. And my occasional attachments to the Court of St James's have been no exception; nurse-maiding little Willy was really the most harrowing job of the lot.

Mind you, the lad was amiable enough in himself, and he took to me from the first.

"You are a brick," he told me as soon as we were alone. "Is that not the word? When I saw you today, I was sure you would tell them of the billiard place, and I would be disgraced. But you said nothing—that was to be a true friend."

"Least said, soonest mended," says I. "But whatever did you run away for that night?—why, I'd have seen you home right enough. We couldn't think what had become of you."

"I do not know myself," says he. "I know that some ruffians set upon me in a dark place, and . . . stole some of my clothes." He blushed crimson, and burst out: "I resisted them fiercely, but they were too many for me! And then the police came, and Dr Winter had to be sent for, and—oh! there was such a fuss! But you were right—he was too fearful of his own situation to inform on me to their highnesses. However, I think it is by his insistence that a special guardian has been appointed for me."

* See Royal Flash.

He gave me his shy, happy smile. "What luck that it should be you!"

Lucky, is it, thinks I, we'll see about that. We'd be off to the war, if ever the damned thing got started—but when I thought about it, it stood to reason they wouldn't risk Little Willy's precious royal skin very far, and his bear-leader should be safe enough, too. All I said was:

"Well, I think Dr Winter's right; you need somebody and a half to look after you, for you ain't safe on your own hook. So look'ee here—I'm an easy chap, as anyone'll tell you, but I'll stand no shines, d'ye see? Do as I tell you, and we'll do famously, and have good fun, too. But no sliding off on your own again— or you'll find I'm no Dr Winter. Well?"

"*Very* well, sir—Harry," says he, prompt enough, but for all his nursery look, I'll swear he had a glitter in his eye.

We started off on the right foot, with a very pleasant round of tailors and gunsmiths and bootmakers and the rest, for the child hadn't a stick or stitch for a soldier, and I aimed to see him—and myself—bang up to the nines. The luxury of being toadied through all the best shops, and referring the bills to Her Majesty, was one I wasn't accustomed to, and you may believe I made the most of it. At my tactful suggestion to Raglan, we were both gazetted in the 17th, who were lancers—no great style as a regiment, perhaps, but I knew it would make Cardigan gnash his elderly teeth when he heard of it, and I'd been a lancer myself in my Indian days. Also, to my eye it was the flashiest rigout in the whole light cavalry, all blue and gold—the darker the better, when you've got the figure for it, which of course I had.

Anyway, young Willy clapped his hands when he saw himself in full fig, and ordered another four like it—no one spends like visiting royalty, you know. Then he had to be horsed, and armed, and given lashings of civilian rig, and found servants, and camp gear—and I spent a whole day on that alone. If we were going campaigning, I meant to make certain we did it with every conceivable luxury—wine at a sovereign the dozen, cigars at ten guineas the pound, preserved foods of the best, tip-top linen, quality spirits by the gallon, and all the rest of the stuff that you need if you're going to fight a war properly. Last of all I insisted on a lead box of biscuits—and Willy cried out with laughter.

"They are ship's biscuits—what should we need those for?"

"Insurance, my lad," says I. "Take 'em along, and it's odds you'll never need them. Leave 'em behind, and as sure as shooting you'll finish up living off blood-stained snow and dead mules." It's God's truth, too.

"It will be exciting!" cries he, gleefully. "I long to be off!"

"Just let's hope you don't find yourself longing to be back," says I, and nodded at the mountain of delicacies we had ordered. "That's all the excitement we want."

His face fell at that, so I cheered him up with a few tales of my own desperate deeds in Afghanistan and elsewhere, just to remind him that a cautious campaigner isn't necessarily a milksop. Then I took him the rounds, of clubs, and the Horse Guards, and the Park, presented him to anyone of consequence whom I felt it might be useful to toady—and, by George, I had no shortage of friends and fawners when the word got about who he was. I hadn't seen so many tuft-hunters since I came home from Afghanistan.

You may imagine how Elspeth took the news, when I notified her that Prince Albert had looked me up and given me a Highness to take in tow. She squealed with delight—and then went into a tremendous flurry about how we must give receptions and soirées in his honour, and Hollands would have to provide new curtains and carpet, and extra servants must be hired, and who should she invite, and what new clothes she must have—"for we shall be in *everyone's* eye now, and I shall be an object of general remark whenever I go out, and everyone will wish to call—oh, it will be famous!—and we shall be receiving all the time, and—"

"Calm yourself, my love," says I. "We shan't be receiving— we shall be being received. Get yourself a few new duds, by all means, if you've room for 'em, and then—wait for the pasteboards to land on the mat."

And they did, of course. There wasn't a hostess in Town but was suddenly crawling to Mrs Flashman's pretty feet, and she gloried in it. I'll say that for her, there wasn't an ounce of spite in her nature, and while she began to condescend most damnably, she didn't cut anyone—perhaps she realized, like me, that it never pays in the long run. I was pretty affable myself, just then, and pretended not to hear one or two of the more jealous remarks that were dropped—about how odd it was that Her Majesty hadn't chosen one of the purple brigade to squire her young cousin, not so much as Guardee even, but a plain Mr— and who the deuce were the Flashmans anyway?

But the Press played up all right; *The Times* was all approval that "a soldier, not a courtier, has been entrusted with the grave responsibility entailed in the martial instruction of the young prince. If war should come, as it surely must if Russian imperial despotism and insolence try our patience further, what better guardian and mentor of His Highness could be found than the Hector of Afghanistan? We may assert with confidence—*none.*" (I could have asserted with confidence, any number, and good luck to 'em.)

Even *Punch,* which didn't have much to say for the Palace, as a rule, and loathed the Queen's great brood of foreign relations like poison, had a cartoon showing me frowning at little Willy under a signpost of which one arm said "Hyde Park" and the other "Honour and Duty", and saying: "What, my boy, do you want to be a stroller or a soldier? You can't be both if you march in step with me." Which delighted me, naturally, although Elspeth thought it didn't make me look handsome enough.

Little Willy, in the meantime, was taking to all this excitement like a Scotchman to drink. Under a natural shyness, he was a breezy little chap, quick, eager to please, and good-natured; he could be pretty cool with anyone over-familiar, but he could charm marvellously when he wanted—as he did with Elspeth when I took him home to tea. Mind you, the man who doesn't want to charm Elspeth is either a fool or a eunuch, and little Willy was neither, as I discovered on our second day together, as we were strolling up Haymarket—we'd been shopping for a pair of thunder-and-lightnings* which he admired. It was latish afternoon, and the tarts were beginning to parade; little Willy goggled at a couple of painted princesses swaying by in all their finery, ogling, and then he says to me in a reverent whisper:

"Harry—I say, Harry—those women—are they—"

"Whores," says I. "Never mind 'em. Now, to-morrow, Willy, we must visit the Artillery Mess, I think, and see the guns limbering up in—"

* Striped trousers.

"Harry," says he. "I want a whore."

"Eh?" says I. "You don't want anything of the sort, my lad." I couldn't believe my ears.

"I do, though," says he, and damme, he was gaping after them like a satyr, this well-brought-up, Christian little princeling. "I have never had a whore."

"I should hope not!" says I, quite scandalized. "Now, look here, young Willy, this won't answer at all. You're not to think of such things for a moment. I won't have this . . . this lewdness. Why, I'm surprised at you! What would—why, what would Her Majesty have to say to such talk? Or Dr Winter, eh?"

"I want a whore," says he, quite fierce. "I . . . I know it is wrong—but I don't care! Oh, you have no notion what it is like! Since I was quite small, they have never even let me talk to girls— at home I was not even allowed to play with my little cousins at kiss-in-the-ring, or anything! They would not let me go to dancing-classes, in case it should excite me! Dr Winter is always lecturing me about thoughts that pollute, and the fearful punishments awaiting fornicators when they are dead, and accusing me of having carnal thoughts! Of course I have, the old fool! Oh, Harry, I know it is sinful—but I don't care! I want one," says this remarkable youth dreamily, with a blissful look coming over his pure, chaste, boyish visage, "with long golden hair, and big, big, round—"

"Stop that this minute!" says I. "I never heard the like!"

"And she will wear black satin boots buttoning up to her thighs," he added, licking his lips.

I'm not often stumped, but this was too much. I know youth has hidden fires, but this fellow was positively ablaze. I tried to cry him down, and then to reason with him, for the thought of his cutting a dash through the London bordellos and trotting back to Buckingham Palace with the clap, or some harpy pursuing him for blackmail, made my blood run cold. But it was no good.

"If you say me nay," says he, quite determined, "I shall find one myself."

I couldn't budge him. So in the end I decided to let him have his way, and make sure there were no snags, and that it was done safe and quiet. I took him off to a very high-priced place I knew in St John's Wood, swore the old bawd to secrecy, and stated the randy little pig's requirements. She did him proud, too, with a strapping blonde wench—satin boots and all—and at the sight of her Willy moaned feverishly and pointed, quivering, like a setter. He was trying to clamber all over her almost before the door closed, and of course he made a fearful mess of it, thrashing away like a stoat in a sack, and getting nowhere. It made me quite sentimental to watch him—reminded me of my own ardent youth, when every coupling began with an eager stagger across the floor trying to disentangle one's breeches from one's ankles.

I had a brisk, swarthy little gypsy creature on the other couch, and we were finished and toasting each other in iced claret before Willy and his trollop had got properly buckled to. She was a knowing wench, however, and eventually had him galloping away like an archdeacon on holiday, and afterwards we settled down to a jolly supper of salmon and cold curry. But before we had reached the ices Willy was itching to be at grips with his girl again—where these young fellows get the fire from beats me. It was too soon for me, so while he walloped along I and the gypsy passed an improving few moments spying through a peephole into the next chamber, where a pair of elderly naval men were cavorting with three Chinese sluts. They were worse than Willy —it's those long voyages, I suppose.

When we finally took our leave, Willy was fit to be blown away by the first puff of wind, but pleased as punch with himself.

"You are a beautiful whore," says he to the blonde. "I am quite delighted with you, and shall visit you frequently." He did, too, and must have spent a fortune on her in tin, of which he had loads, of course. Being of a young and developing nature, as Raglan would have said, he tried as many other strumpets in the establishment as he could manage, but it was the blonde lass as often as not. He got quite spoony over her. Poor Willy.

So his military education progressed, and Raglan chided me for working him too hard. "His Highness appears quite pale," says he. "I fear you have him too much at the grindstone, Flashman. He must have some recreation as well, you know." I could have told him that what young Willy needed was a pair of locked iron drawers with the key at the bottom of the Serpentine, but I nodded wisely and said it was sometimes difficult to restrain a young spirit eager for instruction and experience. In fact, when it came to things like learning the rudiments of staff work and army procedure, Willy couldn't have been sharper; my only fear was that he might become really useful and find himself being actively employed when we went east.

For we were going, there was now no doubt. War was finally declared at the end of March, in spite of Aberdeen's dithering, and the mob bayed with delight from Shetland to Land's End. To hear them, all we had to do was march into Moscow when we felt like it, with the Frogs carrying our packs for us and the cowardly Russians skulking away before Britannia's flashing eyes. And mind you, I don't say that the British Army and the French together couldn't have done it—given a Wellington. They were sound at bottom, and the Russians weren't. I'll tell you something else, which military historians never realize: they call the Crimea a disaster, which it was, and a hideous botch-up by our staff and supply, which is also true, but what they don't know is that even with all these things in the balance against you, the difference between hellish catastrophe and brilliant success is sometimes no greater than the width of a sabre blade, but when all is over no one thinks of that. Win gloriously—and the clever dicks forget all about the rickety ambulances that never came, and the rations that were rotten, and the boots that didn't fit, and the generals who'd have been better employed hawking bedpans round the doors. Lose—and these are the only things they talk about.

But I'll confess I saw the worst coming before we'd even begun. The very day war was declared Willy and I reported ourselves to Raglan at Horse Guards, and it took me straight back to the Kabul cantonment—all work and fury and chatter, and no proper direction whatever. Old Elphy Bey had sat picking at his nails and saying: "We must certainly consider what is best to be done" while his staff men burst with impatience and spleen. You could see the germ of it here—Raglan's ante-room was jammed with all sorts of people, Lucan, and Hardinge, and old Scarlett, and Anderson of the Ordnance, and there were staff-scrapers and orderlies running everywhere and saluting and bustling, and mounds of paper growing on the tables, and great consulting of maps ("Where the devil is Turkey?" someone was saying. "Do they have much rain there, d'ye suppose?"), but in the inner sanctum all was peace and amiability. Raglan was talking about neck-stocks, if I remember rightly, and how they should fasten well up under the chin.

We were kept well up to the collar, though, in the next month before our stout and thick-headed commander finally took his leave for the scene of war—Willy and I were not of his advance party, which pleased me, for there's no greater fag than breaking in new ground. We were all day staffing at the Horse Guards, and Willy was either killing himself with kindness in St John's Wood by night, or attending functions about Town, of which there were a feverish number. It's always the same before the shooting begins—the hostesses go into a frenzy of gaiety, and all the spongers and civilians crawl out of the wainscoting braying with good fellowship because thank God they ain't going, and the young plungers and green striplings roister it up, and their fiancées let 'em pleasure them red in the face out of pity, because the poor brave boy is off to the cannon's mouth, and the dance goes on and the eyes grow brighter and the laughter shriller—and the older men in their dress uniforms look tired, and sip their punch by the fireplace and don't say much at all.

Elspeth, of course, was in her element, dancing all night, laughing with the young blades and flirting with the old ones—Cardigan was still roostering about her, I noticed, with every sign of the little trollop's encouragement. He'd got himself the Light Cavalry Brigade, which had sent a great groan through every hussar and lancer regiment in the army, and was even fuller of bounce than usual—his ridiculous lisp and growling "haw-haw" seemed to sound everywhere you went, and he was full of brag about how he and his beloved Cherrypickers would be the élite advanced force of the army.

"I believe they have given Wucan *nominal* charge of the cavalwy," I heard him tell a group of cronies at one party. "Well, I suppose they had to find him *something*, don't ye know, and he may vewwy well look to wemounts, I dare say. Haw-haw. I hope poor Waglan does not find him too gweat an incubus. Haw-haw."

This was Lucan, his own brother-in-law; they detested each other, which isn't to be wondered at, since they were both detestable, Cardigan particularly. But his mighty lordship wasn't having it all his own way, for the Press, who hated him, revived the old jibe about his Cherrypickers' tight pants, and *Punch* dedicated a poem to him called "Oh Pantaloons of Cherry", which sent him wild. It was all gammon, really, for the pants were no tighter than anyone else's—I wore 'em long enough, and should know —but it was good to see Jim the Bear roasting on the spit of popular amusement again. By God, I wish that spit had been a real one, with me to turn it.

It was a night in early May, I think, that Elspeth was bidden to some great drum in Mayfair to celebrate the first absolute fighting of the war, which had been reported a week or so earlier—our ships had bombarded Odessa, and broken half the windows in the place, so of course the fashionable crowd had to rave and riot in honour of the great victory.[8] I don't remember seeing Elspeth lovelier than she was that night, in a gown of some shimmering white satin stuff, and no jewels at all, but only flowers coiled in her golden hair. I would have had at her before she even set out, but she was all a-fuss tucking little Havvy into his cot—as though the nurse couldn't do it ten times better—and was fearful that I would disarrange her appearance. I fondled her, and promised I would put her through the drill when she came home, but she damped this by telling me that Marjorie had bidden her stay the night, although it was only a few streets away, because the dancing would go on until dawn, and she would be too fatigued to return.

So off she fluttered, blowing me a kiss, and I snarled away to the Horse Guards, where I had to burn the midnight oil over sapper transports; Raglan had set out for Turkey leaving most of the work behind him, and those of us who were left were kept at it until three each morning. By the time we had finished, even Willy was too done up to fancy his usual nightly exercise with his Venus, so we sent out for some grub—it was harry and grass,* I remember, which didn't improve my temper—and then he went home.

I was tired and cranky, but I couldn't think of sleep, somehow, so I went out and started to get drunk. I was full of apprehension about the coming campaign, and fed up with endless files and reports, and my head ached, and my shoes pinched, so I poured down the whistle-belly with brandy on top, and the inevitable result was that I finished up three parts tight in some cellar near Charing Cross. I thought of a whore, but didn't want one—and

* Haricot mutton and asparagus.

then it struck me: I wanted Elspeth, and nothing else. By God, there was I, on the brink of another war, slaving my innards into knots, while she was tripping about in a Mayfair ball-room, laughing and darting chase-me glances at party-saunterers and young gallants, having a fine time for hours on end, and she hadn't been able to spare me five minutes for a tumble! She was my wife, dammit, and it was too bad. I put away some more brandy while I considered the iniquity of this, and took a great drunken resolve—I would go round to Marjorie's at once, surprise my charmer when she came to bed, and make her see what she had been missing all evening. Aye, that was it—and it was romantic, too, the departing warrior tupping up the girl he was going to leave behind, and she full of love and wistful longing and be-damned. (Drink's a terrible thing.) Anyway, off I set west, with a full bottle in my pocket to see me through the walk, for it was after four, and there wasn't even a cab to be had.

By the time I got to Marjorie's place—a huge mansion fronting the Park, with every light ablaze—I was taking the width of the pavement and singing "Villikins and his Dinah".[9] The flunkeys at the door didn't mind me a jot, for the house must have been full of foxed chaps and bemused females, to judge by the racket they were making. I found what looked like a butler, inquired the direction of Mrs Flashman's chamber, and tramped up endless staircases, bouncing off the walls as I went. I found a lady's maid, too, who put me on the right road, banged on a door, fell inside, and found the place was empty.

It was a lady's bedroom, no error, but no lady, as yet. All the candles were burning, the bed was turned down, a fluffy little Paris night-rail which I recognized as one I'd bought my darling lay by the pillow, and her scent was in the air. I stood there sighing and lusting boozily; still dancing, hey? We'll have a pretty little hornpipe together by and by, though—aha, I would surprise her. That was it; I'd hide, and bound out lovingly when she came up. There was a big closet in one wall, full of clothes and linen and what-not, so I toddled in, like the drunken, love-sick ass I was—you'd wonder at it, wouldn't you, with all my experience?—settled down on something soft, took a last pull at my bottle—and fell fast asleep.

How long I snoozed I don't know; not long, I think, for I was still well fuddled when I came to. It was a slow business, in which I was conscious of a woman's voice humming "Allan Water", and then I believe I heard a little laugh. Ah, thinks I, Elspeth; time to get up, Flashy. And as I hauled myself ponderously to my feet, and stood swaying dizzily in the dark of the closet, I was hearing vague confused sounds from the room. A voice? Voices? Someone moving? A door closing? I can't be sure at all, but just as I blundered tipsily to the closet door, I heard a sharp exclamation which might have been anything from a laugh to a cry of astonishment. I stumbled out of the closet, blinking against the sudden glare of light, and my boisterous view halloo died on my lips.

It was a sight I'll never forget. Elspeth was standing by the bed, naked except for her long frilled pantaloons; her flowers were still twined in her hair. Her eyes were wide with shock, and her knuckles were against her lips, like a nymph surprised by Pan, or centaurs, or a boozed-up husband emerging from the wardrobe. I goggled at her lecherously for about half a second, and then realized that we were not alone.

Half way between the foot of the bed and the door stood the 7th Earl of Cardigan. His elegant Cherrypicker pants were about his knees, and the front tail of his shirt was clutched up before him in both hands. He was in the act of advancing towards my wife, and from the expression on his face—which was that of a starving, apoplectic glutton faced with a crackling roast—and from other visible signs, his intention was not simply to compare birthmarks. He stopped dead at sight of me, his mottled face paling and his eyes popping, Elspeth squealed in earnest, and for several seconds we all stood stock still, staring.

Cardigan recovered first, and looking back, I have to admire him. It was not an entirely new situation for me, you understand— I'd been in his shoes, so to speak, many a time, when husbands, traps, or bullies came thundering in unexpectedly. Reviewing Cardigan's dilemma, I'd have whipped up my britches, feinted towards the window to draw the outraged spouse, doubled back with a spring on to the bed, and then been through the door in a twinkling. But not Lord Haw-Haw; his bearing was magnificent. He dropped his shirt, drew up his pants, threw back his head, looked straight at me, rasped: "Good night to you!", turned about, and marched out, banging the door behind him.

Elspeth had sunk to the bed, making little sobbing sounds; I still stood swaying in disbelief, trying to get the booze out of my brain, wondering if this was some drunken nightmare. But it wasn't, and as I glared at that big-bosomed harlot on the bed, all those ugly suspicions of fourteen years came flooding back, only now they were certainties. And I had caught her in the act at last, all but in the grip of that lustful, evil old villain! I'd just been in the nick of time to thwart him, too, damn him. And whether it was the booze, or my own rotten nature, the emotion I felt was not rage so much as a vicious satisfaction that I had caught her out. Oh, the rage came later, and a black despair that sometimes wounds me like a knife even now, but God help me, I'm an actor, I suppose, and I'd never had a chance to play the outraged husband before.

"Well?" It came out of me in a strangled yelp. "Well? What? What? Hey?"

I must have looked terrific, I suppose, for she dropped her squeaking and shuddering like a shot, and hopped over t'other side of the bed like a jack rabbit.

"Harry!" she squealed. "What are you doing here?"

It must have been the booze. I had been on the point of striding —well, staggering—round the bed to seize her and thrash her black and blue, but at her question I stopped, God knows why.

"I was waiting for you! Curse you, you adultress!"

"In that cupboard?"

"Yes, blast it, in that cupboard. By God, you've gone too far, you vile little slut, you! I'll—"

"How could you!" So help me God, it's what she said. "How could you be so inconsiderate and unfeeling as to pry on me in this way? Oh! I was never so mortified! Never!"

"Mortified?" cries I. "With that randy old rip sporting his beef in your bedroom, and you simpering naked at him? You—you shameless Jezebel! You lewd woman! Caught in the act, by George! I'll teach you to cuckold me! Where's a cane? I'll beat the shame out of that wanton carcase, I'll—"

"It is not true!" she cried. "It is not true! Oh, how can you say such a thing!"

I was glaring round for something to thrash her with, but at this I stopped, amazed.

"Not true? Why, you infernal little liar, d'you think I can't see? Another second and you'd have been two-backed-beasting all over the place! And you dare—"

"It is not so!" She stamped her foot, her fists clenched. "You are quite in the wrong—I did not know he was there until an instant before you came out of that cupboard! He must have come in while I was disrobing—Oh!" And she shuddered. "I was taken quite unawares—"

"By God, you were! By me! D'you think I'm a fool? You've been teasing that dirty old bull this month past, and I find him all but mounting you, and you expect me to believe—'' My head was swimming with drink, and I lost the words. "You've dishonoured me, damn you! You've—"

"Oh, Harry, it is not true! I vow it is not! He must have stolen in, without my hearing, and—"

"You're lying!" I shouted. "You were whoring with him!"

"Oh, that is untrue! It is unjust! How can you *think* such a thing? How can you *say* it?" There were tears in her eyes, as well there might be, and now her mouth trembled and drooped, and she turned her head away. "I can see," she sobbed, "that you merely wish to make this an excuse for a quarrel."

God knows what I said in reply to that; sounds of rupture, no doubt. I couldn't believe my ears, and then she was going on, sobbing away:

"You are wicked to say such a thing! Oh, you have no thought for my feelings! Oh, Harry, to have that evil old creature steal up on me—the shock of it—oh, I thought to have died of fear and shame! And then you—you!" And she burst into tears in earnest and flung herself down on the bed.

I didn't know what to say, or do. Her behaviour, the way she had faced me, the fury of her denial—it was all unreal. I couldn't credit it, after what I'd seen. I was full of rage and hate and disbelief and misery, but in drink and bewilderment I couldn't reason straight. I tried to remember what I'd heard in the closet —had it been a giggle or a muted shriek? Could she be telling the truth? Was it possible that Cardigan had sneaked in on her, torn down his breeches in an instant, and been sounding the charge when she turned and saw him? Or had she wheedled him in, whispering lewdly, and been stripping for action when I rolled

out? All this, in a confused brandy-laden haze, passed through
my mind—as you may be sure it has passed since, in sober
moments.

I was lost, standing there half-drunk. That queer mixture of
shock and rage and exultation, and the vicious desire to punish
her brutally, had suddenly passed. With any of my other women,
I'd not even have listened, but taken out my spite on them with a
whip—except on Ranavalona, who was bigger and stronger than I.
But I didn't *care* for the other women, you see. Brute and all that
I am, I wanted to believe Elspeth.

Mind you, it was still touch and go whether I suddenly went
for her or not; but for the booze I probably would have done.
There was all the suspicion of the past, and the evidence of my
eyes tonight. I stood, panting and glaring, and suddenly she
swung up in a sitting position, like Andersen's mermaid, her eyes
full of tears, and threw out her arms. "Oh, Harry! Comfort me!"

If you had seen her—aye. It's so easy, as none knows better
than I, to sneer at the Pantaloons of this world, and the cheated
wives, too, while the rakes and tarts make fools of them—"If only
they knew, ho-ho!" Perhaps they do, or suspect, but would just
rather not let on. I don't know why, but suddenly I was seated on
the bed, with my arm round those white shoulders, while she
sobbed and clung to me, calling me her "jo"—it was that funny
Scotch word, which she hadn't used for years, since she had
grown so grand, that made me believe her—almost.

"Oh, that you should think ill of me!" she sniffled. "Oh, I
could die of shame!"

"Well," says I, breathing brandy everywhere, "there he was,
wasn't he? By God! Well, I say!" I suddenly seized her by the
shoulders at arms' length. "Do you—? No, by God! I saw him—
and you—and—and—"

"Oh, you are cruel!" she cried. "Cruel, cruel!" And then her
arms went round my neck, and she kissed me, and I was sure she
was lying—almost sure.

She sobbed away a good deal, and protested, and I babbled a
great amount, no doubt, and she swore her honesty, and I didn't
know what to make of it. She might be true, but if she was a
cheat and a liar and a whore, what then? Murder her? Thrash
her? Divorce her? The first was lunatic, the second I couldn't do,

not now, and the third was unthinkable. With the trusts that old swine Morrison had left to tie things up, she controlled all the cash, and the thought of being a known cuckold living on my pay —well, I'm fool enough for a deal, but not for that. Her voice was murmuring in my ear, and all that naked softness was in my arms, and her fondling touch was reminding me of what I'd come here for in the first place, so what the devil, thinks I, first things first, and if you don't pleasure her now till she faints, you'll look back from your grey-haired evenings and wish you had. So I did.

I still don't know—and what's more I don't care. But one thing only I was certain of that night—whoever was innocent, it wasn't James Brudenell, Earl of Cardigan. I swore then inwardly, with Elspeth moaning through her kiss, that I would get even with that one. The thought of that filthy old goat trying to board Elspeth—it brought me out in a sweat of fury and loathing. I'd kill him, somehow. I couldn't call him out—he'd hide behind the law, and refuse. Even worse, he might accept. And apart from the fact that I daren't face him, man to man, there would have been scandal for sure. But somehow, some day, I would find a way.

We went to sleep at last, with Elspeth murmuring in my ear about what a mighty lover I was, recalling me in doting detail, and how I was at my finest after a quarrel. She was giggling drowsily about how we had made up our previous tiff, with me tumbling her in the broom closet at home, and what fun it had been, and how I'd said it was the most famous place for rogering, and then suddenly she asked, quite sharp:

"Harry—tonight—your great rage at my misfortune was not all a pretence, was it? You did not—you are sure?—have some ... some female in the cupboard?"

And damn my eyes, she absolutely got out to look. I don't suppose I've cried myself to sleep since I was an infant, but it was touch and go then.

While all these important events in my personal affairs were taking place—Willy and Elspeth and Cardigan and so forth—you may wonder how the war was progressing. The truth is, of course, that it wasn't, for it's a singular fact of the Great Conflict against Russia that no one—certainly no one on the Allied side—had any clear notion of how to go about it. You will think that's one of these smart remarks, but it's not; I was as close to the conduct of the war in the summer of '54 as anyone, and I can tell you truthfully that the official view of the whole thing was:

"Well, here we are, the French and ourselves, at war with Russia, in order to protect Turkey. Ve-ry good. What shall we do, then? Better attack Russia, eh? H'm, yes. (Pause). Big place, ain't it?"

So they decided to concentrate our army, and the Froggies, in Bulgaria, where they might help the Turks fight the Ruskis on the Danube. But the Turks flayed the life out of the Russians without anyone's help, and neither Raglan, who was now out in Varna in command of the allies, nor our chiefs at home, could think what we might usefully do next. I had secret hopes that the whole thing might be called off; Willy and I were still at home, for Raglan had sent word that for safety's sake his highness should not come out until the fighting started—there was so much fever about in Bulgaria, it would not be healthy for him.

But there was never any hope of a peace being patched up, not with the mood abroad in England that summer. They were savage—they had seen their army and navy sail away with drums beating and fifes tootling, and 'Rule Britannia' playing, and the press promising swift and condign punishment for the Muscovite tyrant, and street-corner orators raving about how British steel would strike oppression down, and they were like a crowd come to a prize-fight where the two pugs don't fight, but spar and weave and never come to grips. They wanted blood, gallons of it, and to read of grape-shot smashing great lanes through Russian ranks, and stern and noble Britons skewering Cossacks, and Russian towns in flames—and they would be able to shake their heads over the losses of our gallant fellows, sacrificed to stern duty, and wolf down their kidneys and muffins in their warm breakfast rooms, saying: "Dreadful work this, but by George, England never shirked yet, whatever the price. Pass the marmalade, Amelia; I'm proud to be a Briton this day, let me tell you."[10]

And all they got that summer was—nothing. It drove them mad, and they raved at the Government, and the army, and each other, lusting for butchery, and suddenly there was a cry on every lip, a word that ran from tongue to tongue and was in every leading article—"Sevastopol!" God knows why, but suddenly that was the place. Why were we not attacking Sevastopol, to show the Russians what was what, eh? It struck me then, and still does, that attacking Sevastopol would be rather like an enemy of England investing Penzance, and then shouting towards London: "There, you insolent bastard, that'll teach you!" But because it was said to be a great base, and *The Times* was full of it, an assault on Sevastopol became the talk of the hour.

And the government dithered, the British and Russian armies rotted away in Bulgaria with dysentery and cholera, the public became hysterical, and Willy and I waited, with our traps packed, for word to sail.

It came one warm evening, with a summons to Richmond. Suddenly there was great bustle, and I had to ride post-haste to receive from His Grace the Duke of Newcastle despatches to be carried to Raglan without delay. I remember an English garden, and Gladstone practising croquet shots on the lawn, and dragon-flies buzzing among the flowers, and over on the terrace a group of men lounging and yawning—the members of the Cabinet, no less, just finished an arduous meeting at which most of 'em had dozed off—that's a fact, too, it's in the books.[11] And Newcastle's secretary, a dapper young chap with an ink smudge on the back of his hand, handing me a sealed packet with a "secret" label.

"The *Centaur* is waiting at Greenwich," says he. "You must be aboard tonight, and these are to Lord Raglan, from your hand into

his, nothing staying. They contain the government's latest advices
and instructions, and are of the first urgency."

"Very good," says I. "What's the word of mouth?" He
hesitated, and I went on: "I'm on his staff, you know."

It was the practice of every staff galloper then—and for all
I know, may still be—when he was given a written message, to
ask if there were any verbal observations to add. (As you'll see
later, it is a very vital practice.) He frowned, and then, bidding
me wait, went into the house, and came out with that tall grey
figure that everyone in England knew, and the mobs used to
cheer and laugh at and say, what a hell of an old fellow he was:
Palmerston.

"Flashman, ain't it?" says he, putting a hand on my shoulder.
"Thought you had gone out with Raglan." I told him about
Willy, and he chuckled. "Oh, aye, our aspiring Frederick the
Great. Well, you may take him with you, for depend upon it,
the war is now *under way*. You have the despatches? Well, now,
I think you may tell his lordship, when he has digested them—
I daresay Newcastle has made it plain enough—that the capture
of Sevastopol is held by Her Majesty's Government as being an
enterprise that cannot but be seen as signally advancing the
success of Allied arms. Hum? But that it will be a damned serious
business to undertake. You see?"

I nodded, looking knowing, and he grunted and squinted across
the lawn, watching Gladstone trying to knock a ball through a
hoop. He missed, and Pam grunted again. "Off you go then,
Flashman," says he. "Good luck to you. Come and see me when
you return. My respects to his lordship." And as I saluted and
departed, he hobbled stiffly out on to the lawn, and I watched him
say something to Gladstone, and take his mallet from him.
And that was all.

We sailed that night, myself after a hasty but passionate farewell with Elspeth, and Willy after a frantic foray to St John's
Wood for a final gallop at his blonde. I was beginning to feel that
old queasy rumbling in my belly that comes with any departure,
and it wasn't improved by Willy's chatter as we stood on deck,
watching the forest of shipping slip by in the dusk, and the lights
twinkling on the banks.

"Off to the war!" exclaims the little idiot. "Isn't it capital,

Harry? Of course, it is nothing new to you, but for me, it is the most exciting thing I have ever known! Did you not feel, setting out on your first campaign, like some knight in the old time, going out to win a great name, oh, for the honour of your house and the love of your fair lady?"

I hadn't, in fact—and if I had, it wouldn't have been for a whore in St John's Wood. So I just grunted, à la Pam, and let him prattle.

It was a voyage, like any other, but faster and pleasanter than most, and I won't bore you with it. In fact, I won't deal at any great length at all with those things which other Crimean writers go on about—the fearful state of the army at Varna, the boozing and whoring at Scutari, the way the Varna sickness and the cholera swept through our forces in that long boiling summer, the mismanagement of an untrained commissariat and inexperienced regimental officers, the endless bickering among commanders— like Cardigan for instance. He had left England for Paris within two days of our encounter in Elspeth's bedroom, and on arrival in Bulgaria had killed a hundred horses with an ill-judged patrol in the direction of the distant Russians. All this—the misery and the sickness and the bad leadership and the rest—you can read if you wish elsewhere; Billy Russell of The Times gives as good a picture as any, although you have to be wary of him. He was a good fellow, Billy, and we got on well, but he always had an eye cocked towards his readers, and the worse he could make out a case, the better they liked it. He set half England in a passion against Raglan, you remember, because Raglan wouldn't let the army grow beards. "I like an Englishman to look like an Englishman," says Raglan, "and beards are foreign, and breed vermin. Also, depend upon it, they will lead to filthy habits." He was dead right about the vermin, but Russell wouldn't have it; he claimed this was just stiff-necked parade-ground nonsense and red tape on Raglan's part, and wrote as much. (You may note that Billy Russell himself had a beard like a quickset hedge, and I reckon he took Raglan's order as a personal insult.)

In any event, this memorial isn't about the history of the war, but about me, so I'll confine myself to that all-important subject, and let the war take its chance, just the way the government did.

We got to Varna, and the stink was hellish. The streets were filthy, there were stretcher-parties everywhere, ferrying fever cases from the camps outside town to the sewers they called hospitals, there was no order about anything, and I thought, well, we'll make our quarters on board until we can find decent lodgings at leisure. So leaving Willy, I went off to report myself to Raglan.

He was full of affability and good nature, as always, shook hands warmly, called for refreshment for me, inquired at great length about Willy's health and spirits, and then settled down to read the despatches I'd brought. It was close and warm in his office, even with the verandah doors wide and a nigger working a fan; Raglan was sweating in his shirt-sleeves, and as I drank my whistle-belly at a side-table and studied him, I could see that even a couple of months out east had aged him. His hair was snow-white, the lines on his face were deeper than ever, the flesh was all fallen in on his skinny wrist—he was an old man, and he looked and sounded it. And his face grew tireder as he read; when he had done he summoned George Brown, who had the Light Division, and was his bosom pal. Brown read the despatch, and they looked at each other.

"It is to be Sevastopol," says Raglan. "The government's direction seems quite clear to me."

"Provided," says Brown, "both you and the French commander believe the matter can be carried through successfully. In effect, they leave the decision to you, and to St Arnaud."

"Hardly," says Raglan, and picked up a paper. "Newcastle includes a personal aide memoire in which he emphasizes the wishes of the Ministers—it is all Sevastopol, you see."

"What do we know about Sevastopol—its defences, its garrison? How many men can the Russians oppose to us if we invade Crimea?"

"Well, my dear Sir George," says Raglan, "we know very little, you see. There are no reconnaissance reports, but we believe the defences to be strong. On the other hand, I know St Arnaud thinks it unlikely there can be more than 70,000 Russians mustered in the Crimean peninsula."

"About our own numbers," says Brown.

"Precisely, but that is only conjecture. There may be fewer, there may well be more. It is all so uncertain." He sighed, and kneaded his brow with his left hand, rather abstracted. "I cannot say for sure that they might not field 100,000 men, you know. There has been no blockade, and nothing to prevent their troop movements."

"And we would have to invade across the Black Sea, make a foothold, perhaps face odds of four to three, invest Sevastopol, reduce it speedily—or else carry on a siege through a Russian winter—and all this while relying solely on our fleet for supply, while the Russians may send into the Crimea what strength they choose."

"Exactly, Sir George. Meanwhile, only one fourth of our siege equipment has arrived. Nor is the army in the best of health, and I believe the French to be rather worse."

I listened to this with mounting horror—not so much at what they were saying, but how they said it. Perfectly calmly, reasonably, and without visible emotion, they were rehearsing a formula which even I, ignorant staff-walloper that I was, could see was one for disaster. But I could only keep mum, clutching my pot of beer and listening.

"I should welcome your observations, my dear Sir George," says Raglan.

Brown's face was a study. He was an old Scotch war horse this, and nobody's fool, but he knew Raglan, and he knew something of the politics of power and warfare. He put the despatch back on the table.

"As to the enterprise of Sevastopol which the ministers appear to be suggesting," says he, "I ask myself how our old master the Duke would have seen it. I believe he would have turned it down flat—there is not enough information about the Crimea and the Russians, and our armies are reduced to the point where we have no leeway to work on. He would not have taken the terrible responsibility of launching such a campaign."[12]

You could see the relief spreading over Raglan's old face like water.

"I concur exactly in what you say, Sir George," says he, "in which case—"

"On the other hand," says Brown, "I judge from this despatch that the government are determined on Sevastopol. They have made up their minds at home. Now, if you decline to accept the responsibility, what will they do? In my opinion, they will recall

you; in fine, if you will not do the job, they'll send out someone
who will."

Raglan's face lengthened, and I saw an almost pettish set to his
mouth as he said:

"Dear me, that is to be very precise, Sir George. Do you really
think so?"

"I do, sir. As I see it, things have reached a pass where they
will have action, whatever it may be." He was breathing heavy,
I noticed. "And I believe that with them, one place is as good as
another."

Raglan sighed. "It may be as you say; it may be. Sevastopol.
Sevastopol. I wonder why? Why that, rather than the Danube
or the Caucasus?" He glanced round, as though he expected to see
the answer on the wall, and noticed me. "Ah, Colonel Flashman,
perhaps you can enlighten us a little in this. Are you aware of any
factor in affairs at home that may have determined the government
on this especial venture?"

I told him what I knew—that the Press was yelping Sevastopol
right and left, and that everyone had it on the brain.

"Do they know where it is?" says Brown.

I wasn't too sure myself where it was, but I said I supposed they
did. Raglan tapped his lip, looking at the despatch as though he
hoped it would go away.

"Did you see anyone when the despatch was delivered to you
—Newcastle, or Argyll, perhaps?"

"I saw Lord Palmerston, sir. He remarked that the government
were confident that the occupation of Sevastopol would be an
excellent thing, but that it would be a damned serious business.
Those were his words, sir."

Brown gave a bark of disgust, and Raglan laughed. "We may
agree with him, I think. Well, we must see what our Gallic allies
think, I suppose, before we can reach a fruitful conclusion."

So they did—all the chattering Frogs of the day, with St
Arnaud, the little mountebank from the Foreign Legion, who had
once earned his living on the stage and looked like an ice-cream
vendor, with his perky moustache, at their head. He had the
feverish look of a dying man—which he was—and Canrobert,
with his long hair and ridiculous curling moustaches, wasn't one
to inspire confidence either. Not that they were worse than our

own crew—the ass Cambridge, and Evans snorting and growling, and old England burbling, and Raglan sitting at the table head, like a vicar at a prize-giving, being polite and expressing gratified pleasure at every opinion, no matter what it was.

And there was no lack of opinions. Raglan thought an invasion might well come off—given luck—Brown was dead against it, but at first the Frogs were all for it, and St Arnaud said we should be in Sevastopol by Christmas, death of his life and sacred blue. Our navy people opposed the thing, and Raglan got peevish, and then the Frogs began to have their doubts, and everything fell into confusion. They had another meeting, at which I wasn't present, and then the word came out: the Frogs and Raglan were in agreement again, Brown was over-ruled and the navy with him, we were to go to the Crimea.

"I dare say the sea air will do us good and raise everyone's spirits," says Raglan, and by God, he didn't raise mine. I've wondered since, if I could have done anything about it, and decided I could. But what? If Otto Bismarck had been in my boots and uniform, I daresay he could have steered them away, as even a junior man can, if he goes about it right. But I've never meddled if I could avoid it, where great affairs are concerned; it's too chancy. Mind you, if I could have seen ahead I'd have sneaked into Raglan's tent one night and brained the old fool, but I didn't know, you see.

So there was tremendous sound and fury for the next month, with everyone preparing for the great invasion. Willy and I had established ourselves snugly in a cottage outside the town, and with all our provisions and gear we did comfortably enough, but being staff men we couldn't shirk too much, although Raglan worked Willy lightly, and was forever encouraging him to go riding and shooting and taking it easy. For the rest, it was touch and go, so far as I could see, whether the army, which was still full of fever and confusion, would ever be well enough to crawl on the transports, but as you know, the thing was done in the end. I've written about it at length elsewhere—the fearful havoc of embarking, with ships full of spewing soldiers rocking at anchor for days on end, the weeping women who were ordered to stay behind (although my little pal, Fan Duberly,[12] sneaked aboard disguised as a washerwoman), the horses fighting and smashing in their cramped stalls, the hideous stink, the cholera corpses floating in the bay, Billy Russell standing on the quay with his note-book damning Lord Lucan's eyes—"I have my duty, too, my lord, which is to inform my readers, and if you don't like what you're doing being reported, why then, don't do it! And that's my advice to you!" Of course he was daft and Irish, was Billy, but so was Lucan, and they stood and cussed each other like Mississippi pilots.

I had my work cut out latterly in bagging a berth on the *Caradoc*, which was Raglan's flagship, and managed to get not a bad billet for Willy and myself and Lew Nolan, who was galloper to Airey, the new chief of staff. He was another Irish, with a touch of dago or something, this Nolan, a cavalry maniac who held everybody in contempt, and let 'em feel it, too, although he was a long way junior. Mind you, he came no snuff with me, because I was a better horseman, and he knew it. We three bunked in together, while major-generals and the like had to make do with hammocks—I played Willy's royalty for all it was worth, you may be sure. And then, heigh-ho, we were off on our balmy cruise across the Black Sea, a huge fleet of sixty thousand soldiers, only half of 'em rotten with sickness, British, Frogs, Turks, a few Bashi-bazooks, not enough heavy guns to fire more than a salute or two, and old General Scarlett sitting on top of a crate of hens learning the words of command for manoeuvring a cavalry brigade, closing his book on his finger, shutting his boozy old eyes, and shouting, "Walk, march, trot. Damme, what comes next?"

The only thing was—no one knew where we were going. We ploughed about the Black Sea, while Raglan and the Frogs wondered where we should land, and sailed up and down the Russian coast looking for a likely spot. We found one, and Raglan stood there smiling and saying what a capital beach it was. "Do you smell the lavender?" says he. "Ah, Prince William, you may think you are back in Kew Gardens."

Well, it may have smelled like it at first, but by the time we had spent five days crawling ashore, with everyone spewing and soiling themselves in the pouring rain, and great piles of stores and guns and rubbish growing on the beach, and the sea getting fouler and fouler with the dirt of sixty thousand men—well, you may imagine what it was like. The army's health was perhaps a little better than it had been on the voyage, but not much, and when we finally set off down the coast, and I watched the heavy, plodding tread of the infantry, and saw the stretched looked of the cavalry mounts—I thought, how far will this crowd go, on a few handfuls of pork and biscuit, no tents, devil a bottle of jallop, and the cholera, the invisible dragon, humming in the air as they marched?

Mind you, from a distance it looked well. When that whole army was formed up, it stretched four miles by four, a great glittering host from the Zouaves on the beach, in their red caps and blue coats, to the shakos of the 44th on the far horizon of the plain—and they were a sight of omen to me, for the last time I'd seen them they'd been standing back to back in the bloodied snow of Gandamack, with the Ghazi knives whittling 'em down, and Souter with the flag wrapped round his belly. I never see those 44th facings but I think of the army of Afghanistan dying in the ice-hills, and shudder.

I was privileged, if that is the word, to give the word that started the whole march, for Raglan sent me and Willy to gallop first to the rear guard and then to the advance guard with the order to march. In fact, I let Willy deliver the second message, for the advance guard was led by none other than Cardigan, and it was more than I could bear to look at the swine. We cantered through the army, and the fleeting pictures are in my mind still —the little French canteen tarts sitting laughing on the gun limbers, the scarlet stillness of the Guards, rank on rank, the bearded French faces with their kepis, and Bosquet balancing his belly above a horse too small for him, the sing-song chatter of the Highlanders in their dark green tartans, the sombre jackets of the Light Division, the red yokel faces burning in the heat, the smell of sweat and oil and hot serge, the creak of leather and the jingle of bits, the glittering points of the lances where the 17th sat waiting—and Willy burst out in excitement: "Our regiment, Harry! See how grand they look! What noble fellows they are!" —Billy Russell sitting athwart his mule and shouting "What is it, Flash? Are we off at last?", and I turned away to talk to him while Willy galloped ahead to where the long pink and blue line of the 11th marked the van of the army.

"I haven't seen our friends so close before," says Billy. "Look yonder." And following his pointing finger, far out to the left flank, with the sun behind them, I saw the long silent line of horsemen on the crest, the lances like twigs in the hands of pygmies.

"Cossacks," says Billy. We'd seen 'em before, of course, the first night, scouting our landing, and I'd thought then, it's well seen you ain't Ghazis, my lads, or you'd pitch our whole force back into the sea before we're right ashore. And as the advance was sounded, and the whole great army lumbered forward into the heat haze, with a band lilting "Garryowen", and the chargers of the 17th snorting and fidgeting at the sound, I saw to my horror that Willy, having delivered his message, was not riding back towards me, but was moving off at a smart gallop towards the left flank.

I cut out at once, to head him off, but he was light and his horse was fast, and he was a good three hundred yards clear of the left flank before I came up with him. He was cantering on, his eyes fixed on the distant ridge—and it was none so distant now; as I came up roaring at him, he turned and pointed: "Look, Harry—the enemy!"

"You little duffer, what are you about?" cries I. "D'you want to get your head blown off?"

"They are some way off," says he, laughing, and indeed they were—but close enough to be able to see the blue and white stripes of the lances, and make out the shaggy fur caps. They sat immovable while we stared at them, and I felt the sweat turn icy on my spine in spite of the heat. These were the famous savages of Tartary, watching, waiting—and God knew how many of them there might be, in great hordes advancing on our pathetic little army, as it tootled along with its gay colours by the sea. I pulled Willy's bridle round.

"Out of this, my lad," says I, "and don't stray again without my leave, d'ye hear?"

"Why, it is safe enough. None of them is advancing, or even looking like it. What a bore it is! If this were—oh, the Middle Ages, one of them would ride out and challenge us, and we could have a set-to while the army watched!" He was actually sitting there, with his eyes shining, and his hand twitching at his sabre-hilt, *wanting* a fight! A fine credit to me he was, you'll agree. And before I could rebuke him, there was the boom of gunfire, beyond the ridge, and boom-boom-boom, and the whistle of shot ahead, and a little cloud of pink-panted Hussars broke away and went dashing over towards the ridge, sabres out. There was cries and orders, and a troop of horse artillery came thundering out towards us, and I had to shout at Willy to get him trotting back towards the army, while the horse artillery unlimbered, and wheeled their pieces, and crashed their reply to the Russian guns.

He wanted to stay, but I wouldn't have it. "Gallopers can get killed," says I, "but not sitting with their mouths open staring at a peep-show." To tell truth, the sound of those bloody guns had set my innards quaking again, in the old style. "Now—gallop!" says I.

"Oh, very well," says he. "But you need not be so careful of me, you know—I don't mean to go astray just yet." And seeing my expression, he burst out laughing: "My word, what a cautious old stick you are, Harry—you are getting as bad as Dr Winter!"

And I wish I were with Dr Winter this minute, thinks I, whatever the old whoreson's doing. But I was to remember what Willy had said—and in the next day or so, too, when the army had rolled on down the coast, choking with heat by day and shivering by the fires at night, and we had come at last to the long slope that runs down to a red-banked river with great bluffs and gullies beyond. Just a little Russian creek, and today in any English parish church you may see its name on stone memorials, on old tattered flags in cathedrals, in the metalwork of badges, and on the nameplates of grimy back streets beside the factories. Alma.

You have seen the fine oil-paintings, I dare say—the perfect lines of guardsmen and Highlanders fronting up the hill towards the Russian batteries, with here and there a chap lying looking thoughtful with his hat on the ground beside him, and in the distance fine silvery clouds of cannon smoke, and the colours to the fore, and fellows in cocked hats waving their swords. I dare say some people saw and remember the Battle of the Alma like that, but Flashy is not among them. And I was in the middle of it, too, all on account of a commander who hadn't the sense to realize that generals ought to stay in the rear, directing matters.

It was bloody lunacy, from the start, and bloody carnage, too. You may know what the position was—the Russians, forty thousand strong, on the bluffs south of the Alma, with artillery positions dug on the forward slopes above the river, and our chaps, with the Frogs on the right, advancing over the river and up the slopes to drive the Ruskis out. If Menschikoff had known his work, or our troops had had less blind courage, they'd have massacred the whole allied army there and then. But the Russians fought as badly and stupidly as they nearly always do, and by sheer blind luck on Raglan's part, and idiot bravery among our fellows, the thing went otherwise.

You may read detailed accounts of the slaughter, if you wish, in any military history, but you may take my word for it that the battle was for all practical purposes divided into four parts, as follows. One, Flashy observes preliminary bombardment from his post in the middle of Raglan's staff, consoling himself that there are about twenty thousand other fellows between him and the enemy. Two, Flashy is engaged in what seem like hours of frantic galloping behind the lines of the Frog battalions on the right, keeping as far from the firing as he decently can, and inquiring on Lord Raglan's behalf why the hell the Frogs are not driving the seaward flank of the Russian position before them? Three, Flashy is involved in the battle with Lord Raglan. Four, Flashy reaps the fruits of allied victory, and bitter they were.

It was supposed to begin, you see, with the Frogs turning the Ruskis' flank, and then our chaps would roll over the river and finish the job. So for hours we sat there, sweating in the heat, and watching the powder-puff clouds of smoke popping out of the Russian batteries, and peppering our men in the left and centre. But the Frogs made nothing of their part of the business, and Nolan and I were to and fro like shuttlecocks to St Arnaud; he was looking like death, and jabbering like fury, while a bare half-mile away his little blue-coats were swarming up the ridges, and being battered, and the smoke was rolling back over the river in long grey wreaths.

"Tell milor it will take a little longer," he kept saying, and back we would gallop to Raglan. "We shall never beat the French at this rate," says he, and when he was reminded that the enemy were the Russians, not the French, he would correct himself hurriedly, and glance round to see that no Frog gallopers were near to overhear. And at last, seeing our silent columns being pounded by the Russian shot as they lay waiting for the advance, he gave the word, and the long red lines began rolling down the slope to the river.

There was a great reek of black smoke drifting along the banks from a burning hamlet right before us, and the white discharge of the Russian batteries rolled down in great clouds to meet it. The huge wavering lines of infantry vanished into it, and through gaps we could see them plunging into the river, their pieces above their heads, while the crash-crash-crash of the Russian guns reverberated down from the bluffs, and the tiny white spots of musket-fire began to snap like fire-crackers along the lips of the Russian trenches. And then the ragged lines of our infantry appeared beyond the smoke, clambering up the foot of the bluffs, and we could see the shot ploughing through them, tearing up the ground, and our guns were thundering in reply, throwing great fountains of earth up round the Russian batteries. Willy beside me was squirming in his saddle, yelling his head off with excitement, the little fool; it made no odds, for the din was deafening.

And Raglan looked round, and seeing the boy, smiled, and beckoned to me. He had to shout. "Keep him close, Flashman!" cries he. "We are going across the river presently," which was the worst news I had heard in weeks. Our attack was coming to a standstill; as the Russian firing redoubled, you could see our men milling anywhere at the foot of the bluffs, and the ground already thick with still bodies, in little heaps where the cannon had caught them, or singly where they had gone down before the muskets.

Then Nolan comes galloping up, full of zeal and gallantry, damn him, and shouted a message from the Frogs, and I saw Raglan shake his head, and then he trotted off towards the river, with the rest of us dutifully tailing on behind. Willy had his sabre out, God knows why, for all we had to worry about just then was the Russian shot, which was bad enough. We spurred down to the river, myself keeping Willy at the tail of the group, and I saw Airey throw aside his plumed hat just as we took the water. There were bodies floating in the stream, which was churned up with mud, and the smoke was billowing down and catching at our throats, making the horses rear and plunge—I had to grip Willy's bridle to prevent his being thrown. On our left men of the 2nd

Division were crowded on the bank, waiting to go forward; they were retching and coughing in the smoke, and the small shot and balls were whizzing and whining by in a hideously frightening way. I just kept my head down, praying feverishly, as is my wont, and then I saw one of the other gallopers, just ahead of me, go reeling out of his saddle with the blood spouting from his sleeve. He staggered up, clutching at my stirrup, and bawling, "I am perfectly well, my lord, I assure you!" and then he rolled away, and someone else jumped down to see to him.

Raglan halted, cool as you like, glancing right and left, and then summoned two of the gallopers and sent them pounding away along the bank to find Evans and Brown, whose divisions were being smashed to pieces at the foot of the bluffs. Then he says, "Come along, gentlemen. We shall find a vantage point," and cantered up the gully that opened up before us just there in the bluff-face. For a wonder it seemed empty, all the Ruskis being on the heights to either side, and the smoke was hanging above our heads in such clouds you couldn't see more than twenty yards up the hill. A hell of a fine position for a general to be in, you may think, and Raglan must have thought so, too, for suddenly he spurred his horse at the hill to the left, and we all ploughed up behind him, scrambling on the shale and rough tufts, through the reeking smoke, until suddenly we were through it, and on the top of a little knoll at the bluff foot.

I'll never forget that sight. Ahead and to our left rose the bluffs, bare steep hillside for five hundred feet. We could see the Russian positions clear as day, the plumes of musket smoke spouting down from the trenches, and the bearded faces behind them. Directly to our left was a huge redoubt, packed with enemy guns and infantry; there were other great batteries above and beyond. In front of the big redoubt the ground was thick with the bodies of our men, but they were still swarming up from the river, under a hail of firing. And beyond, along the bluffs, they were still advancing, a great sprawling mass of scarlet coats and white cross belts, clawing their way up, falling, scattering, re-forming and pressing on. For a mile, as far as one could see, they were surging up, over that hellish slope with the dead scattered before them towards the smoking positions of the enemy.

Better here than there, thinks I, until I realized that we were sitting up in full view, unprotected, with the Ruski infantry not a hundred yards away. We were absolutely ahead of our own infantry, thanks to that fool Raglan—and he was sitting there, with his blue coat flapping round him, and his plumed hat on his head, as calm as if it were a review, clinging to his saddle with his knees alone, while he steadied his glass with his single arm. There was so much shot whistling overhead, you couldn't be sure whether they were firing on us with intent or not.

And then right up on the crest, above the batteries, we saw the Russian infantry coming down the slope—a great brown mass, packed like sardines, rank after rank of them. They came clumping slowly, inexorably down towards the batteries, obviously intent on rolling into our infantry below. They looked unstoppable, and Raglan whistled through his teeth as he watched them.

"Too good to miss, by George!" cries he, and turning, caught my eye. "Down with you, Flashman! Guns, at once!" and you may understand that I didn't need telling twice. "Stay there!" shouts I to Willy, and then had my charger down that slope like a jack-rabbit. There were gun-teams labouring and splashing up the bank, and I bawled to them to make haste to the ridge. The horses were lashed up the muddy slope, the guns swinging wildly behind them; one of our gallopers got them positioned, with the gunners hauling them round by main force, and as I came back up the hill—none too swiftly—the first salvoes were screaming away to crash into the flank of the Russian columns.

It was havoc all along the bluffs, and smoking hell on that little hill. There were infantry pouring past us now, sweating, panting, smoke-blackened faces, and bayonets thrust out ahead as they surged by and upwards towards the Russian positions. They were shrieking and bawling like madmen, heedless apparently of the bloody holes torn in their ranks by the Russian firing; I saw two of them suddenly turn into pulp as a fusillade struck them, and another lying screaming with a thigh shot away. I looked for Raglan, and saw him with a couple of gallopers preparing to descend the hill; I looked for Willy, and there he was, his hat gone, shouting like a madman at the passing infantry.

And then, by God, he whirled up his sabre, and went flying along with them, across the face of the slope towards the nearest battery. His horse stumbled and recovered, and he waved his sword

and huzza'd. "Come back, you German lunatic!" I yelled, and
Raglan must have heard me, for he checked his horse and turned.
Even with the shot flying and the screaming and the thunder of
the guns, with the fate of the battle in his hands, those ears which
were normally deaf to sense caught my words. He saw me, he saw
Willy, careering away along the bluffs among the infantry, and
he sang out: "After him, Flashman!"

Probably, addressed to any other man in the army, that order
would have evoked an immediate response. The Eye of the Chief,
and all that. But I took one look along that shell-swept slope, with
the bodies thick on it, and that young idiot riding through the
blood and bullets, and I thought, by God, let him go for me.
I hesitated, and Raglan shouted again, angrily, so I set my charger
towards him, cupping a hand behind my ear, and yelling: "What's
that, my lord?" He shouted and pointed again, stabbing with his
finger, and then a shot mercifully ploughed up the ground between
us, and as the dirt showered over me I took the opportunity to
roll nimbly out of the saddle.

I clambered up again, like a man dazed, and rot him, he was
still there, and looking thoroughly agitated. "The Prince, Flashman!" he bawls, and then one of the gallopers plucked at his coat,
and pointed to the right, and off they went, leaving me clutching
at my horse's head, and Willy a hundred yards away, in the thick
of the advancing infantry, setting his horse to the breastwork of
the battery. It baulked, and he reeled in the saddle, his sabre
falling, and then he pitched straight back, losing his grip, and
went down before the feet of the infantry. I saw him roll a yard or
two, and then he lay still, as the advance passed over him.

Christ, I thought, he's done for, and as our fellows surged into
the battery, and the firing from above slackened, I picked my way
cautiously along, through those dreadful heaps of dead and
dying and wounded, with the stink of blood and powder everywhere, and the chorus of shrieks and moans of agony in my ears.
I dropped on one knee beside the little blue-clad figure among the
crimson; he was lying face down. I turned him over, and vomited.
He had half a face—one glazed eye, and brow, and cheek, and on
the other side, just a gory mash, with his brains running out of it.

I don't know how long I crouched there, staring at him, horror-
struck. Above me, I could hear all hell of firing and shouting still

going on as the battle surged up the slope, and I shook with fear at
it. I wasn't going near that again, not for a pension, but as I
forced myself to look at what was left of Willy, I found myself
babbling aloud: "Jesus, what'll Raglan say? I've lost Willy—my
God, what will they say?" And I began cursing and sobbing—not
for Willy, but out of shock and for the folly and ill-luck that had
brought me to this slaughterhouse and had killed this brainless
brat, this pathetic princeling who thought war was great sport, and
had been entrusted to my safe-keeping. By God, his death could
be the ruin of me! So I swore and wept, crouched beside his corpse.

"Of all the fearful sights I have seen on this day, none has so
wrung my heart as this." That's what Airey told Raglan, when
he described how he had found me with Willy's body above the
Alma. "Poor Flashman, I believe his heart is broken. But to see
the bravest blade on your staff, an officer whose courage is a
byword in the army, weeping like a child beside his fallen comrade—it is a terrible thing. He would have given his own life a
hundred times, I know, to preserve that boy."

I was listening outside the tent-flap, you see, stricken dumb
with manly grief. Well, I thought, that's none so bad; crying with
funk and shock has its uses, provided its mistaken for noble tears.
Raglan couldn't blame me, after all; I hadn't shot the poor little
fool, or been able to stop him throwing his life away. Anyway,
Raglan had a victory to satisfy him, and even the loss of a royal
galloper couldn't sour that, you'd think. Aye, but it could.

He was all stern reproach when finally I stood in front of him,
covered in dust, played out with fear, and doing my damndest to
look contrite—which wasn't difficult.

"What," says he, in a voice like a church bell, "will you tell
her majesty?"

"My lord," says I. "I am sorry, but it was no fault—"

He held up his one fine hand. "Here is no question of fault,
Flashman. You had a sacred duty—a trust, given into your hands
by your own sovereign, to preserve that precious life. You have
failed, utterly. I ask again, what will you tell the Queen?"

Only a bloody fool like Raglan would ask a question like that,
but I did my best to wriggle clear.

"What could I have done, my lord? You sent me for the guns,
and—"

"And you had returned. Your first thought thereafter should have been for your sacred charge. Well, sir, what have you to say? Myself, in the midst of battle, had to point to where honour should have taken you at once; And yet you paused; I saw you, and—"

"My lord!" cries I, full of indignation. "That is unjust! I did not fully understand, in the confusion, what your order was, I—"

"Did you need to understand?" says he, all quivering sorrow. "I do not question your courage, Flashman; it is not in doubt." Not with me, either, I thought, "But I cannot but charge you, heavily though it weighs on my heart to do so, with failing in that . . . that instinct for your first duty, which should have been not to me, or to the army even, but to that poor boy whose shattered body lies in the ambulance. His soul, we may be confident, is with God." He came up to me, and his eyes were full of tears, the maudlin old hypocrite. "I can guess at your own grief; it has moved not only Airey, but myself. And I can well believe that you wish that you, too, could have found an honourable grave on the field, as William of Celle has done. Better, perhaps, had you done so." He sighed, thinking about it, and no doubt deciding that he'd be a deal happier, when he saw the Queen again, to be able to say: 'Oh, Flashy's kicked the bucket, by the way, but your precious Willy is all right.' Well, fearful and miserable as I was, I wasn't that far gone, myself.

He prosed on a bit, about duty and honour and my own failure, and what a hell of a blot I'd put on my copybook. No thought, you'll notice, for the blot *he'd* earned, with those thousands of dead piled up above the Alma, the incompetent buffoon.

"I doubt not you will carry this burden all your life," says he, with gloomy satisfaction. "How it will be received at home— I cannot say. For the moment, we must all look to our duty in the campaign ahead. There, it may be, reparation lies." He was still thinking about Flashy filling a pit, I could see. "I pity you, Flashman, and because I pity you, I shall not send you home. You may continue on my staff, and I trust that your future conduct will enable me to think that this lapse—irreparable though its consequences are—was but one terrible error of judgment, one sudden dereliction of duty, which will never—nay, *can* never— be repeated. But for the moment, I cannot admit you again to that full fellowship of the spirit in which members of my staff are wont to be embraced."

Well, I could stand that. He rummaged on his table, and picked up some things. "These are the personal effects of your . . . your dead comrade. Take them, and let them be an awful reminder to you of duty *undone*, of trust neglected, and of honour—no, I will not say aught of honour to one whose courage, at least, I believe to be beyond reproach." He looked at the things; one of them was a locket which Willy had worn round his neck. Raglan snapped it open, and gave a little gulp. He held it out to me, his face all noble and working. "Look on that fair, pure face," cries he, "and feel the remorse you deserve. More than anything I can say, it will strike to your soul—the face of a boy's sweetheart, chaste, trusting, and innocent. Think of that poor, sweet creature who, thanks to your neglect, will soon be draining the bitterest cup of sorrow."

I doubted it myself, as I looked at the locket. Last time I'd seen her, the poor sweet creature had been wearing nothing but black satin boots. Only Willy in this wide world would have thought of wearing the picture of a St John's Wood whore round his neck; he had been truly wild about her, the randy little rascal. Well, if I'd had my way, he'd still have been thumping her every night, instead of lying on a stretcher with only half his head. But I wonder if the preaching Raglan, or any of the pious hypocrites who were his relatives, would have called him back to life on those terms? Poor little Willy.

Well, if I was in disgrace, I was also in good health, and that's what matters. I might have been one of the three thousand dead, or of the shattered wounded lying shrieking through the dusk along that awful line of bluffs. There seemed to be no medical provision—among the British, anyway—and scores of our folk just lay writhing where they fell, or died in the arms of mates hauling and carrying them down to the beach hospitals. The Russian wounded lay in piles by the hundred round our bivouacs, crying and moaning all through the night—I can hear their sobbing "*Pajalsta! pajalsta!*" still. The camp ground was littered with spent shot and rubbish and broken gear among the pools of congealed blood—my stars, wouldn't I just like to take one of our Ministers, or street-corner orators, or blood-lusting, breakfast-scoffing papas, over such a place as the Alma hills—not to let him *see*, because he'd just tut-tut and look anguished and have a good pray and not care a damn—but to shoot him in the belly with a soft-nosed bullet and let him die screaming where he belonged. That's all they deserve.

Not that I cared a fig for dead or wounded that night. I had worries enough on my own account, for in brooding about the injustice of Raglan's reproaches, I convinced myself that I'd be broke in the end. The loss of that mealy little German pimp swelled out of all proportion in my imagination, with the Queen calling me a murderer and Albert accusing me of high treason, and *The Times* trumpeting for my impeachment. It was only when I realized that the army might have other things to think about that I cheered up.

I was feeling as lonely as the policeman at Herne Bay[14] when I loafed into Billy Russell's tent, and found him scribbling away by a storm lantern, with Lew Nolan perched on an ammunition box, holding forth as usual.

"Two brigades of cavalry!" Nolan was saying. "Two brigades,

enough to have pursued and routed the whole pack of 'em! And
what do they do? Sit on their backsides, because Lucan's too
damned scared to order a bag of oats without a written order from
Raglan. Lord Lucan? Bah! Lord bloody Look-on, more like."

"Hm'm," says Billy, writing away, and glanced up. "Here,
Flash—you'll know. Were the Highlanders first into the redoubt? I say yes, but Lew says not.[15] Stevens ain't sure, and I
can't find Campbell anywhere. What d'ye say?"

I said I didn't know, and Nolan cried what the devil did it
matter, anyway, they were only infantry. Billy, seeing he would
get no peace from him, threw down his pen, yawned, and says to
me:

"You look well used up, Flash. Are you all right? What's the
matter, old fellow?"

I told him Willy was lost, and he said aye, that was a pity, a
nice lad, and I told him what Raglan had said to me, and at this
Nolan forgot his horses for a minute, and burst out:

"By God, isn't that of a piece? He's lost the best part of five
brigades, and he rounds on one unfortunate galloper because some
silly little ass who shouldn't have been here at all, at all, gets
himself blown up by the Russians! If he was so blasted concerned for him, what did he let him near the field for in the first
place? And if you was to wet-nurse him, why did he have you
galloping your arse off all day? The man's a fool! Aye, and a bad
general, what's worse—there's a Russian army clear away, thanks
to him and those idle Frogs, and we could have cut 'em to bits on
this very spot! I tell you, Billy, this fellow'll have to go."

"Come, Lew, he's won his fight," says Russell, stroking his
beard. "It's too bad he's set on you, Flash—but I'd lose no sleep
over it. Depend upon it, he's only voicing his own fears of what
may be said to *him*—but he's a decent old stick, and bears no
grudges. He'll have forgotten about it in a day or so."

"You think so?" says I, brightening.

"I should hope so!" cries Nolan. "Mother of God, if he hasn't
more to think about, he should have. Here's him and Lucan between 'em have let a great chance slip, but by the time Billy here
has finished tellin' the British public about how the matchless
Guards and stern Caledonians swept the Muscovite horde aside
on their bayonet points—"

"I like that," says Billy, winking at me. "I like it, Lew; go on, you're inspiring."

"Ah, bah, the old fool'll be thinking he's another Wellington," says Lew. "Aye, you can laugh, Russell—tell your readers what I've said about Lucan, though—I dare ye! That'd startle 'em!"

This talk cheered me up, for after all, it was what Russell thought—and wrote—that counted, and he never even mentioned Willy's death in his despatches to The Times. I heard that Raglan later referred to it, at a meeting with his generals, and Cardigan, the dirty swine, said privately that he wondered why the Prince's safety had been entrusted to a common galloper. But Lucan took the other side, and said only a fool would blame me for the death of another staff officer, and de Lacy Evans said Raglan should think himself lucky it was Willy he had lost and not me. Sound chaps, some of those generals.

And Nolan was right—Raglan and everyone else had enough to occupy them, after the Alma. The clever men were for driving on hard to Sevastopol, a bare twenty miles away, and with our cavalry in good fettle we could obviously have taken it. But the Frogs were too tired, or too sick, or too Froggy, if you ask me, and days were wasted, and the Ruskis managed to bolt the door in time.

What was worse, the carnage at Alma, and the cholera, had thinned the army horribly, there was no proper transport, and by the time we had lumbered on to Sevastopol peninsula we couldn't have robbed a hen-roost. But the siege had to be laid, and Raglan, looking wearier all the time, was thrashing himself to be cheerful and enthusiastic, with his army wasting, and winter coming, and the Frogs groaning at him. Oh, he was brave and determined and ready to take on all the odds—the worst kind of general imaginable. Give me a clever coward every time (which, of course, is why I'm such a dam' fine general myself).

So the siege was laid, the French and ourselves sitting down on the muddy, rain-sodden gullied plateau before Sevastopol, the dismalest place on earth, with no proper quarters but a few poor huts and tents, and everything to be carted up from Balaclava on the coast eight miles away. Soon the camp, and the road to it, was a stinking quagmire; everyone looked and felt filthy, the rations were poor, the work of preparing the siege was cruel hard (for the men, anyway), and all the bounce there had been in the army after Alma evaporated in the dank, feverish rain by day and the biting cold by night. Soon half of us were lousy, and the other half had fever or dysentery or cholera or all three— as some wag said, who'd holiday at Brighton if he could come to sunny Sevastopol instead?

I didn't take any part in the siege operations myself, not because I was out of favour with Raglan, but for the excellent reason that like so many of the army I spent several weeks on the flat of my back with what was thought at first to be cholera, but was in fact a foul case of dysentery and wind, brought on by my own hoggish excesses. On the march south after the Alma I had been galloping a message from Airey to our advance guard, and had come on a bunch of our cavalry who had bushwacked a Russian baggage train and were busily looting it.[10] Like a good officer, I joined in, and bagged as much champagne as I could carry, and a couple of fur cloaks as well. The cloaks were splendid, but the champagne must have carried the germ of the Siberian pox or something, for within a day I was blown up like a sheep on weeds, and spewing and skittering damnably. They sent me down to a seedy little house in Balaclava, not far from where Billy Russell was established, and there I lay sweating and rumbling, and wishing I were dead. Part of it I don't remember, so I suppose I must have been delirious, but my orderly looked after me well, and since I still had all the late Willy's gear and provisions—not that I ate much, until the last week—I did tolerably well. Better at least than any other sick man in the army; they were being carted down to Balaclava in droves, rotten with cholera and fever, lying in the streets as often as not.

Lew Nolan came down to see me when I was mending, and gave me all the gossip—about how my old friend Fan Duberly was on hand, living on a ship in the bay, and how Cardigan's yacht had arrived, and his noble lordship, pleading a weak chest, had deserted his Light Brigade for the comforts of life aboard, where he slept soft and stuffed his guts with the best. There were rumours, too, Lew told me, of Russian troops moving up in huge strength from the east, and he thought that if Raglan didn't look alive, he'd find himself bottled up in the Sevastopol peninsula. But most of Lew's talk was a great harangue against Lucan and

Cardigan; to him, they were the clowns who had mishandled our cavalry so damnably and were preventing it earning the laurels which Lew thought it deserved. He was a dead bore on the subject, but I'll not say he was wrong—we were both to find out all about that shortly.

For now, although I couldn't guess it, as I lay pampering myself with a little preserved jellied chicken and Rhine wine—of which Willy's store-chest yielded a fine abundance—that terrible day was approaching, that awful thunderclap of a day when the world turned upside down in a welter of powder-smoke and cannon-shot and steel, which no one who lived through it will ever forget. Myself least of all. I never thought that anything could make Alma or the Kabul retreat seem like a charabanc picnic, but *that* day did, and I was through it, dawn to dusk, as no other man was. It was sheer bad luck that it was the very day I returned to duty. Damn that Russian champagne; if it had kept me in bed just one day longer, what I'd have been spared. Mind you, we'd have lost India, for what that's worth.

I had been up a day or two, riding a little up to the Balaclava Plain, and wondering if I was fit enough to look up Fan Duberly, and take up again the attempted seduction which had been so maddeningly frustrated in Wiltshire six years before. She'd ripened nicely, by what Lew said, and I hadn't bestrode anything but a saddle since I'd left England—even the Turks didn't fancy the Crim Tartar women, and anyway, I'd been ill. But I'd convalesced as long as I dared, and old Colin Campbell, who commanded in Balaclava, had dropped me a sour hint that I ought to be back with Raglan in the main camp up on the plateau. So on the evening of October 24 I got my orderly to assemble my gear, left Willy's provisions with Russell, and loafed up to headquarters.

Whether I'd exerted myself too quickly, or it was the sound of the Russian bands in Sevastopol, playing their hellish doleful music, that kept me awake, I was taken damned ill in the night. My bowels were in a fearful state, I was blown out like a boiler, and I was unwise enough to treat myself with brandy, on the principle that if your guts are bad they won't feel any worse for your being foxed. They do, though, and when my orderly suddenly tumbled me out before dawn, I felt as though I were about to give birth. I told him to go to the devil, but he insisted that Raglan wanted me, p.d.q., so I huddled into my clothes in the cold, shivering and rumbling, and went to see what was up.

They were in a great sweat at Raglan's post; word had come from Lucan's cavalry that our advanced posts were signalling enemy in sight to the eastward, and gallopers were being sent off in all directions, with Raglan dictating messages over his shoulder while he and Airey pored over their maps.

"My dear Flashman," says Raglan, when his eye lit on me, "why, you look positively unwell. I think you would be better in your berth." He was all benevolent concern this morning—which was like him, of course. "Don't you think he looks ill, Airey?" Airey agreed that I did, but muttered something about needing every staff rider we could muster, so Raglan tut-tutted and said he much regretted it, but he had a message for Campbell at Balaclava, and it would be a great kindness if I would bear it. (He really did talk like that, most of the time; consideration fairly oozed out of him.) I wondered if I should plead my belly, so to speak, but finding him in such a good mood, with the Willy business apparently forgotten, I gave him my brave, suffering smile, and pocketed his message, fool that I was.

I felt damned shaky as I hauled myself into the saddle, and resolved to take my time over the broken country that lay between headquarters and Balaclava. Indeed, I had to stop several times, and try to vomit, but it was no go, and I cantered on over the filthy road with its litter of old stretchers and broken equipment, until I came out on to the open ground some time after sunrise.

After the downpour of the night before, it was dawning into a beautiful clear morning, the kind of day when, if your innards aren't heaving and squeaking, you feel like a fine gallop with the wind in your face. Before me the Balaclava Plain rolled away like a great grey-green blanket, and as I halted to have another unsuccessful retch, the scene that met my eyes was like a galloping field day. On the left of the plain, where it sloped up to the long line of the Causeway Heights, our cavalry were deployed in full strength, more than a thousand horsemen, like so many brilliant little puppets in the sunny distance, trotting in their squadrons, wheeling and reforming. About a mile away, nearest to me, I

could easily distinguish the Light Brigade—the pink trousers of
the Cherrypickers, the scarlet of Light Dragoons, and the blue
tunics and twinkling lance-points of the 17th. The trumpets were
tootling on the breeze, the words of command drifted across to
me as clear as a bell, and even beyond the Lights I could see,
closer in under the Causeway, and retiring slowly in my direction,
the squadrons of the Heavy Brigade—the grey horses with their
scarlet riders, the dark green of the Skins, and the hundreds of
tiny glittering slivers of the sabres. It was for all the world like
a green nursery carpet, with tiny toy soldiers deployed upon it,
and as pretty as these pictures of reviews and parades that you see
in the galleries.

Until you looked beyond, to where Causeway Heights faded
into the haze of the eastern dawn, and you could see why our
cavalry were retiring. The far slopes were black with scurrying
ant-like figures—Russian infantry pouring up to the gun redoubts which we had established along the three miles of the
Causeway; the thunder of cannon rolled continuously across the
plain, the flashes of the Russian guns stabbing away at the redoubts, and the sparkle of their muskets was all along the far end
of the Causeway. They were swarming over the gun emplacements, engulfing our Turkish gunners, and their artillery was
pounding away towards our retreating cavalry, pushing it along
under the shadow of the Heights.

I took all this in, and looked off across the plain to my right,
where it sloped up into a crest protecting the Balaclava road.
Along the crest there was a long line of scarlet figures, with dark
green blobs where their legs should be—Campbell's Highlanders,
at a safe distance, thank God, from the Russian guns, which
were now ranging nicely on the Heavy Brigade under the Heights.
I could see the shot plumping just short of the horses, and hear
the urgent bark of commands: a troop of the Skins scattered as a
great column of earth leaped up among them, and then they reformed, trotting back under the lee of the Causeway.

Well, there was a mile of empty, unscathed plain between me
and the Highlanders, so I galloped down towards them, keeping a
wary eye on the distant artillery skirmish to my left. But before I'd
got halfway to the crest I came on their outlying picket break-
fasting round a fire in a little hollow, and who should I see but

little Fanny Duberly, presiding over a frying-pan with half a dozen grinning Highlanders round her. She squealed at the sight of me, waving and shoving her pan aside; I swung down out of my saddle, bad belly and all, and would have embraced her, but she caught my hands at arms' length. And then it was Harry and Fanny, and where have you sprung from, and all that nonsense and chatter, while she laughed and I beamed at her. She had grown prettier, I think, with her fair hair and blue eyes, and looking damned fetching in her neat riding habit. I longed to give her tits a squeeze, but couldn't, with all those leering Highlanders nudging each other.

She had ridden up, she said, with Henry, her husband, who was in attendance on Lord Raglan, although I hadn't seen him.

"Will there be a great battle to-day, Harry?" says she. "I am so glad Henry will be safely out of it, if there is. See yonder" —and she pointed across the plain towards the Heights— "where the Russians are coming. Is it not exciting? Why do the cavalry not charge them, Harry? Are you going to join them? Oh, I hope you will take care! Have you had any breakfast? My dear, you look so tired. Come and sit down, and share some of our haggis!"

If anything could have made me sick, it would have been that, but I explained that I hadn't time to tattle, but must find Campbell. I promised to see her again, as soon as the present business was by, and advised her to clear off down to Balaclava as fast as she could go—it was astonishing, really, to see her picnicking there, as fresh as a May morning, and not much more than a mile away the Russian forces pounding away round the redoubts, and doubtless ready to sweep right ahead over the plain when they had regrouped.

The sergeant of Highlanders said Campbell was somewhere off with the Heavy Brigade, which was bad news, since it meant I must approach the firing, but there was nothing for it, so I galloped off north again, through the extended deployment of the Lights, who were now sitting at rest, watching the Heavies reforming. George Paget hailed me; he was sitting with one ankle cocked up on his saddle, puffing his cheroot, as usual.

"Have you come from Raglan?" cries he. "Where the hell are the infantry, do you know? We shall be sadly mauled at this rate, unless he moves soon. Look at the Heavies yonder; why don't Lucan shift 'em back faster, out of harm's way?" And indeed they were retiring slowly, it seemed to me, right under the shadow of the Heights, with the Russian fire still kicking up the clods round them as they came. I ventured forward a little way: I could see Lucan, and his staff, but no sign of Campbell, so I asked Morris, of the 17th, and he said Campbell had gone back across the plain, towards Balaclava, a few minutes since.

Well, that was better, since it would take me down to the Highlanders' position, away from where the firing was. And yet, it suddenly seemed very secure in my present situation, with the blue tunics and lances of the 17th all round me, and the familiar stench of horse-flesh and leather, and the bits jingling and the fellows patting their horses' necks and muttering to steady them against the rumble of the guns; there were troop horse artillery close by, banging back at the Russians, but it was still rather like a field day, with the plain all unmarked, and the uniforms bright and gay in the sunlight. I didn't want to leave 'em—but there were the Highlanders drawn up near the crest across the plain southward: I must just deliver my message as quickly as might be, and then be off back to head-quarters.

So I turned my back to the Heights, and set off again through the ranks of the 17th and the Cherrypickers, and was halfway down the plain to the Highlanders on the crest when here came a little knot of riders moving up towards the cavalry. And who should it be but my bold Lord Cardigan, with Squire Brough and his other toadies, all in great spirits after a fine comfortable boozy night on his yacht, no doubt.

I hadn't seen the man face to face since that night in Elspeth's bedroom, and my bile rose up even at the thought of the bastard, so I cut him dead. When Brough hailed me, and asked what was the news I reined up, not even looking in Cardigan's direction, and told Brough the Ruskis were over-running the far end of the Heights, and our horse were falling back.

"Ya-as," says Cardigan to his toadies, "it is the usual foolish-ness. There are the Wussians, so our cavalry move in the other diwection. Haw-haw. You, there, Fwashman, what does Word Waglan pwopose to do?"

I continued to ignore him. "Well, Squire," says I to Brough, "I must be off; can't stand gossiping with yachtsmen, you know," and I wheeled away, leaving them gaping, and an indignant "Haw-haw" sounding behind me.

But I hadn't time to feel too satisfied, for in that moment there was a new thunderous cannonade from the Russians, much closer now; the whistle of shot sounded overhead, there was a great babble of shouting and orders from the cavalry behind me, the calls of the Lights and Heavies sounded, and the whole mass of our horse began to move off westward, retiring again. The cannonading grew, as the Russians turned their guns southward, I saw columns of earth ploughed up to the east of the Highlanders' position, and with my heart in my mouth I buried my head in the horse's mane and fairly flew across the turf. The shot was still falling short, thank God, but as I reached the crest a ball came skipping and rolling almost up to my horse's hooves, and lay there, black and smoking, as I tore up to the Highlanders' flank.

"Where is Sir Colin?" cries I, dismounting, and they pointed to where he was pacing down between the ranks in my direction. I went forward, and delivered my message.

"Oot o' date," says he, when he had read it. "Ye don't look weel, Flashman. Bide a minute. I've a note here for Lord Raglan." And he turned to one of his officers, but at that moment the shouting across the plain redoubled, there was the thunderous plumping of shot falling just beyond the Highland position, and Campbell paused to look across the plain towards the Causeway Heights.

"Aye," says he, "there it is."

I looked towards the Heights, and my heart came up into my throat.

Our cavalry was now away to the left, at the Sevastopol end of the plain, but on the Heights to the right, near the captured redoubts, the whole ridge seemed to have come alive. Even as we watched, the movement resolved itself into a great mass of cavalry—Russian cavalry, wheeling silently down the side of the Heights in our direction. They've told me since that there were only four squadrons, but they looked more like four brigades, blue uniforms and grey, with their sabres out, preparing to descend the long slope from the Heights that ran down towards our position.

It was plain as a pikestaff what they were after, and if I could have sprouted wings in that moment I'd have been fluttering towards the sea like a damned gull. Directly behind us the road to Balaclava lay open; our own cavalry were out of the hunt, too far off to the left; there was nothing between that horde of Russians and the Balaclava base—the supply line of the whole British army —but Campbell's few hundred Highlanders, a rabble of Turks on our flank, and Flashy, full of wind and horror.

Campbell stared for a moment, that granite face of his set; then he pulled at his dreary moustache and roared an order. The ranks opened and moved and closed again, and now across our ridge there was a double line of Highlanders, perhaps a furlong from end to end, kneeling down a yard or so on the seaward side of the crest. Campbell looked along them from our stance at the right-hand extremity of the line, bidding the officers dress them. While they were doing it, there was a tremendous caterwauling from the distant flank, and there were the Turks, all order gone, breaking away from their positions in the face of the impending Russian charge, flinging down their arms and tearing headlong for the sea road behind us.

"Dross," says Campbell.

I was watching the Turks, and suddenly, to their rear, riding towards us, and then checking and wheeling away southward, I recognized the fair hair and riding fig of Fanny Duberly. She was flying along as she passed our far flank, going like a little jockey—she could ride, that girl.

"Damn all society women," says Campbell. And it occurred to me, even through the misery of my stomach and my rising fear, that Balaclava Plain that morning was more like the Row—Fanny Duberly out riding, and Cardigan ambling about haw-hawing.

I looked towards the Russians; they were rumbling down the slope now, a bare half-mile away; Campbell shouted again, and the long scarlet double rank moved foward a few paces, with a great swishing of their kilts and clatter of gear, and halted on the crest, the front rank kneeling and the second standing behind them. Campbell glanced across at the advancing mass of the Russian horse, measuring the distance.

"Ninety-third!" he shouted. "There is no retreat from here! Ye must stand!"

He had no need to tell *me*; I couldn't have moved if I had wanted to. I could only gape at that wall of horsemen, galloping now, and then back at the two frail, scarlet lines that in a moment must be swept away into bloody rabble with the hooves smashing down on them and the sabres swinging; it was the finish, I knew, and nothing to do but wait trembling for it to happen. I found myself staring at the nearest kneeling Highlander, a huge, swarthy fellow with his teeth bared under a black moustache; I remember noticing the hair matting the back of his right hand as it gripped his musket. Beyond him there was a boy, gazing at the advancing squadrons with his mouth open; his lip was trembling.

"Haud yer fire until I give the wurr-rd!" says Campbell, and then quite deliberately he stepped a little out before the front rank and drew his broadsword, laying the great glittering blade across his chest. Christ, I thought, that's a futile thing to do—the ground was trembling under our feet now, and the great quadruple rank of horsemen was a bare two hundred yards away, sweeping down at the charge, sabres gleaming, yelling and shouting as they bore down on us, a sea of flaring horse heads and bearded faces above them.

"Present!" shouts Campbell, and moved past me in behind the front rank. He stopped behind the boy with the trembling lip. "Ye never saw the like o' that comin' doon the Gallowgate," says he. "Steady now, Ninety-third! Wait for my command!"

They were a hundred yards away now, that thundering tide of men and horses, the hooves crashing like artillery on the turf. The double bank of muskets with their fixed bayonets covered them; the locks were back, the fingers hanging on the triggers; Campbell was smiling sourly beneath his moustache, the madman; he glanced to his left along the silent lines—give the word, damn you, you damned old fool, I wanted to shout, for they were a bare fifty yards off, in a split second they would be into us, he had left it too late—

"Fire!" he bellowed, and like one huge bark of thunder the front-rank volley crashed out, the smoke billowed back in our faces, and beyond it the foremost horsemen seemed to surge up in a great wave; there was a split-second of screaming confusion, with beasts plunging and rearing, a hideous chorus of yells from the riders, and the great line crashed down on the turf before us, the men behind careering into the fallen horses and riders, trying to jump them or pull clear, trampling them, hurtling over them in a smashing tangle of limbs and bodies.

"Fire!" roars Campbell above the din, and the pieces of the standing rank crashed together into the press; it seemed to shudder at the impact, and behind it the Russian ranks wheeled and stumbled in confusion, men screaming and going down, horses lashing out blindly, sabres gleaming and flying. As the smoke cleared there was a great tangled bloody bank of stricken men and beasts wallowing within a few yards of the kneeling Highlanders—they'll tell you, some of our historians, that Campbell fired before they reached close range, but here's one who can testify that one Russian, with a fur-crested helmet and pale blue tunic rolled right to within a foot of us; the swarthy Highlander nearest me didn't have to advance a step to plunge his bayonet into the Russian's body.

A great yell went up from the Ninety-third; the front rank seemed to leap forward, but Campbell was before them, bawling them back. "Damn your eagerness!" cries he. "Stand fast! Reload!"

They dropped back, snarling like dogs, and Campbell turned and calmly surveyed the wreckage of the Russian ranks. There were beasts thrashing about everywhere and men crawling blindly away, the din of screaming and groaning was fearful, and a great reek that you could literally see was steaming up from them. Behind, the greater part of the Russian squadrons was turning, reforming, and for a moment I thought they were coming again, but they moved off back towards the Heights, closing their ranks as they went.

"Good," says Campbell, and his sword grated back into its scabbard.

"Ye niver saw a sight like that goin' back up the Gallowgate, Sir Colin," pipes a voice from somewhere, and they began to laugh and cheer, and yell their heathenish slogans, shaking their muskets, and Campbell grinned and pulled at his moustache again. He saw me—I hadn't stirred a yard since the charge began, I'd been so petrified—and walked across.

"I'll add a line to my message for Lord Raglan," says he, and looks at me. "Ye've mair colour in yer cheeks now, Flashman. Field exercises wi' the Ninety-third must agree wi' ye."

And so, with those kilted devils still holding their ranks, and the Russians dying and moaning before them, I waited while he dictated his message to one of his aides. Now that the terror was past, my belly was aching horribly and I felt thoroughly ill again, but not so ill that I wasn't able to note (and admire) the carriage of the retreating Russian cavalry. In charging, I had noticed how they had opened their ranks at the canter and then closed them at the gallop, which isn't easy; now they were doing the same thing as they retired towards the heights, and I thought, these fellows ain't so slovenly as we thought. I remember thinking they'd perhaps startle Jim the Bear and his Light Brigade—but most of all, from that moment of aftermath, I can still see vividly that tangled pile of Russian dead, and sprawled out before them the body of an officer, a big grey-bearded man with the front of his blue tunic soaked in blood, lying on his back with one knee bent up, and his horse standing above him, nuzzling at the dead face.

Campbell put a folded paper into my hand and stood, shading his eyes with a hand under his bonnet-rim, as he watched the Russian horse canter up the Causeway Heights.

"Poor management," says he. "They'll no' come this way again. In the meantime, I've said to Lord Raglan that in my opeenion the main Russian advance will now be directed north of the Causeway, and will doubtless be wi' artillery and horse against our cavalry. What it is doin' sittin' yonder, I cannae—but, hollo! Is that Scarlett movin'? Hand me that glass, Cattenach. See yonder."

The Russian cavalry were now topping the Causeway ridge, vanishing from our view, but on the plain farther left, perhaps half a mile from us, there was movement in the ranks of our Heavy Brigade: a sudden uniform twinkle of metal as the squadrons nearest to us turned.

"They're coming this way," says someone, and Campbell snapped his glass shut.

"Behind the fair," says he, glumly—I never saw him impatient yet. Where other men would get angry and swear, Campbell simply got more melancholy. "Flashman—on your way to

Lord Raglan, I'll be obliged if you'll present my compliments to General Scarlett, or Lord Lucan, whichever comes first in your road, and tell them that in my opeenion they'll do well to hold the ground they have, and prepare for acteevity on the northern flank. Away wi' ye, sir."

I needed no urging. The farther I could get from that plain, the better I'd be suited, for I was certain Campbell was right. Having captured the eastern end of the Causeway Heights, and run their cavalry over the central ridge facing us, it was beyond doubt that the Russians would be moving up the valley north of the Heights, advancing on the plateau position which we occupied before Sevastopol. God knew what Raglan proposed to do about that, but in the meantime he was holding our cavalry on the southern plain—to no good purpose. They hadn't budged an inch to take the retreating Russian cavalry in flank, as they might have done, and now, after the need for their support had passed, the Heavies were moving down slowly towards Campbell's position.

I rode through their ranks—Dragoon Guards and a few Skins, riding in open order, eyeing me curiously as I galloped through —"That's Flashman, ain't it?" cries someone, but I didn't pause. Ahead of me I could see the little knot of coloured figures, red and blue, of Scarlett and his staff; as I reined up, they were cheering and laughing, and old Scarlett waved his hat to me.

"Ho-ho, Flashman!" cries he. "Were you down there with the Sawnies? Capital work, what? That's a bloody nose for Ivan, I say. Ain't it, though, Elliot? Dam' fine, dam' fine! And where are you off to, Flashman, my son?"

"Message to Lord Raglan, sir," says I. "But Sir Colin Campbell also presents his compliments, and advises that you should move no nearer to Balaclava at present."

"Does he, though? Beatson, halt the Dragoons, will you? Now then, why not? Lord Lucan has ordered us to support the Turks, you know, in case of Russian movement towards Balaclava."

"Sir Colin expects no further movement there, sir. He bids you look to your northern flank," and I pointed to the Causeway Heights, only a few hundred yards away. "Anyway, sir, there are no longer any Turks to support. Most of 'em are probably on the beach by now."

"That's true, bigod!" Scarlett exploded in laughter. He was a fat, cheery old Falstaff, mopping his bald head with a hideously-coloured scarf, and then dabbing the sweat from his red cheeks. "What d'ye think, Elliot? No point in goin' down to Campbell that I can see; he and his red-shanks don't need support, that's certain."

"True, sir. But there is no sign of Russian movement to our north, as yet."

"No," said Scarlett, "that's so. But I trust Campbell's judgment, ye know; clever fella. If he smells Ruskis to our north, beyond the Heights, well, I dunno. I trust an old hound any day, what?" He sniffed and mopped himself again, tugging at his puffy white whiskers. "Tell you what, Elliot, I think we'll just hold on here, and see what breaks cover, hey? What d'ye say to that, Beatson? Flashman? No harm in waitin', is there?"

He could dig trenches for all I cared; I was already measuring the remaining distance across the plain westward; once in the gullies I'd be out of harm's way, and could pick my way to Raglan's head-quarters at my leisure. North of us, the ground sloping up to the heights through an old vineyard was empty; so was the crest beyond, but the thump of cannon from behind it seemed to be growing closer to my nervous imagination. There was an incessant whine and thump of shot; Beatson was scanning the ridge anxiously through his glass.

"Campbell's right, sir," says he. "They must be up there in the north valley in strength."

"How d'ye know?" says Scarlett, goggling.

"The firing, sir. Listen to it—that's not just cannon. There—you hear? That's Whistling Dick! If they have mortars with 'em, they're not skirmishing!"

"By God!" says Scarlett. "Well I'm damned! I can't tell one from another, but if you say so, Beatson, I—"

"Look yonder!" It was one of his young gallopers, up in his stirrups with excitement, pointing. "The ridge, sir! Look at 'em come!"

We looked, and for the second time that day I forgot my gurgling aching belly in a freezing wave of fear. Slowly topping the crest, in a great wave of colour and dancing steel, was a long rank of Russian horsemen, and behind them another, and then another, moving at a walk. They came over the ridge as if they were in review, extended line after extended line, and then slowly closed up, halting on the near slope of the ridge, looking down at us. God knows how far their line ran from flank to flank, but there were thousands of them, hanging over us like an ocean roller frozen in the act of breaking, a huge body of blue and silver hussars on the left, and to the right the grey and white of their dragoons.

"By God!" cries Scarlett. "By God! Those are Russians—damn 'em!"

"Left about!" Beatson was yelling. "Greys, stand fast! Cunningham, close 'em up! Inniskillings—close order! Connor, Flynn, keep 'em there! Curzon, get those squadrons of the Fifth up here, lively now!"

Scarlett was sitting gaping at the ridge, damning his eyes and the Russians alternately until Beatson jerked at his sleeve.

"Sir! We must prepare to receive them! When they take the brake off they'll roll down—"

"Receive 'em?" says Scarlett, coming back to earth. "What's that, Beatson? Damned if I do!" He reared up in his stirrups, glaring along to the left, where the Greys' advanced squadrons were being dressed to face the Russian force. "What? What? Connor, what are you about there?" He was gesticulating to the right now, waving his hat. "Keep your damned Irishmen steady there! Wild devils, those! Where's Curzon, hey?"

"Sir, they have the slope of us!" Beatson was gripping Scarlett by the sleeve, rattling urgently in his ear. "They outflank us, too—I reckon that line's three times the length of ours, and when they charge they can sweep round and take us flank, both sides, and front! They'll swallow us, sir, if we break— we must try to hold fast!"

"Hold fast nothin'!" says Scarlett, grinning all over his great red cheeks. "I didn't come all this way to have some dam' Cossack open the ball! Look at 'em, there, the saucy bastards! What? What? Well, they're there, and we're here, and I'm goin' to chase the scoundrels all the way to Moscow! What, Elliot? Here, you, Flashman, come to my side, sir!"

You may gather my emotions at hearing this; I won't attempt to describe them. I stared at this purpling old lunatic in bewilderment, and tried to say something about my message to Raglan, but the impetuous buffoon grabbed at my bridle and hauled me along as he took post in front of his squadrons.

"You shall tell Lord Raglan presently that I have engaged a force of enemy cavalry on my front an' dispersed 'em!" bawls he. "Beatson, Elliot, see those lines dressed! Where are the Royals, hey? Steady, there, Greys! Steady now! Inniskillings, look to that dressing, Flynn! Keep close to me, Flashman, d'ye hear? Like enough I'll have somethin' to add to his lordship. Where the devil's Curzon, then? Damn the boy, if it's not women it's somethin' else! Trumpeter, where are you? Come to my left side! Got your tootler, have you? Capital, splendid!"

It was unbelievable, this roaring fat old man, waving his hat like some buffer at a cricket match, while Beatson tried to shout sense into him.

"You cannot move from here, sir! It is all uphill! We must hold our ground—there's no other hope!" He pointed up hill frantically. "Look, they're moving sir! We must hold fast!"

And sure enough, up on the heights a quarter of a mile away, the great Russian line was beginning to advance, shoulder to shoulder, blue and silver and grey, with their sabres at the present; it was a sight to send you squealing for cover, but there I was, trapped at this idiot's elbow, with the squadrons of the Greys hemming us in behind.

"You cannot advance, sir!" shouts Beatson again.

"Can't I, by God!" roars Scarlett, throwing away his hat. "You just watch me!" He lugged out his sabre and waved it. "Ready, Greys? Ready, old Skins? Remember Waterloo, you fellas, what? Trumpeter—sound the . . . the thing, whatever it is! Oh, the devil! Come on, Flashman! Tally-ho!"

And he dug in his heels, gave one final yell of "Come on, you fellas!" and set his horse at the hill like a madman. There was a huge, crashing shout from behind, the squadrons leaped forward, my horse reared, and I found myself galloping along, almost up Scarlett's dock, with Beatson at my elbow shouting, "Oh, what the blazes—charge! Trumpeter, charge! charge! charge!"

They were all stark, raving mad, of course. When I think of them—and me, God help me—tearing up that hill, and that overwhelming force lurching down towards us, gathering speed with every step, I realize that there's no end to human folly, or human luck, either. It was ridiculous, it was nonsense, that old red-faced pantaloon, who'd never fired a shot or swung a sabre in action before, and was fit for nothing but whipping off hounds, urging his charger up that hill, with the whole Heavy Brigade at his heels, and poor old suffering Flashy jammed in between, with nothing to do but hope to God that by the time the two irresistible forces met, I'd be somewhere back in the mob behind.

And the brutes were enjoying it, too! Those crazy Ulstermen were whooping like Apaches, and the Greys, as they thundered forward, began to make that hideous droning noise deep in their throats; I let them come up on my flanks, their front rank hemming me in with glaring faces and glittering blades on either side; Scarlett was yards ahead, brandishing his sabre and shouting, the Russian mass was at the gallop, sweeping towards us like a great blue wave, and then in an instant we were surging into them, men yelling, horses screaming, steel clashing all round, and I was clinging like a limpet to my horse's right side, Cheyenne fashion, left hand in the mane and right clutching my Adams revolver. I wasn't breaking surface in that melee if I could help it. There were Greys all round me, yelling and cursing, slashing with their sabres at the hairy blue coats—"Give 'em the point! The point!" yelled a voice, and I saw a Greys trooper dashing the hilt of his sword into a bearded face and then driving his point into the falling man's body. I let fly at a Russian in the press, and the shot took him in the neck, I think; then I was dashed aside and swept away in the whirl of fighting, keeping my head ducked low, squeezing my trigger whenever I saw a blue or grey tunic, and praying feverishly that no chance slash would sweep me from the saddle.

I suppose it lasted five or ten minutes; I don't know. It seemed only a few seconds, and then the whole mass was struggling up the hill, myself roaring and blaspheming with the best of them; my revolver was empty, my hat was gone, so I dragged out my sabre, bawling with pretended fury, and seeing nothing but grey horses, gathered that I was safe.

"Come on!" I roared. "Come on! Into the bastards! Cut 'em to bits!" I made my horse rear and waved my sword, and as a stricken Russian came blundering through the mob I lunged at him, full force, missed, and finished up skewering a fallen horse.

The wrench nearly took me out of my saddle, but I wasn't letting that sabre go, not for anything, and as I tugged it free there was a tremendous cheering set up—"Huzza! huzza! huzza"—and suddenly there were no Russians among us, Scarlett, twenty yards away, was standing in his stirrups waving a blood-stained sabre and yelling his head off, the Greys were shaking their hats and their fists, and the rout of that great mass of enemy cavalry was trailing away towards the crest.

"They're beat!" cries Scarlett. "They're beat! Well done, you fellas! What, Beatson? Hey, Elliot? Can't charge uphill, hey? Damn 'em, damn 'em, we did it! Hurrah!"

Now it is a solemn fact, but I'll swear I didn't see above a dozen corpses on the ground around me as the Greys reordered their squadrons, and the Skins closed in on the right, with the Royals coming up behind. I still don't understand it—why the Russians, with the hill behind 'em, didn't sweep us all away, with great slaughter. Or why, breaking as they did, they weren't cut to pieces by our sabres. Except that I remember one or two of the Greys complaining that they hadn't been able to make their cuts tell; they just bounced off the Russian tunics. Anyway, the Ruskis broke, thank heaven, and away beneath us, to our left, the Light Brigade were setting up a tremendous cheer, and it was echoing along the ridge to our left, and on the greater heights beyond.

"Well done!" shouts Scarlett. "Well done, you Greys! Well done, Flashman, you are a gallant fellow! What? Hey? That'll show that damned Nicholas, what? Now then, Flashman, off with you to Lord Raglan—tell him we've . . . well, set about these chaps and driven 'em off, you see, and that I shall hold my position, what, until further orders. You understand? Capital!" He shook with laughter, and hauled out his coloured scarf for another mop at his streaming face. "Tell ye what, Flashman; I don't know much about fightin', but it strikes me that this Russian business is like huntin' in Ireland—confused and primitive, what, but damned interestin'!"

I reported his words to Raglan, exactly as he spoke them, and the whole staff laughed with delight, the idiots. Of course, they were safe enough, snug on the top of the Sapoune Ridge, which lay at the western end of Causeway Heights, and I promise you

I had taken my time getting there. I'd ridden like hell on my spent horse from the Causeway, across the north-west corner of the plain, when Scarlett dismissed me, but once into the safety of the gullies, with the noise of Russian gunfire safely in the distance, I had dismounted to get my breath, quiet my trembling heart-strings, and try to ease my wind-gripped bowels, again without success. I was a pretty bedraggled figure, I suppose, by the time I came to the top of Sapoune, but at least I had a bloody sabre, artlessly displayed—Lew Nolan's eyes narrowed and he swore enviously at the sight: he wasn't to know it had come from a dead Russian horse.

Raglan was beaming, as well he might be, and demanded details of the action I had seen. So I gave 'em, fairly offhand, saying I thought the Highlanders had behaved pretty well—"Yes, and if we had just followed up with cavalry we might have regained the whole Causeway by now!" pipes Nolan, at which Airey told him to be silent, and Raglan looked fairly stuffy. As for the Heavies—well, they had seen all that, but I said it had been warm work, and Ivan had got his bellyful, from what I could see.

"Gad, Flashy, you have all the luck!" cries Lew, slapping his thigh, and Raglan clapped me on the shoulder.

"Well done, Flashman," says he. "Two actions today, and you have been in the thick of both. I fear you have been neglecting your staff duties in your eagerness to be at the enemy, eh?" And he gave me his quizzical beam, the old fool. "Well, we shall say no more about that."

I looked confused, and went red, and muttered something about not being able to abide these damned Ruskis, and they all laughed again, and said that was old Flashy, and the young gallopers, the pink-cheeked lads, looked at me with awe. If it hadn't been for my aching belly, I'd have been ready to enjoy myself, now that the horror of the morning was past, and the cold sweat of reaction hadn't had a chance to set in. I'd come through again, I told myself—twice, no less, and with new laurels. For although we were too close to events just then to know what would be said later—well, how many chaps have you heard of who stood with the Thin Red Line *and* took part in the Charge of the Heavy Brigade? None, 'cos I'm the only one, damned unwilling and full of shakes, but still, I've dined out on it for years. That—and the other thing that was to follow.

But in the meantime, I was just thanking my stars for safety, and rubbing my inflamed guts. (Someone said later that Flashman was more anxious about his bowels than he was about the Russians, and had taken part in all the charges to try to ease his wind.) I sat there with the staff, gulping and massaging, happy to be out of the battle, and taking a quiet interest while Lord Raglan and his team of idiots continued to direct the fortunes of the day.

Now, of that morning at Balaclava I've told you what I remember, as faithfully as I can, and if it doesn't tally with what you read elsewhere, I can't help it. Maybe I'm wrong, or maybe the military historians are: you must make your own choice. For example, I've read since that there were Turks on both flanks of Campbell's Highlanders, whereas I remember 'em only on the left flank; again, my impression of the Heavy Brigade action is that it began and ended in a flash, but I gather it must have taken Scarlett some little time to turn and dress his squadrons. I don't remember that. It's certain that Lucan was on hand when the charge began, and I've been told he actually gave the word to advance—well, I never even saw him. So there you are; it just shows that no one can see everything.[17]

I mention this because, while my impressions of the early morning are fairly vague, and consist of a series of coloured and horrid pictures, I'm in no doubt about what took place in the late forenoon. That is etched forever; I can shut my eyes and see it all, and feel the griping pain ebbing and clawing at my guts—perhaps that sharpened my senses, who knows? Anyway, I have it all clear; not only what happened, but what caused it to happen. I know, better than anyone else who ever lived, why the Light Brigade was launched on its famous charge, because I was the man responsible, and it wasn't wholly an accident. That's not to say I'm to *blame*—if blame there is, it belongs to Raglan, the kind, honourable, vain old man. Not to Lucan, or to Cardigan, or to Nolan, or to Airey, or even to my humble self: we just played our little parts. But blame? I can't even hold it against Raglan, not now. Of course, your historians and critics and hypocrites are full of virtuous zeal to find out who was "at fault", and wag their heads and say "Ah, you see," and tell him what should have been done, from the safety of their studies and lecture-rooms—but I was there, you see, and while I could have wrung Raglan's neck, or blown him from the muzzle of a gun, at the time—well, it's all by now, and we either survived it or we didn't. Proving someone guilty won't bring the six hundred to life again—most of 'em would be dead by now anyway. And they wouldn't blame anyone. What did that trooper of the 17th say afterwards: "We're ready to go in again." Good luck to him, I say; once was enough for me —but, don't you understand, nobody else has the right to talk of blame, or blunders? Just us, the living and the dead. It was our indaba. Mind you, I could kick Raglan's arse for him, and my own.

I sat up there on the Sapoune crest, feeling bloody sick and tired, refusing the sandwiches that Billy Russell offered me, and listening to Lew Nolan's muttered tirade about the misconduct of the battle so far. I hadn't much patience with him—he hadn't been risking his neck along with Campbell and Scarlett, although he no doubt wished he had—but in my shaken state I wasn't ready to argue. Anyway, he was fulminating against Lucan and Cardigan and Raglan mostly, which was all right by me.

"If Cardigan had taken in the Lights, when the Heavies were breaking up the Ruskis, we'd have smashed 'em all by this," says he. "But he wouldn't budge, damn him—he's as bad as Lucan. Won't budge without orders, delivered in the proper form, with nice salutes, and 'Yes, m'lord' an' 'if your lordship pleases'. Christ—cavalry leaders! Cromwell'd turn in his grave, bad cess to him. And look at Raglan yonder—does he know what to do? He'd got two brigades o' the best horsemen in Europe, itchin' to use their sabres, an' in front of 'em a Russian army that's shakin' in its boots after the maulin' Campbell an' Scarlett have given 'em—but he sits there sendin' messages to the infantry! The infantry, bigod, that're still gettin' out of their beds somewhere. Jaysus, it makes me sick!"

He was in a fine taking, but I didn't mind him much. At the same time, looking down on the panorama beneath us, I could see there was something in what he said. I'm not Hannibal, but I've picked up a wrinkle or two in my time, about ground and move-ment, and it looked to me as though Raglan had it in his grasp to do the Russians some no-good, and maybe even hand them a splendid licking, if he felt like it. Not that I cared, you understand;

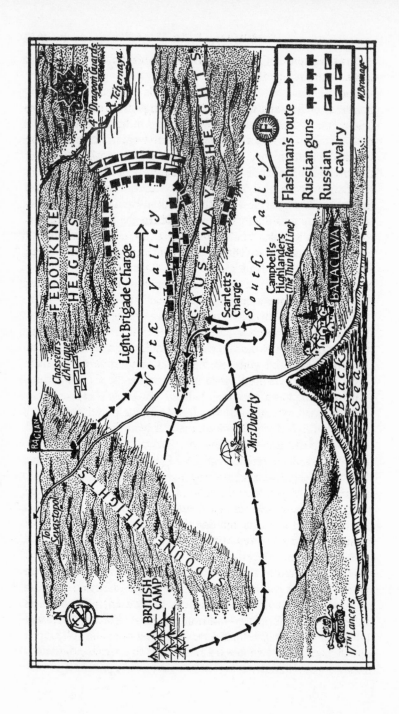

I'd had enough, and was all for a quiet life for everybody. But anyway, this is how the land lay.

The Sapoune, on which we stood, is a great bluff rising hundreds of feet above the plain. Looking east from it, you see below you a shallow valley, perhaps two miles long and half a mile broad; to the north, there is a little clump of heights on which the Russians had established guns to command that side of the valley. On the south the valley is bounded by the long spine of the Causeway Heights, running east from the Sapoune for two or three miles. The far end of the valley was fairly hazy, even with the strong sunlight, but you could see the Russians there as thick as fleas on a dog's back—guns, infantry, cavalry, everything except Tsar Nick himself, tiny puppets in the distance, just holding their ground. They had guns on the Causeway, too, pointing north; as I watched I saw the nearest team of them unlimbering just beside the spot where the Heavies' charge had ended.

So there it was, plain as a pool table—a fine empty valley with the main force of the Russians at the far end of it, and us at the near end, but with Ruskis on the heights to either side, guns and sharpshooters both—you could see the grey uniforms of their infantry moving among their cannon down on the Causeway, not a mile and a half away.

Directly beneath where I stood, at the near end of the valley, our cavalry had taken up station just north of the Causeway, the Heavies slightly nearer the Sapoune and to the right, the Lights just ahead of them and slightly left. They looked as though you could have lobbed a stone into the middle of them—I could easily make out Cardigan, threading his way behind the ranks of the 17th, and Lucan with his gallopers, and old Scarlett, with his bright scarf thrown over one shoulder of his coat—they were all sitting out there waiting, tiny figures in blue and scarlet and green, with here and there a plumed hat, and an occasional bandage: I noticed one trooper of the Skins binding a stocking on to the forefoot of his charger, the little dark-green figure crouched down at the horse's hooves. The distant pipe of voices drifted up from the plain, and from the far end of the Causeway a popping of musketry; for the rest it was all calm and still, and it was this tranquillity that was driving Lew to a frenzy, the bloodthirsty young imbecile.

Well, thinks I, there they all are, doing nothing and taking no harm; let 'em be, and let's go home. For it was plain to see the Ruskis were going to make no advance up the valley towards the Sapoune; they'd had their fill for the day, and were content to hold the far end of the valley and the heights either side. But Raglan and Airey were forever turning their glasses on the Causeway, at the Russian artillery and infantry moving among the redoubts they'd captured from the Turks; I gathered both our infantry and cavalry down in the plain should have been moving to push them out, but nothing was happening, and Raglan was getting the frets.

"Why does not Lord Lucan move?" I heard him say once, and again: "He has the order; what delays him now?" Knowing Look-on, I could guess he was huffing and puffing and laying the blame on someone else. Raglan kept sending gallopers down— Lew among them—to tell Lucan, and the infantry commanders, to get on with it, but they seemed maddeningly obtuse about his orders, and wanted to wait for our infantry to come up, and it was this delay that was fretting Raglan and sending Lew half-crazy.

"Why doesn't Raglan *make* 'em move, dammit?" says he, coming over to Billy Russell and me after reporting back to Raglan. "It's too bad! If he would give 'em one clear simple command, to push in an' sweep those fellows off the Causeway —oh, my God! An' he won't listen to me—I'm a young pup green behind the ears. The cavalry alone could do it in five minutes—it's about time Cardigan earned his general's pay, anyway!"

I approved heartily of that, myself. Every time I heard Cardigan's name mentioned, or saw his hateful boozy vulture face, I remembered that vile scene in Elspeth's bedroom, and felt my fury boiling up. Several times it had occurred to me on the campaign that it would be a capital thing if he could be induced into action where he might well be hit between the legs and so have his brains blown out, but he'd not looked like taking a scratch so far. And there seemed scant chance of it today; I heard Raglan snapping his glass shut with impatience, and saying to Airey: "I despair almost of moving our horse. It looks as though we shall have to rely on Cambridge alone—whenever his infantry come up! Oh, this is vexing! We shall accomplish nothing against the Causeway positions at this rate!"

And just at that moment someone sang out: "My lord! See

there—the guns are moving! The guns in the second redoubt—
the Cossacks are getting them out!"

Sure enough, there were Russian horsemen limbering up away
down the Causeway crest, tugging at a little toy cannon in the
captured Turkish emplacement. They had tackles on it, and were
obviously intent on carrying it off to the main Russian army.
Raglan stared at it through his glass, his face working.

"Airey!" cries he. "This is intolerable! What is Lucan thinking
of—why, these fellows will clear the guns away before our advance
begins!"

"He is waiting for Cambridge, I suppose, my lord," says Airey,
and Raglan swore, for once, and continued to gaze fretfully down
on the Causeway.

Lew was writhing with impatience in his saddle. "Oh, Christ!"
he moaned softly. "Send in Cardigan, man—never mind the
bloody infantry. Send in the Lights!"

Good idea, thinks I—let Jim the Bear skirmish into the redoubts,
and get a Cossack lance where it'll do most good. So you may say
it was out of pure malice towards Cardigan that I piped up—
taking care that my back was to Raglan, but talking loud enough
for him to hear:

"There goes our record—Wellington never lost a gun, you
know."

I've heard since, from a galloper who was at Raglan's side,
that it was those words, invoking the comparison with his God
Wellington, that stung him into action—that he started like a
man shot, that his face worked, and he jerked at his bridle convulsively. Maybe he'd have made up his mind without my help
—but I'll be honest and say that I doubt it. He'd have waited for
the infantry. As it was he went pale and then red, and snapped
out:

"Airey—another message to Lord Lucan! We can delay no
longer—he must move without the infantry. Tell him—ah, he is
to advance the cavalry rapidly to the front, to prevent the enemy
carrying off the guns—ah, to follow the enemy and prevent them.
Yes. Yes. He may take troop horse artillery, at his discretion.
There—that will do. You have it, Airey? Read it back, if you
please."

I see it so clearly still—Airey's head bent over the paper,

jabbing at the words with his pencil, as he read back (more or less in Raglan's words, certainly in the same sense), Nolan's face alight with joy beside me—"At last, at last, thank God!" he was muttering—and Raglan sitting, nodding carefully. Then he cried out: "Good. It is to be acted on at once—make that clear!"

"Ah, that's me darlin'!" whispers Lew, and nudged me. "Well done, Flashy, me boy—you've got him movin'!"

"Send it immediately," Raglan was telling Airey. "Oh, and notify Lord Lucan that there are French cavalry on his left. Surely that should suffice." And he opened his glass again, looking down at Causeway Heights. "Send the fastest galloper."

I had a moment's apprehension at that—having started the ball, I'd no wish to be involved—but Raglan added: "Where is Nolan?—yes, Nolan," and Lew, beside himself with excitement, wheeled his horse beside Airey, grabbed at the paper, tucked it in his gauntlet, smacked down his forage cap, threw Raglan the fastest of salutes, and would have been off like a shot, but Raglan stayed him, repeating that the message was of the utmost importance, that it was to be delivered with all haste to Lucan personally, and that it was vital to act at once, before the Ruskis could make off with our guns.[18] All unnecessary repetition of course, and Lew was in a fever, going pink with impatience.

"Away, then!" cries Raglan at last, and Lew was over the brow in a twinkling, with a flurry of dust—showy devil—and Raglan shouting after him: "At once, Nolan—tell Lord Lucan at once, you understand."

That's how they sent Nolan off—that and no more, on my oath. And so I come to the point with which I began this memoir, with Raglan having a second thought, and shouting to Airey to send after him, and Airey looking round, and myself retiring modestly, you remember, and Airey spotting me and gesturing me violently up beside him.

Well, you know what I thought, of the unreasoning premonition that I had, that this would be the ultimate terror of that memorable day in which I had, much against my will, already been charged at by, and charged against, overwhelming hordes of Russians. There was nothing, really, to be agitated about, up there on the heights—I was merely to be sent after Nolan, with some addition or correction. But I felt the finger of doom on me, I don't know why, as I scrambled aboard a fresh horse with Raglan and Airey clamouring at me.

"Flashman," says Raglan, "Nolan must make it clear to Lord Lucan—he is to behave defensively, and attempt nothing against his better judgment. Do you understand me?"

Well, I understood the words, but what the hell Lucan was expected to make of them, I couldn't see. Told to advance, to attack the enemy, and yet to act defensively. But it was nothing to me; I repeated the order, word for word, making sure Airey could hear me, and then went over the bluff after Lew.

It was as steep as hell's half acre, like a seaside sandcliff shot across by grassy ridges. At any other time I'd have picked my way down nice and leisurely, but with Raglan and the rest looking down, and in full view of our cavalry in the plain, I'd no choice but to go hell-for-leather. Besides, I wasn't going to let that cocky little pimp Nolan distance *me*—I may not be proud of much, but I fancied myself against any galloper in the army, and was determined to overtake him before he reached Lucan. So down I went, with the game little mare under me skipping like a mountain goat, sliding on her haunches, careering headlong, and myself clinging on with my knees aching and my hands on the mane, jolting and swaying wildly, and in the tail of my eye Lew's red cap jerking crazily on the escarpment below.

I *was* the better horseman. He wasn't twenty yards out on the level when I touched the bottom and went after him like a bolt, yelling to him to hold on. He heard me, and reined up, cursing, and demanding to know what was the matter. "On with you!" cries I, as I came alongside, and as we galloped I shouted my message.

He couldn't make it out, but had to pluck the note from his glove and squint at it while he rode. "What the hell does it mean in the first place?" cries he. "It says here, 'advance rapidly to the front'. Well, God love us, the guns ain't in front; they're in flank front if they're anywhere."

"Search me," I shouted. "But he says Look-on is to act defensively, and undertake nothing against his better judgment. So there!"

"Defensive?" cries Lew. "Defensive be damned! He must have said offensive—how the hell could he attack defensively? And this order says nothin' about Lucan's better judgment. For one thing, he's got no more judgment than Mulligan's bull pup!"

"Well, that's what Raglan said!" I shouted. "You're bound to deliver it."

"Ah, damn them all, what a set of old women!" He dug in his spurs, head down, shouting across to me as we raced towards the rear squadrons of the Heavies. "They don't know their minds from one minute to the next. I tell ye, Flash, that ould ninny Raglan will hinder the cavalry at all costs—an' Lucan's not a whit better. What do they think horse-soldiers are for? Well, Lucan shall have his order, and be damned to them!"

I eased up as we shot through the ranks of the Greys, letting him go ahead; he went streaking through the Heavies, and across the intervening space towards the Lights. I'd no wish to be dragged into the discussion that would inevitably ensue with Lucan, who had to have every order explained to him three times at least. But I supposed I ought to be on hand, so I cantered easily up to the 4th Lights, and there was George Paget again, wanting to know what was up.

"You're advancing shortly," says I, and "Damned high time, too," says he. "Got a cheroot, Flash?—I haven't a weed to my name."

I gave him one, and he squinted at me. "You're looking peaky," says he. "Anything wrong?"

"Bowels," says I. "Damn all Russian champagne. Where's Lord Look-on?"

He pointed, and I saw Lucan out ahead of the Lights, with some galloper beside him, and Nolan just reining up. Lew was saluting, and handing him the paper, and while Lucan pored over it I looked about me.

It was drowsy and close down here on the plain after the breezy heights of the Sapoune; hardly a breath of wind, and the flies buzzing round the horses' heads, and the heavy smell of dung and leather. I suddenly realized I was damned tired, and my belly wouldn't lie quiet again; I grunted in reply to George's questions, and took stock of the Brigade, squirming uncomfortably in my saddle—there were the Cherrypickers in front, all very spruce in blue and pink with their pelisses trailing; to their right the mortar-board helmets and blue tunics of the 17th, with their lances at rest and the little red point plumes hanging limp; to their right again, not far from where Lucan was sitting, the 13th Lights, with the great Lord Cardigan himself out to the fore, sitting very aloof and alone and affecting not to notice Lucan and Nolan, who weren't above twenty yards from him.

Suddenly I was aware of Lucan's voice raised, and trotted away from George in that direction; it looked as though Lew would need some help in getting the message into his lordship's thick skull. I saw Lucan look in my direction, and just at that moment, as I was passing the 17th, someone called out:

"Hollo, there's old Flashy! Now we'll see some fun! What's the row, Flash?"

This sort of thing happens when one is generally admired; I replied with a nonchalant wave of the hand, and sang out: "Tally-ho, you fellows! You'll have all the fun you want presently," at which they laughed, and I saw Tubby Morris grinning across at me.

And then I heard Lucan's voice, clear as a bugle. "Guns, sir? What guns, may I ask? I can see no guns."

He was looking up the valley, his hand shading his eyes, and when I looked, by God, you couldn't see the redoubt where the Ruskis had been limbering up to haul the guns away—just the long slope of Causeway Heights, and the Russian infantry uncomfortably close.

"Where, sir?" cries Lucan. "What guns do you mean?"

I could see Lew's face working; he was scarlet with fury, and his hand was shaking as he came up by Lucan's shoulder, pointing along the line of the Causeway.

"There, my lord—there, you see, are the guns! *There's* your enemy!"

He brayed it out, as though he was addressing a dirty trooper, and Lucan stiffened as though he'd been hit. He looked as though he would lose his temper, but then he commanded himself, and Lew wheeled abruptly away and cantered off, making straight for me where I was sitting to the right of the 17th. He was shaking with passion, and as he drew abreast of me he rasped out:

"The bloody fool! Does he want to sit on his great fat arse all day and every day?"

"Lew," says I, pretty sharp, "did you tell him he was to act defensively and at his own discretion?"

"Tell him?" says he, baring his teeth in a savage grin. "By Christ, I told him three times over! As if that bastard needs telling to act defensively—he's capable of nothing else! Well, he's got his bloody orders—now let's see how he carries them out!"

And with that he went over to Tubby Morris, and I thought, well, that's that—now for the Sapoune, home and beauty, and let 'em chase to their hearts content down here. And I was just wheeling my horse, when from behind me I heard Lucan's voice.

"Colonel Flashman!" He was sitting with Cardigan, before the 13th Lights. "Come over here, if you please!"

Now what, thinks I, and my belly gave a great windy twinge as I trotted over towards them. Lucan was snapping at him impatiently, as I drew alongside:

"I know, I know, but there it is. Lord Raglan's order is quite positive, and we must obey it."

"Oh, vewy well," says Cardigan, damned ill-humoured; his voice was a mere croak, no doubt with his roupy chest, or over-boozing on his yacht. He flicked a glance at me, and looked away, sniffing; Lucan addressed me.

"You will accompany Lord Cardigan," says he. "In the event that communication is needed, he must have a galloper."

I stared horrified, hardly taking in Cardigan's comment: "I envisage no necessity for Colonel Fwashman's pwesence, or for communication with your lordship."

"Indeed, sir," says I, "Lord Raglan will need me . . . I dare not wait any longer . . . with your lordship's permission, I—"

"You will do as I say!" barks Lucan. "Upon my word, I have never met such insolence from mere gallopers before this day! First Nolan, and now you! Do as you are told, sir, and let us have none of this shirking!"

And with that he wheeled away, leaving me terrified, enraged, and baffled. What could I do? I couldn't disobey—it just wasn't possible. He had said I must ride with Cardigan, to those damned redoubts, chasing Raglan's bloody guns—my God, after what I had been through already! In an instant, by pure chance, I'd been snatched from security and thrust into the melting-pot again —it wouldn't do. I turned to Cardigan—the last man I'd have

appealed to, in any circumstances, except an extremity like
this.

"My lord," says I. "This is preposterous—unreasonable! Lord
Raglan will need me! Will you speak to his lordship—he must be
made to see—"

"If there is one thing," says Cardigan, in that croaking drawl,
"of which I am tolewably certain in this uncertain world, it is the
total impossibiwity of making my Word Wucan see anything at
all. He makes it cwear, furthermore, that there is no discussion of
his orders." He looked me up and down. "You heard him, sir.
Take station behind me, and to my weft. Bewieve me, I do not
welcome your pwesence here any more than you do yourself."

At that moment, up came George Paget, my cheroot clamped
between his teeth.

"We are to advance, Lord George," says Cardigan. "I shall need
close support, do you hear?—your vewy best support, Lord
George. Haw-haw. You understand me?"

George took the cheroot from his mouth, looked at it, stuck it
back, and then said, very stiff: "As always, my lord, you shall
have my support."

"Haw-haw. Vewy well," says Cardigan, and they turned aside,
leaving me stricken, and nicely hoist with my own petard, you'll
agree. Why hadn't I kept my mouth shut in Raglan's presence?
I could have been safe and comfy up on the Sapoune—but no,
I'd had to try to vent my spite, to get Cardigan in the way of a
bullet, and the result was I would be facing the bullets alongside
him. Oh, a skirmish round gun redoubts is a small enough thing
by military standards—unless you happen to be taking part in it,
and I reckoned I'd used up two of my nine lives today already.
To make matters worse, my stomach was beginning to churn and
heave most horribly again; I sat there, with my back to the Light
Brigade, nursing it miserably, while behind me the orders rattled
out, and the squadrons reformed; I took a glance round and saw
the 17th were now directly behind me, two little clumps of lances,
with the Cherrypickers in behind. And here came Cardigan,
trotting out in front, glancing back at the silent squadrons.

He paused, facing them, and there was no sound now but the
restless thump of hooves, and the creak and jingle of the gear.
All was still, five regiments of cavalry, looking down the valley,

with Flashy out in front, wishing he were dead and suddenly aware that dreadful things were happening under his belt. I moved, gasping gently to myself, stirring on my saddle, and suddenly, without the slightest volition on my part, there was the most crashing discharge of wind, like the report of a mortar. My horse started; Cardigan jumped in his saddle, glaring at me, and from the ranks of the 17th a voice muttered: "Christ, as if Russian artillery wasn't bad enough!" Someone giggled, and another voice said: "We've 'ad Whistlin' Dick—now we got Trumpetin' Harry an' all!"

"Silence!" cries Cardigan, looking like thunder, and the murmur in the ranks died away. And then, God help me, in spite of my straining efforts to contain myself, there was another fearful bang beneath me, echoing off the saddle, and I thought Cardigan would explode with fury.

I could not merely sit there. "I beg your pardon, my lord," says I, "I am not well—"

"Be silent!" snaps he, and he must have been in a highly nervous condition himself, otherwise he would never have added, in a hoarse whisper:

"Can you not contain yourself, you disgusting fellow?"

"My lord," whispers I, "I cannot help it—it is the feverish wind, you see—" and I interrupted myself yet again, thunderously. He let out a fearful oath, under his breath, and wheeled his charger, his hand raised; he croaked out "Bwigade will advance —first squadron, 17th—walk-march—twot!" and behind us the squadrons stirred and moved forward, seven hundred cavalry, one of them palsied with fear but in spite of that feeling a mighty relief internally—it was what I had needed all day, of course, like these sheep that stuff themselves on some windy weed, and have to be pierced to get them right again.

And that was how it began. Ahead of me I could see the short turf of the valley turning to plough, and beyond that the haze at the valley end, a mile and more away, and only a few hundred yards off, on either side, the enclosing slopes, with the small figures of Russian infantry clearly visible. You could even see their artillerymen wheeling the guns round, and scurrying among the limbers—we were well within range, but they were watching, waiting to see what we would do next. I forced myself to look straight ahead down the valley; there were guns there in plenty, and squadrons of Cossacks flanking them; their lance points and sabres caught the sun and threw it back in a thousand sudden gleams of light. Would they try a charge when we wheeled right towards the redoubts? Would Cardigan deploy the 4th Lights? Would he put the 17th forward as a screen when we made our flank movement? If I stuck close by him, would I be all right? Oh, God, how had I landed in this fix again—three times in a day? It wasn't fair—it was unnatural, and then my innards spoke again, resoundingly, and perhaps the Russian gunners heard it, for far down the Causeway on the right a plume of smoke blossomed out as though in reply, there was the crash of the discharge and the shot went screaming overhead, and then from all along the Causeway burst out a positive salvo of firing; there was an orange flash and a huge bang a hundred paces ahead, and a fount of earth was hurled up and came pattering down before us, while behind there was the crash of exploding shells, and a new barrage opening up from the hills on the left.

Suddenly it was, as Lord Tennyson tells us, like the very jaws of hell; I realized that, without noticing, I had started to canter, babbling gently to myself, and in front Cardigan was cantering too, but not as fast as I was (one celebrated account remarks that, "In his eagerness to be first at grips with the foe, Flashman was seen to forge ahead; ah, we can guess the fierce spirit that burned in that manly breast"—I don't know about that, but I'm here to inform you that it was nothing to the fierce spirit that burned in my manly bowels). There was a crash-crash-crash of flaming bursts across the front, and the scream of shell splinters whistling by; Cardigan shouted "Steady!", but his own charger was pacing away now, and behind me the clatter and jingle was being drowned by the rising drum of hooves, from a slow canter to a fast one, and then to a slow gallop, and I tried to rein in that little mare, smothering my own panic, and snarling fiercely to myself: "Wheel, wheel, for God's sake! Why doesn't the stupid bastard wheel?" For we were level with the first Russian redoubt; their guns were levelled straight at us, not four hundred yards away, the ground ahead was being torn up by shot, and then from behind me there was a frantic shout.

I turned in the saddle, and there was Nolan, his sabre out,

charging across behind me, shouting hoarsely, "Wheel, my lord! Not that way! Wheel—to the redoubts!" His voice was all but drowned in the tumult of explosion, and then he was streaking past Cardigan, reining his beast back on its haunches, his face livid as he turned to face the brigade. He flourished his sabre, and shouted again, and a shell seemed to explode dead in front of Cardigan's horse; for a moment I lost Nolan in the smoke, and then I saw him, face contorted in agony, his tunic torn open and gushing blood from shoulder to waist. He shrieked horribly, and his horse came bounding back towards us, swerving past Cardigan with Lew toppling forward on to the neck of his mount. As I stared back, horrified, I saw him careering into the gap between the Lancers and the 13th Light, and then they had swallowed him, and the squadrons came surging down towards me.

I turned to look for Cardigan; he was thirty yards ahead, tugging like damnation to hold his charger in, with the shot crashing all about him. "Stop!" I screamed. "Stop! For Christ's sake, man, rein in!" For now I saw what Lew had seen—the fool was never going to wheel, he was taking the Light Brigade straight into the heart of the Russian army, towards those massive batteries at the valley foot, that were already belching at us, while the cannon on either side were raking us from the flanks, trapping us in a terrible enfilade that must smash the whole command to pieces.

"Stop, damn you!" I yelled again, and was in the act of wheeling to shout at the squadrons behind when the earth seemed to open beneath me in a sheet of orange flame; I reeled in the saddle, deafened, the horse staggered, went down, and recovered, with myself clinging for dear life, and then I was grasping nothing but loose reins. The bridle was half gone, my brute had a livid gash spouting blood along her neck; she screamed and hurtled madly forward, and I seized the mane to prevent myself being thrown from the saddle.

Suddenly I was level with Cardigan; we bawled at each other, he waving his sabre, and now there were blue tunics level with me, either side, and the lance points of the 17th were thrusting forward, with the men crouched low in the saddles. It was an inferno of bursting shell and whistling fragments, of orange flame and choking smoke; a trooper alongside me was plucked from his

saddle as though by an invisible hand, and I found myself
drenched in a shower of blood. My little mare went surging ahead,
crazy with pain; we were outdistancing Cardigan now—and even
in that hell of death and gunfire, I remember, my stomach was
asserting itself again, and I rode yelling with panic and farting
furiously at the same time. I couldn't hold my horse at all; it was
all I could do to stay aboard as we raced onwards, and as I stared
wildly ahead I saw that we were a bare few hundred yards from
the Russian batteries. The great black muzzles were staring me in
the face, smoke wreathing up around them, but even as I saw the
flame belching from them I couldn't hear the crash of their discharge—it was all lost in the fearful continuous reverberating
cannonade that surrounded us. There was no stopping my mad
career, and I found myself roaring pleas for mercy to the distant
Russian gunners, crying stop, stop, for God's sake, cease fire,
damn you, and let me alone. I could see them plainly, crouching
at their breeches, working furiously to reload and pour another
torrent of death at us through the smoke; I raged and swore
mindlessly at them, and dragged out my sabre, thinking, by
heaven, if you finish me I'll do my damndest to take one of you
with me, you filthy Russian scum. ("And then", wrote that
fatuous ass of a correspondent, "was seen with what nobility and
power the gallant Flashman rode. Charging ahead even of his
valiant chief, the death cry of the illustrious Nolan in his ears,
his eye flashing terribly as he swung the sabre that had stemmed
the horde at Jallalabad, he hurtled against the foe.") Well, yes,
you might put it that way, but my nobility and power was
concentrated, in a moment of inspiration, in trying to swerve that
maddened beast out of the fixed lines of the guns; I had just sense
enough left for that. I tugged at the mane with my free hand, she
swerved and stumbled, recovered, reared, and had me half out of
the saddle; my innards were seized with a fresh spasm, and if I
were a fanciful man I'd swear I blew myself back astride of her.
The ground shook beneath us with another exploding shell,
knocking us sideways; I clung on, sobbing, and as the smoke
cleared Cardigan came thundering by, sabre thrust out ahead of
his charger's ears, and I heard him hoarsely shouting:

"Steady them! Hold them in! Cwose up and hold in!"

I tried to yell to him to halt, that he was going the wrong way, but my voice seemed to have gone. I turned in the saddle to shout or signal the men behind, and my God, what a sight it was! Half a dozen riderless horses at my very tail, crazy with fear, and behind them a score—God knows there didn't seem to be any more—of the 17th Lancers, some with hats gone, some streaked with blood, strung out any old how, glaring like madmen and tearing along. Empty saddles, shattered squadrons, all order gone, men and beasts going down by the second, the ground furrowing and spouting earth even as you watched—and still they came on, the lances of the 17th, and behind the sabres of the 11th—just a fleeting instant's thought I had, even in that inferno, remembering the brilliant Cherrypickers in splendid review, and there they were tearing forward like a horde of hell-bound spectres.

I had only a moment to look back—my mare was galloping like a thing demented, and as I steadied, there was Cardigan, waving his sabre and standing in his stirrups; the guns were only a hundred yards away, almost hidden in a great billowing bank of smoke, a bank which kept glaring red as though some Lucifer were opening furnace doors deep inside it. There was no turning, no holding back, and even in that deafening thunder I could hear the sudden chorus of yells behind me as the torn remnant of the Light Brigade gathered itself for the final mad charge into the battery. I dug in my heels, yelling nonsense and brandishing my sabre, shot into the smoke with one final rip from my bowels and a prayer that my gallant little mare wouldn't career headlong into a gun-muzzle, staggered at the fearful concussion of a gun exploding within a yard of me—and then we were through, into the open space behind the guns, leaping the limbers and ammunition boxes with the Russians scattering to let us through, and Cardigan a bare two yards away, reining his beast back almost on its haunches.

And then for a moment everything seemed to happen very slowly. I can see it all so distinctly: immediately to my left, and close enough to toss a biscuit, there was a squadron of Cossacks, with their lances couched, but all immobile, staring as though in amazement. Almost under my mare's hooves there was a Russian gunner, clutching a rammer, sprawling to get out of the way—he was stripped to the waist, I remember, and had a medal round his neck on a string—ahead of me, perhaps fifty yards off, was a brilliant little group of mounted men who could only be staff officers, and right beside me, still stiff and upright as a lance at rest, was Cardigan—by God, I thought, you're through *that* without a scratch on you, damn you! And so, it crossed my mind, was I—for the moment. And then everything jerked into crazy speed again, as the Light Brigade came careering out of the smoke, and the whole battery was suddenly a melee of rearing beasts, yelling maniacs, cracking pieces and flashing steel.

I was in the final moments of Little Big Horn, and the horror of Chillianwallah, which are among my nastiest recollections still, but for sheer murderous fury I recall nothing like the mad few minutes when the battered rabble of the Light Brigade rode over that Russian battery. It was as though they had gone mad— which, in a sense, they had. They slashed those Russian gun-crews apart, sabring, lancing, pounding them down under-hoof—I saw a corporal of the 17th drive his lance point four feet through a gunner's body and then leap from the saddle to tear at the fellow with his hands, Cardigan exchanging cuts with a mounted officer, troopers wrestling with Cossacks in the saddle, one of our Hussars on foot, whirling his sabre round his head and driving into a crowd of half a dozen, a Russian with his arm off at the elbow and a trooper still sabring him about the head—and then a Cossack came lumbering at me, roaring, with his lance couched to drive me through, but he was a handless clown, and missed me by a yard. I howled and slashed him back-handed as he blundered by, and then I was buffeted clean out of the saddle and went rolling away, weaponless, beneath a gun limber.

If I hadn't been scared witless I dare say I'd have stayed where I was, meditating, getting rid of some more wind, and generally taking a detached view, but in my panic I came scurrying out again, and there was George Paget, of all people, leaning from his saddle to grab my arm and swing me towards a riderless horse. I scrambled up, and George shouted:

"Come on, Flash, you old savage—we can't lose *you*! I'll want another of your cheroots presently![19] Close here, 4th Lights! Clo-o-o-se!"

There was a swirl of troopers round us, glaring smoke-blackened, bloody faces, a volley of commands, someone thrust a sabre into my hand, and George was crying:

"What a bloody pickle! We must cut our way home! Follow me!" and off we pounded, gasping and blinded, at his heels. I must have been near stupid with panic, for all I could think was: one more rush, just one more, and we'll be out of this hell-hole and back into the valley—God knows that was a horrifying prospect enough, but at least we were riding in the right direction, and providence or something had been on my side so far, and if only my luck would hold I might come through and reach the Sapoune and the camp beyond it and my bed and a ship and London and never, never go near a bloody uniform again—

"Halt!" bawls George, and I thought, I don't care, this is one gallant cavalryman who isn't halting for anything, I've had enough, and if I'm the only man who goes streaking back up that valley, leaving his comrades in the lurch, to hell with it. I put my head down and my heels in, thrust out my sabre to discourage any fool who got in the way, and charged ahead for all I was worth.

I heard George bawling behind me: "Halt! No, Flash, no!" and thought, carry on, George, and be damned to you. I fairly flew over the turf, the shouting died behind me, and I raised my head and looked—straight at what appeared to be the entire Russian army, drawn up in review order. There were great hideous ranks of the brutes, with Cossacks dead ahead, not twenty yards off— I had only a fleeting glimpse of amazed, bearded faces, there wasn't a hope of stopping, and then with a blasphemous yell of despair I plunged into them, horse, sabre and all.

"Picture, if you can bear it, reader"—as that idiot journalist put it—"the agony of Lord George Paget and his gallant remnant, in that moment. They had fought like heroes in the battery, Lord George himself had plucked the noble Flashman from bloody hand-to-hand conflict, they had rallied and ridden on through the battery, Lord George had given the halt, preparatory to wheeling about and charging back into the battery and the valley beyond, where ultimate safety lay—picture then, their anguish, when that great heart, too full to think of safety, or of aught but the cruel destruction of so many of his comrades, chose instead to launch himself *alone* against the embattled ranks of Muscovy! Sabre aloft, proud defiance on his lips, he chose the course that honour pointed, and rode like some champion of old to find death on the sabres of his enemies."

Well, I've always said, if you get the Press on your side you're half way there. I've never bothered to correct that glowing tribute, until now; it seems almost a shame to do it at last. I don't remember which journal it appeared in—*Bell's Sporting Life*, for all I know—but I don't doubt it caused many a manly tear to start, and many a fair bosom to heave when they read it. In the meantime, I was doing a bit in the manly tear and bosom-heaving line myself, with my horse foundering under me, my sabre flying from my hand, and my sorely-tried carcase sprawling on the turf while all those peasant horsemen shied back, growling and gaping, and then closed in again, staring down at me in that dull, astonished way that Russians have. I just lay there, gasping like a salmon on the bank, waiting for the lance-points to come skewering down on me, and babbling weakly:

"*Kamerad! Ami! Sarte! Amigo!* Oh God, what's the Russian for 'friend'?"

Being a prisoner of war has its advantages, or used to. If you were a British officer, taken by a civilized foe, you could expect to be rather better treated than your adversary would treat his own people; he would use you as a guest, entertain you, be friendly, and not bother overmuch about confining you. He might ask your parole not to try to escape, but not usually—since you would be exchanged for one of his own people at the first opportunity there wasn't much point in running off.

Mind you, I think we British fared rather better than most. They respected us, and knew we didn't make war in a beastly fashion, like these Balkan fellows, so they treated us accordingly. But a Russian taken by the Poles, or an Austrian by the Eyetyes, or even a Confederate by the Yankees—well, he might not come off quite so comfortably. I'm told it's all changing now, and that war's no longer a gentleman's game (as though it ever was), and that among the "new professionals" a prisoner's a prisoner so damned well cage him up. I don't know: we treated each other decently, and weren't one jot more incompetent than this Sandhurst-and-Shop crowd. Look at that young pup Kitchener —what that fellow needs is a woman or two.

At all events, no one has ever treated me better, by and large, than the Russians did, although I don't think it was kindness, but ignorance. From the moment I measured my length among those Cossacks, I found myself being regarded with something like awe. It wasn't just the Light Brigade fiasco, which had impressed them tremendously, but a genuine uncertainty where the English were concerned—they seemed to look on us as though we were men from the moon, or made of dynamite and so liable to go off if scratched. The truth is, they're such a dull, wary lot of peasants —the ordinary folk and soldiers, that is—that they go in fear of anything strange until someone tells 'em what to do about it.

In those days, of course, most of them were slaves—except for the Cossacks—and behaved as such.

I'll have more to say about this, but for the moment it's enough to note that the Cossacks kept away from me, glowering, until one of their officers jumped down, helped me to my feet, and accepted my surrender. I doubt if he understood a word I said, for I was too shocked and confused to be coherent, even if I'd spoken Russian, which I didn't r⋯·h, at that time. He led me through the crowd, and once I had realized that they weren't going to do me violence, and that I was safely out of that hellish maelstrom, I set myself to collect my wits and consider what should be done.

They stuck me in a tent, with two massive Cossacks at the entrance—Black Sea Cossacks, as I learned later, with those stringy long-haired caps, and scarlet lances—and there I sat, listening to the growing chatter outside, and every now and then an officer would stick his face in, and regard me, and then withdraw. I was still feeling fearfully sick and giddy, and my right ear seemed to have gone deaf with the cannonading, but as I leaned against the pole, shuddering, one thought kept crowding gloriously into my mind: I was alive, and in one piece. I'd survived, God knew how, the shattering of the Light Brigade, to say nothing of the earlier actions of the day—it seemed like a year since I'd stood with Campbell's Highlanders, though it was a bare five hours ago. You've come through again, my boy, I kept thinking; you're going to live. That being the case, head up, look alive and keep your eyes open.

Presently in came a little dapper chap in a fine white uniform, black boots, and a helmet with a crowned eagle. "Lanskey," says he, in good French—which most educated Russians spoke, by the way—"Major, Cuirassiers of the Guard. Whom have I the pleasure of addressing?"

"Flashman," says I, "Colonel, 17th Lancers."

"Enchanted," says he, bowing. "May I request that you accompany me to General Liprandi, who is most anxious to make the acquaintance of such a distinguished and gallant officer?"

Well, he couldn't have said fairer; I bucked up at once, and he led me out, through a curious throng of officers and staff hangers-on, into a great tent where about a dozen senior officers were waiting, with a genial-looking, dark-whiskered fellow in a splendid sable coat, whom I took to be Liprandi, seated behind a table. They stopped talking at once; a dozen pairs of eager eyes fixed on me as Lanskey presented me, and I stood up tall, ragged and muck-smeared though I was, and just stared over Liprandi's head, clicking my heels.

He came round the table, right up to me, and said, also in excellent French: "Your pardon, colonel. Permit me." And to my astonishment he stuck his nose up close to my lips, sniffing.

"What the devil?" cries I, stepping back.

"A thousand pardons, sir," says he. "It is true, gentlemen," turning to his staff. "Not a suspicion of liquor." And they all began to buzz again, staring at me.

"You are perfectly sober," says Liprandi. "And so, as I have ascertained, are your troopers who have been taken prisoner. I confess, I am astonished.[20] Will you perhaps enlighten us, colonel, what was the explanation of that . . . that extraordinary action by your light cavalry an hour ago? Believe me," he went on, "I seek no military intelligence from you—no advantage of information. But it is beyond precedent—beyond understanding. Why, in God's name, did you do it?"

Now, I didn't know, at that time, precisely what we had done. I guessed we must have lost three-quarters of the Light Brigade, by a hideous mistake, but I couldn't know that I'd just taken part in the most famous cavalry action ever fought, one that was to sound round the world, and that even eye-witnesses could scarcely believe. The Russians were amazed; it seemed to them we must have been drunk, or drugged, or mad—they weren't to guess that it had been a ghastly accident. And I wasn't going to enlighten them. So I said:

"Ah, well, you know, it was just to teach you fellows to keep your distance."

At this they exclaimed, and shook their heads and swore, and Liprandi looked bewildered, and kept muttering: "Five hundred sabres! To what end?", and they crowded round, plying me with questions—all very friendly, mind, so that I began to get my bounce back, and played it off as though it were just another day's work. What they couldn't fathom was how we'd held together all the way to the guns, and hadn't broken or turned

back, even with four saddles empty out of five, so I just told 'em,
"We're British cavalry," simple as that, and looked them in the
eye. It was true, too, even if no one had less right to say it than I.

At that they stamped and swore again, incredulously, and one
huge chap with a beard began to weep, and insisted on embracing
me, stinking of garlic as he was, and Liprandi called for brandy,
and demanded of me what we, in English, called our light cavalry,
and when I told him they all raised their glasses and shouted
together: "Thee Light Brigedde!" and dashed down their glasses
and ground them underfoot, and embraced me again, laughing
and shouting and patting me on the head, while I, the unworthy
recipient, looked pretty bluff and offhand and said, no, dammit
all, it was nothing, just our usual form, don't you know. (I should
have felt shame, doubtless, at the thought that I, old windy
Harry, was getting the plaudits and the glory, but you know me.
Anyway, I'd been there, hadn't I, all the way; should I be dis-
qualified, just because I was babbling scared?)

After that it was all booze and good fellowship, and when I'd
been washed and given a change of clothes Liprandi gave me a
slap-up dinner with his staff, and the champagne flowed—French,
you may be certain; these Russians know how to go to war—
and they were all full of attention and admiration and a thousand
questions, but every now and then they would fall silent and
look at me in that strange way that every survivor of the charge
has come to recognize: respectfully, and almost with reverence,
but with a hint of suspicion, as though you weren't quite canny.

Indeed their hospitality was so fine, that night, that I began to
feel regretful at the thought that I'd probably be exchanged in the
next day or two, and would find myself back in that lousy, fever-
ridden camp under Sevastopol—it's a curious thing, but my belly,
which had been in such wicked condition all day, felt right as
rain after that dinner. We all got gloriously tight, drinking
healths, and the bearded garlic giant and Lanskey carried me to
bed, and we all fell on the floor, roaring and laughing. As I crawled
on to my blankets I had only a moment's blurred recollection of
the sound of cannonade, and ranks of Highlanders, and Scarlett's
gaudy scarf, and the headlong gallop down the Sapoune, and
Cardigan cantering slowly and erect, and those belching guns, all
whirling together in a great smoky confusion. And it all seemed

past and unimportant as I slid away into unconsciousness and slept like a winter hedgehog.

They didn't exchange me. They kept me for a couple of weeks, confined in a cottage at Yalta, with two musketmen on the door and a Russian colonel of Horse Pioneers to walk the little garden with me for exercise, and then I was visited by Radziwill, a very decent chap on Liprandi's staff who spoke English and knew London well. He was terribly apologetic, explaining that there wasn't a suitable exchange, since I was a staff man, and a pretty rare catch. I didn't believe this; we'd taken senior Russian officers every bit as important as I, at the Alma, and I wondered exactly why they wanted to keep me prisoner, but there was no way of finding out, of course. Not that it concerned me much—I didn't mind a holiday in Russia, being treated as an honoured guest rather than a prisoner, for Radziwill hastened to reassure me that what they intended to do was send me across the Crimea to Kertch, and then by boat to mainland Russia, where I'd be safely tucked away on a country estate. The advantage of this was that I would be so far out of harm's way that escape would be impossible —I tried to look serious and knowing when he said this, as though I'd been contemplating running off to rejoin the bloody battle again—and I could lead a nice easy life without over-many restrictions, until the war was over, which couldn't be long, anyway.

I've learned to make the best of things, so I accepted without demur, packed up my few traps, which consisted of my cleaned and mended Lancer blues and a few shirts and things which Radziwill gave me, and prepared to go where I was taken. I was quite looking forward to it—fool that I was.

Before I went, Radziwill—no doubt meaning to be kind, but in fact just being an infernal nuisance—arranged for me to visit those survivors of the Light Brigade who'd been taken prisoner, and were in confinement down near Yalta. I didn't want to see them, much, but I couldn't refuse.

There were about thirty of them in a big stuffy shed, and not above six of them unwounded. The others were in cots, with bandaged heads and slings, some with limbs off, lying like wax dummies, one or two plainly just waiting to die, and all of them looking desperate hangdog. The moment I went inside I wished

I hadn't come—it's this kind of thing, the stale smell of blood, the wasted faces, the hushed voices, the awful hopeless tiredness, that makes you understand what a hellish thing war is. Worse than a battle-field, worse than the blood and the mud and the smoke and the steel, is the dank misery of a hospital of wounded men—and this place was a good deal better than most. Russians ain't clean, by any means, but the ward they'd made for our fellows was better than our own medical folk could have arranged at Balaclava.

Would you believe it, when I came in they raised a cheer? The pale faces lit up, those that could struggled upright in bed, and their non-com, who wasn't wounded, threw me a salute.

"Ryan, sir," says he. "Troop sergeant-major, Eighth 'Ussars. Sorry to see you're took, sir—but glad to see you well."

I thanked him, and shook hands, and then went round, giving a word here and there, as you're bound to do, and feeling sick at the sight of the pain and disfigurement—it could have been me, lying there with a leg off, or my face stitched like a football.

"Not takin' any 'arm, sir, as you see," says Ryan. "The grub ain't much, but it fills. You're bein' treated proper yourself, sir, if I may make so bold? That's good, that is; I'm glad to 'ear that. You'll be gettin' exchanged, I reckon? No—well, blow me! Who'd ha' thought that? I reckon they doesn't want to let *you* go, though—why, when we heard t'other day as you'd been took, old Dick there—that's 'im, sir, wi' the sabre-cut— 'e says: 'That's good noos for the Ruskis; ole Flashy's worth a squadron any day' —beggin' yer pardon, sir."

"That's mighty kind of friend Dick," says I, "but I fear I'm not worth very much at present, you know."

They laughed—such a thin laugh—and growled and said "Garn!", and Ryan dropped his voice, glancing towards where Lanskey loitered by the door, and says softly:

"I knows better, sir. An' there's 'arf a dozen of us sound enough 'ere to be worth twenty o' these Ruski chaps. If you was to say the word, sir, I reckon we could break our way out of 'ere, grab a few sabres, an' cut our way back to th'Army! It can't be above twenty mile to Sevasto-pool! We could do it, sir! The boys is game fer it, an'—"

"Silence, Ryan!" says I. "I won't hear of it." This was one of these dangerous bastards, I could see, full of duty and desperate notions. "What, break away and leave our wounded comrades? No, no, that would never do—I'm surprised at you."

He flushed. "I'm sorry, sir; I was just—"

"I know, my boy." I put a hand on his shoulder. "You want to do your duty, as a soldier should. But, you see, it can't be. And you can take pride in what you have done already—all of you can." I thought a few patriotic words wouldn't do any harm. "You are stout fellows, all of you. England is proud of you." And will let you go to the poor-house, in time, or sell laces at street corners, I thought to myself.

"Ole Jim the Bear'll be proud, an' all," pipes up one chap with a bandage swathing his head and eye, and I saw the blood-stained Cherrypicker pants at the foot of his cot. "They do say as 'is Lordship got out the battery, sir. Dryden there was picked up by the Ruskis in the valley, an' 'e saw Lord Cardigan goin' back arterwards—says 'e 'ad a bloody sabre, too, but wasn't hurt 'is-self."

That was bad news; I could have borne the loss of Cardigan any day.

"Good ole Jim!"

"Ain't 'e the one, though!"

"'E's a good ole commander, an' a gentleman, even if 'e is an 11th 'Ussar!" says Ryan, and they all laughed, and looked shy at me, because they knew I'd been a Cherrypicker, once.

There was a very pale, thin young face in the cot nearest the door, and as I was turning away, he croaked out, in a little whisper:

"Colonel Flashman, sir—Troop sarn't major was sayin'—it never 'appened afore—cavalry, chargin' a battery wi' no support, an' takin' it. Never 'appened nowheres, in any war, sir. Is that right, sir?"

I didn't know, but I'd certainly never heard of it. So I said: "I believe that's right. I think it may be."

He smiled. "That's good, then. Thank'ee, sir." And he lay back, with his eyelids twitching, breathing very quietly.

"Well," says I. "Good-bye, Ryan. Good-bye, all of you. Ah—keep your spirits up. We'll all be going home soon."

"When the Ruskis is beat," cries someone, and Ryan says:

"Three cheers for the Colonel!" and they all cheered, feebly, and shouted "Good old Flash Harry!" and the man with the patched eye began to sing, and they all took it up, and as I drove off with Lanskey I heard the words of the old Light Brigade canter fading behind me:

> In the place of water we'll drink ale,
> An' pay no reck'ning on the nail,
> No man for debt shall go to jail,
> While he can Garryowen hail.

I've heard it from Afghanistan to Whitehall, from the African veldt to drunken hunting parties in Rutland; heard it sounded on penny whistles by children and roared out in full-throated chorus by Custer's 7th on the day of Greasy Grass—and there were survivors of the Light Brigade singing on that day, too—but it always sounds bitter on my ears, because I think of those brave, deluded, pathetic bloody fools in that Russian shed, with their mangled bodies and lost limbs, all for a shilling a day and a pauper's grave—and yet they thought Cardigan, who'd have flogged 'em for a rusty spur and would see them murdered under the Russian guns because he hadn't wit and manhood enough to tell Lucan to take his order to hell—they thought he was "a good old commander", and they even cheered *me*, who'd have turned tail on them at the click of a bolt. Mind you, I'm harmless, by comparison—I don't send 'em off, stuffed with lies and rubbish, to get killed and maimed for nothing except a politician's vanity or a manufacturer's profit. Oh, I'll sham it with the best in public, and sport my tinware, but I know what I am, and there's no room for honest pride in me, you see. But if there was—just for a little bit, along with the disgust and hatred and selfishness—I'd keep it for them, those seven hundred British sabres.

It must be the drink talking. That's the worst of it; whenever I think back to Balaclava, there's nothing for it but the booze. It's not that I feel guilt or regret or shame—they don't *count* beside feeling alive, anyway, even if I were capable of them. It's just that I don't really understand Balaclava, even now. Oh, I can understand, without sharing, most kinds of courage—that which springs from rage, or fear, or greed or even love. I've had a bit of them myself—anyone can show brave if his children or his woman are threatened. (Mind you, if the hosts of Midian were assailing my little nest, offering to ravish my loved one, my line would be to say to her, look, you jolly 'em along, old girl, and look your best, while I circle round to a convenient rock with my rifle.) But are these emotions, that come of anger or terror or desire, really bravery at all? I doubt it, myself—but what happened in the North Valley, under those Russian guns, all for nothing, that's bravery, and you may take the word of a true-blue coward for it. It's beyond my ken, anyway, thank God, so I'll say no more of it, or of Balaclava, which as far as my Russian adventure is concerned, was really just an unpleasant prelude. Enough's enough; Lord Tennyson may have the floor for me.

*　　*　　*

The journey from Yalta through the woody hills to Kertch was not noteworthy; once you've seen a corner of the Crimea you've seen it all, and it's not really Russia. From Kertch, where a singularly surly and uncommunicative French-speaking civilian took me in charge (with a couple of dragoons to remind me what I was), we went by sloop across the Azov Sea to Taganrog, a dirty little port, and joined the party of an imperial courier whose journey lay the same way as ours. Ah-ha, thinks I, we'll travel in style, which shows how mistaken one can be.

We travelled in two *telegues*, which are just boxes on wheels, with a plank at the front for the driver, and straw or cushions for the passengers. The courier was evidently in no hurry, for we crawled along at an abominably slow pace, although *telegues* can travel at a tremendous clip when they want to, with a bell clanging in front, and everyone scattering out of their way. It always puzzled me, when I later saw the shocking condition of Russian roads, with their ruts and pot-holes, how the highways over which the *telegues* travelled were always smooth and level. The secret was this: *telegues* were used only by couriers and officials of importance, and before they came to a stretch of road, every peasant in the area was turned out to sand and level it.

So as we lumbered along, the courier in state in the first *telegue*, and Flashy with his escort in the second, there were always

peasants standing by the roadside, men and women, in their belted
smocks and ragged puttees, silent, unmoving, staring as we rolled
by. This dull brooding watchfulness got on my nerves, especially
at the post stations, where they used to assemble in silent groups
to stare at us—they were so different from the Crim Tartars I had
seen, who are lively, tall, well-made men, even if their women
are seedy. The steppe Russians were much smaller, and ape-like
by comparison.

Of course, what I didn't realize then was that these people were
slaves—real bound, European white slaves, which isn't easy to
understand until you see it. This wasn't always so; it seems that
Boris Godunov—whom most of you will know as a big fellow
who takes about an hour and a half to die noisily in an opera—imposed serfdom on the Russian peasants, which meant that they
became the property of the nobles and land-owners, who could
buy and sell them, hire them out, starve them, lash them, imprison them, take their goods, beasts and womenfolk whenever
they chose—in fact, do anything short of maiming them permanently or killing them. They did those things, too, of course,
for I saw them, but it was officially unlawful.

The serfs were just like the nigger slaves in the States—worse
off, if anything, for they didn't seem to realize they were slaves.
They looked on themselves as being attached to the soil ("we
belong to the master, but the land is ours", was a saying among
them) and traditionally they had bits of land to work for their
own benefit—three days on their patch each week, three on the
master's, was supposed to be the rule, but wherever I went it
seemed to be six on the master's and one for themselves, if they
were lucky.

It may not seem possible to you that in Europe just forty years
ago white folk could be used like this, that they could be flogged
with rods and whips up to ten times a day, or knouted (which is
something infintely worse), or banished to Siberia for years at their
landlord's whim; all he had to do was pay the cost of their trans-
portation. They could be made to wear spiked collars, the women
could be kept in harems, the men could be drafted off to the army
so that the owners could steal their wives without embarrassment,
their children could be sold off—and in return for this they were
meant to be grateful to their lords, and literally crawl in front of

them, calling them "father", touching their heads on the ground, and kissing their boots. I've watched them do it—just like political candidates at home. I've seen a lot of human sorrow and misery in my time, but the lot of the Russian serf was the most appalling I've ever struck.

Of course, it's all changed now; they freed the serfs in '61, just a few years after I was there, and now, I'm told, they are worse off than ever. Russia depended on slavery, you see, and when they freed them they upset the balance, and there was tremendous starvation and the economy went to blazes—well, in the old days the landlords had at least kept the serfs alive, for their own benefit, but after emancipation, why should they? And it was all nonsense, anyway; the Russians will always be slaves—so will most of the rest of mankind, of course, but it tends to be more obvious among the Ruskis.

For one thing, they look so damned slavish. I remember the first time I really noticed serfs, the first day's drive out of Taganrog. It was at a little village post-station, where some official was thrashing a peasant—don't know why—and this dull clown was just standing and letting himself be caned by a fellow half his size, hardly even wincing under the blows. There was a little crowd of serfs looking on, ugly, dirty-looking rascals in hairy blue smocks and rough trousers, with their women and a few ragged brats—and they were just watching, like cowed, stupid brutes. And when the little official finally broke his cane, and kicked the peasant and screamed at him to be off, the fellow just lumbered away, with the others trailing after him. It was as though they had no feeling whatever.

Oh, it was a cheery place, all right, this great empire of Russia as I first saw it in the autumn of '54—a great ill-worked wilderness ruled by a small landed aristocracy with their feet on the necks of a huge human-animal population, with Cossack devils keeping order when required. It was a brutal, backward place, for the rulers were ever fearful of the serfs, and held back everything educational or progressive—even the railway was discouraged, in case it should prove to be revolutionary—and with discontent everywhere, especially among those serfs who had managed to better themselves a little, and murmurings of revolt, the iron hand of government was pressing ever harder. The "white terror", as they called the secret police, were everywhere; the whole population was on their books, and everyone had to have his "billet", his "ticket to live"—without it you were nobody, you did not exist. Even the nobility feared the police, and it was from a landlord that I heard the Russian saying about being in jail—"Only there shall we sleep sound, for only there are we safe."[21]

The land we travelled through was a fit place for such people—indeed, you have to see it to understand why they are what they are. I've seen big countries before—the American plains on the old wagon-trails west of St Louis, with the whispering grasses waving away and away to the very edge of the world, or the Saskatchewan prairies in grasshopper time, dun and empty under the biggest sky on earth. But Russia is bigger: there is no sky, only empty space overhead, and no horizon, only a distant haze, and endless miles of sun-scorched rank grass and emptiness. The few miserable hamlets, each with its rickety church, only seemed to emphasize the loneliness of that huge plain, imprisoning by its very emptiness —there are no hills for a man to climb into or to catch his imagination, nowhere to go: no wonder it binds its people to it.

It appalled me, as we rolled along, with nothing to do but strain your eyes for the next village, soaked by the rain or sweating in the sun, or sometimes huddling against the first wintry gusts that swept the steppes—they seemed to have all weathers together, and all bad. For amusement, of course, you could try to determine which stink was more offensive—the garlic chewed by the driver or the grease of his axles—or watch the shuttlecocks of the wind-witch plant being blown to and fro. I've known dreary, depressing journeys, but that was the limit; I'd sooner walk through Wales.

The truth is, I was beginning to find Russia a frightening place, with its brooding, brutish people and countryside to match; one began to lose the sense of space and time. The only reliefs were provided by our halts at the way-stations—poor, flea-ridden places with atrocious accommodation and worse food. You'd been able to get decent beef in the Crimea for a penny a pound, but here it was *stchee* and *borsch*, which are cabbage soups, horse-meat porridge, and sweet flour tarts, which were the only palatable things available. That, and their tea, kept me alive; the tea is good, provided you can get "caravan tea", which is Chinese, and the best. The wine they may put back in the *moujiks** for me.

So my spirits continued to droop, but what shook them worst was an incident on the last morning of our journey when we had halted at a large village only thirty versts [twenty miles] from Starotorsk, the estate to which I was being sent. It wasn't so different, really, from the peasant-thrashing I'd already seen, yet it, and the man involved, branded on my mind the knowledge of what a fearful, barbarous, sickeningly cruel land this Russia was.

The village lay on what seemed to be an important cross-roads; there was a river, I remember, and a military camp, and uniforms coming and going from the municipal building where my civilian took me to report my arrival—everything has to be reported to someone or other in Russia, in this case the local registrar, a surly, bull-necked brute in a grey tunic, who pawed over the papers, eyeing me nastily the while.

These Russian civil servants are a bad lot—pompous, stupid and rude at the best. They come in various grades, each with a military title—so that General or Colonel So-and-so turns out to be someone who neglects the parish sanitation or keeps inaccurate records of livestock. The brutes even wear medals, and are immensely puffed-up, and unless you bribe them lavishly they will cause you all the trouble they can.

I was waiting patiently, being eyed curiously by the officials and officers with whom the municipal hall was packed, and the registrar picked his teeth, scowling, and then launched into a great tirade in Russian—I gather it was addressed against all Englishmen in general and me in particular. He made it clear to my escort, and everyone else, that he considered it a gross waste of board and lodging that I should be housed at all—he'd have had me in the salt-mines for a stinking foreigner who had defiled the holy soil of Mother Russia—and so forth, until he got quite worked up, banging his desk and shouting and glaring, so that the noise and talk in the room died away as everyone stopped to listen.

It was just jack-in-office unpleasantness, and I had no choice but to ignore it. But someone else didn't. One of the officers who had been standing to one side, chatting, suddenly strolled forward in front of the registrar's table, paused to drop his cigarette

* Peasants.

and set a foot on it, and then without warning lashed the registrar full across the face with his riding crop. The fellow shrieked and fell back in his chair, flinging up his hands to ward another blow; the officer said something in a soft, icy voice, and the trembling hands came down, revealing the livid whip-mark on the coarse bearded face.

There wasn't a sound in the room, except for the registrar's whimpering, as the officer leisurely raised his crop again, and with the utmost deliberation slashed him across the face a second time, laying the bearded cheek open, while the creature screamed but didn't dare move or protect himself. A third slash sent man and chair over, the officer looked at his whip as though it had been in the gutter, dropped it on the floor, and then turned to me.

"This offal," says he, and to my amazement he spoke in English, "requires correction. With your permission, I shall rein-force the lesson." He looked at the blubbering, bleeding registrar crawling out of the wreck of his chair, and rapped out a string of words in that level, chilly whisper; the stricken man changed course and came wriggling across to my feet, babbling and snuff-ling at my ankles in a most disgusting fashion, while the officer lit another cigarette and looked on.

"He will lick your boots," says he, "and I have told him that if he bleeds on them, I shall have him knouted. You wish to kick him in the face?"

As you know, I'm something in the bullying line myself, and given a moment I dare say I'd have accepted; it isn't every day you have the opportunity. But I was too amazed—aye, and alarmed, too, at the cold, deliberate brutality I'd seen, and the registrar seized the opportunity to scramble away, followed by a shatter-ing kick from my protector.

"Scum—but rather wiser scum," says he. "He will not insult a gentleman again. A cigarette, colonel?" And he held out a gold case of those paper abominations I'd tried at Sevastopol, but hadn't liked. I let him light one for me; it tasted like dung soaked in treacle.

"Captain Count Nicholas Pavlovitch Ignatieff,"[22] says he, in that cold, soft voice, "at your service." And as our eyes met through the cigarette smoke I thought, hollo, this is another of those momentous encounters. You didn't have to look at this chap twice to remember him forever. It was the eyes, as it so often is—I thought in that moment of Bismarck, and Charity Spring, and Akbar Khan; it had been the eyes with them, too. But this fellow's were different from anything yet: one was blue, but the other had a divided iris, half-blue, half-brown, and the oddly fascinating effect of this was that you didn't know where to look, but kept shifting from one to the other.

For the rest, he had gingerish, curling hair and a square, masterful face that was no way impaired by a badly-broken nose. He looked tough, and immensely self-assured; it was in his glance, in the abrupt way he moved, in the slant of the long cigarette between his fingers, in the rakish tilt of his peaked cap, in the immaculate white tunic of the Imperial Guards. He was the kind who knew exactly what was what, where everything was, and precisely who was who—especially himself. He was probably a devil with women, admired by his superiors, hated by his rivals, and abjectly feared by his subordinates. One word summed him up: bastard.

"I caught your name, in that beast's outburst," says he. He was studying me calmly, as a doctor regards a specimen. "You are the officer of Balaclava, I think. Going to Starotorsk, to be lodged with Colonel Count Pencherjevsky. He already has another English officer—under his care." I tried to meet his eye and not keep glancing at the registrar, who had hauled himself up at a nearby table, and was shakily trying to staunch his gashed face: no one moved a finger to help him. For some reason, I found my cigarette trembling between my fingers; it was foolish, with this outwardly elegant, precise, not unfriendly young gentleman doing no more than make civil conversation. But I'd just seen him at work, and knew the kind of soulless, animal cruelty behind the suave mask. I know my villains, and this Captain Count Ignatieff was a bad one; you could feel the savage strength of the man like an electric wave.

"I will not detain you, colonel," says he, in that same cold murmur, and there was all the immeasurable arrogance of the Russian nobleman in the way he didn't look or beckon for my civilian escort, but simply turned his head the merest fraction, and the fellow came scurrying out of the silent crowd.

"We may meet at Starotorsk," says Ignatieff, and with the slightest bow to me he turned away, and my escort was hustling me respectfully out to the *telegue*, as though he couldn't get away fast enough. I was all for it; the less time you spend near folk like that, the better.

It left me shaken, that little encounter. Some people are just terrible, in the true sense of the word—I knew now, I thought, how Tsar Ivan had earned that nickname: it implies something far beyond the lip-licking cruelty of your ordinary torturer. Satan, if there is one, is probably a Russian; no one else could have the necessary soulless brutality; it is just part of life to them.

I asked my civilian who Ignatieff was, and got an unwilling mumble in reply. Russians don't like to talk about their superiors at any time; it isn't safe, and I gathered that Ignatieff was so important, and so high-born—mere captain though he was—that you just didn't mention him at all. So I consoled myself that I'd probably seen the last of him (ha!) and took stock of the scenery instead. After a few miles the bare steppe was giving way to large, well-cultivated fields, with beasts and peasants labouring away, the road improved, and presently, on an eminence ahead of us there was a great, rambling timbered mansion with double wings, and extensive outbuildings, all walled and gated, and the thin smoke of a village just visible beyond. We bowled up a fine gravel drive between well-kept lawns with willow trees on their borders, past the arched entrance of a large courtyard, and on to a broad carriage sweep before the house, where a pretty white fountain played.

Well, thinks I, cheering up a bit, this will do. Civilization in the midst of barbarism, and very fine, too. Pleasant grounds, genteel accommodation, salubrious outlook, company's own water no doubt, to suit overworked military man in need of rest and recreation. Flashy, my son, this will answer admirably until they sign the peace. The only note out of harmony was the Cossack guard lounging near the front steps, to remind me that I was a prisoner after all.

A steward emerged, bowing, and my civilian explained that he would conduct me to my apartment, and thereafter I would doubtless meet Count Pencherjevsky. I was led into a cool, light-panelled hall, and if anything was needed to restore my flagging

spirits it was the fine furs on the well-polished floor, the comfortable leather furniture, the flowers on the table, the cosy air
of civilian peace, and the delightful little blonde who had just
descended the stairs. She was so unexpected, I must have goggled
at her like poor Willy in the presence of his St John's Wood
whore.

And she was worth a long stare. About middle height, perhaps
eighteen or nineteen, plump-bosomed, tiny in the waist, with a
saucy little upturned nose, pink, dimpled cheeks and a cloud of
silvery-blonde hair, she was fit to make your mouth water—
especially if you hadn't had a woman in two months, and had
just finished a long, dusty journey through southern Russia,
gaping at misshapen peasants. I stripped, seized, and mounted her
in a twinkling of my mind's eye, as she tripped past, I bowing
my most military bow, and she disregarding me beyond a quick,
startled glance from slanting grey eyes. May it be a long war,
thinks I, watching her bouncing out of sight, and then my attention was taken by the major-domo, muttering the eternal
"*Pajalsta, excellence,*" and leading me up the broad, creaky
staircase, along a turning passage, and finally halting at a broad
door. He knocked, and an English voice called:

"Come in—no, hang it all—*khadee-tyeh!*"

I grinned at the friendly familiar sound, and strode in, saying:
"Hollo, yourself, whoever you are," and putting out my hand.
A man of about my own age, who had been reading on the bed,
looked up in surprise, swung his legs to the ground, stood up,
and then sank back on the bed again, gaping as though I were a
ghost. He shook his head, stuttering, and then got out:

"Flashman! Good heavens!"

I stopped short. The face was familiar, somehow, but I didn't
know from where. And then the years rolled away, and I saw a
boy's face under a tile hat, and heard a boy's voice saying: "I'm
sorry, Flashman." Yes, it was him all right—Scud East of Rugby.

For a long moment we just stared at each other, and then we both found our voices in the same phrase: "What on earth are you doing here?" And then we stopped, uncertainly, until I said:

"I was captured at Balaclava, three weeks back."

"They took me at Silistria, three months ago. I've been here five weeks and two days."

And then we stared at each other some more, and finally I said:

"Well, you certainly know how to make a fellow at home. Ain't you going to offer me a chair, even?"

He jumped up at that, colouring and apologizing—still the same raw Scud, I could see. He was taller and thinner than I remembered; his brown hair was receding, too, but he still had that quick, awkward nervousness I remembered.

"I'm so taken aback," he stuttered, pulling up a chair for me. "Why—why, I am glad to see you, Flashman! Here, give me your hand, old fellow! There! Well—well—my, what a mountainous size you've grown, to be sure! You always were a big . . . er, a tall chap, of course, but . . . I say, isn't this a queer fix, us meeting again like this . . . after so long! Let's see, it must be fourteen, no fifteen, years since . . . since . . . ah . . ."

"Since Arnold kicked me out for being pissy drunk?"

He coloured again. "I was going to say, since we said goodbye."

"Aye. Well, ne'er mind. What's your rank, Scud? Major, eh? I'm a colonel."

"Yes," says he. "I see that." He gave me an odd, almost shy grin. "You've done well—everyone knows about you—all the fellows from Rugby talk about you, when one meets 'em, you know . . ."

"Do they, though? Not with any great love, I'll be bound, eh, young Scud?"

"Oh, come!" cries he. "What d'you mean? Oh, stuff! We were

all boys then, and boys never get on too well, 'specially when
some are bigger and older and . . . why, that's all done with years
ago! Why—everyone's proud of you, Flashman! Brooke and
Green—and young Brooke—he's in the Navy, you know." He
paused. "The Doctor would have been proudest of all, I'm sure."

Aye, he probably would, thinks I, the damned old hypocrite.

". . . everyone knows about Afghanistan, and India, and all
that," he ran on. "I was out there myself, you know, in the Sikh
campaign, when you were winning another set of laurels. All I
got was a shot wound, a hole in my ribs, and a broken arm."[23]
He laughed ruefully. "Not much to show, I'm afraid—and then
I bought out of the 101st, and—but heavens, how I'm rattling
on! Oh, it is good to see you, old fellow! This is the best, most
famous thing! Let me have a good look at you! By George, those
are some whiskers, though!"

I couldn't be sure if he meant it, or not. God knows, Scud East
had no cause to love me, and the sight of him had so taken me
back to that last black day at Rugby that I'd momentarily forgotten we were men now, and things had changed—perhaps even
his memories of me. For he did seem pleased to see me, now that
he'd got over his surprise—of course, that could just be acting on
his part, or making the best of a bad job, or just Christian
decency. I found myself weighing him up; I'd knocked him about
a good deal, in happier days, and it came as a satisfaction to
realize that I could probably still do it now, if it came to the
pinch; he was still smaller and thinner than I. At that, I'd never
detested him as much as his manly-mealy little pal, Brown; he'd
had more game in him than the others, had East, and now—well,
if he was disposed to be civil, and let bygones be bygones . . . We
were bound to be stuck together for some months at least.

All this in a second's consideration—and you may think, what
a mean and calculating nature, or what a guilty conscience.
Never you mind; I know my own nature hasn't changed in eighty
years, so why should anyone else's? And I never forget an in-
jury—I've done too many of 'em.

So I didn't quite enter into his joyous spirit of reunion, but was
civil enough, and after he had got over his sham-ecstasies at meeting his dear old school-fellow again, I said:

"What about this place, then—and this fellow Pencherjevsky?"

He hesitated a moment, glanced towards the wall, got up, and as he walked over to it, said loudly: "Oh, it is as you see it—a splendid place. They've treated me well—very well indeed." And then he beckoned me to go over beside him, at the same time laying a finger on his lips. I went, wondering, and followed his pointing finger to a curious protuberance in the ornate carving of the panelling beside the stove. It looked as though a small funnel had been sunk into the carving, and covered with a fine metal grille, painted to match the surrounding wood.

"I say, old fellow," says East, "what d'you say to a walk? The Count has splendid gardens, and we are free of them, you know."

I took the hint, and we descended the stairs to the hall, and out on to the lawns. The lounging Cossack looked at us, but made no move to follow. As soon as we were at a safe distance, I asked:

"What on earth was it?"

"Speaking-tube, carefully concealed," says he. "I looked out for it as soon as I arrived—there's one in the next room, too, where you'll be. I fancy our Russian hosts like to be certain we're not up to mischief."

"Well, I'm damned! The deceitful brutes! Is that any way to treat gentlemen? And how the deuce did you know to look for it?"

"Oh, just caution," says he, offhand, but then he thought for a moment, and went on: "I know a little about such things, you see. When I was taken at Silistria, although I was officially with the Bashi-Bazouk people, I was more on the political side, really. I think the Russians know it, too. When they brought me up this way I was most carefully examined at first by some very shrewd gentlemen from their staff—I speak some Russian, you see. Oh, yes, my mother's family married in this direction, a few generations ago, and we had a sort of great-aunt who taught me enough to whet my interest. Anyway, on top of their suspicions of me, that accomplishment is enough to make 'em pay very close heed to H. East, Esq."

"It's an accomplishment you can pass on to me as fast as you like," says I. "But d'you mean they think you're a spy?"

"Oh, no, just worth watching—and listening to. They're the

most suspicious folk in the world, you know; trust no one, not even each other. And for all they're supposed to be thick-headed barbarians, they have some clever jokers among 'em."

Something made me ask: "D'you know a chap called Ignatieff— Count Ignatieff?"   ·

"Do I not!" says he. "He was one of the fellows who ran the rule over me when I came up here. That's Captain Swing with blue blood, that one—why, d'you know him?"

I told him what had happened earlier in the day, and he whistled. "He was there to have a look and a word with you, you may depend on it. We must watch what we say, Flashman— not that our consciences aren't clear, but we may have some information that would be useful to them." He glanced about. "And we won't feed their suspicions by talking too much where they can't hear us. Another five minutes, and we'd better get back to the room. If we want to be private there, at any time, we'll hang a coat over their confounded tube—you may believe me, that works. But before we go in, I'll tell you, as quickly as I may, those things that are better said in the open air."

It struck me, he was a cool, assured hand, this East—of course, he had been all that as a boy, too.

"Count Pencherjevsky—an ogre, loud-mouthed, brutal, and a tyrant. He's a Cossack, who rose to command a hussar regiment in the army, won the Tsar's special favour, and retired here, away from his own tribal land. He rules his estate like a despot, treats his serfs abominably, and will surely have his throat cut one day. I can't abide him, and keep out of his way, although I sometimes dine with the family, for appearance's sake. But he's been decent enough, I'll admit; gives me the run of the place, a horse to ride, that sort of thing."

"Ain't they worried you might ride for it?" says I.

"Where to? We're two hundred miles north of the Crimea here, with nothing but naked country in between. Besides, the Count has a dozen or so of his old Cossacks in his service—they're all the guard anyone needs. Kubans, who could ride down anything on four legs. I saw them bring back four serfs who ran away, soon after I got here—they'd succeeded in travelling twenty miles before the Cossacks caught them. Those devils brought them back tied by the ankles and dragged behind their ponies—

the whole way!" He shuddered. "They were flayed to death in the first few miles!"

I felt my stomach give one of its little heaves. "But, anyway, those were serfs," says I. "They wouldn't do that sort of thing to—"

"Wouldn't they, though?" says he. "Well, perhaps not. But this ain't England, you know, or France, or even India. This is Russia—and these land-owners are no more accountable than . . . than a baron in the Middle Ages. Oh, I dare say he'd think twice about mishandling us—still, I'd think twice about getting on his wrong side. But, I say, I think we'd best go back, and treat 'em to some harmless conversation—if anyone's bothering to listen."

As we strolled back, I asked him a question which had been exercising me somewhat. "Who's the fair beauty I saw when I arrived?"

He went red as a poppy, and I thought, o-ho, what have we here, eh? Young Scud with lecherous notions—or pure Christian passion, I wonder which?

"That would be Valentina," says he, "the Count's daughter. She and her Aunt Sara—and an old deaf woman who is a cousin of sorts—are his only family. He is a widower." He cleared his throat nervously. "One sees very little of them, though—as I said, I seldom dine with the family. Valentina . . . ah . . . is married."

I found this vastly amusing—it was my guess that young Scud had gone wild about the little bundle—small blame to him—and like the holy little humbug he was, preferred to avoid her rather than court temptation. One of Arnold's shining young knights, he was. Well, lusty old Sir Lancelot Flashy had galloped into the lists now—too bad she had a husband, of course, but at least she'd be saddle-broken. At that, I'd have to see what her father was like, and how the land lay generally. One has to be careful about these things.

I met the family at dinner that afternoon, and a most fascinating occasion it turned out to be. Pencherjevsky was worth travelling a long way to see in himself—the first sight of him, standing at his table head, justified East's description of ogre, and made me think of Jack and the Beanstalk, and smelling the blood of

Englishmen, which was an unhappy notion, when you considered it.

He must have been well over six and a half feet tall, and even so, he was broad enough to appear squat. His head and face were just a mass of brown hair, trained to his shoulders and in a splendid beard that rippled down his chest. His eyes were fine, under huge shaggy brows, and the voice that came out of his beard was one of your thunderous Russian basses. He spoke French well, by the way, and you would never have guessed from the glossy colour of his hair, and the ease with which he moved his huge bulk, that he was over sixty. An enormous man, in every sense, not least in his welcome.

"The Colonel Flashman," he boomed. "Be happy in this house. As an enemy, I say, forget the quarrel for a season; as a soldier, I say, welcome, brother." He shook my hand in what was probably only the top joints of his enormous fingers, and crushed it till it cracked. "Aye—you look like a soldier, sir. I am told you fought in the disgraceful affair at Balaclava, where our cavalry were chased like the rabble they are. I salute you, and every good sabre who rode with you. Chased like rabbits, those *tuts** and *moujiks* on horseback. Aye, you would not have chased my Kubans so—or Vigenstein's Hussars[24] when I had command of them—no, by the great God!" He glowered down at me, rumbling, as though he would break into "Fee-fi-fo-fum" at any moment, and then released my hand and waved towards the two women seated at the table.

"My daughter Valla, my sister-in-law, Madam Sara." I bowed, and they inclined their heads and looked at me with that bold, appraising stare which Russian women use—they're not bashful or missish, those ladies. Valentina, or Valla, as her father called her, smiled and tossed her silver-blonde head—she was a plumply pert little piece, sure enough, but I spared a glance for Aunt Sara as well. She'd be a few years older than I, about thirty-five, perhaps, with dark, close-bound hair and one of those strong, masterful, chiselled faces—handsome, but not beautiful. She'd have a moustache in a few years, but she was well-built and tall, carrying her bounties before her.

For all that Pencherjevsky looked like Goliath, he had good

* Renegades.

taste—or whoever ordered his table and domestic arrangements
had. The big dining-room, like all the apartments in the house,
had a beautiful wood-tiled floor, there was a chandelier, and any
amount of brocade and flowered silk about the furnishings.
(Pencherjevsky himself, by the way, was dressed in silk: most
Russian gentlemen wear formal clothes as we do, more or less,
but he affected a magnificent shimmering green tunic, clasped at
the waist by a silver-buckled belt, and silk trousers of the same
colour tucked into soft leather boots—a most striking costume,
and comfortable too, I should imagine.)

The food was good, to my relief—a fine soup being followed
by fried fish, a ragout of beef, and side-dishes of poultry and
game of every variety, with little sweet cakes and excellent coffee.
The wine was indifferent, but drinkable. Between the vittles, the
four fine bosoms displayed across the table, and Pencherjevsky's
conversation, it was a most enjoyable meal.

He questioned me about Balaclava, most minutely, and when
I had satisfied his curiosity, astonished me by rapidly sketching
how the Russian cavalry should have been handled, with the aid of
cutlery, which he clashed about on the table to demonstrate. He
knew his business, no doubt of it, but he was full of admiration
for our behaviour, and Scarlett's particularly.

"Great God, there is an English Cossack!" says he. "Uphill,
eh? I like him! I like him! Let him be captured, dear Lord, and
sent to Starotorsk, so that I can keep him forever, and talk, and
fight old battles, and shout at each other like good companions!"

"And get drunk nightly, and be carried to bed!" says Miss
Valla, pertly—they enter into talk with the men, you know,
these Russian ladies, with a freedom that would horrify our own
polite society. And they drink, too—I noticed that both of
them went glass for glass with us, without becoming more than a
trifle merry.

"That, too, *golubashka*," says Pencherjevsky. "Can he drink,
then, this Scarlett? Of course, of course he must! All good horse-
soldiers can, eh, colonel? Not like your Sasha, though," says he
to Valla, with a great wink at me. "Can you imagine, colonel,
I have a son-in-law who cannot drink? He fell down at his wedding, on this very floor—yes, over there, by God!—after what? A
glass or two of vodka! Saint Nicholas! Aye, me—how I must

have offended the Father God, to have a son-in-law who cannot drink, and does not get me grandchildren."

At this Valla gave a most unladylike snort, and tossed her head, and Aunt Sara, who said very little as a rule, I discovered, set down her glass and observed tartly that Sasha could hardly get children while he was away fighting in the Crimea.

"Fighting?" cries Pencherjevsky, boisterously. "Fighting—in the horse artillery? Whoever saw one of them coming home on a stretcher? I would have had him in the Bug Lancers, or even the Moscow Dragoons, but—body of St Sofia!—he doesn't *ride* well! A fine son-in-law for a Zaporozhiyan *hetman*,* that!"

"Well, dear father!" snaps Valla. "If he had ridden well, and been in the lancers or the dragoons, it is odds the English cavalry would have cut him into little pieces—since you were not there to direct operations!"

"Small loss that would have been," grumbles he, and then leaned over, laughing, and rumpled her blonde hair. "There, little one, he is your man—such as he is. God send him safe home."

I tell you all this to give you some notion of a Russian country gentleman at home, with his family—although I'll own that a Cossack may not be typical. No doubt he wasn't to East's delicate stomach—and I gather he didn't care for East too much, either—but I found myself liking Pencherjevsky. He was gross, loud, boisterous—boorish, if you like, but he was worth ten of your proper gentlemen, to me at any rate. I got roaring drunk with him, that evening, after the ladies had retired—they were fairly tipsy, themselves, and arguing at the tops of their voices about dresses as they withdrew to their drawing-room—and he sang Russian hunting songs in that glorious organ voice, and laughed himself sick trying to learn the words of "The British Grenadiers". I flatter myself he took to me enormously—folk often do, of course, particularly the coarser spirits—for he swore I was a credit to my regiment and my country, and God should send the Tsar a few like me.

"Then we should sweep you English bastards into the sea!" he roared. "A few of your Scarletts and Flashmans and Carragans—that is the name, no?—that is all we need!"

But drunk as he was, when he finally rose from the table he

* Leader.

was careful to turn in the direction of the church, and cross himself devoutly, before stumbling to guide me up the stairs.

I was to see a different side to Pencherjevsky—and to all of them for that matter—in the winter that followed, but for the first few weeks of my sojourn at Starotorsk I thoroughly enjoyed myself, and felt absolutely at home. It was so much better than I had expected, the Count was so amiable in his bear-like, thundering way, his ladies were civil (for I'd decided to go warily before attempting a more intimate acquaintance with Valla) and easy with me, and East and I were allowed such freedom, that it was like a month of week-ends at an English country-house, without any of the stuffiness. You could come and go as you pleased, treat the place as your own, attend at meal-times or feed in your chamber, whichever suited—it was Liberty Hall, no error. I divided my days between working really hard at my Russian, going for walks or rides with Valla and Sara or East, prosing with the Count in the evenings, playing cards with the family—they have a form of whist called "biritsch" which has caught on in England this last few years, and we played that most evenings —and generally taking life easy. My interest in Russian they found especially flattering, for they are immensely proud and sensitive about their country, and I made even better progress than usual. I soon spoke and understood it better than East— "He has a Cossack somewhere in his family!" Pencherjevsky would bawl. "Let him add a beard to those foolish English whiskers and he can ride with the Kubans—eh, colonel?"

All mighty pleasant—until you discovered that the civility and good nature were no deeper than a May frost, the thin covering on totally alien beings. For all their apparent civilization, and even good taste, the barbarian was just under the surface, and liable to come raging out. It was easy to forget this, until some word or incident reminded you—that this pleasant house and estate were like a medieval castle, under feudal law; that this jovial, hospitable giant, who talked so knowledgably of cavalry tactics and the hunting field, and played chess like a master, was also as dangerous and cruel as a cannibal chief; that his ladies, chattering cheerfully about French dressmaking or flower arrangement, were in some respects rather less feminine than Dahomey Amazons.

One such incident I'll never forget. There was an evening when
the four of us were in the salon, Pencherjevsky and I playing
chess—he had handicapped himself by starting without queen or
castle, to make a game of it—and the women at some two-handed
game of cards across the room. Aunt Sara was quiet, as usual, and
Valla prattling gaily, and squeaking with vexation when she lost.
I wasn't paying much attention, for I was happy with the Count's
brandy, and looked like beating him for once, too, but when I
heard them talking about settling the wager I glanced across, and
almost fell from my chair.

Valla's maid and the housekeeper had come into the room.
The maid—a serf girl—was kneeling by the card table, and the
housekeeper was carefully shearing off her long red hair with a
pair of scissors. Aunt Sara was watching idly; Valla wasn't even
noticing until the house-keeper handed her the tresses.

"Ah, how pretty!" says she, and shrugged, and tossed them
over to Aunt Sara, who stroked them, and said:

"Shall I keep them for a wig, or sell them? Thirty roubles in
Moscow or St Petersburg." And she held them up in the light,
considering.

"More than Vera is worth now, at any rate," says Valla,
carelessly. Then she jumped up, ran across to Pencherjevsky,
and put her arms round his shaggy neck from behind, blowing
in his ear. "Father, may I have fifty roubles for a new maid?"

"What's that?" says he, deep in the game. "Wait, child, wait;
I have this English rascal trapped, if only ..."

"Just fifty roubles, father. See, I cannot keep Vera now."

He looked up, saw the maid, who was still kneeling, cropped
like a convict, and guffawed. "She doesn't need hair to hang up
your dresses and fetch your shoes, does she? Learn to count your
aces, you silly girl."

"Oh, father! You know she will not do now! Only fifty roubles
—please—from my kind little *batiushka*!"*

"Ah, plague take you, can a man not have peace? Fifty roubles,
then, to be let alone. And next time, bet something that I will
not have to replace out of my purse." He pinched her cheek.
"Check, colonel."

I've a strong stomach, as you know, but I'll admit that turned

* Father.

it—not the disfigurement of a pretty girl, you understand, although I didn't hold with that, much, but the cheerful unconcern with which they did it—those two cultured ladies, in that elegant room, as though they had been gaming for sweets or counters. And now Valla was leaning on her father's shoulder, gaily urging him on to victory, and Sara was running the hair idly through her hands, while the kneeling girl bowed her pathetically shorn head to the floor and then followed the housekeeper from the room. Well, thinks I, they'd be a rage in London society, these two. You may have noticed, by the way, that the cost of a maid was fifty roubles, of which her hair was worth thirty.

Of course, they didn't think of her as human. I've told you something of the serfs already, and most of that I learned first-hand on the Pencherjevsky estate, where they were treated as something worse than cattle. The more fortunate of them lived in the outbuildings and were employed about the house, but most of them were down in the village, a filthy, straggling place of log huts, called *isbas*, with entrances so low you had to stoop to go in. They were foul, verminous hovels, consisting of just one room, with a huge bed bearing many pillows, a big stove, and a "holy corner" in which there were poor, garish pictures of their saints.

Their food was truly fearful—rye bread for the most part, and cabbage soup with a lump of fat in it, salt cabbage, garlic stew, coarse porridge, and for delicacies, sometimes a little cucumber or beetroot. And those were the well-fed ones. Their drink was as bad—bread fermented in alcohol which they call *qvass* ("it's black, it's thick, and it makes you drunk," as they said), and on special occasions vodka, which is just poison. They'll sell their souls for brandy, but seldom get it.

Such conditions of squalor, half the year in stifling heat, half in unimaginable cold, and all spent in back-breaking labour, are probably enough to explain why they were such an oppressed, dirty, brutish, useless people—just like the Irish, really, but without the gaiety. Even the Mississippi niggers were happier—there was never a smile on the face of your serf, just patient, morose misery.

And yet that wasn't the half of their trouble. I remember the court that Pencherjevsky used to hold in a barn at the back of the house, and those cringing creatures crawling on their bellies along the floor to kiss the edge of his coat, while he pronounced sentence on them for their offences. You may not believe them, but they're true, and I noted them at the time.

There was the local dog-killer—every Russian village is plagued in winter by packs of wild dogs, who are a real danger to life, and this fellow had to chase and club them to death—he got a few kopecks for each pelt. But he had been shirking his job, it seemed.

"Forty strokes of the cudgel," says Pencherjevsky. And then he added: "Siberia," at which a great wail went up from the crowd trembling at the far end of the barn. One of the Cossacks just lashed at them with his *nagaika*,* and the wail died.

There was an iron collar for a woman whose son had run off, and floggings, either with the cudgel or the whip, for several who had neglected their labouring in Pencherjevsky's fields. There was Siberia for a youth employed to clean windows at the house, who had started work too early and disturbed Valla, and for one of the maids who had dropped a dish. You will say, "Ah, here's Flashy pulling the long bow", but I'm not, and if you don't believe me, ask any professor of Russian history.[25]

But here's the point—if you'd suggested to Pencherjevsky or his ladies, or even to the serfs, that such punishments were cruel, they'd have thought you were mad. It seemed the most natural thing in the world to them—why, I've seen a man cudgelled by the Cossacks in Pencherjevsky's courtyard—tied to a post half-naked in the freezing weather, and smashed with heavy rods until he was a moaning lump of bruised and broken flesh, with half his ribs cracked—and through it all Valla was standing not ten yards away, never even glancing in his direction, but discussing a new sledge-harness with one of the grooms.

Pencherjevsky absolutely believed that his *moujiks* were well off. "Have I not given them a stone church, with a blue dome and gilt stars? How many villages can show the like, eh?" And when those he had condemned to years of exile in Siberia were driven off in a little coffle under the *nagaikas* of the Cossacks—they would be taken to the nearest town, to join other unfortunates,

* Cossack whip.

and they would all *walk* the whole way—he was there to give them his blessing, and they would embrace his knees, crying: "*Izvenete, batiushka, veno vat,*"* and he would nod and say "*Horrosho,*"† while the housekeeper gave them bundles of dainties from the "*Sudarinia‡ Valla*". God knows what they were —cucumber rinds, probably.

"From me they have strict justice, under the law," says this amazing gorilla. "And they love me for it. Has anyone ever seen the knout, or the *butuks,*§ used on my estate? No, and never shall. If I correct them, it is because without correction they will become idle and shiftless, and ruin me—and themselves. For without me, where are they? These poor souls, they believe the world rests on three whales swimming in the Eternal Sea! What are you to do with such folk? I will meet with the best, the wisest of them, the spokesman of their *gromada,*¶ driving his *droshky.*|| 'Ha, Ivan,' I will say, 'your axles squeal; why do you not grease them?' And he ponders, and replies, 'Only a thief is afraid to make a noise, *batiushka.*' So the axles remain ungreased—unless I cudgel his foolish head, or have the Cossacks whip and salt his back for him. And he respects me"—he would thump his great fist on his thigh as he said it—"because he knows I am a bread and salt man, and go with my neck open, as he does.²⁶ And I am just—to the inch."

And you may say he was: when he flogged his *dvornik*** for insolence, and the fellow collapsed before the prescribed punishment was finished, they sent him to the local quack—and when he was better, gave him the remaining strokes. "Who would trust me again, if I excused him a single blow?" says Pencherjevsky.

Now, I don't recite all these barbarities to shock or excite your pity, or to pose as one of those holy hypocrites who pretend to be in a great sweat about man's inhumanity to man. I've seen too much of it, and know it happens wherever strong folk have absolute power over spiritless creatures. I merely tell you truly what I saw—as for my own view, well, I'm all for keeping the peasants in order, and if hammering 'em does good, and makes life better for

---

* Pardon, father, I am guilty.   † Very well.
‡ Lady.   § Press for crushing feet.
¶ Village assembly. || Gig.   ** Porter.

the rest of us, you won't find me leaping between the tyrant and his victim crying "Stay, cruel despot!" But I would observe that much of the cruelty I saw in Russia was pure senseless brutishness—I doubt if they even enjoyed it much. They just knew no better.

I wondered sometimes why the serfs, dull, ignorant, superstitious clods though they were, endured it. The truth, as I learned it from Pencherjevsky, was that they didn't, always. In the thirty years just ending when I was in Russia, there had been peasant revolts once every fortnight, in one part of the country or another, and as often as not it had taken the military to put them down. Or rather, it had taken the Cossacks, for the Russian army was a useless thing, as we'd seen in the Crimea. You can't make soldiers out of slaves. But the Cossacks were free, independent tribesmen; they had land, and paid little tax, had their own tribal laws, drank themselves stupid, and served the Tsar from boyhood till they were fifty because they loved to ride and fight and loot—and they liked nothing better than to use their *nagaikas* on the serfs, which was just nuts to them.

Pencherjevsky wasn't worried about revolution among his own *moujiks* because, as I say, he regarded himself as a good master. Also he had Cossacks of his own to strike terror into any malcontents. "And I never commit the great folly," says he. "I never touch a serf-woman—or allow one to be used or sold as a concubine." (Whether he said it for my benefit or not, it was bad news, for I hadn't had a female in ages, and some of the peasants —like Valla's maid—were not half bad-looking once they were washed.) "These uprisings on other estates—look into them, and I'll wager every time the master has ravished some serf wench, or stolen a *moujik's* wife, or sent a young fellow into the army so that he can enjoy his sweetheart. They don't like it, I tell you— and I don't blame them! If a lord wants a woman, let him marry one, or buy one from far afield—but let him slake his lust on one of his own serf-women, and he'll wake up one fine morning with a split head and his roof on fire. And serve him right!"

I gathered he was unusual in this view: most landlords just used the serf-wenches the way American owners used their nigger girls, and pupped 'em all over the place. But Pencherjevsky had his own code, and believed his *moujiks* thought the better of him for it, and were content. I wondered if he wasn't gammoning himself.

Because I paid attention, toady-like, to his proses, and was eager in studying his language, he assumed I was interested in his appalling country and its ways, and was at pains to educate me, as he saw it. From him I learned of the peculiar laws governing the serfs—how they might be free if they could run away for ten years, how some of them were allowed to leave the estates and work in the towns, provided they sent a proportion of earnings to their master; how some of these serfs became vastly rich—richer than their masters, sometimes, and worth millions—but still could not buy their freedom unless he wished. Some serfs even owned serfs. It was an idiotic system, of course, but the landowners were all for it, and even the humanitarian ones believed that if it were changed, and political reforms allowed, the country would dissolve in anarchy. I daresay they were right, but myself I believe it will happen anyway; it was starting even then, as Pencherjevsky admitted.

"The agitators are never idle," says he. "You have heard of the pernicious German-Jew, Marx?" (I didn't like to tell him Marx had been at my wedding, as an uninvited guest.*) "He vomits his venom over Europe—aye, he and other vile rascals like him would spread their poison even to our country if they could.[27] Praise God the *moujiks* are unlettered folk—but they can hear, and our cities crawl with revolutionary criminals of the lowest stamp. What do they understand of Russia, these filth? What do they seek to do but ruin her? And yet countries like your own give harbour to such creatures, to brew their potions of hate against us! Aye, and against you, too, if you could only see it! You think to encourage them, for the downfall of your enemies, but you will reap the wild wind also, Colonel Flashman!"

"Well, you know, Count," says I, "we let chaps say what they like, pretty well, always have done. We don't have any *kabala*,† like you—don't seem to need it, for some reason. Probably because we have factories, and so on, and everyone's kept busy, don't you know? I don't doubt all you say is true—but it suits us, you see. And our *moujiks* are, well, different from yours." I

* See *Royal Flash*   † Slavery.

wondered, even as I said it, if they were; remembering that hospital at Yalta, I doubted it. But I couldn't help adding: "Would your *moujiks* have ridden into the battery at Balaclava?"

At this he roared with laughter, and called me an evil English rascal, and clapped me on the back. We were mighty close, he and I, really, when I look back—but of course, he never really knew me.

So you see what kind of man he was, and what kind of a place it was. Most of the time, I liked it—it was a fine easy life until, as I say, you got an unpleasant reminder of what an alien, brooding hostile land it was. It was frightening then, and I had to struggle to make myself remember that England and London and Elspeth still existed, that far away to the south Cardigan was still croaking "Haw-haw" and Raglan was fussing in the mud at Sevastopol. I would look out of my window sometimes, at the snow-frosted garden, and beyond it the vast, white, endless plain, streaked only by the dark field-borders, and it seemed the old world was just a dream. It was easy then, to get the Russian melancholy, which sinks into the bones, and is born of a knowledge of helplessness far from home.

The thing that bored me most, needless to say, was being without a woman. I tried my hand with Valla, when we got to know each other and I had decided she wasn't liable to run squealing to her father. By George, she didn't need to. I gave her bottom a squeeze, and she laughed at me and told me she was a respectable married woman; taking this as an invitation I embraced her, at which she wriggled and giggled, puss-like, and then hit me an atrocious clout in the groin with her clenched fist, and ran off, laughing. I walked with a crouch for days, and decided that these Russian ladies must be treated with respect.

East felt the boredom of captivity in that white wilderness more than I, and spent long hours in his room, writing. One day when he was out I had a turn through his papers, and discovered he was writing his impressions, in the form of an endless letter to his odious friend Brown, who was apparently farming in New Zealand. There was some stuff about me in it, which I read with interest:

". . . I don't know what to think of Flashman. He is very well liked by all in the house, the Count especially, and I fear that little

Valla admires him, too—it would be hard not to, I suppose, for he is such a big, handsome fellow. (Good for you, Scud; carry on.) I say I fear—because sometimes I see him looking at her, with such an ardent expression, and I remember the kind of brute he was at Rugby, and my heart sinks for her fair innocence. Oh, I trust I am wrong! I tell myself that he has changed—how else did the mean, cowardly, spiteful, bullying toady (steady, now, young East) become the truly brave and valiant soldier that he now undoubtedly is? But I do fear, just the same; I know he does not pray, and that he swears, and has evil thoughts, and that the cruel side of his nature is still there. Oh, my poor little Valla— but there, old fellow, I mustn't let my dark suspicions run away with me. I must think well of him, and trust that my prayers will help to keep him true, and that he will prove, despite my doubts, to be an upright, Christian gentleman at last."

You know, the advantage to being a wicked bastard is that everyone pesters the Lord on your behalf; if volume of prayers from my saintly enemies means anything, I'll be saved when the Archbishop of Canterbury is damned. It's a comforting thought.

So time passed, and Christmas came and went, and I was slipping into a long, bored tranquil snooze as the months went by. And I was getting soft, and thoroughly off guard, and all the time hell was preparing to break loose.

It was shortly before "the old wives' winter", as the Russians call February, that Valla's husband came home for a week's furlough. He was an amiable, studious little chap, who got on well with East, but the Count plainly didn't like him, and once he had given us the news from Sevastopol—which was that the siege was still going on, and getting nowhere, which didn't surprise me—old Pencherjevsky just ignored him, and retired moodily to his study and took to drink. He had me in to help him, too, and I caught him giving me odd, thoughtful looks, which was disconcerting, and growling to himself before topping up another bumper of brandy, and drinking sneering toasts to "the blessed happy couple", as he called them.

Then, exactly a week after Valla's husband had gone back— with no very fond leave-taking from his little spouse, it seemed to me—I was sitting yawning in the salon over a Russian novel, when Aunt Sara came in, and asked if I was bored. I was mildly surprised, for she seldom said much, or addressed one directly. She looked me up and down, with no expression on that fine horse face, and then said abruptly:

"What you need is a Russian steam-bath. It is the sovereign remedy against our long winters. I have told the servants to make it ready. Come."

I was idle enough to be game for anything, so I put on my *tulup*,* and followed her to one of the farthest outbuildings, beyond the house enclosure; it was snowing like hell, but a party of the servants had a great fire going under a huge grille out in the snow, and Aunt Sara took me inside to show me how the thing worked. It was a big log structure, divided down the middle by a high partition, and in the half where we stood was a raised wooden slab, like a butcher's block, surrounded by a trench in the floor. Presently the serfs came in, carrying on metal stretchers great glowing stones which they laid in the trench; the heat was terrific, and Aunt Sara explained to me that you lay on the slab, naked, while the minions outside poured cold water through openings at the base of the wall, which exploded into steam when it touched the stones.

"This side is for men-folk," says she. "Women are through there"—and she pointed to a gap in the partition. "Your clothes go in the sealed closet on the wall, and when you are ready you lie motionless on the slab, and allow the steam to envelope you." She gave me her bored stare. "The door is bolted from within." And off she went, to the other side of the partition.

Well, it was something new, so I undressed and lay on the slab, Aunt Sara called out presently from beyond the partition, and the water came in like Niagara. It hissed and splashed on the stones, and in a twinkling the place was like London fog, choking, scalding, and blotting you in, and you lay there gasping while it sweated into you, turning you scarlet. It was hellish hot and clammy, but not unpleasant, and I lay soaking in it; by and by they pumped in more water, the steam gushed up again, and I was turning over drowsily on my face when Aunt Sara's voice spoke unexpectedly at my elbow.

"Lie still," says she, and peering through the mist, I saw that she was wrapped in a clinging sheet, with her long, dark hair

* Sheepskin coat.

hanging in wet strands on either side of that strong, impassive face. I suddenly choked with what East would have called dark thoughts; she was carrying a bunch of long birch twigs, and as she laid a hot, wet hand on my shoulder she muttered huskily: "This is the true benefit of the baths; do not move."

And then, in that steam-heat, she began to birch me, very lightly at first, up the backs of my legs and to my shoulders, and then back again, harder and harder all the time, until I began to yelp. More steam came belching up, and she turned me over and began work on my chest and stomach. I was fairly interested by now, for mildly painful though it was, it was distinctly stimulating.

"Now, for me," says she, and motioned me to get up and take the birches. "Russian ladies often use nettles," says she, and for once her voice was unsteady. "I prefer the birch—it is stronger." And in a twinkling she was out of her sheet and face down on the slab. I was having a good gloat down at that long, strong, naked body, when the damned serfs blotted everything out with steam again, so I lashed away through the murk, belabouring her vigorously; she began to moan and gasp, and I went at it like a man possessed, laying on so that the twigs snapped, and as the steam cleared again she rolled over on her back, mouth open and eyes staring, and reached out to seize hold of me, pumping away at me and gasping:

"Now! Now! For me! *Pajalsta!* I must have! Now! *Pajalsta!*"

Now, I can recognize a saucy little flirt when I see one, so I gave her a few last thrashes and leaped aboard, nearly bursting. God, it must have been months—so in my perversity, I had to tease her, until she dragged me down, sobbing and scratching at my back, and we whaled away on that wet slab, with the steam thundering round us, and she writhed and grappled fit to dislocate herself, until I began to fear we would slither off on to the hot stones. And when I lay there, utterly done, she slipped away and doused me with a bucket of cold water—what with one thing and another, I wonder I survived that bath.

Mind you, I felt better for it; barbarians they may be, but the Russians have some excellent institutions, and I remain grateful to Sara—undoubtedly my favourite aunt.

I supposed, in my vanity, that she had just proposed our steam-bath romp to help pass the winter, but there was another reason, as I discovered the following day. It was a bizarre, unbelievable thing, really, to people like you and me, but in feudal Russia— well, I shall tell you.

It was after the noon meal that Pencherjevsky invited me to go riding with him. This wasn't unusual, but his manner was; he was curt and silent as we rode—if it had been anyone but this hulking tyrant, I'd have said he was nervous. We rode some distance from the house, and were pacing our beasts through the silent snow-fields, when he suddenly began to talk—about the Cossacks, of all things. He rambled most oddly at first, about how they rode with bent knees, like jockeys (which I'd noticed anyway), and how you could tell a Ural Cossack from the Black Sea variety because one wore a sheepskin cap and the other the long string-haired bonnet. And how the flower of the flock were his own people, the Zaporozhiyan Cossacks, or Kubans, who had been moved east to new lands near Azov by the Empress generations ago, but he, Pencherjevsky, had come back to the old stamping-ground, and here he would stay, by God, and his family after him forever.

"The old days are gone," says he, and I see him so clearly still, that huge bulk in his sheepskin *tulup*, hunched in his saddle, glowering with moody, unseeing eyes across the white wilderness, with the blood-red disc of the winter sun behind him. "The day of the great Cossack, when we thumbed our noses at Tsar and Sultan alike, and carried our lives and liberty on our lance-points. We owed loyalty to none but our comrades and the *hetman* we elected to lead us—I was such a one. Now it is a new Russia, and instead of the *hetman* we have rulers from Moscow to govern the tribe. So be it. I make my place here, in my forefathers' land, I have my good estate, my *moujiks*, my land—the inheritance for the son I never sired." He looked at me. "I would have had one like you, a tall lancer fit to ride at the head of his own *sotnia*.* You have a son, eh? A sturdy fellow? Good. I could wish it were not so—that you had no wife in England, no son, nothing to bind you or call you home. I would say to you then: 'Stay with us here. Be as a son to me. Be a husband to my daughter, and get yourself a son, and me a grandson, who will follow

* Company, band.

after us, and hold our land here, in this new Russia, this empire born of storm, where only a man who is a man can hope to plant himself and his seed and endure.' That is what I would say."

Well, it was flattering, no question, although I might have pointed out to him that Valla had a husband already, and even if I'd been free and willing . . . but it occurred to me that he probably wasn't the man to let a little thing like that stand in the way. Morrison may not have been much of a father-in-law, but this chap would have been less comfortable still.

"As it is," he growled on, "I have a son-in-law—you saw what kind of a thing he is. God knows how any daughter of mine could . . . but there. I have doted on her, and indulged her, for her dear mother's sake—aye, and because I love her. And if he was the last man I would have chosen for her—well, she cared for him, and I thought, their sons will have my blood, they may be Cossacks, horse-and-lance men, grandchildren to be proud of. But I have no grandsons—*he* gets me none!"

And he growled and spat and then swung round to face me. For a moment he wrestled with his tongue, and couldn't speak, and then it came out in a torrent.

"There must be a *man* to follow me here! I am too old now, there are no children left in me, or I would marry again. Valla, my lovely child, is my one hope—but she is tied to this . . . this empty thing, and I see her going childless to her grave. Unless . . ." He was gnawing at his lip, and his face was terrific. "Unless . . . she can bear me a grandson. It is all I have to live for! To see a Pencherjevsky who will take up this inheritance when I am gone—be his father who he will, so long as he is a man! It cannot be her husband, so . . . If it is an offence against God, against the Church, against the law—I am a Cossack, and we were here before God or the Church or the law! I do not care! I will see a male grandchild of mine to carry my line, my name, my land—and if I burn in hell for it, I shall count it worth the cost! At least a Pencherjevsky shall rule here—what I have built will not be squandered piecemeal among the rabble of that fellow's knock-kneed relatives! A man shall get my Valla a son!"

I'm not slow on the uptake, even with a bearded baboon nearly seven feet tall roaring at my face from a few inches away, and what I understood from this extraordinary outburst simply took my breath away. I'm all for family, you understand, but I doubt if I have the dynastic instinct as strong as all that.

"You are such a man," says he, and suddenly he edged his horse even closer, and crushed my arm in his enormous paw. "You can get sons—you have done so," he croaked, his livid face beside mine. "You have a child in England—and Sara has proved you also. When the war is over, you will leave here, and go to England, far away. No one will ever know—but you and I!"

I found my voice, and said something about Valla.

"She is my daughter," says he, and his voice rasped like an iron file. "She knows what this means to the house of Pencherjevsky. She obeys." And for the first time he smiled, a dreadful, crooked grin through his beard. "From what Sara tells me, she may be happy to obey. As for you, it will be no hardship. And"—he took me by the shoulder, rocking me in the saddle—"it may be worth much or little, but hereafter you may call Pencherjevsky from the other side of hell, and he will come to your side!"

If it was an extraordinary proposition, I won't pretend it was unwelcome. Spooky, of course, but immensely flattering, after all. And you only had to imagine, for a split second, what Pencherjevsky's reaction would have been to a polite refusal—I say no more.

"It will be a boy," says he, "I know it. And if by chance it is a girl—then she shall have a *man* for a husband, if I have to rake the world for him!"

An impetuous fellow, this Count—it never occurred to him that it might be his little Valla who was barren, and not her husband. However, that was not for me to say, so I kept mum, and left all the arrangements to papa.

He did it perfectly, no doubt with the connivance of that lustful slut Sara—there was a lady who took pleasure in her experimental work, all right. I sallied forth at midnight, and feeling not unlike a prize bull at the agricultural show—"'ere 'e is, ladies'n' gennelmen, Flashman Buttercup the Twenty-first of Horny Bottom Farm"—tip-toed out of the corridor where my room and East's lay, and set off on the long promenade to the other wing. It was ghostly in that creaky old house, with not a soul about, but true love spurred me on, and sure enough Valla's door was ajar, with a little sliver of light lancing across the passage floor.

I popped in—and she was kneeling beside the bed, praying! I didn't know whether it was for forgiveness for the sin of adultery, or for the sin to be committed successfully, and I didn't stop to ask. There's no point in talking, or hanging back shuffling on these occasions, and saying: "Ah ... well, shall we ...?" On the other hand, one doesn't go roaring and ramping at respectable married women, so I stooped and kissed her very gently, drew off her nightdress, and eased her on to the bed. I felt her plump little body trembling under my hands, so I kissed her long and carefully, fondling her and murmuring nonsense in her ear, and then her arms went round my neck.

Frankly, I think the Count had under-estimated her horse artillery husband, for she had learned a great deal from somewhere. I'd been prepared for her to be reluctant, or to need some jollying along, but she entered into the spirit of the thing like a tipsy widow, and it was from no sense of duty or giving the house of Pencherjevsky its money's worth that I stayed until past four o'clock. I do love a bouncy blonde with a hearty appetite, and when I finally crawled back to my own chilly bed it was with the sense of an honest night's work well done.

But if a job is worth doing, it's worth doing well, and since there seemed to be an unspoken understanding that the treatment should be continued, I made frequent forays to Valla's room in the ensuing nights. And so far as I'm a judge, the little baggage revelled in being a dutiful daughter—they're a damned randy lot, these Russians. Something to do with the cold weather, I dare say. A curious thing was, I soon began to feel as though we were truly married, and no doubt this had something to do with the purpose behind our night games; yet during the day we remained on the same easy terms as before, and if Sara grudged her niece the pleasuring she was getting, she never let on. Pencherjevsky said nothing, but from time to time I would catch him eyeing us with sly satisfaction, fingering his beard at the table head.

East suspected something, I'm certain. His manner to me became nervous, and he avoided the family's society even more than

before, but he didn't dare say anything. Too scared of finding his
suspicions well grounded, I suppose.

The only fly in the ointment that I could see was the possibility that during the months ahead it might become apparent
that I was labouring in vain; however, I was ready to face
Pencherjevsky's disappointment when and if it came. Valla's
yawns at breakfast were proof that I was doing my share man-
fully. And then something happened which made the whole
speculation pointless.

From time to time in the first winter months there had been
other guests at the big house of Starotorsk: military ones. The
nearest township—where I'd encountered Ignatieff—was an important army head-quarters, a sort of staging post for the Crimea,
but as there was no decent accommodation in the place, the more
important wayfarers were in the habit of putting up with Pencherjevsky. On these occasions East and I were politely kept in
our rooms, with a Cossack posted in the corridor, and our meals
sent up on trays, but we saw some of the comings and goings from
our windows—Liprandi, for example, and a grandee with a large
military staff whom East said was Prince Worontzoff. After one
such visit it was obvious to both of us that some sort of military
conference had been held in the Count's library—you could
smell it the next morning, and there was a big map easel leaned up
in a corner that hadn't been there before.

"We should keep our eyes and ears open," says East to me
later. "Do you know—if we could have got out of our rooms
when that confabulation was going on, we might have crept into
the old gallery up yonder, and heard all kinds of useful intelligence."

This was a sort of screened minstrel's gallery that overlooked the
library; you got into it by a little door off the main landing. But
it was no welcome suggestion to me, as you can guess, who am
all for lying low.

"Rot!" says I. "We ain't spies—and if we were, and the whole
Russian general staff were to blab their plans within earshot,
what could we do with the knowledge?"

"Who knows—" says he, looking keen. "That Cossack they put
to watch our doors sleeps half the night—did you know? Reeking of brandy. We could get out, I daresay—I tell you what,

Flashman, if another high ranker comes this way, I think we're bound to try and overhear him, if we can. It's our duty."

"Duty?" says I, alarmed. "Duty to eavesdrop? What kind of company have you been keeping lately? I can't see Raglan, or any other honourable man, thinking much of that sort of conduct." The high moral line, you see; deuced handy sometimes. "Why, we're as good as guests in this place."

"We're prisoners," says he, "and we haven't given any parole. Any information we can come by is a legitimate prize of war—and if we heard anything big enough it might even be worth trying a run for it. We're not that far from the Crimea."

This was appalling. Wherever you go, however snug you may have made yourself, there is always one of these duty-bound, energetic bastards trying to make trouble. The thought of spying on the Russians, and then lighting out in the snow some dark night, with Pencherjevsky's Cossacks after us—my imagination was in full flight in a trice, while Scud stood chewing his lip, muttering his thoughtful lunacies. I didn't argue—it would have looked bad, as though I weren't as eager to strike a blow for Britannia as he was. And it wasn't even worth talking about—we weren't going to get the chance to spy, or escape, or do anything foolish. I'd have given a thousand to one on that—which, as it turned out, would have been very unwise odds to offer.

However, after that small discussion the weeks had slipped by without any other important Russians visiting the place, and then came my diversion with Valla, and East's ridiculous daydream went clean out of my mind. And then, about ten days after I had started galloping her, a couple of Ruski staff captains jingled into the courtyard one morning, to be followed by a large horse-sled, and shortly afterwards comes the Count's major-domo to East and me, presenting his apologies, and chivvying us off to our rooms.

We took the precaution of muffling the hidden speaking-tube, and kept a good watch from East's window that day. We saw more sleds arrive, and from the distant hum of voices in the house and the sound of tramping on the stairs we realized there must be a fair-sized party in the place. East was all excited, but what really stirred him was when a sled arrived late in the afternoon, and Pencherjevsky himself was in the yard to meet it—attired as we'd never seen him before, in full dress uniform.

"This is important," says East, his eyes alight. "Depend upon it, that's some really big wig. Gad! I'd give a year's pay to hear what passes below tonight." He was white with excitement. "Flashman, I'm going to have a shot at it!"

"You're crazy," says I. "With a Cossack mooching about the passage all night? You say he sleeps—he can wake up, too, can't he?"

"I'll chance that," says he, and for all I could try—appeals to his common sense, to his position as a guest, to his honour as an officer (I think I even invoked Arnold and religion) he remained set.

"Well, don't count on me," I told him. "It ain't worth it—they won't be saying anything worth a damn—it ain't safe, and by thunder, it's downright ungentlemanly. So now!"

To my surprise, he patted my arm. "I respect what you say, old fellow," says he. "But—I can't help it. I may be wrong, but I see my duty differently, don't you understand? I know it's St Paul's to a pub it'll be a fool's errand, but—well, you never know. And I'm not like you—I haven't done much for Queen and country. I'd like to try."

Well, there was nothing for it but to get my head under the bed-clothes that night and snore like hell, to let the world know that Flashy wasn't up to mischief. Neither, it transpired, was the bold East: he reported next day that the Cossack had stayed awake all night, so his expedition had to be called off. But the sleds stayed there all day, and the next, and they kept us cooped up all the time, and the Cossack remained vigilant, to East's mounting frenzy.

"Three days!" says he. "Who can it be, down there? I tell you, it must be some important meeting! I *know* it! And we have to sit here, like mice in a cage, when if we could only get out for an hour, we might find out something that would—oh, I don't know, but it might be vital to the war! It's enough to drive a chap out of his wits!"

"It already has," says I. "You haven't been shut up like this before, have you? Well, I've been a prisoner more times than I care to think of, and I can tell you, after a while you don't reason straight any longer. That's what's wrong with you. Also, you're tired out; get to sleep tonight, and forget this nonsense."

He fretted away, though, and I was almost out of patience with him by dinner-time, when who should come up with the servants bearing dinner, but Valla. She had just dropped in to see us, she said, and was very bright, and played a three-handed card game with us, which was a trying one for East, I could see. He was jumpy as a cat with her at the best of times, blushing and falling over his feet, and now in addition he was fighting to keep from asking her what was afoot downstairs, and who the visitors were. She prattled on, till about nine, and then took her leave, and as I held the door for her she gave me a glance and a turn of her pretty blonde head that said, as plain as words: "It's been three nights now. Well?" I went back to my room next door, full of wicked notions, and leaving East yawning and brooding.

If I hadn't been such a lustful brute, no doubt prudence would have kept me abed that night. But at midnight I was peeping out, and there was the Cossack, slumped on his stool, head back and mouth open, reeking like Davis's cellar. Valla's work, thinks I, the charming little wretch. I slipped past him, and he never even stirred, and I padded out of the pool of lamplight round him and reached the big landing.

All was still up here, but there was a dim light down in the hall, and through the banisters I could see two white-tunicked and helmeted sentries on the big double doors of the library, with their sabres drawn, and an orderly officer pacing idly about smoking a cigarette. It struck me that it wasn't safe to be gallivanting about this house in the dark—they might think I was on the East tack, spying—so I flitted on, and two minutes later was stallioning away like billy-o with my modest flower of the steppes—by jingo, she was in a fine state of passion, I remember. We had one violent bout, and then some warm wine from her little spirit lamp, and talked softly and dozed and played, and then went to it again, very slowly and wonderfully, and I can see that lovely white shape in the flickering light even now, and smell the perfume of that silver hair, and—dear me, how we old soldiers do run on.

"You must not linger too long, sweetheart," says she, at last. "Even drunk Cossacks don't sleep forever," and giggled, nibbling at my chin. So I kissed her a long good-night, with endearments, resumed my night-shirt, squeezed her bouncers again for luck, and toddled out into the cold, along her corridor, down the little stairs to the landing—and froze in icy shock against the wall on the second step, my heart going like a hammer.

There was someone on the landing. I could hear him, and then see him by the dim light from the far corridor where my room lay. He was crouched by the archway, listening, a man in a night-shirt, like myself. With a wrenching inward sigh, I realized that it could only be East.

The fool had stayed awake, seen the Cossack asleep, and was now bent on his crack-brained patriotic mischief. I hissed very gently, had the satisfaction of seeing him try to leap through the wall, and then was at his side, shushing him for all I was worth. He seized me, gurgling.

"You! Flashman!" He let out a shuddering breath. "What—? You've been . . . why didn't you tell me?" I wondered what the blazes this meant, until he whispered fiercely: "Good man! Have you heard anything? Are they still there?"

The madman seemed to think I'd been on his eavesdropping lay. Well, at least I'd be spared recriminations for fornicating with his adored object. I shook my head, he bit his lip, and then the maniac breathed in my ear: "Come, then, quickly! Into the gallery—they're still down there!" And while I was peeping, terrified, into the dimness through the banisters, where the white sentries were still on guard, he suddenly flitted from my side across the landing. I daren't even try a loud whisper to call him back; he was fumbling with the catch of the little door in the far shadows, and I was just hesitating before bolting for bed and safety, when from our corridor sounded a cavernous yawn. Panicking, I shot across like a whippet, clutching vainly at East as he slipped through the low aperture into the gallery. Come back, come back, you mad bastard, my lips were saying, but no sound emerged, which was just as well, for with the opening of the little gallery door the clear tones of someone in the library echoed up to us. And light was filtering up through the fine screen which concealed the gallery from the floor below. If our Cossack guard was waking, and took a turn to the landing, he'd see the dim glow from the open gallery door. Gibbering

silently to myself, half-way inside the little opening, I crept
forward, edging the door delicately shut behind me.

East was flat on the dusty gallery floor, his feet towards me;
it stank like a church in the confined space between the carved
wooden screen on the one hand and the wall on the other. My
head was no more than a foot from the screen; thank God it was a
nearly solid affair, with only occasional carved apertures. I lay
panting and terrified, hearing the voice down in the library saying
in Russian:

". . . so there would be no need to vary the orders at present.
The establishment is large enough, and would not be affected."

I remember those words because they were the first I heard,
but for the next few moments I was too occupied with scrabbling
at East's feet, and indicating to him in dumb show that the
sooner we were out of this the better, to pay any heed to what
they were talking about. But damn him, he wouldn't budge, but
kept gesturing me to lie still and listen. So I did, and some first-
rate military intelligence we overheard, too—about the appointment of a commissary-general for the Omsk region, and whether
the fellow who commanded Orianburg oughtn't to be retired.
Horse Guards would give their buttocks to know this, thinks
I furiously, and I had just determined to slide out and leave East
alone to his dangerous and useless foolery, when I became conscious of a rather tired, hoarse, but well-bred voice speaking in
the library, and one word that he used froze me where I lay,
ears straining:

"So that is the conclusion of our agenda? Good. We are grateful to you, gentlemen. You have laboured well, and we are well
pleased with the reports you have laid before us. There is Item
Seven, of course," and the voice paused. "Late as it is, perhaps
Count Ignatieff would favour us with a résumé of the essential
points again."

Ignatieff. My icy bully of the registrar's office. For no reason I
felt my pulse begin to run even harder. Cautiously I turned my
head, and put an eye to the nearest aperture.

Down beneath us, Pencherjevsky's fine long table was agleam
with candles and littered with papers. There were five men
round it. At the far end, facing us, Ignatieff was standing, very
spruce and masterful in his white uniform; behind him there was

the huge easel, covered with maps. On the side to his left was a stout, white-whiskered fellow in a blue uniform coat frosted with decorations—a marshal if ever I saw one. Opposite him, on Ignatieff's right, was a tall, bald, beak-nosed civilian, with his chin resting on his folded hands. At the end nearest us was a high-backed chair whose wings concealed the occupant, but I guessed he was the last speaker, for an aide seated at his side was saying:

"Is it necessary, majesty? It is approved, after all, and I fear your majesty is over-tired already. Perhaps tomorrow . . ."

"Let it be tonight," says the hidden chap, and his voice was dog-weary. "I am not as certain of my tomorrows as I once was. And the matter is of the first urgency. Pray proceed, Count."

As the aide bowed I was aware of East craning to squint back at me. His face was a study and his lips silently framed the words: "Tsar? The Tsar?"

Well, who else would they call majesty?[28] I didn't know, but I was all ears and eyes now as Ignatieff bowed, and half-turned to the map behind him. That soft, metallic voice rang upwards from the library panelling.

"Item Seven, the plan known as the expedition of the Indus. By your majesty's leave."

I thought I must have misheard. Indus—that was in Northern India! What the devil did they have to do with that?

"Clause the first," says Ignatieff. "That with the attention of the allied Powers, notably Great Britain, occupied in their invasion of your majesty's Crimean province, the opportunity arises to further the policy of eastward pacification and civilization in those unsettled countries beyond our eastern and southern borders. Clause the second, that the surest way of fulfilling this policy, and at the same time striking a vital blow at the enemy, is to destroy, by native rebellion aided by armed force, the British position on the Indian continent. Clause the third, that the time for armed invasion by your majesty's imperial forces is now ripe, and will be undertaken forthwith. Hence, the Indus expedition."

I think I had stopped breathing; I couldn't believe what I was hearing.

"Clause the fourth," says Ignatieff. "The invasion is to be made by an imperial force of thirty thousand men, of whom ten thousand will be Cossack cavalry. General Duhamel," and he bowed towards the bald chap, "you majesty's agent in Teheran, believes that it would be assisted if Persia could be provoked into war against Britain's ally, Turkey. Clause the fifth—"

"Never mind the clauses,'" says Duhamel. "That advice has been withdrawn. Persia will remain neutral, but hostile to British interest—as she always has been."

Ignatieff bowed again. "With your majesty's leave. It is so agreed, and likewise approved that the Afghan and Sikh powers should be enlisted against the British, in our imperial invasion. They will understand—as will the natives of India—that our expedition is not one of conquest, but to overthrow the English and liberate India." He paused. "We shall thus be liberating the people who are the source of Britain's wealth."

He picked up a pointer and tapped the map, which was of Central Asia and Northern India. "We have considered five possible routes which the invasion might take. First, the three desert routes—Ust-Yurt-Khiva-Herat, or Raim-Bokhara, or Raim-Syr Daria-Tashkent. These, although preferred by General Khruleff"—at this the stout, whiskered fellow stirred in his seat —"have been abandoned because they run through the unsettled areas where we are still engaged in pacifying the Tajiks, Uzbeks and Khokandians, under the brigand leaders Yakub Beg and Izzat Kutebar. Although stinging reverses have been administered to these lawless bandits, and their stronghold of Ak Mechet occupied, they may still be strong enough to hinder the expedition's advance. The less fighting there is to do before we cross the Indian frontier the better."

Ignatieff lowered his pointer on the map. "So the southern routes, beneath the Caspian, are preferred—either through Tabriz and Teheran, or by Herat. An immediate choice is not necessary. The point is that infantry and artillery may be moved with ease across the South Caspian to Herat, while the cavalry move through Persia. Once we are in Persia, the British will have warning of our attempt, but by then it will be too late—far too late. We shall proceed through Kandahar and Kabul, assisted by the hatred which the Afghans owe the British, and so—to India.

"There are, by reliable report, twenty-five thousand British troops in India, and three hundred thousand native soldiers.

These latter present no problem—once a successful invasion is launched, the majority of them will desert, or join in the rebellion which our presence will inspire. It is doubtful if, six months after we cross the Khyber, a single British soldier, civilian, or settlement will remain on the continent. It will have been liberated, and restored to its people. They will require our assistance, and armed presence, for an indefinite period, to guard against counter-invasion."

At this I heard East mutter, "I'll bet they will." I could feel him quivering with excitement; myself, I was trying to digest the immensity of the thing. Of course, it had been a fear in India since I could remember—the Great Bear coming over the passes, but no one truly believed they'd ever have the nerve or the ability to try it. But now, here it was—simple, direct, and certain. Not the least of the coincidences of our remarkable eavesdrop was that I, who knew as much about Afghan affairs from first hand, and our weakness on the north Indian frontier, as any man living, should be one of the listeners. As I took it in, I could see it happening; yes, they could do it all right.

"That, your majesty," Ignatieff was saying, "is an essential sketch of our purpose. We have all studied the plans in detail, as has your highness, and unless some new points have arisen from my résumé, your majesty will no doubt wish to confirm the royal assent already given." He said it with deference, trying to hide his eagerness—your promoter anxious to get the official seal.

"Thank you, Count." It was the weak voice again. "We have it clear. Gentlemen?" There was a pause. "It is a weighty matter. No such attempt has ever been made before. But we are confident —are we not?"

Khruleff nodded slowly. "It has always been possible. Now it is a certainty. In a stroke, we clear the British from India, and extend your majesty's imperial . . . influence from the North Cape to the isle of Ceylon. No Tsar in history has achieved such an advance for our country. The troops are ample, the planning exact, the conditions ideal. The pick of Britain's army, and of her navy, are diverted in the Crimea, and it is certain that no assistance could be rendered in India within a year. By then— we shall have supplanted England in southern Asia."[29]

"And it can begin without delay?" says the Tsar's voice.

"'Immediately, majesty. By the southern route, we can be at the Khyber, with every man, gun, and item of equipment, seven months from this night." Ignatieff was almost striking an attitude, his tawny head thrown back, one hand on the table. They waited, silently, and I heard the Tsar sigh.

"So be it, then. Forgive us, gentlemen, for desiring to hear it in summary again, but it is a matter for second, and third thoughts, even after the resolve has been given." He coughed, wearily. "All is approved, then—and the other items, with the exception of—yes, Item Ten. It can be referred to Omsk for further study. You have our leave, gentlemen."

At this there was a scrape of chairs, and East was kicking at me, and jabbing a finger at the door behind us. I'd been so spellbound by our enormous discovery, I'd almost forgotten where we were—but, by gad, it was time we were no longer here. I edged back to the door, East crowding behind me, and then we heard Ignatieff's voice again.

"Majesty, with permission. In connection with Item Seven—the Indian expedition—mention was made of possible diversionary schemes, to prevent by all means any premature discovery of our intentions. I mentioned, but did not elaborate, a plan for possibly deluding the enemy with a false scent."

At this we stopped, crouched by the door. He went on:

"Plans have been prepared, but in no considerable detail, for a spurious expedition through your Alaskan province, aimed at the British North American possessions. It was thought that if these could be brought to the attention of the British Government, in a suitably accidental manner, they would divert the enemy's attention from the eastern theatre entirely."

"I don't like it," says Khruleff's voice. "I have seen the plan, majesty; it is over-elaborate and unnecessary."

"There are," says Ignatieff, quite unabashed, "two British officers, at present confined in this house—prisoners from the Crimea whom I had brought here expressly for the purpose. It should not be beyond our wits to ensure that they discovered the false North American plan; thereafter they would obviously attempt to escape, to warn their government of it."

"And then?" says Duhamel.

"They would succeed, of course. It is no distance to the Crimea —it could be arranged without their suspecting they were mere tools of our purpose. And their government would at least be distracted."

"Too clever," says Khruleff. "Playing at spies."

"With submission, majesty," says Ignatieff, "there would be no difficulty. I have selected these two men with care—they are ideal for our purpose. One is an agent of intelligence, taken at Silistria—a clever, dangerous fellow. Show him the hint of a design against his country, and he would fasten on it like a hawk. The other is a very different sort—a great, coarse bully of a man, all brawn and little brain; he has spent his time here lechering after every female he could find." I felt East stiffen beside me, as we listened to this infernal impudence. "But he would be necessary—for even if we permitted, and assisted, their escape here, and saw that they reached the Crimea in safety, they would still have to rejoin their army at Sevastopol, and we could hardly issue orders to our forces in Crimea to let them pass through. This second fellow is the kind of resourceful villain who would find a way."

There was a silence, and then Duhamel says: "I must agree with Khruleff, majesty. It is not necessary, and might even be dangerous. The British are not fools; they smell a rat as soon as anyone. These false plans, these clever stratagems—they can excite suspicion and recoil on the plotter. Our Indus scheme is soundly based; it needs no pretty folly of this kind."

"So." The Tsar's voice was a hoarse murmur. "The opinion is against you, Count. Let your British officers sleep undisturbed. But we thank you for your zeal in the matter, even so. And now, gentlemen, we have worked long enough—"

East was bundling me on to the dark landing before the voice had finished speaking. We closed the door gently, and tip-toed across towards our passage even as we heard the library doors opening down in the hall. I peeped round the corner; the Cossack was snoring away again, and we scuttled silently past him and into East's room. I sank down, shaking, on to his bed, while he fumbled at the candle, muttering furiously till he got it lit. His face was as white as a sheet—but he remembered to muffle the mouth of the hidden speaking-tube with his pillow.

"My God, Flashman," says he, when he had got his wind back. We were staring helplessly at each other. "What are we to do?"

"What can we do?" says I.

"We did hear aright—didn't we?" says he. "They're going for India—while our back's turned? A Russian army over the Khyber—a rebellion! Good God—is the thing possible?"

I thought of '42, and the Afghans—and what they could do with a Russian army to help them. "Aye," says I. "It's possible all right."

"I *knew* we were right to watch and listen!" cries he. "I knew it! But I never dreamed—this is the most appalling thing!" He slapped his hands and paced about. "Look—we've got to do something! We've got to get away—somehow! They must have news of this at Sevastopol. Raglan's there; he's the commander —if we could get this to him, and London, there'd be time— to try to prepare, at least. Send troops out—increase the north-west garrisons—perhaps even an expedition into Persia, or Afghanistan—"

"There isn't time," says I. "You heard them—seven months from tonight they'll be on the edge of the Punjab with thirty thousand men, and God knows how many Afghans ready to join in for a slap at us and the loot of India. It would take a month to get word to England, twice as long again to assemble an army —if that's possible, which I doubt—and then it's four months to India—"

"But that's in time—just in time!" cries he. "If only we can get away—at once!"

"Well, we can't," says I. "The thing's not possible."

"We've got to make it possible!" says he, feverishly. "Look— look at this, will you?" And he snatched a book from his bureau: it was some kind of geography or guide, in Russian script—that hideous lettering that always made me think of black magic recipes for conjuring the Devil. "See here; this map. Now, I've pieced this together over the past few months, just by listening and using my wits, and I've a fair notion where we are, although Starotorsk ain't shown on this map; too small. But I reckon we're about here, in this empty space—perhaps fifty miles from Ekaterinoslav, and thirty from Alexandrovsk, see? It startled me, I tell you; I'd thought we were miles farther inland."

"So did I," says I. "You're sure you're right?—they must have brought me a hell of a long way round, then."

"Of course—that's their way! They'll never do anything straight, I tell you. Confuse, disturb, upset—that's their book of common prayer! But don't you see—we're not much above a hundred miles from the north end of the Crimea—maybe only a couple of hundred from Raglan at Sevastopol!"

"With a couple of Russian armies in between," I pointed out. "Anyway, how could we get away from here?"

"Steal a sled at night—horses. If we went fast enough, we could get changes at the post stations on the way, as long as we kept ahead of pursuit. Don't you see, man—it must be possible!" His eyes were shining fiercely. "*Ignatieff was planning for us to do this very thing!* My God, why did they turn him down! Think of it—if he had had his way, they'd be *helping* us to escape with their bogus information, never dreaming we had the *real* plans! Of all the cursed luck!"

"Well, they did turn him down," says I. "And it's no go. You talk of stealing a sled—how far d'you think we'd get, with Pencherjevsky's Cossacks on our tail? You can't hide sleigh-tracks, you know—not on land as flat as your hat. Even if you could, they know exactly where we'd go—there's only one route"—and I pointed at his map—"through the neck of the Crimean peninsula at—what's it called? Armyansk. They'd over-haul us long before we got there."

"No, they wouldn't," says he, grinning—the same sly, fag grin of fifteen years ago. "Because we won't go that way. There's another road to the Crimea—I got it from this book, but they'd never dream we knew of it. Look, now, old Flashy friend, and learn the advantages of studying geography. See how the Crimean peninsula is joined to mainland Russia—just a narrow isthmus, eh? Now look east a little way along the coast—what d'ye see?"

"A town called Yenitchi," says I. "But if you're thinking of pinching a boat, you're mad—"

"Boat nothing," says he. "What d'ye see in the sea, south of Yenitchi?"

"A streak of fly-dung," says I, impatiently. "Now, Scud—"

"That's what it looks like," says he triumphantly. "But it ain't. That, my boy, is the Arrow of Arabat—a causeway, not more than half a mile across, without even a road on it, that runs from Yenitchi a clear sixty miles *through* the sea of Azov to Arabat in the Crimea—and from there it's a bare hundred miles across to Sevastopol! Don't you see, man? No one ever uses it, according to this book, except a few dromedary caravans in summer. Why, the Russians hardly know it exists, even! All we need is one night of snow, here, to cover our traces, and while they're chasing us towards the isthmus, we're tearing down to Yenitchi, along the causeway to Arabat, and then westward ho to Sevastopol—"

"Through the bloody Russian army!" cries I.

"Through whoever you please! Can't you see—no one will be looking for us there! They've no telegraph, anyway, in this benighted country—we both speak enough Russian to pass! Heavens, we speak it better than most *moujiks*, I'll swear. It's the way, Flashman—the only way!"

I didn't like this one bit. Don't misunderstand me—I'm as true-blue a Briton as the next man, and I'm not unwilling to serve the old place in return for my pay, provided it don't entail too much discomfort or expense. But I draw the line where my hide is concerned—among the many things I'm not prepared to do for my country is die, especially at the end of a rope trailing from a Cossack's saddle, or with his lance up my innards. The thought of abandoning this snug retreat, where I was feeding full, drinking well, and rogering my captivity happily away, and going careering off through the snow-fast Russian wilderness, with those devils howling after me—and all so that we could report this crazy scheme to Raglan! It was mad. Anyway, what did I care for India? I'd sooner we had it than the Russians, of course, and if the intelligence could have been conveyed *safely* to Raglan (who'd have promptly forgotten it, or sent an army to Greenland by mistake, like as not) I'd have done it like a shot. But I draw the line at risks that aren't necessary to my own well-being. That's why I'm eighty years old today, while Scud East has been mouldering underground at Cawnpore this forty-odd years.

But I couldn't say this to him, of course. So I looked profound, and anxious, and shook my head. "Can't be done, Scud. Look now; you don't know much about this Arrow causeway, except what's in that book. Who's to say it's open in winter—or that it's still there? Might have been washed away. Who knows what guards

they may have at either end? How do we get through the
Crimea to Sevastopol? I've done a bit of travelling in disguise,
you know, in Afghanistan and Germany...and, oh, lots of
places, and it's a sight harder than you'd think. And in Russia—
where everyone has to show his damned ticket every few miles—
we'd never manage it. But"—I stilled his protest with a stern
finger—"I'd chance that, of course, if it wasn't an absolute
certainty that we'd be nabbed before we'd got halfway to this
Yenitchi place. Even if we got clear away from here—which
would be next to impossible—they would ride us down in a few
hours. It's hopeless, you see."

"I know that!" he cried. "I can count, too! But I tell you we've
got to try! It's a chance in a million that we've found out this
infernal piece of Russian treachery! We must try to use it, to
warn Raglan and the people at home! What have we got to lose,
except our lives?"

D'you know, when a man talks like that to me, I feel downright
insulted. Why other, unnamed lives, or the East India Company's dividend, or the credit of Lord Aberdeen, or the honour of
British arms, should be held by me to be of greater consequence
than my own shrinking skin, I've always been at a loss to understand.

"You're missing the point," I told him. "Of course, one doesn't
think twice about one's neck when it's a question of duty"—
I don't, anyway—"but one has to be sure where one's duty lies.
Maybe I've seen more rough work than you have, Scud, and I've
learned there's no point in suicide—not when one can wait and
watch and think. If we sit tight, who knows what chance may
arise that ain't apparent now? But if we go off half-cock, and get
killed or something—well, that won't get the news to Raglan.
Here's something: now that Ignatieff don't need us any more,
they may even exchange us. Then the laugh would be on them,
eh?"

At this he cried out that time was vital, and we daren't wait.
I replied that we daren't go until we saw a reasonable chance
(if I knew anything, we'd wait a long time for one), and so we
bandied it to and fro and got no forrarder, and finally went to
bed, played out.

When I thought the thing over, alone (and got into a fine

sweat at the recollection of the fearful risk we'd run, crouching in that musty gallery) I could see East's point. Here we were, by an amazing fluke, in possession of information which any decent soldier would have gone through hell to get to his chiefs. And Scud East was a decent soldier, by anyone's lights but mine. My task, plainly, was to prevent his doing anything rash—in other words, anything at all—and yet appear to be in as big a sweat as he was himself. Not too difficult, for one of my talents.

In the next few days we mulled over a dozen notions for escaping, each more lunatic than the last. It was quite interesting, really, to see at what point in some particular idiocy poor Scud would start to boggle; I remember the look of respectful horror which crept into his eyes when I regretted absently that we hadn't dropped from the gallery that night and cut all their throats, the Tsar's included—"too late, now, of course, since they've all gone," says I. "Pity, though; if we'd finished 'em off, that would have scotched their little scheme. And I haven't had a decent set-to since Balaclava. Aye, well."

Scud began to worry me, though; he was working himself up into a fever of anxiety and impatience where he might do something foolish. "We must try!" he kept insisting. "If we can think of no alternative soon, we're bound to make a run for it some night! I'll go mad if we don't, I tell you! How can you just sit there?—oh, no, I'm sorry, Flashman; I know this must be torturing you too! Forgive me, old fellow. I haven't got your steady nerve."

He hadn't got Valla to refresh him, either, which might have had a calming effect. I thought of suggesting that he take a steam-bath with Aunt Sara, to settle his nerves, but he might have enjoyed it too much, and then gone mad repenting. So I tried to look anxious and frustrated, while he chewed his nails and fretted horribly, and a week passed, in which he must have lost a stone. Worrying about India, stab me. And then the worst happened: we got our opportunity, and in circumstances which even I couldn't refuse.

It came after a day in which Pencherjevsky lost his temper, a rare thing, and most memorable. I was in the salon when I heard him bawling at the front door, and came out to find him standing in the hallway, fulminating at two fellows outside on the steps. One looked like a clergyman; the other was a lean, ugly little fellow dressed like a clerk.

"... effrontery, to seek to thrust yourself between me and my people!" Pencherjevsky was roaring. "Merciful God, how do I keep my hands from you? Have you no souls to cure, you priest fellow, and you, Blank, no pen-pushing or pimping to occupy you? Ah, but no—you have your agitating, have you not, you seditious scum! Well, agitate elsewhere, before I have my Cossacks take their whips to you! Get out of my sight and off my land—both of you!"

He was grotesque in his rage, towering like some bearded old-world god—I'd have been in the next county before him, but these two stood their ground, jeopardizing their health.

"We are no serfs of yours!" cries the fellow Blank. "You do not order us," and Pencherjevsky gave a strangled roar and started forward, but the priest came between.

"Lord Count! A moment!" He was game, that one. "Hear me, I implore. You are a just man, and surely it is little enough to ask. The woman is old, and if she cannot pay the soul-tax on her grandsons, you know what will happen. The officials will block her stove, and she will be driven out—to what? To die in the cold, or to starve, and the little ones with her. It is a matter of only one hundred and seventy silver kopecks—I do not ask you to pay for her, but let me find the money, and my friend here. We will be glad to pay! Surely you will let us—be merciful!"

"Look you," says Pencherjevsky, holding himself in. "Do I care for a handful of kopecks? No! Not if it was a hundred and seventy thousand roubles, either! But you come to me with a pitiful tale of this old crone, who cannot pay the tax on her brats —do I not know her son—worthless bastard!—is a koulak* in Odessa, and could pay it for her, fifty times over! Well, let him! But if he will not, then it is for the government to enforce the law —no man hindering! No, not even me! Suppose I pay, or permit you to pay, on her behalf, what would happen then? I shall tell you. Next year, and every year thereafter, you would have all the moujiks from here to Rostov bawling at my door: 'We cannot pay the soul-tax,[30] batiushka; pay for us, as you paid for so-and-so.' And where does that end?"

* A peasant with money, a usurer.

"But—" the priest was beginning, but Pencherjevsky cut him short.

"You would tell me that you will pay for them all? Aye, Master Blank there would pay—with the filthy money sent by his Communist friends in Germany! So that he could creep among my *moujiks*, sowing sedition, preaching revolution! I know him! So get him hence, priest, out of my sight, before I forget myself!"

"And the old woman, then? Have a little pity, Count!"

"I have explained!" roars Pencherjevsky. "By God, as though I owe you that much! Get out, both of you!"

He advanced, hands clenched, and the two of them went scuttling down the steps. But the fellow Blank[31] had to have a last word:

"You filthy tyrant! You dig your own grave! You and your kind think you can live forever, by oppression and torture and theft—you sow dragon's teeth with your cruelty, and they will grow to tear you! You will see, you fiend!"

Pencherjevsky went mad. He flung his cap on the ground, foaming, and then ran bawling for his whip, his Cossacks, his sabre, while the two malcontents scampered off for their lives, Blank screaming threats and abuse over his shoulder. I listened with interest as the Count raved and stormed:

"After them! I'll have that filthy creature knouted, God help me! Run him down, and don't leave an inch of hide on his carcase!"

Within a few moments a group of his Cossacks were in the saddle and thundering out of the gate, while he stormed about the hall, raging still:

"The dog! The insolent garbage! To beard *me*, at my own door! The priest's a meddling fool—but that Blank! Anarchist swine! He'll be less impudent when my fellows have cut the buttocks off him!"

He stalked away, finally, still cursing, and about an hour later the Cossacks came back, and their leader stumped up the steps to report. Pencherjevsky had simmered down a good deal by this time; he had ordered a brew of punch, and invited East and myself to join him, and we were sipping at the scalding stuff by the hall fire when the Cossack came in, an old, stout, white-

whiskered scoundrel with his belt at the last hole.[12] He was grinning, and had his *nagaika* in his hand.

"Well?" growled Pencherjevsky. "Did you catch that brute
and teach him manners?"

"Aye, *batiushka*," says the Cossack, well pleased. "He's dead.
Thirty cuts—and, pouf! He was a weakling, though."

"Dead, you say?" Pencherjevsky set down his cup abruptly,
frowning. Then he shrugged: "Well, good riddance! No one'll
mourn his loss. One anarchist more or less will not trouble the
prefect."

"The fellow Blank escaped," continued the Cossack. "I'm sorry,
batiushka—"

"Blank escaped!" Pencherjevsky's voice came out in a hoarse
scream, his eyes dilating. "You mean—it was the priest you
killed! The holy man!" He stared in disbelief, crossing himself.
"*Slava Bogu!** The priest!"

"Priest? Do I know?" says the Cossack. "Was it wrong,
batiushka?"

"Wrong, animal? A priest! And you . . . you flogged him to
death!" The Count looked as though he would have a seizure.
He gulped, and clawed at his beard, and then he blundered past
the Cossack, up the stairs, and we heard his door crash behind
him.

"My God!" says East. The Cossack looked at us in wonder,
and then shrugged, as his kind will, and stalked off. We just
stood, looking at each other.

"What will this mean?" says East.

"Search me," I said. "They butcher each other so easily in
this place—I don't know. I'd think flogging a priest to death is
a trifle over the score, though—even for Russia. Old man
Pencherjevsky'll have some explaining to do, I'd say—shouldn't
wonder if they kick him out of the Moscow Carlton Club."

"My God, Flashman!" says East again. "What a country!"

We didn't see the Count at dinner, nor Valla, and Aunt Sara
was uncommunicative. But you could see in her face, and the
servants', and feel in the very air of the house, that Starotorsk
was a place appalled. For once East forgot to talk about escaping,
and we went to bed early, saying good-night in whispers.

* Glory to God!

I didn't rest too easy, though. My stove was leaking, and making the room stuffy, and the general depression must have infected me, for when I dozed I dreamed badly. I got my old nightmare of drowning in the pipe at Jotunberg, probably with the stove fumes,[33] and then it changed to that underground cell in Afghanistan, where my old flame, Narreeman, was trying to qualify me for the Harem Handicap, and then someone started shooting outside the cell, and shrieking, and suddenly I was awake, lathered with sweat, and the shooting was real, and from beneath me in the house there was an appalling crash and the roar of Pencherjevsky's voice, and a pattering of feet, and by that time I was out of bed and into my breeches, struggling with my boots as I threw open the door.

East was in the passage, half-dressed like myself, running for the landing. I reached it on his very heels, crying: "What's happening? What the devil is it?", when there was a terrible shriek from Valla's passage, and Pencherjevsky was bounding up the stairs, bawling over his shoulder to the Cossacks whom I could see in the hall below:

"Hold them there! Hold the door! My child, Valentina! Where are you?"

"Here, father!" And she came hurrying in her night-gown, hair all disordered, eyes starting with terror. "Father, they are everywhere—in the garden! I saw them—oh!"

There was a crash of musket-fire from beyond the front door, splinters flew in the hall, and one of the Cossacks sang out and staggered, clutching his leg. The other were at the hall windows, there was a smashing of glass, and the sound of baying, screaming voices from outside. Pencherjevsky swore, clasped Valla to him with one enormous arm, saw us, and bawled above the shooting:

"That damned priest! They have risen—the serfs have risen! They're attacking the house!"

I've been in a good few sieges in my time, from full-dress affairs like Cawnpore, Lucknow, and the Pekin nonsense a few years ago, to more domestic squabbles such as Kabul residency in '41. But I can't think of one worse managed than the *moujiks*' attack on Starotorsk. I gathered afterwards that several thousand of them, whipped on by Blank's fiery oratory, had just up and marched on the house to avenge their priest's death, seizing what weapons were handiest, and making no attempt at concealment or concerted attack to take the place on all sides at once. They just stamped up the road, roaring, the Cossacks in their little barrack saw them, knocked a few over with rifle fire, and then retired to the main house just as the mob surged into the drive and threw themselves at the front door. And there it was, touch and go, with the *moujiks* beating on the panels, smashing in the downstairs windows on that side to clamber in, waving their trowels and torches and yelling for Pencherjevsky's blood.[34]

As he stood there, clasping Valla and glaring round like a mad thing, I doubt if he fully understood it himself—that his beloved slaves were out to string him from the nearest limb, with his family on either side of him. It was like the sun falling out of the sky for him. But he knew deadly danger when he saw it, and his one thought was for his daughter. He seized me by the arm.

"The back way—to the stables! Quickly! Get her away, both of you! We shall hold them here—the fools, the ingrate clods!" He practically flung her into my arms. "Take a sled and horses, and drive like the wind to the Arianski house—on the Alexandrovsk road! There she will be safe. But hasten, in God's name!"

I'd have been off at the run, but East, the posturing ass, had to thrust in:

"One of us will stay, sir! Or let a Cossack escort your daughter —it is not fitting that British officers should—"

"You numskull!" bawled Pencherjevsky, seizing him and thrusting him violently towards the back corridor. "Go! They will be in, or round the house, while you stand prating! This is no affair of yours—and I command here!" There was a tearing crash from the front door, several pistol shots amid the clamour of the mob and the shouting of the Cossacks, and over the banisters I saw the door cave in, and a torrent of ragged figures pouring in, driving the Cossacks back towards the foot of the stairs. The smoky glare of their torches turned the place suddenly into a struggling hell, as the Cossacks swung their sabres and *nagaikas* to force them back.

"Get her away!" Pencherjevsky encircled both me and Valla for an instant in his bear-like hug, his great, bearded face within an inch of my own, and there were tears in his glaring eyes. "You know what is to do, my son! See to her—and to that other life! God be with you!"

And he bundled us into the corridor, and then rushed to the head of the stairs. I had a glimpse of his towering bulk, with the smoky glare beneath him, and then the chorus of yells and screams from the hall redoubled, there was a rushing of feet, a splintering of timber—and East and I were doubling down the back-stairs at speed, Valla sobbing against my chest as I swept her along.

We tore through the kitchen, East pausing to grab some loaves and bottles, while I hurried out into the yard. It was dead still in the moonlight; nothing but the soft stamp of the beasts in their stalls, and the distant tumult muffled on the other side of the house. I was into the coach-building in a flash, bundled Valla into the biggest sled, and was leading round the first of the horses when East joined me, his arms full.

I don't know the record for harnessing a three-horse sled, but I'll swear we broke it; I wrenched home the last buckle while East scuttled across the snow to unbar the gate. I jumped into the driver's seat and tugged the reins, the horses whinnied and reared and then danced forward, any old how—it's deuced difficult, tooling a sled—and with me swearing at the beasts and East swinging up as we slid past, we scraped through the gateway on to the open road beyond.

There was a bang to our left, and a shot whistled overhead,

causing me to duck and the horses to swerve alarmingly. They were rounding the house wall, a bare thirty yards away, a confused, roaring rabble, torches waving, running to head us off. East seized the whip from its mount and lashed at the beasts, and with a bound that nearly overturned us they tore away, down the road, with the mob cursing at our tail, waving their fists, and one last shot singing wide as we distanced them.

We didn't let up for a mile, though, by which time I had the beasts under control, and we were able to pull up on a gentle rise and look back. It was like a Christmas scene, a great white blanket glittering in the full moon, and the dark house rising up from it, with the red dots of torch-light dancing among the outbuildings, and the thin sound of voices echoing through the frosty air, and the stars twinkling in the purple sky. Very bonny, I suppose—and then East clutched my arm.

"My God! Look yonder!"

There was a dull glow at one corner of the house; it grew into an orange flame, licking upwards with a shower of sparks; the torches seemed to dance more madly than ever, and from the sled behind there was a sudden shrieking sob, and Valla was trying to struggle out—my God, she still had nothing on but her night-dress, and as she half fell out it ripped and sent her tumbling into the snow.

I threw the reins to East, jumped down, and bundled her quickly back into the sled. There were furs there, any amount of them, and I swaddled her in them before the cold could get at her. "Father! Father!" she was moaning, and then she fainted dead away, and I laid her down on the back seat and went forward to East, handing him up one of the furs—for we had nothing but our shirts and breeches and boots, and the cold was crippling.

"Let's get on," says I, wrapping up myself, with my teeth chattering. "The sooner we're out of here, the better. Come on, man, what ails you?"

He was sitting staring ahead, his mouth open, and when he swung round to me, he was positively laughing.

"Flashman!" he cried. "This is our chance! Heaven-sent! The sled—the horses—and a clear start! We're away—old fellow, and no one to stop us!"

It shows you what a hectic scramble it had been, with not a

moment's pause to collect one's wits from the shock of waking
until now, but for a second I didn't see what he was driving at.
And then it struck me—escape. We could light out for Yenitchi,
and East's causeway, and not a living soul would know we had
gone. One couldn't be sure, of course, but I doubted whether any
civilized being would survive what was happening at Starotorsk;
it might be days before the police or the army came on the scene
and realized that there were three persons not accounted for.
And by then we could be in Sevastopol—always assuming we got
through the Russian army. I didn't like it, but I didn't much care
for the Alexandrovsk road, either, wherever that was—God knew
how far the insurrection would spread, and to be caught up in it,
with Pencherjevsky's daughter in tow, would be asking to be torn
limb from limb.

Even as the thoughts rushed through my mind, I was glancing
at the stars, picking out the Plough and judging our line south.
That way, even if we hit the coast fifty versts either side of
Yenitchi, we at least stood a decent chance of finding our road to
it in the end, for we had time on our side.

"Right," says I. "Let's be off. We're sure to hit some farm or
station where we can change horses. We'll drive in turns, and—"

"We must take Valla with us," cries he, and even in that
ghostly light I'll swear he was blushing. "We cannot abandon her
—God knows what kind of villages these will be we shall pass
through—we could not leave her, not knowing what . . . I mean,
if we can reach the camp at Sevastopol, she will be truly safe . . .
and . . . and . . ."

And he would be able to press his suit, no doubt, the poor skirt-
smitten ninny, if he ever plucked up courage enough. I wonder
what he'd have thought if he'd known I had been pupping his
little Ukrainian angel for weeks. And there she was, in the sled,
with not a stitch to her name.

"You're right!" I cried. "We must take her. You are a noble
fellow, Scud! Off we go, then, and I'll take the ribbons as soon as
you're tired."

I jumped in the back, and off we swept, over the snowy plain,
and far behind us the red glow mounted to the night sky. I peered
back at it, wondering if Pencherjevsky was dead yet, and what
had happened to Aunt Sara. Whatever it was, I found myself

hoping that for her, at least, it had been quick. And then I busied myself putting the sled in some order.

They are splendid things, these three-horse sleighs, less like a coach than a little room on runners. They are completely enclosed with a great hood, lashed down all round, with flaps which can be secured on all the window spaces, so that when they are down the whole thing is quite snug, and if you have furs enough, and a bottle or two, you can be as warm as toast. I made sure everything was secure, set out the bread, and a leg of ham, which East had thoughtfully picked up, on the front seat, and counted the bottles—three of brandy, one of white wine. Valla seemed to be still unconscious; she was wrapped in a mountain of furs between the seats, and when I opened the rear window-flap for light to examine her, sure enough, she was in that uneasy shocked sleep that folk sometimes go into when they've been terribly scared. The shaft of moonlight shone on her silvery hair, and on one white tit peeping out saucily from the furs—I had to make sure her heart was beating, of course, but beyond that I didn't disturb her—for the moment. Fine sledges these: the driver is quite walled off.

So there we were; I huddled in my fur, took a pull at the brandy, and then crawled out under the side flap on to the mounting of the runner; the wind hit me like a knife, with the snow furrowing up round my legs from the runner-blades. We were fairly scudding along as I pulled myself up on to the driving seat beside East and gave him a swig at the brandy.

He was chattering with cold, even in his fur wrap, so I tied it more securely round him, and asked how we were going. He reckoned, if we could strike a village and get a good direction, we might make Yenitchi in five or six hours—always allowing for changes of horses on the way. But he was sure we wouldn't be able to stand the cold of driving for more than half an hour at a time. So I took the ribbons and he crept back perilously into the sled—one thing I was sure of: Valla would be safe with him.

It it hadn't been for the biting cold, I'd have enjoyed that moonlight drive. The snow was firm and flat, so that it didn't ball in the horses' hooves, and the runners hissed across the snow —it was strange, to be moving at that speed with so little noise. Ahead were the three tossing manes, with the vapour streaming back in the icy air, and beyond that—nothing. A white sheet to the black horizon, a magnificent silver moon, and that reassuring Pole star dead astern when I looked back.

I was about frozen, though, when I spotted lights to starboard after about twenty minutes, and swerved away to find a tumble-down little village, populated by the usual half-human peasants. After consultation with East, I decided to ask the distance and direction to Osipenke; East was carrying a rough table of places and directions in his head, out of the book he had studied, and from the peasants' scared answers—for they were in awe of any strangers—we were able to calculate our proper course, and swerve away south-west.

East had taken over the reins. Valla had come to while he was in the sled—I wondered if he'd been chancing his arm, but probably not—and had had mild hysterics, about her father, and Aunt Sara, who had been sitting up with a sick Cossack woman in the barracks, and had presumably been cut off there.

"The poor little lamb," says East, as he took the reins. "It tore my heart to see her grief, Flashman—so I have given her a little laudanum from a phial which ... which I carry always with me. She should sleep for several hours; it will be best so."

I could have kicked him, for if there's one thing I'd fancy myself good at, it's comforting a bereaved and naked blonde under a fur rug. But he had put her to sleep, no error, and she was snoring like a walrus. So I had to amuse myself with bread and ham, and try to snatch a nap myself.

We made good progress, and after a couple of hours found a way-station, by great good luck, on what must have been the Mariupol road. We got three new nags, and bowled away famously, but what with lack of sleep it was getting to be hard work now, and a couple of hours after sun-rise we pulled up in the first wood we'd seen—a straggly little affair of stunted bushes, really—and decided to rest ourselves and the horses. Valla was still out to the wide, and East and I took a seat apiece and slept like the dead.

I woke first, and when I put my head out the sky was already dimming in the late afternoon. It was bleak and grey, and freezing starvation, and looking through the twisted branches at the pale, endless waste, I felt a shiver running through me that had nothing to do with cold. Not far away there were two or three of those funny little mounds called *koorgans*, which I believe are the barrows of long-forgotten barbarian peoples; they looked eery and uncanny in the failing light, like monstrous snowmen. The stillness was awful; you could feel it, not even a breath of wind, but just the cold and the weight of emptiness hanging over the steppe. It was unnerving, and suddenly I could hear Kit Carson's strained quiet voice in the dread silence of the wagon road west of Leavenworth: "Nary a sight nor sound anywhere—not even a sniff o' danger. *That's* what frets me."

It fretted me, too, at this minute; I roused East, and then we made all fast, and I took the reins and off we slid silently south-west, past those lonely *koorgans*, into the icy wilderness. I had a bottle, and some bread, but nothing could warm me; I was scared, but didn't know of what—just the silence and the unknown, I suppose. And then from somewhere far off to my right I heard it —that thin, dismal sound that is the terror of the empty steppe, unmistakable and terrifying, drifting through the vast distance: the eldritch cry of the wolf.

The horses heard it too, and whinnied, bounding forward in fear with a stumble of hooves, until we were flying at our uttermost speed. My imagination was flying even faster; I remembered Pencherjevsky's story of the woman who had thrown her children out when those fearful monsters got on the track of her sled, and had been executed for it, and countless other tales of sleds run down by famished packs and their occupants literally eaten alive. I daren't look back for fear of what I might see loping over the snow behind me.

The cry was not repeated, and after a few more miles I breathed easier; there was a twinkle of light dead ahead, and when we reached it, we found it was a *moujik's* cabin, and the man himself at the door, axe in hand, glowering at us. We asked him the nearest town, and could have cried with relief when he said Yenitchi: it was only forty versts away—a couple of hours' driving, if the beasts held up and weren't pressed too hard. East took the reins, I climbed in behind—Valla was sleeping still, uneasily, and mumbling incoherently—and we set off on what I prayed was the last stage of our mainland journey.

For rather more than an hour nothing happened; we drove on

through the silence, I took another turn, and then I halted not far
from another clump of koorgans to let East climb into the driver's
seat again. I had my foot on the runner, and he was just chuckling
to the horses, when it came again—that bloodchilling wail, far
closer this time, and off to the left. The horses shrieked, and the
sled shot forward so fast that for a moment I was dragged along,
clinging to the side by main strength, until I managed to drag
myself inboard, tumbling on to the back seat. Valla was stirring,
muttering sleepily, but I'd no time for her; I thrust out my head,
staring fearfully across the snow, trying to pierce the dusk, but
there was nothing to be seen. East was letting the horses go, and
the sled was swaying with the speed—and then it came again,
closer still, like the sound of a lost soul falling to hell. I heard East
shouting to the horses, cracking his whip; I clutched the side,
feeling the sweat pouring off me in spite of the cold.

Still nothing, as we fairly flew along; there was another cluster
of koorgans just visible in the mirk a quarter of a mile or so to
our left. As I watched them—was that something moving beyond
them? My heart flew to my mouth—no, they stood bleak and
lonely, and I found I was panting with fear as I dashed the sweat
from my eyes and peered again. Silence, save for the muffled
thump of the hooves and the hissing of the runners—and there
was something flitting between the last two koorgans, a low,
long dark shape rushing over the snow, and another behind it,
and another, speeding out now into the open, and swerving
towards us.

"Jesus!" I shrieked. "Wolves!"

East yelled something I couldn't hear, and the sled rocked
horribly as he bore on his offside rein; then we righted, and as I
gazed over the side, the hellish baying broke out almost directly
behind us. There they were—five of them, gliding in our wake;
I could see the leader toss up his hideous snout as he let go his evil
wail, and then they put their heads down and came after us in
dead silence.

I've seen horror in my time, human, animal, and natural, but
I don't know much worse than that memory—those dim grey
shapes bounding behind us, creeping inexorably closer, until I
could make out the flat, wicked heads and the snow spurting up
under their loping paws. I must have been petrified, for God

knows how long I just stared at them—and then my wits came
back, and I seized the nearest rug and flung it out to the side,
as far as I could.

As one beast they swerved, and were on it in a twinkling,
tearing it among them. Only for a second, and then they were
after us again—probably all the fiercer for being fooled. I grabbed
another rug and hurled it, and this time they never even broke
stride, but shot past it, closing in on the sled until they were a
bare twenty paces behind, and I could see their open jaws—
I've never been able to look an Alsatian in the face since—and
delude myself that I could even make out their glittering eyes.
I'd have given my right arm, then, for the feel of my faithful old
Adams in my grip—"You wouldn't run so fast with a forty-four
bullet in you, damn you!" I yelled at them—and they came
streaking up, while the horses screamed with fear and tore ahead,
widening the gap for about ten blessed seconds. I was cursing and
scrabbling in the back looking for something else to throw—a
bottle, that was no use, but by George, if I smashed one at the
bottom it might serve as a weapon when the last moment came
and they were ravening over the tailboard—in desperation I
seized a loaf (we'd finished the ham) and hurled it at the nearest
of them, and I am here to tell you that wolves don't eat bread
—they don't even bloody well look at it, for that matter. I heard
East roaring something, and cracking his whip like a madman, and God help me, I *could* see the eyes behind us now,
glaring in those viciously pointed heads, with their open jaws
and gleaming teeth, and the vapour panting out between them.
The leader was a bare five yards behind, bounding along like
some hound of hell; I grabbed another rug, balled it, prayed,
and flung it at him, and for one joyous moment it enveloped him;
he stumbled, recovered, and came on again, and East sang out
from the box to hold tight. The sled rocked, and we were shooting
along between high snow banks on either side, with those five
devils barely a leap from us—and suddenly they were falling back,
slackening their lope, and I couldn't believe my eyes, and then a
cabin flashed by on the right, and then another, with beautiful,
wonderful light in its windows, and the five awful shapes were
fading into the gloom, and we were gliding up a street, between
rows of cottages on either side, and as East brought the sled slowly

to a halt I collapsed, half-done, on the seat. Valla, I remember, muttered something and turned over in her rugs.

You would not think much of Yenitchi, I dare say, or its single mean street, but to me Piccadilly itself couldn't have looked better. It was five minutes before I crawled out, and East and I faced the curious stares of the folk coming out of the cabins; the horses were hanging in their traces, and we had no difficulty in convincing them that we needed a change. There was a post-station at the end of the street, beside a bridge, and a drunk postmaster who, after much swearing and cajoling, was induced to produce a couple of fairly flea-bitten brutes; East wondered if we should rest for a few hours, and go on with our own nags refreshed, but I said no—let's be off while the going's good. So when we had got some few items of bread and sausage and cheese from the postmaster's wife, and a couple of female garments for Valla to wear when she woke up, we put the new beasts to and prepared to take the road again.

It was a dismal prospect. Beyond the bridge, which spanned a frozen canal, we could see the Arrow of Arabat, a long, bleak tongue of snow-covered land running south like a huge railway embankment into the Azov Sea. The sea proper, which was frozen —at least as far out as we could see—lay to the left; on the right of the causeway lies a stinking inland lagoon, called the Sivache, which is many miles wide in places, but narrows down as you proceed along the Arrow, until it peters away altogether where the causeway reaches Arabat, on the eastern end of the Crimea. The lagoon seems to be too foul to freeze entirely, even in a Russian winter, and the stench from it would poison an elephant.

We were just preparing to set off, when Valla woke up, and after we had told her where she was, and reassured her that all was well, and she had wept a little, and I'd helped her out discreetly to answer a call of nature—well, she'd been asleep for the best of twenty-four hours—we decided after all to have a caulk before setting out again. East and I were both pretty done, but I wouldn't allow more than two hours' rest—having got this far, I'd no wish to linger. We had some food, and now Valla was beginning to come to properly, and wanted to know where we were taking her.

"We're going back to our own army," I told her. "We must

take you with us—we can't leave you here, and you'll be well cared for. I believe your father is all right—we saw him and his Cossacks escaping as we drove away—and I know he would wish us to see you safe, and there's nowhere better than where we're going, d'you see?"

It served, after a deal of questioning and answering; whether she was still under the influence of the laudanum or not, I wasn't certain, but she seemed content enough, in a sleepy sort of way, so we plied her with nips of brandy to keep out the cold—she refused outright the clothes we had got, and stayed curled up in her rugs—and being a Russian girl, she was ready to drink all we offered her.

"If she's half-tight, so much the better," says I to East. "Distressing, of course, but she'll be less liable to give the game away if we run into trouble."

"It is terrible for her—to be subjected to this nightmare," says he. "But that was a noble lie you told, about her father—I wanted to shake your hand on that, old boy." And he wrung it then and there. "I still think I must be dreaming," says he. "This incredible country, and you and I—and this dear girl—fleeing for our lives! But we are nearly home, old fellow—a bare sixty miles to Arabat, and then eight hours at most will see us at Sevastopol, God willing. Will you pray with me, Flashman, for our deliverance?"

I wasn't crawling about in the snow, not for him or anyone, but I stood while he mumped away with his hands folded, beseeching the Lord that we might quit ourselves like men, or something equally useful, and then we climbed in and took our forty winks. Valla was dozing, and the brandy bottle was half-empty—if ever they start the Little White Ribboners in Russia, all the members will have to be boys, for they'll never get the women to take the pledge.

The rest did me little good. The scare we'd had from the wolves, and the perils ahead, had my nerves jangling like fiddle-strings, and after a bare hour of uneasy dozing I roused East and said we should be moving. The moon was up by now, so we should have light enough to ensure we didn't stray from the causeway; I took the driver's seat, and we slid away over the bridge and out on to the Arrow of Arabat.

For the first few miles it was quite wide, and as I kept to the eastern side there was a great expanse of hummocky snow to my right. But then the causeway gradually narrowed to perhaps half a mile, so that it was like driving along a very broad raised road, with the ground falling away sharply on either side to the snow-covered frozen waters of Azov and the Sivache lagoon; the salty charnel reek was awful, and even the horses didn't like it, tossing their heads and pulling awkwardly, so that I had to look sharp to manage them. We passed two empty post-stations, East and I exchanging at each one, and after about four hours he took the reins for what we hoped would be the last spell into Arabat.

I climbed into the back of the sled and made all the fastenings secure as we started off again, and was preparing to curl up on the back seat when Valla stirred sleepily in the darkness, murmuring "Harr-ee?" as she stretched restlessly in her pile of furs on the floor. I knelt down beside her and took her hand, but when I spoke to her she just mumbled and turned over; the laudanum and brandy still had her pretty well foxed, and there was no sense to be got out of her. It struck me she might be conscious enough to enjoy some company, though, so I slipped a hand beneath the furs and encountered warm, plump flesh; the touch of it sent the blood pumping in my head.

"Valla, my love," I whispered, just to be respectable; I could smell the sweet musky perfume of her skin, even over the brandy. I stroked her belly, and she moaned softly, and when I felt upwards and cupped her breast she turned towards me, her lips wet against my cheek. I was shaking as I put my mouth on hers, and then in a trice I was under the rugs, wallowing away like a sailor on shore leave, and half-drunk as she was she clung to me passionately. It was an astonishing business, for the furs were crackling with electricity, shocking me into unprecedented efforts— I thought I knew everything in the galloping line, but I'll swear there's no more alarming way of doing it than under a pile of skins in a sled skimming through the freezing Russian night; it's like performing on a bed of fire-crackers.

Engrossing as the novelty was, it was also exhausting, and I must have dozed off afterwards with Valla purring in her unconsciousness beside me. And then I became dimly conscious that the sled was slowing down, and gliding to a halt; I sat up, wondering what the blazes was wrong, buttoning myself hastily, and then I heard East jump down. I stuck my head out; he was standing by the sled, his head cocked, listening.

"Hush!" says he, sharply. "Do you hear anything?"

It crossed my mind that he'd overheard the heaving and crackling of my contortions with Valla, but his next words drove that idea out of my head, and implanted a new and disturbing one.

"Behind us," says he. "Listen!"

I scrambled out on to the snow, and we stood there, in the silent moonlight, straining our ears. At first there was nothing but the gentle sigh of the wind, the restless movement of the horses, and our own hearts thumping in the stillness—and then? Was there the tiniest murmur from somewhere back on the causeway, an indistinct but regular sound, softly up and down, up and down? I felt the hairs rise on my neck—it couldn't be wolves, not here, but what was it, then? We stared back along the causeway; it was very narrow now, only a couple of hundred yards across, but we had just come on to a stretch where it began to swerve gently towards the east, and it was difficult to make out anything in the gloom beyond the bend about a quarter of a mile behind us. Snow was falling gently, brushing our faces.

"I thought I heard . . ." Scud said slowly. "But perhaps I was wrong."

"Whatever it is, or isn't, there's no sense waiting here for it!" says I. "How far d'you reckon we are from Arabat?"

"Six miles, perhaps—surely not much more. Once there, we should be all right. According to that book of mine, there are little hills and gullies beyond the town, and we can lose ourselves in 'em if we want to, so . . ."

"The devil with dallying here, then!" cries I, in a fine stew. "Why the deuce are we wasting time, man? Let's be off from this blasted place, where there's *nowhere* to hide! Up on the box with you!"

"You're right, of course," says he. "I just . . . Hark, though! what's that?"

I listened, gulping—and there *was* a sound, a sound that I knew all too well. Very faintly, somewhere behind us, there was a gentle but now distinct drumming, and a tiny tinkling with it. There were horsemen on the causeway!

"Quick!" I shouted. "They're after us! Hurry, man—move those horses!"

He tumbled up on to the box, and as I swung myself on to the runner-mounting he cracked his whip and we slid forward across the snow. I clung to the side of the sled, peering back fearfully through the thin snow-fall, trying to make out if anything was showing beyond the bend in the causeway. We increased speed, and with the hiss of the runners it was impossible to listen for that frightening tell-tale sound.

"It may be just other travellers some distance back!" cries Scud from the box. "No one could be pursuing us!"

"Travellers at this time of night?" says I. "For God's sake, man, hurry those beasts!"

We were gathering speed now, cracking along at a good clip, and I was just about to swing myself under the cover—but I paused for another look back along the causeway, and what I saw nearly made me loose my hold. Very dimly through the falling flakes, I could just make out the causeway bend, and there, moving out on to the straight on this side of it, was a dark, indistinct mass —too big and irregular to be anything like a sled. And then the moonlight caught a score of twinkling slivers in the gloom, and I yelled at East in panic:

"It's cavalry—horsemen! They're after us, man!"

At the same time they must have seen us, for a muffled cry reached my ears, and now I could see the mass was indeed made up of separate pieces—a whole troop of them, coming on at a steady hand-gallop, and even as I watched they lengthened their stride, closing the distance. East was flogging at the horses, and the sled swayed and shuddered as we tore along—were they gaining on us? I clung there, trying to measure the distance, but I couldn't be sure; perhaps terror was colouring my judgment, making me see what I wanted to see, but so far as I could judge it looked as though we were holding our own for the moment.

"Faster!" I bawled to East. "Faster, man, or they'll have us!"

If only the bloody ass hadn't halted to listen—if only we hadn't wasted that precious hour dozing at Yenitchi! I couldn't begin to guess who these people were, or how they had got after us—but there they were, scudding along behind as fast as they could ride —four hundred yards, five hundred? Maybe five or more—I couldn't see whether they were hussars or dragoons or what, but I had a feeling they were heavies. Pray God they might be! I swung under the covers and threw myself on to the back seat, peering out through the window-flap. No, they weren't closing the distance—not yet. They were fanned out on the causeway as far as they could—good riding, that, for in column the rear files would have been ploughing into the churned snow of the men in front. Trust Russian cavalry to know about that.

But if they weren't gaining, they weren't dropping back, either. There was nothing in it—it's a queer thing, but where a horseman can easily overhaul a coach, or even a racing phaeton, a good sled on firm snow is another matter entirely. A horse with a load on his back makes heavy weather in snow, but unladen they can spank a sled along at nearly full gallop.

But how long could our beasts keep up their present pace? They were far from fresh—on the other hand, our pursuers didn't look too chipper, either. I watched them, my heart in my mouth, through the falling snow—was it getting thicker? By God, it was! If it really set in, and we could hold them as far as Arabat, we might be able to lose them—and even as the thought crossed my mind I felt the pace of the sled slacken just a little. I stared back at the distant horsemen, my throat dry, fixing on the centre man until my eyes ached and he seemed to be swimming mistily before me. He was just a vague blur—no, I could make out the shape of his head now—they were gaining, ever so little, but still gaining, creeping gradually up behind, yard by yard.

I couldn't stand it. I plunged to the side of the sled, stuck my head out, and bawled at East.

"They're closing, you fool! Faster! Can't you stir those bloody cattle!"

He shot a glance over his shoulder, cracked on the reins, and cried:

"It's no go . . . horses are almost played out! Can't . . . We're too heavy! Throw out some weight . . . the food . . . anything!"

I looked back; they were certainly gaining now, for the pale blobs of their faces were dimly visible even through the driving snow. They couldn't be much more than two hundred yards away, and one of 'em was shouting; I could just catch the voice, but not the words.

"Damn you!" I roared. "Russian bastards!" And fell back into the sled, scrabbling for our supplies, to hurl them out and lighten the sled. It was ridiculous—a few loaves and a couple of bottles— but out they went anyway, and not a scrap of difference did it make. The cover? If I let it go, would that help—it would cut down the wind resistance at least. I struggled with the buckles, stiff with the cold as they were, bruising my fingers and swearing feebly. There were eight of them, two to each side, and I just had the wit to undo the rear ones first, and the front ones last, whereupon the whole thing flew off, billowing away before it flopped on the snow. Perhaps it helped a trifle, but nothing like enough—they were still closing, almost imperceptibly, but closing nonetheless.

I groaned and cursed, while the freezing wind whipped at me, casting about for anything else to jettison. The furs? We'd freeze without them, and Valla didn't have a stitch—Valla! For an instant even I was appalled—but only for an instant. There was eight stone of her if there was an ounce—her loss would lighten us splendidly! And that wasn't all—they'd be bound to check, at least, if she came bouncing over the back. Gallant Russian gentlemen, after all, don't abandon naked girls in the snow. It would gain us seconds, anyway, and the loss of weight would surely do the rest.

I stooped over her, fighting to balance myself in the rocking sled. She was still unconscious, wrapped in her furs, looking truly lovely with her silver hair shining in the moonlight, murmuring a little in her half-drunken sleep. I heaved her upright, keeping the fur round her as best I could, and dragged her to the back seat. She nestled against me, and even in that moment of panic I found myself kissing her goodbye—well, it seemed the least I could do. Her lips were chill, with the snow driving past us in the wind; there'll be more than your lips cold in a moment, thinks I. At least her eyes were shut, and our pursuers would see to her before she froze.

"Good-bye, little one," says I. "Sleep tight," and I slipped my arm beneath her legs and bundled her over the back in one clean movement; there was a flash of white limbs as the furs fell away from her, and then she was sprawling on the snow behind us. The sled leaped forward as though a brake had been released, East yelled with alarm, and I could guess he was clinging to the reins for dear life; I gazed back at the receding dark blur where the fur lay beside Valla in the snow. She was invisible in the white confusion, but I saw the riders suddenly swerve out from the centre, a thin shout reached me, and then the leader and his immediate flankers were reining up, the riders on the wings were checking, too, but then they came on, rot them, while a little knot of the centre men halted and gathered, and I saw a couple of them swinging down from their saddles before they were lost in the snowy night.

And the dozen or so riders from the wings were losing ground, too! The lightened sled was fairly racing along. I yelled with delight, tossing my hands in the air, and scrambled forward, over the front of the sled, heaving myself up beside East on the box.

"On, Scud, on!" I shouted. "We're leaving 'em! We'll beat them yet!"

"What was it?" he cried. "What did you do? What did you throw out?"

"Useless baggage!" shouts I. "Never mind, man! Drive for your life!"

He shouted at the beasts, snapping the reins, and then cries:

"What baggage? We had none!" He glanced over his shoulder, at where the horsemen were dim shapes now in the distance, and his eyes fell on the sled. "Is Valla all—" and then he positively screamed. "Valla! Valla! My God!" He reeled in his seat, and I had to grab the reins as they slipped from his fingers. "You—you—no, you couldn't! Flashman, you . . ."

"Hold on, you infernal fool!" I yelled. "It's too late now!" He made a grab at the reins, and I had to sweep him back by main force, as I clutched the ribbons in one hand. "Stop it, damn you, or you'll have us sunk as well!"

"Rein up!" he bawled, struggling with me. "Rein up—must go back! My God, Valla! You filthy, inhuman brute—oh, God!"

"You idiot!" I shouted, lunging with all my weight to keep him off. "It was her or all of us!" Divine inspiration seized me. "Have you forgotten what we're doing, curse you? We've got to get to Raglan, with our news! If we don't—what about Ignatieff and his cursed plans? By heaven, East, I don't forget my duty, even if you do, and I tell you I'd heave a thousand Russian sluts into the snow for my country's sake!" And ten thousand for my own, but that's no matter. "Don't you see—it was that or be captured? And we've got to get through—whatever the cost!"

It stopped him struggling for the reins, at any rate; I felt him go limp beside me, and then he was sobbing like a man in torment, feebly beating with his fist against his temple.

"Oh, my God! How could you—oh, little Valla! I'd have gone —gladly! Oh, she'll die—freezing in that horrible waste!"

"Stop that damned babbling!" says I, stern duty personified. "Do you think I wouldn't have gone myself? And if I had, and some accident had then happened to you, where would our mission have been? While we're both free we double our hope of success." I snapped the reins, blinking against the driving snow as we sped along, and then stole a glance behind—nothing but whirling snow over the empty causeway; our pursuers were lost in the distance, but they'd still be there; we daren't check for an instant.

East was clinging to the box as we rocked along, a man stricken. He kept repeating Valla's name over and over again, and groaning. 'Oh, it's too much! Too high a price—God, have you no pity, Flashman? Are you made of stone?"

"Where my duty's concerned—aye!" cries I, in a fine patriotic fever. "You may thank God for it! If you'd had your way, we'd have died with Pencherjevsky, or be getting sabred to bits back yonder—and would that have served our country?" I decided a little manly rave would do no harm—not that I gave a damn what East thought, but it would keep him quiet, and stop him doing anything rash even now. "My God, East! Have you any notion what this night's work has cost me? D'you think it won't haunt me forever? D'you think I . . . I have no heart?" I dashed my knuckles across my eyes in a fine gesture. "Anyway, it's odds she'll be all right—they're her people, after all, and they'll wrap her up nice as ninepence."

He heaved a great shuddering breath. "Oh, I pray to God it may be so! But the horror of that moment—it's no good, Flashman—I'm not like you! I have not the iron will—I am not of your metal!"

You're right there, boy, thinks I, turning again to look back.

Still nothing, and then through the dimness ahead there was a faint glimmer of light, growing to a cluster, and the causeway was narrowing to nothing more than a dyke, so that I had to slow the sled for fear we should pitch down the banks to the frozen sea. There was a big square fort looming up on our right, and a straggle of buildings on the left, whence the lights came; between the road ran clear on to broad snowfields.

I snapped the whip, calling to the horses, and we drove through, never heeding a voice that called to us from the fort wall overhead. The horsemen might well have closed on us with our slowing down for the dyke, and there wasn't a second to spare. We scudded across the snowfield, casting anxious glances behind; the ground was becoming broken ahead, with little mounds and valleys, and stunted undergrowth—once into that, with the light snow still falling to blot out our tracks, we could twist away and lose them for certain.

"Bravo!" cries I, "we're almost there!" Behind us, Arabat and its fort were fading into the dark; the glimmer of the lights was diminishing as we breasted the first gentle slope and made for a broad gully in the rising ground. We sped silently into it, the sled rocking on the uneven surface; I reined in gently as we went down the reverse slope—and then the lead horse stumbled, whinnying, and came slithering down, the near-side beast swerved sharply, wrenching the reins from my hands, the sled slewed horribly, struck something with a fearful jar, East went flying over the side, and I was hurled headlong forward. I went somersaulting through the air, roaring, felt my back strike the rump of the near-side horse, and then I was plunging into the snow. I landed on my back, and there above me was the sled, hanging poised: I screamed and flung up my hands to save my head. The sled came lumbering over, slowly almost, on top of me, a fiery pain shot through my left side, a crushing weight was across my chest; I shrieked again, and then it settled, pinning me in the snow like a beetle on a card.

I beat at it with my fists, and tried to heave up, but its weight and the agony in my side stopped me—there was a rib gone for sure, if nothing worse. One of the horses was floundering about in the snow, neighing madly, and then I heard East's voice:

"Flashman! Flashman, are you all right?"

"I'm pinned!" I cried. "The sled—get the damned thing off
me! Ah, God, my back's broken!"

He came blundering through the snow, and knelt beside me.
He put his shoulder to the sled, heaving for all he was worth, but
he might as well have tried to shift St Paul's. It didn't give so
much as an inch.

"Get it off!" I groaned. "It's killing me—oh, Christ! Push,
damn you—are you made of jelly?"

"I can't!" he whispered, straining away. "It won't . . . budge.
Ah!" And he fell back, panting.

"Rot you, it's crushing my guts out!" I cried. "Oh, God—
I know my spine's gone—I can feel it! I'm—"

"Silence!" he hissed, and I could see he was listening, staring
back towards Arabat. "Oh, no! Flashman—they're coming! I can
hear the horsemen on the snow!" He flung himself at the sled,
pushing futilely. "Oh, give me strength, God, please! Please!"
He strove, thrusting at the sled, and groaning: "I can't . . . I can't
shift it! Oh, God, what shall I do?"

"Push, or dig, or anything, curse you!" I cried. "Get me loose,
for God's sake! What are you doing, man? What is it?" For he
was standing up now, staring back over the mouth of the gully
towards Arabat; for half a minute he stood motionless, while I
babbled and pawed at the wreck, and then he looked down at me,
and his voice was steady.

"It's no go, old fellow. I know I can't move it. And they're
coming. I can just see them, dimly—but they're heading this
way." He dropped on one knee. "Flashman—I'm sorry. I'll have
to leave you. I can hide—get away—reach Raglan. Oh, my dear
comrade—if I could give my life, I would, but—"

"Rot you!" cries I. "My God, you can't leave me! Push the
bloody thing—help me, man! I'm dying!"

"Oh, God!" he said. "This is agony! First Valla—now you!
But I must get the news through—you know I must. You have
shown me the way of duty, old chap—depend upon it, I shan't
fail! And I'll tell them—when I get home! Tell them how you
gave . . . But I must go!"

"Scud," says I, babbling, "for the love of—"

"Hush," says he, clapping a hand over my lips. "Don't distress
yourself—there's no time! I'll get there—one of the horses will

serve, and if not—you remember the Big Side run by Brownsover, when we were boys? I finished, you know—I'll finish again, Flash, for your sake! They shan't catch me! Trust an old Rugby hare to distance a Russian pack—I will, and I'll hear you hallooing me on! I'll do it—for you, and for Valla—for both your sacrifices!"

"Damn Valla and you, too!" I squealed feebly. "You can't go! You can't leave me! Anyway, she's a bloody Russian! I'm British, you swine! Help me, Scud!"

But I don't think he so much as heard me. He bent forward, and kissed me on the forehead, and I felt one of his manly bloody tears on my brow. "Good-bye, dear old fellow," says he. "God bless you!"

And then he was ploughing away over the snow, to where the near-side horse was standing; he pulled the traces free of its head, and hurried off, pulling it along into the underbrush, with me bleating after him.

"Scud! For pity's sake, don't desert me! You can't—not your old school-fellow, you callous son-of-a-bitch! Please, stop, come back! I'm dying, damn you! I order you—I'm your superior officer! Scud! Please! Help me!"

But he was gone, and I was pinned, weeping, beneath that appalling weight, with the snow falling on my face, and the cold striking into my vitals. I would die, freezing horribly—unless they found me—oh, God, how would I die then? I struggled feebly, the pain lancing at my side, and then I heard the soft thumping of hooves on the snow, and a shout, and those cursed Russian voices, muffled from the mouth of the gully.

"*Paslusha-tyeh! Ah, tam—skorah!*"*

The jingle of harness was close now, and the pad of hooves —a horse neighed on the other side of· the sled, and I squeezed my eyes shut, moaning. At any moment I expected to feel the agony of a lance-point skewering into my chest; then there was the snorting of a horse almost directly over my face, and I shrieked and opened my eyes. Two horsemen were sitting looking down on me, fur-wrapped figures with those stringy Cossack caps pulled down over their brows; fierce moustached faces peering at me.

* "Listen! Ah, there—quickly!"

"Help!" I croaked. "*Pamagityeh, pajalsta!*"*

One of them leaned forward. "*On syer-yaznuh ranyin,*"†
says he, and they both laughed, as at a good joke. Then, to my
horror, the speaker drew his *nagaika* from his saddle-bow, doubled
it back, and leaned down over me.

"*Nyeh zashta,*"‡ says he, leering. His hand went up, I tried
in vain to jerk my head aside, a searing pain seemed to cleave my
skull, and then the dark sky rushed in on me.

* "Help, please!"
† "He is badly hurt."
‡ "Not at all."

I suppose my life has been full of poetic justice—an expression customarily used by Holy Joes to cloak the vindictive pleasure they feel when some enterprising fellow fetches himself a cropper. They are the kind who'll say unctuously that I was properly hoist with my own petard at Arabat, and serve the bastard right. I'm inclined to agree; East would never have abandoned me if I hadn't heaved Valla out of the sled in the first place. He'd have stuck by me and the Christian old school code, and let his military duty go hang. But my treatment of his beloved made it easy for him to forget the ties of comradeship and brotherly love, and do his duty; all his pious protestations about leaving me were really hypocritical moonshine, spouted out to salve his own conscience.

I know my Easts and Tom Browns, you see. They're never happy unless their morality is being tried in the furnace, and they can feel they're doing the right, Christian thing—and never mind the consequences to anyone else. Selfish brutes. Damned unreliable it makes 'em, too. On the other hand, you can always count on me. I'd have got the news through to Raglan out of pure cowardice and self-love, and to hell with East and Valla both; but your pious Scud had to have a grudge to pay off before he'd abandon me. Odd, ain't it? They'll do for us yet, with their sentiment and morality.

In the meantime he had done for me, handsomely. If you're one of the aforementioned who take satisfaction in seeing the wicked go arse over tip into the pit which they have digged, you'll relish the situation of old Flashy, a half-healed crack in his head, a broken rib crudely strapped up with rawhide, lousy after a week in a filthy cell under Fort Arabat, and with his belly muscles fluttering in the presence of Captain Count Nicholas Pavlovitch Ignatieff.

They had hauled me into the guard-room, and there he was,

the inevitable cigarette clamped between his teeth, those terrible
hypnotic blue-brown eyes regarding me with no more emotion
than a snake's. For a full minute he stared at me, the smoke
escaping in tiny wreaths from his lips, and then without a change
of expression he lashed me across the face with his gloves, back and
forth, while I struggled feebly between my Cossacks guards,
trying to duck my head from his blows.

"Don't!" I cried. "Don't, please! *Pajalsta!* I'm a prisoner!
You've no right to... to treat me so! I'm a British officer...
please! I'm wounded... for God's sake, stop!"

He gave me one last swipe, and then looked at his gloves,
weighing them in his hand. Then, in that icy whisper, he said:
"Burn those," and dropped them at the feet of the aide who
stood beside him.

"You," he said to me, and his voice was all the more deadly
for not bearing the slightest trace of heat or emotion, "plead for
mercy. You need expect none. You are foresworn—a betrayer of
the vilest kind. You were treated with every consideration, with
kindness even, by a man who turned to you in his hour of need,
laying on you the most solemn obligation to protect his daughter.
You repaid him by abducting her, by trying to escape, and by
abandoning her to her death. You..."

"It's a lie!" I shouted. "I didn't—it was an accident! She fell
from the sled—it wasn't my fault! I was driving, I wasn't even
with her!"

His reply to this was a gesture to the aide, who struck me with
the gloves again.

"You are a liar," says Ignatieff. "The officer of the pursuing
troop saw you. Pencherjevsky himself has told me how you and
your comrade East left Starotorsk, how you basely seized the
opportunity to escape..."

"It wasn't base... we'd given no parole... we had the right
of any prisoners of war... in all honour..."

"You talk of honour," says he softly. "You thought to escape
all censure, because you believed Pencherjevsky was doomed.
Fortunately, he was not a *hetman* of Cossacks for nothing. He cut
his way clear, and in spite of your unspeakable treatment of his
daughter, she too survived."

"Thank God for that!" cries I. "Believe me, sir, you are quite mistaken. I intended no betrayal of the Count, and I swear I never mistreated his daughter—it was all an accident..."

"The only accident for you was the one that prevented your escaping. I promise you," he went on, in that level, sibilant voice, "that you will live to wish that sled had crushed your life out. For by your conduct, you understand, you have lost every right to be treated as an honourable man, or even as a common felon. You are beyond the law of nations, you are beyond mercy. One thing alone can mitigate your punishment."

He paused there, to let it sink in, and to take another cigarette. The aide lit it for him, while I waited, quaking and sweating.

"I require an answer to one question," says Ignatieff, "and you will supply it in your own language. Lie to me, or try to evade it, and I will have your tongue removed." His next words were in English. "Why did you try to escape?"

Terrified as I was, I daren't tell him the truth. I knew that if he learned that I'd found out about his expedition to India, it was all up with me.

"Because... because there was the opportunity... and there wasn't any dishonour in it. And we meant... ah, Miss Pencher-jevsky no harm, I swear we didn't..."

"You lie. No one, in your situation, would have attempted such a foolhardy escape, let alone such a dishonourable one, without some pressing reason." The blue-brown eyes seemed to be boring into my brain. "I believe I know what it was—the only thing it could possibly be. And I assure you, in five minutes from now you will be dying, in excruciating agony, unless you can tell me what is meant by—" he paused, inhaling on his cigarette "—Item Seven." He let the smoke trickle down his nostrils. "If, by chance, you *are* unaware of what it means, you will die anyway."

There was nothing for it; I had to confess. I tried to speak, but my throat was dry. Then I stammered out hoarsely, in English:

"It's a plan... to invade India. Please, for God's sake, I found out about it by accident, I..."

"How did you discover it?"

I babbled it out, how we had eavesdropped in the gallery and heard him talking to the Tsar. "It was just by chance... I didn't mean to spy... it was East, and he said we must try to escape...

to get word to our people ... to warn them! I said it was dishonourable, that we were bound as gentlemen ..."

"And Major East was with you, and overheard?"

"Yes, yes ... it was his notion, you see! I didn't like it ... and
when he suggested we escape, when those beastly peasants attacked
Starotorsk ... what could I do? But I swear we meant no harm,
and ... and it's a lie that I mistreated Miss Pencherjevsky—
I'll swear it, by my honour, on the Bible ..."

"Gag him," says Ignatieff. "Bring him to the courtyard.
And bring a prisoner. Any one in the cells will do."

They stuffed a rag into my mouth, and bound it, stifling my
pleas for mercy, for I was sure he was going to make away with
me horribly, now that he had his information. They pinioned my
wrists, and thrust me brutally out into the yard; it was freezing,
and I had nothing but my shirt and breeches. I waited, trembling
with cold and funk, until presently another Cossack appeared,
driving in front of him a scared, dirty-looking peasant with fetters
on his legs. Ignatieff, who had followed us out, and was pinching
the paper of a cigarette, beckoned the Cossack.

"What was this fellow's offence?"

"Insubordination, Lord Count."

"Very good," says Ignatieff, and lit his cigarette.

Two more Cossacks appeared, carrying between them a curious
bench, like a vaulting horse with very short legs and a flat top.
The prisoner shrieked at the sight of it, and tried to run, but
they dragged him to it, tearing off his clothes, and bound him on it
face down, with thongs at his ankles, knees, waist and neck, so
that he lay there, naked and immovable, but still screaming
horribly.

Ignatieff beckoned one of the Cossacks, who held out to him a
curious thick black coil, of what looked for all the world like
shiny liquorice. Ignatieff hefted it in his hands, and then stepped
in front of me and placed it over my head; I shuddered as it
touched my shoulders, and was astonished by the weight of the
thing. At a sign from Ignatieff the Cossack, grinning, drew it
slowly off my shoulders, and I realized in horror as it slithered
off like an obscene black snake that it was a huge whip, over
twelve feet long, as thick as my arm at the butt and tapering to a
point no thicker than a boot-lace.

"You will have heard of this," says Ignatieff softly. "It is called a *knout*. Its use is illegal. Watch."

The Cossack stood opposite the bench with its howling victim, took the *knout* in both hands, and swept it back over his shoulder so that its hideous lash trailed behind him in the snow. Then he struck.

I've seen floggings, and watched with fascination as a rule, but this was horrible, like nothing imaginable. That diabolical thing cut through the air with a noise like a steam whistle, so fast that you couldn't see it; there was a crack like a pistol-shot, a fearful, choked scream of agony, and then the Cossack was snaking it back for another blow.

"Wait," says Ignatieff, and to me: "Come here." They pushed me forward to the bench, the bile nearly choking me behind the gag; I didn't want to look, but they forced me. The wretched man's buttocks were cut clean across, as by a sabre, and the blood was pouring out.

"The drawing stroke," says Ignatieff. "Proceed."

Five more shrieking cuts, five more explosive cracks, five more razor gashes, and the snow beneath the bench was sodden with blood. The most horrible thing was that the victim was conscious still, making awful animal noises.

"Now observe," says Ignatieff, "the effect of a flat blow."

The Cossack struck a seventh time, but this time he didn't snap the *knout*, but let it fall smack across the patient's spine. There was a dreadful sound, like a wet cloth slapped on stone, but from the victim no cry at all. They unstrapped him, and as they lifted the bleeding wreck of his body from the bench, I saw it was hanging horribly limp in the middle.

"The killing stroke," said Ignatieff. "It is debatable how many of the drawing blows a man can endure, but with the flat stroke one is invariably fatal." He turned to look at me, and then at the blood-soaked bench, as though considering, while he smoked calmly. At last he dropped his cigarette in the snow.

"Bring him inside."

I was half-fainting with fear and shock when they dropped me sprawling in a chair, and Ignatieff sat down behind the table and waved them out. He lit himself another cigarette, and then said quietly:

"That was a demonstration, for your benefit. You see now what awaits you—except that when your turn comes I shall take the opportunity of ascertaining how many of the drawing strokes a vigorous and healthy man can suffer before he dies. Your one hope of escaping that fate lies in doing precisely as you are told —for I have a use for you. If I had not, you would be undergoing destruction by the knout at this moment."

He smoked in silence for a minute, never taking his eyes off me, and I watched him like a rabbit before a snake. Not only the hideous butchery I had watched, but the fact that he had condemned a poor devil to it *just to impress me*, appalled me utterly. And I knew I would do anything—anything, to escape that abomination.

"That you had somehow learned of Item Seven I already suspected," says Ignatieff at last. "Nothing else would have led you to flee. Accordingly, for the past week, we have proceeded on the assumption that intelligence of our expedition would reach Lord Raglan—and subsequently your government in London. We can now be certain that it has done so, since your companion, Major East, has not been recaptured. This betrayal is regrettable, but by no means disastrous. Indeed, it can be made to work to our advantage, for your authorities will suppose that they have seven months to prepare against the blow that is coming. They will be wrong. In four months from now our army will be advancing over the Khyber Pass, thirty thousand strong, with at least half as many Afghan allies eager to descend across the Indus. If every British soldier in India were sent to guard the frontier —which is impossible—it would not serve to stem our advance. No adequate help can arrive from England in time, and your troops will have a rebellious Indian population at their backs while we take them by the throat. Our agents are already at work, preparing that insurrection.

"You may wonder how it is possible to advance the moment of our attack by three months. It is simple. General Khruleff's original plan for an attack through the Syr Daria country to Afghanistan and India will be adhered to—our army had been preparing to take this route, which was abandoned only lately because of minor difficulties with native bandits and because the southern road, through Persia, offered a more secure and leisurely progress. The change of plan will thus be simple to effect, since the army is still poised for the northern route, and the arrangements for its transport by sea across Caspian and Aral can proceed immediately. This will ensure progress at twice the speed we could hope for if we went through Persia. And we will consolidate our position among the Syr Daria and Amu Daria tribesmen in passing."

I didn't doubt a word of it—not that I cared a patriotic damn. They could have India, China, and the whole bloody Orient for me, if only I could find a way out for myself.

"It is as well that you should know this," went on Ignatieff, "so that you may understand the part which I intend that you should play in it. A part for which you are providentially qualified. I know a great deal about you—so much, indeed, that you will be astonished at the extent of my knowledge. It is our policy to garner information, and I doubt," went on this cocky bastard, "whether any state in Europe can boast such extensive secret dossiers as we possess. I am especially aware of your activities in Afghanistan fourteen years ago—of your work, along with such agents as Burnes and Pottinger, among the Gilzais and other tribes. I know even of the exploit which earned you the extravagant nickname of 'Bloody Lance', of your dealings with Muhammed Akbar Khan, of your solitary survival of the disaster which befell the British Army*—a disaster in which, you may be unaware, our own intelligence service played some part."

Now, shaken and fearful as I was, one part of my mind was noting something from all this. Master Ignatieff might be a clever and devilish dangerous man, but he had at least one of the besetting weaknesses of youth: he was as vain as an Etonian duke, and it led him to commit the cardinal folly in a diplomatic man. He talked too much.

"It follows," says he, "that you can be of use to us in Afghanistan. It will be convenient, when our army arrives there, to have a British officer, of some small reputation in that country, to assist us in convincing the tribal leaders that the decay of British power is imminent, and that it will be in their interests to join in the conquest of India. They will not need much convincing, but

* See Flashman.

even so your betrayal will add to the impression our armed force
will make."

For all his impassivity, I knew he was enjoying this; it was in
the tilt of his cigarette, and the glitter in his gotch eye.

"It is possible, of course, that you will prefer death—even by
the knout—to betrayal of your country. I doubt it, but I must
take into consideration the facts which are to be found in your
dossier. They tell me of a man brave to the point of recklessness,
of proved resource, and of considerable intelligence. My own
observation of you tends to contradict this—I do not judge you to
be of heroic material, but I may be mistaken. Certainly your conduct at Balaclava, of which I have received eye-witness accounts,
is of a piece with your dossier. It does not matter. If, when you
have been taken to Afghanistan with our army, you decline to
make what the Roman priests call a propaganda on our behalf,
we shall derive what advantage we can from displaying you naked
in an iron cage along the way. The knouting will take place when
we arrive on Indian soil."

He had it all splendidly pat, this icy Muscovite bastard, and
well pleased with himself he was, too. He pinched another
cigarette between his fingers, thinking to himself to see if there
was any other unpleasant detail he could rub into me, and
deciding there wasn't, called to the Cossack guard.

"This man," says he, "is a dangerous and desperate criminal.
He is to be chained wrist and ankle at once, and the keys are to
be thrown away. He will accompany us to Rostov tomorrow, and
if, while he is in your charge he should escape or die"—he
paused, and when he went on it was as casually said as though he
were confining them to barracks—"you will be knouted to death.
And your families also. Take him away."

You may not credit it, but my feelings as they thrust me down
into my underground pit, clamped chains on my wrists and
ankles, and slammed the door on me, were of profound relief.
For one thing, I was out of the presence of that evil madman
with his leery optic—that may seem small enough, but you
haven't been closeted with him, and I have. Point two, I was not
only alive but due to be preserved in good health for at least
four months—and I was old soldier enough to know that a lot
can happen in that time. Point three, I wasn't going into the

unknown: Afghanistan, ghastly place though it is, was a home county hunt to me, and if once I could get a yard start, I fancied I could survive the going a sight better than any Russian pursuers.

It was a mighty "if", of course, but funny things happen north of the Khyber—come to that, I wondered if Ignatieff and his brother-thugs knew exactly what they were tackling in taking an army through that country. We'd tried it, and God knew we were fitter to go to war than the Russians ever were, yet we'd come most horribly undone. I remembered my old sparring chums, the Gilzais and Baluchis and Khels and Afridis—and those fiends of Ghazis—and wondered if the Ruskis knew precisely the kind of folk they'd be relying on for safe-conduct and alliance.

They had their agents in Afghanistan, to be sure, and must have a shrewd notion of how things were; I wondered if they had secured their alliances in advance, perhaps with the King? And one thing was certain, the Afghans hated the British, and would join in an attack on India like Orangemen on the Twelfth. It would be all up with the Honourable East India Company then, and no bones about it.

Thinking about that, I could make a guess that if there was a point where the Russian force might run into trouble, it would be in the wild country that they must pass through before they reached Afghanistan. In my days at Kabul, Sekundar Burnes had told me a bit about it—of the independent Khanates at Bokhara and Samarkand and the Syr Daria country, where the Russians had even then been trying to extend their empire, and getting a bloody nose in the process. Fearsome bastards those northern tribes were, Tajiks and Uzbeks and the remnants of the great hordes, and from the little I'd heard from folk like Pencherjevsky, they were still fiercely resisting Russian encroachment. We'd had a few agents up that way ourselves, in my time, fellows like Burnes and Stoddart, trying to undermine Russian influence, but with our retreat from Afghanistan it was well out of our bailiwick now, and the Russians would no doubt eat up the tribes at their leisure. That's what Ignatieff had hinted, and I couldn't see the wild clans being able to stand up to an army of thirty thousand, with ten thousand Cossack cavalry and artillery trains and the rest of it.

No, setting aside a few minor rubs, this Russian expedition
looked to me to be on a good firm wicket—but that mattered
nothing as far as I was concerned. What I had to bide my time
for was Afghanistan, and the moment when they brought me out
of my blinkers to make what Ignatieff called a propaganda on
Russia's behalf. That would be the moment to lift up mine eyes
unto the hills, or the tall trees, or the nearest hole in the ground
—anywhere at all, so long as it offered a refuge from Ignatieff.
I didn't even think about the price of failure to escape—it was
quite unthinkable.

You may think it strange, knowing me, that even in the hellish
mess I found myself, with the shadow of horrible death hanging
over me, I could think ahead so clearly. Well, it wasn't that I'd
grown any braver as I got older—the reverse, if anything—
but I'd learned, since my early days, that there's no point in
wasting your wits and digestion blubbering over evil luck and
folly and lost opportunities. I'll admit, when I thought how close
I'd been to winning clear, I could have torn my hair—but there it
was. However fearful my present predicament, however horrid the
odds and dangers ahead, they'd get no better with being fretted
over. It ain't always easy, if your knees knock as hard as mine,
but you must remember the golden rule: when the game's going
against you, stay calm—and cheat.

In this state of philosophic apprehension, then, I began my
journey from Fort Arabat the following day—a journey such as
I don't suppose any other Englishman has ever made. You can
trace it on the map, all fifteen hundred miles of it, and your finger
will go over places you never dreamed of, from the edge of
civilization to the real back of beyond, over seas and deserts to
mountains that perhaps nobody will ever climb, through towns
and tribes that belong to the Arabian Nights rather than to the
true story of a reluctant English gentleman (as the guide books
would say) with two enormous scowling Cossacks brooding over
him the whole way.

The first part of the journey was all too familiar, by sled back
along the Arrow of Arabat, over the bridge at Yenitchi, and then
east along that dreary winter coast to Taganrog, where the snow
was already beginning to melt in the foul little streets, and the
locals still appeared to be recovering from the excesses of the great

winter fair at Rostov. Russians, in my experience, are part-drunk most of the time, but if there's a sober soul between the Black Sea and the Caspian for weeks after the Rostov *kermesse* he must be a Baptist hermit; Taganrog was littered with returned revellers. Rostov I don't much remember, or the famous river Don, but after that we took to *telegues*, and since the great Ignatieff was riding at the front of our little convoy of six vehicles, we made good speed. Too good for Flashy, bumping along uncomfortably on the straw in one of the middle wagons; my chains were beginning to be damned uncomfortable, and every jolt of those infernal *telegues* bruised my wrists and ankles. You may think fetters are no more than an inconvenience, but when every move you make means lifting a few pounds of steel, which chafes your flesh and jars your bones, and means you can never lie without their biting into you, they become a real torture. I pleaded to have them removed, if only for an hour or two, and got a kick in my half-mended rib for my pains.

Cossacks, of course, never wash (although they brush their coats daily with immense care) and I wasn't allowed to either, so by the time we were rolling east into the half-frozen steppe beyond Rostov I was filthy, bearded, tangled, and itchy beyond belief, stinking with the garlic of their awful food, and only praying that I wouldn't contract some foul disease from my noisome companions—for they even slept either side of me, with their *nagaikas* knotted into my chains. It ain't like a honeymoon at Baden, I can tell you.

There were four hundred miles of that interminable plain, getting worse as it went on; it took us about five days, as near as I remember, with the *telegues* going like blazes, and new horses at every post-house. The only good thing was that as we went the weather grew slightly warmer, until when we were entering the great salt flats of the Astrakhan, the snow vanished altogether, and you could even travel without your *tulup*.

Astrakhan city itself is a hell-hole. The land all about is as flat as the Wash country, and the town itself lies so low they have a great dyke all round to prevent the Volga washing it into the Caspian, or t'other way round. As you might expect, it's a plague spot; you can smell the pestilence in the air, and before we passed through the dyke Ignatieff ordered everyone to soak his face and hands with vinegar, as though that would do any good. Still, it was the nearest I came to making toilet the whole way.

Mark you, there was one good thing about Astrakhan: the women. Once you get over towards the Caspian the people are more slender and Asiatic than your native Russian, and some of those dark girls, with their big eyes and long straight noses and pouting lips had even me, in my unkempt misery, sitting up and dusting off my beard. But of course I never got near them; it was into the kremlin for Flash and his heavenly twins, and two nights in a steaming cell before they put us aboard a steamer for the trip across the Caspian.

It's a queer sea, that one, for it isn't above twenty feet deep, and consequently the boats are of shallow draught, and bucket about like canoes. I spewed most of the way, but the Cossacks, who'd never sailed before, were in a fearful way, vomiting and praying by turns. They never let go of me, though, and I realized with a growing sense of alarm that if these two watch-dogs were kept on me all the way to Kabul, I'd stand little chance of giving them the slip. Their terror of Ignatieff was if anything even greater than mine, and in the worst of the boat's heaving one of them was always clutching my ankle chains, even if he was rolling about the deck retching at the same time.

It was four days of misery before we began to steam through clusters of ugly, sandy little islands towards the port of Tishkandi, which was our destination. I'm told it isn't there any longer, and this is another strange thing about the Caspian—its coastline changes continually, almost like the Mississippi shores. One year there are islands, and next they have become hills on a peninsula, while a few miles away a huge stretch of coast will have changed into a lagoon.

Tishkandi's disappearance can have been no loss to anyone; it was a dirty collection of huts with a pier, and beyond it the ground climbed slowly through marshy salt flats to two hundred miles of arid, empty desert. You could call it steppe, I suppose, but it's dry, rocky heart-breaking country, fit only for camels and lizards.

"Ust-Yurt," says one of the officers, as he looked at it, and the very name sent my heart into my boots.

It's dangerous country, too. There was a squadron of lancers waiting for us when we landed, to guard us against the wild desert tribes, for this was beyond the Russian frontiers, in land where they were still just probing at the savage folk who chopped up their caravans and raided their outposts whenever they had the chance. When we made camp at night it was your proper little laager, with sangars at each corner, and sentries posted, and half a dozen lancers out riding herd. All very business-like, and not what I'd have expected from Ruskis, really. But this was their hard school, as I was to learn, like our North-west Frontier, where you either soldiered well or not at all.

It was five days through the desert, not too uncomfortable while we were moving, but freezing hellish at night, and the dromedaries with their native drivers must have covered the ground at a fair pace, forty miles a day or thereabouts. Once or twice we saw horsemen in the distance, on the low rocky *barchans*, and I heard for the first time names like "Kazak" and "Turka", but they kept a safe distance. On the last day, though, we saw more of them, much closer, and quite peaceable, for these were people of the Aral coast, and the Russians had them fairly well in order on that side of the sea. When I saw them near I had a strange sense of recognition—those swarthy faces, with here and there a hooked nose and a straggling moustache, the dirty puggarees swathed round the heads, and the open belted robes, took me back to Northern India and the Afghan hills. I found myself stealing a look at my Cossacks and the lancers, and even at Ignatieff riding with the other officers at the head of our caravan, and thinking to myself—these ain't your folk, my lads, but they're mighty close to some I used to know. It's a strange thing, to come through hundreds of miles of wilderness, from a foreign land and moving in the wrong direction, and suddenly find yourself sniffing the air and thinking, "home". If you're British, and have soldiered in India, you'll understand what I mean.

Late that afternoon we came through more salty flats to a long coastline of rollers sweeping in from a sea so blue that I found myself muttering through my beard "Thalassa or thalatta, the former or the latter?," it seemed so much like the ocean that old Arnold's Greeks had seen after their great march. And suddenly I could close my eyes and hear his voice droning away on a summer afternoon at Rugby, and smell the cut grass coming in through the open windows, and hear the fags at cricket outside, and from that I found myself dreaming of the smell of hay in the fields beyond Renfrew, and Elspeth's body warm and yielding, and the birds calling at dusk along the river, and the pony champing at the grass, and it was such a sweet, torturing longing that I groaned aloud, and when I opened my eyes the tears came, and there was a hideous Russian voice clacking "Aralskoe More!",* and bright Asian sunlight, and the chains galling my wrist and ankle-bones, and foreign flat faces all round, and I realized that my earlier thoughts of home had been an illusion, and this was alien, frightening land.

There was a big military camp on the shore, and a handy little steamer lying off, and while the rest of us waited Ignatieff was received with honours by a group of senior officers—and he only a captain, too. Of course, I'd realized before this that he was a big noise, but the way they danced attendance on him you'd have thought he was the Tsar's cousin. (Maybe he was, for all I know.)

They put us aboard the steamer that evening, and I was so tuckered out by the journey that I just slept where I lay down. And in the morning there was a coast ahead, with a great new wooden pier, and a huge river flowing down between low banks to the sea. As far as I could see the coast was covered with tents, and there was another steamer, and half a dozen big wooden transports, and one great warship, all riding at anchor between the pier and the river mouth. There were bugles sounding on the distant shore, and swarms of people everywhere, among the tents, on the pier, and on the ships, and a great hum of noise in the midst of which a military band was playing a rousing march; this is the army, I thought, or most of it, this is their Afghan expedition.

I asked one of the Russian sailors what the river might be, and he said: "Syr Daria," and then pointing to a great wooden stockaded fort on the rising land above the river, he added: "Fort Raim."[35] And then one of the Cossacks pushed him away, cursing, and told me to hold my tongue.

They landed us in lighters, and there was another delegation of smart uniforms to greet Ignatieff, and an orderly holding a horse for him, and all around tremendous bustle of unloading and

* "Aral Sea!"

ferrying from the ships, and gangs of orientals at work, with
Russian non-coms bawling at them and swinging whips, and
gear being stowed in the newly-built wooden sheds along the
shore. I watched gun limbers being swung down from a derrick,
and cursing, half-naked gangs hauling them away; the whole
pier was piled with crates and bundles, and for all the world it
looked like the levee at New Orleans, except that this was a
temporary town of huts and tents and lean-to's. But there were
just as many people, sweating and working in orderly chaos, and
you could feel the excitement in the air.

Ignatieff came trotting down to where I was sitting between
my Cossacks, and at a word they hauled me up and we set off at
his heels through the confusion, up the long, gradual slope to the
fort. It was farther off than I'd expected, about a mile, so that it
stood well back from the camp, which was all spread out like a
sand-table down the shore-line. As we neared the fort he stopped,
and his orderly was pointing at the distant picket lines and identi-
fying the various regiments—New Russian Dragoons, Romiant-
zoff's Grenadiers, Astrakhan Carabiniers, and Aral Hussars, I remember. Ignatieff saw me surveying the camp, and came over.
He hadn't spoken to me since we left Arabat.

"You may look," says he, in that chilling murmur of his,
"and reflect on what you see. The next Englishman to catch sight
of them will be your sentry on the walls of Peshawar. And while
you are observing, look yonder also, and see the fate of all who
oppose the majesty of the Tsar."

I looked where he pointed, up the hill towards the fort, and
my stomach turned over. To one side of the gateway was a series
of wooden gallows, and from each one hung a human figure—
although some of them were hard to recognize as human. A few
hung by their arms, some by their ankles, one or two lucky ones
by their necks. Some were wasted and blackened by exposure; at
least one was still alive and stirring feebly. An awful carrion reek
drifted down on the clear spring air.

"Unteachables," says Ignatieff. "Bandit scum and rebels of the
Syr Daria who have been unreceptive to our sacred Russian
imperial mission. Perhaps, when we have lined their river with
sufficient of these examples, they will learn. It is the only way to
impress recalcitrants. Do you not agree?"

He wheeled his horse, and we trailed up after him towards the fort. It was bigger, far bigger, than I'd expected, a good two hundred yards square, with timber ramparts twenty feet high, and at one end they were already replacing the timber with rough stone. The Russian eagle ensign was fluttering over the roofed gatehouse, there were grenadiers drawn up and saluting as Ignatieff cantered through, and I trudged in, clanking, to find myself on a vast parade, with good wooden barracks around the walls, troops drilling in the dusty square, and a row of two-storey administrative buildings down one side. It was a very proper fort, something like those of the American frontier in the 'seventies; there were even some small cottages which I guessed were officers' quarters.

Ignatieff was getting his usual welcome from a tubby chap who appeared to be the commandant; I wasn't interested in what they said, but I gathered the commandant was greatly excited, and was babbling some great news.

"Not both of them?" I heard Ignatieff say, and the other clapped his hands in great glee and said, yes, both, a fine treat for General Perovski and General Khruleff when they arrived.

"They will make a pretty pair of gallows, then," says Ignatieff. "You are to be congratulated, sir. Nothing could be a better omen for our march through Syr Daria."

"Ah, ha, excellent!" cries the tubby chap, rubbing his hands. "And that will not be long, eh? All is in train here, as you see, and the equipment arrives daily. But come, my dear Count, and refresh yourself."

They went off, leaving me feeling sick and hang-dog between my guards; the sight of those tortured bodies outside the stockade had brought back to me the full horror of my own situation. And I felt no better when there came presently a big, brute-faced sergeant of grenadiers, a coiled *nagaika* in his fist, to tell my Cossacks they could fall out, as he was taking me under his wing.

"Our necks depend on this fellow," says one of the Cossacks doubtfully, and the sergeant sneered, and scowled at me.

"My neck depends on what I've got in the cells already," growls he. "This offal is no more precious than my two birds. Be at peace; he shall join them in my most salubrious cell, from which even the lizards cannot escape. March him along!"

They escorted me to a corner on the landward side of the fort, down an alley between the wooden buildings, and to a short flight of stone steps leading down to an iron-shod door. The sergeant hauled back the massive bolts, thrust back the creaking door, and then reached up, grabbing me by my wrist-chains. "In, *tut!*" he snarled, and yanked me headlong down into the cell. The door slammed, the bolts ground to, and I heard him guffawing brutally as their footsteps died away.

I lay there trembling on the dirty floor, just about done with fatigue and fear. At least it was dim and cool in here. And then I heard someone speaking in the cell, and raised my head; at first I could make nothing out in the faint light that came from a single window high in one wall, and then I started with astonishment, for suspended flat in the air in the middle of the cell, spread-eagled as though in flight, was the figure of a man. As my eyes grew accustomed to the dimness I drew in a shuddering breath, for now I could see that he was cruelly hung between four chains, one to each limb from the top corners of the room. More astonishing still, beneath his racked body, which hung about three feet from the floor, was crouched another figure, supporting the hanging man on his back, presumably to take the appalling strain of the chains from his wrists and ankles. It was the crouching man who was speaking, and to my surprise, his words were in Persian.

"It is a gift from God, brother," says he, speaking with difficulty. "A rather dirty gift, but human—if there is such a thing as a human Russian. At least, he is a prisoner, and if I speak politely to him I may persuade him to take my place for a while, and bear your intolerable body. I am too old for this, and you are heavier than Abu Hassan, the breaker of wind."

The hanging man, whose head was away from me, tried to lift it to look. His voice, when he spoke, was hoarse with pain, but what he said was, unbelievably, a joke.

"Let him . . . approach . . . then . . . and I pray . . . to God . . . that he has . . . fewer fleas . . . than you . . . Also . . . you are . . . a most . . . uncomfortable . . . support . . . God help . . . the woman . . . who shares . . . your bed."

"Here is thanks," says the crouching man, panting under the weight. "I bear him as though I were the Djinn of the Seven

Peaks, and he rails at me. You, *nasrani*,"* he addressed me: "If you understand God's language, come and help me to support this ingrate, this sinner. And when you are tired, we shall sit in comfort against the wall, and gloat over him. Or I may squat on his chest, to teach him gratitude. Come, Ruski, are we not all God's creatures?"

And even as he said it, his voice quavered, he staggered under the burden above him, and slumped forward unconscious on the floor.

* Christian.

The hanging man gave a sudden cry of anguish as his body took the full stretch of the chains; he hung there moaning and panting until, without really thinking, I scrambled forward and came up beneath him, bearing his trunk across my stooped back. His face was hanging backward beside my own, working with pain.

"God . . . thank you!" he gasped at last. "My limbs are on fire! But not for long—not for long—if God is kind." His voice came in a tortured whisper. "Who are you—a Ruski?"

"No," says I, "an Englishman, a prisoner of the Russians."

"You speak . . . our tongue . . . in God's name?"

"Yes," says I, "Hold still, curse you, or you'll slip!"

He groaned again: he was a devilish weight. And then: "Providence . . . works strangely," says he. "An *angliski* . . . here. Well, take heart, stranger . . . you may be . . . more fortunate . . . than you know."

I couldn't see that, not by any stretch, stuck in a lousy cell with some Asiatic nigger breaking my back. Indeed, I was regretting the impulse which had made me bear him up—who was he to me, after all, that I shouldn't let him dangle? But when you're in adversity it don't pay to antagonize your companions, at least until you know what's what, so I stayed unwillingly where I was, puffing and straining.

"Who . . . are you?" says he.

"Flashman. Colonel, British Army."

"I am Yakub Beg,"[36] whispers he, and even through his pain you could hear the pride in his voice. "Kush Begi, Khan of Khokand, and guardian of . . . the White Mosque. You are my . . . guest . . . sent to me . . . from heaven. Touch . . . on my knee . . . touch on my bosom . . . touch where you will."

I recognized the formal greeting of the hill folk, which wasn't appropriate in the circumstances.

"Can't touch anything but your arse at present," I told him, and I felt him shake—my God, he could even laugh, with the arms and legs being drawn out of him.

"It is a . . . good answer," says he. "You talk . . . like a Tajik. We laugh . . . in adversity. Now I tell you . . . Englishman . . . when I go hence . . . you go too."

I thought he was just babbling, of course. And then the other fellow, who had collapsed, groaned and sat up, and looked about him.

"Ah, God, I was weak," says he. "Yakub, my son and brother, forgive me. I am as an old wife with dropsy; my knees are as water."

Yakub Beg turned his face towards mine, and you must imagine his words punctuated by little gasps of pain.

"That ancient creature who grovels on the floor is Izzat Kutebar,"[37] says he. "A poor fellow of little substance and less wit, who raided one Ruski caravan too many and was taken, through his greed. So they made him 'swim upon land', as I am swimming now, and he might have hung here till he rotted—and welcome—but I was foolish enough to think of rescue, and scouted too close to this fort of Shaitan. So they took me, and placed me in his chains, as the more important prisoner of the two—for he is dirt, this feeble old Kutebar. He swung a good sword once, they say—God, it must have been in Timur's time!"

"By God!" cries Kutebar. "Did I lose Ak Mechet to the Ruskis? Was I whoring after the beauties of Bokhara when the beast Perovski massacred the men of Khokand with his grapeshot? No, by the pubic hairs of Rustum! I was swinging that good sword, laying the Muscovites in swathes along Syr Daria, while this fine fighting chief here was loafing in the bazaar with his darlings, saying 'Eyewallah, it is hot today, Give me to drink, Miriam, and put a cool hand on my forehead.' Come out from under him, feringhee, and let him swing for his pains."

"You see?" says Yakub Beg, craning his neck and trying to grin. "A dotard, flown with dreams. A badawi zhazh-kayan* who talks as the wild sheep defecate, at random, everywhere. When you and I go hither, Flashman bahadur, we shall leave him, and even the Ruskis will take pity on such a dried-up husk, and employ

* A wild babbler.

him to clean their privies—those of the common soldiers, you understand, not the officers."

If I hadn't served long in Afghanistan, and learned the speech and ways of the Central Asian tribes, I suppose I'd have imagined that I was in a cell with a couple of madmen. But I knew this trick that they have of reviling those they respect most, in banter, of their love of irony and formal imagery, which is strong in Pushtu and even stronger in Persian, the loveliest of all languages.

"When you go hither!" scoffs Kutebar, climbing to his feet and peering at his friend. "When will that be? When Buzurg Khan remembers you? God forbid I should depend on the good-will of such a one. Or when Sahib Khan comes blundering against this place as you and he did two years ago, and lost two thousand men? Eyah! Why should they risk their necks for you—or me? We are not gold; once we are buried, who will dig us up?"

"My people will come," says Yakub Beg. "And *she* will not forget me."

"Put no faith in women, and as much in the Chinese," says Kutebar cryptically. "Better if this stranger and I try to surprise the guard, and cut our way out."

"And who will cut these chains?" says the other. "No, old one, put the foot of courage in the stirrup of patience. They will come, if not tonight, then tomorrow. Let us wait."

"And while you're waiting," says I, "put the shoulder of friendship beneath the backside of helplessness. Lend a hand, man, before I break in two."

Kutebar took my place again, exchanging insults with his friend, and I straightened up to take a look at Yakub Beg. He was a tall fellow, so far as I could judge, narrow waisted and big shouldered—for he was naked save for his loose *pyjamy* trousers —with great corded arm muscles. His wrists were horribly torn by his manacles, and while I sponged them with water from a *chatti** in the corner I examined his face. It was one of your strong hill figureheads, lean and long-jawed, but straight-nosed for once—he'd said he was a Tajik, which meant he was half-Persian. His head was shaved, Uzbek fashion, with a little scalp-lock to one side, and so was his face, except for a tuft of forked beard on his chin. A tough customer, by the look of him; one of

* Water-jug.

those genial mountain scoundrels who'll tell you merry stories
while he stabs you in the guts just for the fun of hearing his knife-
hilt bells jingle.

"You are an Englishman," says he, as I washed his wrists.
"I knew one, once, long ago. At least I saw him, in Bokhara, the
day they killed him. He was a man, that one—Khan Ali, with the
fair beard. 'Embrace the faith,' they said. 'Why should I?' says
he, 'since you have murdered my friend who forsook his church
and became a Muslim. Ye have robbed; ye have killed; what do
you want of me? And they said, 'Blood'. Says he: 'Then make an
end.' And they killed him. I was only a youth, but I thought,
when I go, if I am far from home, let me go like that one. He was
a *ghazi*,* that Khan Ali."[38]

"Much good it did him," growled Kutebar, underneath. "For
that matter, much good Bokhara ever did anyone. They would
sell us to the Ruskis for a handful of millet. May their goats' milk
turn to urine and their girls all breed Russian bastards—which
they will do, no doubt, with alarming facility."

"You spoke of getting out of here," says I to Yakub Beg. "Is it
possible? Will your friends attempt a rescue?"

"He has no friends," says Kutebar. "Except me, and see the
pass I am brought to, propping up his useless trunk."

"They will come," says Yakub Beg, softly. He was pretty
done, it seemed to me, with his eyes closed and his face ravaged
with pain. "When the light fades, you two must leave me to hang
—no, Izzat, it is an order. You and Flashman *bahadur* must rest,
for when the Lady of the Great Horde comes over the wall the
Ruskis will surely try to kill us before we can be rescued. You two
must hold them, with your shoulders to the door."

"If we leave you to hang you will surely die," says Kutebar,
gloomily. "What will I say to her then?" And suddenly he burst
into a torrent of swearing, slightly muffled by his bent position.
"These Russian apes! These scum of Muscovy! God smite them to
the nethermost pit! Can they not give a man a clean death,
instead of racking him apart by inches? Is this their civilizing
empire? Is this the honour of the soldiers of the White Tsar?
May God the compassionate and merciful rend the bowels from
their bodies and—"

* Champion.

"Do you rest, old groaner," gasps Yakub, in obvious pain from the passionate heaving of his supporter. "Then you may rend them on your own account, and spare the All-wise the trouble. Lay them in swathes along Syr Daria—again."

And in spite of Kutebar's protests, Yakub Beg was adamant. When the light began to fade he insisted that we support him no longer, but let him hang at full stretch in his chains. I don't know how he endured it, for his muscles creaked, and he bit his lip until the blood ran over his cheek, while Kutebar wept like a child. He was a burly, grizzled old fellow, stout enough for all his lined face and the grey hairs on his cropped head, but the tears fairly coursed over his leathery cheeks and beard, and he damned the Russians as only an Oriental can. Finally he kissed the hanging man on the forehead, and clasped his chained hand, and came over to sit by me against the wall.

Now that I had a moment to think, I didn't know what to make of it all. My mind was in a whirl. When you have been tranquil for a while, as I had been at Starotorsk, and then dreadful things begin to happen to you, one after another, it all seems like a terrible nightmare; you have to force your mind to steady up and take it all in, and make yourself understand that it is happening. That flight through the snow with East and Valla—was it only four weeks ago? And since then I'd been harried half-way round the world, it seemed, from those freezing snowy steppes, across sea and desert, to this ghastly fort on the edge of nowhere, and here I was—Harry Flashman, rank of Colonel, 17th Lancers, aide-de-camp to Lord Raglan (God, this time last year I'd been playing pool in Piccadilly with little Willy)—here I was, in a cell with two Tajik-Persian bandits who talked a language[39] I hadn't heard in almost fifteen years, and lived in another world that had nothing to do with Raglan or Willy or Piccadilly or Starotorsk or —oh, aye, it had plenty to do with the swine Ignatieff. But they were talking of rescue and escape, as though it were sure to come, and they chained in a stinking dungeon—I had to grip hard to realize it. It might mean—it just might—that when I had least right to expect it, there was a chance of freedom, of throwing off the horrible fear of the death that Ignatieff had promised me. Freedom, and flight, and perhaps, at the end of it, safety?

I couldn't believe it. I'd seen the fort, and I'd seen the Russian

host down on the shore. You'd need an army—and yet, these
fellows were much the same as Afghans, and I knew *their* way of
working. The sudden raid, the surprise attack, the mad hacking
melee (I shuddered at the recollection), and then up and away
before civilized troops have rubbed the sleep from their eyes. There
were a thousand questions I wanted to ask Kutebar—but what
was the use? They had probably just been talking to keep their
spirits up. Nothing would happen; we were stuck, in the grip of
the bear, and on that despairing conclusion I must have fallen
asleep.

And nothing did happen. Dawn came, and three Russians with
it bearing a dish of nauseating porridge; they jeered at us and
then withdrew. Yakub Beg was half-conscious, swinging in his
fetters, and through that interminable day Kutebar and I took
turns to prop him up. I was on the point, once or twice, of rebelling
at the work, which didn't seem worth it for all the slight relief it
gave his tortured joints, but one look at Kutebar's face made me
think better of it. Yakub Beg was too weak to joke now, or say
much at all, and Kutebar and I just crouched or lay in silence,
until evening came. Yakub Beg somehow dragged himself back to
sense then, just long enough to order Kutebar hoarsely to let him
swing, so that we should save our strength. My back was aching
with the strain, and in spite of my depression and fears I went off
to sleep almost at once, with that stark figure spread horribly
overhead in the fading light, and Kutebar weeping softly beside
me.

As so often happens, I dreamed of the last thing I'd seen before
I went to sleep, only now it was I, not Yakub Beg, who was
hanging in the chains, and someone (whom I knew to be my old
enemy Rudi Starnberg) was painting my backside with boot
blacking. My late father-in-law, old Morrison, was telling him
to spread it thin, because it cost a thousand pounds a bottle, and
Rudi said he had gallons of the stuff, and when it had all been applied they would get Narreeman, the Afghan dancing-girl, to
ravish me and throw me out into the snow. Old Morrison said it
was a capital idea, but he must go through my pockets first; his
ugly, pouchy old face was leering down at me, and then slowly it
changed into Narreeman's, painted and mask-like, and the dream
became rather pleasant, for she was crawling all over me, and we

were floating far, far up above the others, and I was roaring so lustfully that she put her long, slim fingers across my lips, cutting off my cries, and I tried to tear my face free as her grip grew tighter and tighter, strangling me, and I couldn't breathe; she was murmuring in my ear and her fingers were changing into a hairy paw—and suddenly I was awake, trembling and sweating, with Kutebar's hand clamped across my mouth, and his voice hissing me to silence.

It was still night, and the cold in the cell was bitter. Yakub Beg was hanging like a corpse in his chains, but I knew he was awake, for in the dimness I could see his head raised, listening. There wasn't a sound except Kutebar's hoarse breathing, and then, from somewhere outside, very faint, came a distant sighing noise, like a sleepy night-bird, dying away into nothing. Kutebar stiffened, and Yakub Beg's chains clinked as he turned and whispered:

"*Bhisti-sawad!** The sky-blue wolves are in the fold!"

Kutebar rose and moved over beneath the window. I heard him draw in his breath, and then, between his teeth, he made that same strange, muffled whistle—it's the kind of soft, low noise you sometimes think you hear at night, but don't regard, because you imagine it is coming from inside your own head. The Khokandians can make it travel up to a mile, and enemies in between don't even notice it. We waited, and sure enough, it came again, and right on its heels the bang of a musket, shattering the night.

There was a cry of alarm, another shot, and then a positive volley culminating in a thunderous roar of explosion, and the dim light from the window suddenly increased as with a lightning flash. And then a small war broke out, shots, and shrieks and Russian voices roaring, and above all the hideous din of yelling voices—the old Ghazi war-cry that had petrified me so often on the Kabul road.

"They have come!" croaked Yakub Beg. "It is Ko Dali's daughter! Quick, Izzat—the door!"

Kutebar was across the cell in a flash, roaring to me. We threw ourselves against the door, listening for the sounds of our guards.

"They have blown in the main gate with *barut*,"† cries Yakub Beg weakly. "Listen—the firing is all on the other side! Oh, my

* Heavenly!
† Gunpowder.

darling! Eyah! Kutebar, is she not a queen among women, a *najud?** Hold fast the door, for when the Ruskis guess why she has come they will—"

Kutebar's shout of alarm cut him short. Above the tumult of shooting and yelling we heard a rush of feet, the bolts were rasping back, and a great weight heaved at the door on the other side. We strained against it, there was a roar in Russian, and then a concerted thrust from without. With our feet scrabbling for purchase on the rough floor we held them; they charged together and the door gave back, but we managed to heave it shut again, and then came the sound of a muffled shot, and a splinter flew from the door between our faces.

"*Bahnanas!*"† bawled Kutebar. "Monkeys without muscles! Can two weak prisoners hold you, then? Must you shoot, you bastard sons of filth?"

Another shot, close beside the other, and I threw myself sideways; I wasn't getting a bullet in my guts if I could help it. Kutebar gave a despairing cry as the door was forced in; he stumbled back into the cell, and there on the threshold was the big sergeant, torch in one hand and revolver in the other, and two men with bayoneted muskets at his heels.

"That one first!" bawls the sergeant, pointing at Yakub Beg. "Still, you!" he added to me, and I crouched back beside the door as he covered me. Kutebar was scrambling up beyond Yakub Beg; the two soldiers ignored him, one seizing Yakub Beg about the middle to steady him while the other raised his musket aloft to plunge the bayonet into the helpless body.

"Death to all Ruskis!" cries Yakub. "Greetings, Timur—"

But before the bayonet could come down Kutebar had launched himself at the soldier's legs; they fell in a thrashing tangle of limbs, Kutebar yelling blue murder, while the other soldier danced round them with his musket, trying to get a chance with his bayonet, and the sergeant bawled to them to keep clear and give him a shot.

Old dungeon-fighters like myself—and I've had a wealth of experience, from the vaults of Jotunberg, where I was sabre to sabre with Starnberg, to that Afghan prison where I let dear old

* A woman of intelligence and good shape.
† Apes.

Hudson take the strain—know that the thing to do on these occasions is find a nice dark corner and crawl into it. But out of sheer self-preservation I daren't—I knew that if I didn't take a hand Kutebar and Yakub would be dead inside a minute, and where would Cock Flashy be then, poor thing? The sergeant was within a yard of me, side on, revolver hand extended towards the wrestlers on the floor; there was two feet of heavy chain between my wrists, so with a silent frantic prayer I swung my hands sideways and over, lashing the doubled chain at his forearm with all my strength. He screamed and staggered, the gun dropping to the floor, and I went plunging after it, scrabbling madly. He fetched up beside me, but his arm must have been broken, for he tried to claw at me with his far hand, and couldn't reach; I grabbed the gun, stuck it in his face, and pulled the trigger—and the bloody thing was a single-action weapon, and wouldn't fire!

He floundered over me, trying to bite—and his breath was poisonous with garlic—while I wrestled with the hammer of the revolver. His sound hand was at my throat; I kicked and heaved to get him off, but his weight was terrific. I smashed at his face with the gun, and he released my throat and grabbed my wrist; he had a hold like a vice, but I'm strong, too, especially in the grip of fear, and with a huge heave I managed to get him half off me—and in that instant the soldier with the bayonet was towering over us, his weapon poised to drive down at my midriff.

There was nothing I could do but scream and try to roll away; it saved my life, for the sergeant must have felt me weaken, and with an animal snarl of triumph flung himself back on top of me —just as the bayonet came down to spit him clean between the shoulder blades. I'll never forget that engorged face, only inches from my own—the eyes starting, the mouth snapping open in agony, and the deafening scream that he let out. The soldier, yelling madly, hauled on his musket to free the bayonet; it came out of the writhing, kicking body just as I finally got the revolver cocked, and before he could make a second thrust I shot him through the body.

As luck had it, he fell on top of the sergeant, so there was Flashy, feverishly cocking the revolver again beneath a pile of his slain. The sergeant was dead, or dying, and being damned messy about it, retching blood all over me. I struggled as well as I could

with my fettered hands, and had succeeded in freeing myself
except for my feet—those damned fetters were tangled among the
bodies—when Yakub shouted:

"Quickly, *angliski! Shoot!*"

The other soldier had broken free from Kutebar, and was in the
act of seizing his fallen musket; I blazed away at him and missed
—it's all too easy, I assure you—and he took the chance to break
for the door. I snapped off another round at him, and hit him
about the hip, I think, for he went hurtling into the wall. Before
he could struggle up Kutebar was on him with the fallen musket,
yelling some outlandish war-cry as he sank the bayonet to the
locking-ring in the fellow's breast.

The cell was a shambles. Three dead men on the floor, all
bleeding busily, the air thick with powder smoke, Kutebar
brandishing his musket and inviting God to admire him, Yakub
Beg exulting weakly and calling us to search the sergeant for his
fetter keys, and myself counting the shots left in the revolver—
two, in fact.

"The door!" Yakub was calling. "Make it fast, Izzat—then
the keys, in God's name! My body is bursting!"

We found a key in the sergeant's pocket, and released Yakub's
ankles, lowering him gently to the cell floor and propping him
against the wall with his arms still chained to the corners above
his head. He couldn't stand—I doubted if he'd have the use of
his limbs inside a week—and when we tried to unlock his wrist-
shackles the key didn't fit. While Izzat searched the dead man's
clothes, fuming, I kept the door covered; the sounds of distant
fighting were still proceeding merrily, and it seemed to me we'd
have more Russian visitors before long. We were in a damned
tight place until we could get Yakub fully released; Kutebar had
changed his tack now, and was trying to batter open a link in the
chain with his musket butt.

"Strike harder, feeble one!" Yakub encouraged him. "Has all
your strength gone in killing one wounded Ruski?"

"Am I a blacksmith?" says Kutebar. "By the seven pools of
Eblis, do I have iron teeth? I save your life—again—and all you
can do is whine. We have been at work, this *feringhi* and I, while
you swung comfortably—God, what a fool's labour is this!"

"Cease!" cries Yakub. "Watch the door!"

There were feet running, and voices; Kutebar took the other side from me, his bayonet poised, and I cocked the revolver. The feet stopped, and then a voice called "Yakub Beg?" and Kutebar flung up his hands with a crow of delight.

"Inshallah! There is good in the Chinese after all! Come in, little dogs, the work is done! Come and look on the bloody harvest of Kutebar!"

The door swung back, and before you could say Jack Robinson there were half a dozen of them in the cell—robed, bearded figures with grinning hawk faces and long knives—I never thought I'd be glad to see a Ghazi, and these were straight from that stable. They fell on Kutebar, embracing and slapping him, while the others either stopped short at sight of me or hurried on to Yakub Beg, slumped against the far wall. And foremost was a lithe black-clad figure, tight-turbaned round head and chin, with a flowing cloak—hardly more than a boy. He stooped over Yakub Beg, cursing softly, and then shouted shrilly to the tribesmen:

"Hack through those chains! Bear him up—gently—ah, God, my love, my love, what have they done to you?"

He was positively weeping, and then suddenly he was clasping the wounded man, smothering his cheeks with kisses, cupping the lolling head between his hands, murmuring endearments, and finally kissing him passionately on the mouth.

Well, the Pathans are like that, you know, and I wasn't surprised to find these near-relations of theirs similarly inclined to perversion; bad luck on the girls, I always think, but all the more skirt for chaps like me. Disgusting sight, though, this youth slobbering over him like that.

Our rescuers were eyeing me uncertainly, until Kutebar explained whose side I was on; then they all turned their attention to Oscar and Bosie. One of the tribesmen had hacked through Yakub's chains, and four of them were bearing him towards the door, while the black-clad boy flitted alongside, cursing them to be careful. Kutebar motioned me to the door, and I followed him up the steps, still clutching my revolver; the last of the tribesmen paused, even at that critical moment, to pass his knife carefully across the throats of the three dead Russians, and then joined us, giggling gleefully.

"The *hallal!*"* says he. "Is it not fitting, for the proper despatch of animals?"

"Blasphemer!" says Kutebar. "Is this a time for jest?"

The boy hissed at them, and they were silent. He had authority, this little spring violet, and when he snapped a command they jumped to it, hurrying along between the buildings, while he brought up the rear, glancing back towards the sound of shooting from the other side of the fort. There wasn't a Russian to be seen where we were, but I wasn't surprised. I could see the game—a sudden attack, with gunpowder and lots of noise, at the main gate, to draw every Russian in that direction, while the lifting party sneaked in through some rear bolt-hole. They were probably inside before the attack began, marking the sentries and waiting for the signal—but they hadn't bargained, apparently, for the sergeant and his men having orders to kill Yakub Beg as soon as a rescue was attempted. We'd been lucky there.

Suddenly we were under the main wall, and there were figures on the cat-walk overhead; Yakub Beg's body, grotesquely limp, was being hauled up, with the boy piping feverishly at them to be easy with him. Not fifty feet away, to our left, muskets were blazing from one of the guard towers, but they were shooting away from us. Strong lean hands helped me as I scrambled clumsily at a rope-ladder; voices in Persian were muttering around us in the dark, robed figures were crouching at the embrasures, and then we were sliding down the ropes on the outside, and I fell the last ten feet, landing on top of the man beneath, who gave a brief commentary on my parentage, future, and personal habits as only a hillman can, and then called softly:

"All down, Silk One, including the clown Kutebar, your beloved the Atalik Ghazi, and this misbegotten pig of a *feringhi* with the large feet."

"Go!" said the boy's voice from the top of the wall, and as they thrust me forward in the dark a long keening wail broke out from overhead; it was echoed somewhere along the wall, and even above the sound of firing I heard it farther off still. I was stumbling along in my chains, clutching at the hand of the man who led me. "Where are we going?" says I. "Where are you taking me?"

"Ask questions in the council, infidel, not in the battle," says

* Ritual throat-cutting.

he. "Can you ride, you *feringhi* who speaks Persian? Here, Kutebar, he is your friend; do you take him, lest he fall on me again."

"Son of dirt and dung," says Kutebar, lumbering out of the dark. "Did he not assist me in slaying Ruskis, who would undoubtedly have cut our throats before your tardy arrival? What would the Silk One have said to you then, eh? A fine rescue, by God! The whores of Samarkand market could have done it better!"

I thought that a trifle hard, myself; it had been as neat a jail clearance, for my money, as heart could desire, and I doubt if ten minutes had passed since I'd woken with Kutebar's hand on my mouth. I'd killed one man, perhaps two, and their blood was still wet on my face—but I was free! Whoever these fine chaps were, they were taking me out of the clutches of that rascal Ignatieff and his beastly *knouts* and *nagaikas*—I was loose again, and living, and if my fetters were galling me and my joints aching with strain and fatigue, if my body was foul and fit to drop, my heart was singing. You've sold 'em again, old son, I thought; good for you—and these accommodating niggers, of course.

About half a mile from the fort there was a gully, with cypress trees, and horses stamping in the dark, and I just sat on the ground, limp and thankful, beside Kutebar, while he reviled our saviours genially. Presently the boy in black came slipping out of the shadows, kneeling beside us.

"I have sent Yakub away," says he. "It is far to the edge of the Red Sands. We wait here, for Sahib Khan and the others—God grant they have not lost too many!"

"To build the house, trees must fall," says Kutebar complacently. I agreed with him entirely, mind you. "And how is His Idleness, the Falcon on the Royal Wrist—God, my back is broken, bearing him up! How many days did I carry his moping carcase, in that filthy cell, with never a word of complaint from my patient lips? Has my labour been in vain?"

"He is well, God be thanked," says the boy, and then the furious little pansy began to snivel like a girl. "His poor limbs are torn and helpless—but he is strong, he will mend! He spoke to me, Kutebar! He told me how you—cared for him, and fought for him just now—you and the *feringhi* here. Oh, old hawk of the hills, how can I bless you enough?"

And the disgusting young lout flung his arms round Kutebar's neck, murmuring gratefully and kissing him, until the old fellow pushed him away—he was normal, at least.

"Shameless thing!" mutters he. "Respect my grey hairs! Is there no seemliness among you Chinese, then? Away, you bare-faced creature—practise your gratitude on this *angliski* if you must, but spare me!"

"Indeed I shall," says the youth, and turning to me, he put his hands on my shoulders. "You have saved my love, stranger; therefore you have my love, forever and all." He was a nauseatingly pretty one this, with his full lips and slanting Chinese eyes, and his pale, chiselled face framed by the black turban. The tears were still wet on his cheeks, and then to my disgust he leaned forward, plainly intending to kiss me, too.

"No thank'ee!" cries I. "No offence, my son, but I ain't one for your sort, if you don't mind . . ."

But his arms were round my neck and his lips on mine before I could stop him—and then I felt two firm young breasts pressing against my chest, and there was no mistaking the womanliness of the soft cheek against mine. A female, bigad—leading a Ghazi storming-party on a neck-or-nothing venture like this! And such a female, by the feel of her. Well, of course, that put a different complexion on the thing entirely, and I suffered her to kiss away to her heart's content, and mine. What else could a gentleman do?

There are some parts of my life that I'd be glad to relive any time—and some that I don't care to remember at all. But there aren't many that I look back on and have to pinch myself to believe that they really happened. The business of the Khokandian Horde of the Red Sands is one of these, and yet it's one of the few episodes in my career that I can verify from the history books if I want to. There are obscure works on Central Asia by anonymous surveyors and military writers,[40] and I can look in them and find the names and places—Yakub Beg, Izzat Kutebar and Katti Torah; Buzurg Khan and the Seven Khojas, the Great and Middle Hordes of the Black Sands and the Golden Road, the Sky-blue Wolves of the Hungry Steppe, Sahib Khan, and the remarkable girl they called the Silk One. You can trace them all, if you are curious, and learn how in those days they fought the Russians inch by inch from the Jaxartes to the Oxus, and if it reads to you like a mixture of Robin Hood and the Arabian Nights—well, I was there for part of it, and even I look back on it as some kind of frightening fairy-tale come true.

And when I've thumbed through the books and maps, and mumbled the names aloud as an old man does, looking out of my window at the cabs clopping past by the Park in twentieth-century London, and the governesses stepping demurely with their little charges (deuced smart, some of these governesses), I'll go and rummage until I've found that old clumsy German revolver that I took from the Russian sergeant under Fort Raim, and for a threadbare scarf of black silk with the star-flowers embroidered on it—and I can hear again Yakub's laughter ringing behind me, and Kutebar's boastful growling, and the thunder of a thousand hooves and the shouting of the turbanned Tajik riders that makes me shiver still. But most of all I smell the wraith of her perfume, and see those slanting black eyes—"Lick up the honey, stranger, and ask no questions." That was the best part.

On the night of the rescue from Fort Raim, of course, I knew next to nothing about them—except that they were obviously of the warlike tribes constantly warring with the Russians who were trying to invade their country and push the Tsar's dominions south to Afghanistan and east to the China border. It was a bloody, brutal business that, and the wild people—the Tajiks, the Kirgiz-Kazaks, the Khokandians, the Uzbeks and the rest—were being forced back up the Syr Daria into the Hungry Steppe and the Red Sands, harrying all the way, raiding the new Russian outposts and cutting up their caravans.

But they weren't just savages by any means. Behind them, far up the Syr Daria and the Amu Daria, were their great cities of Tashkent and Khokand and Samarkand and Bokhara, places that had been civilized when the Russians were running round bare-arsed—these were the spots that Moscow was really after, and which Ignatieff had boasted would be swept up in the victorious march to India. And leaders like Yakub and Kutebar were waging a desperate last-ditch fight to stop them in the no-man's-land east of the Aral Sea along the Syr Daria.

It was to the brink of that no-man's-land that they carried us on the night of our deliverance from Fort Raim—a punishing ride, hour after hour, through the dark and the silvery morning, over miles of desert and gully and parched steppe-land. They had managed to sever my ankle chain, so that I could back a horse, but I rode in an exhausted dream, only half-conscious of the robed figures flanking me, and when we finally halted I remember only arms supporting me, and the smell of camel-hair robes, and sinking on to a blessed softness to sleep forever.

It was a good place, that—an oasis deep in the Red Sands of the Kizil Kum, where the Russians still knew better than to venture. I remember waking there, to the sound of rippling water, and crawling out of the tent in bright sunlight, and blinking at a long valley, crowded with tents, and a little village of beautiful white houses on the valley side, with trees and grass, and women and children chattering, and Tajik riders everywhere, with their horses and camels—lean, ugly, bearded fellows, bandoliered and booted, and not the kind of company I care to keep, normally. But one of them sings out: "Salaam, angliski!" as he clattered by, and one of the women gave me bread and coffee, and all seemed very friendly.

Somewhere—I believe it's in my celebrated work, *Dawns and Departures of a Soldier's Life*—I've written a good deal about that valley, and the customs and manners of the tribesfolk, and what a little Paradise it seemed after what I'd been through. So it was, and some fellows would no doubt have been content to lie back, wallowing in their freedom, thanking Providence, and having a rest before thinking too hard about the future. That's not Flashy's way; given a moment's respite I have to be looking ahead to the next leap, and that very first morning, while the local smith was filing off my fetters in the presence of a grinning, admiring crowd, I was busy thinking, aye, so far so good, but where next? That Russian army at Fort Raim was still a long sight too close for comfort, and I wouldn't rest easy until I'd reached real safety—Berkeley Square, say, or a little ale-house that I know in Leicestershire.

Afghanistan looked the best bet—not that it's a place I'd ever venture into gladly, but there was no other way to India and my own people, and I figured that Yakub Beg would see me safe along that road, as a return for services rendered to him in our cell at Fort Raim. We jail-birds stick together, and he was obviously a man of power and influence—why, he was probably on dining-out terms with half the *badmashes** and cattle-thieves between here and Jallalabad, and if necessary he'd give me an escort; we could travel as horse-copers, or something, for with my Persian and Pushtu I'd have no difficulty passing as an Afghan. I'd done it before. And there would be no lousy Russians along the road just yet, thank God—and as my thoughts went bounding ahead it suddenly struck me, the magnificent realization—I was free, within reach of India, and I had Ignatieff's great secret plan of invasion! Oh, East might have taken it to Raglan, but that was nothing in the gorgeous dream that suddenly opened up before me—the renowned Flashy, last seen vanishing into the Russian army at Balaclava with boundless energy, now emerging in romantic disguise at Peshawar with the dreadful news for the British garrison.

"You might let the Governor-General know," I would tell my goggling audience, "that there's a Russian army of thirty thousand coming down through the Khyber shortly, with half Afghan-

* Ruffians.

istan in tow, and if he wants to save India he'd better get the
army up here fairly smart. Yes, there's no doubt of it—got it from
the Tsar's secret cabinet. They probably know in London by
now—fellow called East got out through the Crimea, I believe
—I'd been wounded, you see, and told him to clear out and get
the news through at any price. So he left me—well, you take
your choice, don't you? Friendship or duty?—anyway, it don't
signify. I'm here, with the news, and it's here we'll have to
stop 'em. How did I get here? Ha-ha, my dear chap, if I told you,
it wouldn't make you any wiser. Half-way across Russia, through
Astrakhan, over the Aral Sea (Caspian, too, as a matter of fact)
and across the Hindu Kush—old country to me, of course.
Rough trip? No-o, not what I'd call rough, really—be glad when
these fetter-marks have healed up, though—Russian jailers, I
don't mind telling you, have a lot to learn from English
chambermaids, what? Yes, I assure you, I am Flashman—yes, the
Flashman, if you like. Now, do be a good fellow and get it on the
telegraph to Calcutta, won't you? Oh, and you might ask them to
forward my apologies to Lord Raglan that I wasn't able to rejoin him at Balaclava, owing to being unavoidably detained.
Now, I'd give anything for a bath, and a pair of silk socks and a
hairbrush, if you don't mind. . . ."

Gad, the Press would be full of it. Hero of Afghanistan, and
now Saviour of India—assuming the damned place was saved.
Still, I'd have done my bit, and East's scuttle through the snow
would look puny by comparison. I'd give him a careful pat on the
back, of course, pointing out that he'd only done his duty, even
if it did mean sacrificing his old chum. "Really, I think that in
spite of everything, I had the easier part," I would say gravely.
"I didn't have that kind of choice to make, you see." Modest, offhand, self-deprecatory—if I played it properly, I'd get a knighthood out of it.

And all I had to do to realize that splendid prospect was have
a chat with Yakub Beg, as soon as he had recovered from his
ordeal, point out that the Russians were our mutual enemies and
I was duty bound to get to India at once, thank him for his hospitality, and be off with his blessing and assistance. Not to waste
time, I broached the thing that afternoon to Izzat Kutebar, when
he invited me to share a dish of *kefir* with him in the neighbouring

tent where he was recovering, noisily, from his captivity and escape.

"Eat, and thank Providence for such delights as this, which you infidels call ambrosia," says he, while one of his women put the dish of honey-coloured curds before me. "The secret of its preparation was specially given by God to Abraham himself. Personally, I prefer it even to a Tashkent melon—and you know the proverb runs that the Caliph of the Faithful would give ten pearl-breasted beauties from his hareem for a single melon of Tashkent. Myself, I would give five, perhaps, or six, if the melon were a big one." He wiped his beard. "And you would go to Afghanistan, then, and to your folk in India? It can be arranged —we owe you a debt, Flashman *bahadur*, Yakub and I and all our people. As you owe one to us, for your own deliverance," he added gently.

I protested my undying gratitude at once, and he nodded gravely.

"Between warriors let a word of thanks be like a heart-beat —a small thing, hardly heard, but it suffices," says he, and then grinned sheepishly. "What do I say? The truth is, we all owe our chief debt to that wild witch, Ko Dali's daughter. She whom they call the Silk One." He shook his head. "God protect me from a wayward child, and a wanton that goes bare-faced. There will be no holding her in after this—or curbing Yakub Beg's infatuation with her, either. And yet, my friend, would you and I be sitting here, eating this fine *kefir*, but for her?"

"Who is she?" I asked, for I'd seen—and felt—just enough of that remarkable female last night to be thoroughly intrigued. She'd have been a phenomenon anywhere, but in a Muslim country, where women are kept firmly in their place, and never dream of intruding in men's work, her apparent authority had astounded me. "Do you know, Izzat, last night until she . . . er, kissed me—I was sure she was a man."

"So Ko Dali must have thought, when the fierce little bitch came yelping into the world," says he. "Who is Ko Dali?—a Chinese war lord, who had the good taste to take a Khokandian wife, and the ill luck to father the Silk One. He governs in Kashgar, a Chinese city of East Turkestan a thousand miles east of here, below the Issik Kul and the Seven Rivers Country. Would

to God he could govern his daughter as well—so should we be
spared much shame, for is it not deplorable to have a woman who
struts like a khan among us, and leads such enterprises as that
which freed you and me last night? Am I, Kutebar, to hold up
my head and say: 'A woman brought me forth of Fort Raim
jail'? Aye, laugh, you old cow," he bellowed at the ancient
serving-woman, who had been listening and cackling. "You
daughter of shame, is this respect? You take her side, all you
wicked sluts, and rejoice to see us men put down. The trouble
with the Silk One," he went on to me, "is that she is always
right. A scandal, but there it is. Who can fathom the ways of
Allah, who lets such things happen?"

"Well," says I, "it happened among the Ruskis, you know,
Kutebar. They had an empress—why, in my own country, we are
ruled by a queen."

"So I have heard," says he, "but you are infidels. Besides, does
your Sultana, Vik Taria, go unveiled? Does she plan raid and
ambush? No, by the black tomb of Timur, I'll wager she does not."

"Not that I've heard, lately," I admitted. "But this Silk One—
where does she come from? What's her name, anyway?"

"Who knows? She is Ko Dali's daughter. And she came, on a
day—it would be two years ago, after the Ruskis had built that
devil's house, Fort Raim, and were sending their soldiers east of
the Aral, in breach of all treaty and promise, to take our country
and enslave our people. We were fighting them, as we are fighting still, Yakub and I and the other chiefs—and then she was
among us, with her shameless bare face and bold talk and a dozen
Chinese devil-fighters attending on her. It was a troubled time,
with the world upside down, and we scratching with our finger-
nails to hold the Ruskis back by foray and ambuscade; in such
disorders, anything is possible, even a woman fighting-chief. And
Yakub saw her, and. . . ." He spread his hands. "She is beautiful,
as the lily at morning—and clever, it is not to be denied.
Doubtless they will marry, some day, if Yakub's wife will let
him—she lives at Julek, on the river. But he is no fool, my
Yakub—perhaps he loves this female hawk, perhaps not, but he is
ambitious, and he seeks such a kingdom for himself as Kashgar.
Who knows, when Ko Dali dies, if Yakub finds the throne of
Khokand beyond his reach, he may look to Ko Dali's daughter to

help him wrest Kashgar province from the Chinese. He has spoken of it, and she sits, devouring him with those black Mongolian eyes of hers. It is said," he went on confidentially, "that she devours other men also, and that it was for her scandalous habits that the governor of Fort Raim, Engmann the Ruski—may wild hogs mate above his grave!—had her head shaved when she was taken last year, after the fall of Ak Mechet. They say—"

"They lie!" screeched the old woman, who had been listening. "In their jealousy they throw dirt on her, the pretty Silk One!"

"Will you raise your head, mother of discord and ruiner of good food?" says Izzat. "They shaved her scalp, I say, which is why she goes with a turban about her always—for she has kept it shaved, and vowed to do so until she has Engmann's own head on a plate at her feet. God, the perversity of women! But what can one do about her? She is worth ten heads in the council, she can ride like a Kazak, and is as brave as . . . as . . . as I am, by God! If Yakub and Buzurg Khan of Khokand—and I, of course— hold these Russian swine back from our country, it will be because she has the gift of seeing their weaknesses, and showing us how they may be confounded. She is touched by God, I believe —which is why our men admit her, and heed her—and turn their heads aside lest they meet her eye. All save Yakub Beg, who has ever championed her, and fears nothing."

"And you say she'll make him a king one day, and be his queen? An extraordinary girl, indeed. Meanwhile she helps you fight the Ruskis."

"She helps not me, by God! She may help Yakub, who fights as chief of the Tajiks and military governor under Buzurg Khan, who rules in Khokand. They fight for their state, for all the Kirgiz-Kazak people, against an invader. But I, Izzat Kutebar, fight for myself and my own band. I am no statesman, I am no governor or princeling. I need no throne but my saddle. I," says this old ruffian, with immense pride, "am a bandit, as my fathers were. For upwards of thirty years—since I first ambushed the Bokhara caravan, in fact—I have robbed the Russians. Let me wear the robe of pride over the breastplate of distinction, for I have taken more loot and cut more throats of theirs since they put their thieving noses east of the Blue Lake* than any—"

* The Aral Sea.

"And a chit of a girl had to lift you from Fort Raim prison," cries the crone, busy among her pots. "Was it an earthquake they had in Samarkand last year—nay, it was Timur turning in his grave for the credit of the men of Syr Daria! Heh-heh!"

". . . and it is as a bandit that I fight the Ruskis," says he, ignoring the interruption. "Shall I not be free to rob, in my own country? Is that not as just a cause as Yakub's, who fights for his people's freedom, or Buzurg's, who fights for his throne and his fine palace and revenue and dancing-women? Or Sahib Khan, who fights to avenge the slaughter of his family at Ak Mechet? Each to his own cause, I say. But you shall see for yourself, when we go to greet Yakub tonight—aye, and you shall see the Silk One, too, and judge what manner of thing she is. God keep me from the marriage-bed of such a demon, and when I find Paradise, may my *houris* not come from China."

So that evening, when I had bathed, trimmed my beard, and had the filthy rags of my captivity replaced by shirt, *pyjamy* trousers, and soft Persian boots, Kutebar took me through the crowded camp, with everyone saluting him as he strutted by, with his beard oiled and his silver-crusted belt and broad gold medal worn over his fine green coat, and the children crowding about him for the sweets which he carried for them. A robber he might be, but I never saw a man better liked—mind you, I liked him myself, and the thought struck me that he and Pencherjevsky and old Scarlett would have got on like a house on fire. I could see them all three hunting in Rutland together, chasing poachers, damning the government, and knocking the necks off bottles at four in the morning.

We climbed up to the white houses of the village, and Izzat led me through a low archway into a little garden where there was a fountain and an open pillared pavilion such as you might find in Aladdin's pantomime. It was a lovely little place, shaded by trees in the warm evening, with birds murmuring in the branches, the first stars beginning to peep in the dark blue sky overhead, and some flute-like instrument playing softly beyond the wall. It's strange, but the reality of the East is always far beyond anything the romantic poets and artists can create in imitation.

Yakub Beg was lying on a pile of cushions beneath the pavilion, bare-headed and clad only in his *pyjamys*, so that his shoulders could be massaged by a stout woman who was working at them with warmed oil. He was tired and hollow-eyed still, but his lean face lit up at the sight of us—I suppose he was a bit of a demon king, with his forked beard and skull-lock, and that rare thing in Central Asia, which they say is a legacy of Alexander's Greek mercenaries—the bright blue eyes of the European. And he had the happiest smile, I think, that ever I saw on a human face. You only had to see it to understand why the Syr Daria tribes carried on their hopeless struggle against the Russians; fools will always follow the Yakub Begs of this world.

He greeted me eagerly, and presented me to Sahib Khan, his lieutenant, of whom I remember nothing except that he was un-usually tall, with moustaches that fell below his chin; I was try-ing not to look too pointedly at the third member of the group, who was lounging on the cushions near Yakub, playing with a tiny Persian kitten on her lap. Now that I saw her in full light, I had a little difficulty in recognizing the excitable, passionate creature I had taken for a boy only the night before; Ko Dali's daughter this evening was a very self-possessed, consciously feminine young woman indeed—of course, girls are like that, squealing one minute, all assured dignity the next. She was dressed in the tight-wrapped white trousers the Tajik women wear, with curled Persian slippers on her dainty feet, and any illusion of boyishness was dispelled by the roundness of the cloth-of-silver blouse beneath her short embroidered jacket. Round her head she wore a pale pink turban, very tight, framing a striking young face as pale as alabaster—you'll think me susceptible, but I found her incredibly fetching, with her slanting almond eyes (the only Chinese thing about her), the slightly-protruding milk-white teeth which showed as she teased and laughed at the kitten, the determined little chin, and the fine straight nose that looked as though it had been chiselled out of marble. Not as perfectly beauti-ful as Montez, perhaps, but with the lithe, graceful gift of move-ment, that hint of action in the dark, unfathomable eyes which —aye, well, well. As Yakub Beg was saying:

"Izzat tells me you are eager to rejoin your own people in India, Flashman *bahadur*. Before we discuss that, I wish to make a small token sign of my gratitude to you for . . . well, for my life, no less. There are perhaps half a dozen people in the world who

have saved Yakub Beg at one time or another—three of them you
see here. . . ."

"More fool us," growls Kutebar. "A thankless task, friends."

". . . but you are the first *feringhi* to render me that service.
So"—he gave that frank impulsive grin, and ducked his shaven
head—"if you are willing, and will do me the great honour to
accept. . . ."

I wondered what was coming, and caught my breath when, at
a signal from Sahib Khan, a servant brought in a tray on which
were four articles—a little bowl containing salt, another in which
an ember of wood burned smokily, a small square of earth with
a shred of rank grass attaching to it, and a plain, wave-bladed
Persian dagger with the snake-and-hare design on its blade. I
knew what this meant, and it took me aback, for it's the ultimate
honour a hillman can do to you: Yakub Beg wanted to make me
his blood brother. And while you could say I had saved his life
—still, it was big medicine, on such short acquaintance.

However, I knew the formula, for I'd been blood brother to
young Ilderim of Mogala years before, so I followed him in tasting
the salt, and passing my hand over the fire and the earth, and
then laying it beside his on the knife while he said, and I repeated:

"By earth, and salt, and fire; by hilt and blade; and in the name
of God in whatever tongue men call Him, I am thy brother in
blood henceforth. May He curse me and consign me to the pit forever, if I fail thee, my friend."

Funny thing—I don't hold with oaths, much, and I'm not by
nature a truthful man, but on the three occasions that I've sworn
blood brotherhood it has seemed a more solemn thing than swearing on the Bible. Arnold was right; I'm damned beyond a doubt.

Yakub Beg had some difficulty, his shoulders were still crippled,
and Sahib Khan had to lift his hand to the tray for him. And then
he had to carry both his hands round my neck as I stooped for
the formal embrace, after which Kutebar and Ko Dali's daughter
and Sahib Khan murmured their applause, and we drank hot
black coffee with lemon essence and opium, sweetened with sherbet.

And then the serious business began. I had to recite, at Yakub
Beg's request, my own recent history, and how I had come into

the hands of the Russians. So I told them, in brief, much of what I've written here, from my capture at Balaclava to my arrival in Fort Raim—leaving out the discreditable bits, of course, but telling them what they wanted to hear most, which was why there was a great Russian army assembling at Fort Raim, for the march to India. They listened intently, the men only occasionally exploding in a "Bismillah!" or "Eyah!", with a hand-clap by way of emphasis, and the woman silent, fondling the kitten and watching me with those thoughtful, almond eyes. And when I had done, Yakub Beg began to laugh—so loud and hearty that he hurt his torn muscles.

"So much for pride, then! Oh, Khokand, what a little thing you are, and how insignificant your people in the sight of the great world! We had thought, in our folly, that this great army was for us, that the White Tsar was sending his best to trample us flat—and we are just to be licked up in the bygoing, like a mosquito brushed from the hunter's eye when he sights his quarry. And the Great Bear marches on India, does he?" He shook his head. "Can your people stop him at the Khyber gate?"

"Perhaps," says I, "if I get word to them in time."

"In three weeks you might be in Peshawar," says he, thoughtfully. "Not that it will profit us here. The word is that the Ruskis will begin their advance up Syr Daria within two weeks, which means we have a month of life left to us. And then—" he made a weary little gesture. "Tashkent and Khokand will go; Perovski will drink his tea in the serai by Samarkand bazaar, and his horses will water in the See-ah stream. The Cossacks will ride over the Black Sands and the Red." He smiled wryly. "You British may save India, but who shall save us? The wise men were right: 'We are lost when Russia drinks the waters of Jaxartes'. They have been tasting them this four years, but now they will sup them dry."

There was silence, the men sitting glum, while the Silk One toyed with her cat, and from time to time gave me a slow, disturbing glance.

"Well," says I, helpfully, "perhaps you can make some sort of ... accommodation with them. Terms, don't you know."

"Terms?" says Yakub. "Have you made terms with a wolf lately, Englishman? Shall I tell you the kind of terms they make?

When this scum Perovski brought his soldiers and big guns to my city of Ak Mechet two years ago, invading our soil for no better reason than that he wished to steal it, what did he tell Mahomed Wali, who ruled in my absence?" His voice was still steady, but his eyes were shining. "He said: 'Russia comes not for a day, not for a year, but forever'. Those were his terms. And when Wali's people fought for the town, even the women and children throwing their *kissiaks** against the guns, and held until there was no food left, and the swords were all broken, and the little powder gone, and the walls blown in, and only the citadel remained, Wali said: 'It is enough. We will surrender'. And Perovski tore up the offer of surrender and said: 'We will take the citadel with our bayonets'. And they did. Two hundred of our folk they mowed down with grape, even the old and young. That is the honour of a Russian soldier; that is the peace of the White Tsar."[41]

"My wife and children died in Ak Mechet, beneath the White Mosque," says Sahib Khan. "They did not even know who the Russians were. My little son clapped his hands before the battle, to see so many pretty uniforms, and the guns all in a row."

They were silent again, and I sat uncomfortably, until Yakub Beg says:

"So you see, there will be no terms. Those of us whom they do not kill, they will enslave: they have said as much. They will sweep us clean, from Persia to Balkash and the Roof of the World. How can we prevent them? I took seven thousand men against Ak Mechet two winters since, and saw them routed; I went again with twice as many, and saw my thousands slain. The Russians lost eighteen killed. Oh, if it were sabre to sabre, horse to horse, man to man, I would not shirk the odds—but against their artillery, their rifles, what can our riders do?"

"Fight," growls Kutebar. "So it is the last fight, let it be one they will remember. A month, you say? In that time we can run the horse-tail banner to Kashgar and back; we can raise every Muslim fighting-man from Turgai to the Killer-of-Hindus,† from Khorassan to the Tarm Desert." His voice rose steadily from a growl to a shout. "When the Chinese slew the Kalmucks in the

---

* Hard dung balls used as missiles.
† Hindu Kush range.

old time, what was the answer given to the faint hearts: 'Turn east, west, north, south, there you shall find the Kirgiz'. Why should we lie down to a handful of strangers? They have arms, they have horses—so have we. If they come in their thousands, these infidels, have we not the Great Horde of the far steppes, the people of the Blue Wolf,[42] to join our *jihad*?* We may not win, but by God, we can make them understand that the ghosts of Timur and Chinghiz Khan still ride these plains; we can mark every yard of the Syr Daria with a Russian corpse; we can make them buy this country at a price that will cause the Tsar to count his change in the Kremlin palace!"

Sahib Khan chimed in again: "So runs the proverb: 'While the gun-barrel lies in its stock, and the blade is unbroken'. It will be all that is left to us, Yakub."

Yakub Beg sighed, and then smiled at me. He was one of your spirited rascals who can never be glum for more than a moment. "It may be. If they overrun us, I shall not live to see it; I'll make young bones somewhere up by Ak Mechet. You understand, Flashman *bahadur*, we may buy you a little time here, in Syr Daria—no more. Your red soldiers may avenge us, but only God can help us."

"And He has a habit of choosing the winning side, which will not be ours," says Kutebar. "Well, I'm overdue for Paradise; may I find it by a short cut and a bloody one."

Ko Dali's daughter spoke for the first time, and I was surprised how high and yet husky her voice was—the kind that makes you think of French satin sofas, with the blinds down and purple wall-paper. She was lying prone now, tickling the kitten's belly and murmuring to it.

"Do you hear them, little tiger, these great strong men? How they enjoy their despair! They reckon the odds, and find them heavy, and since fighting is so much easier than thinking they put the scowl of resignation on the face of stupidity, and swear most horribly." Her voice whined in grotesque mimicry. " 'By the bowels of Rustum, we shall give them a battle to remember—hand me my scimitar, Gamal, it is in the woodshed. Aye, we shall make such-and-such a slaughter, and if we are all blown to the ends of Eblis—may God protect the valorous!—we shall at least be blown

* Holy war.

like men. Eyewallah, brothers, it is God's will; we shall have done our best'. This is how the wise warriors talk, furry little sister—which is why we women weep and children go hungry. But never fear—when the Russians have killed them all, I shall find myself a great, strong Cossack, and you shall have a lusty Russian tom, and we shall live on oranges and honey and cream forever."

Yakub Beg just laughed, and silenced Kutebar's angry growl. "She never said a word that was not worth listening to. Well, Silk One, what must we do to be saved?"

Ko Dali's daughter rolled the kitten over. "Fight them now, before they have moved, while they have their backs to the sea. Take all your horsemen, suddenly, and scatter them on the beach."

"Oh, cage the wind, girl!" cries Kutebar. "They have thirty thousand muskets, one-third of them Cossack cavalry. Where can we raise half that number?"

"Send to Buzurg Khan to help you. At need, ask aid from Bokhara."

"Bokhara is lukewarm," says Yakub Beg. "They are the last to whom we can turn for help."

The girl shrugged. "When the Jew grows poor, he looks to his old accounts. Well, then, you must do it alone."

"How, woman? I have not the gift of human multiplication; they outnumber us."

"But their ammunition has not yet come—this much we know from your spies at Fort Raim. So the odds are none so great— three to one at most. With such valiant sabres as Kutebar here, the thing should be easy."

"Devil take your impudence!" cries Kutebar. "I could not assemble ten thousand swords within a week, and by then their powder and cartridge ships will have arrived."

"Then you should have assembled them before this," was the tart rejoinder.

"Heaven lighten your understanding, you perverse Chinese bitch! How could I, when I was rotting in jail?"

"That was clever," says she, "that was sound preparation, indeed. Hey, puss-puss puss, are they not shrewd, these big strong fellows?"

"If there were a hope of a surprise attack on their camp suc-
ceeding, I should have ordered it," says Yakub Beg. "To stop
them here, before their advance has begun. . . ." He looked at me.
"That would solve your need as well as ours, Englishman. But I
see no way. Their powder ships will arrive in a week, and three
days, perhaps four thereafter, they will be moving up Syr Daria.
If something is to be done, it must be done soon."

"Ask her, then," says Kutebar sarcastically. "Is she not waiting to be asked? To her, it will be easy."

"If it were easy, even you would have thought of it by now,"
says the girl. "Let me think of it instead." She rose, picking up
her cat, stroking it and smiling as she nuzzled it. "Shall we think,
little cruelty? And when we have thought, we shall tell them,
and they will slap their knees and cry: 'Mashallah, but how
simple! It leaps to the eye! A child could have conceived it.' And
they will smile on us, and perhaps throw us a little jumagi,* or a
sweetmeat, for which we shall be humbly thankful. Come, butcher
of little mice."

And without so much as a glance at us, she sauntered off, with
those tight white pants stirring provocatively, and Izzat cursing
under his breath.

"Ko Dali should have whipped the demons out of that baggage
before she grew teeth! But then, what do the Chinese know of
education? If she were mine, by death, would I not discipline
her?"

"You would not dare, father of wind and grey whiskers," says
Yakub genially. "So let her think—and if nothing comes of it,
you may have the laugh of her."

"A bitter laugh it will be, then," says Kutebar. "By Shaitan,
it will be the last laugh we have."

Now their discussion had been all very well, no doubt, but it
was of no great interest to me whether they got themselves cut
up by the Russians now or a month hence. The main thing was
to get Flashy on his way to India, and I made bold to raise the
subject again. But Yakub Beg disappointed me.

"You shall go, surely, but a few days will make no difference.
By then we shall have made a resolve here, and it were best your
chiefs in India knew what it was. So they may be the better

* Pocket-money.

prepared. In the meantime, Flashman *bahadur*, blood brother, take your ease among us."

I couldn't object to that, and for three days I loafed about, wandering through the camp, observing the great coming and going of couriers, and the arrival each day of fresh bands of horsemen. They were coming in from all parts of the Red Sands, and beyond, from as far as the Black Sands below Khiva, and Zarafshan and the Bokhara border—Uzbeks with their flat yellow faces and scalp-locks, lean, swarthy Tajiks and slit-eyed Mongols, terrible-looking folk with their long swords and bandy legs—until there must have been close on five thousand riders in that valley alone. But when you thought of these wild hordes pitted against artillery and disciplined riflemen, you saw how hopeless the business was; it would take more than the Silk One to think them out of this.

An extraordinary young woman that—weeping passionately over Yakub's wounds on the night of the rescue, but in council with the men as composed (and bossy) as a Mayfair mama. A walking temptation, too, to a warm-blooded chap like me, so I kept well clear of her in those three days. She might be just the ticket for a wet week-end, but she was also Yakub Beg's intended—and that apart, I'm bound to confess that there was something about the cut of her shapely little jib that made me just a mite uneasy. I'm wary of strong, clever women, however beddable they may be, and Ko Dali's daughter was strong and too clever for comfort. As I was to find out to my cost—God, when I think what that Chinese-minded mort got me into!

I spent my time, as I say, loafing, and getting more impatient and edgy by the hour. I wanted to get away for India, and every day that passed brought nearer the moment when those Russian brutes (with Ignatieff well to the fore, no doubt) came pouring up the Syr Daria valley from Fort Raim, guns, Cossacks, foot and all, and spread like a tide over the Khokand country. I wanted to be well away before that happened, bearing the glad tidings to India and reaping the credit; Yakub Beg and his hairy fellows could fight the Russians how they liked, for although I'll own I'd conceived an affection for him and his Tajiks and Uzbeks, and wished them no harm, it was all one to me how *they* fared, so long as I was safely out of it. But Yakub still seemed uncertain

how to prepare for the fight that was coming; he'd tried his overlord, Buzurg Khan, for help, and got little out of him, and egged
on by Kutebar, he was coming round to the Silk One's notion of
one mad slash at the enemy before they had got under way from
Fort Raim with their magazines full. It was a doomed enterprise, of course, but he figured he'd do them more damage on the
beach than when they were upcountry on the march; good luck,
thinks I, just give me a horse and an escort first, and I'll bless your
enterprise as I wave farewell.

And it would have fallen out like that, too, but for the infernal
ingenuity of that kitten-tickling besom—Kutebar was right: Ko
Dali should have whaled the wickedness out of her years ago.

It was the fourth day, and I was lounging in the camp's little
market, improving my Persian by learning the ninety-nine names
of God (only the Bactrian camels know the hundredth, which is
why they look so deuced superior) from an Astrabad caravan-
guard-turned-murderer, when Kutebar came in a great bustle to
take me to Yakub Beg at once. I went, thinking no evil, and found
him in the pavilion with Sahib Khan and one or two others,
squatting round their coffee table. Ko Dali's daughter was
lounging apart, listening and saying nothing, feeding her kitten
with sweet jelly. Yakub, whose limbs had mended to the point
where he could move with only a little stiffness, was wound up
like a fiddle-string with excitement; he was smiling gleefully as he
touched my hand in greeting and motioned me to sit.

"News, Flashman *bahadur*! The Ruski powder boats come tomorrow. They have loaded at Tokmak, the *Obrucheff* steamer
and the *Mikhail*, and by evening they will be at anchor off Syr
Daria's mouth, with every grain of powder, every cartridge, every
pack for the artillery in their holds! The next day their cargoes
will be dispersed through the Ruski host, who at the moment have
a bare twenty rounds to each musket." He rubbed his hands
joyfully. "You see what it means, *angliski*? God has put them in
our hands—may his name be ever blessed!"

I didn't see what he was driving at, until Sahib Khan enlightened me.

"If those two powder boats can be destroyed," says he, "there
will be no Ruski army on the Syr Daria this year. They will be a
bear without claws."

"And there will be no advance on India this year, either!" cries Yakub. "What do you say to that, Flashman!"

It was big news, certainly, and their logic was flawless—so far as it went: without their main munitions, the Russians couldn't march. From my detached point of view, there was only one small question to ask.

"Can you do it?"

He looked at me, grinning, and something in that happy bandit face started the alarms rumbling in my lower innards.

"That you shall tell us," says he. "Indeed, God has sent you here. Listen, now. What I have told you is sure information; every slave who labours on that beach at Fort Raim, unloading and piling baggage for those Ruski filth, is a man or a woman of our people— so that not a word is spoken in that camp, not a deed done, not a sentry relieves himself, but we know of it. We know to the last peck of rice, to the last horse-shoe, what supplies already lie on that beach, and we know, too, that when the powder-ships anchor off Fort Raim, they will be ringed about with guard-boats, so that not even a fish can swim through. So we cannot hope to mine or burn them by storm or surprise."

Well, that dished him, it seemed to me, but on he went, happily disposing of another possibility.

"Nor could we hope to drag the lightest of the few poor cannon we have to some place within shot of the ships. What then remains?" He smiled triumphantly and produced from his breast a roll of papers, written in Russian; it looked like a list.

"Did I not say we were well served for spies? This is a manifest of stores and equipment already landed, and lying beneath the awnings and in the sheds. My careful Silk One"—he bowed in her direction—"has had them interpreted, and has found an item of vast interest. It says—now listen, and bless the name of your own people, from whom this gift comes—it says: 'Twenty stands of British rocket artillery; two hundred boxes of cases.' "

He stopped, staring eagerly at me, and I was aware that they were all waiting expectantly.

"Congreves?" says I. "Well, what—"

"What is the range of such rockets?" asked Yakub Beg.

"Why—about two miles." I knew a bit about Congreves from my time at Woolwich. "Not accurate at that distance, of course;

if you want to make good practice, then half a mile, three-quarters, but—"

"The ships will not be above half a mile from the shore," says he, softly. "And these rockets, from what I have heard, are fiercely combustible—like Greek fire! If one of them were to strike the upperworks of the steamer, or the wooden hull of the Mikhail—"

"We would have the finest explosion this side of Shaitan's lowest pit!" exulted Kutebar, thumping the table.

"And then—a Russian army without powder, with cannon that would be so much useless lumber, with soldiers armed for nothing better than a day's hunting!" cries Yakub. "They will be an army bahla dar!"*

For the life of me, I couldn't understand all this excitement.

"Forgive me," says I. "But the Ruskis have these rockets—you don't. And if you're thinking of stealing some of 'em, I'm sorry, Yakub, but you're eating green corn. D'ye know how much a single Congreve rocket-head weighs, without its stick? Thirty-two pounds. And the stick is fifteen feet long—and before you can fire one you have to have the firing-frame, which is solid steel weighing God knows what, with iron half-pipes. Oh, I daresay friend Kutebar here has some pretty thieves in his fighting-tail, but they couldn't hope to lug this kind of gear out from under the Russians' noses—not unseen. Dammit, you'd need a mule-train. And if, by some miracle, you did get hold of a frame and rockets, where would you find a firing-point close enough? For that matter, at two miles —maximum range, trained at fifty-five degrees—why, you could blaze away all night and never score a hit!"

I suddenly stopped talking. I'd been expecting to see their faces fall, but Yakub was grinning broader by the second, Kutebar was nodding grimly, even Sahib Khan was smiling.

"What's the joke, then?" says I. "You can't do it, you see."

"We do not need to do it," says Yakub, looking like a happy crocodile. "Tell me: these things are like great sky-rockets, are they not? How long would it take unskilled men—handless creatures like the ancient Kutebar, for example—to prepare and fire one?"

"To erect the frame?—oh, two minutes, for artillerymen. Ten

* Literally, "wearing hunting gloves in one's belt", i.e. unarmed.

times as long, probably, for your lot. Adjust the aim, light the fuse, and off she goes—but dammit, what's the use of this to you?"

"Yallah!" cries he, clapping his hands delightedly. "I should call you *saped-pa*—white foot, the bringer of good luck and good news, for what you have just told us is the sweetest tidings I have heard this summer." He reached over and slapped my knee. "Have no fear—we do not intend to steal a rocket, although it was my first thought. But, as you have pointed out, it would be impossible; this much we had realised. But my Silk One, whose mind is like the puzzles of her father's people, intricately simple, has found a way. Tell him, Kutebar."

"We cannot beat the Ruskis, even if we launch our whole power, five or six thousand riders, upon their beach camp and Fort Raim," says the old bandit. "They must drive us back with slaughter in the end. But"—he wagged a finger like an eagle's talon under my nose—"we can storm their camp by night, in one place, where these *feringhi* ra-kets are lying—and that is hard by the pier, in a little go-down.* This our people have already told us. It will be a strange thing if, descending out of the night past Fort Raim like a thunderbolt, we cannot hold fifty yards of beach for an hour, facing both ways. And in our midst, we shall set up this ra-ket device, and while our riders hold the enemy at bay, our gunners can launch this fire of Eblis against the Ruski powder ships. They will be in fair range, not half a mile—and in such weather, with timbers as dry as sand, will not one ra-ket striking home be sufficient to burn them to Jehannum?"

"Why—yes, I suppose so—those Congreves burn like hell. But, man," I protested, "you'll never get off that beach alive— any of you! They'll ring your storming party in, and cut it down by inches—there are thirty thousand of them, remember? Even if you do succeed in blowing their ships to kingdom come, you'll lose—I don't know, a thousand, two thousand swords doing it."

"We shall have saved our country, too," says Yakub Beg, quietly. "And your India, Flashman *bahadur*. Like enough many will die on that beach—but better to save Khokand for a year, or perhaps even for a generation, and die like men, than see our country trampled by these beasts before the autumn comes." He paused. "We have counted the odds and the cost, and I ask your

* Warehouse.

advice, as a soldier of experience, not on the matter of holding the beach and fighting off the Ruskis, for that is an affair we know better than you, but only as to these rockets. From what you have told us, I see that it can be done. Silk One"—he turned towards her, smiling and touching his brow—"I salute your woman's wit —again."

I looked at her with my skin crawling. She'd schemed up this desperate, doomed nonsense, in which thousands of men were going to be cut up, and there she sat, dusting her kitten's whiskers. Mind you, I didn't doubt, when I thought of the thing, that they could bring it off, given decent luck. Five thousand sabres, with the likes of Kutebar roaring about in the dark, could create havoc in that Russian camp, and probably secure a beachhead just long enough for them to turn the Russians' own rockets on the powder ships. And I knew any fool could lay and fire a Congreve. But afterwards? I thought of the shambles of that beach in the dark —and those rows of gallows outside Fort Raim.

And yet, there they sat, those madmen, looking as pleased as if they were going to a birthday party, Yakub Beg calling for coffee and sherbet, Kutebar's evil old face wreathed in happy smiles. Well, it was no concern of mine, if they wanted to throw their lives away—and if they did succeed in crippling the Russian invasion before it had even started, so much the better. It would be glad news to bring into Peshawar—by jove, I might even hint that I'd engineered the whole thing: if I didn't, the Press probably would. "British Officer's Extraordinary Adventure. Russian Plot Foiled by His Ingenuity. Tribal Life in the Khokand. Colonel Flashman's Remarkable Narrative." Yes, a few helpings of that would go down well ... Elspeth would be in raptures ... I'd be the lion of the day yet again. . . .

And then Yakub Beg's voice broke in on my day-dreams.

"Who shall say there is such a thing as chance?" he was exulting. "All is as God directs. He sends the Ruski powder ships. He sends the means of their destruction. And"—he reached out to pass me my coffee cup—"best of all, he sends you, blood brother, without whom all would be naught."

You may think that until now I'd been slow on the uptake— that I should have seen the danger signal as soon as this lunatic mentioned Congreve rockets. But I'd been so taken aback by the scheme, and had it so fixed in my mind that I had no part in it, anyway, that the fearful implication behind his last words came like a douche of cold water. I nearly dropped my coffee cup.

"Naught?" I echoed. "What d'you mean?"

"Who among us would have the skill or knowledge to make use of these rockets of yours?" says he. "I said you were sent by God. A British officer, who knows how these things are employed, who can ensure success where our bungling fingers would . . ."

"You mean you expect me to fire these bloody things for you?" I was so appalled that I said it in English, and he looked at me in bewilderment. Stammering, and no doubt going red in the face, I blundered back into Persian.

"Look, Yakub Beg—I'm sorry, but it cannot be. You know I must go to India, to carry the news of this Russian invasion . . . this army . . . I can't risk such news going astray . . . it's my bounden duty, you see . . ."

"But there will be no invasion," says he, contentedly. "We will see to that."

"But if we—you—I mean, if it doesn't work?" I cried. "I can't take the risk! I mean—it's not that I don't wish to help you— I would if I could, of course. But if I were killed, and the Russians marched in spite of your idiotic—I mean, your daring scheme, they would catch my people unprepared!"

"Rest assured," says he, "the news will go to Peshawar. I pledge my honour, just as I pledge my people to fight these Ruskis tooth and nail from here to the Killer-of-Hindus. But we will stop them here—" and he struck the ground beside him. "I know it! And your soldiers in India will be prepared, for a blow that never comes. For we will not fail. The Silk One's plan is sound. Is she not the *najud*?"

And the grinning ape bowed again in her direction, pleased as Punch.

By George, this was desperate. I didn't know what to say. He was bent on dragging me into certain destruction, and I had to weasel out somehow—but at the same time I daren't let them see the truth, which was that the whole mad scheme terrified me out of my wits. That might well be fatal—you've no idea what those folk are like, and if Yakub Beg thought I was letting him down . . . well, one thing I could be sure of: there'd be no excursion train ordered up to take me to the coral strand in a hurry.

"Yakub, my friend," says I. "Think but a moment. I would ask nothing better than to ride with you and Kutebar on this affair. I have my own score to settle with these Ruski pigs, believe me. And if I could add one asper in the scale of success, I would be with you heart and soul. But I am no artilleryman. I know something of these rockets, but nothing to the purpose. Any fool can aim them, and fire them—Kutebar can do it as easily as he breaks wind—" that got them laughing, as I intended it should. "And I have my duty, which is to my country. I, and I alone, must take that news—who else would be believed? Don't you see—you may do this thing without me?"

"Not as surely," says he. "How could we? An artilleryman you may not be, but you are a soldier, with those little skills that mean the difference between success and failure. You know this— and think, blood brother, whether we stand or fall, when those ships flame like the rising sun and sink into destruction, we will have shattered the threat to your folk and mine! We will have lit a fire that will singe the Kremlin wall! By God, what a dawn that will be!"

Just the glitter in those eyes, the joyful madness on that hawk face, sent my spirits into my boots. Normally I'll talk myself hoarse in my skin's interest, and grovel all the way to Caesar's throne, but in that moment I knew it would be no use. You see, even with the saliva pumping into my mouth, I knew that his reasoning was right—ask Raglan or the Duke or Napoleon: they'd have weighed it and said that I should stay. And it's no use trying to defeat an Oriental's logic—let alone one who has the fire in his guts. I tried a little more, as far as I dared, and then let it lie, while the coffee went round again, and Kutebar speculated gloatingly on how many Russians he would kill, and Yakub sat with his hand on my shoulder, praising God and giving thanks for the opportunity to confound the politics of the Tsar. And the cause of it all, that slant-eyed witch in the tight trousers, said nothing at all, but sauntered across to a bird cage hanging on the pavilion trellis, murmuring and pursing her lips to the nightingale to coax it to sing.

I sat pretty quiet myself, feverishly trying to plot a way out of this, and getting nowhere. The others got down to the details of the business, and I had to take part and try to look happy about it. I must say, looking back, they had it well schemed out: they would take five thousand riders, under Yakub and Kutebar and Sahib Khan, each commanding a division, and just go hell for leather past Fort Raim at four in the morning, driving down to the beach and cutting off the pier. Sahib Khan's lot would secure the northern flank beyond the pier, facing the Syr Daria mouth; Yakub would take the south side, fronting the main beach, and their forces would join up at the landward end of the pier, presenting a ring of fire and steel against the Russian counter-attacks. Kutebar's detachment would be inside the ring, in reserve, and shielding the firing party—here they looked at me with reverent eyes, and I managed an offhand grin that any dentist would have recognized first go.

The rockets and stands were in a go-down, Kutebar had said; they would have their spies—the impressed labourers who slept on the beach—on hand to guide us to them. And then, while all hell was breaking loose around us, the intrepid Flashy and his assistants would set the infernal things up and blaze away at the powder ships. And when the great Guy Fawkes explosion occurred—supposing that it did—we would take to the sea; it was half a mile across Syr Daria mouth, and Katti Torah—a horrible little person with yellow teeth and a squint, who was one of the council that night—would be waiting on the other side to cover all who could escape that way. Well, it was at least a glimmer of hope; I'd swum the Mississippi in my time.*

But the more I considered the thing, the more appalling it looked. Indeed, my mind was already running on a different tack entirely: if I could get a horse tonight, and ride for it—anywhere, but south towards Persia for preference, where they wouldn't expect me to go—could I make a clean getaway? Anywhere else, I'd have chanced it, but south was pure desert—for that matter, it was all bloody wilderness, on every side—and if I didn't lose myself and perish horribly, I'd be run down for certain. And blood brother or not, I couldn't see Yakub Beg condoning desertion. Even the beach and the rockets offered a little hope—it couldn't

* See *Flash for Freedom!*

be worse than Balaclava, surely? (God, what a fearful thought that was.) So I looked as steady as I could, while those grinning wolves chuckled over their plan, and when the Silk One broke silence to announce that she personally would go with Kutebar's detachment, and assist with the rockets, I even managed to join in the hum of approval, and say how jolly it would be to have her along. One thing tribulation teaches you, and that is to wear the mask when there's nothing else for it. She gave me a thoughtful glance, and then went back to her nightingale.

As you can guess, I slept fitfully that night. Here I was again, with my essentials trapped in the mangle, and devil a thing to do but grin and bear it—but it was such madness, I kept swearing to myself as I thumped the pillow. Once on a day I'd have wept, or even prayed, but not now; I'd never had any good from either in the past. I could only sweat and hope—I'd come through so much, so often, perhaps my luck would hold again. One thing I was sure of—the first man into the water tomorrow night was going to be H. Flashman, and no bones about it.

I loafed about my tent, worrying, next morning, while the camp hummed around me—you never saw so many happy faces at the prospect of impending dissolution. How many of them would be alive next day? Not that I cared—I'd have seen 'em all dead and damned if only I could come off safe. My guts were beginning to churn in earnest as the hours went by, and finally I was in such a sweat I couldn't stand it any longer. I decided to go up to the pavilion and have a last shot at talking some sense into Yakub Beg—I didn't know what I could say, but if the worst came to the worst I might even chance a flat refusal to have any-thing to do with his mad venture, and see what he would do about it. In this desperate frame of mind I made my way up through the village, which was quiet with everyone being down in the camp below, went through the little archway and past the screen to the garden—and there was Ko Dali's daughter, alone, sitting by the fountain, trailing her fingers in the water, with that damned kitten watching the ripples.

In spite of my fearful preoccupations—which were entirely her fault, in the first place—I felt the old Adam stir at the sight of her. She was wearing a close-fitting white robe with a gold-embroidered border, and her shapely little bare feet peeping out beneath it; round her head was the inevitable turban, also of white. She looked like Sheherazade in the caliph's garden, and didn't she know it, just?

"Yakub is not here," says she, before I'd even had time to state my business. "He has ridden out with the others to talk with Buzurg Khan; perhaps by evening he will have returned." She stroked the kitten. "Will you wait?"

It was an invitation if ever I heard one—and I'm used to them. But it was unexpected, and as I've said, I was something wary of this young woman. So I hesitated, while she watched me, smiling with her lips closed, and I was just on the point of making my apology and withdrawing, when she leaned down to the kitten and said:

"Why do you suppose such a tall fellow is so afraid, little sister? Can you tell? No? He would be wise not to let Yakub Beg know it—for it would be a great shame to the Atalik Ghazi to find fear in his blood brother."

I don't know when I've been taken more aback. I stood astonished as she went on, with her face close to the kitten's:

"We knew it the first night, at Fort Raim—you remember I told you? We felt it even in his mouth. And we both saw it, last night, when Yakub Beg pressed him into our venture—the others did not, for he dissembles well, this *angliski*. But we knew, you and I, little terror of the larder. We saw the fear in his eyes when he tried to persuade them. We see it now." She picked the kitten up and nuzzled it against her cheek. "What are we to make of him, then?"

"Well, I'm damned!" I was beginning, and took a stride forward, red in the face, and stopped.

"Now he is angry, as well as frightened," says she, pretending to whisper in the brute's ear. "Is that not fine? We have stirred him to rage, which is one of the seven forbidden sins he feels against us. Yes, pretty tiger, he feels another one as well. Which one? Come, little foolish, that is easy—no, not envy, why should he envy us? Ah, you have guessed it, you wanton of the night walls, you trifler in *jimai najaiz*.* Is it not scandalous? But be at ease—we are safe from him. For does he not fear?"

Kutebar was undoubtedly right—this one should have had the mischief tanned out of her when she was knee-high. I stood there,

* Illicit love.

wattling, no doubt, and trying to think of a cutting retort—but interrupting a conversation between a woman and a cat ain't as easy as it might seem. One tends to look a fool.

"You think it a pity, scourge of the milk bowls? Well ... there it is. If lechery cannot cast out fear, what then? What does he fear, you ask? Oh, so many things—death, as all men do. That is no matter, so that they do not cross the line from 'will' to 'will not'. But he fears also Yakub Beg, which is wisdom—although Yakub Beg is far away, and we are quite alone here. So ... still he wavers, although desire struggles with fear in him. Which will triumph, do you suppose? Is it not exciting, little trollop of the willow-trees? Are your male cats so timorous? Do they fear even to sit beside you?"

I wasn't standing for that, anyway—besides, I was becoming decidedly interested. I came round the fountain and sat down on the grass. And, damme, the kitten popped its face round her head and miaowed at me.

"There, brave little sister!" She cuddled it, turned to look at me out of those slanting black eyes, and returned to her conversation. "Would you protect your mistress, then? Eyah, it is not necessary —for what will he do? He will gnaw his lip, while his mouth grows dry with fear and desire—he will think. Oh, such thoughts —there is no protection against them. Do you not feel them touching us, embracing us, enfolding us, burning us with their passion? Alas, it is only an illusion—and like to remain one, so great is his fear."

I've seduced—and been seduced—in some odd ways, but never before with a kitten pressed into service as pimp. She was right, of course—I was scared, not only of Yakub Beg, but of her: she knew too much, this one, for any man's comfort, and if I knew anything at all it wasn't just for love of my brawny frame and bonny black whiskers that she was taunting me into attempting her. There was something else—but with that slim white shape tantalizing me within arm's length, and that murmuring voice, and the drift of her perfume, subtle and sweet as a garden flower, I didn't care. I reached out—and hesitated, sweating lustfully. My God, I wanted her, but—

"And now he pants, and trembles, and fears to touch, my furry sweet. Like the little boys at the confectioner's stall, or a beardless

youth biting his nails outside a brothel, and he such a fine, strong
—nothing of a man. He—"

"Damn you!" roars I, "and damn your Yakub Beg! Come here!"

And I grabbed her round the body, one hand on her breast,
the other on her belly, and pulled her roughly to me. She came
without resistance, her head back, and those almond eyes looking
up at me, her lips parted; I was shaking as I brought my mouth
down on them, and pulled the robe from her shoulders, gripping
her sharp-pointed breasts in my hands. She lay quivering against
me for a moment, and then pulled free, pushing the kitten gently
aside with her foot.

"Go find a mouse, little idleness. Will you occupy your mistress
all day with silly chatter?"

And then she turned towards me, pushing me back and down
with her hands on my chest, and sliding astride of me while her
tongue flickered out against my lips and then my eyelids and
cheeks and into my ear. I grappled her, yammering lustfully, as
she shrugged off the robe and began working nimbly at my girdle
—and no sooner had we set to partners and commenced heaving
passionately away, than up comes that damned kitten beside my
head, and Ko Dali's daughter had to pause and lift her face to
blow at it.

"Does no one pay heed to you, then? Fie, selfish little inquisi-
tive! Can your mistress not have a moment to pleasure herself
with an *angliski*—a thing she has never done before?" And they
purred at each other while I was going mad—I've never been
more mortified in my life.

"I shall tell you all about it later," said she, which is an
astonishing thing to hear, when you're at grips.

"Never mind telling the blasted cat!" I roared, straining at her.
"Dammit, if you're going to tell anyone, tell me!"

"Ah," says she, sitting back. "You are like the Chinese—you
wish to talk as well? Then here is a topic of conversation." And
she reached up and suddenly plucked off her turban, and there she
was, shaved like a Buddhist monk, staring mischievously down at
me.

"Good God!" I croaked. "You're bald!"

"Did you not know? It is my vow. Does it make me—" she
stirred her rump deliciously "—less desirable?"

"My God, no!" I cried, and fell to again with a will, but every time I became properly engrossed, she would stop to chide the cat, which kept loafing around miaowing, until I was near crazy, with that naked alabaster beauty squirming athwart my hawse, as the sailors say, and nothing to be done satisfactorily until she had left off talking and come back to work. And once she nearly unmanned me completely by stopping short, glancing up, and crying "Yakub!" and I let out a frantic yelp and near as anything heaved her into the fountain as I strained my head round to look at the archway and see—nothing. But before I could remonstrate, or swipe her head off, she was writhing and plunging away again, moaning with her eyes half-closed, and this time, for a wonder, the thing went on uninterrupted until we were lying gasping and exhausted, in each other's arms—and the kitten was there again, purring censoriously in my ear.

By then I was too blissfully sated to care. A teasing, wicked-minded sprite she might be, but Ko Dali's daughter had nothing to learn about killing a chap with kindness, and one of my fondest recollections is of lying there ruined in the warmth of that little garden, with the leaves rustling overhead, watching her slip into her robe and turban again, sleek and satisfied as the kitten which she picked up and cuddled against her cheek. (If only the English dowagers of my acquaintance could know what I'm remembering when I see them pick up their gross fat tabbies in the drawing-room. "Ah, General Flashman has gone to sleep again, poor dear old thing. How contented he looks. Ssh-hh.")

Presently she got up and went off, returning with a little tray on which there were cups of sherbet, and two big bowls of *kefir* —just the thing after a hot encounter, when you're feeling well and contented, and wondering vaguely whether you ought not to slide out before the man of the house comes back, and deciding the devil with him. It was good *kefir*, too—strangely sweet, with a musky flavour that I couldn't place, and as I spooned it down gratefully she sat watching me, with those mysterious dark eyes, and murmuring to her kitten as it played with her fingers.

"Did cruel mistress neglect her darling?" says she. "Ah, do not scold—do I reproach you when you come home with your ears scratched and your fur bedraggled? Do I pester you with impertinent questions? Mmm? Oh, shameless—it is not proper to ask, in his presence. Besides, some little evil bird might hear, and talk . . . and what then? What of me—and Yakub Beg—and fine dreams of a throne in Kashgar some day? Ah, indeed. And what of our fine *angliski*? It would go hard with all of us, if certain things were known, but hardest of all with him . . ."

"Capital *kefir*, this," says I, cleaning round the bowl. "Any more?"

She gave me another helping, and went on whispering to the cat—taking care that I could hear.

"Why did we permit him to make love, then? Oh, such a question! Because of his fine shape and handsome head, you think, and the promise of a great *baz-baz**—oh, whiskered little harlot, have you no blushes? What—because he was fearful, and we women know that nothing so drives out a man's fear as passion and delight with a beautiful darling? That is an old wisdom, true —is it the poet Firdausi who says 'The making of life in the shadow of death is the blissful oblivion . . .'?"

"Stuff and nonsense, beautiful darling," says I, wolfing away. "The poet Flashman says that a good gallop needs no philosophic excuse. You're a lusty little baggage, young Silk One, and that's all about it. Here, leave that animal a moment, and give us a kiss."

"You enjoy your kefir?" says she.

"The blazes with the *kefir*," says I, putting down my spoon. "Here a minute, and I'll show you."

She nuzzled the kitten, watching me thoughtfully. "And if Yakub should return?"

"Blazes with him, too. Come here, can't you?"

But she slipped quickly out of harm's way, and stood slim and white and graceful, cradling the kitten and smiling at it.

"You were right, curious tiny leopard—you and Firdausi both. He is much braver now—and he is so very strong, with his great powerful arms and thighs, like the black djinn in the story of es-Sinbad of the sea—he is no longer safe with delicate ladies such as we. He might harm us." And with that mocking smile she went quickly round the fountain, before I could stop her. "Tell me, *angliski*," she said, looking back, but not stopping. "You who speak Persian and know so much of our country—have you ever heard of the Old Man of the Mountains?"

* An indelicate synonym for virility.

"No, by jove, I don't think I have," says I. "Come back and tell me about him."

"After tonight—when the work has been done," says she, teasing. "Perhaps then I shall tell you."

"But I want to know now."

"Be content," says she. "You are a different man from the fearful fellow who came here seeking Yakub an hour ago. Remember the Persian saying: 'Lick up the honey, stranger, and ask no questions'."

And then she was gone, leaving me grinning foolishly after her, and cursing her perversity in a good-humoured way. But, do you know, she was right? I couldn't account for it, but for some reason I felt full of buck and appetite and great good humour, and I couldn't even remember feeling doubts or fears or anything much—of course, I knew there was nothing like a good lively female for putting a chap in trim, as her man Firdausi had apparently pointed out. Clever lads, these Persian poets. But I couldn't recall ever feeling so much the better for it—a new man, in fact, as she'd said.

Now, you who know me may find what I've just written, and what I am about to tell you, extremely strange, coming from me at such a time. But as I've said before, there's nothing in these memoirs that isn't gospel true, and you must just take my word for it. My memory's clear, even if my understanding isn't always perfect, and I'm in no doubt of what happened on that day, or on the night that followed.

I went striding back down to the valley, then, singing "A-hunting we will go", if I remember rightly, and was just in time to see Yakub and Kutebar return from their meeting with Buzurg Khan in a fine rage: the overlord had refused to risk any of his people in what he, the shirking recreant, regarded as a lost hope. I couldn't believe such poltroonery, myself, and said so, loudly. But there it was: the business was up to us and our five thousand sabres, and when Yakub jumped on a pile of camel bales in the valley market, and told the mob it was do or die by themselves for the honour of Old Khokand, and explained how we were going to assault the beach that night and blow up the powder-ships, the whole splendid crowd rose to him as a man. There was just a sea of faces, yellow and brown, slit-eyed and hook-nosed, bald-pated and scalp-locked or turbanned and hairy, all yelling and laughing and waving their sabres, with the wilder spirits cracking off their pistols and racing their ponies round the outskirts of the crowd in an ecstasy of excitement, churning up the dust and whooping like Arapahoes.

And when Kutebar, to a storm of applause, took his place beside Yakub, and thundered in his huge voice: "North, south, east, and west—where shall you find the Kirgiz? By the silver hand of Alexander, they are *here!*" the whole place exploded in wild cheering, and they crowded round the two leaders, promising ten Russian dead for every one of ours, and I thought, why not give 'em a bit of civilized comfort, too, so I jumped up myself, roaring "Hear, hear!", and when they stopped to listen I gave it to them, straight and manly.

"That's the spirit, you fellows!" I told them. "I second what these two fine associates of mine have told you, and have only this to add. We're going to blow these bloody Russians from Hell to Huddersfield—and I'm the chap who can do it, let me tell you! So I shall detain you no longer, my good friends—and Tajiks, and niggers, and what-not—but only ask you to be upstanding and give a rousing British cheer for the honour of the dear old School-house—hip, hip, hip, hurrah!"

And didn't they cheer, too? Best speech I ever made, I remember thinking, and Yakub clapped me on the back, grinning all over, and said by the beard of Mohammed, if we had proposed a march on Moscow every man-jack would have been in his saddle that minute, riding west. I believed him, too, and said it was a damned good idea, but he said no, the powder ships were enough for just now, and I must take pains to instruct the band of assistants whom he'd told off to help me with the rockets when we got to the beach.

So I got them together—and Ko Dali's daughter was there, too, lovely girl and so attentive, all in black, now, shirt, *pyjamys*, boots and turban, very business-like. And I lectured them about Congreves—it was remarkable how well I remembered each detail about assembling the firing-frame and half-pipes, and adjusting the range-screws and everything; the excellent fellows took it all in, spitting and exclaiming with excitement, and you could see that even if they weren't the kind to get elected to the Royal Society for their mechanical aptitude, their hearts were in the right place. I tried to get Ko Dali's daughter aside afterwards for some special instruction, but she excused herself, so I went off to the grindstone merchant to get a sabre sharpened, and got Kutebar to find me a few rounds for my German revolver.

"The only thing that irks me," I told him, "is that we are going to be stuck in some stuffy go-down, blazing away with rockets, while Yakub and the others have got the best of the evening. Damn it, Izzat, I want to put this steel across a few Ruski necks —there's a wall-eyed rascal called Ignatieff, now, have I told you about him? Two rounds from this pop-gun into his midriff, and then a foot of sabre through his throat—that's all he needs. By gad, I'm thirsty tonight, I tell you."

"It is a good thirst," says he approvingly. "But think, *angliski*, of the countless hundreds infidel pigs—your pardon, when I say infidels, I mean Ruskis—whom we shall send to the bottom of Aral with these fine ra-kets. Is that not worthy work for a warrior?"

"Oh, I daresay," I grumbled. "But it ain't the same as jamming a sword in their guts and watching 'em wriggle. That's my sort, now. I say, have I ever told you about Balaclava?"

I didn't know when I'd felt so blood-lusty, and it got worse as the evening wore on. By the time we saddled up I was full of hate against a vague figure who was Ignatieff in a Cossack hat with the Tsar's eagle across the front of his shirt; I wanted to settle him, gorily and painfully, and all the way on our ride across the Kizil Kum in the gathering dark I was dreaming fine nightmares in which I despatched him. But from time to time I felt quite jolly, too, and sang a few snatches of "The Leather Bottel" and "John Peel" and other popular favourites, while the riders grinned and nudged each other, and Kutebar muttered that I was surely bewitched. And all the way the Silk One rode knee to knee with me —not so close that I could give her a squeeze, unfortunately, and silent most of the time, although she seemed to be watching me closely. Well, what girl doesn't—especially when she's just had her first taste of Flashy? I recalled it fondly, and promised myself I would continue her education, for she deserved it, the dear child —but not until I'd satisfied my yearning for slaughter of Russians. That was the main thing, and by the time we had trotted silently into the scrubby wood that lies a bare half-mile from Fort Raim, I was fairly dribbling to be at them.

It took a good hour in the cold dark to bring all the riders quietly into the safety of the wood, each man holding his horse's nostrils or blanketing its head, while I fidgeted with impatience. It was the waiting that infuriated me, when we could have been down on the beach killing Russians, and I spoke pretty sharp to Yakub Beg about it when he emerged out of the shadows, very brave in spiked helmet and red cloak, to say that we should move when the moon hid behind the cloud bank.

"Come along, come along, come along," says I. "What are we about, then? The brutes'll be sounding reveille in a moment."

"Patience, blood brother," says he, giving me a puzzled look, and then a grin. "You shall have your rockets at their throats

presently. God keep you. Kutebar, preserve that worthless carcase
if you can, and you, beloved Silk One—" he reached out and
pressed her head to his breast, whispering to her. Bully for some,
thinks I: wonder if you can do it on a trotting horse? Have to try
some time—and then Yakub was calling softly into the dark:

"In the name of God and the Son of God! Kirgiz, Uzbek, Tajik,
Kalmuk, Turka—remember Ak Mechet! The morning rides behind us!" And he made that strange, moaning Khokand whistle,
and with a great rumbling growl and a drumming of hooves the
whole horde went surging forward beneath the trees and out on
to the empty steppe towards Fort Raim.

If I'd been a sentry on those walls I'd have had apoplexy. One
moment an empty steppe, and the next it was thick with mounted
men, pouring down on the fort; we must have covered quarter of
a mile before the first shot cracked, and then we were tearing at
full tilt towards the gap between fort and river, with the shouts of
alarm sounding from the walls, and musketry popping, and then
with one voice the yell of the Ghazi war-cry burst from the riders
(one voice, in fact, was crying "Tally-ho! Ha-ha!"), five thousand
mad creatures thundering down the long slope with the glittering
sea far ahead, and the ships riding silent and huge on the water,
and on to the cluttered beach, with men scattering in panic as we
swept in among the great piles of bales, sabring and shooting,
leaping crazily in the gloom over the boxes and low shelters,
Yakub's contingent streaming out to the left among the sheds and
go-downs, while our party and Sahib Khan's drove for the pier.

God, what a chaos it was! I was galloping like a dervish at
Kutebar's heels, roaring "Hark forrard! Ha-ha, you bloody
foreigners, Flashy's here!", careering through the narrow spaces
between the sheds, with the muskets banging off to our left,
startled sleepers crying out, and everyone yelling like be-damned.
As we burst headlong onto the last stretch of open beach, and
swerved past the landward end of the pier, some stout Russian was
bawling and letting fly with a pistol; I left off singing "Rule,
Britannia" to take a shot at him, but missed, and there ahead
someone was waving a torch and calling, and suddenly there were
dark figures all around us, clutching at our bridles, almost pulling
us from the saddles towards a big go-down on the north side of the
pier.

I was in capital fettle as I strode into the go-down, which was full of half-naked natives with torches, all in a ferment of excitement.

"Now, then, my likely lads," cries I, "where are these Congreves, eh? Look alive, boys, we haven't got all night, you know."

"Here is the devil-fire, oh slayer of thousands," says someone, and there sure enough was a huge pile of boxes, and in the smoky torchlight I could see the broad arrow, and make out the old familiar lettering on them: "Royal Small Arms Factory. Handle with Extreme Care. Explosives. Danger. This side up."

"And how the deuce did this lot get here, d'ye suppose?" says I to Kutebar. "Depend upon it, some greasy bastard in Birmingham with a pocketful of dollars could tell us. Right-o, you fellows, break 'em out, break 'em out!" And as they set to with a will, I gave them another chorus of "John Peel" and strode to the sea end of the go-down, which of course was open, and surveyed the bay.

Ko Dali's daughter was at my elbow, with a chattering nigger pointing out which ship was which. There were two steamers, the farther one being the *Obrucheff*, three vessels with masts, of which the *Mikhail* was farthest north, and a ketch, all riding under the moon on the glassy sea, pretty as paint.

"That's the ticket for soup!" says I. "We'll have 'em sunk in half a jiffy. How are you, my dear—I say, that's a fetching rig you're wearing!" And I gave her a squeeze for luck, but she wriggled free.

"The firing-frame, *angliski*—you must direct them," says she, and I turned reluctantly from surveying the bay and listening to the war that was breaking out along the beach—hell of a din of shooting and yelling, and it stirred my blood to action. I strode in among the toilers, saw the firing-frame broken from its crate, and showed them where to position it, at the very lip of the go-down, just above the small boats and barges which were rocking gently at their moorings on the water six feet below our feet.

Putting up the frame was simple—it's just an iron fence, you see, with supports both sides, and half-pipes running from the ground behind to the top of the fence, to take the rockets. I've never known my fingers so nimble as I tightened the screws and adjusted the half-pipes in their sockets; everyone else seemed slow

by comparison, and I cursed them good-naturedly and finally left
Ko Dali's daughter to see to the final adjustments while I went off
to examine the rockets.

They had them broken out by now, the dull grey three-foot
metal cylinders with their conical heads—I swore when I saw
that, as I'd feared, they were the old pattern, without fins and
needing the fifteen-foot sticks.⁴⁸ Sure enough, there were the
sticks, in long canvas bundles; I called for one, and set to work to
fit it into a rocket head, but the thing was corroded to blazes.

"Now blast these Brummagem robbers!" cries I. "This is too bad
—see how British workmanship gets a bad name! At this rate the
Yankees will be streets ahead of us. Break out another box!"

"Burst it open! off with the lid, sons of idleness!" bawls Kutebar,
fuming with impatience. "If it was Russian gold within, you'd
have them open fast enough!"

"They will open in God's time, father of all wisdom," says one
of the riders. "See, there they lie, like the silver fish of See-ah—
are they not pretty to behold?"

"Prettier yet when they strike those Ruski ships of Eblis!" roars
Kutebar. "Bring me a stick that I may arm one of these things!
What science is here! Wisdom beyond that of the great astronomer
of Samarkand has gone to the making of these fine instruments.
I salute you, Flashman *bahadur*, and the genius of your infidel
professors of Anglistan. See, there it stands, ready to blow the
sons of pigs straight up Shaitan's backside!" And he flourished
the stick, with the rockethead secured—upside down, which made
me laugh immoderately.

I was interrupted by the Silk One, tugging urgently at my
sleeve, imploring me to hurry—I couldn't see what all the fuss
was, for I was enjoying things thoroughly. The battle was going
great guns outside, with a steady crackle of gunfire, but no regular
volleys, which meant, as I pointed out, that the Ruskis hadn't
come to order yet.

"Lots of time, darling," I soothed her. "Now, how's the frame?
Very creditable, very handy, you fellows—well done. Right-ho,
Izzat, let's have some of those rockets along here, sharp now!
Mustn't keep ladies waiting, what?" And I took a slap at her
tight little backside—I don't know when I've felt so full of
beans.

It was a fine, sweaty confusion in the go-down as they dragged the rockets down to the firing-frame, and I egged 'em on, and showed them how to lay a rocket in the half-pipe—no corrosion there, thank God, I noted, and the Silk One fairly twitched with impatience—strange girl, she was, tense as a telegraph wire at moments like this, but all composure when she was at home— while I lectured her on the importance of unrusted surfaces, so that the rockets flew straight.

"In God's name, *angliski!*" cries Kutebar. "Let us be about it! See the *Mikhail* yonder, with enough munitions aboard to blow the Aral dry—for the love of women, let us fire on her!"

"All right, old fellow," says I. "Let's see how we stand." I squinted along the half-pipe, which was at full elevation. "Give us a box beneath the pipe, to lift her. So—steady." I adjusted the ranging-screw, and now the great conical head of the rocket was pointing just over her main-mast. "That's about it. Right, give me a slow-match, someone."

Suddenly there wasn't a sound in the go-down, apart from me whistling to myself as I took a last squint along the rocket and glanced round to see that everything was ready. I can see them still—the eager, bearded hawk-faces, the glistening half-naked bodies running sweat in the stuffy go-down, even Kutebar with his mouth hanging open, quiet for once, Ko Dali's daughter with her face chalk-white and her eyes fixed on me. I gave her a wink.

"Stand clear, boys and girls," I sang out. "Papa's going to light the blue touch-paper and retire immediately!" And in that instant before I touched the match to the firing-vent, I had a sudden vivid memory of November the Fifth, with the frosty ground and the dark, and little boys chattering and giggling and the girls covering their ears, and the red eye of the rocket smouldering in the black, and the white fizz of sparks, and the chorus of admiring "oohs" and "aahs" as the rocket bursts overhead— and it was something like that now, if you like, except that here the fizzing was like a locomotive funnel belching sparks, filling the go-down with acrid, reeking smoke, while the firing-frame shuddered, and then with an almighty whoosh like an express tearing by the Congreve went rushing away into the night, clouds of smoke and fire gushing from its tail, and the boys and

girls cried "By Shaitan!" and "Istagfarullah!", and Papa skipped
nimbly aside roaring "Take that, you sons of bitches!" And we all
stood gaping as it soared into the night like a comet, reached the
top of its arc, dipped towards the Mikhail—and vanished miles
on the wrong side of it.

"Bad luck, dammit! Hard lines! Right, you fellows, let's have
another!" And laughing heartily, I had another box shoved under
the pipe to level it out. We let fly again, but this time the rocket
must have been faulty, for it swerved away crazily into the night,
weaving to and fro before plunging into the water a bare three
hundred yards out with a tremendous hiss and cloud of steam. We
tried three more, and all fell short, so we adjusted the range
slightly, and the sixth rocket flew straight and true, like a great
scarlet lance searching for its target; we watched it pass between
the masts of the Mikhail, and howled with disappointment. But
now at least we had the range, so I ordered all the pipes loaded,
and we touched off the whole battery at once.

It was indescribable, and great fun—like a volcano erupting
under your feet, and a dense choking fog filling the go-down;
the men clinging to steady the firing-frame were almost torn
from their feet, the rush of the launching Congreves was deafening,
and for a moment we were all staggering about, weeping and
coughing in that filthy smoke. It was a full minute before the reek
had cleared sufficiently to see how our shots had fared, and then
Kutebar was flinging himself into the air and rushing to embrace
me.

"Ya'allahah! Wonder of God! Look—look yonder, Flashman!
Look at the blessed sight! Is it not glorious—see, see how they
burn!"

And he was right—the Mikhail was hit! There was a red ball
of fire clinging to her timbers just below the rail amidships, and
even as we watched there was a climbing lick of flame—and over
to the right, by some freakish chance, the ketch had been hit,
too: there was a fire on her deck, and she was slewing round at
anchor. All about me they were dancing and yelling and clapping
hands, like school girls when Popular Penelope has won the
sewing prize.

All except Ko Dali's daughter. While Kutebar was roaring and
I was chanting "For we are jolly good fellows," she was barking

shrill commands at the men on the frame, having them swivel the pipes round for a shot at the *Obrucheff*—trust women to interfere, thinks I, and strode over.

"Now then, my dear, what's this?" says I, pretty short. "I'll decide when we leave off shooting at our targets, if you don't mind. You, there—"

"We have hit one, *angliski*—it is time for the other." She rapped it out, and I was aware that her face was strained, and her eyes seemed to be searching mine anxiously. "There is no time to waste—listen to the firing! In a few moments they will have broken through Yakub's line and be upon us!"

You know, I'd been so taken up with our target practice, I'd almost forgotten about the fighting that was going on outside. But she was right; it was fiercer than ever, and getting closer. And she was probably right about the *Mikhail*, too—with any luck that fire aboard her would do the business.

"You're a clever girl, Silk One, so you are," says I. "Right-ho, bonny boys, heave away!" And I flung my weight on the frame, chanting "Yo-ho", while the gleeful niggers dragged up more rockets—they were loving this as much as I was, grinning and yelling and inviting God and each other to admire the havoc we had wrought.

"Aye, now for the steamer!" shouts Kutebar. "Hasten, Flashman *bahadur*! Fling the fire of God upon them, the spawn of Muscovy! Aye, we shall burn you here, and Eblis will consume your souls thereafter, you thieves, you disturbers, you dunghill sons of whores and shameless women!"

It wasn't quite as easy as that. Perhaps we'd been lucky with the *Mikhail*, but I fired twenty single rockets at the *Obrucheff* and never came near enough to singe her cable—they snaked over her, or flew wide, or hit the water short, until the smoky trails of their passing blended into a fine mist across the bay; the go-down was a scorching inferno of choking smoke in which we shouted and swore hoarsely as we wrestled sticks and canisters into pipes that were so hot we had to douse them with water after every shot. My good humour didn't survive the twentieth miss; I raged and swore and kicked the nearest nigger—I was aware, too, that as we laboured the sounds of battle outside were drawing closer still, and I was in half a mind to leave these infernal rockets that wouldn't fly straight, and pitch into the fighting on the beach. It was like hell, outside and in, and to add to my fury one of the ships in the bay was firing at us now; the pillar of cloud from the go-down must have made a perfect target, and the rocket trails had long since advertised to everyone on that beach exactly what was going on. The smack of musket balls on the roof and walls was continuous—although I didn't know it then, detachments of Russian cavalry had tried three times to drive through the lumbered beach in phalanx to reach the go-down and silence us, and Yakub's riders had halted them each time with desperate courage. The ring round our position was contracting all the time as the Khokandian riders fell back; once a shot from the sea pitched right in front of the go-down, showering us with spray, another howled overhead like a banshee, and a third crashed into the pier alongside us.

"Damn you!" I roared, shaking my fist. "Come ashore, you swine, and I'll show you!" I seemed to be seeing everything through a red mist, with a terrible, consuming rage swelling up inside me; I was swearing incoherently, I know, as we dragged another rocket into the reeking pipe; half-blinded with smoke and sweat and fury I touched it off, and this time it seemed to drop just short of the *Obrucheff*—and then, by God, I saw that the ship was moving; they must have got steam up in her at last, and she was veering round slowly, her stern-wheel churning as she prepared to draw out from the shore.

"Ah, God, she will escape!" It was Ko Dali's daughter, shrill beside me. "Quickly, quickly, *angliski*! Try again, with all the rockets! Kutebar, all of you, load them all together before she has gone too far!"

"Cowardly rascals!" I hollered. "Turn tail, will you? Why don't you stand and fight, you measly hounds? Load 'em up, you idle bastards, there!" And savagely I flung myself among them as they hauled up the five rockets—one of 'em was still half off its stick, I remember, with a little nigger still wrestling to fix it home even as the man with the match was touching the fuse. I crammed the burning remnant of my match against a vent, and even as the trail of sparks shot out the whole go-down seemed to stand on end, I felt myself falling, something hit me a great crack on the head, and my ears were full of cannonading that went on and on until the pain of it seemed to be bursting my brain before blackness came.

I've reckoned since that I must have been unconscious for only a few minutes, but for all I knew when I opened my eyes it might have been hours. What had happened was that a cannon shot had hit the go-down roof just as the rockets went off, and a falling slat had knocked me endways; when I came to the first thing I saw was the firing-frame in ruins, with a beam across it, and I remember thinking, ah well, no more Guy Fawkes night until next year. Beyond it, through the smoke, I could see the *Mikhail*, burning quite nicely now, but not exploding, which I thought strange; the ketch was well alight, too, but the *Obrucheff* was under way, with smoke pouring from her funnel and her wheel thrashing great guns. There was a glow near her stern, too, and I found myself wondering, in a confused way, if one of the last salvo had got home. "Serve you right, you Russian scoundrels," I muttered, and tried to pull myself up, but I couldn't; all the strength had gone from my limbs.

But the strangest thing was, that my head seemed to have floated loose from my shoulders, and I couldn't seem to focus properly on things around me. The great berserk rage that had possessed me only a moment since seemed to have gone, and I felt quite tranquil, and dreamy—it wasn't unpleasant, really, for I felt that nothing much mattered, and there was no pain or anxiety, or even inclination to do anything, but just lie there, resting body and brain together.

And yet I have a pretty clear recollection of what was happening around me, although none of it was important at the time. There were folk crawling about the go-down, among the smoke and wreckage, and Kutebar was thundering away blasphemously, and then Ko Dali's daughter was kneeling beside me, trying to raise my head, which was apparently swollen as big as a house. Outside, the fight was raging, and among the shots and yells I could hear the actual clash of steel—it didn't excite me now, though, or even interest me. And then Yakub Beg was there, his helmet gone, one arm limp with a great bloodied gash near the shoulder, and a naked sabre in his good hand. Strange, thinks I, you ought to be out on the beach, killing Russians; what the deuce are you doing here?

"Away!" he was shouting. "Away—take to the water!" And he dropped his sabre and took Ko Dali's daughter by the shoulder. "Quickly, Silk One—it is done! They have driven us in! Swim for it, beloved—and Kutebar! Get them into the sea, Izzat! There are only moments left!"

Ko Dali's daughter was saying something that I couldn't catch, and Yakub was shaking his head.

"Sahib Khan can hold them with his Immortals—but only for minutes. Get you gone—and take the Englishman. Do as I tell you, girl! Yes, yes, I will come—did I not say Sahib Khan is staying?"

"And you will leave him?" Her voice seemed faint and far away.

"Aye, I will leave him. Khokand can spare him, but it cannot spare me; he knows it, and so do I. And he seeks his wife and little ones. Now, in God's name, get out quickly!"

She didn't hesitate, but rose, and two of the others half-dragged, half-carried me to the mouth of the go-down. I was so dazed I don't think it even crossed my mind that I was in no case to swim; it didn't matter, anyway, for some clever lads were cutting loose the lighter that swung under the edge of the go-down, and men were tumbling into it. I remember a fierce altercation was going on between Yakub Beg and Kutebar, the latter protesting that he wanted to stay and fight it out with Sahib Khan and the others, and Yakub more or less thrusting him down into the lighter with his sound arm, and then jumping in himself. I was aware that one wall of the go-down was burning, and in the glare and the smoke I caught a glimpse of a swirling mass of figures at the doors, and I think I even made out a Cossack, laying about him with a sabre, before someone tumbled down on top of me and knocked me flat on the floor of the lighter.

Somehow they must have poled the thing off, for when I had recovered my breath and pulled myself up to the low gun-wale, we were about twenty yards from the go-down, and drifting away from the pier as the eddy from the river mouth, I suppose, caught the lighter and tugged it out to sea. I had only a momentary sight of the interior of the go-down, looking for all the world like a mine-shaft, with the figures of miners hewing away in it, and then I saw a brilliant light suddenly glowing on its floor, growing in intensity, and then the rush-rush-rush sound of the Congreves as the flames from the burning wall reached them, and I just had sense enough to duck my head below the gunwale before the whole place dissolved in a blinding light—but strangely enough, without any great roar of explosion, just the rushing noise of a huge whirlwind. There were screams and oaths from the lighter all around me, but when I raised my head there was just one huge flame where the go-down had been, and the pier beside it was burning at its landward end, and the glare was so fierce that beyond there was nothing to be seen.

I just lay, with my cheek on the thwart, wondering if the eddy would carry us out of range before they started shooting at us, and thinking how calm and pleasant it was to be drifting along here, after all the hellish work in the go-down. I still wasn't feeling any sense of urgency, or anything beyond a detached, dreamy interest, and I can't say even now whether we were fired on or not, for I suddenly became aware that Ko Dali's daughter was crouched down beside me at the gunwale, staring back, and people were pressed close about us, and I thought, this is a splendid opportunity to squeeze that lovely little rump of hers. There it was, just nicely curved within a foot of me, so I took a handful and kneaded away contentedly, and she never even noticed—or if she did, she didn't mind. But I think she was too preoccupied with the inferno we had left behind us; so were the others, craning and muttering as we drifted over the dark water. It's queer, but in my memory that drifting and bum-fondling seems to have gone on for the deuce of a long time—I suppose I was immensely preoccupied with it, and a capital thing, too. But some other things I remember: the flames of the go-down and pier seen at a distance, and a wounded man groaning near me in the press of bodies; Ko Dali's daughter speaking to Yakub Beg, and Kutebar saying something which involved an oath to do with a camel; and a water-skin being pressed against my lips, and the warm, brackish water making me choke and cough. And Yakub Beg saying that the *Mikhail* was burning to a wreck, but the *Obrucheff* had got away, so our work was only half-done, but better half-done than not done at all, and Kutebar growling that, by God, it was all very well for those who had been loafing about on the beach, building sand-castles, to talk, but if Yakub and his saunterers had been in the go-down, where the real business was . . .

And pat on his words the sun was suddenly in the sky—or so it seemed, for the whole place, the lighter, the sea around, and sky itself, were suddenly as bright as day, and it seemed to me that the lighter was no longer drifting, but racing over the water, and then came the most tremendous thundering crash of sound I've ever heard, reverberating over the sea, making the head sing and shudder with the deafening boom of it, and as I tried to put up my hands to my ears to shut out the pain, I heard Kutebar's frantic yell:

"The *Obrucheff*! She has gone—gone to the pit of damnation! Now whose work is half-done? By God!—it is done, it is done, it is done! A thousand times done! Ya, Yakub—is it not done? Now the praise to Him and to the foreign professors!"

More than two thousand Khokandians were killed in the battle of Fort Raim, which shows you what a clever lad Buzurg Khan was to keep out of it. The rest escaped, some by cutting their way eastward off the beach, some by swimming the Syr Daria mouth, and a favoured few travelling in style, by boat and lighter. How many Russians died, no one knows, but Yakub Beg later estimated about three thousand. So it was a good deal bigger than many battles that are household words, but it happened a long way away, and the Russians doubtless tried to forget it, so I suppose only the Khokandians remember it now.

It achieved their purpose, anyhow, for it destroyed the Russian munition ships, and prevented the army marching that year. Which saved British India for as long as I've lived—and preserved Khokand's freedom for a few years more, before the Tsar's soldiers came and stamped it flat in the 'sixties. I imagine the Khokandians thought the respite was worth while, and the two thousand lives well lost—what the two thousand would say, of course, is another matter, but since they went to fight of their own free will (so far as any soldier ever does), I suppose they would support the majority.

Myself, I haven't changed my opinion since I came back to my senses two days afterwards, back in the valley in Kizil Kum. I remember nothing of our lighter being hauled from the water by Katti Torah's rescue party, or of the journey back through the desert, for by that time I was in the finest hallucinatory delirium since the first Reform Bill, and I came out of it gradually and painfully. The terrible thing was that I remembered the battle very clearly, and my own incredible behaviour—I knew I'd gone bawling about like a Viking in drink, seeking sorrow and raving heroically in murderous rage, but I couldn't for the life of me understand why. It had been utterly against nature, instinct and judgement—and I knew it hadn't been booze, because I hadn't had any, and anyway the liquor hasn't been distilled that can make me oblivious of self-preservation. It appalled me, for what security does a right-thinking coward have, if he loses his sense of panic?

At first I thought my memory of that night's work must be playing me false, but the admiring congratulations I got from Yakub Beg and Kutebar (who called me "Ghazi", of all things) soon put paid to that notion. So I must have been temporarily deranged—but why? The obvious explanation, for some reason, never occurred to me—and yet I knew Ko Dali's daughter was at the bottom of it somehow, so I sought her out first thing when I had emerged weak and shaky from my brief convalescence. I was too upset to beat about the bush, and although she played the cool arch tart at first, and pretended not to understand what I was talking about, I went at it so hard that at last she told me —not to put my mind at rest, you may be sure, but probably because she knew that the only fun to be had from a secret lies in betraying it, especially if it makes someone wriggle.

"You remember I spoke to you about the Old Man of the Mountains, of whom you had never heard?"

"What's he got to do with me rushing about like a lunatic?"

"He lived many years ago, in Persia, beyond the Two Seas and the Salt Desert. He was the master of the mad fighting-men— the *hasheesheen*—who nerved themselves to murder and die by drinking the *hasheesh* drug—what the Indians call *bhang*. It is prepared in many ways, for many purposes—it can be so concocted that it will drive a man to any lengths of hatred and courage—and other passions."

And she said it as calm as a virgin discussing flower arrangement, sitting there gravely cross-legged on a *charpai** in a corner of her garden, with her vile kitten gorging itself on a saucer of milk beside her. I stared at her astounded.

"The *hasheesheen*—you mean the Assassins?" Great God, woman, d'you mean to say you filled me with an infernal drug, that sent me clean barmy?"

"It was in your *kefir*," says she, lightly. "Drink, little tiger, there is more if you need it."

"But . . . but . . ." I was almost gobbling. "What the devil for?"

* Bed platform.

"Because you were afraid. Because I knew, from the moment I first saw you, that fear rules you, and that in the test, it will always master you." The beautiful face was quite impassive, the voice level. "And I could not allow that to happen. If you had proved a coward that night, when all depended on you, we would have been lost—Yakub's enterprise would have failed, and Khokand with it. I would do—anything, rather than see him fail. So I drugged you—has it done any harm, in the end?"

"I never heard of such infernal impudence in my life!" I stormed. By George, I was angry, and resentful, and bursting with it. "Blast you, I might have got myself killed!"

She suddenly laughed, showing those pretty teeth. "You are sometimes an honest man, *angliski!* Is he not, puss? And he does wrong to rage and abuse us—for is he not alive? And if he had turned coward, where would he have been?"

A sound argument, as I've realized since, but it didn't do much to quieten me just then. I detested her in that moment, as only a coward can when he hears the truth to his face, and I didn't have to look far to see how to vent my spite on her.

"If I'm honest, it's more than you are. All this fine talk of not failing your precious Yakub Beg—we know how much that's worth! You pretend to be devoted to him—but it doesn't stop you coupling like a bitch in heat with the first chap that comes along. Hah! That shows how much you care for him!"

She didn't even blush, but smiled down at the kitten, and stroked it. "Perhaps it does, eh, puss? But the *angliski* would not be pleased if we said as much. But then—"

"Stop talking to the blasted cat! Speak plain, can't you?"

"If it pleases you. Listen *angliski*, I do not mock—now, and I do not seek to put shame on you. It is no sin to be fearful, any more than it is a sin to be one-legged or red-haired. All men fear —even Yakub and Kutebar and all of them. To conquer fear, some need love, and some hate, and some greed, and some even—*hasheesh*. I understand your anger—but consider, is it not all for the best? You are here, which is what matters most to you—and no one but I knows what fears are in your heart. And that I knew from the beginning. So—" she smiled, and I remember it still as a winning smile, curse her. "'Lick up the honey, stranger, and ask no questions'."

And that was all I could get from her—but somewhere in it I detected a tiny mite of consolation. I've got my pride in one direction, you know—or had then. So before I left her, I asked the question:

"Why did you goad me into making love to you?"

"Call that a drug, too, if you will—to make certain you ate my *kefir*."

"Just that, eh? Lot of trouble, you Chinese girls go to."

She laughed aloud at that, and gave a little pout. "And I had never met an *angliski* before, you remember. Say I was curious."

"May I ask if your curiosity was satisfied?"

"Ah, you ask too much, *angliski*. That is one tale I tell only to my kitten."

I daresay I've no cause to remember her with much affection, but I do, like the old fool I am. As indeed I do all my girls, now that they're at a safe distance. Perhaps she was right, and I owed it to her that I'd come out with a whole skin—but that was blind luck, and anyway, she had plunged me into the stew in the first place. But it's all by now, and I have only to hold that faded flower scarf that she gave me as a parting gift, and I'm back in the bright garden behind the ranges, looking into those black almond eyes, and feeling the sun's warmth and those soft lips against my cheek, and—aye, but she knew too much, the Silk One. Kutebar was decidedly right.

Still, I had no cause for complaint, once I'd recovered from the shock of realizing that I'd fought a do-or-die action by means of a bellyful of some disgusting Oriental potion. I've often wondered since, if chaps like Chinese Gordon and Bobs and Custer *always* went about feeling the way I did that night—not knowing what fear was? It would account for a lot, you know. But God help anyone who's born that way; I'm sorry for 'em. You can't know real peace of mind, I think, unless you've got a windy streak in you.

But I didn't think too long about it just then. The danger was past, all right, I was safe out of the Russians' reach, and among friendly folk who thought I was the best thing to come their way since Tamburlaine—but I'd no wish to linger. When I took stock of what I'd been through in the past year, from the hell of Balaclava and the snow-sodden nightmare of Russia, with its wolves and knouts and barbarous swine like Ignatieff, to the shocking perils of Fort Raim and the go-down (I shudder to this day at the mention of Guy Fawkes), I had only one notion in my head: India, and a hero's welcome, no doubt, and after that home, and the sounds of London and Leicestershire, and the comfort of clubs and taverns and English bed-clothes and buttered toast, and above all my beautiful blonde Elspeth—who didn't have the wit to converse with kittens, and could be relied on not to lace my kidneys and bacon with opium. By God, though, I wondered if Cardigan had been mooching round in my absence—unless he'd got himself killed, with luck? For that matter, was the war over, or what? Decidedly I must get back to civilization quickly.

Yakub Beg was deuced good about it—as well he might have been, considering the risks I'd run on his behalf—and after a tremendous feast in the Kizil Kum valley, at which we celebrated the Russians' confusion, and the salvation of Khokand—oh, and India, too—we set out for Khiva, where he was moving his folk out of reach of Russian reprisals. From there we went east to Samarkand, where he had promised to arrange for some Afghan pals of his to convoy me over the mountains and through Afghanistan to Peshawar. I wasn't looking forward, much, to that part of the journey, but our trip to Samarkand was like a holiday outing. It was clear air and good horses, with Kutebar and Yakub snarling happily at each other, and Ko Dali's daughter, though I never entirely trusted that leery glint in her eye, was as cheerful and friendly as you could wish. I tried to board her at Khiva, but the caravanserai was too crowded, and on the Samarkand road there wasn't the opportunity, which was a pity. I'd have liked another tussle with her, but Yakub Beg was too much with us.

He was a strange, mad, mystic-cheery fellow, that one. I don't know how much he knew, or what Ko Dali's daughter told him, but for some reason he talked to me a good deal on our journey —about Khokand, and whether the British would help him maintain its independence, and his ambitions to found a state of his own, and always his talk would turn to the Silk One, and Kashgar, far over the deserts and mountains, where even the Russians could never reach. The very last words he said to me were on that score.

We had passed the night in Samarkand, in the little serai near the market, under the huge turquoise walls of the biggest mosque in the world, and in the morning they rode out with me and my new escort a little way on the southern road. It was thronged with folk—bustling crowds of Uzbeks in their black caps, and big-nosed hillmen with their crafty faces, and veiled women, and long lines of camels with their jingling bells shuffling up the yellow dust, and porters staggering under great bales, and children underfoot, and everywhere the babbling of twenty different languages. Yakub and I were riding ahead, talking, and we stopped at a little river running under the road to water our beasts.

"The stream of See-ah," says Yakub, laughing. "Did I say the Ruskis would water their horses in it this autumn? I was wrong —thanks to you—and to my silk girl and Kutebar and the others. They will not come yet, to spoil all this"—and he gestured round at the crowds streaming by—"or come at all, if I can help it. And if they do—well, there is still Kashgar, and a free place in the hills."

" 'Where the wicked cease from troubling,' eh," says I, because it seemed appropriate.

"Is that an English saying?" he asked.

"I think it's a hymn." If I remember rightly, we used to sing it in chapel at Rugby before the miscreants of the day got flogged.

"All holy songs are made of dreams," says he. "And this is a great place for dreams, such as mine. You know where we are, Englishman?" He pointed along the dusty track, which wound in and out of the little sand-hills, and then ran like a yellow ribbon across the plain before it forked towards the great white barrier of the Afghan mountains. "This is the great Pathway of Expectation, as the hill people say, where you may realize your hopes just by hoping them. The Chinese call it the Baghdad Highway, and the Persians and Hindus know it as the Silk Trail, but we call it the Golden Road." And he quoted a verse which, with considerable trouble, I've turned into rhyming English:

> To learn the age-old lesson day by day:
> It is not in the bright arrival planned,
> But in the dreams men dream along the way,
> They find the Golden Road to Samarkand.

"Very pretty," says I. "Make it up yourself?"

He laughed. "No—it's an old song, perhaps Firdausi or Omar. Anyway, it will take me to Kashgar—if I live long enough. But here are the others, and here we say farewell. You were my guest, sent to me from heaven: touch upon my hand in parting."

So we shook, and then the others arrived, and Kutebar was gripping me by the shoulders in his great bear-hug and shouting: "God be with you, Flashman—and my compliments to the scientists and doctors in Anglistan." And Ko Dali's daughter approached demurely to give me the gift of her scarf and kiss me gently on the lips—and just for an instant the minx's tongue was half-way down my throat before she withdrew, looking like St Cecilia. Yakub Beg shook hands again and wheeled his horse.

"Goodbye, blood brother. Think of us in England. Come and visit us in Kashgar some day—or better still, find a Kashgar of your own!"

And then they were thundering away back on the Samarkand road, cloaks flying, and Kutebar turning in the saddle to give me a wave and a roar. And it's odd—but for a moment I felt lonely, and wondered if I should miss them. It was a deeply-felt sentimental mood which lasted for at least a quarter of a second, and has never returned, I'm happy to say. As to Kashgar, and Yakub's invitation—well, if I could get guaranteed passports from the Tsar, and the Empress of China, and every hill-chief between Astrakhan and Lake Baikal, and a private Pullman car the whole way with running buffet, bar, and waitresses in constant attendance—I might think quite hard about it before declining. I've too many vivid memories of Central Asia; at my time of life Scarborough is far enough east for me.

It was strange, though, to go back into Afghanistan again, with my escort—heaven knows where Yakub had got 'em from, but one look at their wolfish faces and well-stuffed cartridge belts reassured me that this was one party that no right-minded badmash would dream of attacking. It took us a week over the Hindu-Killer, and another couple of days through the hills to Kabul—and suddenly there was the old Bala Hissar again, and I sat in disbelief looking across to the overgrown orchards where Elphy Bey's cantonment had been, so many years ago, and the Kabul River, and the hillside where Akbar had spread his carpet and McNaghten had died—I could close my eyes and almost hear the drums of the 44th beating "Yankee Doodle" and old Lady Sale berating some unfortunate bearer for brewing tea before the water was *thoroughly* boiling.

I even took a turn up by the ruined Residency, and found my heart beating faster as I looked at the bullet-pocked walls, and marked the window where Broadfoot had tumbled to his death —and from there I turned and tried to find the spot where the Ghazis had set on me and the Burnes brothers, but I couldn't find it.

It was strange—everything the same and yet different. I stood looking round at the close-packed houses, and wondered in which one Gul Shah had tried to murder me with his infernal snakes— and at that I found myself shivering and hurrying back to the market where my escort were waiting: sometimes ghosts can hover in too close for comfort. I didn't want to linger in Kabul any longer, and to the astonishment of my escort I insisted that we journey on to Peshawar by the north bank of the Kabul River although, as the leader pointed out, there was a fine road by way of Boothak and Jallalabad to the south.

"There are serais, huzoor," says he, "and all comfort for us and our beasts—this way is broken country, where we must lie out by night in the cold. Truly, the south road is better."

"My son," says I, "when you were a *chotah wallah** gurgling your mother's milk, I travelled that south road, and I didn't like it one little bit. So we'll stick to the river, if you don't mind."

"Aye-ee!" says he, grinning with his jagged teeth. "Perchance you owe money to someone in Jallalabad? "

"No," says I, "not money. Lead on, friend of all travellers—to the river."

So that way we went, and cold it was by night, but I didn't have nightmares, waking or sleeping, all the way to the Khyber and the winding road down to Peshawar, where I said goodbye to my escort and rode under the arch where Avitabile used to hang the Gilzais, and so into the presence of a young whipper-snapper of a Company ensign.

"A very good day to you, old boy," says I. "I'm Flashman."

He was a fishy-looking, fresh young lad with a peeling nose, and he goggled at me, going red.

* Little fellow.

"Sergeant!" he squeaks. "What's this beastly-looking nigger doing on the office verandah?" For I was attired à la Kizil Kum still, in cloak and pyjamys and puggaree, with a bigger beard than Dr Grace.

"Not at all," says I, affably, "I'm English—a British officer, in fact. Name of Flashman—Colonel Flashman, 17th Lancers, but slightly detached for the moment. I've just come from—up yonder, at considerable personal expense, and I'd like to see someone in authority. Your commanding officer will do."

"It's a madman!" cries he. "Sergeant, stand by!"

And would you believe it, it took me half an hour before I could convince him not to throw me in the lock-up, and he summoned a peevish-looking captain, who listened, nodding irritably while I explained who and what I was.

"Very good," says he. "You've come from Afghanistan?"

"By way of Afghanistan, yes. But—"

"Very good. This is a customs post, among other things. Have you anything to declare?"

(The end of the fourth packet of the Flashman Papers).

APPENDIX I: Balaclava

So much has been written about this battle, by its survivors, by journalists and historians, and even by propagandists and poets, that it is hardly necessary to say more than that Flashman's account, while it adds certain graphic details that have not been recorded hitherto, agrees substantially with other eyewitness descriptions. Much of what he says of the actual charge of the Light Brigade, for example, may be verified by comparison with the accounts of those who survived the action, such as Paget, Trooper Farquharson, Captain Morgan, Cardigan, and others.

But the great controversy of Balaclava, which will probably never be settled satisfactorily, is why the Light Brigade attacked the battery at all. Experts and amateurs of history alike, who have read Russell, Kinglake, Woodham-Smith, Fortescue and a host of others, and who are familiar with the points of view of Raglan, Lucan, and Cardigan, may decide for themselves whether Flashman casts valuable light on the subject or not. Many believe that Raglan and Airey were principally at fault for issuing an imprecise order, that Nolan's excitement in transmitting it to Lucan led to the final fatal confusion, and that neither Cardigan nor Lucan can be fairly blamed for what followed. These are conclusions with which Flashman himself would obviously not disagree. The whole question hinges dramatically on the moment when Nolan made his wild gesture (down the valley? towards the redoubts? how great was the angle of difference anyway? did he say "*our* guns" or "*your* guns" or what?) and if he was at fault, he paid the highest price for it. So too, perhaps, did Raglan; he died in the Crimea, like the six hundred sabres, and if there was a blunder, it was buried with them.

APPENDIX II: Yakub Beg and Izzat Kutebar

Yakub (Yakoob) Beg, who became the greatest chief in Central
Asia and the leading resistance fighter against Russian imperialism,
was born in Piskent in 1820. He was one of the Persian–Tajik
people, and a descendant of Tamerlaine the Great (Timur)—
Flashman's description of him corresponds closely to the recon-
struction of features recently made from Timur's skull by the
Russian expert, Professor Gerasimov.

In 1845 Yakub became chamberlain to the Khan of Khokand,
and then Pansad Bashi (commander of 500). He was made Kush
Begi (military commander) and Governor of Ak Mechet, an
important fortress on the Syr Daria, in 1847, and in the same year
married a girl from Julek, a river town; she is described as "a
Kipchak lady of the Golden Horde". Yakub was active in raiding
the new Russian outposts on the Aral coast, and after the fall of
Ak Metchet in 1853 he made strenuous efforts to retake it from
the Russians, without success.

After the Russian invasion, Yakub eventually turned his attention to making his own state in Kashgar. In 1865, as commander-
in-chief to the decadent Buzurg Khan, he took Kashgar, then
dispossessed his own overlord, and assumed the throne himself as
Amir and Atalik Ghazi; in this same year he married "the
beautiful daughter of Ko Dali, an officer in the Chinese army", by
whom he had several children.

As ruler of Kashgar and East Turkestan, Yakub Beg was the
most powerful monarch of Central Asia. He remained a bitter
enemy of Russia and a close friend of the British, whose envoys
were received in Kashgar, where a British–Kashgari commercial
treaty was concluded in 1874. It was Russia's fear that he would
eventually unite all the Muslims of Central Asia in a holy war
against the Tsar, but in 1876 Kashgar was attacked by China, and
Yakub was driven out; he was assassinated on May 1, 1877, by
Hakim Khan, a son of Buzurg Khan.

His biographer has described Yakub Beg as "a great man born
centuries too late". Certainly, as a nationalist leader and resistance

fighter he was unique in his time and country, for "alone in Central Asia he remained free", and he fought his campaigns and ruled his independent state without wealth or any large following; his great gifts, according to contemporaries, were a keen intelligence, a winning and handsome appearance, and a refusal to be panicked—he also seems to have had a sense of timing, as witness the neatness with which he betrayed Buzurg Khan.

Anywhere else in the world he would probably be remembered as William Wallace, Hereward, and Crazy Horse are remembered, but not in modern Russia. In Tashkent recently I asked an educated Russian what kind of place Yakub Beg occupied in local history: his name was not even known. (See D. C. Boulger's *Yakoob Beg*, 1878.)

Izzat Kutebar, brigand, rebel, and guerrilla leader, was a Kirgiz, born probably in 1800. He first robbed the Bokhara caravan in 1822, and was at his height as a raider and scourge of the Russians in the 1840s. They eventually persuaded him to suspend his bandit activities, and rewarded him with a gold medal (see page 231), but he cut loose again in the early fifties, was captured in 1854, escaped or was released, raised a revolt, and lived as a rebel in the Ust-Yurt until 1858, when he finally surrendered to Count Ignatieff and made his peace with Russia.

NOTES

1. Possibly because of the war scare, as Flashman suggests, there was a craze for growing moustaches, in addition to beards and whiskers, in the early months of 1854. Another fashion among the young men was for brilliantly-coloured shirts with grotesque designs, skulls, snakes, flowers, and the like. Both fads bore an interesting resemblance to modern "hippy" fashions," not least in the reactions they provoked: Bank of England clerks were expressly forbidden to join "the moustache movement", as it was called.

2. The "eunuchs". The open-range musketry target in use at this time consisted of the usual concentric circles, but with a naked human figure in the centre; the bull was a black disc discreetly placed below the figure's waist-line.

3. Although Britain was not formally at war until March 28, 1854, the preparations for conflict had been going on for many weeks amid growing popular determination for a showdown with Russia. The Scots (3rd) Guards had embarked a month earlier, and Palmerston, the Home Secretary, and Sir James Graham, First Lord of the Admiralty, made their jingoistic Reform Club speeches on March 7. These were brilliantly parodied by *Punch* ("Shomeshay we're norrawar. Norrawar! Hash-ha! No! Norrawar! Noshexactly awar. But...") But while the war fever was strong in Britain it was not as universal as Flashman suggests; there was an active peace movement, and anti-war sentiments could be passionate. For an extreme but interesting view, see J. McQueen's *The War: who's to blame?* (1854).

4. The play was almost certainly Balzac's "The Married Unmarried", which caused a minor controversy.

5. Shell-out, skittle pool, go-back, etc. The rules of these early variations on pool (and forerunners of snooker) are to be found in "Captain Crawley's" standard Victorian work, *Billiards*, which is a mine of practical information and billiards lore, and contains much information on pool-room sharks and swindles. Joe Bennet was a champion player of the time. A jenny is a difficult in-off shot to the middle pocket, usually with the object ball close to the side-cushion; a pair of breeches is a simultaneous in-off and pot red in the top pockets.

6. Sir William Molesworth's Commons committee met in March, 1854, to consider small arms production. Lord Paget was among the members, and Lt-Col. Sam Colt, the American inventor of the Colt revolver, was among those who gave evidence.

7. Quite apart from the popular criticism he had been receiving for allegedly meddling in State affairs, Prince Albert's zeal for designing military clothing attracted considerable ridicule in the spring of 1854. In fact, judging from contemporary sketches, the so-called "Albert Bonnet" for the Guards was a sensible, if ugly, multi-purpose forage cap. But there was growing controversy at this time about British uniforms—the traditional tight stocks and collars being a principal target—and any suggestions from H.R.H. were, as usual, unwelcome.

8. The main bombardment of Odessa by British ships took place on April 22, but without doing great damage.

9. "Villikins and his Dinah" was the hit song of 1854.
10. From this, and one later reference, it seems obvious that Flashman was particularly impressed by a *Punch* cartoon, published shortly after Balaclava, showing a stout British father brandishing a poker with patriotic zeal in the morning-room as he reads news of the Charge of the Light Brigade.
11. The Cabinet did meet at Pembroke Lodge, Richmond, on the evening of June 28, 1854, and agreed on important orders to be sent to Lord Raglan for the invasion of the Crimea. "Agreed" may be too strong a word, since most of the Cabinet were asleep during the meeting, and were not fully aware of what orders were being sent; they woke up once, when someone knocked over a chair, and then dozed off again. The authority for this is no less than A. W. Kinglake, the great Crimea historian, who devotes a separate appendix to the incident in his massive history of the war, *The Invasion of the Crimea*. Kinglake was obviously uneasy about disclosing that the Cabinet had taken the vital decision of the war while in a state of torpor, and speculated about the possibility "of a narcotic substance having been taken by some mischance" in their food. He was too tactful or charitable to mention the obvious conclusion, which is that they had had too much to drink.
12. Flashman's account of this important meeting between Raglan and Sir George Brown is largely corroborated by Brown's own version in Kinglake. Both Newcastle's despatch and his personal note to Raglan were definite on the need to besiege Sevastopol, while leaving the final responsibility with Raglan and his French colleagues.
13. Mrs Duberly, wife of an officer of the 8th Hussars, and an old friend of Flashman's (see *Flash for Freedom!*), left a vivid journal of her experiences in the Crimea, including the incident described here, when she boarded a transport "wrapped up in an old hat and shawl . . . an extraordinary figure" to avoid detection by Lord Lucan. (See E. E. P. Tisdall's *Mrs Duberly's Campaigns*.)
14. "The policeman at Herne Bay". This mythical policeman was a humorous by-word of the time.
15. It is interesting to note that William Howard Russell, in his original despatch to *The Times*, made the mistake of reporting that the Highlanders were involved in the attack on the Redoubt, but corrected this in later despatches. His histories of the Crimea are the work of a brilliant newspaperman, and even those who question his criticism of Raglan and other British leaders (see Colonel Adye's *The Crimean War*) acknowledge the quality of his reporting. Anyone interested in verifying Flashman's statements cannot do better than refer to Russell, or to Kinglake, who was also an eye-witness. Incidentally, Flashman's account of the Alma action is extremely accurate, especially where Lord Raglan's movements are concerned, but his memory has surely played him false in a slightly earlier passage when he suggests that the Russian gunners fired on the army at the start of its march down the Crimea coast: this took place some hours later.
16. For an account of this incident, see Russell's *The War from the landing at Gallipoli to the death of Lord Raglan* (1855).
17. Generally Flashman disagrees with other eye-witnesses no more than they disagree among themselves, and these discrepancies are minor ones. For example, some authorities suggest that the Highlanders fired three volleys against the Russian cavalry, not two, and at fairly long range (E. H. Nolan actually says that there was properly speaking "no cavalry charge upon the Highlanders", but this is not borne out by others). Again, as to casualties in the Heavy Brigade charge, Flashman saw comparatively few, but Trooper Farquharson of the 4th Light

Dragoons, who rode over the ground immediately afterwards, "saw dozens . . . with the ugliest gashes about their heads and faces." (See R. S. Farquharson, *Reminiscences of Crimean Campaigning*).

18. The original pencilled order, scribbled by Airey, is still preserved. It reads: "Lord Raglan wishes the Cavalry to advance rapidly to the front, follow the Enemy & try to prevent the Enemy carrying away the guns. Troop Horse Attily may accompany. French Cavalry is on yr left. Immediate." As to what verbal instructions may have been added, there is no certainty, but one of the rumours which later arose (see H. Moyse-Bartlett's *Louis Edward Nolan*) was that Nolan had been told to tell Lucan to act on the *defensive*, but had passed on the vital word as *offensive*.

19. It is one of the true curiosities of the charge of the Light Brigade that Lord George Paget rode into action smoking a cheroot—obviously the one which Flashman gave him—and did not actually draw his sabre until the moment of entering the battery, when his orderly, Parkes, advised him to do so. Paget's coolness, which as much as anything saved the remnants of the Light Brigade, was notorious; Trooper Farquharson, who rode with him in the charge, recalled how earlier in the battle Paget was hit by a shell splinter, and reacted only by telling his orderly to collect it as a souvenir.

20. The recklessness of the British cavalry charge so amazed the Russians that Liprandi's immediate conclusion was that the Light Brigade must have been drunk. (See Cecil Woodham-Smith's *The Reason Why*, and Kinglake.)

21. Whatever may be said of his opinions, Flashman's information about the plight of the Russian serfs in the 1850s is entirely accurate, and is borne out by several other contemporary authorities. The best of these are perhaps Baron von Haxthausen, whose *The Russian Empire* appeared in 1856, and Shirley Brooks's *The Russians of the South* (1854). They also corroborate his descriptions of Russian life in general, as does *The Englishwoman in Russia*, by "a Lady ten years resident in that country", published in 1855. *Savage and Civilised Russia*, by "W.R." (1877), is an informative work; two largely political tracts by S. Stepniak, *Russia under the Tsars* (1885) and *The Russian Peasantry* (1888), contain useful material and interesting bias; and the *Memoirs* of the celebrated Russian radical, Alexander Herzen (1812–70), give an illuminating insight into the serf mentality. Like Flashman, he observed how his family's land serfs "somehow succeed in not believing in their complete slavery", and contrasted this with the plight of the house serfs who, although they were paid wages, had their existence destroyed and poisoned by "the terrible consciousness of serfdom".

22. Captain Count Nicholas Pavlovitch Ignatieff was later to become one of Russia's most brilliant agents in the Far East. He served in China, undertook daring missions into Central Asia, and was also for a time military attaché in London. There is evidence that early in the Crimean War he was serving on the Baltic, and this must have been shortly before his encounter with Flashman. He was twenty-two at this time.

23. For confirmation, and other details of Harry East's military career, see *Tom Brown at Oxford*, by Thomas Hughes (1861).

24. The commander of Prince Vigenstein's Hussars in 1837 was, in fact, Colonel Pencherjevsky.

25. If anything, Flashman's description of the punishments meted out to Russian serfs by their owners appears to be on the mild side. The works cited earlier in these notes contain examples of fearful cruelty and the carelessness with which extraordinary penalties were some-

times imposed—Alexander Herzen gives instances of atrocities, and also recalls the psychological misery caused when his father, a nobleman, ordered a village patriarch's beard to be shaved off. Turgenev the novelist, another nobleman who saw serfdom at first hand, described how his mother banished two young serfs to Siberia because they failed to bow to her in passing—and how they came to bid her farewell before leaving for exile. (See A. Yarmolinsky's *Turgenev the Man*.)

26. It was a folk-saying—and may still be—that one could tell a true Russian by that fact that he would go with his neck open and unprotected, even in the coldest weather.

27. It is interesting that Pencherjevsky had heard of Marx at this time, for although the great revolutionary had already gained an international notoriety, his influence was not to be felt in Russia for many years. Non-Communist agitators were, however, highly active in the country, and no doubt to the Count they all looked alike.

28. Flashman seems to suggest that this incident took place in February, 1855. If it did, then Tsar Nicholas I had only weeks, and possibly days, to live: he died on March 2 in St Petersburg, after influenza which had lasted about a fortnight. There is no evidence that he visited the south in the closing weeks of his life; on the other hand Flashman's account seems highly circumstantial. Possibly he has confused the dates, and Nicholas came to Starotorsk earlier than February. However, anyone scenting a mystery here may note that while the Tsar died on March 2, he was last seen *in public* on February 22 at an infantry review. (See E. H. Nolan's *History of the War against Russia*.)

29. The Khruleff and Duhamel plans were only two in a long list of proposed Russian invasions of British India. As far back as 1801 Tsar Paul, hoping to replace British rule by his own, agreed to a joint Franco-Russian invasion through Afghanistan (Napoleon was at that time in Egypt, and the French Government were to pave the invaders' way by sending "rare objects" to be "distributed with tact" among native chiefs on the line of march.) The Russian part of the expedition actually got under way, but with the death of the Tsar and the British victory at Copenhagen the scheme was abandoned.

General Duhamel's plan for an invasion through Persia was first put to the Tsar in 1854, and was followed in early 1855 by General Khruleff's proposed Afghan-Khyber expedition. The details of the two plans, as given by Flashman, correspond almost exactly with the versions subsequently published as a result of British intelligence work (see *Russia's March to India*, published anonymously by an Indian Army officer in 1894). Indeed, at various points in Flashman's account Ignatieff repeats passages from Duhamel and Khruleff almost verbatim.

30. The "soul tax" was simply a tax on each male, of 86 silver kopecks annually (see J. Blum's *Lord and Peasant in Russia*). If a serf died, his family had to continue to pay the tax until he was officially declared dead at the next census. Blocking the family stove was a common inducement to pay.

31. It is probably mere coincidence, but one of V. I. Lenin's immediate ancestors bore the surname Blank.

32. ". . . with his belt at the last hole". Obviously a corpulent Cossack, or one near retiring age. It was a rule that the Cossacks wore belts of a standard length, and were not permitted to grow stouter than the belt allowed.

33. Leaking Russian stoves could be highly poisonous. At least three British officers were killed by fumes ("smothered in charcoal") at Balaclava in the first week of January 1855. (See General Gordon's letters from the Crimea, Jan. 3–8, 1855.)

34. The serf rising at Starotorsk may have astonished Flashman, but such rebellions were exceedingly common (as he himself remarks elsewhere in his narrative). More than 700 such revolts took place in Russia during the thirty years of Nicholas I's reign.

35. Fort Raim was built on the Syr Daria (the Jaxartes) in 1847, the year after Russia's first occupation on the Aral coast, and was immediately raided by Yakub Beg. The Russian policy of expansion followed the fort's establishment, and their armed expeditions eastward began in 1852 and 1853.

36. Yakub Beg (1820–77), fighting leader of the Tajiks, chamberlain to the Khan of Khokand, warlord of the Syr Daria, etc. (See Appendix II.)

37. Izzat Kutebar, bandit, guerrilla fighter, so-called "Rob Roy of the Steppe". (See Appendix II.)

38. "Khan Ali" was Captain Arthur Conolly, a British agent executed at Bokhara in 1842, along with another Briton, Colonel Charles Stoddart. They had been kept in terrible conditions in the Shah's dungeons, but Conolly was told his life would be spared if he became a Muslim, as Stoddart had done. He refused—his words quoted by an eye-witness were: "Do your work."

39. The language would not be pure Persian, as Flashman suggests, but the Tajik dialect of that language—the Tajiks, being of Persian origin, considered themselves a cut above other Central Asians, and clung to their traditional language and customs.

40. Presumably such works as *England and Russia in Central Asia* (1879), *Central Asian Portraits* (1880), by D. C. Boulger, and *Caravan Journeys and Wanderings*, by J. P. Ferrier. These, and companion volumes, give in addition to biographical details an account of the occupation of the Eastern lands by Russia, which had its origins in the agreement of 1760, when the Kirgiz-Kazak peoples, under their khan, Sultan Abdul Faiz, became nominal subjects of the Tsar, receiving his protection in return for their promise to safeguard the Russian caravans. Neither side kept its bargain.

41. The Russian expansion into Central Asia in the middle of the last century, which swallowed up all the independent countries and khanates east of the Caspian as far as China and south to Afghanistan, was conducted with considerable brutality. The massacre at Ak Mechet (the White Mosque), by General Perovski, on August 8, 1853, took place as Yakub Beg describes it, but it was surpassed by such atrocities as Denghil Tepe, in the Kara Kum, in 1879, when the Tekke women and children, attempting to escape from the position which their menfolk were holding, were deliberately shot down by Lomakin's troops. In this, as in other places, the Russian commanders made it clear that they were not interested in receiving surrenders.

It is customary nowadays for Russians to refer to this expansion as "Tsarist imperialism"; however, it will be noted that while the much-abused Western colonial powers have now largely divested themselves of their empires, the modern Russian Communist state retains an iron grip on the extensive colonies in Central Asia which the old Russian empire acquired.

42. The Mongols were said to be descended from a sky-blue wolf. Flashman's Khokandian friends seem to have used the term rather loosely, possibly because many of them were part Mongol by descent. Incidentally, much of Kutebar's speech at this point is almost word for word with a rallying-call heard in the Syr Daria country at the time of the Russian advance.

43. The military rockets devised by Sir William Congreve were used in the War of 1812, and those described by Flashman were obviously similar to this early pattern, which continued in use for many years.

The Congreve was a gigantic sky-rocket, consisting of an iron cylinder four inches in diameter and over a yard long, packed with powder and attached to a fifteen-foot stick. It was fired from a slanting trough or tube, and travelled with a tremendous noise and a great trail of smoke and sparks, exploding on impact. Although they could fly two miles, the rockets were extremely erratic, and throughout the first half of the nineteenth century frequent modifications were made, including William Hale's spinning rocket, and the grooved and finned rocket, which could be fired without a stick.

44. The secret society of Assassins, founded in Persia in the eleventh century by Hassan el Sabbah, "the Old Man of the Mountains", were notorious for their policy of secret murder and their addiction to the hashish drug from which they took their name. At their height they operated from hill strongholds, mostly in Persia and Syria, and were active against the Crusaders before being dispersed by the Mongol invasion of Hulagu Khan in the thirteenth century. Traces of the sect exist today in the Middle East.

George MacDonald Fraser

Flashman
in the Great Game

From The Flashman Papers 1856-1858
Edited and Arranged by
George MacDonald Fraser

For the Mad White Woman
of Papar River

Explanatory note

One of the most encouraging things about editing the first four volumes of the Flashman Papers has been the generous response from readers and students of history in many parts of the world. Since the discovery of Flashman's remarkable manuscript in a Leicestershire saleroom in 1965, when it was realised that it was the hitherto-unsuspected autobiographical memoir of the notorious bully of *Tom Brown's Schooldays*, letters have reached the editor from such diverse places as Ascension Island, a G.I. rest camp in Vietnam, university faculties and campuses in Britain and America, a modern caravanserai on the Khyber Pass road, a police-station cell in southern Australia, and many others.

What has been especially gratifying has been not only the interest in Flashman himself, but the close historical knowledge which correspondents have shown of the periods and incidents with which his memoirs have dealt so far—the first Afghan War, the solution of the Schleswig-Holstein Question (involving as it did Count Bismarck and Lola Montez), the Afro-American slave trade, and the Crimean War. Many have contributed interesting observations, and one or two have detected curious discrepancies in Flashman's recollections which, regrettably, escaped his editor. A lady in Athens and a gentleman in Flint, Michigan, have pointed out that Flashman apparently saw the Duchess of Wellington at a London theatre some years after her death, and a letter on Foreign Office notepaper has remarked on his careless reference to a "British Ambassador" in Washington in 1848, when in fact Her Majesty's representative in the American capital held a less exalted diplomatic title. Such lapses are understandable, if not excusable, in a hard-living octogenarian.

Equally interesting have been such communications as those from a gentleman in New Orleans who claims to be Flashman's illegitimate great-grandson (as the result of a liaison in a military hospital at Richmond, Va., during the U.S. Civil War), and from a British serving officer who asserts that his grandfather lent fifty dollars and a horse to Flashman during the same campaign; neither, apparently, was returned.

It is possible that these and other matters of interest will be resolved when the later papers are edited. The present volume deals with Flashman's adventures in the Indian Mutiny, where he witnessed many of the dramatic moments of that terrible struggle, and encountered numerous Victorian celebrities—monarchs, statesmen, and generals among them. As in previous volumes, his narrative tallies closely with accepted historical fact, as well as furnishing much new information, and there has been little for his editor to do except correct his spelling, deplore his conduct, and provide the usual notes and appendices.

G.M.F.

They don't often invite me to Balmoral nowadays, which is a blessing; those damned tartan carpets always put me off my food, to say nothing of the endless pictures of German royalty and that unspeakable statue of the Prince Consort standing knock-kneed in a kilt. King Teddy's company is something I'd sooner avoid than not, anyway, for he's no better than an upper-class hooligan. Of course, he's been pretty leery of me for forty-odd years (ever since I misguided his youthful footsteps into an actress's bed, in fact, and brought Papa Albert's divine wrath down on his fat head) and when he finally wheezed his way on to the throne I gather he thought of dropping me altogether—said something about my being Falstaff to his Prince Hal. Falstaff, mark you—from a man with piggy eyes and a belly like a Conestoga wagon cover. Vile taste in cigars he has, too.

In the old Queen's time, of course, I was at Balmoral a great deal. She always fancied me, from when she was a chit of a girl and pinned the Afghan medal on my manly breast, and after I had ridden herd on that same precious Teddy through the Tranby Croft affair and saved him from the worst consequences of his own folly, she couldn't do enough for me. Each September after that, regular as clockwork, there would come a command for "dear General Flashman" to take the train north to Kailyard Castle, and there would be my own room, with a bowl of late roses on the window-sill, and a bottle of brandy on the side-table with a discreet napkin over it—they knew my style. So I put up with it; she was all right, little Vicky, as long as you gave her your arm to lean on, and let her prattle on endlessly, and the rations were adequate. But even then, I never cottoned to the place. Not only, as I've said, was it furnished in a taste that would have offended the sensibilities of a nigger costermonger, it had the most awful Highland gloom about it—all drizzle and mist and draughts under the door and holy melancholy: even the billiard-room had a print on the wall of a dreadful ancient Scotch couple glowering devoutly. Praying, I don't doubt, for me to be snookered.

But I think what really turns me against Balmoral in my old age is its memories. It was there that the Great Mutiny began for me, and on my rare excursions north nowadays there's a point on the line where the rhythm of the wheels changes, and in my imagination they begin to sing: "Mera-*Jhansi*-denge-nay, mera-*Jhansi*-denge-nay", over and over, and in a moment the years have dropped away, and I'm remembering how I first came to Balmoral half a century ago; aye, and what it led to—the stifling heat of the parade ground at Meerut with the fettering-hammers clanging; the bite of the muzzle of the nine-pounder jammed into my body and my own blood steaming on the sun-scorched iron; old Wheeler bawling hoarsely as the black cavalry sabres come thundering across the maidan towards our flimsy rampart ("No surrender! One last volley, damn 'em, and aim at the horses!"); the burning bungalows, a skeleton hand in the dust, Colin Campbell scratching his grizzled head, the crimson stain spreading in the filthy water below Suttee Ghat, a huge glittering pile of silver and gold and jewels and ivory bigger than anything you've ever seen—and two great brown liquid eyes shadowed with kohl, a single pearl resting on the satin skin above them, open red lips trembling . . . and, blast him, here's the station-master, beaming and knuckling his hat and starting me out of the only delightful part of that waking nightmare, with his cry of "Welcome back tae Deeside, Sir Harry! here we are again, then!"

And as he hands me down to the platform, you may be sure the local folk are all on hand, bringing their brats to stare and giggle at the big old buffer in his tweed cape and monstrous white whiskers ("There he is! The V.C. man, Sir Harry Flashman—aye, auld Flashy, him that charged wi' the Light Brigade and killed a' the niggers at Kau-bool—Goad, but isnae he the auld yin?—hip, hooray!"). So I acknowledge the cheers with a wave, bluff and hearty, as I step into the dog-cart, stepping briskly to escape the inevitable bemedalled veteran who comes shuffling after me, hoping I'll slip him sixpence for a dram when he assures me that we once stood together in the Highlanders' line at Balaclava. Lying old bastard, he was probably skulking in bed.

Not that I'd blame him if he was, mark you; given the chance I'd have skulked in mine—and not just at Balaclava, neither, but at every battle and skirmish I've sweated and scampered through during fifty inglorious years of unwilling soldiering. (Leastways, I know they were inglorious, but the country don't, thank heaven, which is why they've rewarded me with general rank and the knighthood and a double row of medals on my left tit. Which shows you what cowardice and roguery can do, given a stalwart appearance, long legs, and a thumping slice of luck. Aye, well, whip up, driver, we mustn't keep royalty waiting.)

But to return to the point, which is the Mutiny, and that terrible, incredible journey that began at Balmoral—well, it was as ghastly a road as any living man travelled in my time. I've seen a deal of war, and agree with Sherman that it's hell, but the Mutiny was the Seventh Circle under the Pit. Of course, it had its compensations: for one, I came through it, pretty whole, which is more than Havelock and Harry East and Johnny Nicholson did, enterprising lads that they were. (What's the use of a campaign if you don't survive it?) I did, and it brought me my greatest honour (totally undeserved, I needn't tell you), and a tidy enough slab of loot which bought and maintains my present place in Leicestershire—I reckon the plunder's better employed keeping me and my tenants in drink, than it was decorating a nigger temple for the edification of a gang of blood-sucking priests. And along the Mutiny road I met and loved that gorgeous, wicked witch Lakshmibai—there were others, too, naturally, but she was the prime piece.

One other thing about the Mutiny, before I get down to cases —I reckon it must be about the only one of my campaigns that I was pitched into through no fault of mine. On other occasions, I'll own, I've been to blame; for a man with a white liver a yard wide I've had a most unhappy knack of landing myself neck-deep in the slaughter through my various follies—to wit, talking too much (*that* got me into the Afghan débâcle of '41); playing the fool in pool-rooms (the Crimea); believing everything Abraham Lincoln told me (American Civil War); inviting a half-breed

Hunkpapa whore to a regimental ball (the Sioux Rising of '76), and so on; the list's as long as my arm. But my involvement in the Mutiny was all Palmerston's doing (what disaster of the fifties wasn't?).

It came out of as clear and untroubled a sky as you could wish, a few months after my return from the Crimea, where, as you may know, I'd won fresh laurels through my terrified inability to avoid the most gruelling actions. I had stood petrified in the Thin Red Streak, charged with the Heavies and Lights, been taken prisoner by the Russians, and after a most deplorable series of adventures (in which I was employed as chief stud to a nobleman's daughter, was pursued by hordes of wolves and Cossacks, and finally was caught up in a private war between Asian bandits and a Ruski army bound for India—it's all in my memoirs somewhere) had emerged breathless and lousy at Peshawar.*

There, as if I hadn't had trouble enough, I was restoring my powers by squandering them on one of those stately, hungry Afghan Amazons, and she must have been a long sight better at coupling than cooking, for something on her menu gave me the cholera. I was on the broad of my back for months, and it took a slow, restful voyage home before I was my own man again, in prime fettle for the reunion with my loving Elspeth and to enjoy the role of a returned hero about town. And, I may add, a *retired* hero; oxen and wainropes weren't going to drag Flashy back to the Front again. (I've made the same resolve a score of times, and by God I've meant it, but you can't fight fate, especially when he's called Palmerston.)

However, there I was in the summer of '56, safely content on half-pay as a staff colonel, with not so much as a sniff of war in sight, except the Persian farce, and that didn't matter. I was comfortably settled with Elspeth and little Havvy (the first fruit of our union, a guzzling lout of seven) in a fine house off Berkeley Square which Elspeth's inheritance maintained in lavish style, dropping by occasionally at Horse Guards, leading the social life, clubbing and turfing, whoring here and there as an occasional change from my lawful brainless beauty, and being lionised by all London—well, I'd stood at Armageddon and battled for the

* See *Flashman at the Charge.*

Lord (ostensibly) hadn't I, and enough had leaked out about my subsequent secret exploits in Central Asia (though government was damned cagey about them, on account of our delicate peace negotiations with Russia) to suggest that Flashy had surpassed all his former heroics. So with the country in a patriotic fever about its returning braves, I was ace-high in popular esteem—there was even talk that I'd get one of the new Victoria Crosses (for what that was worth) but it's my belief that Airey and Cardigan scotched it between them. Jealous bastards.

I suspect that Airey, who'd been chief of staff to Raglan in Crimea, hadn't forgotten my minor dereliction of duty at the Alma, when the Queen's randy little cousin Willy got his fool head blown off while under my care. And Cardigan loathed me, not least because I'd once emerged drunk, in the nick of time, from a wardrobe to prevent him cocking his lustful leg over my loving Elspeth. (She was no better than I was, you know.) And since coming home, I hadn't given him cause to love me any better.

You see, there was a deal of fine malicious tittle-tattle going about that summer, over Cardigan's part in the Light Brigade fiasco—not so much about his responsibility for the disaster, which was debatable, if you ask me, but for his personal behaviour at the guns. He'd been at the head of the charge, right enough, with me alongside on a bolting horse, farting my fearful soul out, but after we'd reached the battery he'd barely paused to exchange a cut or two with the Ruski gunners before heading for home and safety again. Shocking bad form in a commander, says I, who was trying to hide under a gun limber at the time—not that I think for a moment that he was funking it; he hadn't the brains to be frightened, our Lord Haw-Haw. But he *had* retreated without undue delay, and since he was never short of enemies eager to believe the worst, the gossips were having a field day now. There were angry letters in the press, and even a law-suit,[1] and since I'd been in the thick of the action, it was natural that I should be asked about it.

In fact, it was George Paget, who'd commanded the 4th Lights in the charge, who put the thing to me point-blank in the card-room at White's (can't imagine what I was doing there; must have been somebody's guest) in front of a number of people, civilians mostly, but I know Spottswood was there, and old Scarlett of the Heavies, I think.

"You were neck and neck with Cardigan," says Paget, "and in the battery before anyone else. Now, God knows he's not my soul-mate, but all this talk's getting a shade raw. Did you see him in the battery or not?"

Well, I had, but I wasn't saying so—far be it from me to clear his lordship's reputation when there was a chance of damaging it. So I said offhand:

"Don't ask me, George; I was too busy hunting for your cigars," which caused a guffaw.

"No gammon, Flash," says he, looking grim, and asked again, in his tactful way: "Did Cardigan cut out, or not?"

There were one or two shocked murmurs, and I shuffled a pack, frowning, before I answered. There are more ways than one of damning a man's credit, and I wanted to give Cardigan of my best. So I looked uncomfortable, and then growled, slapped the pack down as I rose, looked Paget in the eye, and said:

"It's all by and done with now, ain't it? Let's drop it, George, shall we?" And I went out then and there, leaving behind the impression that bluff, gallant Flashy didn't want to talk about it—which convinced them all that Cardigan had shirked, better than if I'd said so straight out, or called him a coward to his face.

I had a chance to do that, too, a bare two hours later, when the man himself came raging up to me with a couple of his toadies in tow, just as Spottswood and I were coming out of the Guards Club. The hall was full of fellows, goggling at the sensation.

"Fwashman! You there, sir!" he croaked—they were absolutely the first words between us since the Charge, nearly two years before. He was breathing frantically, like a man who has been running, his beaky face all mottled and his grey whiskers quaking with fury. "Fwashman—this is intolewable! My honour is impugned—scandalous lies, sir! And they tell me that you don't deny them! Well, sir? Well? Haw-haw?"

I tilted back my tile with a forefinger and looked him up and down, from his bald head and pop eyes to his stamping foot. He looked on the edge of apoplexy; a delightful sight.

"What lies are these, my lord?" says I, very steady.

"You know vewy well!" he cried. "Bawacwava, sir—the storming of the battewy! Word George Paget has asked you, in pubwic, whether you saw me at the guns—and you have the effwontewy to tell him you don't know! Damnation, sir! And one of my own officers, too—"

"A former member of your regiment, my lord—I admit the fact."

"Blast your impudence!" he roared, frothing at me. "Will you give me the lie? Will you say I was not at the guns?"

I settled my hat and pulled on my gloves while he mouthed.

"My lord," says I, speaking deliberately clear, "I saw you in the advance. In the battery itself—I was otherwise engaged, and had no leisure nor inclination to look about me to see who was where. For that matter, I did not see Lord George himself until he pulled me to my feet. I assumed—" and I bore on the word ever so slightly "—that you were on hand, at the head of your command. But I do not know, and frankly I do not care. Good day to you, my lord." And with a little nod I turned to the door.

His voice pursued me, cracking with rage.

"Colonel Fwashman!" he cried. "You are a viper!"

I turned at that, making myself go red in the face in righteous wrath, but I knew what I was about; he was getting no blow or challenge from me—he shot too damned straight for that.

"Indeed, my lord," says I. "Yet I don't wriggle and turn." And I left him gargling, well pleased with myself. But, as I say, it probably cost me the V.C. at the time; for all the rumours, he was still a power at Horse Guards, and well insinuated at Court, too.

However, our little exchange did nothing to diminish my popularity at large; a few nights later I got a tremendous cheer at the Guards Dinner at Surrey Gardens, with chaps standing on the table shouting "Huzza for Flash Harry!" and singing "Garryowen" and tumbling down drunk—how they did it on a third of a bottle of bubbly beat me.[2] Cardigan wasn't there, sensible fellow; they'd have hooted him out of the kingdom. As it was, *Punch* carried a nasty little dig about his absence, and wondered that he hadn't sent along his spurs, since he'd made such good use of them in retiring from the battery.

Of course, Lord Haw-Haw wasn't the only general to come

under the public lash that summer; the rest of 'em, like Lucan and Airey, got it too for the way they'd botched the campaign. So while we gallant underlings enjoyed roses and laurels all the way, our idiot commanders were gainfully employed exchanging recriminations, writing furious letters to the papers saying 'twasn't their fault, but some other fellow's, and there had even been a commission set up to investigate their misconduct of the war.

Unfortunately, government picked the wrong men to do the investigating—MacNeill and Tulloch—for they turned out to be honest, and reported that indeed our high command hadn't been fit to dig latrines, or words to that effect. Well, *that* plainly wouldn't do, so another commission had to be hurriedly formed to investigate afresh, and this time get the right answer, and no nonsense about it. Well, they did, and exonerated everybody, hip-hip-hurrah and Rule, Britannia. Which was what you'd have expected any half-competent government to stage-manage in the first place, but Palmerston was in the saddle by then, and he wasn't really good at politics, you know.

To crown it all, in the middle of the scandal the Queen herself had words about it with Hardinge, the Commander-in-Chief, at the Aldershot Review, and poor old Hardinge fell down paralysed and never smiled again. It's true; I was there myself, getting soaked through, and Hardinge went down like a shanghaied sailor, with all his faculties gone, not that he had many to start with. Some said it was a judgement on the Army and government corruption, so there.

All of which mattered rather less to me than the width of Elspeth's crinolines, but if I've digressed it is merely to show you how things were in England then, and also because I can never resist the temptation to blackguard Cardigan as he deserves. Meanwhile, I was going happily about my business, helping my dear wife spend her cash—which she did like a clipper-hand in port, I'm bound to say—and you would have said we were a blissful young couple, turning a blind eye to each other's infidelities and galloping in harness when we felt like it, which was frequent, for if anything she got more beddable with the passing years.

And then came the invitation to Balmoral, which reduced

Elspeth to a state of nervous exultation close to hysterics, and took me clean aback. I'd have imagined that if the Royal family ever thought of me at all, it was as the chap who'd been remiss enough to lose one of the Queen's cousins—but mind you, she had so many of 'em she probably didn't notice, or if she did, hadn't heard that I was to blame for it. No, I've puzzled over it sometimes, and can only conclude that the reason we were bidden to Balmoral that September was that Russia was still very much the topic of the day, what with the new Tsar's coronation and the recent peace, and I was one of the most senior men to have been a prisoner in Russia's hands.

I didn't have leisure to speculate at the time, though, for Elspeth's frenzy at the thought of being "in attendance", as she chose to call it, claimed everyone's attention within a mile of Berkeley Square. Being a Scotch tradesman's daughter, my darling was one degree more snobbish than a penniless Spanish duke, and in the days before we went north her condescension to her middle-class friends would have turned your stomach. Between gloating, and babbling about how she and the Queen would discuss dress-making while Albert and I boozed in the gunroom (she had a marvellous notion of court life, you see), she went into declines at the thought that she would come out in spots, or have her drawers fall down when being presented. You must have endured the sort of thing yourself.

"Oh, Harry, Jane Speedicut will be *green*! You and I—guests of her majesty! It will be the finest thing—and I have my new French dresses—the ivory, the beige silk, the lilac satin, and the lovely, lovely green which old Admiral Lawson *so* admired—if you think it is not a *leetle* low for the Queen? And my *barrege* for Sunday—will there be members of the nobility staying also?—will there be ladies whose husbands are of lower rank than you? Ellen Parkin—*Lady* Parkin, indeed!—was *consumed* with spite when I told her—oh, and I must have another maid who can manage my hair, for Sarah is too *maladroit* for words, although she is very passable with dresses—what shall I wear to picnics?—for we shall be bound to walk in the lovely Highland countryside —oh, Harry, what do you suppose the Queen reads?—and shall I call the Prince 'highness' or 'sir'?"

I was glad, I can tell you, when we finally reached Abergeldie, where we had rooms in the castle where guests were put up—for Balmoral was very new then, and Albert was still busy having the finishing touches put to it. Elspeth by this time was too nervous even to talk, but her first glimpse of our royal hosts reduced her awe a trifle, I think. We took a stroll the first afternoon, in the direction of Balmoral, and on the road encountered what seemed to be a family of tinkers led by a small washerwoman and an usher who had evidently pinched his headmaster's clothes. Fortunately, I recognised them as Victoria and Albert out with their brood, and knew enough simply to raise my hat as we passed, for they loathed to be treated as royalty when they were playing at being commoners. Elspeth didn't even suspect who it was until we were past, and when I told her she swooned by the roadside. I revived her by threatening to carry her into the bushes and molest her, and on the way back she observed that really her majesty had looked *quite* royal, but in a *common* sort of way.

By the time we were presented at Balmoral, though, the next day, she was high up the scale again, and the fact that we shared the waiting-room beforehand with some lord or other and his beak-nosed lady, who looked at us as though we were riff-raff, reduced my poor little scatterbrain to quaking terror. I'd met the royals before, of course, and tried to reassure her, whispering that she looked a stunner (which was true) and not to be put out by Lord and Lady Puffbuttock, who were now ignoring us with that icy incivility which is the stamp of our lower-class aristocracy. (I know; I'm one myself nowadays.)

It was quite handy that our companions kept their noses in the air, though, for it gave me the chance to loop a ribbon from the lady's enormous crinoline on to an occasional table without her knowing, and when the doors to the royal drawing-room were opened she set off and brought the whole thing crashing down, crockery and all, in full view of the little court circle. I kept Elspeth in an iron grip, and steered her round the wreckage, and so Colonel and Mrs Flashman made their bows while the doors were hurriedly closed behind us, and the muffled sounds of the Puffbuttocks being extricated by flunkeys was music to my ears, even if it did make the Queen look more pop-eyed than usual. The moral is: don't put on airs with Flashy, and if you do, keep your crinolines out of harm's way.

And, as it turned out, to Elspeth's lifelong delight and my immense satisfaction, she and the Queen got on like port and nuts from the first. Elspeth, you see, was one of those females who are so beautiful that even other women can't help liking 'em, and in her idiot way she was a lively and engaging soul. The fact that she was Scotch helped, too, for the Queen was in one of her Jacobite moods just then, and by the grace of God someone had read *Waverley* to Elspeth when she was a child, and taught her to recite "The Lady of the Lake".

I had been dreading meeting Albert again, in case he mentioned his whoremongering Nephew Willy, now deceased, but all he did was say:

"Ah, Colonel Flash-mann—haff you read Tocqueville's *L'Ancien Régime?*"

I said I hadn't, yet, but I'd be at the railway library first thing in the morning, and he looked doleful and went on:

"It warns us that bureaucratic central government, far from curing the ills of revolution, can actually arouse them."

I said I'd often thought that, now that he mentioned it, and he nodded and said: "Italy is very unsatisfactory," which brought our conversation to a close. Fortunately old Ellenborough, who'd been chief in India at the time of my Kabul heroics, was among those present, and he buttonholed me, which was a profound relief. And then the Queen addressed me, in that high sing-song of hers:

"Your *dear* wife, Colonel Flashman, tells me that you are *quite* recovered from the rigours of your *Russian* adventures, which you shall tell us of *presently.* They seem to be a quite *extraordinary* people; Lord Granville writes from Petersburg that Lady Wodehouse's Russian maid was found *eating* the contents of one of her ladyship's dressing-table pots—it was castor oil pomatum for the *hair!* What a *remarkable* extravagance, was it not?"

That was my cue, of course, to regale them with a few domestic anecdotes of Russia, and its primitive ways, which went down well, with the Queen nodding approval and saying: "How barbarous! How strange!" while Elspeth glowed to see her hero holding the floor. Albert joined in in his rib-tickling way to observe that no European state offered such fertile soil for the seeds of socialism as Russia did, and that he feared that the new Tsar had little intellect or character.

"So Lord Granville says," was the Queen's prim rejoinder, "but I do not *think* it is *quite* his place to make such observations on a *royal* personage. Do you not agree, Mrs Flashman?"

Old Ellenborough, who was a cheery, boozy buffer, said to me that he hoped I had tried to civilise the Russians a little by teaching them cricket, and Albert, who had no more humour than the parish trough, looked stuffy and says:

"I am sure Colonel Flash-mann would do no such thing. I cannot unner-stend this passion for cricket; it seems to me a great waste of time. What is the proff-it to a younk boy in crouching motionless in a field for hourss on end? Em I nott right, Colonel?"

"Well, sir," says I, "I've looked out in the deep field myself long enough to sympathise with you; it's a great fag, to be sure. But perhaps, when the boy's a man, his life may depend on crouching motionless, behind a Khyber rock or a Burmese bush— so a bit of practice may not come amiss, when he's young."

Which was sauce, if you like, but I could never resist the temptation, in grovelling to Albert, to put a pinch of pepper down his shirt. It was in my character of bluff, no-nonsense Harry, too, and a nice reminder of the daring deeds I'd done. Ellenborough said "Hear, hear", and even Albert looked only half-sulky, and said all diss-cipline was admirable, but there must be better ways of instilling it; the Prince of Wales, he said, should nott play cricket, but some more constructiff game.

After that we had tea, very informal, and Elspeth distinguished herself by actually prevailing on Albert to eat a cucumber sandwich; she'll have him in the bushes in a minute, thinks I, and on that happy note our first visit concluded, with Elspeth going home on a cloud to Abergeldie.

But if it was socially useful, it wasn't much of a holiday, although Elspeth revelled in it. She went for walks with the Queen, twice (calling themselves Mrs Fitzjames and Mrs Marmion, if you please), and even made Albert laugh when charades were played in the evening, by impersonating Helen of Troy with a

Scotch accent. I couldn't even get a grin out of him; we went shooting with the other gentlemen, and it was purgatory having to stalk at his pace. He was keen as mustard, though, and slaughtered stags like a Ghazi on hashish—you'll hardly credit it, but his notion of sport was that a huge long trench should be dug so that we could sneak up on the deer unobserved; he'd have done it, too, but the local ghillies showed so much disgust at the idea that he dropped it. He couldn't understand their objections, though; to him all that mattered was killing the beasts.

For the rest, he prosed interminably and played German music on the piano, with me applauding like hell. Things weren't made easier by the fact that he and Victoria weren't getting on too well just then; she had just discovered (and confided to Elspeth) that she was in foal for the ninth time, and she took her temper out on dear Albert—the trouble was, he was so bloody patient with her, which can drive a woman to fury faster than anything I know. And he was always *right*, which was worse. So they weren't dealing at all well, and he spent most of the daylight hours tramping up Glen Bollocks, or whatever they call it, roaring "Ze gunn!" and butchering every animal in view.

The only thing that seemed to cheer up the Queen was that she was marrying off her oldest daughter, Princess Vicky—the best of the whole family, in my view, a really pretty, green-eyed little mischief. She was to wed Frederick William of Prussia, who was due at Balmoral in a few weeks, and the Queen was full of it, Elspeth told me.

However, enough of the court gossip; it will give you some notion of the trivial way in which I was being forced to pass my time—toadying Albert, and telling the Queen how many acute accents there were on "déterminés". The trouble with this kind of thing is that it dulls your wits, and your proper instinct for self-preservation, so that if a blow falls you're caught clean offside, as I was on the night of September 22, 1856: I recollect the date absolutely because it was the day after Florence Nightingale came to the castle.[3]

I'd never met her, but as the leading Crimean on the premises I was summoned to join in the tête-à-tête she had with the Queen in the afternoon. It was a frost, if you like; pious platitudes from

the two of 'em, with Flashy passing the muffins and joining in
when called on to agree that what our wars needed was more
sanitation and texts on the wall of every dressing-station. There
was one near-facer for me, and that was when Miss Nightingale
(a cool piece, that) asked me calm as you like what regimental
officers could do to prevent their men from contracting certain indelicate social infections from—hem-hem—female camp-
followers of a certain sort; I near as dammit put my tea-cup in the
Queen's lap, but recovered to say that I'd never heard of any such
thing, not in the Light Cavalry, anyway—French troops another
matter, of course. Would you believe it, I actually made her blush,
but I doubt if the Queen even knew what we were talking about.
For the rest, I thought La Nightingale a waste of good woman-
hood; handsome face, well set up and titted out, but with that
cold don't-lay-a-lecherous-limb-on-me-my-lad look in her eye—the
kind, in short, that can be all right if you're prepared to spend
time and trouble making 'em cry "Roger!", but I seldom have the
patience. Anywhere else I might have taken a squeeze at her, just
by way of research, but a queen's drawing-room cramps your
style. (Perhaps it's a pity I didn't; being locked up for indecent
assault on a national heroine couldn't have been worse than the
ordeal that was to begin a few hours later.)

Elspeth and I spent the following evening at a birthday party
at one of the big houses in the neighbourhood; it was a cheery
affair, and we didn't leave till close on midnight to drive back to
Abergeldie. It was a close, thundery night, with big rain-drops
starting to fall, but we didn't mind; I had taken enough drink on
board to be monstrously horny, and if the drive had been longer
and Elspeth's crinoline less of a hindrance I'd have had at her on
the carriage-seat. She got out at the lodge giggling and squeaking,
and I chased her through the front door—and there was the
messenger of doom, waiting in the hall. A tall chap, almost a
swell, but with a jaw too long and an eye too sharp; very
respectable, with a hard hat under his arm and a billy in his hip-
pocket, I'll wager. I know a genteel strong man from a government
office when I see one.

He asked could he speak to me, so I took my arm from Elspeth's
waist, patted her towards the stairs with a whispered promise that

I'd be up directly to sound the charge, and told him to state his business. He did that smart enough.

"I am from the Treasury, Colonel Flashman," says he. "My name is Hutton. Lord Palmerston wishes to speak with you."

It took me flat aback, slightly foxed that I was. My first thought was that he must want me to go back to London, but then he said: "His lordship is at Balmoral, sir. If you will be good enough to come with me—I have a coach."

"But—but ... you said Lord Palmerston? The Prime ... what the deuce? Palmerston wants *me?*"

"At once, sir, if you please. The matter is urgent."

Well, I couldn't make anything of it. I never doubted it was genuine—as I've said, the man in front of me had authority written all over him. But it's a fair start when you come rolling innocently home and are told that the first statesman of Europe is round the corner and wants you at the double—and now the fellow was positively ushering me towards the door.

"Hold on," says I. "Give me a moment to change my shoes"— what I wanted was a moment to put my head in the wash-bowl and think, and despite his insistence I snapped at him to wait, and hurried upstairs.

What the devil was Pam doing here—and what could he want with me? I'd only met him once, for a moment, before I went to the Crimea; I'd leered at him ingratiatingly at parties, too, but never spoken. And now he wanted me urgently—me, a mere colonel on half-pay. I'd nothing on my conscience, either— leastways, not to interest him. I couldn't see it, but there was nothing but to obey, so I went to my dressing-room, fretting, donned my hat and topcoat against the worsening weather, and remembered that Elspeth, poor child, must even now be waiting for her cross-buttocking lesson. Well, it was hard lines on her, but duty called, so I just popped my head round her door to call a chaste farewell—and there she was, dammit, reclining languorously on the coverlet like one of those randy classical goddesses, wearing nothing but the big ostrich-plume fan I'd brought her from Egypt, and her sniggering maid turning the lamp down low. Elspeth clothed could stop a monk in his tracks; naked and pouting expectantly over a handful of red feathers, she'd have made the Grand Inquisitor burn his books. I hesitated between love and duty for a full second, and then "The hell with Palmerston, let him wait!" cries I, and was plunging for the bed before the abigail was fairly out of the room. Never miss the chance, as the Duke used to say.

"Lord Palmerston? Oooo-ah! Harry—what *do* you mean?"

"Ne'er mind!" cries I, taking hold and bouncing away.

"But Harry—such impatience, my love! And, dearest—you're wearing your hat!"

"The next one's going to be a boy, dammit!" And for a few glorious stolen moments I forgot Palmerston and minions in the hall, and marvelled at the way that superb idiot woman of mine could keep up a stream of questions while performing like a harem houri—we were locked in an astonishing embrace on her dressing-table stool, I recall, when there was a knock on the door, and the maid's giggling voice piped through to say the gentleman downstairs was getting impatient, and would I be long.

"Tell him I'm just packing my baggage," says I. "I'll be down directly", and presently, keeping my mouth on hers to stem her babble of questions, I carried my darling tenderly back to the bed. Always leave things as you would wish to find them.

"I cannot stay longer, my love," I told her. "The Prime Minister is waiting." And with bewildered entreaties pursuing me I skipped out, trousers in hand, made a hasty toilet on the landing, panted briefly against the wall, and then stepped briskly down. It's a great satisfaction, looking back, that I kept the government waiting in such a good cause, and I set it down here as a deserved tribute to the woman who was the only real love of my life and as the last pleasant memory I was to have for a long time ahead.

It's true enough, too, as Ko Dali's daughter taught me, that there's nothing like a good rattle for perking up an edgy chap like me. It had shaken me for a moment, and it still looked rum, that Palmerston should want to see me, but as we bowled through the driving rain to Balmoral I was telling myself that there was probably nothing in it after all; considering the good odour I stood in just then, hob-nobbing with royalty and being admired for my Russian heroics, it was far more likely to be fair news

than foul. And it wasn't like being bidden to the presence of one
of your true ogres, like the old Duke or Bismarck or Dr Wrath-of-
God Arnold (I've knocked tremulously on some fearsome doors in
my time, I can tell you).

No, Pam might be an impatient old tyrant when it came to
bullying foreigners and sending warships to deal with the dagoes,
but everyone knew he was a decent, kindly old sport at bottom,
who put folk at their ease and told a good story. Why, it was
notorious that the reason he wouldn't live at Downing Street, but
on Piccadilly, was that he liked to ogle the good-lookers from his
window, and wave to the cads and crossing-sweepers, who loved
him because he talked plain English, and would stump up a
handsome subscription for an old beaten prize-pug like Tom Sayers.
That was Pam—and if anyone ever tells you that he was a
politically unprincipled old scoundrel, who carried things with a
high and reckless hand, I can only say that it didn't seem to work
a whit worse than the policies of more high-minded statesmen.
The only difference I ever saw between them and Pam was that
he did his dirty work bare-faced (when he wasn't being deeper
than damnation) and grinned about it.

So I was feeling pretty easy as we covered the three miles to
Balmoral—and even pleasantly excited—which shows you how
damned soft and optimistic I must have grown; I should have
known that it's never safe to get within range of princes or prime
ministers. When we got to the Castle I followed Hutton smartly
through a side-door, up some back-stairs, and along to heavy
double doors where a burly civilian was standing guard; I gave
my whiskers a martial twitch as he opened the door, and stepped
briskly in.

You know how it can be when you enter a strange room—
everything can look as safe and merry as ninepence, and yet
there's something in the air that touches you like an electric
shock. It was here now, a sort of bristling excitement that put my
nerves on edge in an instant. And yet there was nothing out of
the ordinary to see—just a big, cheerful panelled room with a
huge fire roaring under the mantel, a great table littered with
papers, and two sober chaps bustling about it under the direction
of a slim young fellow—Barrington, Palmerston's secretary. And

over by the fire were three other men—Ellenborough, with his great flushed face and his belly stuck out; a slim, keen-looking old file whom I recognised as Wood, of the Admiralty; and with his back to the blaze and his coat-tails up, the man himself, peering at Ellenborough with his bright, short-sighted eyes and looking as though his dyed hair and whiskers had just been rubbed with a towel—old Squire Pam as ever was. As I came in, his brisk, sharp voice was ringing out (he never gave a damn who heard him):

"... so if he's to be Prince Consort, it don't make a ha'porth of difference, you see. Not to the country—or me. However, as long as Her Majesty *thinks* it does—that's what matters, what? Haven't you found that telegraph of Quilter's yet, Barrington?— well, look in the Persian packet, then."

And then he caught sight of me, and frowned, sticking out his long lip. "Ha, that's the man!" cries he. "Come in, sir, come in!"

What with the drink I'd taken, and my sudden nervousness, I tripped over the mat—which was an omen, if you like—and came as near as a toucher to oversetting a chair.

"By George," says Pam, "is he drunk? All these young fellows are, nowadays. Here, Barrington, see him to a chair, before he breaks a window. There, at the table." Barrington pulled out a chair for me, and the three at the fireplace seemed to be staring ominously at me while I apologised and took it, especially Pam in the middle, with those bright steady eyes taking in every inch of me as he nursed his port glass and stuck a thumb into his fob— for all the world like the marshal of a Kansas trail-town surveying the street. (Which is what he was, of course, on a rather grand scale.)

He was very old at this time, with the gout and his false teeth forever slipping out, but he was evidently full of ginger tonight, and not in one of his easygoing moods. He didn't beat about, either.

"Young Flashman," growls he. "Very good. Staff colonel, on half-pay at present, what? Well, from this moment you're back on the full list, an' what you hear in this room tonight is to go no further, understand? Not to anyone—not even in this castle. You follow?"

I followed, sure enough—what he meant was that the Queen

wasn't to know: it was notorious that he never told her anything. But that was nothing; it was his tone, and the solemn urgency of his warning, that put the hairs up on my neck.

"Very good," says he again. "Now then, before I talk to you, Lord Ellenborough has somethin' to show you—want your opinion of it. All right, Barrington, I'll take that Persian stuff now, while Colonel Flashman looks at the damned buns."

I thought I'd misheard him, as he limped past me and took his seat at the table-head, pawing impatiently among his papers. But sure enough, Barrington passed over to me a little lead biscuit-box, and Ellenborough, seating himself beside me, indicated that I should open it. I pushed back the lid, mystified, and there, in a rice-paper wrapping, were three or four greyish, stale-looking little scones, no bigger than captain's biscuits.

"There," says Pam, not looking up from his papers. "Don't eat 'em. Tell his lordship what you make of those."

I knew, right off; that faint eastern smell was unmistakable, but I touched one of them to make sure.

"They're chapattis, my lord," says I, astonished. "Indian chapattis."

Ellenborough nodded. "Ordinary cakes of native food. You attach no signal significance to them, though?"

"Why . . . no, sir."

Wood took a seat opposite me. "And you can conjecture no situation, colonel," says he, in his dry, quiet voice, "in which the sight of such cakes might occasion you . . . alarm?"

Obviously Ministers of the Crown don't ask damnfool questions for nothing, but I could only stare at him. Pam, apparently deep in his papers at the table-head, wheezing and sucking his teeth and muttering to Barrington, paused to grunt: "Serve the dam' things at dinner an' they'd alarm me," and Ellenborough tapped the biscuit box.

"These chapattis came last week from India, by fast steam sloop. Sent by our political agent at a place called Jhansi. Know it? It's down below the Jumna, in Maharatta country. For weeks now, scores of such cakes have been turning up among the sepoys of our native Indian garrison at Jhansi—not as food, though. It seems the sepoys pass them from hand to hand as tokens—"

"Have you ever heard of such a thing?" Wood interrupted.

I hadn't, so I just shook my head and looked attentive, wondering what the devil this was all about, while Ellenborough went on:

."Our political knows where they come from, all right. The native village constables—you know, the *chowkidars*—bake them in batches of ten, and send one apiece to ten different sepoys—and each sepoy is bound to make ten *more*, and pass *them* on, to his comrades, and so on, ad infinitum. It's not new, of course; ritual cake-passing is very old in India. But there are three remarkable things about it: firstly, it happens only rarely; second, even the natives themselves don't know *why* it happens, only that the cakes must be baked and passed; and third—" he tapped the box again "—they believe that the appearance of the cakes foreshadows terrible catastrophe."

He paused, and I tried to look impressed. For there was nothing out of the way in all this—straight from *Alice in Wonderland*, if you like, but when you know India and the amazing tricks the niggers can get up to (usually in the name of religion) you cease to be surprised. It seemed an interesting superstition—but what was more interesting was that two Ministers of the Government, and a former Governor-General of India, were discussing it behind closed doors—and had decided to let Flashy into the secret.

"But there's something more," Ellenborough went on, "which is why Skene, our political man at Jhansi, is treating the matter as one of urgency. Cakes like these have circulated among native *troops*, quite apart from civilians, on only three occasions in the past fifty years—at Vellore in '06, at Buxar, and at Barrackpore. You don't recall the names? Well, at each place, when the cakes appeared, the same reaction followed among the sepoys." He put on his House of Lords face and said impressively, "Mutiny."

Looking back, I suppose I ought to have thrilled with horror at the mention of the dread word—but in fact all that occurred to me was the facetious thought that perhaps they ought to have varied the sepoys' rations. I didn't think much of the political man Skene's judgement, either; I'd been a political myself, and it's part of the job to scream at your own shadow, but if he—or Ellenborough, who knew India outside in—was smelling a sepoy

revolt in a few mouldy biscuits—well, it was ludicrous. I knew
John Sepoy (we all did, didn't we?) for the most loyal ass who
ever put on uniform—and so he should have been, the way the
Company treated him. However, it wasn't for me to venture an
opinion in such august company, particularly with the Prime
Minister listening: he'd pushed his papers aside and risen, and
was pouring himself some more port.

"Well, now," says he briskly, taking a hearty swig and rolling
it round his teeth, "you've admired his lordship's cakes, what?
Damned unappetisin' they look, too. All right, Barrington, your
assistants can go—our special leaves at four, does it? Very well."
He waited till the junior secretaries had gone, muttered something
about ungodly hours and the Queen's perversity in choosing a
country retreat at the North Pole, and paced stiffly over to the
fire, where he set his back to the mantel and glowered at me from
beneath his gorse-bush brows, which was enough to set my dinner
circulating in the old accustomed style.

"Tokens of revolution in an Indian garrison," says he. "Very
good. Been readin' that report of yours again, Flashman—the one
you made to Dalhousie last year, in which you described the
discovery you made while you were a prisoner in Russia—about
their scheme for invadin' India, while we were busy in Crimea.
Course, we say nothin' about *that* these days—peace signed with
Russia, all good fellowship an' be damned, et cetera—don't have
to tell you. But somethin' in your report came to mind when this
cake business began." He pushed out his big lip at me. "You wrote
that the Russian march across the Indus was to be accompanied
by a native risin' in India, fomented by Tsarist agents. Our
politicals have been chasin' that fox ever since—pickin' up some
interestin' scents, of which these infernal buns are the latest.
Now, then," he settled himself, eyes half-shut, but watching me,
"tell me precisely what you heard in Russia, touchin' on an Indian
rebellion. Every word of it."

So I told him, exactly as I remembered it—how Scud East and
I had lain quaking in our nightshirts in the gallery at Starotorsk,
and overheard about "Item Seven", which was the Russian plan
for an invasion of India. They'd have done it, too, but Yakub
Beg's riders scuppered their army up on the Syr Daria, with

Flashy running about roaring with a bellyful of *bhang*, performing unconscious prodigies of valour. I'd set it all out in my report to Dalhousie, leaving out the discreditable bits (you can find *those* in my earlier memoirs, along with the licentious details). It was a report of nicely-judged modesty, that official one, calculated to convince Dalhousie that I was the nearest thing to Hereward the Wake he was ever likely to meet—and why not? I'd suffered for my credit.

But the information about an Indian rebellion had been slight. All we'd discovered was that when the Russian army reached the Khyber, their agents in India would rouse the natives—and particularly John Company's sepoys—to rise against the British. I didn't doubt it was true, at the time; it seemed an obvious ploy. But that was more than a year ago, and Russia was no threat to India any longer, I supposed.

They heard me out, in a silence that lasted a full minute after I'd finished, and then Wood says quietly:

"It fits, my lord."

"Too dam' well," says Pam, and came hobbling back to his chair again. "It's all pat. You see, Flashman, Russia may be spent as an armed power, for the present—but that don't mean she'll leave us at peace in India, what? This scheme for a rebellion—by George, if I were a Russian political, invasion or no invasion, I fancy I could achieve somethin' in India, given the right agents. Couldn't I just, though!" He growled in his throat, heaving restlessly and cursing his gouty foot. "Did you know, there's an Indian superstition that the British Raj will come to an end exactly a hundred years after the Battle of Plassey?" He picked up one of the chapattis and peered at it. "Dam' thing isn't even sugared. Well, the hundredth anniversary of Plassey falls next June the twenty-third. Interestin'. Now then, tell me—what d'you know about a Russian nobleman called Count Nicholas Ignatieff?"

He shot it at me so abruptly that I must have started a good six inches. There's a choice collection of ruffians whose names you can mention if you want to ruin my digestion for an hour or two —Charity Spring and Bismarck, Rudi Starnberg and Wesley Hardin, for example—but I'd put N. P. Ignatieff up with the leaders any time. He was the brute who'd nearly put paid to me

in Russia—a gotch-eyed, freezing ghoul of a man who'd dragged
me halfway to China in chains, and threatened me with exposure
in a cage and knouting to death, and like pleasantries. I hadn't
cared above half for the conversation thus far, with its bloody
mutiny cakes and the sinister way they kept dragging in my
report to Dalhousie—but at the introduction of Ignatieff's name
my bowels began to play the Hallelujah Chorus in earnest. It
took me all my time to keep a straight face and tell Pam what I
knew—that Ignatieff had been one of the late Tsar's closest
advisers, and that he was a political agent of immense skill and
utter ruthlessness; I ended with a reminiscence of the last time
I'd seen him, under that hideous row of gallows at Fort Raim.
Ellenborough exclaimed in disgust, Wood shuddered delicately,
and Pam sipped his port.

"Interestin' life you've led," says he. "Thought I remembered
his name from your report—he was one of the prime movers
behind the Russian plan for invasion an' Indian rebellion, as I
recall. Capable chap, what?"

"My lord," says I, "he's the devil, and that's a fact."

"Just so," says Pam. "An' the devil will find mischief." He
nodded to Ellenborough. "Tell him, my lord. Pay close heed to
this, Flashman."

Ellenborough cleared his throat and fixed his boozy spaniel eyes
on me. "Count Ignatieff," says he, "has made two clandestine
visits to India in the past year. Our politicals first had word of
him last autumn at Ghuznee; he came over the Khyber disguised
as an Afridi horse-coper, to Peshawar. There we lost him—as you
might expect, one disguised man among so many natives—"

"But my lord, that can't be!" I couldn't help interrupting.
"You can't lose Ignatieff, if you know what to look for. However
he's disguised, there's one thing he can't hide—his eyes! One of
'em's half-brown, half-blue!"

"He can if he puts a patch over it," says Ellenborough. "India's
full of one-eyed men. In any event, we picked up his trail again—
and on both occasions it led to the same place—Jhansi. He spent
two months there, all told, usually out of sight, and our people
were never able to lay a hand on him. What he was doing, they
couldn't discover—except that it was mischief. Now, we see what

the mischief was—" and he pointed to the chapattis. "Brewing insurrection, beyond a doubt. And having done his infernal work —back over the hills to Afghanistan. This summer he was in St Petersburg—but from what our politicals did learn, he's expected back in Jhansi again. We don't know when."

No doubt it was the subject under discussion, but there didn't seem to be an ounce of heat coming from the blazing fire behind me; the room felt suddenly cold, and I was aware of the rain slashing at the panes and the wind moaning in the dark outside. I was looking at Ellenborough, but in his face I could see Ignatieff's hideous parti-coloured eye, and hear that soft icy voice hissing past the long cigarette clenched between his teeth.

"Plain enough, what?" says Pam. "The mine's laid, in Jhansi— an' if it explodes ... God knows what might follow. India looks tranquil enough—but how many other Jhansis, how many other Ignatieffs, are there?" He shrugged. "We don't know, but we can be certain there's no more sensitive spot than this one. The Russians have picked Jhansi with care—we only annexed it four years ago, on the old Raja's death, an' we've still barely more than a foothold there. Thug country, it used to be, an' still pretty wild, for all it's one of the richest thrones in India. Worst of all, it's ruled by a woman—the Rani, the Raja's widow. She was old when she married him, I gather, an' there was no legitimate heir, so we took it under our wing—an' she didn't like it. She rules under our tutelage these days—but she remains as implacable an enemy as we have in India. Fertile soil for Master Ignatieff to sow his plots."

He paused, and then looked straight at me. "Aye—the mine's laid in Jhansi. But precisely when an' where they'll try to fire it, an' whether it'll go off or not ... this we must know—an' prevent at all costs."

The way he said it went through me like an icicle. I'd been sure all along that I wasn't being lectured for fun, but now, looking at their heavy faces, I knew that unless my poltroon instinct was sadly at fault, some truly hellish proposal was about to emerge. I waited quaking for the axe to fall, while Pam stirred his false teeth with his tongue—which was a damned unnerving sight, I may tell you—and then delivered sentence.

"Last week, the Board of Control decided to send an extra-ordinary agent to Jhansi. His task will be to discover what the Russians have been doing there, how serious is the unrest in the sepoy garrison, and to deal with this hostile beldam of a Rani by persuadin' her, if possible, that loyalty to the British Raj is in her best interest." He struck his finger on the table. "An' if an' when this man Ignatieff returns to Jhansi again—to deal with *him*, too. Not a task for an ordinary political, you'll agree."

No, but I was realising, with mounting horror, who they *did* think it was a task for. But I could only sit, with my spine dissolving and my face set in an expression of attentive idiocy, while he went inexorably on.

"The Board of Control chose you without hesitation, Flashman. I approved the choice myself. You don't know it, but I've been watchin' you since my time as Foreign Secretary. You've been a political—an' a deuced successful one. I dare say you think that the work you did in Middle Asia last year has gone un-recognised, but that's not so." He rumbled at me impressively, wagging his great fat head. "You've the highest name as an active officer, you've proved your resource—you know India—fluent in languages—includin' Russian, which could be of the first importance, what? You know this man Ignatieff, by sight, an' you've bested him before. You see, I know all about you, Flashman," you old fool, I wanted to shout, you don't know any-thing of the bloody sort; you ain't fit to be Prime Minister, if that's what you think, "and I know of no one else so fitted to this work. How old are you? Thirty-four—young enough to go a long way yet—for your country and yourself." And the old buffoon tried to look sternly inspiring, with his teeth gurgling.

It was appalling. God knows I've had my crosses to bear, but this beat all. As so often in the past, I was the victim of my own glorious and entirely unearned reputation—Flashy, the hero of Jallalabad, the last man out of the Kabul retreat and the first man into the Balaclava battery, the beau sabreur of the Light Cavalry, Queen's Medal, Thanks of Parliament, darling of the mob, with a liver as yellow as yesterday's custard, if they'd only known it. And there was nothing, with Pam's eye on me, and Ellenborough and Wood looking solemnly on, that I could do about it. Oh, if

I'd followed my best instincts, I could have fled wailing from the room, or fallen blubbering at some convenient foot—but of course I didn't. With sick fear mounting in my throat, I knew that I'd have to go, and that was that—back to India, with its heat and filth and flies and dangers and poxy niggers, to undertake the damndest mission since Bismarck put me on the throne of Strackenz.

But this was infinitely worse—Bismarck's crew had been as choice a collection of villains as ever jumped bail or slit a throat, but they were civilised by comparison with Ignatieff. The thought of *dealing* with that devil, as Pam so nicely put it, was enough to send me into a decline. And if that wasn't enough, I was to sneak about some savage Indian kingdom (Thug country, for a bonus), spying on some withered old bitch of an Indian princess and trying to wheedle her to British interest against her will—and she probably the kind of hag whose idea of fun would be to chain malefactors to a rogue elephant's foot. (Most Indian rulers are mad, you know, and capable of anything.) But there wasn't the slightest chance to wriggle; all I could do was put on my muscular Christian expression, look Palmerston fearlessly in the eye, like Dick Champion when the headmaster gives him the job of teaching the fags not to swear, and say I'd do my best.

"Well enough," says he. "I know you will. Who knows—perhaps the signs are false, what? Tokens of mutiny, in a place where Russia's been stirrin' the pot, an' the local ruler's chafin' under our authority—it's happened before, an' it may amount to nothin' in the end. But if the signs are true, make no mistake—" and he gave me his steady stare "—it's the gravest peril our country has faced since Bonaparte. It's no light commission we're placin' in your hands, sir—but they're the safest hands in England, I believe."

So help me God, it's absolutely what he said; it makes you wonder how these fellows ever get elected. I believe I made some manly sounds, and as usual my sick terror must have been manifesting itself by making me red in the face, which in a fellow of my size is often mistaken for noble resolution. It must have satisfied Pam, anyway, for suddenly he was smiling at me, and sitting back in his chair.

"Now you know why you're sittin' here talkin' to the Prime Minister, what? Been sittin' on eggshells, haven't you? Ne'er mind—I'm glad to have had the opportunity of instructin' you myself—of course, you'll be more fully informed, before you sail, of all the intelligence you'll need—his lordship here, an' Mangles at the Board in London, will be talkin' to you. When d'you take leave of her majesty? Another week? Come, that's too long. When does the India sloop sail, Barrington? Monday —you'd best be off to Town on Friday, then. Leave pretty little Mrs Flashman to take care of royalty, what? Stunnin' gal, that— never see her from my window on Piccadilly but it sets me in humour—must make her acquaintance when you come home. Bring her along to Number 96 some evenin'—dinner, an' so forth, what?"

He sat there, beaming like Pickwick. It turned my stomach at the time, and small wonder, considering the stew he was launching me into—and yet, when I think back on Pam nowadays, that's how I see him, painted whiskers, sloppy false teeth and all, grinning like a happy urchin. You never saw such young peepers in a tired old face. I can say it now, from the safety of my declining years: in spite of the hellish pickle he landed me in, I'd swap any politician I ever met for old Pam—damn him.[4]

However, now that he'd put the doom on me, he couldn't get rid of me fast enough; before I'd been properly shooed out of the room he was snapping at Barrington to find some American telegraph or other, and chivvying at Wood that they must soon be off to catch their special train at Aberdeen. It must have been about three in the morning, but he was still full of bounce, and the last I saw of him he was dictating a letter even as they helped him into his coat and muffler, with people bustling around him, and he was breaking off to peer again at the chapattis on the table and ask Ellenborough did the Hindoos eat 'em with meat, or any kind of relish.

"Blasted buns," says he. "Might do with jam, d'you think, what? No ... better not ... crumble an' get under my confounded teeth, probably ..." He glanced up and caught sight of me bowing my farewell from the doorway. "Good night to you, Flashman," he sings out, "an' good huntin'. You look out sharp for yourself, mind."

So that was how I got my marching orders—in a snap of the fingers almost. Two hours earlier I'd been rogering happily away, with not a care in the world, and now I was bound for India on the most dangerous lunatic mission I'd ever heard of—by God, I cursed the day I'd written that report to Dalhousie, glorifying myself into the soup. And fine soup it promised to be—rumours of mutiny, mad old Indian princesses, thugs, and Ignatieff and his jackals lurking in the undergrowth.

You can imagine I didn't get much rest in what was left of the night. Elspeth was fast asleep, looking glorious with the candlelight on her blonde hair tumbled over the pillow, and her rosebud lips half open, snoring like the town band. I was too fretful to rouse her in her favourite way, so I just shook her awake, and I must say she bore the news of our impending parting with remarkable composure. At least, she wept inconsolably for five minutes at the thought of being bereft while her Hector (that's me) was Braving the Dangers of India, fondled my whiskers and said she and little Havvy would be quite *desolate*, whimpered sadly while she teased me, in an absent-minded way, into mounting her, and then remembered she had left her best silk gloves behind at the evening's party and that she had a spot on her left shoulder which no amount of cream would send away. It's nice to know you're going to be missed.

I had three days still left at Balmoral, and the first of them was spent closeted with Ellenborough and a sharp little creature from the Board of Control, who lectured me in maddening detail about my mission to Jhansi, and conditions in India—I won't weary you with it here, for you'll learn about Jhansi and its attendant horrors and delights in due course. Sufficient to say it did nothing but deepen my misgivings—and then, on the Wednesday morning, something happened which drove everything else clean out of my mind. It was such a shock, such an unbelievable coincidence in view of what had gone before (or so it seemed at the time) that I can still think back to it with disbelief—aye, and start sweating at the thought.

I'd had a thoroughly drunken night at Abergeldie, to take my mind off the future, and when I woke cloth-headed and surly on the Wednesday morning, Elspeth suggested that instead of breakfast I'd be better going for a canter. I damned her advice and sent for a horse, left her weeping sulkily into her boiled egg, and ten minutes later was galloping the fumes away along the Balmoral road. I reached the castle, and trotted up as far as the carriage entrance; beyond it, on the far side of the gravel sweep, one of the big castle coaches that brought quality visitors from Aberdeen station was drawn up, and flunkies were handing down the arrivals and bowing them towards the steps leading to the side door.

Some more poor fools of consequence about to savour the royal hospitality, thinks I, and was just about to turn my horse away when I happened to glance again at the group of gentlemen in travelling capes who were mounting the steps. One of them turned to say something to the flunkies—and I nearly fell from the saddle, and only saved myself by clutching the mane with both hands. I believe I nearly fainted—for it was something infinitely worse than a ghost; it was real, even if it was utterly impossible. The man on the steps, spruce in the rig of an English country gentleman, and now turning away into the castle, was the man I'd last seen beside the line of carrion gallows at Fort Raim—the man Palmerston was sending me to India to defeat and kill: Count Nicholas Pavlevitch Ignatieff.

"You're sure?" croaked Ellenborough. "No, no, Flashman—it can't be! Count Ignatieff—whom we were discussing two nights since—here? Impossible!"

"My lord," says I, "I've good cause to know him better than most, and I tell you he's in the castle now, gotch-eye and all. Cool as damn-your-eyes, in a tweed cape and deer-stalker hat, so help me! He was there, at the door, not ten minutes ago!"

He plumped down on a chair, mopping at the shaving-soap on his cheeks—I'd practically had to manhandle his valet to be admitted, and I'd left a trail of startled minions on the back-stairs in my haste to get to his room. I was still panting from exertion, to say nothing of shock.

"I want an explanation of this, my lord," says I, "for I'll not believe it's chance."

"What d'ye mean?" says he, goggling.

"Two nights ago we talked of precious little else but this Russian monster—how he'd been spying the length and breadth of India, in the very place to which I'm being sent. And now he turns up—the very man? Is that coincidence?" I was in such a taking I didn't stand on ceremony. "How comes he in the country, even? Will you tell me Lord Palmerston didn't know?"

"My God, Flashman!" His big mottled face looked shocked. "What d'you mean by that?"

"I mean, my lord," says I, trying to hold myself in, "that there's precious little that happens anywhere, let alone in England, that Lord Palmerston doesn't know about—is it possible that he's unaware that the most dangerous agent in Russia —and one of their leading nobles, to boot—is promenading about as large as life? And never a word the other night, when—"

"Wait! Wait!" cries he, wattling. "That's a monstrous suggestion! Contain yourself, sir! Are you positive it's Ignatieff?"

I was ready to burst, but I didn't. "I'm positive."

"Stay here," says he, and bustled out, and for ten minutes I chewed my nails until he came back, shutting the door behind him carefully. He had got his normal beetroot colour back, but he looked damned rattled.

"It's true," says he. "Count Ignatieff is here with Lord Aberdeen's party—as a guest of the Queen. It seems—you know we have Granville in Petersburg just now, for the new Tsar's coronation? Well, a party of Russian noblemen—the first since the war —have just arrived in Leith yesterday, bringing messages of good will, or God knows what, from the new monarch to the Queen. Someone had written to Aberdeen—I don't know it all yet—and he brought them with him on his way north—with this fellow among 'em. It's extraordinary! The damndest chance!"

"Chance, my lord?" says I. "I'll need some convincing of that!"

"Good God, what else? I'll allow it's long odds, but I'm certain if Lord Palmerston had had the least inkling ..." He trailed off, and you could see the sudden doubt of his own precious Prime Minister written on his jowly face. "Oh, but the notion's preposterous ... what purpose could it serve not to tell us? No—he would certainly have told me—and you, I'm sure."

Well, I wasn't sure—from what I'd heard of Pam's sense of humour I'd have put nothing past him. And yet it would have been folly, surely, with me on the point of setting off for India, ostensibly to undo Ignatieff's work, to have let him come face to face with me. And then, the wildest thought—was it possible Ignatieff *knew* about my mission?

"Never!" trumpets Ellenborough. "No, that couldn't be! The decision to send you out was taken a bare two weeks since—it would be to credit the Russian intelligence system with superhuman powers—and if he did, what could he accomplish here? —dammit, in the Queen's own home! This isn't Middle Asia—it's a civilised country—"

"My lord, that's not a civilised man," says I. "But what's to be done? I can't meet him!"

"Let me think," says he, and strode about, heaving his stomach around. Then he stopped, heavy with decision.

"I think you must," says he. "If he has seen you—or finds out that you were here and left before your time ... wait, though, it might be put down to tact on your part ... still, no!" He snapped his fingers at me. "No, you must stay. Better to behave as though there was nothing untoward—leave no room to excite suspicion—after all, former enemies meet in time of peace, don't they? And we'll watch him—by George, we will! Perhaps we'll learn something ourselves! Hah-ha!"

And this was the port-sodden clown who had once governed India. I'd never heard such an idiot suggestion—but could I shift him? I pleaded, in the name of common sense, that I should leave at once, but he wouldn't have it—I do believe that at the back of his mind was the suspicion that Pam *had* known Ignatieff was coming, and Ellenborough was scared to tinker with the Chief's machinations, whatever they were.

"You'll stay," he commanded, "and that's flat. What the devil—it's just a freak of fate—and if it's not, there's nothing this Russian rascal can do. I tell you what, though—I'm not going to miss his first sight of you, what? The man he threatened with torture and worse—disgusting brute! Aye, and the man who bested him in the end. Ha-ha!" And he clapped me on the shoulder. "Aye—hope nothing happens to embarrass the Queen, though. You'll mind out for that, Flashman, won't you—it wouldn't do—any unpleasantness, hey?"

I minded out, all right. Strangely enough, by the time I came back to the Castle with Elspeth that afternoon, my qualms about coming face to face again with that Russian wolf had somewhat subsided; I'd reminded myself that we weren't meeting on his ground any more, but on mine, and that the kind of power he'd once had over me was a thing quite past. Still, I won't pretend I was feeling at ease, and I'd drummed it into Elspeth's head that not a hint must be let slip about my ensuing departure for India, or Pam's visit. She took it in wide-eyed and assured me she would not *dream* of saying a word, but I realised with exasperation that you couldn't trust any warning to take root in that beautiful empty head: as we approached the drawing-room doors she was prattling away about what wedding present she should suggest to the Queen for Mary Seymour, and I, preoccupied, said offhand, why not a lusty young coachman, and immediately regretted it—you

couldn't be sure she wouldn't pass it on—and then the doors
opened, we were announced, and the heads in the room were all
turning towards us.

There was the Queen, in the middle of the sofa, with a lady
and gentleman behind; Albert, propping up the mantelpiece, and
lecturing to old Aberdeen, who appeared to be asleep on his feet,
half a dozen assorted courtiers—and Ellenborough staring across
the room. As we made our bows, and the Queen says: "Ah
Mrs Flashman, you are come *just* in time to help with the service
of tea", I was following Ellenborough's glance, and there was
Ignatieff, with another Russian-looking grandee and a couple of
our own gentry. He was staring at me, and by God, he never so
much as blinked or twitched a muscle; I made my little bow
towards Albert, and as I turned to face Ignatieff again I felt, God
knows why, a sudden rush of to-hell-with-it take hold of me.

"My—dear—Count!" says I, astonished, and everyone stopped
talking; the Queen looked pop-eyed, and even Albert left off
prosing to the noble corpse beside him.

"Surely it's Count Ignatieff?" cries I, and then broke off in
apology. "Your pardon, ma'am," says I to Vicky. "I was quite
startled—I had no notion Count Ignatieff was here! Forgive me,"
but of course by this time she was all curiosity, and I had to
explain that Count Ignatieff was an old comrade-in-arms, so to
speak, what? And beam in his direction, while she smiled uncertainly, but not displeased, and Ellenborough played up well,
and told Albert that he'd heard me speak of being Ignatieff's
prisoner during the late war, but had had no idea this was the
same gentleman, and Albert looked disconcerted, and said that
was most remarkable.

"Indeed, highness, I had that honour," says Ignatieff, clicking
his heels, and the sound of that chilly voice made my spine tingle.
But there was nothing he could do but take the hand I stretched
out to him.

"This is splendid, old fellow!" says I, gripping him as though
he were my long-lost brother. "Wherever have you been keeping
yourself?" One or two of them smiled, to see bluff Flash Harry so
delighted at meeting an old enemy—just what they'd have
expected, of course. And when the Queen had been made quite

au fait with the situation, she said it was *exactly* like Fitzjames
and Roderick Dhu.

So after that it was quite jolly, and Albert made a group with
Ignatieff and Ellenborough and me, and questioned me about our
acquaintance, and I made light of my captivity and escape, and
said what a charming jailer Ignatieff had been, and the brute just
stood impassive, with his tawny head bowed over his cup, and
looking me over with that amazing half-blue, half-brown eye.
He was still the same handsome, broken-nosed young iceberg I
remembered—if I'd closed my eyes I could have heard the lash
whistling and cracking in Arabat courtyard, with the Cossacks'
grip on my arms.

Albert, of course, was much struck by the coincidence of our
meeting again, and preached a short sermon about the brotherhood of men-at-arms, to which Ignatieff smiled politely and I
cried "Hear, hear!" It was difficult to guess, but I judged my
Muscovite monster wasn't enjoying this too much; he must have
been wondering why I pretended to be so glad to see him. But I
was all affability; I even presented him to Elspeth, and he
bowed and kissed her hand; she was very demure and cool, so I
knew she fancied him, the little trollop.

The truth is, my natural insolence was just asserting itself, as it
always does when I feel it's safe; when a moment came when
Ignatieff and I were left alone together, I thought I'd stick a pin
in him, just for sport, so I asked, quietly:

"Brought your knout with you, Count?"

He looked at me a moment before replying. "It is in Russia,"
says he. "Waiting. So, I have no doubt, is Count Pencherjevsky's
daughter."

"Oh, yes," says I. "Little Valla. Is she well, d'you know?"

"I have no idea. But if she is, it is no fault of yours." He
glanced away, towards Elspeth and the others. "Is it?"

"She never complained to me," says I, grinning at him. "On
that tack—if I'm well, it's no fault of yours, either."

"That is true," says he, and the eye was like a sword-point.
"However, may I suggest that the less we say about our previous
acquaintance, the better? I gather from your ... charade, a little
while ago—designed, no doubt, to impress your Queen—that you

are understandably reluctant that the truth of your behaviour there should be made public."

"Oh, come now," says I. "'Twasn't a patch on yours, old boy. What would the Court of Balmoral think if they knew that the charming Russian nobleman with the funny eye, was a murderous animal who flogs innocent men to death and tortures prisoners of war? Thought about that?"

"If you think you were tortured, Colonel Flashman," says he, poker-faced, "then I congratulate you on your ignorance." He put down his cup. "I find this conversation tedious. If you will excuse me," and he turned away.

"Oh, sorry if you're bored," says I. "I was forgetting—you probably haven't cut a throat or burned a peasant in a week."

It was downright stupid of me, no doubt—two hours earlier I'd been quaking at the thought of meeting him again, and here I was sassing him to my heart's content. But I can never resist a jibe and a gloat when the enemy's hands are tied, as Thomas Hughes would tell you. Ignatieff didn't seem nearly as fearsome here, among the tea-cups, with chaps toadying the royals, and cress sandwiches being handed round, and Ellenborough flirting ponderously with Elspeth while the Queen complained to old Aberdeen that it was the *press* which had killed Lord Hardinge, in her Uncle Leopold's *opinion*. No, not fearsome at all—without his chains and gallows and dungeons and power of life and death, and never so much as a Cossack thug to bless himself with. I should have remembered that men like Nicholas Ignatieff are dangerous anywhere—usually when you least expect it.

And I was far from expecting anything the next day, the last full one I was to spend at Balmoral. It was a miserable, freezing morning, I remember, with flurries of sleet among the rain, and low clouds rolling down off Lochnagar; the kind of day when you put your nose out once and then settle down to punch and billiards with the boys, and build the fire up high. But not Prince Albert; there were roe deer reported in great numbers at Balloch Buie, and nothing would do but we must be drummed out, cursing, for a stalk.

I'd have slid back to Abergeldie if I could, but he nailed me in the hall with Ellenborough. "Why, Colonel Flash-mann, where

are your gaiters? Haff you nott called for your loader yet? Come,
gentlemen, in this weather we haff only a few hours—let us be
off!"

And he strutted about in his ridiculous Alpine hat and tartan
cloak, while the loaders were called and the brakes made ready,
and the ghillies loafed about grinning on the terrace with the
guns and pouches—they knew I loathed it, and that Ellenborough couldn't carry his guts more than ten yards without a
rest, and the brutes enjoyed our discomfiture. There were four
or five other guns in the party, and presently we drove off into
the rain, huddling under the tarpaulin covers as we jolted away
from the castle on the unmade road.

The country round Balmoral is primitive at the best of times;
on a dank autumn day it's like an illustration from Bunyan's
'Holy War', especially near our destination, which was an eery,
dreary forest of firs among the mountains, with great patches of
bog, and gullies full of broken rocks, and heather waist-deep on
the valley sides. The road petered out there, and we clambered
out of the brakes and stood in the pouring wet while Albert, full
of energy and blood-lust, planned the campaign. We were to
spread out singly, with our loaders, and drive ahead up to the
high ground, because the mist was hanging fairly thick by this
time, and if we kept together we might miss the stags altogether.

We were just about to start on our squelching climb, when
another brake came rolling up the road, and who should pile out
but the Russian visitors, with one of the local bigwigs, all dressed
for the hill. Albert of course was delighted.

"Come, gentlemen," cries he, "this is capital! What? There
are no bearss in our Scottish mountains, but we can show you
fine sport among the deer. General Menshikof, will you accompany me? Count Ignatieff—ah, where iss Flash-mann?" I was
having a quick swig from Ellenborough's flask, and as the Prince
turned towards me, and I saw Ignatieff at his elbow, very trim in
tweeds and top boots, with a fur cap on his head and a heavy
piece under his arm, I suddenly felt as though I'd been kicked in
the stomach. In that second I had a vision of those lonely, gully-
crossed crags above us, with their great reaches of forest in which
you could get lost for days, and mist blotting out sight and sound

of all companions—and myself, alone, with Ignatieff down-wind of me, armed, and with that split eye of his raking the trees and heather for a sight of me. It hadn't even occurred to me that he might be in the shooting party, but here he came, strolling across, and behind him a great burly unmistakable *moujik*, in smock and boots, carrying his pouches.

Ellenborough stiffened and shot a glance at me. For myself, I was wondering frantically if I could plead indisposition at the last minute. I opened my mouth to say something, and then Albert was summoning Ellenborough to take the left flank, and Ignatieff was standing watching me coolly, with the rain beating down between us.

"I have my own loader," says he, indicating the *moujik*. "He is used to heavy game—bears, as his royal highness says, and wolves. However, he has experience of lesser animals, and vermin, even."

"I ... I ..." It had all happened so quickly that I couldn't think of what to say, or do. Albert was dispatching the others to their various starting-points; the first of them were already moving off into the mist. As I stood, dithering, Ignatieff stepped closer, glanced at my own ghillie, who was a few yards away, and said quietly in French:

"I did not know you were going to India, Colonel. My congratulations on your ... appointment? A regimental command, perhaps?"

"Eh? What d'you mean?" I started in astonishment.

"Surely nothing less," says he, "for such a distinguished campaigner as yourself."

"I don't know what you're talking about," I croaked.

"Have I been misinformed? Or have I misunderstood your charming wife? When I had the happiness to pay my respects to her this morning, I understood her to say—but there, I may have been mistaken. When one encounters a lady of such exceptional beauty, I fear one tends to look rather than to listen." He smiled —something I'd never seen him do before: it reminded me of a frozen river breaking up. "But I think his royal highness is calling you, Colonel."

"Flash-mann!" I tore myself away from the hypnotic stare of

that split eye; there was Albert waving at me impatiently. "Will
you take the lead on the right flank? Come, sir, we are losing
time—it will be dark before we can come up to the beasts!"

If I'd had any sense I'd have bolted, or gone into a swoon, or
claimed a sprained ankle—but I didn't have time to think. The
royal nincompoop was gesticulating at me to be off, my loader
was already ploughing into the trees just ahead, one or two of the
others had turned to look, and Ignatieff was smiling coldly at my
evident confusion. I hesitated, and then started after the loader;
as I entered the trees, I took one quick glance back; Ignatieff was
standing beside the brake, lighting a cigarette, waiting for Albert
to set him on his way. I gulped, and plunged into the trees.

The ghillie was waiting for me under the branches; he was
one of your grinning, freckled, red-haired Highlanders, called
MacLehose, or something equally unpronounceable. I'd had him
before, and he was a damned good shikari—they all are, of course.
Well, I was going to stick to him like glue this trip, I told myself,
and the farther we got away from our Russian sportsmen in
quick time, the better. As I strode through the fir wood, ducking
to avoid the whippy branches, I heard Albert's voice faintly
behind us, and pressed on even harder.

At the far side of the wood I paused, staring up at the hillside ahead of us. What the devil was I getting in such a stew for?
—my heart racing like a trip-hammer, and the sweat running
down me, in spite of the chill. This wasn't Russia; it was a
civilised shooting-party in Scotland. Ignatieff wouldn't dare to
try any devilment here—it had just been the surprise of his sudden appearance at the last minute that had unmanned me...
wouldn't he, though? By God, he'd try anything, that one—and
he knew about my going to India, thanks to that blathering idiot
I'd married in an evil hour. Shooters had been hit before, up on
the crags, in bad light ... it could be made to look like an accident ... mistaken for a stag ... heavy mist ... tragic error ...
never forgive himself....

"Come on!" I yammered, and stumbled over the rocks for a
gully that opened to our left—there was another one straight
ahead, but I wasn't having that. The ghillie protested that if we
went left we might run into the nearest shooters; that was all

right with me, and I ignored him and clambered over the rubble at the gully foot, plunging up to the knee in a boggy patch and almost dropping my gun. I stole a glance back, but there was no sign of anyone emerging from the wood; I sprang into the gully and scrambled upwards.

It was a gruelling climb, through the huge heather-bushes that flanked the stream, and then it was bracken, six feet high, with a beaten rabbit-path that I went up at a run. At the top the gully opened out into another great mass of firs, and not until we were well underneath them did I pause, heaving like a bellows, and the ghillie padded up beside me, not even breathing hard, and grinning surprise on his face.

"Crackey good gracious," says he, "you're eager to be at the peasties the day. What's the great running, whatever?"

"Is this piece loaded?" says I, and held it out.

"What for would it be?" says the clown. "We'll no' be near a deer for half an hour yet. There's no occasion."

"Load the dam' thing," says I.

"And have you plowing your pluidy head off, the haste you're in? She'll look well then, right enuff."

"Damn you, do as you're told!" says I, so he shrugged and spat and looked his disgust as he put in the charge.

"Mind, there's two great pullets in there now," says he as he handed it back. "If you've as much sense as a whaup's neb you'll keep the caps in your pooch until we sight the deer." They've no respect, those people.

I snatched it from him and made off through the wood, and for ten minutes we pushed on, always upwards, through another long gully, and along a rocky ledge over a deep stream, where the mist hung in swirls among the rowan trees, and the foam drifted slowly by on the brown pools. It was as dark as dusk, although it was still early afternoon; there was no sound of another living soul, and nothing moving on the low cliffs above us.

By this time I was asking myself again if I hadn't been over-anxious—and at the same time wondering if it wouldn't be safest to lie up here till dark, and buy the ghillie's silence with a sovereign, or keep moving to our left to reach the other guns. And then he gave a sudden exclamation and stopped, frowning, and putting a hand on his belly. He gave a little barking cough, and his ruddy face was pale as he turned to me.

"Oh!" says he. "What's this? All of a sudden, my pudden's is pad."

"What is it?" says I, impatiently, and he sat down on a rock, holding himself and making strained noises.

"I—I don't know. It's my belly—there's some mischief in herself—owf!"

"Are you ill?"

"Oh, goad—I don't know." His face was green. "What do these foreign puggers tak' to drink? It's—it must be the spirits yon great hairy fella gave me before we cam' up—oh, mither, isn't it hellish? Oh, stop you, till I vomit!"

But he couldn't, try as he would, but leaned against the rock, in obvious pain, rubbing at himself and groaning. And I watched him in horror, for there was no doubt what had happened—Ignatieff's man had drugged or poisoned him, so that I'd be alone on the hill. The sheer ruthlessness of it, the hellish calculation, had me trembling to my boots—they would come on me alone, and—but wait, whatever he'd been given, it couldn't be fatal: two corpses on one shoot would be too much to explain away, and one of them poisoned, at that. No, it must just be a drug, to render him helpless, and of course I would turn back down the hill to get help, and they'd be there. . . .

"Stay where you are—I'll get help," says I, and lit out along the ledge, but not in the direction we'd come; it was up and over the hills for Flashy, and my groaning ghillie could be taken care of when time served. I scudded round the corner of rock at the ledge's end, and through a forest of bracken, out into a clear space, and then into another fir wood, where I paused to get my bearings. If I bore off left—but which way *was* left? We'd taken so many turnings, among the confounded bogs and gullies, I couldn't be sure, and there was no sun to help. Suppose I went the wrong way, and ran into them? God knows, in this maze of hills and heather it would be easy enough. Should I go back to the stricken ghillie, and wait with him? I'd be safer, in his company—but they might be up with him by now, lurking on the gully-side, waiting. I stood clutching my gun, sweating.

It was silent as death under the fir-trees, close as a tomb, and dim. I could see out one side, where there was bracken—that would be the place to lie up, so I stole forward on tip-toe, making no noise on the carpet of mould and needles. Near the wood's edge I waited, listening: no sound, except my own breathing. I turned to enter the bracken—and stood frozen, biting back a yelp of fear. Behind me, on the far side of the wood, a twig had snapped.

For an instant I was paralysed, and then I was across the open space of turf and burrowing into the bracken for dear life. I went a few yards, and then writhed round to look back; through the stems and fronds I could see the trees I'd just left, gloomy and silent. But I was deep in cover; if I lay still, not to shake the bracken above me, no one could hope to spot me unless he trod on me. I burrowed down in the sodden grass, panting, and waited, with my ears straining.

For five minutes nothing happened; there was only the dripping of the fronds, and my own heart thumping. What made the suspense so hellish was the sheer unfairness of my predicament— I'd been in more tight corners before than I cared to count, but always in some godless, savage part of the world like Afghanistan or Madagascar or Russia or St Louis—it was damnable that I should be lurking in fear of my life in England—or Scotland, even. I hadn't been in this kind of terror on British soil since I'd been a miserable fag at Rugby, carrying Bully Dawson's game bag for him, and we'd had to hide from keepers at Brownsover. They'd caught me, too, and I'd only got off by peaching on Dawson and his pals, and showing the keepers where . . . and suddenly, where there had been nothing a moment ago, a shadow moved in the gloom beneath the trees, stopped, and took on form in the half-light. Ignatieff was standing just inside the edge of the fir wood.

I stopped breathing, while he turned his head this way and that, searching the thickets; he had his gun cocked, and by God he wasn't looking for stags. Then he snapped his fingers, and the *moujik* came padding out of the dimness of the wood; he was heeled and ready as well, his eyes glaring above his furze of beard. Ignatieff nodded to the left, and the great brute went prowling off that way, his piece presented in front of him; Ignatieff waited a few seconds and then took the way to the right. They both disappeared, noiselessly, and I was left fumbling feverishly for my caps. I slipped them under the hammers with trembling fingers, wondering whether to stay where I was or try to wriggle farther back into the undergrowth. They would be on either side of me shortly, and if they turned into the bracken they might easily ... and with the thought came a steady rustling to my left, deep in the green; it stopped, and then started again, and it sounded closer. No doubt of it, someone was moving stealthily and steadily towards my hiding place.

It takes a good deal to stir me out of petrified fear, but that did it. I rolled on my side, trying to sweep my gun round to cover the sound; it caught in the bracken, and I hauled frantically at it to get it clear. God, what a din I must be making—and then the damned lock must have caught on a stem, for one barrel went off like a thunderclap, and I was on my feet with a yell, tearing downhill through the bracken. I fairly flung myself through the high fronds, there was the crack of a shot behind me, and a ball buzzed overhead like a hornet. I went bounding through, came out in a clearing with firs on either side, sprang over a bank of ferns—and plunged straight down into a peat cutting. I landed belly first in the stinking ooze, but I was up and struggling over the far side in an instant, for I could hear crashing in the bracken above me, and knew that if I lost an instant he'd get a second shot. I was plastered with muck like a tar-and-feather merchant, but I still had my gun, and then I must have trod on a loose stone, for I pitched headlong, and went rolling and bumping down the slope, hit a rock, and finished up winded and battered in a burn, trying frantically to scramble up, and slithering on the slimy gravel underfoot.

There was a thumping of boots on the bank, I started round, and there was the *moujik*, not ten yards away. I didn't even have time to look for my gun; I was sprawling half out of the burn, and the bastard had his piece at his shoulder, the muzzle looking me straight in the face. I yelled and grabbed for a stone, there was the crash of a gunshot—and the *moujik* dropped his piece, shrieking, and clutched at his arm as he toppled backwards among the rocks.

"Careful, colonel," says a voice behind me. "He's only winged."

And there, standing not five yards off, with a smoking revolver in his hand, was a tall fellow in tweeds; he just gave me a nod, and then jumped lightly over the rocks and stood over the *moujik*, who was groaning and clutching his bleeding arm.

"Murderous swine, ain't you?" says the newcomer conversationally, and kicked him in the face. "It's the only punishment he'll get, I'm afraid," he added, over his shoulder. "No diplomatic scandals, you see." And as he turned towards me, I saw to my amazement who it was—Hutton, the tall chap with the long jaw who'd taken me to Palmerston only a few nights before. He put his pistol back in his arm-pit and came over to me.

"No bones broken? Bless me, but you're a sight." He pulled me to my feet. "I'll say this, colonel—you're the fastest man over rough country I ever hope to follow. I lost you in five minutes, but I kept track of our friends, all right. Nice pair, ain't they, though? I wish to God it had been the other one I pulled trigger on—oh, we won't see him again, never fret. Not until everyone's down the hill, and he'll turn up cool as you like, never having been near you all day, what?"

"But—but . . . you mean, you expected this?"

"No-o—not exactly, anyway. But I've been pretty much on hand since the Russian brotherhood arrived, you know. We don't believe in taking chances, eh? Not with customers like Master Ignatieff—enterprising chap, that. So when I heard he'd decided to join the shoot today, I thought I'd look along—just as well I did, I think," says this astonishing fellow. "Now, if you've got your wind back, I suggest we make our way down. Never mind our little wounded bird yonder—if he don't bleed to death he'll find his way back to his master. Pity he shot himself by accident, ain't it? That'll be their story, I dare say—and we won't contradict it—here, what are you about, sir?"

I was lunging for my fallen gun, full of murderous rage now that the danger was past. "I'm going to blow that bloody peasant's head off!" I roared, fumbling with the lock. "I'll teach—"

"Hold on!" cries he, catching my arm, and he was positively grinning. "Capital idea, I agree—but we mustn't, you see. One bullet in him can be explained away by his own clumsiness—but not two, eh? We mustn't have any scandal, colonel—not involving her majesty's guests. Come along now—let's be moving down, so that Count Ignatieff, who I've no doubt is watching us this minute, can come to his stricken servant's assistance. After you, sir."

He was right, of course; the irony of it was that although Ignatieff and his brute had tried to murder me, we daren't say so, for diplomacy's sake. God knows what international complications there might have been. This didn't sink in with me at once—but his reminder that Ignatieff was still prowling about was enough to lend me wings down the hill. Not that even he'd have tried another shot, with Hutton about, but I wasn't taking chances.

I'll say this for the secret service—which is what Hutton was, of course—they're damned efficient. He had a gig waiting on the road, one of his assistants was dispatched to the help of my ghillie, and within a half-hour I was back in Balmoral through the servants' entrance, being cleaned up and instructed by Hutton to put it about that I'd abandoned the shoot with a strained muscle.

"I'll inform my chiefs in London that Colonel Flashman had a fortunate escape from an unexpected danger, arising from a chance encounter with an old Russian friend," says he, "and that he is now fit and well to proceed on the important task ahead of him. And that, in the meantime, I'm keeping an eye on him. No, sir, I'm sorry—I can't answer any of your questions, and I wouldn't if I could."

Which left me in a fine state of consternation and bewilderment, wondering what to make of it all. My immediate thought was that Palmerston had somehow arranged the whole thing, in the hope that I'd kill Ignatieff, but even in my excited condition that didn't make sense. A likelier explanation was that Ignatieff, coming innocently to Balmoral and finding me on the premises, had decided to take advantage of the chance to murder me, in revenge for the way I'd sold him the previous year. That, knowing the man and his ice-cold recklessness, was perfectly sound reasoning—but there was also the horrid possibility that he had found out about the job Palmerston had given me (God alone knew how—but he'd at least discovered from the idiot Elspeth that I was going to India) and had been out to dispose of me in the way of business.

"A preposterous notion," was Ellenborough's answer when I

voiced my fears to him that night. "He could *not* know—why, the Board decision was highly secret, and imparted only to the Prime Minister's most intimate circle. No, this is merely another example of the naked savagery of the Russian bear!" He was full of port, and wattling furiously. "And virtually in her majesty's presence, too! Damnable! But, of course, we can say nothing, Flashman. It only remains," says he, booming sternly, "for you to mete out conclusive justice to this villain, if you chance to encounter him in India. In the meantime, I'll see that the Lord Chamberlain excludes him from any diplomatic invitations which may be extended to St Petersburg in future. By gad, I will!"

I ventured the cautious suggestion that it might be better, after what had happened, to send someone else to Jhansi—just in case Ignatieff had tumbled to me—but Ellenborough wasn't even listening. He was just full of indignation at Ignatieff's murderous impudence—not on my account, you'll note, but because it might have led to a scandal involving the Queen. (Admittedly, you can't have it getting about that her guests have been trying to slaughter each other; the poor woman probably had enough trouble getting people to visit, with Albert about the place.)

So, of course, we kept mum, and as Hutton had foreseen, it was put about and accepted that Ignatieff's loader had had an accident with a gun, and everyone wagged their heads in sympathy, and the Queen sent the poor unfortunate fellow some shortbread and a tot of whisky. Ignatieff even had the crust to thank her after dinner, and I could feel Ellenborough at my elbow fairly bubbling with suppressed outrage. And to cap it all, the brute had the effrontery to challenge me to a game of billiards—and beat me hollow, too, in the presence of Albert and half a dozen others: I had to be certain there was a good crowd on hand, for God knows what he'd have tried if we'd gone to the pool-room alone. I'll say it for Nicholas Ignatieff—he was a bear-cat for nerve. He'd have been ready to brain me and claim afterwards that it was a mis-cue.

So now—having heard the prelude to my Indian Mutiny adventure, you will understand why I don't care much for Balmoral. And if what happened there that September was trivial by comparison with what followed—well, I couldn't foresee that. Indeed, as I soothed my bruised nerves with brandy fomentations that night, I reflected that there were worse places than India; there was Aberdeenshire, with Ignatieff loose in the bracken, hoping to hang my head on his gunroom wall. I hadn't been able to avoid him here, but if we met again on the coral strand, it wasn't going to be my fault.

I've never been stag-shooting from that day to this, either. Ellenborough was right: the company's too damned mixed.

I remember young Fred Roberts (who's a Field-Marshal now, which shows you what pull these Addiscombe wallahs have got) once saying that everyone hated India for a month and then loved it forever. I wouldn't altogether agree, but I'll allow that it had its attractions in the old days; you lived like a lord without having to work, waited on hand and foot, made money if you set your mind to it, and hardly exerted yourself at all except to hunt the beasts, thrash the men, and bull the women. You had to look sharp to avoid active service, of course, of which there was a lot about; I never fell very lucky that way. But even so, it wasn't a half-bad station, most of the time.

Personally, I put that down to the fact that in my young days India was a middle-class place for the British, where society people didn't serve if they could help it. (Cardigan, for example, took one look and fled.) It's different now, of course; since it became a safe place many of our best and most highly-connected people have let the light of their countenances shine on India, with the results you might expect—prices have gone up, service has gone down, and the women have got clap. So they tell me.

Mind you, I could see things were changing even in '56, when I landed at Bombay. My first voyage to India, sixteen years before, had lasted four months on a creaking East Indiaman; this time, in natty little government steam sloops, it had taken just about half that time, even with a vile journey by camel across the Suez isthmus in between. And even from Bombay you could get the smell of civilisation; they'd started the telegraph, and were pushing ahead with the first railways, there were more white faces and businesses to be seen, and people weren't talking, as they'd used to, of India as though it were a wild jungle with John Company strongholds here and there. In my early days, a journey from Calcutta to Peshawar had seemed half round the world, but no longer. It was as though the Company was at last seeing India as one vast country—and realising that now the wars with the Sikhs and Maharattas and Afghans were things of the past, it was an empire that had to be ruled and run, quite apart from fighting and showing a nice profit in Leadenhall Street.

It was far busier than I remembered it, and somehow the civilians seemed more to the fore nowadays than the military. Once the gossip on the verandahs had all been about war in the north, or the Thugs, or the bandit chiefs of the Ghats who'd have to be looked up some day; now it was as often as not about new mills or factories, and even schools, and how there would be a railroad clear over to Madras in the next five years, and you'd be able to journey from Mrs Blackwell's in Bombay to the Auckland in Calcutta without once putting on your boots.

"All sounds very peaceful and prosperous," says I, over a peg and a whore at Mother Sousa's—like a good little political, you see, I was conducting my first researches in the best gossip-mart I could find (fine mixed clientele, Mother Sousa's, with nothing blacker than quarter-caste and exhibition dances that would have made a Paris gendarme blench—well, if it's scuttle-butt you want, you don't go to a cathedral, do you?). The chap who'd bought me the peg laughed and said:

"Prosperous? I should just think so—my firm's divvy is up forty per cent., and we'll have new factories at Lahore and Allahabad working before Easter. Building churches—and when the universities come there'll be contracts to last out my service, I can tell you."

"Universities?" says I. "Not for the niggers, surely?"

"The native peoples," says he primly—and the little snirp hadn't been out long enough to get his nose peeled—"will soon be advanced beyond those of any country on earth. Heathen countries, that is. Lie still, you black bitch, can't you see I'm fagged out? Yes, Lord Canning is very strong on education, I believe, and spreading the gospel, too. Well, that's bricks and mortar, ain't it?—that's where to put your money, my boy."

"Dear me," says I, "at this rate I'll be out of a job, I can see."

"Military, are you? Well, don't fret, old fellow; you can always apply to be sent to the frontiers."

"Quiet as that, is it? Even round Jhansi?"

"Wherever's that, my dear chap?"

He was just a pipsqueak, of course, and knew nothing; the little yellow piece I was exercising hadn't heard of Jhansi either, and when I asked her at a venture what chapattis were good for except eating, she didn't bat an eye, but giggled and said I was a verree fonnee maan, and must buy her meringues, not chapattis, yaas? You may think I was wasting my time, sniffing about in Bombay, but it's my experience that if there's anything untoward in a country—even one as big as India—you can sometimes get a scent in the most unexpected places, just from the way the natives look and answer. But it was the same whoever I talked to, merchant or military, whore or missionary; no ripples at all. After a couple of days, when I'd got the old Urdu *bat* rolling familiarly off my palate again, I even browned up and put on a puggaree and coat and pyjamys, and loafed about the Bund bazaar, letting on I was a Mekran coast trader, and listening to the clack. I came out rotten with fleas, stinking of nautch-oil and cheap perfume and cooking *ghee*, with my ears full of beggars' whines and hawkers' jabbering and the clang of the booths—but that was all. Still, it helped to get India back under my hide again, and that's important, if you intend to do anything as a political.

Hullo, says you, what's this?—not Flashy taking his duty seriously for once, surely. Well, I was, and for a good reason. I didn't take Pam's forebodings seriously, but I knew I was bound to go to Jhansi and make some sort of showing in the task he'd given me—the thing was to do it quickly. If I could have a couple of official chats with this Rani woman, look into the business of the sepoys' cakes, and conclude that Skene, the Jhansi political, was a nervous old woman, I could fire off a report to Calcutta and withdraw gracefully. What I must not do was linger—because if there *was* any bottom to Pam's anxieties, Jhansi might be full of Ignatieff and his jackals before long, and I wanted to be well away before that happened.

So I didn't linger in Bombay. On the third day I took the road north-east towards Jhansi, travelling in good style by bullock-hackery, which is just a great wooden room on wheels, in which you have your bed and eat your meals, and your groom and cook and bearer squat on the roof. They've gone out now, of course, with the railway, but they were a nice leisurely way of travelling, and I stopped off at messes along the road, and kept my ears open. None of the talk chimed with what I'd heard at Balmoral, and the general feeling was that the country had never been so quiet. Which was heartening, even if it was what you'd expect, down-country.

I purposely kept clear of any politicals, because I wanted to form my own judgements without getting any uncomfortable news that I didn't want to hear. However, up towards Mhow, who should I run into but Johnny Nicholson, whom I hadn't seen since Afghanistan, fifteen years before, trotting along on a Persian pony and dressed like a Baluchi robber with a beard down to his belly, and a couple of Sikh lancers in tow. We fell on each other like old chums—he didn't know me well, you see, but mostly by my fearsome reputation; he was one of your play-up-and-fear-God paladins, full of zeal and athirst for glory, was John, and said his prayers and didn't drink and thought women were either nuns or mothers. He was very big by now, I discovered, and just coming down for leave before he took up as resident at Peshawar.

By rights I shouldn't have mentioned my mission to anyone, but this was too good a chance to miss. There wasn't a downier bird in all India than Nicholson, or one who knew the country better, and you could have trusted him with anything, money even. So I told him I was bound for Jhansi, and why—the chapattis, the Rani, and the Russians. He listened, fingering his beard and squinting into the distance, while we squatted by the road drinking coffee.

"Jhansi, eh?" says he. "Pindari robber country—Thugs, too. Trust you to pick the toughest nut south of the Khyber. Maharatta chieftains—wouldn't turn my back on any of 'em, and if you tell me there have been Russian agitators at work, I'm not surprised. Any number of ugly-looking copers and traders have been sliding south with the caravans up our way this year past, but not many guns, you see—that's what we keep our accounts by. But I don't like this news about chapattis passing among the sepoys."

"You don't think it amounts to anything, surely?" I found all his cheerful references to Thugs and Pindaris damned disconcerting; he was making Jhansi sound as bad as Afghanistan.

"I don't know," says he, very thoughtful. "But I do know that this whole country's getting warm. Don't ask me how I know—Irish instinct if you like. Oh, I know it looks fine from Bombay or Calcutta, but sometimes I look around and ask myself what we're sitting on, out here. Look at it—we're holding a northern frontier against the toughest villains on earth: Pathans, Sikhs, Baluchis, and Afghanistan thrown in, with Russia sitting on the touchline waiting their chance. In addition, down-country, we're nominal masters of a collection of native states, half of them wild as Barbary, ruled by princes who'd cut our throats for three-pence. Why? Because we've tried to civilise 'em—we've clipped the tyrants' wings, abolished abominations like *suttee* and *thugee*, cancelled their worst laws and instituted fair ones. We've reformed 'em until they're sick—and started the telegraph, the railroad, schools, hospitals, all the rest of it."

This sounded to me like a man riding his pet hobby; I couldn't see why any of this should do anything but please the people.

"The people don't count! They never do. It's the rulers that matter, the rajas and the nabobs—like this rani of yours in Jhansi. They've squeezed this country for centuries, and Dalhousie put a stop to it. Of course it's for the benefit of the poor folk, but they don't know that—they believe what their princes tell 'em. And what they tell 'em is that the British Sirkar is their enemy, because it stops them burning their widows, and murdering each other in the name of Kali, and will abolish their religion and force Christianity on them if it can."

"Oh, come, John," says I, "they've been saying that for years."

"Well, there's something in it." He looked troubled, in a stuffy religious way. "I'm a Christian, I hope, or try to be, and I pray I shall see the day when the Gospel is the daily bread of every poor benighted soul on this continent, and His praise is sung in a thousand churches. But I could wish our people went more carefully about it. These are a devout people, Flashman, and their beliefs, misguided though they are, must not be taken lightly. What do they think, when they hear Christianity taught in the schools—in the jails, even—and when colonels preach to their

regiments?⁵ Let the prince, or the agitator, whisper in their ears
'See how the British will trample on thy holy things, which they
respect not. See how they will make Christians of you.' They will
believe him. And they are such simple folk, and their eyes are
closed. D'you know," he went on, "there's a sect in Kashmir that
even worships *me?*"

"Good for you," says I. "D'ye take up a collection?"

"I try to reason with them—but it does no good. I tell you,
India won't be converted in a day, or in years. It must come
slowly, if surely. But our missionaries—good, worthy men—press
on apace, and cannot see the harm they may do." He sighed. "Yet
can one find it in one's heart to blame them, old fellow, when one
considers the blessings that God's grace would bring to this
darkened continent? It is very hard." And he looked stern and
nobly anguished; Arnold would have loved him. Then he frowned
and growled, and suddenly burst out:

"It wouldn't be so bad, if we weren't so confounded soft! If we
would only carry things with a high hand—the reforms, and the
missionary work, even. Either let well alone, or do the thing
properly. But we don't, you see; we take half-measures, and are
too gentle by a mile. If we are going to pull down their false gods,
and reform their old and corrupt states and amend their laws, and
make 'em worthy men and women—then let us do it with
strength! Dalhousie was strong, but I don't know about Canning.
I know if I were he, I'd bring these oily, smirking, treacherous
princes under my heel—" his eyes flashed as he ground his boot
in the dust. "I'd give 'em government, firm and fair. I'd be less
soft with the sepoys, too—and with some of our own people.
That's half the trouble—you haven't been back long enough, but
depend upon it, we send some poor specimens out to the army
nowadays, and to the Company offices. 'Broken-down tapsters and
serving men's sons', eh? Well, you'll see 'em—ignorant, slothful
fellows of poor class, and we put 'em to officer high-caste Hindoos
of ten years' service. They don't know their men, and treat 'em
like children or animals, and think of nothing but drinking and
hunting, and—and . . ." he reddened to the roots of his enormous
beard and looked aside. "Some of them consort with . . . with the
worst type of native women." He cleared his throat and patted

my arm. "There, I'm sorry, old fellow; I know it's distasteful to talk of such things, but it's true, alas."

I shook my head and said it was heart-breaking.

"Now you see why your news concerns me so? These omens at Jhansi—they may be the spark to the tinder, and I've shown you, I hope, that the tinder exists in India, because of our own blindness and softness. If we were stronger, and dealt firmly with the princes, and accompanied our enlightenment of the people with proper discipline—why, the spark would be stamped out easily enough. As it is—" he shook his head again. "I don't like it. Thank God they had the wit to send someone like you to Jhansi—I only wish I could come with you, to share whatever perils may lie ahead. It's a strange, wild place, from all I've heard," says this confounded croaker with pious satisfaction, as he shook my hand. "Come, old fellow, shall we pray together— for your safety and guidance in whatever dangers you may find yourself?"

And he plumped down there and then on his knees, with me alongside, and gave God his marching orders in no uncertain fashion, telling him to keep a sharp eye on his servant. I don't know what it was about me, but holy fellows like Nicholson were forever addressing heaven on my behalf—even those who didn't know me well seemed to sense that there was a lot of hard graft to be done if Flashy was ever to smell salvation. I can see him yet—his great dark head and long nose against the sunset, his beard quivering with exhortation, and even the freckles on the back of his clasped hands. Poor wild John—he should have canvassed the Lord on his own behalf, perhaps, for while I'm still here after half a century, he was stiff inside the year, shot in the midriff by a pandy sniper in the attack on Delhi, and left to die by inches at the roadside. That's what his duty earned for him; if he'd taken proper precautions he'd have made viceroy. And Delhi would have fallen just the same.[6]

Whatever his prayers accomplished for my solid flesh, his talk about Jhansi had done nothing for my spirits. "A strange wild place," he'd said, and talked of the Pindari bandits and Thugs and Maharatta scoundrels—well, I knew it had been hell's punch-bowl in the old days, but I'd thought since we'd annexed it that it must be quieter now. Mangles, at the Board of Control in London, had described it as "tranquil beneath the Company's benevolent rule", but he was a pompous ass with a talent for talking complete bosh about subjects on which he was an authority.

As I pushed on into Bandelkand it began to look as though he was wrong and Nicholson was right—it was broken, hilly country, with jungle on the slopes and in the valleys, never a white face to be seen, and the black ones getting uglier by the mile. The roads were so atrocious, and the hackery jolted and rolled so sickeningly, that I was forced to take to my Pegu pony; there was devil a sign of civilisation, but only walled villages and every so often a sinister Maharatta fort squatting on a hilltop to remind you who really held the power in this land. "The toughest nut south of the Khyber"—I was ready to believe it, as I surveyed those unfriendly jungly hills, seeing nothing cheerier than a distant tiger skulking among the waitabit thorn. And this was the country that we were "ruling"—with one battalion of suspect sepoy infantry and a handful of British civilians to collect the taxes.

My first sight of Jhansi city wasn't uplifting either. We rounded a bend on the hill road, and there it was under a dull evening sky—a massive fort, embattled and towered, on a great steep rock, and the walled city clustered at its foot. It was far bigger than I'd imagined; the walls must have been four miles round at least, and the air over the city was thick with the smoke of a thousand cooking fires. On this side of the city lay the orderly white lines of the British camp and cantonment—God, it looked tiny and feeble, beneath that looming vastness of Jhansi fort. My mind went back to Kabul, and how our camp had seemed dwarfed by the Bala Hissar—and even at Kabul, with an army of ten thousand, only a handful of us had escaped. I told myself that here it was different—that less than a hundred miles ahead of me there were our great garrisons along the Grand Trunk, and that however forbidding Jhansi might look, it was a British state nowadays, and under the Sirkar's protection. Only there wasn't much sign of that protection—just our pathetic little village like a flea on the lion's lip, and somewhere in that great citadel, where our troops never went, that brooding old bitch of a Rani scheming against us, with her thousands of savage subjects waiting for her word. Thus my imagination—as if it hadn't been full enough already, what with Ignatieff and Thugs and wild Pindaris and dissident sepoys and Nicholson's forebodings.

My first task was to look up Skene, the political whose reports had started the whole business, so I headed down to the cantonment, which was a neat little compound of perhaps forty bungalows, with decent gardens, and the usual groups already meeting on the verandahs for sundown pegs and cordials; there were a few carriages waiting with their grooms and drivers to take people out for dinner, and one or two officers riding home, but I drove straight through, and got a *chowkidar's* direction to the little Star Fort, where Skene had his office—he'd still be there, the *chowkidar* said, which argued a very conscientious political indeed.

Frankly, I hoped to find him scared or stupid; he wasn't either. He was one of these fair, intent young fellows who fall over themselves to help, and will work all the hours God sends. He hopped from one leg to another when I presented myself, and seemed fairly overwhelmed to meet the great Flashy, but the steady grey eye told you at once that here was a boy who didn't take alarm at trifles. He had clerks and bearers running in all directions to take my gear to quarters, saw to it that I was given a bath, and then bore me off for dinner at his own bungalow, where he lost no time in getting down to business.

"No one knows why you're here, sir, except me," says he. "I believe Carshore, the Collector, suspects, but he's a sound man, and will say nothing. Of course, Erskine, the Commissioner at Saugor, knows all about it, but no one else." He hesitated. "I'm not quite clear myself, sir, why they sent you out, and not someone from Calcutta."

"Well, they wanted an assassin, you see," says I, easily, just for bounce. "It so happens I'm acquainted with the Russian gentleman who's been active in these parts—and dealing with him ain't a job for an ordinary political, what?" It was true, after all; Pam himself had said it. "Also, it seems Calcutta and yourself and Commissioner Erskine—with all respect—haven't been too successful with this titled lady up in the city palace. Then there

are these cakes; all told, it seemed better to Lord Palmerston to
send me."

"Lord Palmerston?" says he, his eyes wide open. "I didn't know
it had gone that far."

I assured him he'd been the cause of the Prime Minister's losing
a night's sleep, and he whistled and reached for the decanter.

"That's neither here nor there, anyway," says I. "You cost *me*
a night's sleep, too, for that matter. The first thing is: have any
of these Russian fellows been back this way?"

To my surprise, he looked confused. "Truth is, sir—I never
knew they'd been near. That came to me from Calcutta—our
frontier people traced them down this way, three times, I believe,
and I was kept informed. But if they hadn't told me, I'd never
have known."

That rattled me, if you like. "You mean, if they *do* come back—
or if they're loose in your bailiwick now—you won't know of it
until Calcutta sees fit to tell you?"

"Oh, our frontier politicals will send me word as soon as any
suspected person crosses over," says he. "And I have my own
native agents on the look-out now—some pretty sharp men, sir."

"They know especially to look out for a one-eyed man?"

"Yes, sir—he has a curious deformity which he hides with a
patch, you know—one of his eyes is half-blue, half-brown."

"You don't say," says I. By George, I hadn't realised our
political arrangements were as ramshackle as this. "That, Captain
Skene, is the man I'm here to kill—so if any of your...sharp
men have the chance to save me the trouble, they may do it with
my blessing."

"Oh, of course, sir. Oh, they will, you know. Some of them,"
says he, impressively, "are Pindari bandits—or used to be, that is.
But we'll know in good time, sir, before any of these Ruski fellows
get within distance."

I wished I could share his confidence. "Calcutta has no notion
what the Russian spies were up to down here?" I asked him, but
he shook his head.

"Nothing definite at all—only that they'd been here. We were
sure it must be connected with the chapattis going round, but
those have dried up lately. None have passed since October, and

the sepoys of the 12th N.I.—that's the regiment here, you know—seem perfectly quiet. Their colonel swears they're loyal—has done from the first, and was quite offended that I reported the cakes to Calcutta. Perhaps he's right; I've had some of my men scouting the sepoy lines, and they haven't heard so much as a murmur. And Calcutta was to inform me if cakes passed at any other place, but none have, apparently."

Come, thinks I, this is decidedly better; Pam's been up a gum-tree for nothing. All I had to do was make a show of brief activity here, and then loaf over to Calcutta after a few weeks and report nothing doing. Give 'em a piece of my mind, too, for causing me so much inconvenience.

"Well, Skene," says I, "this is how I see it. There's nothing to be done about what the Prime Minister calls 'those blasted buns' —unless they make a reappearance, what? As to the Russians— well, *when* we get word of them, I'll probably drop out of sight, d'you see?" I would, too—to some convenient haven which the Lord would provide, and emerge when the coast was clear. But I doubted it would even come to that. "Yes, you won't see me— but I'll be about, never fear, and if our one-eyed friend, or any of his creatures, shows face . . . well . . ."

He looked suitably impressed, with a hint of that awe which my fearsome reputation inspires. "I understand, sir. You'll wish to . . . er, work in your own way, of course." He blinked at me, and then exclaimed reverently: "By jove, I don't envy those Ruski fellows above half—if you don't mind my saying so, sir."

"Skene, old chap," says I, and winked at him. "Neither do I." And believe me, he was my slave for life, from that moment.

"There's the other thing," I went on. "The Rani. I have to try to talk some sense into her. Now, I daresay there isn't much I can do, since I gather she's shown you and Erskine that she's not disposed to be friendly, but I'm bound to try, you see. So I'll be obliged to you if you'll arrange an audience for me the day after tomorrow—I'd like to rest and perhaps look around the city first. For the present, you can tell me your own opinion of her."

He frowned, and filled my glass. "You'll think it's odd, sir, I daresay, but in all the time I've been here, I've never even seen her. I've met her, frequently, at the palace, but she speaks from behind a purdah, you know—and as often as not her chamberlain does the talking for her. She's a stickler for form, and since government granted her diplomatic immunity after her husband died—as a sop, really, when we assumed suzerainty—well, it makes it difficult to deal with her satisfactorily. She was friendly enough with Erskine at one time—but I've had no change out of her at all. She's damned bitter, you see—when her husband died, old Raja Gangadar, he left no children of his own—well, he was an odd bird, really," and Skene blushed furiously and avoided my eye. "Used to go about in female dress most of the time, and wore bangles and . . . and perfume, you see—"

"No wonder she was bitter," says I.

"No, no, what I mean is, since he left no legitimate heir, but only a boy whom he'd adopted, Dalhousie wouldn't recognise the infant. The new succession law, you know. So the state was annexed—and the Rani was furious, and petitioned the Queen, and sent agents to London, but it was no go. The adopted son, Damodar, was dispossessed, and the Rani, who'd hoped to be regent, was deprived of her power—officially. Between ourselves, we let her rule pretty well as she pleases—well, we can't do otherwise, can we? We've one battalion of sepoys, and thirty British civilians to run the state administration—but she's the law, where her people are concerned, absolute as Caesar."

"Doesn't that satisfy her, then?"

"Not a bit of it. She detests the fact that officially she only holds power by the Sirkar's leave, you see. And she's still wild about the late Raja's will—you'd think that with a quarter of a million in her treasury she'd be content, but there was some jewellery or other that Calcutta confiscated, and she's never forgiven us."

"Interesting lady," says I. "Dangerous, d'you think?"

He frowned. "Politically, yes. Given the chance, she'd pay our score off, double quick—that's why the chapatti business upset me. She's got no army, as such—but with every man in Jhansi a born fighter, and robber, she don't need one, do she? And they'll jump if she whistles, for they worship the ground she treads on. She's proud as Lucifer's sister, and devilish hard, not to say cruel, in her own courts, but she's uncommon kind to the poor folk, and highly thought of for her piety—spends five hours a day meditating, although she was a wild piece, they say, when she was a girl. They brought her up like a Maharatta prince at the old Peshwa's court—taught her to ride and shoot and fence with the best of them. They say she still has the fiend's own temper," he added, grinning, "but she's always been civil enough to me— at a distance. But make no mistake, she's dangerous; if you can sweeten her, sir, we'll all sleep a deal easier at nights."

There was that, of course. However withered an old trot she might be, she'd be an odd female if she was altogether impervious to Flashy's manly bearing and cavalry whiskers—which was probably what Pam had in mind in the first place. Cunning old devil. Still, as I turned in that night I wasn't absolutely looking forward to poodle-faking her in two days' time, and as I glanced from my bungalow window and saw Jhansi citadel beetling in the starlight, I thought, we'll take a nice little escort of lancers with us when we go to take tea with the lady, so we will.

But that was denied me. I had intended to pass the next day looking about the city, perhaps having a discreet word with Carshore the Collector and the colonel of the sepoys, but as the *syce*** was bringing round my pony to the dak-bungalow, up comes Skene in a flurry. When he'd sent word to the palace that Colonel Flashman, a distinguished soldier of the Sirkar, was seeking an audience for the following day, he'd been told that distinguished visitors were expected to present themselves immediately as a token of proper respect to her highness, and Colonel Flashman could shift his distinguished rump up to the palace forthwith.

"I . . . I thought in the circumstances of your visit," says Skene, apologetically, "that you might think it best to comply."

"You did, did you?" says I. "Does every Briton in Jhansi leap to attention when this beldam snaps her fingers, then?"

"Shall we say, we find it convenient to humour her highness," says he—he was more of a political than he looked, this lad, so I blustered a bit, to be in character, and then said he might find me an escort of lancers to convoy me in.

"I'm sorry, sir," says he. "We haven't any lancers—and if we had, we've agreed not to send troop formations inside the city

* Groom.

walls. Also, since I was excluded from the, er ... invitation, I
fear you must go alone."

"What?" says I. "Damnation, who governs here—the Sirkar
or this harridan?" I didn't fancy above half risking my hide
unguarded in that unhealthy-looking fortress, but I had to cover
it with dignity. "You've made a rod for your own backs by being
too soft with this ... this woman. She's not Queen Bess, you know!"

"She thinks she is," says he cheerfully, so in the end of course
I had to lump it. But I changed into my lancer fig first, sabre,
revolver and all—for I could guess why she was ensuring that I
visited her alone: up-country, on the frontier, they judge a man
on his own looks, but down here they go on the amount and
richness of your retinue. One mounted officer wasn't going to
impress the natives with the Sirkar's power—well, then, he'd look
his best, and be damned to her. So I figged up, and when I
regarded myself in Skene's cracked mirror—blue tunic and
breeches, gold belt and epaulettes, white gauntlets and helmet,
well-bristled whiskers, and Flashy's stalwart fourteen stone inside
it all, it wasn't half bad. I took a couple of packages from my
trunk, stowed them in my saddle-bag, waved to Skene, and trotted
off to meet royalty, with only the syce to show me the way.

Jhansi city lies about a couple of miles from the cantonment,
and I had plenty of time to take in the scenery. The road, which
was well-lined with temples and smaller buildings, was crowded
into the city, with bullock-carts churning up the dust, camels,
palankeens, and hordes of travellers both mounted and on foot.
Most of them were country folk, on their way to the bazaars, but
every now and then would come an elephant with red and gold
fringed howdah swaying along, carrying some minor nabob or
rich lady, or a portly merchant on his mule with a string of porters
behind, and once the syce pointed out a group who he said were
members of the Rani's own bodyguard—a dozen stalwart Khyberie
Pathans, of all things, trotting along very military in double file,
with mail coats and red silk scarves wound round their spiked
helmets. The Rani might not have an army, but she wasn't short
of force, with those fellows about: there was a hundred years'
Company service among them if there was a day.

And her city defences were a sight to see—massive walls twenty

feet high, and beyond them a warren of streets stretching for near
a mile to the castle rock, with its series of curtain walls and round
towers—it would be the deuce of a place to storm, after you'd
fought through the city itself; there were guns in the embrasures,
and mail-clad spearmen on the walls, all looking like business.

We had to force our horses through a crowded inferno of heat
and smells and noise and jostling niggers to get to the palace,
which stood apart from the fort near a small lake, with a shady
park about it; it was a fine, four-square building, its outer walls
beautifully decorated with huge paintings of battles and hunting
scenes. I presented myself to another Pathan, very splendid in
steel back-and-breast and long-tail *puggaree*,* who commanded
the gate guard, and sat sweating in the scorching sun while he
sent off a messenger for the chamberlain. And as I chafed
impatiently, the Pathan walked slowly round me, eyeing me up
and down, and presently stopped, stuck his thumbs in his belt,
and spat carefully on my shadow.

Now, close by the gate there happened to be a number of booths
and side-shows set up—the usual things, lemonade-sellers, a fakir
with a plant growing through his palm, sundry beggars, and a
kind of punch-and-judy show, which was being watched by a
group of ladies in a palankeen. As a matter of fact, they'd already
taken my eye, for they were obviously Maharatta females of
quality, and four finer little trotters you never saw. There was a
very slim, languid-looking beauty in a gold sari reclining in the
palankeen, another plump piece in scarlet trousers and jacket
beside her, and a third, very black, but fine-boned as a Swede,
with a pearl headdress that must have cost my year's pay, sitting
in a kind of camp-chair alongside—even the ladies' maid standing
beside the palankeen was a looker, with great almond eyes and a
figure inside her plain white sari like a Hindoo temple goddess. I
was in the act of touching my hat to them when the Pathan
started expectorating. At this the maid giggled, the ladies looked,
and the Pathan sniffed contemptuously and spat again.

Well, as a rule anyone can insult me and see how much it pays
him, especially if he's large and ugly and carrying a *tulwar*.† But

* Turban.
† A sword.

for the credit of the Sirkar, and my own face in front of the
women, I had to do something, so I looked the Pathan up and
down, glanced away, and said quietly in Pushtu:

"You would spit more carefully if you were still in the Guides,
hubshi."*

He opened his eyes at that, and swore. "Who calls me hubshi?
Who says I was in the Guides? And what is it to thee, feringheet
pig?"

"You wear the old coat under your breastplate," says I. "But
belike you stole it from a dead Guide. For no man who had a right
to that uniform would spit on Bloody Lance's shadow."

That set him back on his heels. "Bloody Lance?" says he.
"Thou?" He came closer and stared up at me. "Art thou that
same Iflass-man who slew the four Gilzais?"

"At Mogala," says I mildly. It had caused a great stir at the
time, in the Gilzai country, and won me considerable fame (and
my extravagant nickname) along the Kabul road—in fact, old
Mohammed Iqbal had killed the four horsemen, while I lit out
for the undergrowth, but nobody living knew that.‡ And
obviously the legend endured, for the Pathan gaped and swore
again, and then came hastily to attention and threw me a barra
salaam§ that would have passed at Horse Guards.

"Sher Khan, havildar,¶ lately of Ismeet Sahib's company of the
Guides,⁷ as your honour says," croaks he. "Now, shame on me
and mine that I put dishonour on Bloody Lance, and knew him
not! Think not ill of me, husoor,‖ for—"

"Let the ill think ill," says I easily. "The spittle of a durwan**
will not drown a soldier." I was watching out of the corner of my
eye to see how the ladies were taking this, and noted with
satisfaction that they were giggling at the Pathan's discomfiture.
"Boast to your children, O Ghazi††-that-was-a-Guide-and-is-now-a-
Rani's-porter, that you spat on Bloody Lance Iflass-man's shadow—

* Literally "woolly-haired"—a negro.
† Christian, a white man.
‡ See Flashman.
§ Great salute.
¶ Sergeant.
‖ Sir, Lord.
** Door-keeper.
†† Hero.

and lived." And I walked my horse past him into the courtyard, well pleased; it would be all round Jhansi inside the hour.

It was a trifling enough incident, and I forgot it with my first glance at the interior of the Rani's palace. Outside it had been all dust and heat and din, but here was the finest garden courtyard you ever saw—a cool, pleasant enclosure where little antelopes and peacocks strutted on the lawns, parrots and monkeys chattered softly in the surrounding trees, and a dazzling white fountain played; there were shaded archways in the carved walls, where well-dressed folk whom I took to be her courtiers sat and talked, waited on by bearers. One of the richest thrones in India, Pam had said, and I could believe it—there were enough silks and jewellery on view there to stuff an army with loot, the statuary was of the finest, in marble and coloured stones that I took to be jade, and even the pigeons that pecked at the spotless pavements had silver rings on their claws. Until you've seen it, of course, you can't imagine the luxury in which these Indian princes keep themselves—and there are folk at home who'll tell you that John Company were the robbers!

I was kept waiting there a good hour before a major-domo came, salaaming, to lead me through the inner gate and up a narrow winding stair to the durbar room on the first storey; here again all was richness—splendid silk curtains on the walls, great chandeliers of purple crystal hanging from the carved and gilded ceiling, magnificent carpets on the floor (with good old Axminster there among the Persian, I noticed) and every kind of priceless ornament, gold and ivory, ebony and silverwork, scattered about. It would have been in damned bad taste if it hadn't all been so bloody expensive, and the dozen or so men and women who lounged about on the couches and cushions were dressed to match; the ones down in the courtyard must have been their poor relations. Handsome as Hebe the women were, too—I was just running my eye over one alabaster beauty in tight scarlet trousers who was reclining on a shawl, playing with a parakeet, when a gong boomed somewhere, everyone stood up, and a fat little chap in a huge turban waddled in and announced that the durbar had begun. At which music began to play, and they all turned and bowed to the wall, which I suddenly realised wasn't a wall at all, but a colossal ivory screen, fine as lace, that cut the room in two. Through it you could just make out movement in the space beyond, like shadows behind thick gauze; this was the Rani's purdah screen, to keep out prying heathen eyes like mine.

I seemed to be first man in, for the chamberlain led me to a little gilt stool a few feet from the screen, and there I sat while he stood at one end of the screen and cried out my name, rank, decorations, and (it's a fact) my London clubs; there was a murmur of voices beyond, and then he asked me what I wanted, or words to that effect. I replied, in Urdu, that I brought greetings from Queen Victoria, and a gift for the Rani from her majesty, if she would graciously accept it. (It was a perfectly hellish photograph of Victoria and Albert looking in apparent stupefaction at a book which the Prince of Wales was holding in an attitude of sullen defiance; all in a silver frame, too, and wrapped up in muslin.) I handed it over, the chamberlain passed it through, listened attentively, and then asked me who the fat child in the picture was. I told him, he relayed the glad news, and then announced that her highness was pleased to accept her sister-ruler's gift—the effect was spoiled a trifle by a clatter from behind the screen which suggested the picture had fallen on the floor (or been thrown), but I just stroked my whiskers while the courtiers tittered behind me. It's hell in the diplomatic, you know.

There was a further exchange of civilities, through the chamberlain, and then I asked for a private audience with the Rani; he replied that she never gave them. I explained that what I had to say was of mutual but private interest to Jhansi and the British government; he looked behind the screen for instructions, and then said hopefully:

"Does that mean you have proposals for the restoration of her highness's throne, the recognition of her adopted son, and the restitution of her property—all of which have been stolen from her by the Sirkar?"

Well, it didn't, of course. "What I have to say is for her highness alone," says I, solemnly, and he stuck his head round the screen and conferred, before popping back.

"There are such proposals?" says he, and I said I could not talk in open durbar, at which there were sounds of rapid female muttering from behind the screen. The chamberlain asked what I could have to say that could not be said by Captain Skene, and I said politely that I could tell that to the Rani, and no other. He conferred again, and I tried to picture the other side of the screen, with the Rani, sharp-faced and thin in her silk shawl, muttering her instructions to him, and puzzled to myself what the odd persistent noise was that I could hear above the soft pipes of the hidden orchestra—a gentle, rhythmic swishing from beyond the screen, as though a huge fan were being used. And yet the room was cool and airy enough not to need one.

The chamberlain popped out again, looking stern, and said that her highness could see no reason for prolonging the interview; if I had nothing new from the Sirkar to impart to her, I was permitted to withdraw. So I got to my feet, clicked my heels, saluted the screen, picked up the second package which I had brought, thanked him and his mistress for their courtesy, and did a smart about-turn. But I hadn't gone a yard before he stopped me.

"The packet you carry," says he. "What is that?"

I'd been counting on this; I told him it was my own.

"But it is wrapped as the gift to her highness was wrapped," says he. "Surely it also is a present."

"Yes," says I, slowly. "It was." He stared, was summoned behind the screen, and came out looking anxious.

"Then you may leave it behind," says he.

I hesitated, weighing the packet in my hand, and shook my head. "No, sir," says I. "It was my own personal present, to her highness—but in my country we deliver such gifts face to face, as honouring both giver and receiver. By your leave," and I bowed again to the screen and walked away.

"Wait, wait!" cries he, so I did; the rhythmic sound from behind the screen had stopped now, and the female voice was talking quickly again. The chamberlain came out, red-faced, and to my astonishment he bustled everyone else from the room, shooing the silken ladies and gentlemen like geese. Then he turned to me, bowed, indicated the screen, and effaced himself through one of the archways, leaving me alone with my present in my hand. I listened a moment; the swishing sound had started again.

I paused to give my whiskers a twirl, stepped up to the end of

the screen, and rapped on it with my knuckles. No reply. So I
said: "Your highness?", but there was nothing except that damned
swishing. Well, here goes, I thought; this is what you came to
India for, and you must be civil and adoring, for old Pam's sake.
I stepped round the screen, and halted as though I'd walked into
a wall.

It wasn't the gorgeously-carved golden throne, or the splendour
of the furniture which outshone even what I'd left, or the
unexpected sensation of walking on the shimmering Chinese quilt
on the floor. Nor was it the bewildering effect of the mirrored
ceiling and walls, with their brilliantly-coloured panels. The
astonishing thing was that from the ceiling there hung, by silk
ropes, a great cushioned swing, and sitting in it, wafting gently
to and fro, was a girl—the only soul in the room. And such a
girl—my first impression was of great, dark, almond eyes in a
skin the colour of milky coffee, with a long straight nose above
a firm red mouth and chin, and hair as black as night that hung
in a jewelled tail down her back. She was dressed in a white silk
bodice and sari which showed off the dusky satin of her bare
arms and midriff, and on her head was a little white jewelled cap
from which a single pearl swung on her forehead above the caste-
mark.

I stood and gaped while she swung to and fro at least three
times, and then she put a foot on the carpet and let the swing
drag to a halt. She considered me, one smooth dusky arm up on
the swing rope—and then I recognised her: she was the ladies'
maid who had been standing by the palankeen at the palace gate.
The Rani's maid?—then the lady of the palankeen must be . . .

"Your mistress?" says I. "Where is she?"

"Mistress? I have no mistress," says she, tilting up her chin and
looking down her nose at me. "I am Lakshmibai, Maharani of
Jhansi."

For a moment I didn't believe it: I had become so used to picturing her over the past three months as a dried-up old shrew with skinny limbs that I just stood and gaped.[8] And yet, as I looked at her, there couldn't be any doubt: the richness of her clothes shouted royalty at you, and the carriage of her head, with its imperious dark eyes, told you as nothing else could that here was a woman who'd never asked permission in her life. There was strength in every line of her, too, for all her femininity—by George, I couldn't remember when I'd seen bouncers like those, thrusting like pumpkins against the muslin of her blouse, which was open to the jewelled clasp at her breast bone—if it hadn't been for a couple of discreetly embroidered flowers on either side, there would have been nothing at all to hide. I could only stand speechless before such queenly beauty, wondering what it would be like to tear the muslin aside, thrust your whiskers in between 'em, and go brrrrr!

"You have a gift to present," says she, speaking in a quick, soft voice which had me recollecting myself and clicking my heels as I presented my packet. She took it, weighed it in her hand, still half-reclining in her swing, and asked sharply: "Why do you stare at me so?"

"Forgive me, highness," says I. "I did not expect to find a queen who looked so..." I'd been about to say "young and lovely", but changed it hurriedly for a less personal compliment. "So like a queen."

"Like that queen?" says she, and indicated the picture of Vicky and Albert, which was lying on a cushion.

"Each of your majesties," says I, with mountainous diplomacy, "looks like a queen in her own way."

She considered me gravely, and then held the packet out to me. "You may open it."

I pulled off the wrapping, opened the little box, and took out the gift. You may smile, but it was a bottle of perfume—you see, Flashy ain't as green as he looks; it may be coals to Newcastle to take perfume to India, but in my experience, which isn't inconsiderable, there's not a woman breathing who isn't touched by a gift of scent, and it don't matter what age she is, either. And it was just the gift a blunt, honest soldier would choose, in his simplicity—furthermore, it was from Paris, and had cost the dirty old goat who presented it to Elspeth a cool five sovs. (She'd never miss it.) I handed it over with a little bow, and she touched the stopper daintily on her wrist.

"French," says she. "And very costly. Are you a rich man, colonel?"

That took me aback; I muttered something about not calling on a queen every day of my life.

"And why have you called?" says she, very cool. "What is there that you have to say that can be said only face to face?" I hesitated, and she suddenly stood up in one lithe movement—by jove, they jumped like blancmanges in a gale. "Come and tell me," she went on, and swept off out on to the terrace at that end of the room, with a graceful swaying stride that stirred the seat of her sari in a most disturbing way. She jingled as she walked—like all rich Indian females, she seemed to affect as much jewellery as she could carry, with bangles at wrist and ankle, a diamond collar beneath her chin, and even a tiny pearl cluster at one nostril. I followed, admiring the lines of the tall, full figure, and wondering for the umpteenth time what I *should* say to her, now that the moment had come.

Pam and Mangles, you see, had given me no proper directions at all: I was supposed to wheedle her into being a loyal little British subject, but I'd no power to make concessions to any of her grievances. And it wasn't going to be easy; an unexpected stunner she might be, and therefore all the easier for me to talk to, but there was a directness about her that was daunting. This was a queen, and intelligent and experienced (she even knew French perfume when she smelled it); she wasn't going to be impressed by polite political chat. So what must I say? The devil with it, thinks I, there's nothing to lose by being as blunt as she is herself.

So when she'd settled herself on a daybed, and I'd forced myself to ignore that silky naked midriff and the shapely brown ankle peeping out of her sari, I set my helmet on the ground and stood up four-square.

"Your highness," says I, "I can't talk like Mr Erskine, or Captain Skene even. I'm a soldier, not a diplomat, so I won't mince words." And thereafter I minced them for all I was worth, telling her of the distress there was in London about the coolness that existed between Jhansi on the one hand and the Company and Sirkar on the other; how this state of affairs had endured for four years to the disadvantage of all parties; how it was disturbing the Queen, who felt a sisterly concern for the ruler of Jhansi not only as a monarch, but as a woman, and so on—I rehearsed Jhansi's grievances, the willingness of the Sirkar to repair them so far as was possible, threw in the information that I came direct from Lord Palmerston, and finished on a fine flourish with an appeal to her to open her heart to Flashy, plenipotentiary extraordinary, so that we could all be friends and live happy ever after. It was the greatest gammon, but I gave it my best, with noble compassion in my eye and a touch of ardour in the curl shaken down over my brow. She heard me out, not a muscle moving in that lovely face, and then asked:

"You have the power to make redress, then? To alter what has been done?"

I said I had the power to report direct to Pam, and she said that so, in effect, had Skene. Her agents in London had spoken direct to the Board of Control, without avail.

"Well," says I, "this is a little different, highness, don't you see? His lordship felt that if I heard from you at first-hand, so to speak, and we talked—"

"There is nothing to talk about," says she. "What can I say that has not been said—that the Sirkar does not know? What can you—"

"I can ask, maharaj', what actions by the Sirkar, short of removing from Jhansi and recognising your adopted son, would satisfy your grievances—or go some way to satisfying them."

She came up on one elbow at that, frowning at me with those magnificent eyes. For what I was hinting at—without the least authority, mind you—was concessions, and devil a smell of those she'd had in four years.

"Why," says she, thoughtfully. "They know well enough. They have been told my grievances, my just demands, for four years now. And yet they have denied me. How can repetition serve?"

"A disappointed client may find a new advocate," says I, with my most disarming smile, and she gave me a long stare, and then got up and walked over to the balustrade, looking out across the city. "If your highness would speak your mind to me, openly—"

"Wait," says she, and stood for a moment, frowning, before she turned back to me. She couldn't think what to make of this; she was suspicious, and didn't dare to hope, and yet she was wondering. God, she was a black beauty, sure enough—if I'd been the Sirkar, she could have had Jhansi and a pound of tea with it, just for half an hour on the daybed.

"If Lord Palmerston," says she at last—and old Pam himself would have been tempted to restore her throne just to hear the pretty way she said "Lud Pammer-stan"—"wishes me to restate the wrongs that have been done me, it can only be because he has discovered some interest to serve by redressing them—or promising redress. I do not know what that interest is, and you will not tell me. It is no charitable desire to set right injustices done to my Jhansi—" and she lifted her head proudly. "That is certain. But if he wishes my friendship, for whatever purpose of his own, he may give an earnest of his good will by restoring the revenues which should have come to me since my husband's death, but which the Sirkar has confiscated." She stopped there, chin up, challenging, so I said:

"And after that, highness? What else?"

"Will he concede as much? Will the Company?"

"I can't say," says I. "But if a strong case can be made—when I report to Lord Palmerston . . ."

"And you will put the case, yourself?"

"That is my mission, maharaj'."

"And such other . . . cases . . . as I may advance?" She looked the question, and there was just a hint of a smile on her mouth. "So. And I must first put them to you—and no doubt you will suggest to me how they may best be phrased . . . or modified. You will advise, and . . . persuade?"

"Well," says I, "I'll help your highness as I can . . ."

To my astonishment she laughed, with a flash of white teeth, her head back, and shaking most delightfully.

"Oh, the subtlety of the British!" cries she. "Such delicacy, like an elephant in a swamp! Lord Palmerston wishes, for his own mysterious reasons of policy, to placate the Rani of Jhansi. So he invites her to repeat the petition which has been repeatedly denied for years. But does he send a lawyer, or an advocate, or even an official of the Company? No—just a simple soldier, who will discuss the petition with her, and how it may best be presented to his lordship. Could not a lawyer have advised her better?" She folded her hands and came slowly forward, sauntering round me. "But how many lawyers are tall and broad-shouldered and . . . aye, quite handsome—and persuasive as Flashman *bahadur*?* Not a doubt but *he* is best fitted to convince a silly female that a modest claim is most likely to succeed—and she will abate her demands for *him*, poor foolish girl, and be less inclined to insist on fine points, and stand upon her rights. Is this not so?"

"Highness, you misunderstand entirely . . . I assure you—"

"Do I?" says she, scornfully, but laughing still. "I am not sixteen, colonel; I am an old lady of twenty-nine. And I may not know Lord Palmerston's purpose, but I understand his methods. Well, well. It may not have occurred to his lordship that even a poor Indian lady may be persuasive in her turn." And she eyed me with some amusement, confident in her own beauty, the damned minx, and the effect it was having on me. "He paid me a poor compliment, do you not think?"

What could I do but grin back at her? "Do his lordship justice, highness," says I. "He'd never seen you. How many have, since you are *purdah-nishin*?"†

"Enough to have told him what I am like, I should have hoped. How did he instruct you—humour her, whatever she is, fair or foul, young and silly or old and ugly? Charm her, so that she keeps her demands cheap? Captivate her, as only a hero can." She

---

* Title of honour, champion.
† Literally, "one who sits behind a curtain".

stirred an eyebrow. "Who could resist the champion who killed the four Gilzais—where was it?"

"At Mogala, in Afghanistan—as your highness heard at the gate. Was it to test me that you had the Pathan spit on my shadow?"

"His insolence needed no instruction," says she. "He is now being flogged for it." She turned away from me and sauntered back into the durbar-room. "You may have the tongue which insulted you torn out, if you wish," she added over her shoulder.

That brought me up sharp, I can tell you. We'd been rallying away famously, and I'd all but forgotten who and what she was —an Indian prince, with all the capricious cruelty of her kind under that lovely hide. Unless she was just mocking me with the reminder—whether or no, I would play my character.

"Not necessary, highness," says I. "I had forgotten him."

She nodded, and struck a little silver gong with her wrist-bangle. "It is time for my noon meal, and this afternoon I hold my court. You may return tomorrow, and we shall discuss the representations you are to make to the subtle Lord Palmerston." She smiled slightly in dismissal. "And I thank you for your gift, colonel."

Her maids were coming in, and the little fat chamberlain, so I made my bow.

"Maharaj'," says I. "Your most humble obedient."

She inclined her head regally, and turned away, but as I backed out round the screen I noticed that she had picked up my perfume-bottle from the table, and was inviting her maids to have a sniff at it.

I came away from that audience thinking no small diplomatic beer of myself. At least I seemed to have got further with her than any other representative of the Sirkar had ever done, even if I'd had to lie truth out of Jhansi to do it. God knew I'd not the slightest right to promise redress of any of her grievances against the Raj, and if I trotted back a list of them to London the Board would turn 'em down flat again, no question. But she didn't know that, and if I could jolly her along for a week or two, hinting at this or that possible concession, she might grow more friendly disposed—which was what Pam wanted, after all. Her hopes would revive, and while they were sure to be dashed in the end, I'd be back snug in England by then.

That was the official aspect, of course; the important thing was the delightful surprise that the old beldam of Jhansi was as prime a goer as ever wriggled a hip, and just ripe for my kind of diplomacy. She was a cocky bitch, with a fine sense of her queenly consequence, but I wasn't fooled by her airs, or the set-down she'd tried to give me by warning me not to try to come round her with whiskery blandishments. That was pure flirtation, to put me on my mettle—I know these beauties, you see, and it don't matter whether they're queens or commoners, when they start to play the cool, mocking grand dame it's a sure sign that they're wondering what kind of a mount you'll make. I'd seen the glint in this one's eye when she walked round me, and thought quietly to myself, we'll have you gasping for more, my girl, before this fortnight's out.

You may think me a presumptuous ambassador on short notice, especially where the object of my carnal ambitions was royal, clever, dangerously powerful, and a high-caste Hindoo lady of reputed purity to boot. But that means nothing when a woman fancies a buck like me; besides, I knew about these high-born Indian wenches—randy as ferrets, the lot of them, and with all the opportunity to gratify it, too. A woman with a shape and face like Lakshmibai's hadn't let it go to waste in four years' widowhood (after being married to some prancing old quean, too), not with the stallions of her palace guard available at the crook of her little finger. Well, I'd make a rare change of bedding for her—and if her lusty inclinations needed any prompting, she might find it in the thought that being amiable to ambassador Flashy was the likeliest way of getting what she wanted for herself and her state. Dulce et decorum est pro patria rogeri, she could say to herself—and I cantered back to the cantonments full of cheery thoughts, imagining what that voluptuous tawny body would look like when I peeled the sari off it, and speculating on the novel uses to which the pair of us could put that swing of hers, in the interests of diplomatic relations.

In the meantime, I had Pam's other business to attend to, so I spent the afternoon in the Native Infantry lines, looking at the

Company sepoys to gauge for myself what their temper was. I did it idly enough, for they seemed a properly smart and docile lot, and yet it was a momentous visit. For it led to an encounter that was to save my life, and set me on one of the queerest and most terrifying adventures of my career, and perhaps shaped the destiny of British India, too.

I had just finished chatting to a group of the *jawans*,* and telling 'em that in my view they'd never be called on to serve overseas, in spite of the new act,⁹ when the officer with me— fellow called Turnbull—asked me if I'd like to look at the irregular horse troop who had their stables close by. Being a cavalryman, I said yes, and a fine mixed bunch they were, too, Punjabis and frontiersmen mostly, big, strapping ruffians with oiled whiskers and their shirts inside their breeches, laughing and joking as they worked on their leather, and as different from the smooth-faced infantry as Cheyennes are from hottentots. I was having a good crack with them, for these were the kind of scoundrels with whom I'd ridden (albeit reluctantly) in my Afghan days, when their *rissaldar*† came up—and at the sight of me he stopped dead in the stable door, gaping as though he couldn't believe his eyes. He was a huge, bearded Ghazi of a fellow, Afghan for certain by the devil's face of him—I'd have said Gilzai or Dourani —with a skull cap on the back of his head, and the old yellow coat of Skinner's riders over his shoulders.¹⁰

"Jehannum!" says he, and stared again, and then stuck his hands on his hips and roared with laughter.

"Salaam, *rissaldar*," says I, "what do you want with me?"

"A sight of thy left wrist, Bloody Lance," says he, grinning like a death's head. "Is there not a scar, there, to match this?—" and he pulled up his sleeve, while I stared in disbelief at the little puckered mark, for the man who bore it should have been dead, fifteen years ago—and he'd been a mere slip of a Gilzai boy when it had been made, with his bleeding fore-arm against mine, and his mad father, Sher Afzul, doing the honours and howling to heaven that his son's life was pledged eternally to the service of the White Queen.

* Soldiers.
† Native officer commanding a cavalry troop.

"Ilderim?" says I, flabbergasted. "Ilderim Khan, of Mogala?" And then he flung his arms round me, roaring, and danced me about while the *sowars** grinned and nudged each other.

"Flashman!" He pounded my back. "How many years since ye took me for the Sirkar? Stand still, old friend, and let me see thee! Bismillah, thou hast grown high and heavy in the service —such a *barra sahib*,† and a colonel, too! Now praise God for the sight of thee!"

And then he was showing me off to his fellows, telling them how we'd met in the old Kabul days, when his father had held the passes south, and how I'd killed the four Gilzais (strange, the same lying legend coming up twice in a day), and he'd been pledged to me as a hostage, and we'd lost sight of each other in the Great Retreat. It's all there, in my earlier memoirs, and pretty gruesome, too, even if it was the basis of my glorious career.‡

So now it was Speech Day with a vengeance, while we relived old memories and slapped each other on the shoulder for half an hour or so. And then he asked me what I was doing here, and I answered vaguely that I was on a mission to the Rani, but soon to go home again; and at this he looked at me shrewdly, but said nothing more until I was leaving.

"It will be *palitikal*, beyond doubt," says he. "Do not tell me. Listen, instead, to a friend's word. If ye speak with the Rani, be wary of her; she is a Hindoo woman, and knows too much for a woman's good."

"What d'you know about her?" says I.

"Little enough," says he, "except that she is like the silver krait, in that she is beautiful and cunning and loves to bite the sahibs. The Company have made a *cutch-rani*¶ of her, Flashman, but she still has fangs. This," he added bitterly, "comes of soft government in Calcutta, by *ducks* and *mulls*‖ who have been too

* Troopers.
† Great lord, important man.
‡ See *Flashman*.
¶ "Cutch" in this sense means inferior, as opposed to "pukka", meaning first-rate. E.g. *pukka road*, a macadam surface, *cutch road*, a mere track. Thus *cutch-rani*, a nominal queen, without power.
‖ *Ducks* and *mulls*—Bombay Anglo-Indians and Madras Anglo-Indians. Slang expressions current among the British in India, but probably seldom used by Indians themselves.

long in the heat. So beware of her, and go with God, old friend.
And remember, while thou art in Jhansi, Ilderim is thy shadow—
or if not me, then these *loose-wallahs* and *jangli-admis** of mine.
They have their uses—" And he jerked a thumb towards his
troopers.

That, coming from an Afghan *upper roger*† who was also a
friend, was the best kind of insurance policy you could wish—
not that I now had any fears, fool that I was, about my stay in
Jhansi. As to what he'd said of the Rani—well, I knew it already,
and Afghans' views on women are invariably sour—beastly brutes.
Anyway, I didn't doubt my ability to handle Lakshmibai, in every
sense of the word.

Still, I found his simile coming to mind next day, when I
attended her durbar again, and watched her sitting enthroned to
hear petitions, dressed in a cloth-of-silver sari that fitted her like a
skin, with a silver-embroidered shawl framing that fine dark face;
when she moved it was for all the world like a great gleaming
snake stirring. She was very grave and queenly, and her courtiers
and suppliants fairly grovelled, and scuttled about if she raised her
pinky; when the last petitioner had been heard, and a gong had
boomed to end the durbar, she sat with her chin in the air while the
mob bowed itself out backwards, leaving only me and her two chief
councillors standing there—and then she slipped out of her throne
with a little cry of relief, hissed at one of her pet monkeys and
chased it out on to the terrace, clapping her hands in mock anger,
and then returned, perfectly composed, to lounge on her swing.

"Now we can talk," says she, "and while my *vakeel*‡ reads out
the matter of my 'petition', you may refresh yourself, colonel—"
and she indicated a little table with flasks and cups on it. "Ah,
and see," she added, flicking a flimsy little handkerchief from her
sari, "I am wearing French perfume today—do you care for it?
My lady Vashki thinks I am no better than an infidel."

It was my perfume, right enough; I bowed acknowledgement
while she smiled and settled herself, and the *vakeel* began to drone
out her petition in formal Persian.

---

* Thieves and jungle-men.
† A young chief—Sansk., "yuva rajah". For this and other curiosities of
Anglo-Indian slang, see *Hobson-Jobson*, by H. Yule (1886).
‡ Legal representative (possibly used here ironically).

It's worth repeating, perhaps, for it was a fair sample of the objections that many Indian princes had to British rule—the demand for restoration of her husband's revenues, compensation for the slaughter of sacred cows, reappointment of court hangers-on dismissed by the Sirkar, restitution of confiscated temple funds, recognition of her authority as regent, and the like. All a waste of time, had she but known it, but splendid stuff for me to talk to her about over the next week or two while I pursued the really important work of charming her into a recumbent position.

I had no doubt she was willing enough for me to make the running there—she was wearing my scent, and letting me know it, and she was as pleasant as pie in her cool way at that meeting —nodding graciously as I talked to her wise men about the petition, smiling if I ventured a joke, inviting them to admire my reasoning (which they fell over themselves to do, absolutely), even asking my advice occasionally, and always considering me languidly with those dark slanting eyes as I talked. All of which might have seemed suspiciously amiable after her frankness at our first encounter—but since then she'd had time to weigh the political advantages of being pleasant to me, and was setting out to make me enjoy my work.

But I knew politics wasn't the half of it—I know when a woman's got that little flutter in her midriff about me, and in our ensuing meetings I could watch her enjoying using her beauty on me—and she could do that with a touch that Montez might have envied. I'll admit it now, I found her enchanting; she had the advantage of being a queen, of course, which makes a beauty all the more tantalising—well, even I, on short acquaintance, could hardly have taken her belly in one hand, her bum in the other, and fondled her flat on her back with passionate murmurs, as one would do in ordinary circumstances. No, with royalty you have to wait a little. Not that I wasn't tempted, in those early talks, when she had dismissed her councillors, and we were alone, and just once or twice, from the warm gleam in her eye as she swayed on her swing or lay on her daybed, I wondered if perhaps ... but I decided to make haste slowly, and play the bowling as it came down.

It came mighty fast, too, sometimes, for if she was generally content just to politick flirtatiously, I soon discovered that she could be dead serious where Jhansi and her own ambitions were concerned; let the talk turn that way, and you saw the passion of her feeling.

"Five years ago, how many beggars were on the streets?" she rounded on me once. "One for every ten today. And who has accomplished this? Who but the Sirkar, by assuming the affairs of the state, so that one white sahib comes to do the work that employed a dozen of our people, who must be turned out to starve. Who guards the state? Why, the Company soldiers—so Jhansi's army must be disbanded, and they, too, can shift or steal or go hungry!"

"Well now, highness," says I, "it's hard to blame the Sirkar for being efficient, and as for your unemployed soldiers, they'll be more than welcome in the Company service—"

"In a foreign army? And will there be room in its ranks, too, for the Indian craftsmen whom the Sirkar's efficiency has put out of work? For the traders whose commerce has decayed under the benevolent rule of the Raj?"

"You must give us a little time, maharaj'," says I, humouring her. "And it ain't all bad, you know. Banditry has ceased; the poor folk are safe from dacoits and Thugs—why, your own throne is secure against greedy neighbours like Kathe Khan and the Dewan of Orcha—"

"My throne is safe?" says she, stopping the swing on which she had been swaying, and lifting her brows at me. "Oh, very safe—for the Sirkar to enjoy its revenues, and usurp my place, and disinherit my son—ha! As to Kathe Khan and that jackal of Orcha, whom the Company in their wisdom allow to live—if I ruled this state, and had my soldiers, Kathe Khan and his fellow-viper would come against me once—" she picked up a fruit from the tray at her elbow, considered it, and nibbled daintily "—and crawl home again— without their hands and feet."

"No doubt, ma'am," says I. "But the fact is that when Jhansi ruled itself, it couldn't deal with these foes. Nor were the Thugs put down—"

"Oh, aye—we hear much of them, and how the Company suppressed their wickedness. And why—because they slew tra-

vellers, or was it because they served a Hindoo god and so offended
the Christian Company?" She eyed me contemptuously. "Belike
had the Thugs been Jesus-worshippers, they would have been
roaming yet—especially if they had chosen Hindoo victims."

You can't argue with gross prejudice, so I just looked amiable
and said:

"And doubtless had *suttee*, that fine old Hindoo custom whereby
widows were tortured to death, been a Christian practice, we
would have encouraged it? But in our ignorance and spite, we
forbade it—along with the law which condemned those widows
who had escaped burning to a life of slavery and degradation with
their heads shaved and heaven knows what else. Come, maharaj'—
can we do nothing right?" And without thinking I added: "I'd
have thought your highness, as a widow, would have cause to
thank the Sirkar for that at least."

As soon as the words were out, I saw I'd put my foot in it. The
swing stopped abruptly, and she sat upright, with a face like a
mask, staring at me.

"I?" says she. "I? Thank the Sirkar?" And she suddenly flung
her fruit across the room and stood upright, blazing at me. "You
dare to suggest that?"

Well, I could grovel, or face it out—but I don't hold with
grovelling to pretty women, not unless the danger's desperate or
I'm short of cash. So I started to hum and haw placatingly, while
she snapped in a voice like ice:

"I owe the Company nothing! If the Company had never been,
do you think I would have submitted to *suttee*, or allowed myself
to be made a menial? Do you take me for a fool?"

"By God, no, ma'am," says I hastily. "Anything but, and if
I've offended, I beg your pardon. I simply thought that the law
was binding on all, ah . . . ladies, you see, and . . ."

"The Maharani makes the law," says she, all Good Queen Bess
damning the dagoes, and I hurriedly cried thank heaven for that,
at which she looked down her nose at me.

"That is not the view of your Company or your country. Why
should you be different? Why should you care?"

That was my cue, of course; I hesitated a second, and then
looked at her, very frank and manly. "Because I've seen your

highness," says I quietly. "And ... well ... I do care, a great deal, you see." I stopped there, giving her my steadiest smile, with a touch of ardent admiration thrown in, and after a long moment her stare softened, and she even smiled as she sat down again and said:

"Shall we return to the confiscated temple funds?"

Altogether it was a rum game in those first few days—rum for her, because she was a fair natural tyrant, yet whenever a disagreement in our discussions arose, she would allow it to smooth over, with that warm mysterious smile, and rum for me, because here I was day after day closeted with this choice piece of rump, and not so much as touching her, let alone squeezing and grappling. But I had to bide my time, and since she took such obvious and natural pleasure in my company, I contained my horniness for the moment, in the interests of diplomacy.

In the meantime, I occasionally paid attention to the other side of Pam's business, talking with Skene, and Carshore the Collector, and reassuring myself that all continued to go well among the sepoys. There wasn't a hint of agitation now, my earlier fears about Ignatieff and his scoundrels were beginning to seem like a distant nightmare, and now that I was so well established in the Rani's good graces, the last cloud over my mission appeared to have been dispelled. Laughable, you may think, when you recollect that this was 1856 drawing to a close—you will ask how I, and the others, could have been so blind to the fact that we were living on the very edge of hell, but if you'd been there, what would you have seen? A peaceful native state, ruled by a charming young woman whose grievances were petty enough, and who gave most of her time to seducing the affections of a dashing British colonel; a contented native soldiery; and a tranquil, happy, British cantonment.

I was about it a great deal, and all our people were so placid and at ease—I remember a dinner at Carshore's bungalow, with his family, and Skene and his pretty little wife so nervous and pleased in her new pink gown, and jolly old Dr McEgan with his fund of Irish stories, and the garrison men with their red jackets, slung on the backs of their chairs, matching their smiling red faces, and their gossipy wives, and myself raising a laugh by coaxing one of the Wilton girls to eat a "country captain"* with the promise that it would make her hair curl when she grew older.

It was all so comfy and easy, it might have been a dinner-party at home, except for the black faces and gleaming eyes of the bearers standing silent against the chick-screens, and the big moths fluttering round the lamps; afterwards there was a silly card game, and Truth or Consequences, and local scandal, and talk of leave and game-shooting with our cheroots and port on the verandah. Trivial enough memories, when you think what happened to all of them—I can still feel the younger Wilton chit pulling at my arm and crying:

"Oh, Colonel Flashman, Papa says if I ask you ever so nicely you will sing us 'The Galloping Major'—will you please, oh, please do!" And see those shining eyes, and the ringlets, as she tugged me to where her sister was sitting at the piano.

We couldn't see ahead, then, and life was pleasant—especially for me, with my diplomatic duties to attend to, and they became more enjoyable by the hour; I'll say that for Rani Lakshmibai, she knew how to make business a pleasure. Much of the time we didn't talk in the palace at all; she was, as Skene had told me, a fine horsewoman, and loved nothing better than to put on her jodhpurs and turban, with two little silver pistols in her sash, and gallop on the maidan, or go hawking along a wooded river not far from the city. There was a charming little pavilion there, of about a dozen rooms on two storeys, hidden among the trees, and once or twice I was taken on picnics with a few of her courtiers and attendants. At other times we would talk in the palace garden, among the scores of pet beasts and birds which she kept, and once she had me in to one of her hen-parties in the durbar room, at which she entertained all the leading ladies of Jhansi to tea and cakes, and I found myself called on to discourse on European fashions to about fifty giggling Indian females in saris and bangles and kohl-dark eyes—excellent fun, too, although the questions they asked about crinolines and panniers would have made a sailor blush.

But her great delight was to be out of doors, riding or playing with her adopted son Damodar, a grave-faced imp of eight, or

* A type of curry.

inspecting her guards at field exercise; she even watched their
wrestling-matches in the courtyard, and a race-meeting in which
some of our garrison officers took part—I was intrigued to see that
on this occasion she wore a purdah veil and an enveloping robe,
for about the palace she went bare-faced—and pretty bare-bodied,
too. And if she could be as formal as a stockbroker with a new-
bought peerage, she had a delightful way with the ordinary folk—
she was never so gay and happy as when she held a party for
children from the city in her garden, letting them run among the
birds and monkeys, and at one of her alms-givings I saw her quite
concerned as her treasurer scattered coins among the mob of
hideous and stinking beggars clamouring at her gate. Not at all like
a Rani, sometimes—she was a queer mixture of schoolgirl and
sophisticated woman, all scatter one moment, all languor and
dignity the next. Damned unpredictable—oh, and captivating;
there were times when even I found myself regarding her with an
interest that wasn't more than four-fifths lustful—and that ain't
like me. It was directly after that alms-giving, when we rode out
to her pavilion among the trees, and I had just remarked that what
was needed for India was a Poor Law and a few parish workuses,
that she suddenly turned in her saddle, and burst out:

"Can you not see that that is not our way—that none of our
ways are your ways? You talk of your reforms, and the benefits
of British law and the Sirkar's rule—and never think that what
seems ideal to you may not suit others; that we have our own
customs, which you think strange and foolish, and perhaps they
are—but they are ours—our own! You come, in your strength,
and your certainty, with your cold eyes and pale faces, like ... like
machines marching out of your northern ice, and you will have
everything in order, tramping in step like your soldiers, whether
those you conquer and civilise—as you call it— whether they will
or no. Do you not see that it is better to leave people be—to let
them alone?"

She wasn't a bit angry, or I'd have agreed straight off, but she
was as intense as I'd known her, and the great dark eyes were
almost appealing, which was most unusual. I said that all I'd
meant was that instead of thousands going sick and ragged and
hungry about her city, it might be better to have some system of

relief; come cheaper on her, too, if they had the beggars picking yarn or mending roads for their dole.

"You talk of a system!" says she, striking her riding crop on the saddle. "We do not care for systems. Oh, we admire and respect those which you show us—but we do not want them; we would not choose them for ourselves. You remember we spoke of how twelve Indian babus* did the work of one white clerk—"

"Well, that's waste, ma'am," says I respectfully. "There's no point—"

"Wasteful or not, does it matter—if people are happy?" says she, impatiently. "Where lies the virtue of your boasted progress, your telegraphs, your railway trains, when we are content with our sandals and our ox-carts?"

I could have pointed out that the price of *her* sandals would have kept a hundred Jhansi coolie families all their lives, and that she'd never been within ten yards of an ox-cart, but I was tactful.

"We can't help it, maharaj'," says I. "We have to do the best we can, don't you know, as we see it. And it ain't just telegraphs and trains—though you'll find those useful enough, in time— why, I'm told there are to be universities, and hospitals—"

"To teach philosophies that we do not want, and sciences that we do not need. And a law that is foreign to us, which our people cannot understand."

"Well, that doesn't leave 'em far behind the average Englishman," says I. "But it's fair law—and with respect that's more than you can say for most of your Indian courts. Look now— when there was a brawl in the street outside your palace two days since, what happened? Your guards didn't catch the culprits—so they laid hands on the first poor soul they met, haled him into your *divan*,† guilty or not—and you have him hanging by his thumbs and sun-drying at the scene of the crime for two solid days. Fellow near died of it—and he'd done nothing! I ask you, ma'am, is that justice?"

"He was a *badmash*,‡ and well known," says she, wide-eyed. "Would you have let him go?"

* Clerks.
† Court.
‡ Scoundrel.

"For that offence, yes—since he was innocent of it. We punish only the guilty."

"And if you cannot find them? Is there to be no example made? There will be no more brawls outside the palace, I think." And seeing my look, she went on: "I know it is not your way, and it seems unfair and even barbarous to you. But we understand it—should that not be enough? You find it strange—like our religions, and our forbidden things, and our customs. But can your Sirkar not see that they are as precious to us as yours are to you? Why is it not enough to your Company to drive its profit? Why this greed to order people's lives?"

"It isn't greed, highness," says I. "But you can't drive trade on a battlefield, now can you? There has to be peace and order, surely, and you can't have 'em without ... well, a strong hand, and a law that's fair for all—or for most people, anyway." I knew she wouldn't take kindly if I said the law was as much for her as for her subjects. "And when we make mistakes, well, we try to put 'em right, you see—which is what I'm here for, to see that justice—our justice, if you like—is done to you—"

"Do you think that is all that matters?" says she. We had stopped in the pavilion garden, and the horses were cropping while her attendants waited out of earshot. She was looking at me, frowning, and her eyes were very bright. "Do you think it is the revenues, and the jewels—even my son's rights; do you think that is all I care for? These are the things that can be redressed—but what of the things that cannot? What of this life, this land, this country that you will change—as you change everything you touch? Today, it is still bright—but you will make it grey; today, it is still free—oh, and no doubt wrong and savage by your lights—and you will make it tame, and orderly, and bleak, and the people will forget what they once were. That is what you will do—and that is why I resist as best I can. As you, and Lord Palmerston would. Tell him," says she, and by George, her voice was shaking, but the pretty mouth was set and hard, "when you go home, that whatever happens, I will not give up my Jhansi. *Mera Jhansi denge nay.* I will not give up my Jhansi!"

I was astonished; I'd never been in doubt that under the delectable feminine surface there was a tigress of sorts, but I hadn't thought it was such a passionately sentimental animal. D'you know, for a moment I was almost moved, she seemed such a damned spunky little woman; I felt like saying "There, there", or stroking her hand, or squeezing her tits, or something—and then she had taken a breath, and sat upright in the saddle, as though recovering herself, and she looked so damned royal and so damned lovely that I couldn't help myself.

"Maharaj'—you don't need me to say it. Go to London yourself, and tell Lord Palmerston—and I swear he'll not only give you Jhansi but Bombay and Hackney Wick as well." And I meant it; she'd have been a sensation—had 'em eating out of her dusky little palm. "See the Queen herself—why don't you?"

She stared thoughtfully ahead for a moment, and then murmured under her breath: "The Queen . . . God save the Queen—what strange people you British are."

"Don't you worry about the British," says I, "they'll sing 'God save the Queen', all right—and they'll be thinking of the Queen of Jhansi."

"Now that is disloyal, colonel," says she, and the languid smile was back in her eyes, as she turned her horse and trotted off with me following.

Now, you may be thinking to yourself, what's come over old Flash? He ain't going soft on this female, surely? Well, you know, I think the truth is that I was a bit soft on all my girls—Lola and Cassie and Valla and Ko Dali's Daughter and Susie the Bawd and Takes-Away-Clouds-Woman and the rest of 'em. Don't mistake me; it was always the meat that mattered, but I had a fair affection for them at the same time—every now and then, weather permitting. You can't help it; feeling randy is a damned romantic business, and it's my belief that Galahad was a bigger beast in bed than ever Lancelot was. That's by the way, but worth remembering if you are to understand about me and Lakshmibai—and I've told you a good deal about her on purpose, because she was such a mysterious, contrary female that I can't hope to explain her (any more than historians can) but must just leave you to judge for yourselves from what I've written—and from what was to follow.

For on the morning after that talk at the pavilion—two weeks to the day since I'd arrived in Jhansi—things began to happen in earnest. To me, at any rate.

I sensed there was something up as soon as I presented myself in the durbar room; she was perfectly pleasant, vivacious even, as she told me about some new hunting-cheetah she'd been given, but her *vakeel* and chief minister weren't meeting her eye, and her foot was tap-tapping under the edge of her gold sari; ah, thinks I, someone's been getting the sharp side of missy's tongue. She didn't have much mind to business, either, and once or twice I caught her eyeing me almost warily, when she would smile quickly—with anyone else I would have said it was nervousness. Finally she cut the discussion off abruptly, saying enough for today, and we would watch the guardsmen fencing in the courtyard.

Even there, I noticed her finger tapping on the balcony as we looked down at the Pathans sabring away—damned active, dangerous lads they looked, too—but in a little while she began to take notice, talking about the swordplay and applauding the hits, and then she glanced sidelong at me, and says:

"Do you fence as well as you ride, colonel?"

I said, pretty fair, and she gave me her lazy smile and says:

"Then we shall try a bout", and blow me if she didn't order a couple of foils up to the durbar room, and go off to change into her jodhpurs and blouse. I waited, wondering—of course, Skene had said she'd been brought up with boys, and could handle arms with the best of them, but it seemed deuced odd—and then she was back, ordering her attendants away, tying up her hair in a silk scarf, and ordering me on guard very business-like. They'll never believe this at home, thinks I, but I obeyed, indulgently enough, and she touched me three times in the first minute. So I settled down, in earnest, and in the next minute she hit me only once, laughing, and told me to try harder.

That nettled me, I confess; I wasn't having this, royalty or not, so I went to work—I'm a strong swordsman, but not too academic— and I pushed her for all I was worth. She was better-muscled than she looked, though, and fast as a cat, and I had to labour to make her break ground, gasping with laughter, until her back was against one of the glass walls. She took to the point, holding me off, and then unaccountably her guard seemed to falter, I jumped in with the old heavy cavalry trick, punching my hilt against the forte of her blade, her foil spun out of her hand—and for a moment we were breast to breast, with me panting within inches of that dusky face and open, laughing mouth—the great dark eyes were wide and waiting—and then my foil was clattering on the floor and I had her in my arms, crushing my lips on hers and tasting the sweetness of her tongue, with that soft body pressed against me, revelling in the feel and fragrance of her. I felt her hands slip up my back to my head, holding my face against hers for a long delicious moment, and then she drew her lips away, sighing, opened her eyes, and said:

"How well do you shoot, colonel?"

And then she had slipped from my arms and was walking quickly towards the door to her private room, with me grunting endearments in pursuit, but as I came after her she just raised a hand, without turning or breaking stride, and said firmly:

"The durbar is finished . . . for the moment." The door closed behind her, and I was left with the fallen foils, panting like a bull before business, but thinking, my boy, we're home—the damned little teaser. I hesitated, wondering whether to invade her boudoir, when the little chamberlain came pottering in, eyeing the foils in astonishment, so I took my leave and presently was riding back to the cantonment, full of buck and anticipation—I'd known she'd call "Play!" in the end, and now there was nothing to do but enjoy the game.

That was why she'd been jumpy earlier, of course, wondering how best to bring me to the boil, the cunning minx. "How well do you shoot?" forsooth—she'd find out soon enough, when we finished the durbar—tomorrow, no doubt. So by way of celebration I drank a sight more bubbly than was good for me at dinner, and even took a magnum back to my bungalow for luck. It was as well I did, for about ten Ilderim dropped by for a prose—as he'd taken to doing—and there's nobody thirstier than a dry Gilzai— if you think all Muslims abstain, I can tell you of one who didn't. So we popped the cork, and gassed about the old days, and smoked, and I was enjoying myself with carnal thoughts about my Lucky Lakshmibai and thinking about turning in, when there came a scraping on the chick at the back of the bungalow, and the *khitmagar** appeared to tell me that there was a *bibi†* who insisted on seeing me.

Ilderim grinned and wagged his ugly head, and I cursed, thinking here was some bazaar houri plying her trade where it was least wanted, but I staggered out, and sure enough at the foot of the steps was a veiled woman in a sari, but with a burly-looking escort standing farther back at the gate. She didn't look like a slut, somehow, and when I asked what she wanted she came quickly up the steps, salaamed, and held out a little leather pouch. I took it, wondering; inside there was a handkerchief, and even through the champagne fumes there was no mistaking—it was heavy with my perfume.

"From my mistress," says the woman, as I goggled at it.

"By God," says I, and sniffed it again. "Who the blazes—"

"Name no names," says she, and it was a well-spoken voice, for a Hindoo. "My mistress sends it, and bids you come to the river pavilion in an hour." And with that she salaamed again, and slipped down the steps. I called after her, and took an unsteady step, but she didn't stop, and she and her escort vanished in the dark.

Well, I'm damned, thinks I, surprise giving way to delight—she couldn't wait, by heaven . . . and of course the river pavilion at night was just the place . . . far better than the palace, where all sorts of folk were prying. Nice and secluded, very discreet—just the place for a rowdy little Rani to entertain. "*Syce!*" I shouted, and strode back inside, a trifle unsteadily, damning the champagne, but chortling as I examined my chin in the glass, decided it would do, and roared for a clean shirt.

"Now where away?" says Ilderim, who was squatting on the rug. "Not after some trollop from the bazaar, at this time?"

"No, brother," says I. "Something much better than a trollop. If you could see this one you'd forswear small boys and melons for good." By jove, I was feeling prime; I dandied myself up in no time, rinsed my face to clear some of the booze away, and was out champing on the verandah as the *syce* brought my pony round.

"You're mad," growls Ilderim. "Do you go alone—where to?"

* Bearer, waiter.
† Lady.

"I'm not sharing her, if that's what you mean. I'll take the *syce*." For I wasn't too sure of the way at night, and it was pitch black. I must have been drunker than I felt, for it took me three shots to mount, and then, with a wave to Ilderim, who was glowering doubtfully from the verandah, I trotted off, with the *syce* scrambling up behind.

Now, I'll admit I was woozy, and say at the same time that I'd have gone if I'd been cold sober. I don't know when I've been pawing the ground quite so hard for a woman—probably the two weeks' spooning had worked me up, and I couldn't cover the two miles to the pavilion fast enough. Fortunately the *syce* was a handy lad, for he not only guided us but held me from tumbling out of the saddle; I don't remember much of the journey except that it lasted for ages, and then we were among trees, with the hooves padding on grass, the *syce* was shaking my arm, and there ahead was the pavilion, half-hidden by the foliage.

I didn't want the *syce* spying, so I slid down and told him to wait, and then I pushed on. In spite of the night air, the booze seemed to have increased its grip, but I navigated well enough, leaning on a trunk every now and then. I surveyed the pavilion; there were dim lights on the ground floor, and in one room upstairs, and by George, there was even the sound of music on the slight breeze. I beamed into the dark—what these Indians don't know about the refinements of romping isn't worth knowing. An orchestra underneath, privacy and soft lights upstairs, and no doubt refreshments to boot—I rubbed my face and hurried forward through the garden to the outside staircase leading to the upper rooms, staggering quietly so as not to disturb the hidden musicians, who were fluting sweetly away behind the screens.

I mounted the staircase, holding on tight, and reached the little landing. There was a small passage, and a slatted door at the end, with light filtering through it. I paused, to struggle out of my loose trousers—at least I wasn't so tight that I'd been fool enough to come out in boots—took a great lusty breath, padded unsteadily forward, and felt the door give at my touch. The air was heavy with perfume as I stepped in, stumbled into a muslin curtain, swore softly as I disentangled myself, took hold of a wooden pillar for support, and gazed round into the half-gloom.

There were dim pink lamps burning, on the floor against the walls, giving just enough light to show the broad couch, shrouded in mosquito net, against the far wall. And there she was, silhou-etted against the glow, sitting back among the cushions, one leg stretched out, the other with knee raised; there was a soft tinkle of bangles, and I leaned against my pillar and croaked:

"Lakshmibai? Lucky?—it's me, darling...*chabeli**...I'm here!"

She turned her head, and then in one movement raised the net and slipped out, standing motionless by the couch, like a bronze statue. She was wearing bangles, all right, and a little gold girdle round her hips, and some kind of metal headdress from which a flimsy veil descended from just beneath her eyes to her chin—not another stitch. I let out an astonishing noise, and was trying to steady myself for a plunge, but she checked me with a lifted hand, slid one foot forward, crooked her arms like a nautch-dancer, and came gliding slowly towards me, swaying that splendid golden nakedness in time to the throbbing of the music beneath our feet.

I could only gape; whether it was the drink or admiration or what, I don't know, but I seemed paralysed in every limb but one. She came writhing up to me, bangles tinkling and dark eyes gleaming enormously in the soft light; I couldn't see her face for the veil, but I wasn't trying to; she retreated, turning and swaying her rump, and then approached again, reaching forward to brush me teasingly with her fingertips; I grabbed, gasping, but she slid away, faster now as the tempo of the music increased, and then back again, hissing at me through the veil, lifting those splendid breasts in her hands, and this time I had the wit to seize a tit and a buttock, fairly hooting with lust as she writhed against me and lifted the veil just enough to bring her mouth up to mine. Her right foot was slipping up the outside of my left leg, past the knee, up to the hip, and round so that her heel was in the small of my back—God knows how they do it, double joints or something—and then she was thrusting up and down like a demented monkey on a stick, raking me with her nails and giving little shrieks into my mouth, until the torchlight procession which was marching

* Sweetheart.

through my loins suddenly exploded, she went limp in my arms, and I thought, oh Lord, now lettest thou thy servant depart in peace, as I slid gently to the floor in ecstatic exhaustion with that delightful burden clinging and quivering on top of me.

The instructors who taught dancing to young Indian royalty in those days must have been uncommon sturdy; she had just about done for me, but somehow I must have managed to crawl to the couch, for the next I knew I was there with my face cradled against those wonderful perfumed boobies—I tried feebly to go brrr! but she turned my head and lifted a cup to my lips. As if I hadn't enough on board already, but I drank greedily and sank back, gasping, and was just deciding I might live, after all, when she set about me again, lips and hands questing over my body, fondling and plaguing, writhing her hips across my groaning carcase until she was astride my thighs with her back to me, and the torchlight procession staggered into marching order once more, eventually erupting yet again with shattering effect. After which she left me in peace for a good half-hour, as near as I could judge in my intoxicated state—one thing I'm certain of, that if I'd been sober and in my right mind she could never have teased me into action a third time, as she did, by doing incredible things which I still only half-believe as I recall them. But I remember those great eyes, over the veil, and the pearl on her brow, and her perfume, and the tawny velvet skin in the half-light. . . .

I came awake in an icy sweat, my limbs shivering, trying to remember where I was. There was a cold wind from somewhere out in the dark, and I turned my aching head; the pink lamps were burning, casting their shadows, but she was no longer there. Someone was, though, surely, over by the door; there was a dark figure, but it wasn't naked, for I could see a white loin-cloth, and instead of the gold headdress, there was a tight white turban. A man? And he was holding something—a stick? No, it had a strange curved head on it—and there was another man, just behind him, and even as I watched they were gliding stealthily into the room, and I saw that the second one had a cloth in his right hand.

For perhaps ten seconds I lay motionless, gazing—and then it rushed in on me that this wasn't a dream, that they were moving towards the couch, and that this was horrible, inexplicable danger. The net was gone from the couch, and I could see them clearly, the white eyes in the black faces—I braced for an instant and then hurled myself off the couch away from them, slipped, recovered, and rushed at the shutters in the screen-wall. There was a snarl from behind me, something swished in the air and thudded, and I had a glimpse of a small pick-axe quivering in the shutter as I flung myself headlong at the screen, yelling in terror. Thank God I'm fourteen stone—it came down with a splintering crash, and I was sprawling on the little verandah, thrashing my way out of the splintered tangle and heaving myself on to the verandah rail.

From the tail of my eye I saw a dark shape springing for me over the couch; there was a tree spreading its thick foliage within five feet of the verandah, and I dived straight into it, crashing and scraping through the branches, clutching vainly and taking a tremendous thump across the hips as I struck a limb. For a second I seemed suspended, and then I shot down and landed flat on my back with a shock that sickened me. I rolled over, trying to heave myself up, as two black figures dropped from the tree almost on top of me; I blundered into one of them, smashed a fist into its face, and then something flicked in front of my eyes, and I only just got a hand up in time to catch the garotte as it jerked back on to my throat.

I shrieked, hauling at it; my wrist was clamped under my chin by the strangler's scarf, but my right arm was free, and as I staggered back into him I scrabbled behind me, was fortunate enough to grab a handful of essentials, and wrenched for all I was worth. He screamed in agony, the scarf slackened, and he went down, but before I could flee for the safety of the wood the other one was on my back, and he made no mistake; the scarf whipped round my windpipe, his knee was into my spine, and I was flailing helplessly with his breath hissing in my ear. Five seconds, it flashed across my mind, is all it takes for an expert garotter to kill a man—oh, Jesus, my sight was going, my head was coming off, with a horrible pain tearing in my throat, I was dying even as I fell, floating down to the turf—and then I was on my back, gasping down huge gulps of air, and the faces that were swimming

in front of my eyes, glaring horribly, were merging into one—
Ilderim Khan was gripping my shoulders and urging:

"Flashman! Be still! There—now lie a moment, and breathe!
Inshallah! The strangler's touch is no light thing." His strong
fingers were massaging my throat as he grinned down at me. "See
what comes of lusting after loose women? A moment more, and
we would have been sounding retreat over thee—so give thanks
that I have a suspicious mind, and followed with my *badmashes*
to see what kind of *cunchunee** it was who bade thee to her bed
so mysteriously. How is it, old friend—can you stand?"

"What happened?" I mumbled, trying to rise.

"Ask why, rather. Has she a jealous husband, perhaps? We saw
the lights, and heard music, but presently all was still, and many
came out, to a palankeen in which ladies travel, and so away. But
no sign of thee, till we heard thee burst out, with these hounds of
hell behind thee." And following his nod, I saw there were two of
his ruffians squatting in the shadows over two dark shapes lying
on the grass—one was ominously still, but the other was gasping
and wheezing, and from the way he clutched himself I imagine
he was the assassin whose courting-tackle I'd tried to rearrange.
One of Ilderim's *sowars* was ostentatiously cleaning his Khyber
knife with a handful of leaves, and presently a third came
padding out of the dark.

"The sahib's *syce* is dead yonder," says he. "Bitten with a tooth
from Kali's mouth!"†

"What?" says Ilderim, starting up. "Now, in God's name—"
and he went quickly to the body of the dead strangler, snatching
a lantern from one of his men, and peering into the dead face. I
heard him exclaim, and then he beckoned me. "Look there," says
he, and pulled down the dead man's eyelid with his finger; even
in the flickering light I could see the crude tattoo on the skin.

"Thug!"[11] says Ilderim through his teeth. "Now, Flashman,
what does this mean?"

I was trying to take hold of my senses, with my head splitting
and my neck feeling as though it had been through the mangle.
It was a nightmare—one moment I'd been in a drunken frenzy

* Dancing-girl.
† Stabbed with a Thug pick-axe.

of fornication with Lakshmibai, with a houseful of musicians
beating time—and the next I was being murdered by professional
stranglers—and Thugs at that. But I was too shocked to think, so
Ilderim grunted and turned to the groaning prisoner.

"This one shall tell us," says he, and seized him by the throat.
"Look now—thou art dead already. But it can be swift, or I can
trim off the appurtenances and extremities from thy foul carcase
and make thee eat them. That, for a beginning. So choose—who
sent thee, and why?"

The Thug snarled, and spat at him, so Ilderim says: "Take him
to the trees yonder," and while they did he hauled out his knife,
stropped it on his sole, says "Bide here, *husoor*," and then strode
grimly after them.

I couldn't have moved, if I'd wanted to. It was a nightmare,
unbelievable, but in those few minutes, while dreadful grunts and
an occasional choked-off scream came out of the dark, I strove to
make some sense of it. Lakshmibai had plainly left me asleep—
or drunk, or drugged, or both—in the pavilion, and shortly after
the Thugs had arrived. But why—why should she seek my death?
It made no sense—no, by God, because if she *had* just been luring
me out for assassination, she'd have had me ambushed on the
way—she'd certainly not have pleasured me like a crazy spinster
first. And there was no earthly reason why she should want me
killed—what had I done to merit that? She'd been so friendly and
straight and kind—I could have sworn she'd been falling in love
with me for two weeks past. Oh, I've known crafty women, sluts
who'd tickle your buttons with one hand and reach for a knife
with the other—but not her. I couldn't swallow that; I wouldn't.

I could even understand her slipping out and leaving me—it
had been a clandestine gallop, after all; she had a reputation to
consider. What better way of concluding it than by vanishing
swiftly back to the palace, leaving her partner to find his own
way home—I reflected moodily that she'd probably done the same
thing, countless times, in that very pavilion, whenever she felt
like it. She was no novice, that was certain—no wonder her late
husband had lost interest and curled up and died: the poor devil
must have been worn to a shadow.

But who then had set Thugs on me? Or were they just stray,

indiscriminate killers—as Thugs usually were, slaying anyone who happened in their way, for fun and religion? Had they just spotted me, out at night, and decided to chalk up another score for Kali— and then Ilderim came striding out of the dark, whipping his knife into the turf, and squatting down beside me.

"Stubborn," says he, rubbing his beard, "but not too stubborn. Flashman—it is ill news." He stared at me with grave eyes. "There is a fellowship—hunting thee. They have been out this week past —the brotherhood of deceivers, whom everyone thought dead or disbanded these years past—with orders to seek out and slay the Colonel Flashman sahib at Jhansi. That one yonder is a chief among them—six nights since he was at Firozabad, where his lodge met to hear a strange fakir who offered them gold, and—" he tapped my knee "—an end to the Raj in due time, and a rebirth of their order of *thugee*. They were to prepare against the day—and as grace before meat they were to sacrifice thee to Kali. I knew all along," says he with a grim satisfaction, "that this was *palitikal*, and ye walked a perilous road. Well, thou art warned in time—but it must be a fast horse to the coast, and ship across the *kala pani*,* for if these folk are riding thy tail, then this land is death to thee; there will not be a safe nook from the Deccan to the Khyber Gate."

I sat limp and trembling, taking this horror in; I was afraid to ask the question, but I had to know.

"This fakir," I croaked. "Who is he?"

"No one knows—except that he is from the north, a one-eyed man with a fair skin from beyond the passes. There are those who think he is a sahib, but not of thy people. He has money, and followers in secret, and he preaches against the *sahib-log*† in whispers . . ."

Ignatieff—I almost threw up. So it had happened, as Pam had thought it might: the bastard was back, and had tracked me down —and devil a doubt he knew all about my mission, too, somehow— and he and his agents were spreading their poison everywhere, and seeking to revive the devilish *thugee* cult against us, with me at the top of the menu—and Ilderim was right, there wasn't a

* Black water, i.e., the ocean.
† Lord-people, i.e., the British.

hope unless I could get out of India—but I couldn't! This was
what I was meant to be here for—why Pam in his purblind folly
had sent me out: to tackle Ignatieff at his own game and dispose
of him. I couldn't run squealing to Bombay or Calcutta bawling
"Gangway—and a first-class ticket home, quick!" This was the
moment I was meant to earn my corn—against bloody dacoits and
Ruski agents? I gulped and sweated—and then another thought
struck me.

Was Lakshmibai part of this? God knew she'd no cause to
love the Sirkar—was she another of the spiders in this devilish
web, playing Delilah for the Russians?—but no, no, even to
my disordered mind one thing remained clear: she'd never have
walloped the mattress with me like that if she'd been false. No,
this was Ignatieff, impure and anything but simple, and I had to
think as I'd never thought before, with Ilderim's eye on me while
I took my head in my hands and wondered, Christ, how can I
slide out this time. And then inspiration dawned, slowly—I
couldn't leave India, or be seen to be running away, but I'd told
Skene that if the crisis came I might well vanish from sight,
locally, to go after Ignatieff in my own way—well, now I would
vanish, right enough; that shouldn't be difficult. I schemed it fast,
as I can when I'm truly up against it, and turned to Ilderim.

"Look, brother," says I. "This is a great *palitikal* affair, as you
guessed. I cannot tell thee, and I cannot leave India—"

"Then thou art dead," says he, cheerfully. "Kali's hand will be
on thee, through these messengers—" and he pointed at the dead
Thug.

"Hold on," says I, sweating. "They're looking for Colonel
Flashman—but if Colonel Flashman becomes, say—a Khyekeen
pony-pedlar, or an Abizai who has done his time in the Guides
or lancers, how will they find him then? I've done it before,
remember? Dammit, I speak Pushtu as well as you do, and Urdu
even better—wasn't I an agent with Sekundar Sahib? All I need
is a safe place for a season, to lie up and sniff the wind before—"
and I started lying recklessly, for effect "—before I steal out again,
having made my plans, to break this one-eyed fakir and his rabble
of stranglers and *loose-wallahs*. D'you see?"

"Inshallah!" cries he, grinning all over his evil face. "It is the great game! To lie low in disguise, and watch and listen and wait, and conspire with the other *palitikal* sahibs of the Sirkar, until the time is ripe—and then go against these evil subverters in a secret *razzia!** And when that time comes—I may share the sport, and *hallal*† these Hindoo and foreign swine, with my lads?—thou wouldst not forget thy old friend then?" He grabbed my hand, the bloodthirsty devil. "Thou'd send me word, surely, when the knives are out—thy brother Ilderim?"

You'll wait a long time for it, my lad, thinks I; give me a good disguise and a pony and you'll not see me again—not until everything has safely blown over, and some other idiot has disposed of Ignatieff and his bravos. That's when I'd emerge, with a good yarn to spin to Calcutta (and Pam) about how I'd gone after him secretly, and dammit, I'd missed the blighter, bad luck. That would serve, and sound sufficiently mysterious and convincing—but for the moment my urgent need was a disguise and a hiding-place at a safe distance. Some jungly or desert spot might be best; I'd lived rough that way before, and as I'd told Ilderim, I could pass as a frontiersman or Afghan with any of 'em.

"When there are Ruski throats to be cut, you'll be the first to know," I assured him, and he embraced me, chuckling, and swearing I was the best of brothers.

The matter of disguise reminded me that I was still stark naked, and shivering; I told him I wanted a kit exactly like that of his *sowars*, and he swore I'd have it, and a pony, too.

"And you may tell Skene sahib from me," says I, "that the time has come—and he can start feeling sorry for the Ruskis—he'll understand." For I wasn't going back to the cantonment; I wanted to ride out tonight, wherever I was going. "Tell him of the one-eyed fakir, that the Thugs are abroad again, and the axles are getting hot. You may say I've had a brush with the enemy already—but you needn't tell him what else I was doing tonight." I winked at him. "Understand? Oh, aye—and if he has inquiries after me from the Rani of Jhansi, he may say I have been called away, and present my apologies."

"The Rani?" says he, and his eye strayed towards the pavilion.

* An attack on unbelievers.
† Ritual throat-cutting.

"Aye." He coughed and grinned. "That was some rich lady's palankeen I saw tonight, and many servants. Perchance, was it—"

" 'A Gilzai and a grandmother for scandal'," I quoted. "Mind your own dam' business. And now, be a good lad, and get me that outfit and pony."

He summoned one of his rascals, and asked if the tortured Thug was dead yet.

"Nay, but he has no more to tell," says the other. "For he said nothing when I—" You wouldn't wish to know what he said next. "Shall I pass him some of his own tobacco?"[12] he added.

"Aye," says Ilderim. "And tell Rafik Tamwar I want all his clothes, and his knife, and his horse. Go thou."

For answer the *sowar* nodded, took out his Khyber knife, and stepped back under the trees to where his companions were guarding the prisoner, or what was left of him. I heard him address the brute—even at that time and place it was an extraordinary enough exchange to fix itself in my mind; one of the most astonishing things I ever heard, even in India.

"It is over, deceiver," says he. "Here is the knife—in the throat or the heart? Choose."

The Thug's reply was hoarse with agony. "In the heart, then— quickly!"

"You're sure? As you wish."

"No—wait!" gasps the Thug. "Put the point . . . behind . . . my ear—so. Thrust hard—thus I will bleed less, and go undisfigured. Now!"

There was a pause, and then the *sowar's* voice says: "He was right—he bleeds hardly at all. Trust a deceiver to know."

A few moments later and Rafik Tamwar appeared, grumbling, in a rag of loin-cloth, with his clothes over his arm, and leading a neat little pony. I told Ilderim that Skene sahib must see his kit replaced, and he could have my own Pegu pony, at which the good Tamwar grinned through his beard, and said he would willingly make such an exchange every day. I slipped into his shirt and cavalry breeches, drew on the soft boots, donned his hairy *poshteen*,* stuck the Khyber cleaver in my sash, and was

---

* Sheepskin coat.

winding the *puggaree* round my head and wishing I had a revolver as well, when Ilderim says thoughtfully:

"Where wilt thou go, Flashman—have ye an eyrie to wait in where no enemy can find thee?"

I confessed I hadn't, and asked if he had any suggestions, at which he frowned thoughtfully, and then smiled, and then roared with laughter, and rolled on his back, and then stood up, peering and grinning at me.

"Some juice for thy skin," says he. "Aye, and when thy beard has grown, thou'lt be a rare Peshawar ruffler—so ye swagger enough, and curl thy hair round thy finger, and spit from the back of thy throat—"

"I know all about that," says I, impatiently. "Where d'you suggest I do all these things?"

"In the last place any ill-willer would ever look for a British colonel sahib," says he, chortling. "Look now—wouldst thou live easy for a spell, and eat full, and grow fat, what time thou art preparing to play the game against these enemies of the Raj? Aye, and get well paid for it—24 rupees a month, and *batta**   also?" He slapped his hands together at my astonishment. "Why not— join the Sirkar's army! What a recruit for the native cavalry— why, given a month they'll make thee a *daffadar!*"† He stuck his tongue in his cheek. "Maybe a *rissaldar* in time—who knows?"

"Are you mad?" says I. "Me—enlist as a *sowar*? And how the devil d'you expect me to get away with that?"

"What hinders? Thou hast passed in Kabul bazaar before today, and along the Kandahar road. Stain thy face, as I said, and grow thy beard, and thou'lt be the properest Sirkar's bargain in India! Does it not meet thy need—and will it not place thee close to affairs—within reach of thine own folk, and ready to move at a finger-snap?"

It was ridiculous—and yet the more I thought of it, the more obvious it was. How long did I want to hide—a month? Two or three perhaps? I would have to live, and for the life of me I couldn't think of a more discreet and comfortable hiding-place than the ranks of a native cavalry regiment—I had all the

* Field allowance.
† Cavalry commander of ten.

qualifications and experience ... if I was careful. But I'd have to
be that, whatever I did. I stood considering while Ilderim urged
me, full of enthusiasm.

"See now—there is my mother's cousin, Gulam Beg, who was
malik* in one of my father's villages, and is now *woordy-major*†
in the 3rd Cavalry at Meerut garrison. If thou goest to him, and
say Ilderim sent thee, will he not be glad of such a fine sturdy
trooper—ye may touch the hilt, and eat the salt, and belike he'll
forget the *assami*‡ for my sake. Let me see, now," says this mad
rascal, chuckling as he warmed to his work, "thou art a Yusufzai
Pathan of the Peshawar Valley—no, no, better still, we'll have
thee a Hasanzai of the Black Mountain—they are a strange folk,
touched, and given to wild fits, so much may be excused thee. Oh,
it is rare! Thou art—Makarram Khan, late of the Peshawar
police, and so familiar with the ways of the sahibs; thou hast
skirmished along the line, too. Never fear, there was a Makarram
Khan,[13] until I shot him on my last furlough; he will give thee a
shabash¶ from hell, for he was a stout rider in his time. Careless, though—or he'd have watched the rocks as he rode. Well,
Makarram—" says he, grinning like a wolf in the gloom "—wilt
thou carry a lance for the Sirkar?"

I'd been determining even as he talked; I was in the greatest
fix, and there was no other choice. If I'd known what it would
lead to, I'd have damned Ilderim's notion to his teeth, but it
seemed inspired at the time.

"Bind thy *puggaree* round thy jaw at night, lest thou babble
in English in thy sleep," says he at parting. "Be sullen, and speak
little—and be a good soldier, blood-brother, for the credit of
Ilderim Khan." He laughed and slapped my saddle as we shook
hands in the dark under the trees. "When thou comest this way
again, go to Bull Temple, beyond the Jokan Bagh—I will have a
man waiting for an hour at sunrise and sunset. Salaam, *sowar!*"
cries he, and saluted, and I dug my heels into my pony and
cantered off in the dawn, still like a man in a wild dream.

---

* Headman.
† Native adjutant of Indian irregular cavalry. (Since the 3rd were not
irregulars, Flashman seems to have misused the term here.)
‡ In this sense, a deposit paid by a recruit on enlistment.
¶ Hurrah, bravo.

You might think it impossible for a white man to pass himself off as a native soldier in John Company's army, and indeed I doubt if anyone else has ever done it. But when you've been called on to play as many parts as I have, it's a bagatelle. Why, I've been a Danish prince, a Texas slave-dealer, an Arab sheik, a Cheyenne Dog Soldier, and a Yankee navy lieutenant in my time, among other things, and none of 'em was as hard to sustain as my lifetime's impersonation of a British officer and gentleman. The truth is we all live under false pretences much of the time; you just have to put on a bold front and brazen it through.

I'll admit my gift of languages has been my greatest asset, and I suppose I'm a pretty fair actor; anyway, I'd carried off the role of an Asian-Afghan nigger often enough, and before I was more than a day's ride on the way to Meerut I was thoroughly back in the part, singing Kabuli bazaar songs through my nose, sneering sideways at anyone I passed, and answering greetings with a grunt or a snarl. I had to keep my chin and mouth covered for the first three days, until my beard had sprouted to a disreputable stubble; apart from that, I needed no disguise, for I was dark and dirty-looking enough to start with. By the time I struck the Grand Trunk my own mother wouldn't have recognised the big, hairy Border ruffian jogging along so raffishly with his boots out of his stirrups, and his love-lock curling out under his *puggaree*; on the seventh day, when I cursed and shoved my pony through the crowded streets of Meerut City, spurning the rabble aside as a good Hasanzai should, I was even *thinking* in Pushtu, and if you'd offered me a seven-course dinner at the Café Royal I'd have turned it down for mutton-and-rice stew with boiled dates to follow.

My only anxiety was Ilderim's cousin, Gulam Beg, whom I had to seek out in the native cavalry lines beyond the city; he would be sure to run a sharp eye over a new recruit, and if he spotted anything queer about me I'd have a hard job keeping up the imposture. Indeed, at the last minute my nerve slackened a little, and I rode about for a couple of hours before I plucked up the courage to go and see him—I rode on past the native infantry lines, and over the Nullah Bridge up to the Mall in the British town; it was while I was sitting my pony, brooding under the trees, that a dog-cart with two English children and their mother went by, and one of the brats squealed with excitement and said I looked just like Ali Baba and the Forty Thieves. That cheered me up, for some reason—anyway, I had to have a place to eat and sleep while I shirked my duty, so I finally presented myself at the headquarters of the 3rd Native Light Cavalry, and demanded to see the *woordy-major*.

I needn't have worried. Gulam Beg was a stout, white-whiskered old cove with silver-rimmed spectacles on the end of his nose, and when I announced that Ilderim Khan of Mogala was my sponsor he was all over me. Hasanzai, was I, and late of the *polis?* That was good—I had the look of an able man, yes—doubtless the Colonel Sahib would look favourably on such a fine upstanding recruit. I had seen no military service, though?—hm . . . he looked at me quizzically, and I tried to slouch a bit more.

"Not in the Guides, perhaps?" says he, with his head on one side. "Or the *cutch*-cavalry? No? Then doubtless it is by chance that you stand the regulation three paces from my table, and clench your hand with the thumb forward—and that the pony I see out yonder is girthed and bridled like one of ours." He chuckled playfully. "A man's past is his own affair, Makarram Khan—what should it profit us to pry and discover that a new 'recruit' had once quit the Sirkar's service over some small matter of feud or blood-letting, eh? You come from Ilderim—it is enough. Be ready to see the Colonel Sahib at noon."

He'd spotted me for an old soldier, you see, which was all to the good; having detected me in a small deception, it never occurred to him to look for a large one. And he must have passed on his conclusion to the Colonel, for when I made my *salaam* to that worthy officer on the orderly-room verandah, he looked me up and down and says to the *woordy-major* in English:

"Shouldn't wonder if you weren't right, Gulam Beg—he's

heard Boots and Saddles before, that's plain. Probably got bored
with garrison work and slipped off one night with half-a-dozen
rifles on his back. And now, having cut the wrong throat or lifted
the wrong herd, he's come well south to avoid retribution." He
sat back, fingering the big white moustache which covered
most of his crimson face. "Ugly-looking devil, ain't he though?
Hasanzai of the Black Mountain, eh?—yes, that's what I'd have
thought. Very good . . ." He frowned at me and then said, very
carefully:

"*Company cavalry apka mangta?*"
which abomination of bad Urdu I took to mean: did I want to
join the Company cavalry? So I showed my teeth and says: "*Han,
sahib,*" and thought I might as well act out my part by betraying
some more military knowledge—I ducked my head and leaned
over and offered him the hilt of my sheathed Khyber knife, at
which he burst out laughing and touched it,[14] saying that Gulam
Beg was undoubtedly right, and I wasn't half knowledgeable for
a chap who pretended never to have been in the Army before. He
gave instructions for me to be sworn in, and I took the oath on
the sabre-blade, ate a pinch of salt, and was informed that I was
now a skirmisher of the 3rd Native Light Cavalry, that my
daffadar was Kudrat Ali, that I would be paid one rupee per day,
with a quarter-anna dyeing allowance, and that since I had
brought my own horse I would be excused the customary recruit
deposit. Also that if I was half as much a soldier as the Colonel
suspected, and kept my hands off other people's throats and
property, I might expect promotion in due course.

Thereafter I was issued with a new *puggaree,* half-boots and
pyjamy breeches, a new and very smart silver-grey uniform coat,
a regulation sabre, a belt and bandolier, and a tangle of saddlery
which was old and stiff enough to have been used at Waterloo
(and probably had), and informed by a betel-chewing *havildar*
that if I didn't have it reduced to gleaming suppleness by next
morning, I had best look out. Finally, he took me to the armoury,
and I was shown (mark this well) a new rifled Enfield musket,
serial number 4413—some things a soldier never forgets—which
I was informed was mine henceforth, and more precious than my
own mangy carcase.

Without thinking, I picked it up and tested the action, as I'd done a score of times at Woolwich—and the Goanese store-wallah gaped.

"Who taught you that?" says he. "And who bade you handle it, *jangli* pig? It is for you to see—you touch it only when it is issued on parade." And he snatched it back from me. I thought another touch of character would do no harm, so I waited till he had waddled away to replace it in the rack, and then whipped out my Khyber knife and let it fly, intending to plant it in the wall a foot or so away from him. My aim was off though—the knife imbedded itself in the wall all right, but it nicked his arm in passing, and he squealed and rolled on the floor, clutching at his blood-smeared sleeve.

"Bring the knife back," I snarled, baring my fangs at him, and when he had scrambled up, grey-faced and terrified, and returned it, I touched the point on his chest and says: "Call Makarram Khan a pig just once more, *ulla kabaja*,* and I will carry thine eyes and genitals on this point as kebabs." Then I made him lick the blood off the blade, spat in his face, and respectfully asked the *havildar* what I should do next. He, being a Mussulman, was all for me, and said, grinning, that I should make a fair recruit; he told my *daffadar*, Kudrat Ali, about the incident, and presently the word went round the big, airy barrack-room that Makarram Khan was a genuine saddle-and-lance man, from up yonder, who would strike first and inquire after—doubtless a Border lifter, and a feud-carrier, but a man who knew how to treat Hindoo insolence, and therefore to be properly respected.

So there I was—Colonel Harry Paget Flashman, late of the 11th Hussars, 17th Lancers and the Staff, former aide to the Commander-in-Chief, and now acting-*sowar* and rear file in the skirmishing squadron, 3rd Cavalry, Bengal Army, and if you think it was a mad-brained train of circumstance that had taken me there—well, so did I. But once I had got over the unreality of it all, and stopped imagining that everyone was going to see through my disguise, I settled in comfortably enough.

It was an eery feeling, though, at first, to squat on my *charpai*†

* Son of an owl.
† Cot.

against the wall, with my *puggaree* off, combing my hair or oiling
my light harness, and look round that room at the brown, half-
naked figures, laughing and chattering—of all the things that
soldiers talk about, women, and officers, and barrack gossip, and
women, and rations, and women— but in a foreign tongue which,
although I spoke it perfectly and even with a genuine frontier
accent, was still not my own. While I'd been by myself, as I say,
I'd even been thinking in Pushtu, but here I had to hold on tight
and remember what I was meant to be—for one thing, I wasn't
used to being addressed in familiar terms by native soldiers, much
less ordered about by an officious *naik** who'd normally have
leaped to attention if I'd so much as looked in his direction. When
the man who bunked next to me, Pir Ali, a jolly rascal of a
Baluch, tapped my shoulder in suggesting that we might visit the
bazaar that first evening, I absolutely stared at him and just
managed to bite back the "Damn your impudence" that sprang to
my tongue.

It wasn't easy, for a while; quite apart from remembering
obeisances at the prescribed times, and making a show at cooking
my own dinner at the *choola*,† there were a thousand tiny details
to beware of—I must remember not to cross my legs when sitting,
or blow my nose like a European, or say "Mmh?" if someone
said something I couldn't catch, or use the wrong hand, or clear
my throat in the discreet British fashion, or do any of the things
that would have looked damned odd in an Afghan frontiersman.[15]

Of course I made mistakes—once or twice I was just plain
ignorant of things that I ought to have known, like how to chew
a *majoon*‡ when Pir Ali offered me one (you have to spit into
your hand from time to time, or you'll end up poisoned), or how
to cut a sheep-tail for curry, or even how to sharpen my knife in
the approved fashion. When I blundered, and anyone noticed, I
found the best way was to stare them down and growl sullenly.

But more often than not my danger lay in betraying knowledge
which Makarram Khan simply wouldn't have had. For example,
when Kudrat Ali was giving us sword exercise I found myself

---

* Corporal.
† Cooking-place, camp oven of clay.
‡ Green sweetmeat containing *bhang.*

once falling into the "rest" position of a German schlager-fencer (not that anyone in India was likely to recognise that), and again, day-dreaming about fagging days at Rugby while cleaning my boots one evening, I found myself humming "Widdicombe Fair"— fortunately under my breath. My worst blunder, though, was when I was walking near a spot where the British officers were playing cricket, and the ball came skipping towards me—without so much as thinking I snapped it up, and was looking to throw down the wicket when I remembered, and threw it back as clumsily as I could. One or two of them stared, though, and I heard someone say that big nigger was a deuced smart field. That rattled me, and I trod even more carefully than before.

My best plan, I soon discovered, was to do and say as little as possible, and act the surly, reserved hillman who walked by himself, and whom it was safest not to disturb. The fact that I was by way of being a protégé of the woordy-major's, and a Hasanzai (and therefore supposedly eccentric), led to my being treated with a certain deference; my imposing size and formidable looks did the rest, and I was left pretty much alone. Once or twice I walked out with Pir Ali, to lounge in the Old Market and ogle the bints, or dally with them in the boutique doorways, but he found my grunts a poor return for his own cheery prattle, and abandoned me to my own devices.

It wasn't, as you can guess, the liveliest life for me at first—but I only had to think of the alternative to resign myself to it for the present. It was easy enough soldiering, and I quickly won golden opinions from my naik and jemadar* for the speed and intelligence with which I appeared to learn my duties. At first it was a novelty, drilling, working, eating, and sleeping with thirty Indian troopers—rather like being on the other side of the bars of a monkey zoo—but when you're closed into a world whose four corners are the barrack-room, the choola, the stables, and the maidan, it can become maddening to have to endure the society of an inferior and foreign race with whom you've no more in common than if they were Russian moujiks or Irish bog-trotters. What makes it ten times worse is the outcast feeling that comes of knowing that within a mile or two your own kind are enjoying

* Under-officer.

all the home comforts, damn 'em—drinking *barra* pegs, smoking decent cigars, flirting and ramming with white women, and eating ices for dessert. (I was no longer so enamoured of mutton *pilau* in *ghee*,* you gather.) Within a fortnight I'd have given anything to join an English conversation again, instead of listening to Pir Ali giggling about how he'd bullocked the headman's wife on his last leave, or the endless details of Sita Gopal's uncle's law-suit, or Ram Mangal's reviling of the *havildar*, or Gobinda Dal's whining about how he and his brothers, being soldiers, had lost much of the petty local influence they'd formerly enjoyed in their Oudh village, now that the Sirkar had taken over.

When it got too bad I would loaf up to the Mall, and gape at the mem-sahibs with their big hats and parasols, driving by, and watch the officers cantering past, flicking their crops as I clumped my big boots and saluted, or squat near the church to listen to them singing "Greenland's Icy Mountains" of a Sunday evening. Dammit, I missed my own folk then—far worse than if they'd been a hundred miles away. I missed Lakshmibai, too—odd, ain't it, but I think what riled me most was the knowledge that if she'd seen me as I now was—well, she wouldn't even have noticed me. However, it had to be stuck out—I just had to think of Ignatieff —so I would trudge back to barracks and lie glowering while the *sowars* chattered. It had this value—I learned more about Indian soldiers in three weeks than I'd have done in a lifetime's ordinary service.

You'll think I'm being clever afterwards, but I soon realised that all wasn't as well with them as I'd have thought at first sight. They were Northern Muslims, mostly, with a sprinkling of high-caste Oudh Hindoos—the practice of separating the races in different companies or troops hadn't come in then. Good soldiers, too; the 3rd had distinguished itself in the last Sikh War, and a few had frontier service. But they weren't happy—smart as you'd wish on parade, but in the evening they would sit about and croak like hell—at first I thought it was just the usual military sore-headedness, but it wasn't.

At first all I heard was vague allusions, which I didn't inquire about for fear of betraying a suspicious ignorance—they talked a

* Native butter, cooking-fat.

deal about one of the padres in the garrison, Reynolds sahib, and
how Colonel Carmik-al-Ismeet (that was the 3rd's commander,
Carmichael-Smith) ought to keep him off the post, and there was
a fairly general repeated croak about polluted flour, and the
Enlistment Act, but I didn't pay much heed until one night, I
remember, an Oudh *sowar* came back from the bazaar in a
tremendous taking. I don't even remember his name, but what
had happened was that he'd been taking part in a wrestling match
with some local worthy, and before he'd got his shirt back on
afterwards, some British troopers from the Dragoon Guards who
were there at the time had playfully snapped the sacred cord
which he wore over his shoulder next the skin—as his kind of
Hindoos did.

"*Banchuts!** Scum!" He was actually weeping with rage. "It
is defiled—I am unclean!" And for all that his mates tried to
cheer him up, saying he could get a new one, blessed by a holy
man, he went on raving—they take these things very seriously,
you know, like Jews and Muslims with pork. If it seems foolish
to you, you may compare it with how you'd feel if a nigger pissed
in the font at your own church.

"I shall go to the Colonel sahib!" says he finally, and one of the
Hindoos, Gobinda Dal, sneered:

"Why should he care—the man who will defile our *atta*† will
not rebuke an English soldier for this!"

"What's all this about the *atta*?" says I to Pir Ali, and he
shrugged.

"The Hindoos say that the sahibs are grinding cow bones into
the sepoys' flour to break their caste. For me, they can break any
Hindoo's stupid caste and welcome."

"Why should they do that?" says I, and Sita Gopal, who
overheard, spat and says:

"Where have you lived, Hasanzai? The Sirkar will break every
man's caste—aye, and what passes for caste even among you
Muslims: there are pig bones in the *atta*, too, in case you didn't
know it. *Naik* Shere Afzul in the second troop told me; did he not
see them ground at the sahibs' factory at Cawnpore?"

* A highly offensive term.
† Flour.

"Wind from a monkey's backside," says I. "What would it profit the sahibs to pollute your food—since when do they hate their soldiers?"

To my astonishment about half a dozen of them scoffed aloud at this—"Listen to the Black Mountain *munshi!*"* "The sahibs love their soldiers—and so the *gora*-cavalry broke Lal's string for him tonight!" "Have you never heard of the Dum-Dum sweeper, Makarram Khan?" and so on. Ram Mangal, who was the noisiest croaker of them all, spat out:

"It is of a piece with the padre sahib's talk, and the new regulation that will send men across the *kala pani*—they will break our caste to make us Christians! Do they not know this even where you come from, hillman? Why, it is the talk of the army!"

I growled that I didn't put any faith in latrine-gossip—especially if the latrine was a Hindoo one, and at this one of the older men, Sardul something-or-other, shook his head and says gravely:

"It was no latrine-rumour, Makarram Khan, that came out of Dum-Dum arsenal." And for the first time I heard the astonishing tale that was, I discovered, accepted as gospel by every sepoy in the Bengal army—of the sweeper at Dum-Dum who'd asked a caste sepoy for a drink from his dish, and on being refused, had told the sepoy that he needn't be so dam' particular because the sahibs were going to do away with caste by defiling every soldier in the army by greasing their cartridges with cow and pig fat.

"This thing is known," says old Sardul, positively, and he was the kind of old soldier that men listen to, thirty years' service, Aliwal medal, and clean conduct sheet, damn your eyes. "Is not the new Enfield musket in the armoury? Are not the new greased cartridges being prepared? How can any man keep his religion?"

"They say that at Benares the *jawans* have been permitted to grease their own loads," says Pir Ali,[16] but they hooted him down.

"They say!" cries Ram Mangal. "It is like the tale they put about that all the grease was mutton-fat—if that were so, where is the need for anyone to make his own grease? It is a lie—just as the Enlistment Act is a lie, when they said it was a provision only,

* Teacher.

and no one would be asked to do foreign service. Ask the 19th at Behrampore—where their officers told them they must serve in Burma if they refused the cartridge when it was issued! Aye, but they will refuse—then we'll see!" He waved his hands in passion. "The polluted *atta* is another link in the chain—like the preaching of that owl Reynolds sahib with his Jesus-talk, which Carmik-al-Ismeet permits to our offence. He *wants* to put us to shame!"

"It is true enough," says old Sardul, sadly. "Yet I would not believe it if such a sahib as my old Colonel MacGregor—did he not take a bullet meant for me at Kandahar?—were to look in my eye and say it was false. The pity is that Carmik-al-Ismeet is not such a sahib—there are none such nowadays," says he with morbid satisfaction, "and the Army is but a poor ruin of what it was. You do not know today what officers were—if you had seen Sale sahib or Larrinsh* sahib or Cotton sahib, you would have seen men!" (Since he'd served in Afghanistan I'd hoped he would mention Iflass-man sahib, but he didn't, the croaking old bastard.) "They would have died before they would have put dishonour on their sepoys; their children, they used to call us, and we would have followed them to hell! But now," he wagged his head again, "these are *cutch*-sahibs, not *pakka*-sahibs—and the English common soldiers are no better. Why, in my young day, an English trooper would call me brother, give me his hand, offer me his water-bottle (not realising that I could not take it, you understand). And now—these common men spit on us, call us monkeys and *hubshis*—and break Lal's string!"

Most of their talk was just patent rubbish, of course, and I'd no doubt it was the work of agitators, spreading disaffection with their nonsense about greased cartridges and polluted food. I almost said so, but decided it would be unwise to draw attention to myself—and anyway it wasn't such a burning topic of conversation most of the time that one could take it seriously. I knew they put tremendous store by their religion—the Hindoos especially—and I supposed that whenever an incident like Lal's string stirred them up, all the old grievances came out, and were soon forgotten. But I'll confess that what Sardul had said about the British officers

* "Lawrence"—any one of the famous Lawrence brothers who served on the frontier, and later in the Mutiny.

and troops reminded me of John Nicholson's misgivings. I had hardly seen a British officer on parade since my enlistment; they seemed content to leave their troops to the *jemadars* and n.c.o.s— Addiscombe[17] tripe, of course—and there was no question the British rankers in the Meerut garrison were a poorer type than, say, the 44th whom I'd known in the old Afghan days, or Campbell's Highlanders.

I got first-hand evidence of this a day or two later, when I accidentally jostled a Dragoon in the bazaar, and the brute turned straight round and lashed out with his boot.

"Aht the way, yer black bastard!" says he. "Think yer can shove a sahib arahnd—*banchut!*" And he would have taken a swipe at me with his fist, too, but I just put my hand on my knife-hilt and glared at him—it wouldn't have been prudent to do more. "Christ!" says he, and took to his heels until he got to the end of the street, where he snatched up a stone and flung it at me—it smashed a plate on a booth nearby—and then made off. I'll remember you, my lad, thinks I, and the day'll come when I'll have you triced up and flogged to ribbons. (And I did, as good luck had it.) I've never been so wild—that the scum of a White-chapel gutter should take his boot to *me!* I'll be honest and say that if I'd seen him do it to a native two months earlier I wouldn't have minded a bit—and still wouldn't, much: it's a nigger's lot to be kicked. But it ain't mine, and I can't tell you how I felt afterwards—filthy, in a way, because I hadn't been able to pay the swine back. That's by the way; the point is that old Sardul was right. There wasn't the respect for *jawans* among the British that there had been in my young day; we probably lashed and kicked niggers just as much (I know I did), but there was a higher regard for the sepoys at least, on the whole.

I doubt if any commander in the old days would have done what Carmichael-Smith did in the way of preaching-parades, either. I hadn't believed it in the barrack gossip, but sure enough, the next Sunday this coffin-faced Anglican *fakir*, the Rev. Reynolds, had a muster on the maidan, and we had to listen to him expounding the Parable of the Prodigal Son, if you please. He did it through a brazen-lunged *rissaldar* who interpreted for him, and you never heard the like. Reynolds lined it out in English, from the Bible, and the *rissaldar* stood there with his staff under his arm, at attention, with his whiskers bristling, bawling his own translation:

"There was a *zamindar*,* with two sons. He was a mad *zamindar*, for while he yet lived he gave to the younger his portion of the inheritance. Doubtless he raised it from a money-lender. And the younger spent it all whoring in the bazaar, and drinking *sherab*.† And when his money was gone he returned home, and his father ran to meet him, for he was pleased—God alone knows why. And in his foolishness, the father slew his only cow—he was evidently not a Hindoo—and they feasted on it. And the older son, who had been dutiful and stayed at home, was jealous, I cannot tell for what reason, unless the cow was to have been part of his inheritance. But his father, who did not like him, rebuked the older son. This story was told by Jesus the Jew, and if you believe it you will not go to Paradise, but instead will sit on the right-hand side of the English Lord God Sahib who lives in Calcutta. And there you will play musical instruments, by order of the Sirkar. Parade—dismiss!"

I don't know when I've been more embarrassed on behalf of my church and country. I'm as religious as the next man—which is to say I'll keep in with the local parson for form's sake and read the lessons on feast-days because my tenants expect it, but I've never been fool enough to confuse religion with belief in God. That's where so many clergymen, like the unspeakable Reynolds, go wrong—and it makes 'em arrogant, and totally blind to the harm they may be doing. This idiot was so drunk with testaments that he couldn't conceive how ill-mannered and offensive he was making himself look; I suppose he thought of high-caste Hindoos as being like wilful children or drunken costermongers—perverse and misguided, but ripe for salvation if he just pointed 'em the way. He stood there, with his unctuous fat face and piggy eyes, blessing us soapily, while the Muslims, being worldly in their worship, tried not to laugh, and the Hindoos fairly seethed. I'd have found it amusing enough, I dare say, if I hadn't been irritated by the thought that these irresponsible Christian zealots were

* Farmer.
† Strong drink.

only making things harder for the Army and Company, who had important work to do. It was all so foolish and unnecessary—the heathen creeds, for all their nonsensical mumbo-jumbo, were as good as any for keeping the rabble in order, and what else is religion for?

In any event, this misguided attempt to cure Hindoo souls took place, not just at Meerut but elsewhere, according to the religious intoxication of the local commanders, and in my opinion was the most important cause of the mischief that followed.[18] I didn't appreciate this at the time—and couldn't have done anything if I had. Besides, I had more important matters to engage my attention.

A few days after that parade, there was a gymkhana on the maidan, and I rode for the skirmishers in the *nezabazi*.* Apart from languages and fornication, horsemanship is my only accomplishment, and I'd been well-grounded in tent-pegging by the late Muhammed Iqbal, so it was no surprise that I took the greatest number of pegs, and would have got even more if I'd had a pony that I knew, and my lance hadn't snapped in a touch peg on the last round. It was enough to take the cup, though, and old Bloody Bill Hewitt, the garrison commander, slipped the handle over my broken lance-point in front of the marquee where all the top numbers of Meerut society were sitting applauding politely, the ladies in their crinolines and the men behind their chairs.

"*Shabash, sowar*," says Bloody Bill. "Where did you learn to manage a lance?"

"Peshawar Valley, *husoor*," says I.

"Company cavalry?" says he, and I said no, Peshawar police.

"Didn't know they was lancers," says he, and Carmichael-Smith, who was on hand, laughed and said to Hewitt in English:

"No more they are, sir. It's a rather delicate matter, I suspect—this bird here pretends he's never served the Sirkar before, but he's got Guide written all over him. Shouldn't wonder if he wasn't *rissaldar*—*havildar* at least. But we don't ask embarrassing questions, what? He's a dam' good recruit, anyway."

"Ah," says Hewitt, grinning; he was a fat, kindly old buffer.

* Tent-pegging with a lance.

" 'Nough said, then." And I was in the act of saluting when a little puff of wind sprang up, scattering the papers which were on the table behind him, and blowing them under the pony's hooves. Like a good little toady, I slipped out of the saddle and gathered them up, and without thinking set them on the table and put the ink-pot on top of them, to hold them steady—a simple, ordinary thing, but I heard an exclamation, and looked up to see Duff Mason, one of the infantry colonels, staring at me in surprise. I just salaamed and saluted and was back in my saddle in a second, while they called up the next man for his prize, but as I wheeled my pony away I saw that Mason was looking after me with a puzzled smile on his face, and saying something to the officer next to him.

Hollo, thinks I, has he spotted something? But I couldn't think I'd done anything to give myself away—until next morning, when the *rissaldar* called me out of the ranks, and told me to report to Mason's office in the British lines forthwith. I went with my heart in my mouth, wondering what the hell I was going to do if he had seen through my disguise, only to find it was the last thing my guilty conscience might have suspected.

"Makarram Khan, isn't it?" says Mason, when I stood to attention on his verandah and went through the ritual of hilt-touching. He was a tall, brisk, wiry fellow with a sharp eye which he cast over me. "Hasanzai, Peshawar policeman—but only a few weeks' Army service?" He spoke good Urdu, which suggested he was smarter than most, and my innards quaked.

"Well, now, Makarram," says he, pleasantly, "I don't believe you. Nor does your own Colonel. You're an old soldier—you ride like one, you stand like one, and what's more you've held command. Don't interrupt—no one's trying to trap you, or find out how many throats you've cut in the Khyber country in your time: that's nothing to me. You're here now, as an ordinary *sowar* —but a sowar who gathers up papers as though he's as used to handling 'em as I am. Unusual, in a Pathan—even one who's seen service, don't you agree?"

"In the police, husoor," says I woodenly, "are many *kitabs** and papers."

* Books.

"To be sure there are," says he, and then added, ever so easily, in English, "What's that on your right hand?"

I didn't look, but I couldn't help my hand jerking, and he chuckled and leaned back in his chair, pleased with himself.

"I guessed you understood English when the commander and your Colonel were talking in front of you yesterday," says he. "You couldn't keep it out of your eyes. Well, never mind; it's all to the good. But see here, Makarram Khan—whatever you've done, whatever you've been, where's the sense in burying yourself in the ranks of a native cavalry *pultan*?* You've got education and experience; why not use 'em? How long will it take you to make *subedar*,† or *havildar* even, in your present situation? Twenty years, thirty—with down-country cavalry? I'll tell you what—you can do better than that."

Well, it was a relief to know my disguise was safe enough, but the last thing I wanted was to be singled out in any way. However, I listened respectfully, and he went on:

"I had a Pathan orderly, Ayub Jan; first-class man, with me ten years, and now he's gone back home, to inherit. I need someone else—well, you're younger than he was, and a sight smarter, or I'm no judge. And he wasn't a common orderly—never did a menial task, or anything of that order; wouldn't have asked him to, for he was Yusufzai—and a gentleman, as I believe you are, d'you see?" He looked at me very steady, smiling. "So what I want is a man of affairs who is also a man of his hands—someone I can trust as a soldier, messenger, steward, aide, guide, shield-on-shoulder—" He shrugged. "When I saw you yesterday, I thought 'That's the kind of man.' Well—what d'ye say?"

I had to think quickly about this. If I could have looked at myself in the mirror, I suppose I was just the sort of ruffian I'd have picked myself, in Duff Mason's shoes. Pathans make the best orderly-bodyguards-comrades there are, as I'd discovered with Muhammed Iqbal and Ilderim. And it would be a pleasant change from barracks—but it was risky. It would draw attention to me; on the other hand my character was established by now, and any lapses into Englishness might be explained from the past which

* Regiment.
† Native officer.

Mason and Carmichael-Smith had wished upon me. I hesitated, and he said quietly:

"If you're thinking that coming out of the ranks may expose you to greater danger of—being recognised by the police, say, or some inconvenient acquaintance from the past . . . have no fear of that. At need, there'll always be a fast horse and a *dustuck** to see you back to the Black Mountain again."

It was ironic—he thought I went in fear of discovery as a deserter or Border raider, when my only anxiety was that I'd be unmasked as a British officer. Bit of a lark, really—and on that thought I said very good, I'd accept his offer.

"Thank you, Makarram Khan," says he, and nodded to a table that was set behind his chair, against the chick: there was a drawn sabre lying on it, and I knew what was expected of me. I went past him, and put my hand on the blade—it had been so arranged that with my body in between, he couldn't see from where he sat whether I was touching the steel or not. The old dodge, thinks I, but I said aloud:

"On the haft and hilt, I am thy man and soldier."

"Good," says he, and as I turned he held out his hand. I took it, and just for devilment I said:

"Have no fear, *husoor*—you will smell the onion on your fingers." I knew, you see, that in anticipation of the oath, he would have rubbed onion on the blade, so that he could tell afterwards if I'd truly touched it while I swore. A Pathan who intended to break his oath wouldn't have put his hand on the steel, and consequently wouldn't have got the onion-smell on his fingers.

"By Jove!" says he, and quickly sniffed his hand. Then he laughed, and said I was a Pathan for wiliness, all right, and we would get along famously.

Which I'm bound to say we did—mind you, our association wasn't a long one, but while it lasted I thoroughly enjoyed myself, playing major-domo in his household, for that's what it amounted to, as I soon discovered. His bungalow was a pretty big establishment, you see, just off the east end of the Mall, near the British infantry lines, with about thirty servants, and since there was no

* Permit.

proper mem-sahib, and his *khansamah** was almost senile, there
was no order about the place at all. Rather than have me spend
my time dogging him about his office, where there wasn't much
for me to do except stand looking grim and impressive, Duff
Mason decided I should make a beginning by putting his house
and its staff into *pakka* order (as I gathered Ayub Jan had done in
his time) and I set about it. Flashy, Jack-of-all-trades, you see: in
the space of a few months I'd already been a gentleman of leisure,
staff officer, secret political agent, ambassador, and sepoy, so why
not a nigger butler for a change?

You may think it odd—and looking back it seems damned queer
to me, too—but the job was just nuts to me. I was leading such
an unreal existence, anyway, and had become so devilish bored in
the sepoy barracks, that I suppose I was ready enough for anything
that occupied my time without too much effort. Duff Mason's
employ was just the ticket: it gave me the run of a splendid
establishment, the best of meat and drink, a snug little bunk of
my own, and nothing to do but bully menials, which I did with
a hearty relish that terrified the brutes and made the place run
like clockwork. All round, I couldn't have picked a softer billet for
my enforced sojourn in Meerut if I'd tried. (Between ourselves,
I've a notion that had I been born in a lower station in life I'd
have made a damned fine butler for some club or Town house, yes-
me-lording the Quality, ordering flunkeys about, putting upstarts in
their place, and pinching the port and cigars with the best of them.)

I've said there were no proper mem-sahibs in the house, by
which I mean that there was no colonel's lady to supervise it—
hence the need for me. But in fact there were two white women
there, both useless in management—Miss Blanche, a thin, twitchy
little spinster who was Duff Mason's sister, and Mrs Leslie, a
vague relative who was either a grass widow or a real one, and
reminded me rather of a sailor's whore—she was a plumpish, pale-
skinned woman with red frizzy hair and a roving eye for the
garrison officers, with whom she went riding and flirting when
she wasn't lolling on the verandah eating sweets. (I didn't do
more than run a brisk eye over either of 'em when Duff Mason
brought me to the house, by the way—we nigger underlings

* Butler.

know our place, and I'd already spotted a nice fat black little kitchen-maid with a saucy lip and a rolling stern.)

However, if neither of the resident ladies was any help in setting me about my duties, there was another who was—Mrs Captain MacDowall, who lived farther down the Mall, and who bustled in on my first afternoon on the pretext of taking tea with Miss Blanche, but in fact to see that Duff Mason's new orderly started off on the right foot. She was a raw-boned old Scotch trot, not unlike my mother-in-law; the kind who loves nothing better than to interfere in other folk's affairs, and put their lives in order for them. She ran me to earth just as I was stowing my kit; I salaamed respectfully, and she fixed me with a glittering eye and demanded if I spoke English.

"Now then, Makarram Khan, this is what you'll do," says she. "This house is a positive disgrace; you'll make it what it should be—the best in the garrison after General Hewitt's, mind that. Ye can begin by thrashing every servant in the place—and if you're wise you'll do it regularly. My father," says she, "believed in flogging servants every second day, after breakfast. So now. Have you the slightest—the slightest notion—of how such an establishment as this should be run? I don't suppose ye have."

I said, submissively, that I had been in a sahib's house before.

"Aye, well," says she, "attend to me. Your first charge is the kitchen—without a well-ordered kitchen, there's no living in a place. Now—I dined here two nights since, *and I was disgusted.* So I have lists here prepared—" she whipped some papers from her bag. "Ye can't read, I suppose? No, well, I'll tell you what's here, and you'll see to it that the cook—who is none too bad, considering—prepares her menus accordingly. I shouldn't need to be doing this—" she went on, with a withering glance towards the verandah, where Miss Blanche and Mrs Leslie were sitting (reading "The Corsair" aloud, I recall) "—but if I don't, who will, I'd like to know? Hmf! Poor Colonel Mason!" She glared at me. "That's none of your concern—you understand?" She adjusted her spectacles. "Breakfast ... aye. Chops-steaks-quail-fried-fish-baked-minced-chicken-provided-the-bird's-no-more-than-a-day-old. No servants in the breakfast room—it can all be placed on the buffet. Can ye make tea—I mean tea that's fit to drink?"

Bemused by these assaults, I said I could.

"Aye," says she, doubtfully. "A mistress should always make the tea herself, but here . . ." She sniffed. "Well then, always two tea-pots, with no more than three spoonfuls to each, and a pinch of carbonate of soda in the milk. See that the cook makes coffee, very strong, first thing in the morning, and adds *boiling* water during the course of the day. *Boiling*, I said—and *fresh* hot milk, or cold whipped cream. Now, then—" and she consulted another list.

"Luncheon—also on the buffet. Mutton - broth - almond - soup - mulligatawny - white - soup - cold - clear - soup - milk - pudding - stewed - fruit. No *heavy cooked dishes*—" this with a glare over her spectacles. "They're unhealthy. Afternoon tea—brown bread and butter, scones, Devonshire cream, and cakes. Have ye any apostle spoons?"

"Mem-sahib," says I, putting my hands together and ducking my head, "I am only a poor soldier, I do not know what—"

"I'll have two dozen sent round. Dinner—saddle-of-mutton-boiled-fowls-roast-beef . . . ach!" says she, "I'll tell the cook myself. But you—" she wagged a finger like a marlin-spike "—will mind what I've said, and see that my instructions are followed and that the food is cleanly and promptly served. And see that the salt is changed every day, and that no one in the kitchen wears woollen clothes. And if one of them cuts a finger—straight round with them to my bungalow. Every inch of this house will be dusted twice a day, before callers come between noon and two, and before dinner. Is that clear?"

"*Han* mem-sahib, *han* mem-sahib," says I, nodding vigorously, heaven help me. She regarded me grimly, and said she would be in from time to time to see that all was going as it should, because Colonel Mason *must* be properly served, and if *she* didn't attend to it, and see that I kept the staff *hard* at their duties, well . . . This with further sniffy looks towards the verandah, after which she went to bully the cook, leaving me to reflect that there was more in an orderly's duties than met the eye.[19]

I tell you this, because although it may seem not to have much to do with my story, it strikes me it has a place; if you're to understand India, and the Mutiny, and the people who were

caught up in it, and how they fared, then women like Mrs Captain
MacDowall matter as much as Outram or Lakshmibai or old
Wheeler or Tantia Tope. Terrible women, in their way—the mem-
sahibs. But it would have been a different country without 'em—
and I'm not sure the Raj would have survived the year '57, if they
hadn't been there, interfering.

At all events, under her occasional guidance and blistering
rebukes, I drove Mason's menials until the place was running like
a home-bound tea clipper. You'll think it trivial, perhaps, but I
got no end of satisfaction in this supervising—there was nothing
else to occupy me, you see, and as Arnold used to say, what thy
hand findeth to do ... I welted the backsides off the sweepers,
terrorised the *mateys*,* had the bearers parading twice a day with
their dusters, feather brooms, and polish bottles, and stalked
grimly about the place pleased as punch to see the table-tops and
silver polished till they gleamed, the floors bone-clean, and the
chota hazri† and *darwazaband*‡ trays carried in on the dot.
Strange, looking back, to remember the pride I felt when Duff
Mason gave a dinner for the garrison's best, and I stood by the
buffet in my best grey coat and new red sash and *puggaree*, with
my beard oiled, looking dignified and watching like a hawk as the
khansamah and his crew scuttled round the candle-lit table with
the courses. As the ladies withdrew Mrs Captain MacDowall
caught my eye, and gave just a little nod—probably as big a
compliment, in its way, as I ever received.

So a few more weeks went by, and I was slipping into this nice
easy life, as is my habit whenever things are quiet. I reckoned I'd
give it another month or so, and then slide out one fine night for
Jhansi, where I'd surprise Skene by turning up à la Pathan and
pitch him the tale about how I'd been pursuing Ignatieff in secret
and getting nowhere. I'd see Ilderim, too, and find if the Thugs
were still out for me; if it seemed safe I'd shave, become Flashy
again, and make tracks for Calcutta, protesting that I'd done all
that could be done. Might even pay my respects to Lakshmibai on
the way ... however, in the meantime I'd carry on as I was,

---

* Waiters.
† Lit. "little breakfast"—early morning tea.
‡ "*Darwazaband*", not at home. Presumably the salver used for calling-
cards.

eating Duff Mason's rations, seeing that his bearer laid out his kit, harrying his servants, and tupping his kitchen-maid—she was a poor substitute for my Rani, and once or twice, when it seemed to me that Mrs Leslie's eye lingered warmly on my upstanding Pathan figure or my swarthy bearded countenance, I toyed with the idea of having a clutch at her. Better not, though—too many prying eyes in a bungalow household, which is what made life hard for grass widows and unattached white females in Indian garrisons—they couldn't do more than flirt in safety.

Every now and then I had to go back to barracks. Carmichael-Smith had been willing enough to detach me to Duff Mason, but I still had to muster on important parades, when all sepoys on the regimental strength were called in. It was on one of these that I heard the rumour flying that the 19th N.I. had rioted at Behrampore over the greased cartridge, as sepoy Ram Mangal had predicted.

"They have been disbanded by special court," says he to me out of the corner of his mouth as we clattered back to the armoury to hand in our rifles; he was full of excitement. "The sahibs have sent the *jawans* home, because the Sirkar fears to keep such spirited fellows under arms! So much for the courage of your British colonels—they begin to fear. Aye, presently they will have real cause to be fearful!"

"It will need to be better cause than a pack of whining monkeys like the 19th," says Pir Ali. "Who minds if a few Hindoos get cow-grease on their fingers?"

"Have you seen this, then?" Mangal whipped a paper from under his jacket and thrust it at him. "Here are your own people —you Mussulmen who so faithfully lick the sahibs' backsides— even they are beginning to find their manhood! Read here of the great *jihad** that your *mullahs*† are preaching against the infidels —not just in India, either, but Arabia and Turkestan. Read it— and learn that an Afghan army is preparing to seize India, with Ruski guns and artillerymen—what does it say? 'Thousands of Ghazis, strong as elephants'." He laughed jeeringly. "They may come to help—but who knows, perhaps they will be behind the

* Holy war.
† Preachers.

fair? The goddess Kali may have destroyed the British already—as the wise men foretold."

It was just another scurrilous pamphlet, no doubt, but the sight of that grinning black ape gloating over his sedition riled me; I snatched the paper and rubbed it deliberately on the seat of my trousers. Pir Ali and some of the sepoys grinned, but the rest looked pretty glum, and old Sardul shook his head.

"If the 19th have been false to their salt, it is an ill thing," says he, and Mangal broke in excitedly to say hadn't the sahibs broken faith first, by trying to defile the sepoys' caste?

"First Behrampore—then where?" cries he. "Which *pultan* will be next? It is coming, brothers—it is coming!" And he nodded smugly, and went off chattering with his cronies.[20]

I didn't value this, at the time, but it crossed my mind again a couple of nights later, when Duff Mason had Archdale Wilson, the *binky-nabob*,* and Hewitt and Carmichael-Smith and a few others on his verandah, and I heard Jack Waterfield, a senior man in the 3rd Native Cavalry, talking about Behrampore, and wondering if it was wise to press ahead with the issue of the new cartridge.

"Of course it is," snaps Carmichael-Smith. "Especially now, when it's been refused at Behrampore. Give way on this—and where will it end? It's a piece of damned nonsense—some crawling little agitator fills the sepoys' heads with rubbish about beef-grease and pig-fat, when it's been made perfectly plain by the authorities that the new cartridge contains nothing that could possibly offend Muslim or Hindoo. But it serves as an excuse for the trouble-makers—and there are always some."

"Fortunately not in our regiment," says another—Plowden, who commanded my own company. By God, thinks I, that's all you know, and then Carmichael-Smith was growling on that he'd like to see one of his sepoys refuse the issue, by God he would.

"No chance of that, sir," says another major of the 3rd, Richardson. "Our fellows are too good soldiers, and no fools. Can't think what happened with the 19th—too many senior officers left regimental service for the staff, I shouldn't wonder. New men haven't got the proper grip."

* Artillery commander.

"But suppose our chaps did refuse?" says one young fellow in the circle. "Mightn't it—"

"That is damned croaking!" says Carmichael-Smith angrily. "You don't know sepoys, Gough, and that's plain. I do, and I won't countenance the suggestion that my soldiers would have their heads turned by this . . . this seditious bosh. What the devil —they know their duty! But if they get the notion that any of us have doubts, or might show weakness—well, that's the worst thing imaginable. I'll be obliged if you'll keep your half-baked observations to yourself!"

That shut up Gough, sharp enough, and Duff Mason tried to get the pepper out of the air by saying he was sure Carmichael-Smith was right, and if Gough had misgivings, why not settle them then and there.

"Your colonel won't mind, I'm sure, if I put it to one of his own *sowars*—don't fret, Smith, he's a safe man." And he beckoned me from where I stood in the shadows by the serving-table from which the bearers kept the glasses topped up.

"Now, Makarram Khan," says he. "You know about this cartridge nonsense. Well—you're a Muslim . . . will you take it?"

I stood respectfully by his chair, glancing round the circle of faces—Carmichael-Smith red and glistening, Waterfield thin and shrewd, young Gough flustered, old Hewitt grinning and belching quietly.

"If it will drive a ball three hundred yards, and straight, *husoor*," says I, "I shall take it."

They roared, of course, and Hewitt said there was a real Pathan answer, what?

"And your comrades?" asks Archdale Wilson.

"If they are told, truly, by the colonel sahib, that the cartridge is clean, why should they refuse?" says I, and they murmured agreement. Well, thinks I, that's a plain enough hint, and Carmichael-Smith can put Master Mangal's croaking into the shade.

He might have done, too, but the very next day the barracks was agog with a new rumour—and we heard for the first time a name that was to sweep across India and the world.

"Pandy?" says I to Pir Ali. "Who may he be?"

"A sepoy of the 34th, at Barrackpore," says he. "He shot at his captain sahib on the parade-ground—they say he was drunk with *sharab* or *bhang*, and called on the sepoys to rise against their officers.[21] What do I know? Perhaps it is true, perhaps it is rumour —Ram Mangal is busy enough convincing those silly Hindoo sheep that it really happened."

So he was, with an admiring crowd round him in the middle of the barrack-room, applauding as he harangued them.

"It is a lie that the sepoy Pandy was drunk!" cries he. "A lie put about by the sahibs to dishonour a hero who will defend his caste to the death! He would not take the cartridge—and when they would have arrested him, he called to his brothers to beware, because the British are bringing fresh battalions of English soldiers to steal away our religion and make slaves of us. And the captain sahib at Barrackpore shot Pandy with his own hands, wounding him, and they keep him alive for torture, even now!"

He was working himself into a terrific froth over this—what surprised me was that no one—not even the Muslims—contradicted him, and *Naik* Kudrat Ali, who was a good soldier, was standing by chewing his lip, but doing nothing. Eventually, when Mangal had raved himself hoarse, I thought I'd take a hand, so I asked him why he didn't go to the Colonel himself, and find out the truth, whatever it was, and ask for reassurance about the cartridge.

"Hear him!" cries he scornfully. "Ask a sahib for the truth? Hah! Only the *gora-colonel*'s lapdog would suggest it! Maybe I will speak to Karmik-al-Ismeet, though—in my own time!" He looked round at his cronies with a significant, ugly grin. "Yes, maybe I will . . . we shall see!"

Well, one swallow don't make a summer, or one ill-natured agitator a revolt—no doubt what I'm telling you now about barrack-room discontent among the sepoys looks strong evidence of trouble brewing, but it didn't seem so bad then. Of course there was discontent, and Ram Mangal played on it, and every rumour, for all he was worth—but you could go into any barracks in the world, you know, at any time, and find almost the same thing happening. No one *did* anything, just sullen talk; the parades went on, and the sepoys did their duty, and the British officers seemed content enough—anyway, I was only occasionally in the barracks myself, so I didn't hear much of the grumbling. When the word came through that Sepoy Pandy had been hanged at Barrackpore for mutiny, I thought there might be some kind of stir among our men, but they never let cheep.

In the meantime, I had other things to claim my attention: Mrs Leslie of the red hair and lazy disposition had begun to take a closer interest in me. It started with little errands and tasks that put me in her company, then came her request to Duff Mason that I should ride escort on her and Miss Blanche when they drove out visiting ("it looks so much better to have Makarram Khan attending us than an ordinary *syce*"), and finally I found myself accompanying her when she went riding alone—the excuse was that it was convenient to her to have an attendant who spoke English, and could answer her questions about India, in which she professed a great interest.

I know what interests you, my girl, thinks I, but you'll have to make the first move. I didn't mind; she was a well-fleshed piece in her way. It was amusing, too, to see her plucking up her courage; I was a black servant to her, you see, and she was torn between a natural revulsion and a desire to have the big hairy Pathan set about her. On our rides, she would flirt a very little, in a hoity-toity way, and then think better of it; I maintained my correct and dignified noble animal pose, with just an occasional ardent smile, and a slight squeeze when I helped her dismount. I knew she was getting ready for the plunge when she said one day:

"You Pathans are not truly . . . Indian, are you? I mean . . . in some ways you look . . . well, almost . . . white."

"We are not Indian at all, mem-sahib," says I. "We are descended from the people of Ibrahim, Ishak and Yakub, who were led from the Khedive's country by one Moses."

"You mean—you're Jewish?" says she. "Oh." She rode in silence for a while. "I see. How strange." She thought some more. "I . . . I have Jewish acquaintances . . . in England. Most respectable people. And quite white, of course."

Well, the Pathans believe it, and it made her happy, so I hurried the matter along by suggesting next day that I show her the ruins at Aligaut, about six miles from the city; it's a deserted

temple, very overgrown, but what I hadn't told her was that the
inside walls were covered with most artistically-carved friezes
depicting all the Hindoo methods of fornicating—you know
the kind of thing: effeminate-looking lads performing incredible
couplings with fat-titted females. She took one look and gasped; I
stood behind with the horses and waited. I saw her eyes travel
round from one impossible carving to the next, while she gulped
and went crimson and pale by turns, not knowing whether to
scream or giggle, so I stepped up behind her and said quietly that
the forty-fifth position was much admired by the discriminating.
She was shivering, with her back to me, and then she turned, and
I saw that her eyes were wild and her lips trembling, so I gave
my swarthy ravisher's growl, swept her up in my arms, and then
down on to the mossy floor. She gave a little frightened moan,
opened her eyes wide, and whispered:

"You're sure you're Jewish ... not ... not Indian?"

"*Han*, mem-sahib," says I, thrusting away respectfully, and
she gave a contented little squeal and grappled me like a wrestler.

We rode to Aligaut quite frequently after that, studying Indian
social customs, and if the forty-fifth position eluded us, it wasn't
for want of trying. She had a passion for knowledge, did Mrs
Leslie, and I can think back affectionately to that cool, dim, musty
interior, the plump white body among the ferns, and the thoughtful way she would gnaw her lower lip while she surveyed the
friezes before pointing to the lesson for today. Pity for some chap
she never re-married. Aye, and more of a pity for her she never
got the chance.

For by now April had turned into May, the temperature was
sweltering, and there was a hot wind blowing across the Meerut
parade-ground and barracks that had nothing to do with the
weather. You could feel the tension in the air like an electric
cloud; the sepoys of the 3rd N.C. went about their drill like sullen
automatons, the native officers stopped looking their men in the
eye, the British officers were quiet and wary or explosively short-
tempered, and there were more men on report than anyone could
remember. There were ugly rumours and portents: the 34th N.I.
—the executed Sepoy Pandy's regiment—had been disbanded at
Barrackpore, a mysterious fakir on an elephant had appeared in

Meerut bazaar predicting that the wrath of Kali was about to fall
on the British, chapattis were said to be passing in some barrack-
rooms, the Plassey legend was circulated again. Out of all the
grievances and mistrust that folk like Ram Mangal had been
voicing, a great, discontented unease grew in those few weeks—
and one thing suddenly became known throughout the Meerut
garrison: without a word said, the certainty was there. When the
new greased cartridge was issued, the 3rd Native Cavalry would
refuse it.

Now, you may say, knowing what followed, something should
have been done. I, with respect, will ask: what? The thing was,
while everyone *knew* that feeling was rising by the hour, no one
could foresee for a moment what was about to happen. It was
unimaginable. The British officers couldn't conceive that their
beloved sepoys would be false to their salt—dammit, neither could
the sepoys. If there's one thing I will maintain, it is that not a
soul—not even creatures like Ram Mangal—thought that the
bitterness could explode in violence. Even if the cartridge was
refused—well, the worst that could follow was disbandment, and
even that was hard to contemplate. I didn't dream of what lay
ahead—not even with all my forewarning over months. And I
was there—and no one can take fright faster than I. So when I
heard that Carmichael-Smith had ordered a firing-parade, at which
the skirmishers (of whom I was one) would demonstrate the new
cartridge, I simply thought: well, this will settle it—either they'll
accept the new loads, and it'll all blow over, or they won't and
Calcutta will have to think again.

Waterfield tried to smooth things beforehand, singling out the
older skirmishers and reassuring them that the loads were not
offensively greased, but they wouldn't have it—they even pleaded
with him not to ask them to take the cartridge. I think he tried to
reason with Carmichael-Smith—but the word came out that the
firing-parade would take place as ordered.

After Waterfield's failure, this was really throwing down the
gauntlet, if you like—I'd not have done it, if I'd been Carmichael-
Smith, for one thing I've learned as an officer is never to give an
order unless there's a good chance of its being obeyed. And if
you'd fallen in with the skirmishers that fine morning, having

seen the sullen faces as they put on their belts and bandoliers and drew their Enfields from the armoury, you'd not have wagered a quid to a hundred on their taking the cartridge. But Carmichael-Smith, the ass, was determined, so there we stood, in extended line between the other squadrons of the regiment facing inwards, the native officers at ease before their respective troops, and the *rissaldar* calling us to attention as Carmichael-Smith, looking thunderous, rode up and saluted.

We waited, with our Enfields at our sides, while he rode along the extended rank, looking at us. There wasn't a sound; we stood with the baking sun at our backs; every now and then a little puff of warm wind would drive a tiny dust-devil across the ground; Plowden's horse kept shying as he cursed and tried to steady it. I watched the shadows of the rank swaying with the effort of standing rigid, and the sweat rivers were tickling my chest. *Naik* Kudrat Ali on my right was straight as a lance; on my other side old Sardul's breathing was hoarse enough to be audible. Carmichael-Smith completed his slow inspection, and reined up almost in front of me; his red face under the service cap was as heavy as a statue's. Then he snapped an order, and the *havildar-major* stepped forward, saluted, and marched to Carmichael-Smith's side, where he turned to face us. Jack Waterfield, sitting a little in rear of the colonel, called out the orders from the platoon exercise manual.

"Prepare to load!" says he, adding quietly: "Rifle-at-full-extent-of-left-arm." The *havildar-major* shoved out his rifle.

"Load!" cries Jack, adding again: "Cartridge-is-brought-to-the-left-hand-right-elbow-raised-tear-off-top-of-cartridge-with-fingers-by-dropping-elbow."

This was the moment; you could feel the rank sway forward ever so little as the *havildar-major*, his bearded face intent, held up the little shiny brown cylinder, tore it across, and poured the powder into his barrel. A hundred and eighty eyes watched him do it; there was just a suspicion of a sigh from the rank as his ram-rod drove the charge home; then he came to attention again. Waterfield gave him the "present" and "fire", and the single demonstration shot cracked across the great parade-ground. On either side, the rest of the regiment waited, watching us.

"Now," says Carmichael-Smith, and although he didn't raise his voice, it carried easily across the parade. "Now, you have seen the loading drill. You have seen the *havildar-major*, a soldier of high caste, take the cartridge. He knows the grease with which it is waxed is pure. I assure you again—nothing that could offend Hindoo or Muslim is being offered to you—I would not permit it. Carry on, *havildar-major*."

What happened was that the *havildar-major* came along the rank, with two *naiks* carrying big bags of cartridges, of which he offered three to each skirmisher. I was looking straight to my front, sweating and wishing the back of my leg would stop itching; I couldn't see what was happening along the rank, but I heard a repeated murmur as the *havildar-major* progressed —"*Nahin, havildar-major sahib; nahin, havildar-major sahib.*" Carmichael-Smith's head was turned to watch; I could see his hand clenched white on his rein.

The *havildar-major* stopped opposite Kudrat Ali, and held out three cartridges. I could feel Kudrat stiffen—he was a big, rangy Punjabi Mussulman, a veteran of Aliwal and the frontier, proud as Lucifer of his stripes and himself, the kind of devoted ass who thinks his colonel is his father and even breaks wind by numbers. I stole a glance at him; his mouth was trembling under his heavy moustache as he muttered:

"*Nahin, havildar-major sahib.*"

Suddenly, Carmichael-Smith broke silence; his temper must have boiled higher with each refusal.

"What the devil do you mean?" His voice cracked hoarsely. "Don't you recognise an order? D'you know what insubordination means?"

Kudrat started violently, but recovered. He swallowed with a gulp you could have heard in Poona, and then says:

"Colonel sahib—I cannot have a bad name!"

"Bad name, by God!" roars Smith. "D'you know a worse name than mutineer?" He sat there glowering and Kudrat trembled; then the *havildar-major's* hand was thrust out to me, his bloodshot brown eyes glaring into mine; I looked at the three little brown cylinders, aware that Waterfield was watching me intently, and old Sardul was breathing like a walrus on my other side.

I took the cartridges—there was a sudden exclamation farther along the rank, but I stuffed two of them into my belt, and held up the third. As I glanced at it, I realised with a start that it wasn't greased—it was waxed. I tore it across with a shaky hand, poured the powder into the barrel, stuffed the cartridge after it, and rammed it down.[22] Then I returned to attention, waiting.

Old Sardul was crying. As the cartridges were held out to him he put up a shaking hand, but not to take them. He made a little, feeble gesture, and then sings out:

"Colonel sahib—it is not just! Never—never have I disobeyed —never have I been false to my salt! Sahib—do not ask this of me—ask anything—my life, even! But not my honour!" He dropped his Enfield, wringing his hands. "Sahib, I—"

"Fool!" shouts Carmichael-Smith. "D'you suppose I would ask you to hurt your honour? When did any man know me do such a thing? The cartridges are clean, I tell you! Look at the havildar-major—look at Makarram Khan! Are they men of no honour? No—and they're not mutinous dogs, either!"

It wasn't the most tactful thing to say, to that particular sepoy; I thought Sardul would go into a frenzy, the way he wept—but he wouldn't touch the cartridges. So it went, along the line; when the end had been reached only four other men out of ninety had accepted the loads—four and that stalwart pillar of loyalty, Flashy Makarram Khan (he knew his duty, and which side his bread was buttered).

So there it was. Carmichael-Smith could hardly talk for sheer fury, but he cussed us something primitive, promising dire retribution, and then dismissed the parade. They went in silence—some stony-faced, others troubled, a number (like old Sardul) weeping openly, but mostly just sullen. For those of us who had taken the cartridges, by the way, there were no reproaches from the others —proper lot of long-suffering holy little Tom Browns they were.

That, of course, was something that Carmichael-Smith didn't understand. He thought the refusal of the cartridges was pure pig-headedness by the sepoys, egged on by a few malcontents. So it was, but there was a genuine religious feeling behind it, and a distrust of the Sirkar. If he'd had his wits about him, he'd have seen that the thing to do now was to drop the cartridge for the moment, and badger Calcutta to issue a new one that the sepoys could grease themselves (as was done, I believe, in some garrisons). He might even have made an example of one or two of the older disobedients, but no, that wasn't enough for him. He'd been defied by his own men, and by God, he wasn't having that. So the whole eighty-five were court-martialled, and the court, composed entirely of native officers, gave them all ten years' hard labour.

I can't say I had much sympathy with 'em—anyone who's fool enough to invite ten years on the rock-pile for his superstitions deserves all he gets, in my view. But I'm bound to say that once the sentence had been passed, it couldn't have been worse carried out—instead of shipping the eighty-five quietly off to jail the buffoon Hewitt decided to let the world—and other sepoys especially—see what happened to mutineers, and so a great punishment parade was ordered for the following Saturday.

As it happened, I quite welcomed this myself, because I had to attend, and so was spared an excursion to Aligaut with Mrs Leslie —that woman's appetite for experiment was increasing, and I'd had a wearing if pleasurable week of it. But from the official point of view, that parade was a stupid, dangerous farce, and came near to costing us all India.

It was a red morning, oppressive and grim, with a heavy, over-cast sky, and a hot wind driving the dust in stinging volleys across the maidan. The air was suffocatingly close, like the moment before thunder. The whole Meerut garrison was there— the Dragoon Guards with their sabres out; the Bengal Artillery, with their British gunners and native assistants in leather breeches standing by their guns; line on line of red-coated native infantry completing the hollow square, and in the middle Hewitt and his staff with Carmichael-Smith and the regimental officers, all mounted. And then the eighty-five were led out in double file, all in full uniform, but for one thing—they were in their bare feet.

I don't know when I've seen a bleaker sight than those two grey ranks standing there hangdog, while someone bawled out the court's findings and sentence, and then a drum began to roll, very slow, and the ceremony began.

Now I've been on more punishment parades than I care to

remember, and quite enjoyed 'em, by and large. There's a
fascination about a hanging, or a good flogging, and the first
time I saw a man shot from a gun—at Kabul, that was—I
couldn't take my eyes off it. I've noticed, too, that the most pious
and humanitarian folk always make sure they get a good view,
and while they look grim or pitying or shocked they take care to
miss none of the best bits. Really, what happened at Meerut
was tame enough—and yet it was different from any other
drumming-out or execution I remember; usually there's excitement, or fear, or even exultation, but here there was just a
doomed depression that you could feel, hanging over the whole
vast parade.

While the drum beat slowly, a *havildar* and two *naiks* went
along the ranks of the prisoners, tearing the buttons off the
uniform coats; they had been half cut off beforehand, to make
the tearing easy, and soon in front of the long grey line there
were little scattered piles of buttons, gleaming dully in the
sultry light; the grey coats hung loose, like sacks, each with a
dull black face above it.

Then the fettering began. Groups of armourers, each under a
British sergeant, went from man to man, fastening the heavy
lengths of irons between their ankles; the fast clanging of the
hammers and the drum-beat made the most uncanny noise,
clink-clank-boom! clink-clank-clink-boom! and a thin wailing
sounded from beyond the ranks of the native infantry.

"Keep those damned people quiet!" shouts someone, and
there was barking of orders and the wailing died away into a
few thin cries. But then it was taken up by the prisoners themselves; some of them stood, others squatted in their chains,
crying; I saw old Sardul, kneeling, smearing dust on his head and
hitting his fist on the ground; Kudrat Ali stood stiff at attention,
looking straight ahead; my half-section, Pir Ali—who to my
astonishment had refused the cartridge in the end—was jabbering angrily to the man next to him; Ram Mangal was actually
shaking his fist and yelling something. A great babble of noise
swelled up from the line, with the *havildar-major* scampering
along the front, yelling "*Chubbarao!* Silence!" while the hammers
clanged and the drum rolled—you never heard such an infernal

din. Old Sardul seemed to be appealing to Carmichael-Smith, stretching out his hands; Ram Mangal was bawling the odds louder than ever; close beside where I was an English sergeant of the Bombay Artillery knocked out his pipe on the gun-wheel, spat, and says:

"There's one black bastard I'd have spread over the muzzle o' this gun, by Jesus! Scatter his guts far enough, eh, Paddy?"

"Aye," says his mate, and paced about, scratching his head. "'Tis a bad business, though, Mike, right enough. Dam' niggers! Bad business!"

"Oughter be a bleedin' sight worse," says Mike. "Pampered sods—lissen 'em squeal! If they 'ad floggin' in the nigger army, they'd 'ave summat to whine about—touch o' the cat'd 'ave them bitin' each other's arses, never mind cartridges. But all they get's the chokey, an' put in irons. That's what riles me— Englishmen get flogged fast enough, an' these black pigs can stand by grinnin' at it, but somebody pulls their buttons off an' they yelp like bleedin' kids!"[23]

"Ah-h," says the other. "Disgustin'. An' pitiful, pitiful."

I suppose it was, if you're the pitying kind—those pathetic-looking creatures in their shapeless coats, with the irons on their feet, some yelling, some pleading, some indifferent, some silently weeping, but mostly just sunk in shame—and out in front Hewitt and Carmichael-Smith and the rest sat their horses and watched, unblinking. I'm not soft, but I had an uneasy feeling just then—you're making a mistake, Hewitt, thinks I, you're doing more harm than good. He didn't seem to know it, but he was trampling on their pride (I may not have much my-self, but I recognise it in others, and it's a chancy thing to tamper with). And yet he could have seen the danger, in the sullen stare of the watching native infantry; they were feeling the shame, too, as those fetters went on, and the prisoners wept and clamoured, and old Sardul grovelled in the dust for one of his fallen buttons, and clenched it against his chest, with the tears streaming down his face.

He was one, I confess, that I felt a mite sorry for, when the fettering was done, and the band had struck up "The Rogues March", and they shuffled off, dragging their irons as they were herded away to the New Jail beyond the Grand Trunk Road. He kept turning and crying out to Carmichael-Smith—it reminded me somehow of how my old guv'nor had wept and pleaded when I saw him off for the last time to the blue-devil factory in the country where he died bawling with delirium tremens. Damned depressing—and as I walked my pony off with the four other loyal skirmishers, and glanced at their smug black faces, I thought, well, you bloody toadies—after all, they were Hindoos; I wasn't.

However, I soon worked off my glums back at Duff Mason's bungalow, by lashing the backside off one of the bearers who'd lost his oil-funnel. And then I had to be on hand for the dinner that was being given for Carmichael-Smith that night (doubtless to celebrate the decimation of his regiment), and Mrs Leslie, dressed up to the nines for the occasion, was murmuring with a meaning look that she intended to have a long ride in the country next day, so I must see picnic prepared, and there were the *mateys* to chase, and the kitchen-staff to swear at, and little Miss Langley, the riding-master's daughter, to chivvy respectfully away—she was a pretty wee thing, seven years old, and a favourite of Miss Blanche's, but she was the damnedest nuisance when she came round the back verandah in the evenings to play, keeping the servants from their work and being given sugar cakes.

With all this, I'd soon forgotten about the punishment parade, until after dinner, when Duff Mason and Carmichael-Smith and Archdale Wilson had taken their pegs and cheroots on to the verandah, and I heard Smith's voice suddenly raised unusually loud. I stopped a *matey* who was taking out a tray to them, and took it myself, so I was just in time to hear Smith saying:

"... of all the damned rubbish I ever heard! Who is this *havildar*, then?"

"Imtiaz Ahmed—and he's a good man, sir." It was young Gough, mighty red in the face, and carrying his crop, for all he was in dinner kit.

"Damned good croaker, you mean!" snaps Smith, angrily. "And you stand there and tell me that he has given you this cock-and-bull about the cavalry plotting to march on the jail and set the prisoners free? Utter stuff—and you're a fool for listening to—"

"I beg your pardon, sir," says Gough, "but I've been to the jail—and it looks ugly. And I've been to barracks; the men are in a bad way, and—"

"Now, now, now," says Wilson, "easy there, young fellow. You don't know 'em, perhaps, as well as we do. Of course they're in a bad way—what, they've seen their comrades marched off in irons, and they're upset. They're like that—they'll cry their eyes out, half of 'em... All right, Makarram Khan," says he, spotting me at the buffet, "you can go." So that was all I heard, for what it was worth, and since nothing happened that night, it didn't seem to be worth too much.[24]

Next morning Mrs Leslie wanted to make an early start, so I fortified myself against what was sure to be a taxing day with half a dozen raw eggs beaten up in a pint of stout, and we rode out again to Aligaut. She was in the cheeriest spirits, curse her, climbing all over me as soon as we reached the temple, and by the end of the afternoon I was beginning to wonder how much more Hindoo culture I could endure, delightful though it was. I was a sore and weary native orderly by the time we set off back, and dozing pleasantly in my saddle as we passed through the little village which lies about a mile east of the British town—indeed, I could just hear the distant chiming of the church bell for evening service—when Mrs Leslie gave an exclamation and reined in her pony.

"What's that?" says she, and as I came up beside her, she hushed me and sat listening. Sure enough, there was another sound—a distant, indistinct murmur, like the sea on a far shore. I couldn't place it, so we rode quickly forward to where the trees ended, and looked across the plain. Straight ahead in the distance were the bungalows at the end of the Mall, all serene; far to the left, there was the outline of the Jail, and beyond it the huge mass of Meerut city—nothing out of the way there. And then beyond the Jail, I saw it as I peered at the red horizon—where the native cavalry and infantry lines lay, dark clouds of smoke were rising against the orange of the sky, and flickers of flame showed in the dusk. Buildings were burning, and the distant murmur was resolving itself into a thousand voices shouting, louder and ever louder. I sat staring, with a horrid suspicion growing in my mind, half-aware that Mrs Leslie was tugging at my sleeve, demanding to know what was happening. I couldn't tell her, because I didn't know; nobody knew, in that first moment, on a peaceful, warm May evening when the great Indian Mutiny began.

If I'd had my wits about me, or more than an inkling of what was happening, I'd have turned our ponies north and ridden for the safety of the British infantry lines a mile away. But my first thought was: Gough was right, some crazy bastards are rioting and trying to break the prisoners loose—and of course they'll fail, because Hewitt'll have British troops marching down to the scene at once; maybe they're there already, cutting up the niggers. I was right—and wrong, you see, but above all I was curious, once my first qualms had settled. So it wasn't in any spirit of chivalry that I sang out to Mrs Leslie:

"Ride to the bungalow directly, mem-sahib! Hold tight, now!" and cut her mare hard across the rump. She squealed as it leaped forward, and called to me, but I was already wheeling away down towards the distant Jail—I wanted to see the fun, whatever it was, and I had a good horse under me to cut out at the first sign of danger. Her plaintive commands echoed after me, but I was putting my pony to a bank, and clattering off towards the outlying buildings of the native city bazaar, skirting south so that I'd pass the Jail at a distance and see what was happening.

At first there didn't seem to be much; this side of the bazaar was strangely empty, but in the gathering dark I could hear rather than see confused activity going on between the Jail and the Grand Trunk—shouting and the rush of hurrying feet, and sounds of smashing timber. I wheeled into the bazaar, following the confusion of noise ahead; the whole of the sky to my front beyond the bazaar was glowing orange now, whether with fire or sundown you couldn't tell, but the smoke was hanging in a great pall beyond the city—it's a hell of a fine fire, thinks I, and forged on into the bazaar, between booths where dim figures seemed to be trying to get their goods away, or darting about in the shadows, chattering and wailing. I bawled to a fat vendor, who was staring down the street, asking what was up, but he just waddled swiftly into his shop, slamming his shutters—try to get sense out of an excited Indian, if you like. Then I reined up, with a *chico** scampering almost under my hooves, and the mother after it, crouching and shrieking, and before I knew it there was a swarm of folk in the street, all wailing and running in panic; stumbling into my pony, while I cursed and lashed out with my quirt; behind them the sounds of riot were suddenly closer—hoarse yelling and chanting, and the sudden crack of a shot, and then another.

Time to withdraw to a safer distance, thinks I, and wheeled my pony through the press into a side-alley. Someone went down beneath my hooves, they scattered like sheep—and then down the alley ahead of me, running pell-mell for his life, was a man in the unmistakable stable kit of the Dragoon Guards, bare-headed and wild-eyed, and behind him, like hounds in full cry, a screaming mob of niggers.

He saw me ahead, and yelled with despair—of course, what he saw was a great hairy native villain blocking his way. He darted for a doorway, and stumbled, and in an instant they were on him, a clawing, animal mob, tearing at him while he lashed out, yelling obscenities. For an instant he broke free, blood pouring from a wound in his neck, and actually scrambled under my pony; the mob was round us in a trice, dragging him out bodily while I struggled to keep my seat—there was no question of helping him, even if I'd been fool enough to try. They bore him up, everyone shrieking like madmen, and smashed him down on the table of a pop-shop, holding his limbs while others broke the pop-bottles and slashed and stabbed at him with the shards.

It was a nightmare. I could only clutch my reins and stare at that screaming, thrashing figure, half-covered in the pop foam, as those glittering glass knives rose and fell. In seconds he was just a hideous bloody shape, and then someone got a rope round him, and they swung him up to a beam, with his life pouring out of him.[25] In panic I drove my heels into the pony, blundered to the corner, and rode for dear life.

It was the shocking unexpectedness of it that had unmanned

* Child.

me—to see a white man torn to pieces by natives. Perhaps you can't imagine what that meant in India; it was something you could not believe, even when you saw it. For a few moments I must have ridden blind, for the next thing I knew I was reining up on the edge of the Grand Trunk where it comes north out of Meerut city, gazing at a huge rabble pouring up towards the British town; to my amazement half of them were sepoys, some of them just in their jackets, others in full fig down to the cross-belts, brandishing muskets and bayonets, and yelling in unison: "Mat karo! Mat karo!* Sipahi jai!" and the like—slogans of death and rebellion. There was one rascal on a cart, brandishing ankle-irons above his head, and a heaving mass of sepoys and bazaar-wallahs pushing his vehicle along, yelling like drunkards.

Beyond the road the native cavalry barracks were in full flame; even as I watched I saw one roof cave in with an explosion of sparks. Behind me there were buildings burning in the bazaar, and even as I turned to look I saw a gang of ruffians hurling an oil-lamp into a booth, while others were steadily thrashing with clubs at the fallen body of the owner; finally they picked him up and tossed him into the blaze, dancing and yelling as he tried vainly to struggle out; he was a human torch, his mouth opening and closing in unheard screams, and then he fell back in the burning ruin.

I don't know how long I sat there, staring at these incredible things, but I know it was dark, with flames leaping up every-where, and an acrid reek pervading the air, before I came to my senses enough to realise that the sooner I lit out the better—of course, I was safe enough in that I was to all outward appearance a native, and a big, ugly one at that, but it made no sense to linger; any moment there must be the sound of bugles up the road, heralding a British detachment, and I didn't want to be caught up in the ensuing brawl. So I put my pony's nose north, and trotted along the edge of the road, with that stream of mad humanity surging in the same direction at my elbow.

Even then I hadn't determined what it all meant, but any doubts I might have had were resolved as I came level with the Jail, and there was a huge crowd, clamouring and applauding

* "Kill!"

round a bonfire, and forming up, in their prison *dhotis*,* but with their ankles freed, were some of the prisoners—I recognised Gobinda, and one or two others, and a sepoy whom I didn't know was standing on a cart, haranguing the mob, although you could hardly hear him for the din:

"It is done!... Death to the *gora-log*!†... sahibs are already running away...see the broken chains!... On, brothers, kill! kill! To the white town!"

The whole mob screamed as one man, leaping up and down, and then bore the prisoners shoulder-high, streaming out on to the Grand Trunk towards the distant Mall—God, I could see flames up there already, out towards the eastern end. There must be bungalows burning on this side of the Mall, beyond the Nullah.

There was only one way for me to go. Behind was Meerut city and the bazaar, which was being smashed up and looted by the sound of things; to my left lay the burning native barracks; ahead, between me and the British Town, the road was jammed with thousands of crazy fanatics, bent on blood and destruction. I waited till the press thinned a little, and swung right, heading for the Nullah north of the Jail; I would cross the east bridge, and make a long circle north past the Mall to come to the British camp lines.

The first part was easy enough; I crossed the Nullah, and skirted the east end of the British Town, riding carefully in the half-dark, for the moon wasn't up yet. It was quiet here, in the groves of trees; the tumult was far off to my left, but now and then I saw little groups of natives—servant-women, probably, scurrying among the bushes, and one ominous sign that some of the killers had come this way—an old *chowkidar*, with his broken staff beside him, lying with his skull beaten in. Were they butchering anyone, then—even their own folk? Of course—any natives suspected of loyalty would be fair game—including the *gora-colonel*'s lapdog, as Ram Mangal had charmingly called me. I pressed on quickly; not far behind me, I could hear chanting voices, and see torch-light among the trees. The sooner I ...

* Loin-cloths.
† British.

"Help! Help! In God's name, help us!"

It came from my right; a little bungalow, behind a white gate, and as I stopped, uncertain, another voice cried:

"Shut up, Tommy! God knows who it is . . . see the lights yonder!"

"But Mary's dead!" cries the first voice, and it would have made your hair stand up. "She's dead, I tell you—they've—"

They were English, anyway, and without thinking I slipped from the saddle, vaulted the gate, and cried:

"It's a friend! Who are you?"

"Oh, thank God!" cries the first voice. "Quickly—they've killed Mary . . . Mary!"

I glanced back; the torches were still two hundred yards away among the trees. If I could get the occupants of the bungalow moving quickly, they might get away. I strode up the verandah steps, looked through the space where a chick had been torn down, and saw a wrecked room, with an oil-lamp burning feebly, and a white man, his left leg soaked in blood, lying against the wall, a sabre in his hand, staring at me with feverish eyes.

"Are you . . . ?" he began, and then yelled. "Christ—it's a mutineer—3rd Cavalry! Jim!"

And I hadn't got my mouth open when out of the shadows someone sprang; I had an instant's vision of a white face, red moustache, staring eyes, and whirling sabre, and then I was locked with him, crashing to the floor, while I yelled:

"You bloody idiot! I'm English, damn you!"

But he seemed to have gone mad; even as I wrested his sabre from him and sprang away he yelled to his pal, who feebly shoved his sabre towards him; the next thing he was slashing at me, yelling curses, and I was guarding and trying to shout sense at him. I broke ground, fell over something soft, and realised as I struck the ground that it was a white woman, in evening dress— or rather it was her body, for she was lying in a pool of blood. I flung up my sabre to guard another maniac slash, but too late; I felt a fiery pain across my skull, just above the left ear, and the fellow on the floor screams:

"Go it, Jim! Finish him, finish—"

The crash of musketry filled the room; the fellow above me

twisted grotesquely, dropping his sabre, and tumbled down across my legs; there were black faces grinning at the window above me through the powder smoke, and then they were in the room, yelling with triumph as they drove their bayonets into the wounded Tommy, hacking at him, smashing the furniture, and finally one of them was helping me up, shouting:

"Just in time, brother! Thank the 11th N.I., *sowar*! Aieee! Three of the pigs! God be praised—have ye been at their goods, then?"

I was dizzy with pain, so he dropped me, and while they ransacked the bungalow, growling like beasts, I crawled out on to the verandah and into the bushes. I lay there, staunching the blood that was running down my cheek; it wasn't a bad wound—no worse than the schlager cut beside it, which de Gautet had given me years ago. But I didn't come out, even after they'd gone, taking my pony with them; I was too shaken and scared—that idiot Jim had come within an ace of finishing me—my God, it had been Jim Lewis, of course—the veterinary. I'd bowed him out of Mason's bungalow only a couple of nights before. And now, he was dead, and his wife Mary—and I was alive, saved by the mutineers who'd murdered them.

I lay there, still half-dazed, trying to make sense of it. This was mutiny, no doubt of it, and on the grand scale—the 3rd Cavalry were out, of course, and I'd seen 20th N.I. men under arms on the Grand Trunk; the fellows who'd inadvertently saved me were 11th N.I., so that was the whole Indian garrison of Meerut. But where the devil were the two British regiments?—their lines weren't more than a half-mile from where I was lying, beyond the Mall, but although two or three hours must have passed since the rioting started, there wasn't a sign of any activity by the authorities. I lay listening to the crackle of firing, and the distant tumult of voices and wrecking and burning—there were no bugle calls, no sound of volleys, no shouted orders, no heavy gunfire amidst the confusion. Hewitt couldn't just be sitting doing nothing—a terrible thought struck me: they couldn't have been wiped out, surely? No, you can't beat two thousand disciplined soldiers with a mutinous mob—but what the hell was keeping 'em quiet, then?[26]

In the long run I decided I'd have to make a break for it, up to the Mall and across towards the British infantry lines; it would take me past Duff Mason's bungalow, and the MacDowalls', so I could see what was happening there, though no doubt the people would have withdrawn already to the safety of the British camps. Yes, I could see, when I stood up, that some of the bungalows south of the Mall were burning, and there was a hell of a din and shooting coming from the British Town farther west; I would have to keep well clear of that.

I moved cautiously through the trees, and found the little drive that led up to the eastern end of the Mall. There was a bungalow burning like blazes a hundred yards ahead, and half a dozen sepoys standing by its fence, cursing and occasionally firing a shot into it; on the other side of the road, a crowd of servants were huddled under a tree, and as I stole quietly towards them in the shadows I could hear them wailing. That was Surgeon Dawson's bungalow; as I came level with it, I remembered that Dawson had been down with smallpox—he and his wife and children had all been confined to the house—and there was its roof caving in with a thunderous whoosh of sparks. I felt giddy and ill at the thought—and then hurried on, past that hellish scene; the drive ahead was deserted as far as I could see in the light of the rising moon.

Our bungalow wasn't burning, anyway—but just before I reached it my eye was caught by something on the verandah of the Courtneys' place across the way. Something was moving; it was a human figure, trying to crawl. I hesitated fearfully, and then slipped through the gate and up the path; the figure was wheezing horribly; it suddenly rolled over on its back, and I saw it was a native servant, with a bayonet buried in his chest. As I stood appalled his head rolled, and he saw me; he tried to lift a hand, pointing towards the house, and then he flopped back, groaning.

For the life of me I can't think what made me go inside, and I wish I hadn't. Mrs Courtney was dead in her chair, shot and bayonetted, with her head buried in the cushions, and when I looked beyond I vomited on the spot—her three children were there as well. It was a sight to blast your eyes; the place was like a slaughter-house, stinking with blood—I turned and ran, retching, and didn't stop until I found myself stumbling on to Duff Mason's verandah.

The place was still as death—but I had to go in, for I knew that in Duff Mason's bottom desk-drawer there was a Colt and a box of ammunition, and I wanted them both as I wanted my next breath. I glanced through the trees towards the Dawsons' burning home, but there was no sign of approaching mutineers, so I slipped through the chick-door into the hall. And there I fainted dead away—something I haven't done more than twice in my life.

The reason I'll tell you quickly—Mrs Leslie's head was lying on the hall table. Her body, stripped naked—that same plump white body that I'd fondled only a few hours earlier, was lying a few feet beyond, unspeakably gashed. And in the doorway to the dining-room, Mrs Captain MacDowall was huddled grotesquely against the jamb, with a *tulwar* pinning her to the wall; clenched in one hand was a small vase, with the flowers it had held scattered on the boards—I realised that she must have snatched it up as a weapon.

I don't remember getting Duff Mason's revolver, but I know that later I was standing in the hall, keeping my eyes away from those ghastly things on the floor, loading it with cartridges and weeping and cursing to myself together. Why—why the hell should they do this?—I found myself blubbering it aloud. I've seen death and horror more than most men, but this was worse than anything—it was beyond bestiality. Gobinda? Pir Ali? Old Sardul? Ram Mangal, even? They couldn't have done this—they wouldn't have done it to the wives of their bitterest enemies. But it had been done—if not by them, then by men like them. It was mad, senseless, incredible—but it was there, and if I tell you of it now, it is not to horrify, but to let you understand what happened in India in '57, and how it was like nothing that any of us had ever seen before. And none of us—not even I—was ever the same again.

You know me, and what a damned coward and scoundrel I am, and not much moved by anything—but I did an odd thing in that house. I couldn't bring myself to touch Mrs Leslie, or even to look again at that ghastly head, with its frizzy red hair and staring eyes—but before I left I went to Mrs Captain MacDowall, and forced the vase from her fingers, and I collected the flowers and put them in it. I was going to set it on the floor beside her, and then I remembered that carping Scotch voice, and her contemptuous sniff—so I set it on a little table instead, with a napkin under it, just so. I took one more look round—at the wreckage of the place that my bearers had made the finest house on the station; the polished wood scarred and broken, the ornaments smashed, the rug matted with blood, the fine chandelier that had been Miss Blanche's pride wantonly shattered in a corner—and I went out of that house with such hate in my heart as I've never felt before or since. There was something I wanted to do—and quickly; I had my chance in the next five minutes, as I slipped up to the corner of the drive, and looked westward along the Mall.

The shots were still crackling in the British Town—were there any of our folk left alive down there, I wondered. How many bungalows, burned or whole, contained the same horrors that I'd found? I wasn't going to look—and I wasn't going a step farther, either. Burning buildings, screaming mobs, death and wreckage—they were all there, ahead of me; as I looked north through the trees I could see torchlight and hear yelling between me and the British lines. Whatever Hewitt and Carmichael-Smith and the rest of them were doing—supposing they were still alive—I'd now decided they could do without me: all I wanted was to get out of Meerut, and away from that hell, as fast as I could, and find peace and safety, and rest the hellish pain in my wounded head. But first I must do what I lusted above all things to do—and here came the chance, in the shape of a trooper, cantering along the Mall, swaying in his saddle, singing drunkenly to himself as he rode. Behind him, against the distant flames, there were a few parties of sepoys straggling on the Mall; eastward the road was quite empty.

I stepped into the Mall as he rode up; he had a bloody *tulwar* in one hand, a foolish animal grin on his filthy black face, and the grey coat of the 3rd Cavalry on his back. Seeing me in the same rig he let out a whoop and reined in unsteadily.

"*Ram-ram,** sowar*," says I, and forced myself to leer at him.
"Have you slain as many as I have, eh? And whose blood is
that?" I pointed at his sword.

"Hee-hee-hee-hee," giggles he, lurching in the saddle. "Is it
blood? It is? Whose—why, maybe it is Karmik-al-Ismeet's?" He
waved the blade, goggling drunkenly. "Or Hewitt Sahib's? Nay,
nay, nay!"

"Whose, then?" says I, genially, and laid a hand on his crupper.

"Ah, now," says he, studying the blade. "The Riding-Master
Langley Sahib's—eh? That son of a stinking mangy pork-eating
dog! Nay, nay, nay!" He leaned precariously from the saddle.
"Not Langley. Hee-hee-hee-hee! He will have no grand-children
by his daughter! Hee-hee-hee-hee!"

And I'd chased her growling, off the verandah, just the previous
night. I had to hold on to his leather to keep my balance, biting
back the bile that came into my mouth. I took another quick
glance along the Mall; the nearest sepoys were still some distance
off.

"*Shabash!*" says I. "That was a brave stroke." And as he
leered and chortled I brought my hand up with the Colt in it,
aimed carefully just above his groin, and fired.

He reared up, and I clutched the bridle to steady the horse as
he went flying from the saddle; a second and I had it managed,
then I was up and in his place, and he was threshing on the
ground, screaming in agony—with luck he would take days to die.
I circled him once, snarling down at him, looked back along the
Mall, at those distant black figures like Dante's demons against
the burning inferno behind them, and then I was thundering
eastward, past the last bungalows, and the sights and sounds of
horror were fading behind me.[27]

*   *   *

God knows how far I rode that night—probably no great distance. I don't think I was quite right in the head, partly from
the shock of what I'd seen, but much more from the pain of my
wound, which began to act up most damnably. It felt as though
my left temple was wide open, and white heat was getting into

* Hello.

my brain; I could hardly see out of my left eye, and was haunted
by the fear that the cut would send me blind. I had enough sense,
though, to know which way I wanted to go—south by east at
first to skirt Meerut city, and then south by west until I struck
the Delhi road at a safe distance. Delhi meant the safety of a
great British garrison (or so I thought), and since there were telegraph lines between it and Meerut I felt certain that I'd meet help
coming along it. I wasn't to know that the fool Hewitt hadn't
even sent a message to tell of the Meerut outbreak.

So that was the course I followed, half-blind with pain, and
constantly losing my bearings, even in the bright moonlight, so
that I had to stop and cast about among the groves and hamlets.
I forged ahead, and when I came on the Delhi road at last, what
did I see but two companies of sepoys tramping along under the
moon, in fair order, singing and chanting as they went, with
their muskets slung and the *havildars* calling the step. For an
instant I thought they must be reliefs from Delhi, and then it
dawned on me that they were marching in the wrong direction—
but I was too done up to care; I just sat my pony by the roadside,
and when they spotted me half a dozen of them broke ranks,
crying that it was a 3rd Cavalryman, and cheering me until they
saw the blood on my face and coat. Then they helped me down,
and sponged my head and gave me a drink, and their *havildar* says:

"You're in no case to catch your *pultan* tonight, bhai.* They
must be half-way to Delhi by now," at which the rest of them
cheered and threw up their hats.

"Are they so?" says I, wondering what the devil he meant.

"Aye, first among the loot, as usual," cries another. "They
have the advantage of us, on their ponies—but we'll be there,
too!" And they all cheered and laughed again, black faces with
grinning white teeth looking down at me. Even in my bemused
state this seemed to mean only one thing.

"Has Delhi fallen, then?" I asked, and the *havildar* says, not
yet, but the three regiments there would surely rise, and with the
whole of the Meerut garrison marching to help them the sahibs
would be overthrown and slaughtered within the day.

"We were only the beginning!" says he, sponging away at my

* Brother.

wound. "Soon Delhi—then Agra, Cawnpore, Jaipur—aye, and Calcutta itself! The Madras army is on the move also, and from one end of the Grand Trunk to the other the sahibs have been driven into their compounds like mice into their holes. The North is rising—there, lie still, man—there will be sahibs enough for your knife-edge, when your wound is healed. Best come with us, if you can travel; see, we hold together in good company, like soldiers—lest the sahibs send out riders who may snap us up piecemeal."

"No—no," says I, struggling up. The pain made me dizzy, but I had to get away from them. "I'll ride on to join my *pultan*." And despite their protests I clambered on to my pony again.

"He thirsts for white blood!" shouts one. "*Shabash, sowar!* But leave enough for the rest of us to drink!"

I shouted something incoherent, about wanting to be first in at the death, and as they halloed encouragement after me I put my pony to a trot, hanging on grimly, and set off down the road. The other company was yelling and singing as I passed—I remember noting that they were wearing flower garlands round their necks. I carried on until I had distanced them, my head splitting at every step and swelling up like a balloon, and then I remember swinging off into the forest, and blundering until I slumped out of the saddle and lay where I fell, utterly exhausted.

When I came to—if you can call it that—I was extremely ill. I've no clear idea of what followed, except that there were long periods of confused dreaming, and moments of vivid clarity, but it's difficult to tell one from the other. I'm sure that at one point I was lying face-down in a tank, gulping down brackish water while a little girl with a goat stood and watched me—I can even remember that the goat had a red thread round its horns. On the other hand, I doubt if Dr Arnold truly did come striding through the trees in an enormous turban, crying: "Flashman, you have been fornicating with Lakshmibai during first lesson; how often must I tell you there is to be no galloping after morning prayers, sir!" Or that John Charity Spring stood there four-square shouting: "Amo, amas, amat! Lay into him, doctor! The horny young bastard is always amo-ing! *Hae nugae in seria ducent mala,** by God!" And then they changed into a wrinkled old

* These trifles will lead to grave evils.

native woman and a scrawny nigger with a white moustache;
she was holding a *chatti** to my mouth—it felt hard and cold,
but it became suddenly soft and warm, and the *chatti* was Mrs
Leslie's lips against mine, and what was running into my mouth
wasn't water, but blood, and I screamed silently while all the
grinning faces whirled round me, and the whole world was burning while a voice intoned: "Cartridge is brought to the left hand
with right elbow raised"... and then the old man and woman
were there again, peering anxiously down at me while I slipped
into black unconsciousness.

It was in their hut that I finally came to myself, with a half-
healed wound on my temple, having lost heaven knows how
much blood and weight, verminous and stinking and weak as a
kitten—but with my head just clear enough to remember what
had happened. Unfortunately, it wasn't to prove quite so clear
about thinking ahead.

I've since calculated that I lay ill and delirious in their hovel
for nearly three weeks, perhaps longer. They didn't seem to know
—apart from being the lowest kind of creatures, they were scared
stiff of me, and it wasn't until I'd prevailed on them to fetch
someone from a nearby village that I could get any notion of
what was happening. They finally drummed up an ancient
pensioner, who shied off as soon as he saw me—my cavalry coat
and gear, and my filthy appearance must have marked me as a
mutineer par excellence—but before he could get out of the door
I had soothed him with my revolver, held in a shaky hand, and in
no time he was crouching beside my charpoy, babbling like the
man from Reuters, while the rest of his village peeped through
cracks in the walls, shivering.

Delhi had fallen—he had been there, and there had been a
terrible slaughter of sahibs, and all their folk. The King of Delhi
had been proclaimed and now ruled all India. It had been the
same everywhere—Meerut, Bareilly, Aligarh, Etawah, Mainpuri
(all of which were within a hundred miles or so), the splendid
sepoys had triumphed all along the line, and soon every peasant
in the land would receive a rupee and a new chicken. (Sensation.)
The sahibs had tried to fall treacherously on the native soldiers at

* Pot, drinking cup.

Agra, Cawnpore and Lucknow, but there was no doubt that these places would succumb also—two regiments of mutineers had passed through his own village last night, with cannon, to assist in the overthrow of Agra—everywhere there were dead sahibs, obviously there would soon be none left in the world. Bombay had risen, Afghan fighters were pouring in from the north, a great Muslim *jihad* had been proclaimed, fort after fort of the hated *gora-log* was going down, with fearful slaughter. Doubtless I had already borne my part?—excellent, I would certainly be rewarded with a nawab's throne and treasure and flocks of amorous women. What less did I deserve? 3rd Cavalry, was I not? Doughty fighters—he had been in the Bombay Sappers, himself, thirty-one years' service, and not so much as a *naik's* stripes to swell his miserable *pinshun*—aieee, it was time the mean, corrupt and obscene Sirkar was swept away . . .

Some of his news would be exaggerated bosh, of course, but I couldn't judge how much, and I didn't doubt his information about the local mutinies (which proved accurate enough, by the way: half the stations between Meerut and Cawnpore had been overrun by this time). Perhaps I was too ready to swallow his gammon about Afghan invasion and Bombay being in flames— but remember, I'd *seen* the stark, staring impossible happen at Meerut—after that, anything was credible. After all, there was only one British soldier in India for every fifty sepoys, to say nothing of banditti, frontiersmen, dacoits, bazaar ruffians and the like—dear God, if the thing spread there wasn't an earthly damned reason why they shouldn't swallow every British garri-son, cantonment and residency from Khyber to Coromandel. And it would spread—I didn't doubt it, as I sat numb and shaking on my *charpai*.

Coward's reasoning, if you like, but I don't know any other kind, thank heaven; at least it prepares you for the worst. And there couldn't be much worse than my present situation, plumb in the eye of the storm—damnation, of all the places to hide in, what malign fate had taken me to Meerut? And how to get away? —my native disguise was sound enough, but I couldn't skulk round India forever as a footloose nigger. I'd have to find a British garrison—a large, safe one. . . . Cawnpore? Not by a mile—the whole Jumna valley seemed to be ablaze. North wasn't any good, Delhi was gone and Agra on the brink. . . . South? Gwalior? Jhansi? Indore? I found myself chattering the names aloud, and repeating one over and over—"Jhansi, Jhansi!"

Now, you must remember I was in my normal state of great pusillanimity, and half-barmy to boot, as a result of shock and the clout I'd taken. Otherwise I'd never have dreamed of Jhansi, two hundred and fifty miles away—but Ilderim was at Jhansi, and if there was one thing certain in this dreadful world, it was that he'd keep his tryst, and would either wait for me at Bull Temple as he'd promised, or leave word. And Jhansi must be safe —dammit, I'd spent weeks with its ruler, in civilised discussion and hectic banging; she was a lovely, wonderful girl, and would have her state well in hand, surely? Yes, Jhansi—it was madness, and I know it now, but in my weak, feverish state it seemed the only course at the time.

So south I went, talking to myself most of the time, and shying away from everyone and everything except the meanest villages, where I put in for provisions; I didn't stand on ceremony, but just lurched in snarling and brandishing my Colt, kicking the cowed inhabitants aside, and lifting whatever I fancied—I've never been more grateful for my English public school upbringing than I was then. Whether I was unlucky or not I don't know, but as I worked my way south past Khurjah and Hathras and Firozabad, over the river and down past Gohad to the Jhansi border, everything I saw confirmed my worst fears. I must have skulked in the brush a dozen times to avoid bands of sepoys—one of 'em a full regiment, blow me, with colours and band tootling away, but plainly mutineers from the din they made and the slovenly way they marched. I know now that there were British-held towns and stations along the way, and even bands of our cavalry scouring the country, but I never ran across them. What I did see was a sickening trail of death—burned-out bungalows, looted villages, bodies all swollen up and half-eaten by vultures and jackals. I remember one little garden, beside a pretty house, and three skeletons among the flowers—picked clean by ants, I daresay. Two were full-grown, and one was a baby. Now and then I would see smoke on the horizon, or over the trees, and crowds of

villagers fleeing with their miserable belongings—it was like the
end of the world to me, then, and if you'd known India you'd
have thought the same—imagine it in Kent or Hampshire, for
that's how it seemed to us.

Fortunately, thanks to my curiously light-headed condition,
my recollections of that wandering ride are not too clear; it
wasn't until the very morning that I came down out of the low
hills to Jhansi city, and saw the distant fort-crowned rock above
the town, that my mind seemed to give a little snap—I remember
sitting my pony, with my brain clearing, understanding what I'd
done, and why I was here, breaking out in a sweat at my own
temerity, and then realising that I'd perhaps done the wise thing,
after all. It all looked peaceful enough, although I was on the
wrong side of the city to see the British cantonment; I decided to
lie up during the afternoon, and then slip into Bull Temple, which
was not far from the Jokan Bagh, a garden of little beehive temples
not far outside the town. If Ilderim's messenger wasn't there by
sundown, I'd scout the cantonment, and if all was well I'd ride in
and report myself to Skene.

The sun was just slipping away and the shadows lengthening
when I skirted the woods where Lakshmibai's pavilion lay—who
knows, thinks I, perhaps we'll dance another Haymarket hornpipe
before long—and came down to Bull Temple just after dusk. I
didn't see a soul as I came, but I was cheered by the sound of a
bugle-call in the distance, and I was pressing ahead more boldly
up towards the temple ruin when someone clicked his tongue in
the shadows, and I reined up sharply.

"Who goes there?" says I, fingering the Colt, and a man
lounged out, spreading his hands to show they were empty. He
was a Pathan, skull-cap and *pyjamys* and all, and as he came to
my horse's head I recognised the *sowar* who'd given me his gear
and pony when I'd left Jhansi—Rafik Tamwar.

"Flashman *husoor*," says he, softly. "Ilderim said you would
come." And without another word he jerked his thumb towards
the temple itself, put his hands to his mouth, and hooted softly
like an owl; there was an answering hoot from the ruins, and
Tamwar nodded to me to go ahead.

"Ilderim is yonder," says he, and before I could ask him what the devil it meant, he had dissolved into the shadows and I was staring uneasily across the tangle of weeds and broken masonry that marked the old temple garden; there was a glare of fire-light from the doorway in the half-fallen shell of the dome, and a man was standing waiting—even at that distance I knew it was Ilderim Khan, and a moment later I was face to bearded grinning face with him, shaking with very relief as his one sound arm clasped me round the shoulders—the other was bound up in a sling—and he was chuckling in his throat and growling that I must have a pact with Shaitan since I was alive to keep the rendezvous.

"For we have heard of Meerut," says he, as he drew me in to the fire, and the half-dozen *sowars* crouched round it made space for us. "And Delhi, Aligarh and the rest—"

"But what the blazes are you doing here?" says I. "Since when have irregular cavalry taken to bivouacking in ruins when they have their own quarters?"

He stared at me, stopping in the act of throwing a billet on the fire, and something in that look turned my blood to ice. They were all staring at me; I glanced from one grim bearded face to another, and in a voice suddenly hoarse I asked:

"What does it mean? Your officer—Henry sahib? Has any-thing—"

Ilderim threw the billet on the fire, and squatted down beside me. "Henry sahib is dead, brother," says he quietly. "And Skene sahib. And the Collector sahib. And all their women, and their children also. They are all dead."

I can see it now as vividly as I saw it then—the dark hawk-face silhouetted against the temple wall that glowed ruddy in the firelight, and the bright stream of a tear on his cheek. You don't often see a Pathan cry, but Ilderim Khan cried as he told me what had happened at Jhansi.

"When the news came of Meerut, that black Hindoo bitch who calls herself Maharani summoned Skene sahib, and says she needs must enlarge her bodyguard, for the safety of her person and the treasure in her palace. These being unquiet times. She spoke very sweetly, and Skene, being young and foolish, gave her what she wished—aye, he even said that we of the free cavalry might serve her, and Kala Khan (may he rot in hell) took her salt and her money, and two others with him. But most of her new guard were the scum of the bazaar—*badmashes* and *klifti-wallahs** and street-corner ten-to-one assassins and the sweepings of the jail.

"Then, two weeks ago, there was stirring among the sepoys of the 12th N.I., and chapattis and lotus flowers passed, and some among them burned a bungalow by night. But the colonel sahib spoke with them, and all seemed well, and a day and a night passed. Then Faiz Ali and the false swine Kala Khan, with a great rabble of sepoys and these new heroes of the Rani's guard, fell on the Star Fort, and made themselves masters of the guns and powder, and marched on the cantonment to put it to the fire, but Skene sahib had warning from a true sepoy, and while some dozen sahibs were caught and butchered by these vermin, the rest escaped into the little Town Fort, and the mem-sahibs and little ones with them, and made it good against the mutineers. And for five days they held it—do I not know? For I was there, with Rafik Tamwar and Shadman Khan and Muhammed Din, whom you see here. And I took this—" he touched his wounded arm "—the seventh time they tried to storm the wall."

* Thieves.

"They came like locusts," growls one of the *sowars* round the fire. "And like locusts they were driven."

"Then the food was gone, and the water, and no powder remained for the *bundooks*,"* says Ilderim. "And Skene sahib— have ye seen a young man grow old in a week, brother?—said we could hold no longer, for the children were like to die. So he sent three men, under a white flag, to the Rani, to beg her help. And she—she told them she had no concern for the English swine."

"I don't believe it," says I.

"Listen, brother—and believe, for I was one of the three, and Muhammed Din here another, and we went with Murray sahib to her palace gate. Him only they admitted, and flung us two in a stinking pit, but they told us what passed afterwards—that she had spurned Murray sahib, and afterwards he was racked to pieces in her dungeon." He turned to stare at me with blazing eyes. "I do not know—it is what I was told; only hear what followed, and then—judge thou."

He stared into the fire, clenching and unclenching his fist, and then went on:

"When no word went back to Skene sahib, and seeing the townsfolk all comforting the mutineers, and jeering at his poor few, he offered to surrender. And Kala Khan agreed, and they opened the fort gates, and trusted to the mercy of the mutineers."

It was then I saw the tear run down into his beard; he didn't look at me, but just continued gazing at the flames and speaking very softly:

"They took them all—men, and women, and children—to the Jokan Bagh, and told them they must die. And the women wept, and threw themselves on their knees, and begged for the children's lives—mem-sahibs, brother, you understand, such ladies as you know of, grovelled at the boots of the filth of the bazaar. I saw it!" He suddenly shouted. "And the untouchable scum— these high-caste worms who call themselves men, and will shudder away if a real man's shadow falls across their *chattis*—these creatures laughed and mocked the mem-sahibs and kicked them aside.

"I saw it—I, and Muhammed Din here, for they brought us

* Firearms.

out to the Jokan Bagh saying, 'See thy mighty sahibs; see thy proud mem-sahibs who looked on us as dirt; see them crawl to us before they die.'"

"There is a furnace thrice-heated waiting," says one of the *sowars*. "Remember that, *rissaldar* sahib."

"If they burn forever it will not be hot enough," says Ilderim. "They killed the sahibs first—the Collector sahib, Andrews sahib—Gordon, Burgess, Taylor, Turnbull—all of them. They held them in a row, and chopped them down with cleavers. Skene sahib they slew last of all; he asked to embrace his wife, but they laughed at him and struck him, and bade him kneel for the knife. 'I will die on my feet,' says he, 'with no regret save that I am polluted by the touch of dishonoured lice like you. Strike, coward —see, my hands are tied.' And Bakshish Ali, the jail daroga, cut him down. And through all this they made the women and children watch, crying 'See, thy husband's blood! See, baby, it is thy father's head—ask him to kiss thee, baby!' And then they killed the mem-sahibs, in another row, while the townsfolk watched and cheered, and threw marigolds at the executioners. And Skene mem-sahib said to Faiz Ali, 'If it pleases you, you may burn me alive, or do what you will, if you will spare the children.' But they threw dirt in her face, and swore the children should die."

One of the *sowars* says: "There will be a red thread round her wrist, as for a *Ghazi*."

"And I," says Ilderim, "fought like a tiger and foamed and swore as they held me. And I cried out: '*Shabash*, mem-sahib!' and 'Heep-heep-heep-hoora', as the sahibs do, to comfort her. And they cut her down." He was crying openly now, his mouth working. "And then they took the children—twenty of them— little children, that cried out and called for their dead mothers, and they cut them all in pieces, with axes and butchers' knives. And there they left them all, in the Jokan Bagh, without burial."[28]

Hearing something, however horrible, can never be as ghastly as seeing it; the mind may take it in, but mercifully the imagination can't. Even while I shuddered and felt sickened, listening, I couldn't conjure up the hideous scene he was describing—all I could think of was McEgan's jolly red face as he told his awful jokes, and little Mrs Skene so anxious in case her dress was wrong for the Collector's dinner, and Andrews talking about Keats's poetry, and Skene saying it wasn't a patch on Burns, and that dainty little Wilton girl singing "bobbity-bobbity-bob" along with me and laughing till she was breathless. It didn't seem possible they were all dead—cut down like beasts in a slaughter-house. Yet what shocked me most, I think, was to see that great Gilzai warrior, whom you could have roasted alive and got nothing but taunts and curses, sobbing like a child. There was nothing to say; after a moment I asked him how he came to be still alive.

"They put Muhammed and me in the jail, with promises of death by torture, but these others of my troop broke us out at night, and we escaped. Until yesterday we hid in the woods, but then the mutineers departed, God knows whither, and we came here. Shadman and two others have gone for horses; we wait for them—and for thee, brother." He wiped his face and forced a grin, and gripped me by the shoulder.

"But the Rani, then?"

"God send that fair foulness a lover made of red-hot metal to bed her through eternity," says he, and spat. "She is in her citadel yonder, while Kala Khan marshals her guard on the maidan—perchance ye heard his bugles?—and sends out for levies to raise her an army. For why?—hear this and laugh. Some of the mutineers chose Sadasheo Rao of Parola as their leader—he has taken Karera Fort, and calls himself Raja of Jhansi in defiance of her." He laughed harshly. "They say she will crucify him with his own bayonets—God send she does. Then she will march against Kathe Khan and the Dewan of Orcha, to bring them under her pretty heel. Oh, an enterprising lady, this Rani, who knows how to take advantage of a world upside down—and meanwhile they say she sends messages to the British protesting her loyalty to the Sirkar—rot her for a lying, faithless, female pi-dog!"

"Maybe she is," says I. "Loyal, I mean. Very well, I don't doubt your story, or what you saw and were told—but, look here, Ilderim. I know something of her—and while I'll allow she's deep, I'll not credit that she would have children slaughtered—it isn't in her. Do you know for a fact that she joined the mutineers,

or encouraged them—or could have prevented them?" The fact is,
I didn't want to believe she was an enemy, you see.

Ilderim glanced at me witheringly, and bit his nail in scorn.

"Bloody Lance," says he, "ye may be the bravest rider in the
British Army, and God knows thou art no fool—but with women
thou art a witless infant. Thou hast coupled this Hindoo slut, hast
thou not?"

"Damn your impudence—"

"I thought as much. Tell me, blood-brother, how many women
hast thou covered, in thy time?" And he winked at his mates.

"What the devil d'you mean?" I demanded.

"How many? Come, as a favour to thy old friend."

"Eh? What's it to you, dammit? Oh, well, let's see . . . there's
the wife, and . . . er . . . and, ah—"

"Aye—ye have fornicated more times than I have passed
water," says this elegant fellow. "And just because they let thee
have thy way, didst thou trust them therefore? Because they were
beautiful or lecherous—wert thou fool enough to think it made
them honest? Like enough. This Rani has beglamoured thee—
well then, go thou up and knock on her palace gate tonight, and
cry 'Beloved, let me in.' I shall stand under the wall to catch the
pieces."

When he put it that way, of course, it was ridiculous. Whether
she was loyal or not—and I could hardly credit that she wasn't—
it didn't seem quite the best time to test the matter, with her
state running over at the edges with mutineers. Good God, was
there nowhere safe in this bloody country? Delhi, Meerut, Jhansi
—how many garrisons remained, I asked Ilderim, and told him
the stories I'd heard, and the sights I'd seen, on my way south.

"No one knows," says he grimly. "But be sure the sepoys have
not won, as they would have the world believe. They have made
the land between Ganges and Jumna a ruin of fire and blood, and
gone undefeated—as yet. They range the country in strength—
but already there is word that the British are marching on Delhi,
and bands of sahibs who escaped when their garrisons were overthrown are riding abroad in growing numbers. Not only men
who have lost their regiments, but civilian sahibs also. The Sirkar
still has teeth—and there are garrisons that hold out in strength.

Cawnpore for one—a bare four days' ride from here. They say the old General Wheeler sahib is in great force there, and has shattered an army of sepoys and *badmashes*. When Shadman brings our horses, it is there we will ride."

"Cawnpore?" I almost squeaked the word in consternation, for it was back in the dirty country with a vengeance. Having come out of that once, I'd no wish to venture in again.

"Where else?" says he. "There is no safer road from Jhansi. Farther south ye dare not go, for there are few sahib places, and no great garrisons. Nor are there to the west. Over the Jumna the country may be hot with mutineers, but it is where thine own folk are—and they are mine, too, and my lads'."

I looked at the ugly villains round the fire, hard-bitten frontier rough-necks to a man in their dirty old poshteens and the big Khyber knives in their belts—by George, I'd be a sight safer going north again in their company than striking out anywhere else on my own. What Ilderim said was probably true, too; Cawnpore and the other river strongholds would be where our generals would concentrate—I could get back among my own kind, and shed this filthy beard and sepoy kit and feel civilised again. Wouldn't have to spin any nonsense about why I'd disappeared from Jhansi, either, in supposed pursuit of Ignatieff— my God, I'd forgotten him entirely, and the Thugs, and all the rest. My mission to Jhansi—Pam and his cakes and warnings—it was all chaff in the wind now, forgotten in this colossal storm that was sweeping through India. No one was going to fret about where I'd sprung from, or what I'd been doing. I felt my spirits rising by the minute—when I thought of the escape I'd had, leaving Jhansi in the first place, I could say that even my horrible experience at Meerut had been worth while.

That's another thing about being a windy beggar—if you scare easily, you usually cheer up just as fast when the danger is past. Well, not past yet, perhaps—but at least I was with friends again, and by what Ilderim said the Mutiny wasn't by any means such a foregone thing as I'd imagined—why, once our people got their second wind, it would be the bloody rebels who'd be doing the running, no doubt, with Flashy roaring on the pursuit from a safe distance. And I might have been rotting out yonder with the others at Jokan Bagh—I shuddered at the ghastly memory of Ilderim's story—or burned alive with the Dawsons at Meerut. By Jove, things weren't so bad after all.

"Right," says I. "Cawnpore let it be." How was I to know I was almost speaking my own epitaph?

In the meantime, I had one good night's sleep, feeling safe for the first time in weeks with Ilderim's rascals around me, and next day we just lay up in the temple ruins while one *sowar* went to scout for Shadman Khan, who was meant to be out stealing horses for us. It was the rummest fix to be in, for all day we could hear the bugles tootling out on the plain where the Rani's army was mustering for her own private little wars with Jhansi's neighbours; Ilderim reported in the evening that she had assembled several hundred foot soldiers, and a few troops of Maharatta riders, as well as half a dozen guns—not a bad beginning, in a troubled time, but of course with a treasury like Jhansi's she could promise regular pay for her soldiers, as well as the prospect of Orcha's loot when she had dealt with the Dewan.

With the second dawn came Shadman himself, cackling at his own cleverness: he and his pals had laid hands on six horses already, they were snug in a thicket a couple of miles from the town, and he had devised a delightful plan for getting another half dozen mounts as well.

"The Hindoo bitch needs riders," says he. "So I marched into her camp on the maidan this afternoon and offered my services. 'I can find six old Company *sowars* who will ride round Jehannum and back for a rupee a day and whatever spoil the campaign promises,' says I to the noseless pig who is master of her cavalry, 'if ye have six good beasts to put under them.' 'We have horses and to spare,' says he, 'bring me your six *sowars* and they shall have five rupees a man down payment, and a carbine and embroidered saddle-cloth apiece.' I beat him up to ten rupees each —so tomorrow let six of us join her cavalry, and at nightfall we shall unjoin, and meet thee, *rissaldar*, and all ride off rejoicing. Is it not a brave scheme—and will cost this slut of a Rani sixty rupees as well as her steeds and furniture?"

There's nothing as gleeful as a Pathan when he's doing the dirty; they slapped their knees in approval and five of them went

off with him that afternoon. Ilderim and I and the remaining
three waited until nightfall, and then set off on foot to the
thicket where we were to rendezvous; there were the first six
horses and a *sowar* waiting, and round about midnight Shadman
and his companions came clattering out of the dark to join us,
crowing with laughter. Not only had they lifted the six horses,
they had cut the lines of a score more, slit the throat of the
cavalry-master as he lay asleep, and set fire to the fodder-store,
just to keep the Rani's army happy.

"Well enough," growls Ilderim, when he had snarled them to
silence. "It will do—till we ride to Jhansi again, some day. There
is a debt to pay, at the Jokan Bagh. Is there not, blood-brother?"
He gripped my shoulder for a moment as we sat our mounts
under the trees, and the others fell in two by two behind us. In
the distance, very black against the starlit purple of the night
sky, was the outline of the Jhansi fortress with the glow of the
city beneath it; Ilderim was staring towards it bright-eyed—I
remember that moment so clearly, with the warm gloom and the
smell of Indian earth and horse-flesh, the creak of leather and the
soft stamping of the beasts. I was thinking of the horror that lay
in the Jokan Bagh—and of that lovely girl, in her mirrored palace
yonder with its swing and soft carpets and luxurious furniture,
and trying to make myself believe that they belonged in the same
world.

"It will take more than one dead rebel and a few horses to settle
the score for Skene sahib and the others," says he. "Much more.
So—to Cawnpore? Walk-march, trot!"

He had said it was a bare four days' ride, but it took us that
long to reach the Jumna above Haminpur, for on my advice we
steered clear of the roads, and kept to the countryside, where we
sighted nothing bigger than villages and poor farms. Even there,
though, there was ample sign of the turbulence that was sweeping the land; we passed hamlets that were just smoking, blackened
ruins, with buzzing carcases, human and animal, lying where
they had been shot down, or strung up to branches; and several
times we saw parties of mutineers on the march, all heading
north-east like ourselves. That was enough to set me wondering
if I wasn't going in the wrong direction, but I consoled myself

that there was safety in numbers—until the morning of the fourth day, when Ilderim aroused me in a swearing passion with the news that eight of our party had slipped off in the night, leaving only the two of us with Muhammed Din and Rafik Tamwar.

"That faithless thieving, reiving son of a Kabuli whore, Shadman Khan, has put them up to this!" He was livid with rage. "He and that other dung-beetle Asaf Yakub had the dawn watch —they have stolen off and left us, and taken the food and fodder with them!"

"You mean they've gone to join the mutineers?" I cried.

"Not they! We would never have woken again if that had been their aim. No—they will be off about their trade, which is loot and murder! I should have known! Did I not see Shadman licking his robber's lips when we passed the sacked bungalows yesterday? He and the others see in this broken countryside a chance to fill their pockets, rather than do honest service according to their salt. They will live like the bandits they were before the Sirkar enlisted them in an evil hour, and when they have ravaged and raped their fill they will be off north to the frontier again. They have not even the stomach to be honest mutineers!" And he spat and stamped, raging.

"Never trust an Afridi," says Tamwar philosophically. "I knew Shadman was a *badmash* the day he joined. At least they have left us our horses."

That was little consolation to me as we saddled up; with eleven hardy riders round me I'd felt fairly secure, but now that they were reduced to three—and only one of those really trustworthy —I fairly had the shakes again. However, having come this far there was nothing for it but to push on; we weren't more than a day's ride from Cawnpore by my reckoning, and once we were behind Wheeler's lines we would be safe enough. My chief anxiety was that the closer we got, the more likely we would be to find mutineers in strength, and this was confirmed when, a few hours after sun-up, we heard, very faint in the distance, the dull thump of gunfire. We had stopped to water our beasts at a tank beside the road, which at that point was enclosed by fairly thick forest either side; Ilderim's head came up sharp at the sound.

"Cawnpore!" says he. "Now what shall that shooting mean? Can Wheeler sahib be under siege? Surely—"

Before I could reply there was a sudden drumming of hooves, and round a bend in the road not two hundred yards ahead came three horsemen, going like hell's delight; I barely had time to identify them as native cavalrymen of some sort, and therefore probably mutineers, when into view came their pursuers—and I let out a yell of delight, for out in the van was an undoubted white officer, with his sabre out and view-hallooing like a good 'un. At his heels came a motley gang of riders, but I hadn't time to examine them—I was crouched down at the roadside with my Colt out, drawing a bead on the foremost fugitive. I let blaze, and his horse gave a gigantic bound and crashed down, thrashing in the dust; his two companions swung off to take to the woods, but one of the mounts stumbled and threw its rider, and only the other won to the safety of the trees, with a group of the pursuers crashing after him.

The others pounced on the two who'd come to grief, while I ran towards them, yelling:

"Hurrah! Bravo, you fellows! It's me, Flashman! Don't shoot!"

I could see now that they were Sikh cavalry, mostly, although there were at least half a dozen white faces among them, staring at me as I came running up; suddenly one of them, with a cry of warning, whips out his revolver and covers me.

"Don't move" he bawls. "Drop that pistol—sharp, now!"

"No, no!" cries I. "You don't understand! I'm a British officer! Colonel Flashman!"

"The devil you are!" He stared from me to Ilderim, who had come up behind me. "You look like it, don't you? And who the hell is he—the Duke of Cambridge?"

"He's a *rissaldar* of irregular cavalry. And I, old fellow, believe it or not, beneath this fine beard and homely native garb, am Colonel Harry Paget Flashman—of whom I dare say you've heard?" I was positively burbling with relief as I held out my hand to him.

"You look bloody like a pandy* to me," says he. "Keep your distance!"

* Mutineer (see Note 21).

"Well, you don't exactly look straight from Horse Guards yourself, you know," says I, laughing. None of them did; apart from the Sikhs, who were a fairly wild-looking bunch, his white companions were the oddest crowd, in bits and pieces of uniform from half a dozen regiments, with their gear slung any old how. Some had *puggarees*, some helmets, and one fat chap with a white beard had a straw hat and frock coat; they were all dirty and unshaven after weeks in the saddle, and the only thing uniform about them was that they were fairly bristling with weapons— pistols, carbines, swords, knives in their belts, and one or two with pig spears.

"May I ask who I have the honour of addressing?" says I, as they crowded up. "And if you have a commanding officer, perhaps you might convey my compliments to him."

That impressed him, although he still looked suspicious.

"Lieutenant Cheeseman, of Rowbotham's Mosstroopers," says he. "But if you're one of us, what the dooce are you going about dressed as a nigger for?"

"You say you're Flashman?" says another—he was wearing a pith helmet and spectacles, and what looked like old cricket flannels tucked into his top-boots. "Well, if you are—an' I must say you don't look a bit like him—you ought to know me. Because Harry Flashman stood godfather to my boy at Lahore in '42 —what's my name, eh?"

I had to close my eyes and think—it had been on my triumphal progress south after the Jalallabad business. An Irish name—yes, by God, it was unforgettable.

"O'Toole!" says I. "You did me the honour of having your youngster christened Flashman O'Toole—I trust he's well?"

"By God I did!" says he, staring. "It must be him, Cheeseman! Here, where's Colonel Rowbotham?"

I confess I was curious myself—Rowbotham's Mosstroopers was a new one on me, and if their commander was anything like his followers he must be a remarkable chap. There was a great rumpus going on in the road behind the group who surrounded me, and I saw that one of the fugitives was being dragged up between two of the Sikhs, and thrown forward in the dust before one of the riders, who was leaning down from his saddle looking at the still form of the fellow whose horse I'd shot.

"Why, this one's dead!" he exclaimed, peevishly. "Of all the confounded bad luck! Hold on to that other scoundrel, there! Here, Cheeseman, what have you got—is it some more of the villains?"

He rode over the dead man, glaring at me, and I don't think I've ever seen an angrier-looking man in my life. Everything about him was raging—his round red face, his tufty brindle eyebrows, his bristling sandy whiskers, even the way he clenched his crop, and when he spoke his harsh, squeaky voice seemed to shake with suppressed wrath. He was short and stout, and sat his pony like a hog on a hurdle; his pith helmet was wrapped in a long *puggaree*, and he wore a most peculiar loose cape, like an American poncho, clasped round with a snake-clasp belt. Altogether a most ridiculous sight, but there was nothing funny about the pale, staring eyes, or the way his mouth worked as he considered me.

"Who's this?" he barked, and when Cheeseman told him, and O'Toole, who had been eyeing me closely, said he believed I was Flashman after all, he growled suspiciously and demanded to know why I was skulking about dressed as a native, and where had I come from. So I told him, briefly, that I was a political, lately from Jhansi, where I and my three followers had escaped the massacre.

"What's that you say?" cries he. "Massacre—at Jhansi?" And the others crowded their horses round, staring and exclaiming, while I reported what had happened to Skene and the rest—even as I told it, I was uncomfortably aware of something not quite canny in the way they listened: it was a shocking story enough, but there was an excitement about them, in the haggard faces and the bright eyes, as though they had some fever, that I couldn't account for. Usually, when Englishmen listen to a dreadful tale, they do it silently, at most with signs of disgust or disbelief, but this crowd stirred restlessly in their saddles, muttering and exclaiming, and when I'd finished the little chap burst into tears, gritting his teeth and shaking his crop.

"God in Heaven!" cries he. "Will it never cease? How many

innocents—twenty children, you say? And all the women? My God!" He rocked in his saddle, dashing the tears away, while his companions groaned and shook their fists—it was an astonishing sight, those dozen scarecrows who looked as though they'd fought a long campaign in fancy-dress costume, swearing and addressing heaven; it occurred to me that they weren't quite right in the head. Presently the little chap regained his composure, and turned to me.

"Your pardon, colonel," says he, and if his voice was low it was shaking with emotion. "This grievous news—this shocking intelligence—it makes me forget myself. Rowbotham, James Kane Rowbotham, at your service; these are my mosstroopers—my column of volunteer horse, sir, banded after the rebellion at Delhi, and myself commissioned by Governor Colvin at Agra."

"Commissioned . . . by a civilian?" It sounded deuced odd, but then he and his gang looked odd. "I gather, sir, that you ain't . . . er, Army?"

He flew up at that. "We are soldiers, sir, as much as you! A month ago I was a doctor, at Delhi . . ." His mouth worked again, and his tongue seemed to be impeding his speech. "My . . . my wife and son, sir . . . lost in the uprising . . . murdered. These gentlemen . . . volunteers, sir, from Agra and Delhi . . . merchants, lawyers, officials, people of all classes. Now we act as a mobile column, because there are no regular cavalry to be spared from the garrisons; we strive to keep the road open between Agra and Cawnpore, but since the mutineers are now before Cawnpore in force, we scour the country for news of their movements and fall on them when we can. Vermin!" He choked, glaring round, and his eye fell on the prisoner, prone in the dust with a Sikh keeping a foot on his neck. "Yes!" cries he, "we may not be soldiers, sir, in your eyes, but we have done some service in putting down this abomination! Oh, yes! You'll see—you'll see for yourself! Cheeseman! How many have we now?"

"Seven, sir, counting this one." Cheeseman nodded at the prisoner. "Here comes Fields with the others now."

What I took to be the rest of Rowbotham's remarkable regiment was approaching down the road at a brisk trot, a dozen Sikhs and two Englishmen in the same kind of outlandish rig as the others. Running or staggering behind, their wrists tied to the Sikhs' stirrup-leathers, were half a dozen niggers in the last stages of exhaustion; three or four of them were plainly native infantrymen, from their coats and breeches.

"Bring them up here!" cries Rowbotham violently, and when they had been untied and ranged in a straggled line in front of him, he pointed to the trees behind them. "Those will do excellently—get the ropes, Cheeseman! Untie their hands, and put them under the branches." He was bouncing about in his saddle in excitement, and there were little flecks of spittle among the stubble of his chin. "You'll see, sir," says he to me. "You'll see how we deal with these filthy butchers of women and children! It has been our custom to hang them in groups of thirteen, as an appropriate warning—but this news of Jhansi which you bring—this new horror—makes it necessary ... makes it necessary...."
He broke off incoherently, twisting the reins in his hands. "We must make an immediate example, sir! This cancer of mutiny ... what? Let these serve as a sacrifice to those dead innocent spirits so cruelly released at Jhansi!"

He wasn't mad, I'd decided; he was just an ordinary little man suddenly at war. I've seen it scores of times. He had reason, too; I, who had been at Meerut and Jhansi, was the last to deny that. His followers were the same; while the Sikhs threw lines over the branches, they sat and stared their hatred at the prisoners; I glanced along and noted the bright eyes, the clenched teeth, the tongues moistening the lips, and thought to myself, you've taken right smartly to nigger-killing, my boys. Well, good luck to you; you'll make the pandies sorry they ever broke ranks before you're done.

They didn't look sorry at the moment, mind, just sullen as the Sikhs knotted the ropes round their necks—except for one of them, a fat scoundrel in a *dhoti* who shrieked and struggled and blubbered and even broke free for a moment and flung himself grovelling before Rowbotham until they dragged him back again. He collapsed in the dust, beating the earth with his hands and feet while the others stood resigned; Cheeseman says:

"Shall we put 'em on horses, sir—makes it quicker?"

"No!" cries Rowbotham. "How often must I tell you—I do

not wish to make it quicker for these . . . these villains! They are being hanged as a punishment, Mr Cheeseman—it is not my design to make it easy for them! Let them suffer—and the longer the better! Will it atone for the atrocities they have wrought? No, not if they were flayed alive! You hear that, you rascals?" He shook his fist at them. "You know now the price of mutiny and murder—in a moment you shall pay it, and you may thank whatever false God you worship that you obtain a merciful death —you who did not scruple to torture and defile the innocent!" He was raving by now, with both hands in the air, and then he noticed again the dead fellow lying in the road, and roared to the Sikhs to string him up as well, so that they should all hang together as a token of justice. While they were manhandling the corpse he rode along behind the prisoners, examining each knot jealously, and then, so help me, he whipped off his hat and began to pray aloud, beseeching a Merciful God, as he put it, to witness what just retribution they were meting out in His name, and putting in a word for the condemned, although he managed to convey that a few thousand years in hell wouldn't do them any harm.

Then he solemnly told the Sikhs to haul away, and they tailed on the ropes and swung the pandies into the air, the fat one screeching horribly. He wasn't a mutineer, I was certain, but it probably wouldn't have been tactful to mention that just then. The others gasped and thrashed about, clutching at their halters —now I saw why they hadn't tied their hands, for three of them managed to clutch the ropes and haul themselves up, while the others choked and turned blue and presently hung there, twitching and swaying gently in the sunlight. Everyone was craning to watch the struggles of the three who had got their hands on the ropes, pulling themselves up to take the choking strain off their necks; they kicked and screamed now, swinging wildly to and fro; you could see their muscles quivering with the appalling strain.

"Five to one on the Rajput," says O'Toole, fumbling in his pockets.

"Gammon," says another. "He's no stayer; I'll give evens on the little 'un—less weight to support, you see."

"Neither of 'em's fit to swing alongside that artillery *havildar* we caught near Barthana," says a third. "Remember, the one old J.K. found hiding under the old woman's charpoy. I thought he'd hang on forever—how long was it, Cheese?"

"Six and a half minutes," says Cheeseman. He had his foot cocked up on his saddle and was scribbling in a notebook. "That's eighty-six, by the way, with today's batch—" he nodded towards the struggling figures. "Counting the three shot last night, but not the ones we killed in the Mainpuri road ambush. Should knock up our century by tomorrow night, with luck."

"I say, that's not bad—hollo, O'Toole, there goes your Rajput! Bad luck, old son—five chips, what? Told you my bantam was the form horse, didn't I?"

"Here—he'll be loose in a moment, though! Look!" O'Toole pointed to the small sepoy, who had managed to pull himself well up his rope, getting his elbow in the bight of it, and was tugging at the noose with his other hand. One of the Sikhs sprang up to haul at his ankles, but Rowbotham barked an order and then, drawing his revolver, took careful aim and shot the sepoy through the body. The man jerked convulsively and then fell, his head snapping back as the rope tightened; someone laughed and sang out "Shame!" while another huzzaed, and then they all had their pistols out, banging away at the hanging figures which twitched and swung under the impact of the bullets.

"Take that, you bastard!" "There—that's for little Jane! And that—and that!" "How d'ye like it now, you black pig of a mutineer? I wish you had fifty lives to blow away!" "Die, damn you—and roast in hell!" "That's for Johnson—that's for Mrs Fox —that, that, and that for the Prices!" They wheeled their mounts under the corpses, which were running with blood now, blasting at them point-blank.

"Too bloody good for 'em!" cries the white-bearded chap in the straw hat, as he fumbled feverishly to reload. "The colonel's right —we ought to be flaying 'em alive, after what they've done! Take that, you devil! Or burning the brutes. I say, J.K., why ain't we burnin' 'em?"

They banged away, until Rowbotham called a halt, and their frenzy died down; the smoking pistols were put away, and the

column fell in, with the flies buzzing thickly over the eight
growing pools of blood beneath the bodies. I wasn't surprised to
see the riders suddenly quiet now, their excitement all spent;
they sat heavy in their saddles, breathing deeply, while Cheeseman checked their dressing. It's the usual way, with civilians
suddenly plunged into war and given the chance to kill; for the
first time, after years spent pushing pens and counting pennies,
they're suddenly free of all restraint, away from wives and
families and responsibility, and able to indulge their animal
instincts. They go a little crazy after a while, and if you can
convince 'em they're doing the Lord's work, they soon start
enjoying it. There's nothing like a spirit of righteous retribution
for kindling cruelty in a decent, kindly, God-fearing man—I, who
am not one, and have never needed any virtuous excuse for my
bestial indulgences, can tell you that. Now, having let off steam,
they were sated, and some a little shocked at themselves, just as if
they'd been whoring for the first time—which, of course, was
something they'd never have dreamed of doing, proper little
Christians that they were. If you ask me what I think of what
I'd just witnessed—well, personally, I'd have backed O'Toole's
Rajput, and lost my money.

However, now that the bloody assizes was over, and Rowbotham and his merry men were ready to take the road again, I
was able to get back to the business in hand, which was getting
myself safely into Cawnpore. Fortunately they were headed that
way themselves, since two weeks spent slaughtering pandies in
the countryside had exhausted their forage and ammunition (the
way they shot up corpses, I wasn't surprised). But when, as we
rode along, I questioned Rowbotham about how the land lay, and
what the cannonading to the north signified, I was most disagree-
ably surprised by his answer; it couldn't have been much worse
news.

Cawnpore was under siege, right enough, and had been for two
weeks. It seemed that Wheeler, unlike most commanders, had
seen the trouble coming; he didn't trust his sepoys a damned
inch, and as soon as he heard of the Meerut rising he'd prepared
a big new fortification in barracks on the eastern edge of Cawnpore city, with entrenchments and guns, so that if his four native

regiments mutinied he could get inside it with every British civilian and loyal rifle in the place. He knew that the city itself, a great straggling place along the Ganges, was indefensible, and that he couldn't have hoped to secure the great numbers of white civilians, women and children and all, unless he packed them into his new stronghold, which was by the racecourse, and had a good level field of fire all round.

So when the pandies did mutiny, there he was, all prepared, and for a fortnight he'd been giving them their bellyful, in spite of the fact that the mutineers had been reinforced by the local native prince, Nana Dondu Pant Sahib, who'd turned traitor at the last minute. Rowbotham hadn't the least doubt that the place would hold; rumours had reached him that help was already on its way, from Lucknow, forty miles to the north, and from Allahabad, which lay farther off, east along the Ganges.

This was all very well, but we were going to have to run the gauntlet to get inside, as I pointed out; wouldn't it be better to skirt the place and make for Lucknow, which by all accounts was still free from mutiny? He wouldn't have that, though; his troops needed supplies badly, and in the uncertain state of the country he must make for the nearest British garrison. Besides, he anticipated no difficulty about getting in; his Sikhs had already scouted the pandy besiegers, and while they were in great strength there was no order about their lines, and plenty of places to slip through. He'd even got a message in to Wheeler, giving him a time and signal for our arrival, so that we could win to the entrenchment without any danger of being mistaken for the enemy.

For a sawbones he was a most complete little bandolero, I'll say that for him, but what he said gave me the blue fits straight off. Plainly, I'd jumped from the Jhansi frying-pan into the Cawnpore fire, but what the devil could I do about it? From what Rowbotham said, there wasn't a safe bolt-hole between Agra and Allahabad; no one knew how many garrisons were still holding, and those that were couldn't offer any safer refuge than Cawnpore; I daren't try a run for Lucknow with Ilderim (God knew what state it might be in when we got there). A rapid, fearful calculation convinced me that there wasn't a better bet than to stick with this little madman, and pray to God he knew what he was doing. After all, Wheeler was a good man—I'd known him in the Sikh war—and Rowbotham was positive he'd hold out easily and be relieved before long.

"And that will be the end of this wicked, abominable insurrection," says he, when we made camp that night ten miles closer to Cawnpore, with the distant northern sky lighting to the flashes of gunfire, rumbling away unceasingly. "We know that our people are already investing Delhi, and must soon break down the rebel defences and pull that unclean creature who calls himself King off his traitor's throne—that will be to root out the mischief at its heart. Then, when Lawrence moves south from Lucknow, and our other forces push up the river, this nest of rebels about Cawnpore will be trapped; destroy them, and the thing is done. Then it will only remain to restore order, and visit a merited punishment upon these scoundrels; they must be taught such a lesson as will never be forgotten—aye, if we have to destroy them by tens of thousands—" he was away again on that fine, rising bray which reminded me of the hangings that afternoon; his troopers, round the camp-fire, growled enthusiastically "—hundreds of thousands, even. Nothing less will serve if this foulness is to be crushed once for all. Mercy will be folly—it will be construed as mere weakness."

This sermon provoked a happy little discussion on whether, when all the mutineers had been rounded up, they should be blown from guns, or hanged, or shot. Some favoured burning alive, and others flogging to death; the chap in the straw hat was strong for crucifixion, I remember, but another fellow thought that would be blasphemous. They got quite heated about it—and before you throw up your hands in pious horror, remember that many of them had seen their own families butchered in the kind of circumstances I'd witnessed myself at Meerut, and were thirsting to pay the pandies back with interest, which was reasonable enough. Also, they were convinced that if they didn't make a dreadful example, it would lead to more outbreaks, and the slaughter of every white person in India—the fear of that, and the knowledge of the kind of wantonly cruel foe they were up against, hardened them as nothing else could have done.

It was all one to me, I may say; I was too anxious about coming safe into Cawnpore to worry about how they disposed of the mutineers—it seemed a trifle premature to me. They were the rummest lot, though; when they'd tired of devising means of execution they got into a great argument about whether hacking and carrying should be allowed in football, and as I was an old Rugby boy my support was naturally enlisted by the hackers—it must have been the strangest sight, when I come to think of it, me in my garb of hairy Pathan with *poshteen* and *puggaree*, maintaining that if you did away with scrimmaging you'd be ruining the manliest game there was (not that I'd go near a scrimmage if you paid me), and the white-bearded wallah, with the blood splashes still on his coat, denouncing the handling game as a barbarism. Most of the others joined in, on one side or the other, but there were some who sat apart brooding, reading their Bibles, sharpening their weapons, or just muttering to themselves; it wasn't a canny company, and I can get the shivers thinking about them now.

They could soldier, though; how Rowbotham had licked them into shape in less than a month (and where *he'd* got the genius from) beat me altogether, but you never saw anything more workmanlike than the way they disposed their march next day, with flank riders and scouts, a twenty-pound forage bag behind each saddle, all their gear and arms padded with cloth so that they didn't jingle, and even leather night-shoes for the horses slung on their cruppers. Pencherjevsky's Cossacks and Custer's scalp-hunters couldn't have made a braver show than that motley gang of clerks and counter-jumpers that followed Rowbotham to Cawnpore.

We were coming in from the east, and since the pandy army was all concentrated close to Wheeler's stronghold and in the city itself, we got within two or three miles before Rowbotham said we must lie up in a wood and wait for dark. Before then, by the way, we'd pounced on an outlying pandy picket in a grove and killed two of them, taking three more prisoner: they were strung up on the spot. Two more stragglers were caught farther on, and since there wasn't a tree handy Rowbotham and the Sikh *rissaldar* cut their heads off. The Sikh settled his man with one swipe, but Rowbotham took three; he wasn't much with a sabre. (Ninety-three not out, as Cheeseman put it.)

We lay up in the stuffy, sweltering heat of the wood all after-noon, listening to the incessant thunder of the cannonading; one consolation was the regular crash of the artillery salvoes, which indicated that Wheeler's gunners were making good practice, and must still be well stocked with powder and shot. Even after night-fall they still kept cracking away, and one of the Sikhs, who had wormed his way up to within a quarter-mile of the entrenchment, reported that he had heard Wheeler's sentries singing out "All's well!" regular as clockwork.

About two in the morning Rowbotham called us together and gave his orders. "There is a clear way to the Allahabad road," says he, "but before we reach it we must bear right to come in behind the rebel gun positions, no more than half a mile from the entrenchment. At precisely four o'clock I shall fire a rocket, on which we shall burst out of cover and ride for the entrench-ment at our uttermost speed; the sentries, having seen our rocket, will pass us through. The word is 'Britannia'. Now, remember, for your lives, that our goal lies to the left of the church, so keep that tower always to your right front. Our rush will take us past the racecourse and across the cricket pitch—"

"Oh, I say!" says someone. "Mind the wicket, though."

"—and then we must put our horses to the entrenchment bank, which is four feet high. Now, God bless us all, and let us meet again within the lines or in Heaven."

That's just the kind of pious reminder of mortality I like, I must say; while the rest of 'em were shaking hands in the dark I was carefully instructing Ilderim that at all costs he must stick by my shoulder. I was in my normal state of chattering funk, and my spirits weren't raised as we were filing out of the wood and I heard someone whisper:

"I say, Jinks, what's the time?"

"Ten past three," says Jinks, "on the bright summer morning of June the twenty-second—and let's hope to God we see the twenty-third."

June twenty-third; I knew that date—and suddenly I was back in the big panelled room at Balmoral, and Pam was saying

". . . the Raj will come to an end a hundred years after the battle of Plassey . . . next June twenty-third." By George, there was an omen for you! And now all round was the gloom, and the soft pad of the walking horses, and the reins sweating in my palms as we advanced interminably, my eyes glued to the faint dark shape of the rider ahead; there was a mutter of voices as we halted, and then we waited in the stifling dark between two rows of ruined houses—five minutes, ten, fifteen, and then a voice called "Ready, all!" There was the flare of a match, a curse, then a brighter glare, and suddenly a rush of sparks and an orange rocket shot up into the purple night sky, weaving like a comet, and as it burst to a chorus of cries and yells from far ahead Rowbotham shouts "Advance!" and we dug in our heels and fairly shot forward in a thundering mass.

There was a clear space ahead, and then a grove of trees, and beyond more level ground with dim shapes moving. As we bore down on them I realised that they must be pandies; we were charging the rear of their positions, and it was just light enough to make out the guns parked at intervals. There were shrieks of alarm and a crackle of shots, and then we were past, swerving between the gun-pits; there were horsemen ahead and either side and Ilderim crouched low in the saddle at my elbow. He yelled something and pointed right, and I saw an irregular tumbled outline which must be the church; to its left, directly ahead, little sparks of light were flashing in the distance—the entrenchment defenders were firing to cover us.

Someone sang out: "Bravo, boys!" and then all hell burst loose behind us; there was a crashing salvo of cannon, the earth ahead rose up in fountains of dust, and shot was whistling over our heads. A horse screamed, and I missed by a whisker a thrashing tangle of man and mount which I passed so close that a lashing limb caught me smack on the knee. Voices were roaring in the dark, I heard Rowbotham's frantic "Close up! Ride for it!" A dismounted man plunged across my path and was hurled aside by my beast; behind me I heard the shriek of someone mortally hit, and a riderless horse came neighing and stretching frantically against my left side. Another shattering volley burst from the guns in our rear, and that hellish storm swept through us—it was

Balaclava all over again, and in the dark, to boot. Suddenly my
pony stumbled, and I knew from the way he came up that he was
hit; a stinging cloud of earth and gravel struck me across the
face, a shot howled overhead, and Ilderim was sweeping past
ahead of me.

"Stop!" I bawled. "My screw's foundered! Stop, blast you—
give me a hand!"

I saw his shadowy form check, and his horse rear; he swung
round, and as my horse sank under me his arm swept me out of
the saddle—by God, he was strong, that one. My feet hit the
ground, but I had hold of his bridle, and for a few yards I was
literally dragged along, with Ilderim above hauling to get me
across the crupper. Someone cannoned into us, and then as I
pulled myself by main force across the crupper I felt a sudden
shock, and Ilderim pitched over me and out of the saddle.

Even as I righted myself on the horse's back the whole scene
was suddenly bathed in glaring light—some swine had fired a
flare, and its flickering illumination shone on a scene that looked
like a mad artist's hell. Men and horses seemed to be staggering
and going down all round me under the hail of fire, throwing
grotesque shadows as they fought and struggled. I saw Rowbotham pinned under a fallen horse only a few yards away;
Cheeseman, his face a bloody mask, was stretched supine beside
him, his limbs asprawl; Ilderim, with his left arm dangling, was
half-up on one knee, clutching at my stirrup. A bare hundred
yards ahead the entrenchment was in plain view, with the
defenders' heads visible, and some ass standing atop of it waving
his hat; behind us, the red explosions of the cannon suddenly
died, and to my horror I saw, pounding out under the umbrella
of light cast by the flare, a straggling line of riders—sepoy
cavalry with their sabres out, bearing down at the charge, and
not more than a furlong away. Ilderim seized my stirrup and
bawled:

"On, on! Ride, brother!"

I didn't hesitate. He'd turned back to rescue me, and his noble
sacrifice wasn't going to be in vain if I could help it. That was
certain death bearing down on us; I jammed in my heels, the
horse leaped forward, and Ilderim was almost jerked off his feet.

For perhaps five paces he kept up, with the yells and hoof-beats growing behind us, and then he stumbled and went down. I did my damnedest to shake him free, but in that instant the bloody bridle snapped, and I hurtled out of the saddle and hit the ground with a smash that jarred every bone in my body. A shocking pain shot through my left ankle—Christ, it was caught in the stirrup, and the horse was tearing ahead, dragging me behind at the end of a tangle of leatherwork which somehow was still attached to its body.

If any of you young fellows ever find yourself in this predicament, where you're dragged over rough, iron-hard ground, with or without a mob of yelling black fiends after you, take a word of advice from me. Keep your head up (screaming helps), and above all try to be dragged on your back—it will cost you a skinned arse, but that's better than having your organs scraped off. Try, too, to arrange for some stout lads to pour rapid fire into your pursuers, and for a handy Gilzai friend to chase after you and slash the stirrup-leather free in the nick of time before your spine falls apart. I was half-conscious and virtually buttockless when Ilderim—God knows, wounded as he was, where he'd got the speed and strength—hauled me up below the entrenchment and pitched me almost bodily over the breastwork. I went over in a shocking tangle, roaring: "Britannia! Britannia, for Christ's sake! I'm a friend!" and then a chap was catching me and lowering my battered carcase to earth and inquiring:

"Will you have nuts or a cigar, sir?"

Then a musket was being pushed into my hand, and in shocked confusion I found myself at the rampart, banging away at red-coated figures who came out of the smoke and dust, and I know Ilderim was alongside me, relieving me of my revolver and loosing off shots into the brown. All round there was the crash of volleys, and a great bass voice was yelling "Odds, fire! Reload! Evens, fire! Reload!" The pain from my ankle was surging up my leg, into my body, making me sick and dizzy, I was coughing with the reek of powder smoke, there was a bugle sounding, and a confused roar of cheering—and the next thing I remember I was lying in the half-light of dawn, with my back against a sandbagged wall, staring at a big, shot-torn barrack building, while a tall, bald-headed cove with a pipe was getting my boot off, and applying a damp cloth to my swollen ankle.

There were a couple of chaps with muskets looking on, and Ilderim was having his arm bandaged by a fellow in a kepi and spectacles. There were others, moving about, carrying people towards the barrack, and along the parapet there were haggard-looking fellows, white and sepoy, with their pieces at the ready. A horrid smell seemed to hang over the place, and everything was filthy, with gear and litter all over the dusty ground, and the people seemed to be moving slowly. I was still feeling pretty dazed, but I guessed it must all be a dream anyway, for the chap third along the parapet to my left, with a handkerchief knotted round his head, was undoubtedly young Harry East. There couldn't be two snub noses like that in the world, and since the last time I'd seen him I'd been pinned under a sledge in the snows of southern Russia, and he had been lighting out for safety, it didn't seem reasonable that he should have turned up here.

I'll tell you a strange thing about pain—and Cawnpore. That ankle of mine, which I'd thought was broken, but which in fact was badly sprained, would have kept me flat on my back for days anywhere else, bleating for sympathy; in Cawnpore I was walking on it within a few hours, suffering damnably, but with no choice but to endure it. That was the sort of place it was; if you'd had both legs blown off you were rated fit for only light duties.

Imagine a great trench, with an earth and rubble parapet five feet high, enclosing two big single-storey barracks, one of them a burned-out shell and the other with half its roof gone. All round was flat plain, stretching hundreds of yards to the encircling pandy lines which lay among half-ruined buildings and trees; a mile or less to the north-west was the great straggling mass of Cawnpore city itself, beside the river—but when anyone of my generation speaks of Cawnpore he means those two shattered barracks with the earth wall round them.

That was where Wheeler, with his ramshackle garrison, had been holding out against an army for two and a half weeks. There were nine hundred people inside it when the siege began, nearly half of them women and children; of the rest four hundred were British soldiers and civilians, and a hundred loyal natives. They had one well, and three cannon; they were living on two handfuls of mealies a day, fighting off a besieging force of more than three thousand mutineers who smashed at them constantly with fifteen cannon, subjected them to incessant musket-fire, and tried to storm the entrenchment. The defenders lost over two hundred dead in the first fortnight, men, women, and children, from gunfire, heat and disease; the hospital barrack had been burned to ashes with the casualties inside, and of the three hundred left fit to fight, more than half were wounded or ill.

They worked the guns and manned the wall with muskets and bayonets and whatever they could lay hands on.

This, I discovered to my horror, was the place I'd fled to for safety, the stronghold which Rowbotham had boasted was being held with such splendid ease. It was being held—by starved ghosts half of whom had never fired a musket before, with their women and children dying by inches in the shot-torn, stifling barrack behind them, in the certainty that unless help came quickly that entrenchment would be their common grave. Rowbotham never lived to discover how mistaken he'd been; he and half his troop were lying stark out on the plain—his final miscalculation having been to time our rush to coincide with a pandy assault.

I was the senior officer of those who'd got safely (?) inside, and when they'd discovered who I was and bound up my ankle I was helped into the little curtained corner of the remaining barrack where Wheeler had his office. We stared at each other in disbelief, he because I was still looking like Abdul the Bulbul, and I because in place of the stalwart, brisk commander I'd known ten years ago there was now a haggard, sunken ancient; with his grimy, grizzled face, his uniform coat torn and filthy, and his breeches held up with string, he looked like a dead gardener.

"Good God, you're never young Harry Flashman!" was his greeting to me. "Yes, you are though! Where the dooce did you spring from?" I told him—and in the short time I took to tell him about Meerut and Jhansi, no fewer than three round-shot hit the building, shaking the plaster; Wheeler just brushed the debris absently off his table, and then says:

"Well, thank God for twenty more men—though what we'll feed you on I cannot think. Still, what matter a few more mouths?—you see the plight we're in. You've heard nothing of . . . our people advancing from Allahabad, or Lucknow?" I said I hadn't and he looked round at his chief officers, Vibart and Moore, and gave a little gesture of despair.

"I suppose it was not to be expected," says he. "So . . . we can only do our duty—how much longer? If only it was not for the children, I think we could face it well enough. Still—no croaking, eh?" He gave me a tired grin. "Don't take it amiss if I say I'm glad to see you, Flashman, and will welcome your presence in our council. In the meantime, the best service you can do is to take a place at the parapet. Moore here will show you—God bless you," says he, shaking hands, and it was from Moore, a tall, fair-haired captain with his arm in a blood-smeared sling, that I learned of what had been happening in the past two weeks, and how truly desperate our plight was.

It may read stark enough, but the sight of it was terrible. Moore took me round the entrenchment, stooping as he walked and I hobbled, for the small-arms fire from the distant sepoy lines kept whistling overhead, smacking into the barrack-wall, and every so often a large shot would plump into the enclosure or smash another lump out of the building. It was terrifying—and yet no one seemed to pay it much attention; the men at the parapet just popped up for an occasional look, and those moving in the enclosure, with their heads hunched down, never even broke step if a bullet whined above them. I kept bobbing nervously, and Moore grinned and said:

"You'll soon get used to it—pandy marksmen don't hit a dam' thing they aim at. It's the random shots that do the damage— damnation!" This as a cloud of dust, thrown up by a round-shot hitting the parapet, enveloped us. "Stretcher, there! Lively now!" There was a body twitching close by where the shot had struck; at Moore's shout two fellows doubled out from the barrack to attend to it. After a brief look one of them shook his head, and then they picked up the body between them and carried it off towards what looked like a well; they just pitched it in, and Moore says:

"That's our cemetery. I've worked it out that we put someone in there every two hours. Over there—that's the wet well, where we get our water. We won't go too close—the pandy sharp-shooters get a clear crack at it from that grove yonder, so we draw our water at night. Jock McKillop worked it for a week, until they got him. Heaven only knows how many we've lost on water-drawing since."

What seemed so unreal about it, and still does, was the quiet conversational way he talked. There was this garrison, being steadily shot to bits, and starving in the process, and he went on

pointing things out, cool as dammit, with the crackle of desultory
firing going on around us. I stomached it so long, and then burst
out:

"But in God's name—it's hopeless! Hasn't Wheeler tried to
make terms?"

He laughed straight out at that. "Terms? Who with? Nana
Sahib? Look here, you were at Meerut, weren't you? Did they
make terms? They want us dead, laddie. They slaughtered everything white up in the city yonder, and God knows how many of
their own folk as well. They tortured the native goldsmiths to
death to get at their loot; Nana's been blowing loyal Indians from
guns as fast as they can trice 'em over the muzzles! No," he shook
his head, "there'll be no terms."

"But what the devil—I mean, what...?"

"What's going to come of it? Well, I don't need to tell you, of
all people—either a relief column wins through from Allahabad
in three days at most, or we'll be so starved and short of cartridge
that the pandies will storm over that wall. Then . . ." He
shrugged. "But of course, we don't admit that—not in front of
the ladies, anyway, however much some of 'em may guess. Just
grin and assure 'em that Lawrence will be up with the rations
any day, what?"

I won't trouble to describe my emotions as this sank in, along
with the knowledge that for once there was nowhere to bolt to—
and I couldn't have run anyway, with my game ankle. It was
utterly hopeless—and what made it worse, if anything, was that
as a senior man I had to pretend, like Wheeler and Moore and
Vibart and the rest, that I was ready to do or die with the best.
Even I couldn't show otherwise—not with everyone else steady
and cheery enough to sicken you. I'll carry to my grave the
picture of that blood-sodden ground, with the flies droning
everywhere, and the gaunt figures at the parapet; the barrack wall
honeycombed with the shots that slapped into it every few
seconds; the occasional cry of a man struck; the stretcher-parties
running—and through it all Moore walking about with his
bloody arm, grinning and calling out jokes to everyone; Wheeler,
with his hat on the back of his head and the pistol through the
cord at his waist, staring grim-faced at the pandy lines and

scratching his white moustache while he muttered to the aide scribbling notes at his elbow; a Cockney sergeant arguing with a private about the height of the pillars at Euston Square station, while they cut pieces from a dead horse for the big copper boiler against the barrack wall.

"Stew today," says Moore to me. "That's thanks to you fellows coming in. Usually, if we want meat, we have to let a pandy cavalryman charge up close, and then shoot the horse, not the rider,"

"More meat on the 'orse than there is on the pandy, eh, Jasper?" says the sergeant, winking, and the private said it was just as well, since some non-coms of his acquaintance, namin' no names, would as soon be cannibals as not.

These are the trivial things that stick in memory, but none clearer than the inside of that great barrack-room, with the wounded lying in a long, sighing, groaning line down one wall, and a few yards away, behind roughly improvised screens of chick and canvas, four hundred women and children, who had lived in that confined, sweating furnace for two weeks. The first thing that struck you was the stench, of blood and stale sweat and sickness, and then the sound—the children's voices, a baby crying, the older ones calling out, some even laughing, while the firing cracked away outside; the quiet murmur of the women; the occasional gasp of pain from the wounded; the brisk voices from the curtained corner where Wheeler had his office. Then the gaunt patient faces—the weary-looking women, some in ragged aprons, others in soiled evening dresses, nursing or minding the children or tending the wounded; the loyal sepoys, slumped against the wall, with their muskets between their knees; an English civilian sitting writing, and staring up in thought, and then writing again; beside him an old babu in a *dhoti*, mouthing the words as he read a scrap of newspaper through steel-rimmed spectacles; a haggard-looking young girl stitching a garment for a small boy who was waiting and hitting out angrily at the flies buzzing round his head; two officers in foul suits that had once been white, talking about pig-sticking—I remember one jerking his arm to shoot his linen, and him with nothing over his torso but his jacket; an *ayah** smiling as she piled toy bricks for a little

* Native nursemaid.

girl; a stocky, tow-headed corporal scraping his pipe; a woman whispering from the Bible to a pallid Goanese-looking fellow lying on a blanket with a bloody bandage round his head; an old, stern, silver-haired mem-sahib rocking a cradle.

They were all waiting to die, and some of them knew it, but there was no complaint, no cross words that I ever heard. It wasn't real, somehow—the patient, ordinary way they carried on. "It beats me," I remember Moore saying, "when I think how our dear ladies used to slang and back-bite on the verandahs, to see 'em now, as gentle as nuns. Take my word for it, they'll never look at their fellow-women the same way again, if we get out of this."

"Don't you believe it," says another, called Delafosse. "It's just lack of grub that's keeping 'em quiet. A week after it's all over, they'll be cutting Lady Wheeler dead in the street, as usual."

It's all vague memory, though, with no sense of time to it; I couldn't tell you when it was that I came face to face with Harry East, and we spoke, but I know that it was near Wheeler's curtain, where I'd been talking with two officers called Whiting and Thomson, and a rather pretty girl called Bella Blair was sitting not far away reading a poem to some of the children. I must have got over my funks to some extent, for I know I was sufficiently myself to be properly malicious to him.

"Hallo, Flashman," says he.

"Hallo, young Scud East," says I, quite cool. "You got to Raglan, I hear."

"Yes," says he, blushing. "Yes, I did."

"Good for you," says I. "Wish I could have come along—but I was delayed, you recollect."

This was all Greek to the others, of course, so the young ass had to blurt it out for their benefit—how we'd escaped together in Russia, and he'd left me behind wounded (which, between ourselves, had been the proper thing to do, since there was vital news to carry to Raglan at Sevastopol), and the Cossacks had got me. Of course, he hadn't got the style to make the tale sound creditable to himself, and I saw Whiting cock an eyebrow and sniff. East stuttered over it, and blushed even redder, and finally says:

"I'm so glad you got out, in the end, though, Flashman. I . . . I hated leaving you, old fellow."

"Yes," says I. "The Cossacks were all for it, though."

"I . . . I hope they didn't—I mean, they didn't use you too badly . . . that they didn't . . ." He was making a truly dreadful hash of it, much to my enjoyment. "It's been on my conscience, you know . . . having to go off like that."

Whiting was looking at the ceiling by this, Thomson was frowning, and the delectable Bella had stopped reading to listen.

"Well," says I, after a moment, "it's all one now, you know." I gave a little sigh. "Don't fret about it, young Scud. If the worst comes to the worst here—I won't leave *you* behind."

It hit him like a blow; he went chalk-white, and gasped, and then he turned on his heel and hurried off. Whiting said, "Good God!" and Thomson asked incredulously: "Did I understand that right? He absolutely cut out and left you—saved his own skin?"

"Um? What's that?" says I, and frowned. "Oh, now, that's a bit hard. No use both of us being caught and strung up in a dungeon and . . ." I stopped there and bit my lip. "That would just have meant the Cossacks would have had two of us to . . . play with, wouldn't it? Doubled the chance of one of us cracking and telling 'em what they wanted to know. That's why I wasn't sorry he cleared out. . . . I knew I could trust myself, you see. . . . But, Lord, what am I rambling about? It's all past." I smiled bravely at them. "He's a good chap, young East; we were at school together, you know."

I limped off then, leaving them to discuss it if they wanted to, and what they said I don't know, but later that evening Thomson sought me out at my place on the parapet, and shook my hand without a word, and then Bella Blair came, biting her lip, and kissed me quickly on the cheek and hurried off. It's truly remarkable, if you choose a few words carefully, how you can enhance your reputation and damage someone else's—and it was the least I could do to pay back that pious bastard East. Between me and his own precious Arnold-nurtured conscience he must have had a happy night of it.

I didn't sleep too well myself. A cupful of horse stew and a handful of flour don't settle you, especially if you're shaking with the horrors of your predicament. I even toyed with the idea of resuming my Pathan dress—which I had exchanged for army shirt and breeches—slipping over the parapet, lame as I was, and trying to escape, but the thought of being caught in the pandy lines was more than I could bear. I just lay there quaking, listening to the distant crack of the rebel snipers, and the occasional crump of a shot landing in the enclosure, tortured by thirst and hunger cramps, and I must have dozed off, for suddenly I was being shaken, and all round me people were hurrying, and a brazen voice was bawling "Stand to! Stand to! Loading parties, there!" A bugle was blaring, and orders were being shouted along the parapet—the fellow next me was ramming in a charge hurriedly, and when I demanded what was the row he just pointed out over the barricade, and invited me to look for myself.

It was dawn, and across the flat maidan, in front of the pandy gun positions, men were moving—hundreds of them. I could see long lines of horsemen in white tunics, dim through the light morning mist, and in among the squadrons were the scarlet coats and white breeches of native infantry. Even as I looked there was the red winking of fire from the gun positions, and then the crash of the explosions, followed by the whine of shot and a series of crashes from the barracks behind. Clouds of dust billowed down from the wall, to the accompaniment of yells and oaths, and a chorus of wails from the children. A kettle-drum was clashing, and here were the loading parties, civilians and followers and even some of the women, and a couple of bhistis,* and then Wheeler himself, with Moore at his heels, bawling orders, and behind him on the barrack-roof the torn Union Jack was being hauled up to flap limply in the warm dawn air.

"They're coming, rot 'em!" says the man next to me. "Look at 'em, yonder—56th N.I., Madras Fusiliers. An' Bengal Cavalry, too—don't I know it! Those are my own fellows, blast the scoundrels—or were. All right, my bucks, your old riding-master's waiting for you!" He slapped the stock of his rifle. "I'll give you more pepper than I ever did at stables!"

The pandy guns were crashing away full tilt now, and the whistle of small arms shot was sounding overhead. I was fumbling

* Native water-carriers.

with my revolver, pressing in the loads; all down the parapet
there was the scraping of ram-rods, and Wheeler was shouting:

"Every piece loaded, mind! Loading parties be ready with
fresh charges! Three rifles to each man! All right, Delafosse!
Moore, call every second man from the south side—smartly, now!
Have the fire-parties stand by! Sergeant Grady, I want an orderly
with bandages every ten yards on this parapet!"

He could hardly be heard above the din of the enemy firing
and the crash of the shots as they plumped home; the space
between the parapet and the barracks was swirling with dust
thrown up by the shot, and we lay with our heads pressed into
the earth below the top of the barrier. Someone came forward at
a crouching run and laid two charged muskets on the ground
beside me; to my astonishment I saw it was Bella Blair—the fat
babu I'd seen reading the previous night was similarly arming
the riding-master, and the chap on t'other side of me had as his
loader a very frail-looking old civilian in a dust-coat and cricket
cap. They lay down behind us; Bella was pale as death, but she
smiled at me and pushed the hair out of her eyes; she was wearing a yellow calico dress, I recall, with a band tied round her
brows.

"All standing to!" roars Wheeler. He alone was on his feet,
gaunt and bare-headed, with his white hair hanging in wisps
down his cheeks; he had his revolver in one hand, and his sabre
stuck point-first in the ground before him. "Masters—I want a
ration of flour and half a cup of water to each—"

A terrific concerted salvo drowned out the words; the whole
entrenchment seemed to shake as the shots ploughed into it and
smashed clouds of brickdust from the barracks. Farther down the
line someone was screaming, high-pitched, there was a cry for
the stretchers, the dust eddied round us and subsided, and then
the noise gradually ebbed away, even the screams trailed off into a
whimper, and a strange, eery stillness fell.

"Steady, all!" It was Wheeler, quieter now. "Riflemen—up to
the parapet! Now hold your fire, until I give the word! Steady,
now!"

I peered over the parapet. Across the maidan there was silence,
too, suddenly broken by the shrill note of a trumpet. There they

were, looking like a rather untidy review—the ranks of red-coated infantry, in open order, just forward of the ruined build-ings, and before them, within shot, the horse squadrons, half a dozen of them well spaced out. A musket cracked somewhere down the parapet, and Wheeler shouted:

"Confound it, hold that fire! D'you hear?"

We waited and watched as the squadrons formed, and the riding-master cursed under his breath.

"Sickenin'," says he, "when you think I taught 'em that. As usual—C Troop can't dress! That's *Havildar* Ram Hyder for you! Look at 'em, like a bloody Paul Jones! Take a line from the right-hand troop, can't you? Rest of 'em look well enough, though, don't they? There now, steady up. That's better, eh?"

The man beyond him said something, and the riding-master laughed. "If they must charge us I'd like to see 'em do it proper, for my own credit's sake, that's all."

I tore my eyes away from that distant mass of men, and glanced round. The babu, flat on the ground, was turning his head to polish his spectacles; Bella Blair had her face hidden, but I noticed her fists were clenched. Wheeler had clapped his hat on, and was saying something to Moore; one of the *bhistis* was crawling on hands and knees along the line, holding a chaggle for the fellows to drink from. Suddenly the distant trumpet sounded again, there was a chorus of cries from across the maidan, a volley of orders, and now the cavalry were moving, at a walk, and then at a trot, and there was a bright flicker along their lines as the sabres came out.

Oh, Christ, I thought, this is the finish. There seemed to be hordes of them, advancing steadily through the wisps of mist, the dust coming up in little clouds behind them, and the crackle of the sharpshooters started up again, the bullets whining overhead.

"Steady, all!' roars Wheeler again. "Wait for the word, remember!"

I had laid by my revolver and had my musket up on the para-pet. My mouth was so dry I couldn't swallow—I was remembering those masses of horsemen that had poured down from the Cause-way Heights at Balaclava, and how disciplined fire had stopped them in their tracks—but those had been Campbell's Highlanders shooting then, and we had nothing but a straggling line of sick crocks and civilians. They must break over us like a wave, brushing past our feeble volleys—

"Take aim!" yells Wheeler, "make every shot tell, and wait for my command!"

They were coming at the gallop now, perhaps three hundred yards off, and the sabres steady against the shoulders; they were keeping line damned well, and I heard my riding-master muttering:

"Look at 'em come, though! Ain't that a sight?—and ain't they shaping well! Hold 'em in there, *rissaldar*, mind the dressing—"

The thunder of the beating hooves was like surf; there was a sudden yell, and all the points came down, with the black blobs of faces behind them as the riders crouched forward and the whole line burst into the charge. They came sweeping in towards the entrenchment, I gripped my piece convulsively, and Wheeler yelled "Fire!"

The volley crashed out in a billow of smoke—but it didn't stop them. Horses and men went down, and then we were seizing our second muskets and blazing away, and then our third—and still they came, into that hell of smoke and flame, yelling like madmen; Bella Blair was beside me, thrusting a musket into my hand, and hurrying feverishly to reload the others. I fired again, and as the smoke cleared we looked out onto a tangle of fallen beasts and riders, but half of them were still up and tearing in, howling and waving their sabres. I seized my revolver and blasted away; there were three of them surging in towards my position, and I toppled one from the saddle, another went rolling down with his mount shot under him, and the third came hurtling over the entrenchment, with the man on my right slashing at him as he passed.

Behind him pressed the others—white coats, black faces, rearing beasts, putting their horses to the parapet; I was yelling incoherent obscenities, scrabbling up the muskets as fast as they were reloaded, firing into the mass; men were struggling all along the entrenchment, bayonets and swords against sabres, and still the firing crashed out. I heard Bella scream, and then there was a dismounted rider scrambling up the barrier directly before me; I had a vision of glaring eyes in a black face and a sabre upraised to strike, and then he fell back shrieking into the smoke. Behind me Wheeler was roaring, and I was grabbing for another musket, and then they were falling back, thank God, wheeling and riding back into the smoke, and the *bhisti* was at my elbow, thrusting his chaggle at my lips.

"Stand to!" shouts Wheeler, "they're coming again!"

They were re-forming, a bare hundred yards off; the ground between was littered with dead and dying beasts and men. I had barely time to gulp a mouthful of warm, muddy water and seize my musket before they were howling in at us once more, and this time there were pandy infantrymen racing behind them.

"One more volley!" bawls Wheeler. "Hold your fire, there! Aim for the horses! No surrender! Ready, present—fire!"

The whole wall blasted fire, and the charge shook and wavered before it came rushing on again; half a dozen of them were rearing and plunging up to the entrenchment, the sabres were swinging about our heads, and I was rolling away to avoid the smashing hooves of a rider coming in almost on top of me. I scrambled to my feet, and there was a red-coated black devil leaping at me from the parapet; I smashed at him with my musket butt and sent him flying, and then another one was at me with his sabre, lunging. I shrieked as it flew past my head, and then we had closed, and I was clawing at his face, bearing him down by sheer weight. His sabre fell, and I plunged for it; another pandy was rushing past me, musket and bayonet extended, but I got my hand on the fallen hilt, slashing blindly; I felt a sickening shock on my head, and fell, a dead weight landed on top of me, and the next thing I knew I was on my hands and knees, with the earth swimming round me, and Wheeler was bawling,

"Cease fire! Cease fire! Stretchers, there!"

and the noise of yelling and banging had died away, while the last of the smoke cleared above the ghastly shambles of the parapet.

There seemed to be dead and dying everywhere. There must have been at least a dozen pandies sprawled within ten yards of where I knelt; the ground was sticky with blood. Wheeler himself was down on one knee, supporting the fat babu, who was wailing with a shattered leg; the frail civilian was lying asprawl, his cricket cap gone and his head just a squashed red mess. One of the pandies stirred, and pulled himself up on one knee; Wheeler, his arm still round the babu, whipped up his revolver and fired, and the pandy flopped back in the dust. The stretcher parties were hurrying up; I looked out over the parapet, across a maidan littered with figures of men that crawled or lay still; there were screaming horses trying to rise, and others that lay dead among the fallen riders. Two hundred yards off there were men running—the other way, thank God; farther down the parapet someone sent up a cheer, and it gradually spread along the entrenchment in a ghastly, croaking yell. My mouth was too dry, and I was too dazed to cheer—but I was alive.

Bella Blair was dead. She was lying on her side, her hands clutched on the stock of a musket whose bayonet was buried in her body. I heard a moan behind me, and there was the riding-master, flopped against the parapet, his shirt soaked in blood, trying to reach for the fallen water-chaggle. I stumbled over to him, and held it up to his lips; he sucked at it, groaning, and then let his head fall back.

"Beat 'em, did we?" says he, painfully. I could only nod; I took a gulp at the chaggle myself, and offered him another swig, but he turned his head feebly aside. There was nothing to be done for him; his life was running out of him where he lay.

"Beat 'em," says he again. "Dam' good. Thought . . . they was going to ride . . . clean over us there . . . for a moment." He coughed blood, and his voice trailed away into a whisper. "They shaped well, though . . . didn't they . . . shape well? My Bengalis . . ." He closed his eyes. "I thought they shaped . . . uncommon well . . ."

I looked down the entrenchment. About half the defenders were on their feet at the parapet, I reckoned. In between, the sprawled, silent figures, the groaning, writhing wounded waiting for the stretchers, the tangle of gear and fallen weapons, the bloody rags—and now the pandy guns again, pounding anew at the near-dead wreck of the Cawnpore garrison, with its tattered flag still flapping from the mast. Well, thinks I, they can walk in now, any time they like. There's nothing left to stop 'em.

But they didn't. That last great assault of June twenty-third,

which had come within an ace of breaking us, had sickened the
pandies. The maidan was strewn with their dead, and although
they pounded us with gunfire for another two terrible days, they
didn't have the stomach for another frontal attack. If only they'd
known it, half the men left on our parapet were too done up with
fatigue and starvation to lift a musket, the barrack was choked
with more than three hundred wounded and dying, the well was
down to stinking ooze, and our remaining flour was so much
dust. We couldn't have lasted two minutes against a determined
assault—yet why should they bother, when hunger and heat and
the steady rate of casualties from bombardment were sure to finish
us soon anyway?

Three folk went mad, as I remember, in those forty-eight
hours; I only wonder now that we all didn't. In the furnace of
the barrack the women and children were too reduced by famine
even to cry; even the younger officers seemed to be overcome by
the lethargy of approaching certain death. For that, Wheeler now
admitted, was all that remained.

"I have sent a last message out to Lawrence," he told us senior
men on the second night. "I have told him that we have nothing
left but British spirit, and that cannot last forever. We are like
rats in a cage. Our best hope is that the rebels will come in again,
and give us a quick end; better that than watch our women and
little ones die by inches."[29]

I can still see the gaunt faces in the flickering candlelight
round his table; someone gave a little sob, and another swore
softly, and after a moment Vibart asked if there was no hope that
Lawrence might yet come to our relief.

Wheeler shook his head. "He would come if he could, but even
if he marched now he could not reach us in under two days. By
then . . . well, you know me, gentlemen. I haven't croaked in
fifty years' soldiering, and I'm not croaking now, when I say that
short of a miracle it is *all up*. We're in God's hands, so let each
one of us make his preparations accordingly."

I was with him there, only my preparations weren't going to
be spiritual. I still had my Pathan rig-out stowed away, and I
could see that the time was fast approaching when, game ankle or
no, Flashy was going to have to take his chance over the wall. It

was that or die in this stinking hole, so I left them praying and went to my place on the parapet to think it out; I was in a blue funk at the thought of trying to decamp, but the longer I waited, the harder it might become. I was still wrestling with my fears when someone hove up out of the gloom beside me, and who should it be but East.

"Flashman," says he, "may I have a word with you?"

"If you must," says I. "I'll be obliged if you'll make it a brief one."

"Of course, of course," says he. "I understand. As Sir Hugh said, it is time for each of us to make his own soul; I won't intrude on your meditations a moment longer than I must, I promise. The trouble is . . . my own conscience. I . . . I need your help, old fellow."

"Eh?" I stared at him, trying to make out his face in the dark. "What the deuce—?"

"Please . . . bear with me. I know you're bitter, because you think I abandoned you in Russia . . . left you to die, while I escaped. Oh, I know it was my duty, and all that, to get to Raglan . . . but the truth is—" he broke off and had a gulp to himself "—the truth is, I was *glad* to leave you. There—it's out at last . . . oh, if you knew how it had been tormenting me these two years past! That weight on my soul—that I abandoned you in a spirit of hatred and sinful vengeance. No . . . let me finish! I hated you then . . . because of the way you had treated Valla . . . when you flung her from that sledge, into the snow! I could have killed you for it!"

He was in a rare taking, no error; a Rugby conscience pouring out is a hell of a performance. He wasn't telling me a thing I hadn't guessed at the time—I know these pious bastards better than they know themselves, you see.

"I loved her, you see," he went on, talking like an old man with a hernia. "She meant everything to me . . . and you had cast her away so . . . brutally. Please, please, hear me out! I'm confessing, don't you see? And . . . and asking for your forgiveness. It's late in the day, I know—but, well, it looks as though we haven't much longer, don't it? So . . . I wanted to tell you . . . and shake your hand, old school-fellow, and hear from you that my . . . my sin is forgiven me. If you can find it in your heart, that is." He choked resoundingly. "I . . . I trust you can."

I've heard some amazing declarations in my time, but this babbling was extraordinary. It comes of Christian upbringing, of course, and taking cold baths, all of which implants in the impressionable mind the notion that repentance can somehow square the account. At any other time, it would have given me some malicious amusement to listen to him; even in my distracted condition, it was interesting enough for me to ask him:

"D'ye mean that if I *hadn't* given you cause to detest me, you'd have stayed with me, and let Raglan's message go hang?"

"What's that?" says he. "I . . . I don't know what you mean. I . . . I . . . please, Flashman, you must see my agony of spirit . . . I'm trying to . . . make you understand. Please—tell me, even now, what I can do."

"Well," says I, thoughtfully, "you could go and fart in a bottle and paint it."

"What?" says he, bewildered. "What did you say?"

"I'm trying to indicate that you can take yourself off," says I. "You're a selfish little swine, East. You admit you've behaved like a scoundrel to me, and if that wasn't enough, you have the cheek to waste my time—when I need it for prayer. So go to hell, will you?"

"My God, Flashman . . . you can't mean it! You can't be so hard. It only needs a word! I own I've wronged you, terribly . . . maybe in more ways than I know. Sometimes . . . I've wondered if perhaps you too loved Valla . . . if you did, and placed duty first . . ." He gulped again, and peered at me. "Did you . . . love her, Flashman?"

"About four or five times a week," says I, "but you needn't be jealous; she wasn't nearly as good a ride as her Aunt Sara. You should have tried a steam-bath with that one."

He gave a shocked gasp, and I absolutely heard his teeth chatter. Then: "God, Flashman! Oh . . . oh, you are unspeakable! You are vile! God help you!"

"Unspeakable and vile I may be," says I, "but at least I'm no hypocrite, like you: the last thing you want is for God to help me. You don't want my forgiveness, either; you just want to be able to forgive yourself. Well, you run along and do it, Scud, and thank me for making it easy for you. After what you've heard tonight, your conscience needn't trouble you any longer about having left old Flashy to his fate, what?"

He stumbled off at that, and I was able to resume my own debate about whether it was best to slide out or stay. In the end, my nerve failed me, and I curled up in the lee of the parapet for the night. Thank God I did, for on the next morning Wheeler got his miracle.

She was the most unlikely messenger of grace you ever saw—a raddled old *chee-chee** biddy with clanking earrings and a parasol, drawn in a rickshaw *ghari* by two pandies, with another couple marching as guard, and a *havildar* out in front brandishing a white flag. Wheeler ordered a stand-to when this strange little procession was seen approaching the east corner of the entrenchment, and went off himself with Moore to meet it, and a few minutes later word was passed for me and Vibart, who was up at my end of the parapet, to present ourselves.

Wheeler and the other senior men were grouped inside the parapet, while the old wife, fanning herself with a leaf and sipping at a *chatti*, was sitting just outside with her escort squatting round her. Wheeler was holding a paper, and glancing in bewilderment from it to the old woman; as we came up someone was saying: "I wouldn't trust it a blasted inch! Why should they want to treat, at this time o'day? Tell me that!", and Wheeler shook his head and passed the paper to Vibart.

"Read that," says he. "If what it says is true, the Nana wishes to make terms."

It didn't sink in, at first; I studied the paper over Vibart's shoulder, while he read it out half-aloud. It was a brief, simple note, written in a good hand, in English, and addressed to Wheeler. As near as I recall, it said:

To subjects of Her Most Gracious Majesty, Queen Victoria— all who are not connected with the acts of Lord Dalhousie and are willing to lay down their arms, shall receive a safe passage to Allahabad.

It was signed on behalf of Nana Sahib, with a name I couldn't make out, until Vibart muttered it out: "Azeemoolah Khan". He

* Half-caste.

looked at Wheeler, then at the old woman, and Wheeler flapped
a hand and says:

"This is Mrs Jacobs, of ... ah, Cawnpore city. She has this
note from Azeemoolah himself, in the presence of the Nana."

"How-dee-do, gentlemen," says Mrs Jacobs, bowing with a
great creak of stays from her seat in the *ghari*. "Such jolly
weather we are having, yess?"

"I don't like it," says Wheeler quietly, turning his back so that
she shouldn't hear; the others grouped round us. "As Whiting
says, why should he offer terms when he must know we're at his
mercy? All he needs do is wait."

"Perhaps, sir," says Vibart, "he don't know how reduced we
are." He let out a deep breath. "And we have our women and
children to think of—"

At this the others broke in, in a fierce babble of low voices:
"It's a plot!" "No, it ain't!" "We've stood the bastards off this
long—" "It's false—I can smell nigger treachery a mile away."
"Why should it be treachery—my God, what have we to lose?
We're done for as it is ...", while I tried to keep my face straight
and the delicious hope began to break over me—we were saved!
For it seemed to me in that moment that whatever anyone said,
whatever Wheeler felt, he was going to have to accept any terms
the pandies offered—he couldn't refuse, and doom the women and
children in that stinking barrack to certain death, however fearful
of treachery he might be. We were being offered at least a chance
of life against the certainty of death: he had to take it.

So I said nothing, while they wrangled in whispers there by
the parapet, with every drawn face along the entrenchment on
either side turned anxiously in our direction, and that painted
old harridan sitting under the canopy of her *ghari*, nodding and
bowing whenever anyone glanced at her. And sure enough,
Wheeler finally says:

"What's your opinion, Colonel Flashman?"

The temptation to sing out: "Take it, you bloody old fool—
offer to crawl on your belly the whole way to Allahabad!" was
strong, but I mastered it and looked pretty cool. "Well, sir," says
I. "It's an offer—no more. There's nothing to be decided until
we've tested it."

That shut them up. "True enough," says Wheeler, "but—"

"Someone must talk to Nana Sahib," says I. "It may be that all isn't well with him, or that he thinks this siege ain't worth the candle. Maybe his precious pandies have had enough—"

"That's it, by God!" broke in Delafosse, but I went on, very steady:

"But we can't accept—or turn him down flat—till we've heard more than is written here," and I tapped the paper in Vibart's hand. "He hasn't approached us out of charity, we may be sure— well, it may be treachery, or it may be weakness. Let's look him in the eye."

It must have sounded well—bluff Flashy talking calm sense while others went pink in the face. They weren't to know I'd made up my trembling mind in the moment I'd read the note; the trick now was to make sure that Wheeler made up his, and in the right direction. For he was obviously full of suspicion about the Nana, and half-inclined to listen to the hotheads who were urging him to throw the offer back in the mutineers' teeth— you never heard such appalling nonsense in your life. Here we were, doomed for certain, being offered an eleventh-hour reprieve, and more than half the idiots in that impromptu council were for rejecting it out of hand. It made my innards heave to listen; thinks I, this is going to need delicate handling.

However, Wheeler saw the sense of what I'd said, and decided that Moore and I should go to see the Nana and hear precisely what he had to say. Thank God he chose me—I don't care, as a rule, to put my head into the lion's den, even under a flag of truce, but this was one negotiation I wanted to have a large hand in. I didn't want any hitches about the surrender—for surrender, if I had anything to do with it, was what it was going to be. All that mattered besides was that I should keep my credit intact.

So at noon Moore and I were escorted through the pandy lines, with Mrs Jacobs in her *ghari* jabbering about what a shame it was, oah yess, that the present unsettled state of affairs had prevented her getting up to the hills during the hot weather. Who she was, by the way, I never discovered; she looked like a typical half-caste bawd who'd been employed as a go-between because she was obviously neutral and inoffensive. But I may be misjudging the lady.

The notorious Nana Sahib was waiting for us in front of a great day-tent in a grove of trees, with a pack of servitors and minions attending him, and a score of Maharatta guardsmen, in breastplates and helmets, ranged either side of the great Afghan carpet before his chair. That carpet gave me an uneasy twinge—it reminded me of the one on which I'd seen McNaghten seized and chopped up outside Kabul, at just such a meeting as this; however, Moore and I put out our chests and looked down our noses, as true Britons ought to do in the presence of rebellious niggers who happen to have the drop on them.

Nana himself was a burly, fat-faced rascal with curly mustachioes and a shifty look—what they call a *tung admi*,* dressed in more silks and jewels than a French whore, sliding his eyes across Moore and me and whispering behind a plump hand to the woman beside him. She was worth a lewd thought or two, by the way; one of your tall, heavy-hipped beauties with a drooping lower lip—Sultana Adala, they called her, and I'm sorry I never got closer to her than twenty feet. We exchanged a glance or two during that interview, and let our mutual imaginations work; ten minutes alone together would have done the rest. On Nana's other side sat a nondescript and nasty-looking rascal, who I gather was his brother-in-crime, Tantia Tope.

However, the man who took things in hand was Azeemoolah Khan, a tall, handsome, light-skinned exquisite in a cloth-of-gold coat and with a jewelled aigret in his turban, who stepped smiling across the carpet with his hand out. Moore promptly put his hands behind his back, I contented myself by hooking my thumbs into my belt, and Azeemoolah smiled even wider and withdrew his hand with a graceful flutter—Rudi Starnberg couldn't have done it better. I gave him our names, and he opened his eyes wide.

"Colonel Flashman! But this is an honour indeed! It has always been my regret that I missed you in the Crimea," says he, flashing his teeth. "And how is my dear old friend, Mr William Howard Russell?"

It was my turn to stare, at that; I didn't know then that this Azeemoolah was a travelled man, who spoke French and English as well as I did, had done diplomatic work in London—and gone

* Literally, "a tight man".

through our sillier society women like a mad stallion at the same time. A charming, clever politician, whose urbanity masked a nature as appealing as a hooded cobra's;[30] for the occasion he was acting as interpreter for the Nana, who spoke no English.

I told him, fairly cool, that we were there to receive his master's proposals, at which he sighed and spread his hands.

"Well, gentlemen, it is a most distressing business, and no one is more deeply troubled by it than his highness, which is why he has sent his note to General Wheeler, in the hope that we can put an end to all this bloodshed and suffering—"

Moore interrupted at this to say that in that case it was a pity he hadn't sent his message earlier, or stayed loyal in the first place. Azeemoolah just smiled.

"But we are not talking politics, are we, Captain Moore? We are looking at military reality—which is that your gallant resistance is at an end, one way or another. His highness deplores the thought of useless slaughter; he is willing, if you will quit Cawnpore, to allow your garrison to depart with the honours of war; you shall have all necessary food and comforts for your women and children (for whom his highness is particularly concerned), and safe passage to Allahabad. It seems to me not an ungenerous offer."

The Nana, who obviously knew the purport of what was being said, leaned forward at this, smiling greasily, and gabbled in Maharatta. Azeemoolah nodded, and went on:

"He says that baggage animals are already being collected to carry your wounded to the river, where boats will be waiting to take you all to Allahabad."

I asked the question Wheeler wanted asked. "What guarantees of safe-conduct does he offer?"

Azeemoolah lifted his brows. "But are any necessary? If we intended you harm, we have only to attack, or wait. We know your situation, you see. Believe me, gentlemen, his highness is moved simply by humanity, the spirit of mercy—"

Whether it was deliberately timed or not, I don't know, but his words were interrupted by the most hideous scream of agony— a drawn-out, bubbling wail from behind the grove of trees. It rang out again, and then died into an awful whimper of pain, and I felt the hairs rise on my neck. Moore almost jumped out of his boots.

"What in God's name was that?" says he.

"Maharatta diplomacy, I imagine," says I, with a straight face and my innards dissolving. "Someone being flayed alive, probably, for our benefit—so that we could hear, and take note."

". . . but if his highness's word is not sufficient," Azeemoolah went on blandly, "he would raise no objection to your carrying away your personal arms and . . . shall we say, twenty rounds a man? With that, you will hardly be at a greater disadvantage in the open than behind that pathetic breastwork. But I repeat, gentlemen, his highness has nothing to gain by treachery—quite the reverse. It is repugnant to him, and would be politically damaging."

I didn't trust the bastard an inch, but I was privately inclined to agree with him. Wiping out a British garrison entire was one thing, but he could do that anyway, without luring us into the open. On the other hand, getting a British garrison to haul down its flag would be a real feather in his cap—but Azeemoolah was a mile too shrewd to say so, for nothing would have been better calculated to stiffen Wheeler's resistance.

Nana started to chatter again in Maharatta, while I tried to efface the memory of that awful scream by exchanging a long look or two with Sultana Adala—it never does any harm. Azeemoolah heard him out, and then addressed us again.

"His highness asks you to reassure General Wheeler, and to add that while you are considering his most generous proposal, he is instructing our troops to observe an armistice. I myself will come tomorrow for General Wheeler's answer."

And that was that. Moore and I trudged back through the pandy lines—and if anything was needed to convince me that surrender was imperative it was the sight of those glowering black faces at the gun emplacements and round the bivouacs. They might look less smart and orderly than they'd done as loyal Company troops, but by God there were plenty of them, and no signs of weakening or desertion.

It was touch and go, though, when we got back to the entrenchment and reported to Wheeler what Nana's proposals were. He called a council of all the officers, and we sat or stood crowded into the stifling corner of the barrack which was his office, with the moaning of the wounded beyond the partition, and the wailing of the children, while we heard rehearsed again all the arguments that had been whispered to and fro that morning. It frightened me, I may tell you, for Wheeler was still smelling treachery, and our younger sparks were in full cry against the notion of surrender.

"We've held out this long," cries Delafosse, "and now they're weakening. Tell him to go to blazes, I say, and ten to one he'll raise the siege."

There were growls of approval at this, until Vibart says: "And if he don't raise it? What then? We'll not have a child or woman alive in this hellish place three days hence. Are you prepared to accept that?"

"Are you prepared to accept a rebel's word?" retorts Delafosse. "While we're in a defensive position here, at least we can make some show against him—and he may raise the siege, or Lawrence may march. But once we accept his terms and step into the open, we're at his mercy."

"And we'll have hauled down our flag to a pack of rebels," says Thomson bitterly. "How do we go home to England and tell 'em that?"

At this some cried "Bravo!" and urged Wheeler to answer Nana with defiance, but old Ewart, who was so sick that he had to attend the council lying on a stretcher, wondered what England would say if we condemned hundreds of women and children to die in the useless defence of a couple of ruined mud buildings. The older men nodded agreement, but the youngsters shouted him down, and Delafosse repeated the argument, red in the face, that Nana must be weakening or he'd never have made the offer.

Wheeler, who'd been sitting tugging his moustache while they bickered, looks at Moore and me.

"You saw his camp, gentlemen; what opinion did you form? Is he negotiating from weakness, because his troops have lost heart?"

I'd said nothing throughout; I was biding my time, and let Moore answer. He said we'd seen no signs of flagging morale, which was true enough. Wheeler looked glum, and shook his head.

"I cannot think the Nana is to be trusted," says he. "And yet . . . it is a cruel choice. All my nature, every instinct, tells me to fight this command to the last; to die in my duty as a soldier should do, and let my country avenge me. But to do that at the cost of our loved ones' lives . . . already, so many . . ."

He broke off, and there was an uneasy silence; everyone knew that Wheeler's own son had died the day before. Finally he rubbed his face and looked round.

"If it were ourselves alone, there could be but one answer. As it is, I confess I should be tempted, for our women and children's sake, to accept this murderer's terms, were it not that my judgement tells me he will play us false. I . . ."

"Forgive me, sir," says Moore, quietly, "but if he does, we've lost nothing. For if we don't trust him, we're dead anyway—all of us. We know that, and—"

"At least we can die with honour!" cries some fool, and the younger chaps cheered like the idiots they were. At this Wheeler's head came up, and I saw his stubborn lip go out, and I thought, now, Flashy, now's your time, or the stupid old bastard will damn us all in the name of Duty and Honour. So I growled in my throat, and scraped my heel, and that caught his attention, just in time, and he looked at me.

"You've said nothing, Flashman," says he. "What is your thought?"

I felt all their eyes turn to me, and deliberately took my time, for I knew Wheeler was within an ace of deciding to fight it out to a finish, and I was going to have to humbug him, and the rest of them, into surrendering. But it was going to require my most artistic handling.

"Well, sir," says I, "like you, I wouldn't trust the Nana as far as the tuck-shop." (Someone laughed; homely old Flashy, you see, with his schoolboy metaphors.) "But as Moore here says—that don't matter. What does—or so it seems to me—is the fate of our ladies—" (here I looked red-faced and noble) "—and the . . . the youngsters. If we accept the Nana's offer, at least there's a chance they'll come off safe."

"You'd surrender?" says Wheeler, in a strained voice.

"For myself?" growls I, and looked at the floor. "Well, I never quite got the habit . . . goes against the grain, I reckon. Matter of honour—as someone said just now. And I suppose it can be said that honour demands we fight it out to the last—"

"*Shabash!*" cries Delafosse. "Well done, Flashy!"

"—but, d'ye know, sir," I went on, "the day my honour has to be maintained by sacrificing Vibart's little boy—or Tunstall's mother—or Mrs Newnham's daughter, well . . ." I raised my head and stared at the circle of faces, a strong, simple man stirred to his depths; you could have heard a pin drop. "I don't know—I may be wrong . . . but I don't think my honour's worth that much, d'ye know?"

The beauty of it was, while it was the most fearful gammon, coming from me—it was stark truth for the rest of them, gallant and honourable souls that they were. The irony was that for my own cowardly, selfish reasons, I was arguing the sane and sensible course, and having to dress it up in high-sounding bilge in order to break down their fatuous notions of Duty. Reason wouldn't have done it, but to suggest that the true honour demanded surrender, for the women and children's sake—that shamed 'em into sanity.

Old Ewart put the final touch to it. "And that, gentlemen, you would do well to bear in mind—" he glared almost defiantly at Delafosse "—is the opinion of the man who held Piper's Fort, and led the Light Brigade."

Wheeler put it to the formality of a vote, but it was foregone now. When Moore and Whiting voted to surrender, even the firiest of the younger men gave way, and inside half an hour Wheeler's answer was on its way to Nana, agreeing to capitulate with the honours of war.[31] But he added the condition that we should not only keep our arms, but sixty rounds a man instead of the proposed twenty—"then, if there is treachery, it will profit him little," he told us, and echoed the thought Azeemoolah had expressed in the afternoon: "We can fight as well in the open as in this death-trap." That was all he knew.

He was still fearful of treachery, you see. I was not—you may think I was deluding myself, but the fact was I couldn't see that the Nana had anything to gain by playing us false. I state that honestly now, and I've explained the details of the Cawnpore surrender because it was a momentous thing, not only in the Mutiny, but in Indian history. I had spoken—and, as I've said, I believe mine was the decisive voice—for surrender, because I saw it as the only way to save my skin. But apart from that vital consideration, I still believe that surrender was right, by every canon of soldiering and common sense. Call me a fool if you like, and shake your heads in the light of history—nothing could have been worse than fighting on in that doomed entrenchment.

Whatever misgivings Wheeler may have had, hardly anyone else shared them when word got round of what had been decided, and Azeemoolah and Jwala Pershad had come to the entrenchment with the Nana's undertakings all signed and witnessed: draught animals were to arrive at dawn for the mile-long journey to the river where boats would be waiting, and throughout the night there was bustle and eagerness and thanksgiving all through the garrison. It was as though a great shadow had been lifted; cooking fires blazed outside the barrack for the first time in weeks, the wounded were brought out of that stinking oven to lie in the open air, and even the children frolicked on the parapet where we'd been slashing at the sepoys two days before. Tired, worn faces were smiling, no one minded the dirt and stench any longer, or gave a thought to the rebels' massed guns and infantry a few hundred yards away; the firing had stopped, the fear of death had lifted, we were going out to safety, and throughout the night, over the din of packing and preparation, the sound of hymns rolled up to the night sky.

One of the few croakers was Ilderim. Wheeler had told those sepoys who had remained loyal and fought in the garrison to slip away over the southern rampart, for fear of reprisals from their mutinous fellows in the morning, but Ilderim wouldn't have it. He came to me in the dark at the north entrenchment, where I was smoking a cheroot and enjoying my peace of mind.

"Do I slip away like a cur when someone throws a stone at it?" says he. "No—I march with Wheeler Sahib and the rest of you tomorrow. And so that no pi-dog of a mutineer will take me

for anything but what I am, I have put this on, for a *killut**—"
and as he stepped closer in the gloom, I saw he was in the full fig
of a native officer of cavalry, white coat, gauntlets, long-tailed
puggaree and all. "It is just a down-country regiment's coat,
which I took from one of those we slew the other day, but it will
serve to mark me as a soldier." He grinned, showing his teeth.
"And I shall take my sixty rounds—do thou likewise, blood-
brother."

"We're not going to need 'em, though," says I, and he
shrugged.

"Who knows? When the tiger has its paw on the goat's neck,
and then smiles in friendship . . . Wheeler Sahib does not trust
the Nana. Dost thou?"

"There's no choice, is there?" says I. "But he's signed his
name to a promise, after all—"

"And if he breaks it, the dead can complain," says he, and
spat. "So I say—keep thy sixty rounds to hand, Flashman
sahib."

I didn't heed him much, for Pathans are notoriously suspicious
of everyone, reason or none, and when day broke there was too
much to do to waste time in thinking. The mutineers came in the
first mists of dawn, with bullocks and elephants and carts to carry
us to the river, and we had the herculean task of getting everyone
into the convoy. There were two hundred wounded to be moved,
and all the women and children, some of them just babes-in-arms,
and old people who'd have been feeble enough even without
three weeks on starvation rations. Everyone was tired and filthy
and oddly dispirited now that the first flush of excitement had
died away. As the sun came up it shone on a strange, nightmare
sight that lives with me now only as a series of pictures as the
evacuation of Cawnpore began.

I can see the straggling mass of the procession, the bullock-
carts with their stretchers carrying the blood-stained figures of
the wounded, gaunt and wasted; bedraggled white women, either
sitting in the carts or standing patiently alongside, with children
who looked like Whitechapel waifs clinging to their skirts; our
own men, ragged and haggard, with their muskets cradled,

* Dress of honour, usually on ceremonial occasions.

taking up station along the convoy; the red coats and sullen faces of the mutineers who were to shepherd us across the maidan and down to the river ghat beyond the distant trees where the boats were waiting. The dawn air was heavy with mist and suspicion and hatred, as Wheeler, with Moore at his elbow as always, stood up on the rampart and reviewed the battered remnants of his command, strung out along the entrenchment, waiting listlessly for the word to move while all around was the confused babble of voices, orders being shouted, officers hurrying up and down, elephants squealing, the carts creaking, children crying, and the kites beginning to swoop down on the emptying barracks.

Incidents and figures remain very clear—two civilians hauling down the tattered flag from the barrack roof, rolling it up carefully and bringing it to Wheeler, who stood absent-mindedly with it trailing from one hand while he shouted: "Sarn't Grady! Is the south entrenchment clear, Sarn't Grady?" A little boy with curly hair, laughing and shouting "Plop-plop!" as one of the elephants dropped its dung; his mother, a harassed young woman in a torn ball-gown (it had rosebuds embroidered, I recall) with a sleeping infant in her arms, slapped and shook him with her free hand, and then straightened her hair. A group of mutineers walking round the barracks, belabouring one of our native cooks who was limping along under a great load of pans. A British private, his uniform unrecognisable, being railed at by an old mem-sahib as he helped her into a cart, until she was settled, when she said, "Thank you, my good man, thank you very much", and began searching her reticule for a tip. Four mutineers were hurrying up and down the untidy convoy, calling out and searching, until they spotted Vibart and his family—and then they ran hallooing and calling "Colonel sahib! Mem-sahib!", and seized on the family's baggage, and one of them, beaming and chuckling, lifted Vibart's little lad on to his shoulders, piggy-back, while the others shouted and shoved and made room for Mrs Vibart in a wagon. Vibart was dumbfounded, and two of the mutineers were weeping as they took his hand and carried his gear—I saw another one at it, too, an old grizzled *havildar* of the 56th, standing on the entrenchment gazing down into the ruin of the barracks with tears running down his white beard; he was shaking his head in grief, and then he would look no more, but turned about and stared across the maidan, still crying.

Most of the mutineers weren't so sentimental, though. One tried to snatch a musket from Whiting, and Whiting flung him off snarling and shouting: "You want it, do you? I'll give you its contents fast enough, you damned dog, if you don't take care!" The pandies fell back, growling and shaking their fists, and another gang of them stood and jeered while old Colonel Ewart was carried on a *palki* to his place in the line. "Is it not a fine parade, colonel sahib?" they were jeering. "Is it not well drawn up?" And they cackled and made mock of the drill, prancing up and down.

I didn't like the look of this a bit, or of the menacing-looking crowd of pandies which was growing across the maidan. Promises or no promises, it don't take much to touch off a crowd like that, and I was relieved when Moore, who had hurried to the head of the column, shouted and blew his whistle, and the procession began to move, creaking slowly, away from the entrenchment, and out on to the plain. I was near the rear of the line, where Vibart had charge of the supply-wagons; behind us the pandies were already scavenging in the deserted barracks—by God, they were welcome to anything they could find.

It was about a mile to the river, where the boats were, but we were so exhausted, and the convoy so haphazard and cumbersome, that it took us the best part of an hour to cross the maidan alone. It was a hellish trek, with the mutineers trying to drive us along, swearing and thrusting, and our fellows cursing 'em back, while wagons foundered, and one or two of the garrison collapsed and had to be loaded aboard, and the drivers thrashed at the beasts. Crowds of natives had come down from Cawnpore city to watch and jeer at us and get in the way; some of them, and the more hostile pandies, kept sneaking in close to shout taunts, or even to strike at us and try to steal our belongings. Something's going to crack in a moment, thinks I, and sure enough, just as we were trying to manhandle one of the store-wagons over a little white bridge at the far side of the maidan, where the trees began, there was a crackle of firing off to one side, and sudden shouting, and then more shots.

The driver of my store-wagon tried to whip up in alarm, a
wheel caught on the bridge, and I and two civilians were
struggling to keep it steady when Whiting comes up at the run,
cocking his musket and demanding to know what the row was.
In the same moment one of our corporals came flying out of the
wood, rolled clean under the wagon in front of us, and jumps up
yelling:

"Quick, sir—come quick! Them devils is murthering Colonel
Ewart! They got 'im in the trees yonder, an'—"

Whiting sprang forward with an oath, but quick as light one
of the mutineers who'd been watching us at the bridge jumps in
his way and flung his arm round him. For a moment I thought,
oh God, now they're going to ambush us, and the corporal must
have thought the same, for he whipped out his bayonet, but the
mutineer holding Whiting was just trying to keep him back and
shouting:

"*Nahin*, sahib, *khabadar!** If you go there, they will kill you!
Let be, sahib! Go on—to the river!"

Whiting swore, and struggled with him, but the mutineer—a
big, black-moustached *havildar* with a Chillianwallah medal—
threw him down and wrested his musket away. Whiting came up,
furious, but the corporal understood, and grabbed his wrist.

"'E's right, sir! Them swine'll just *sarf karot*† you, like they
done the colonel! We got to git on to the river, like 'e says!
Otherwise, maybe they'll do for everybody—the wimmen an'
kids an' all, sir!"

He was right, of course—I'd been through the same sort of
retreat as this, back in Afghanistan, and you've got to allow for a
few stray slaughters and turn a blind eye, or the next thing you
know you'll have a battle on your hands. Even Whiting realised
it, I think, for he wheeled on the *havildar* and says:

"I must see. Will you come with me?"

The fellow says "*Han*, sahib", and they strode into the trees.
It seemed a sensible time to be getting on down to the river, so I
told the corporal I must inform Wheeler of what was happening,
ordered him to see the store-wagon safely over the bridge, and

* Take care!
† To make clean—i.e., clean you up.

jumped up on to the coping, running past the carts ahead, with their passengers demanding to know what was happening. I hurried on through the trees, and found myself looking down the slope to the Suttee Choura Ghat, and beyond it the broad, placid expanse of the Ganges.

The slope was alive with people. The foremost wagons had reached the landing-stage, and our folk were already getting out and making their way to the water's edge, where a great line of thatched, clumsy-looking barges were anchored in the shallows. The wagons nearer me were splitting away from the convoy to get closer to the water, and everything was in confusion, with some people getting out and others sitting tight. Already the ground was littered with abandoned gear, the stretchers with the wounded were being unloaded just anywhere; groups of women and children were waiting, wondering which way to go, while their menfolk, red in the face and shouting, demanded to know what the orders for embarkation were. Someone was calling, "All ladies with small children are to go in numbers twelve to sixteen!" but no one knew which barges were which, and you couldn't hear yourself think above the elephants squealing and the babble of voices.

On either side of the slope there were groups of pandies with their bayonets fixed, glowering but doing nothing to help, and off to one side I saw a little gaily-dressed group of natives by a temple on a knoll—Azeemoolah was there, talking to Wheeler, who was gesturing towards the barges, so I walked across towards them, through the silent groups of pandy riflemen, and as I came up Azeemoolah was saying:

". . . but I assure you general, the flour is already in the boats —go and see for yourself. Ah, Colonel Flashman, good morning, sir; I trust I see you in good health. Perhaps, general, Colonel Flashman could be asked to examine the boats, and see that all is as I have told you?"

So I was dispatched down to the water, and had to wade out through the shallows to the barges; they were great, musty-smelling craft, but clean enough, with half-naked nigger boatmen in charge, and sure enough there were grain sacks in most of them, as Azeemoolah had said. I reported accordingly, and then we set to with the embarkation, which simply meant telling people off at random to the various barges, carrying the women and children through the water, bearing the stretchers of the wounded head-high, stumbling and swearing in the stinking ooze of the shallows—I went under twice myself, but thank God I didn't swallow any; the Ganges is one river you don't want to take the waters of. It was desperate work, gasping in the steamy heat as the sun came up; the worst of it was getting the women and children and wounded properly stowed inboard—I remember thinking it was ironic that my experience of packing howling niggers into the slave-ship *Balliol College* some years before should come in so handy now. But there you are—any special knowledge comes in useful, sooner or later.

By God, though, the niggers had been easier to handle. I reckon I must have carried twenty females to the barges (and none of 'em worth even a quick fumble, just my luck), plucked one weeping child from the water's edge, where she was crying for her mama, put my fist into the face of a pandy who was pestering Mrs Newnham and trying to snatch her parasol, quieted an old crone who refused to be embarked until she was positive the barge she was going to was Number 12 ("Mr Turner said I *must* go to Number 12; I will go to *no other*"—it might have been the *Great Eastern* for all I knew, or cared), and stood neck deep wrestling to replace a rotted rudder rope. Strange, when you're working all out with things like that, sweating and wrestling to make sense out of chaos, you forget about death and danger and possible treachery—all that matters is getting that piece of hemp knotted through the rudder stem, or finding the carpetbag that Mrs Burtenshaw's maid has left in the cart.

I was about done when I stumbled up through the litter of the bank for the last time, and looked about me. Nearly all the command was loaded, the barges were floating comfortably high on the oily surface, and beyond them the last dawn mists were receding across the broad expanse of the river to the far bank half a mile distant, with the eastern sun turning the water to a great crimson mirror.

There weren't above fifty of our folk, Vibart's rearguard mostly, left on the wreck-strewn, mud-churned slope; Wheeler and Moore and Vibart were all together, and as I came to them I heard Whiting's voice, shaking with anger:

"—and he was shot on his *palki*, I tell you—half a dozen times, at least! Those foresworn swine up yonder—" and he shook his fist towards the temple on the knoll, where Azeemoolah was sitting with Tantia Tope in a little group of the Nana's officers. There was no sign of Nana himself, though.

"There is nothing to be done, Captain Whiting!" Wheeler's voice was hoarse, and his gaunt face was crimson and sweating. He looked on the edge of collapse. "I know, sir, I know—it is the basest treachery, but there is no remedy now! Let us thank God we have come this far—no, no, sir, we are in no case to protest, let alone punish—we must make haste down the river before worse befalls!"

Whiting stamped and cursed, but Vibart eased him away. The pandies who had lined the slope were moving down now, through the abandoned wagons, converging on the landing-place.

"Hollo, Flash," says Moore, wearily. Like me, he was plastered with mud, and the sling was gone from his wounded arm. "They settled Massie, too—did you know? He and Ewart protested when the pandies dragged off four of our loyal sepoys—so they shot 'em all, out o' hand—"

"Like dogs, beside the road!" cries Whiting. "By God, if I'd a gun!" He dashed the sweat from his eyes, glaring at the pandies on the slope. Then he saw me. "Flashman—one of the sepoys was that Pathan orderly of yours—the big chap in the *havildar's* coat —they shot him in the ditch!"

For a moment I didn't comprehend; I just stared at his flushed, raging face. "Like a dog in the ditch!" cries he again, and then it hit me like a blow: he was telling me that Ilderim was dead. I can't describe what I felt—it wasn't grief, or horror, so much as disbelief. Ilderim couldn't die—he was indestructible, always had been, even as the boy I'd first met at Mogala years ago, one of those folk whose life is fairly bursting out of them; I had a vision of that grinning, bearded hawk-face of just a few hours ago—"No pi-dog of a mutineer will take me for anything but what I am!" And he'd been right, and it had been the death of him—but not the kind of death the great brave idiot had always looked for, just a mean, covert murder at the roadside. Oh, you stupid Gilzai bastard, I thought—why didn't you go over the wall when you had the chance . . .

"Come on!" Moore was pushing at my shoulder. "We'll be last aboard. We're in the—hollo, what's that?"

From the trees on the top of the slope a bugle sounded, the notes floating clearly down to us. I looked up the hill, and saw a strange thing happening—I suppose I was still shocked by the news of Ilderim's death, but what I saw seemed odd rather than menacing. The pandies on the slope, and there must have been a couple of hundred of them, were dropping to the kneeling firing position, their muskets were at their shoulders, and they were pointing at us.

"For Christ's—" a voice shouted, and then the hillside seemed to explode in a hail of musketry, the balls were howling past, I heard someone scream beside me, and then Moore's arm flailed me to the ground, and I was plunging through the ooze, into the water. I went under, and struck out for dear life, coming up with a shattering crash of my head against the middle barge. Overhead women were shrieking and muskets were cracking, and then there was the crash of distant cannon, and I saw the narrow strip of water between me and the shore ploughed up as the storm of grape hit it. I reached up, seizing the gunwale, and heaved myself up, and then the whole barge shook as though in a giant hand, and I was hurled back into the water again.

I came up gasping. The pandies were tearing down the slope now, sabres and muskets and bayonets at the ready, charging into the last of our shore-party, who were struggling in the shallows. Up on the slope others were firing at the boats, and in the shade beneath the trees there was the triple flash of cannon, sending grape and round-shot smashing down into the helpless lumbering boats. Men were struggling in the water only a few yards from me—I saw a British soldier sabred down, another floundering back as a sepoy shot him point-blank through the body, and a third, thrust through with a bayonet, sinking down slowly on the muddy shore. Wheeler, white-faced and roaring "Treachery! Shove off—quickly! Treachery!", was stumbling out into the shallows, his sabre drawn; he slashed at a pursuing sepoy, missed

his footing and went under, but a hand reached out from the
gunwale near me and pulled him up, coughing and spewing
water. Moore was in the water close by, and Vibart was trying
to swim towards us with his wounded arm trailing. As Moore
plunged towards him I sank beneath the surface, dived, and struck
out beneath the boat, and as I went I was thinking, clear enough,
well, Flashy my lad, you were wrong again—Nana Sahib wasn't
to be trusted after all.

I came up on the other side, and the first thing I saw was a
body falling from the boat above me. Overhead its thatch was
burning, and as a great chunk of the stuff fell hissing into the
water I shoved away. I trod water, looking about me: in the next
two barges the thatches were alight as well, and people were
screaming and tumbling into the water—I saw one woman jumping with a baby in her arms: I believe it was the one who had
cuffed the little boy for laughing at the elephant's dung. The
shore was hidden from me by the loom of the barge, but the
crash of firing was redoubling, and the chorus of screams and
yells was deafening. People were firing back from the barges, too,
and in the one down-river from me two chaps were beating at
the burning thatch, and another was heaving at its tiller; very
slowly it seemed to be veering from the bank. That's the boy for
me, thinks I, and in the same moment the thatch of the barge
immediately above me collapsed with a roar and a whoosh of
sparks, with shrieks of the damned coming from beneath it.

It was obvious, even in that nightmare few moments, what had
happened. Nana had been meaning to play false all along; he had
just waited until we were in the boats before opening up with
musketry, grape, and every piece of artillery he had. From where
I was I could see one barge already sinking, with people
struggling in the water round it; at least four others were on fire;
two were drifting helplessly into midstream. The pandies were in
the water round the last three boats, where most of the women
and children were, but then a great gust of smoke blotted the
scene from my view, and at the same time I heard the crackle of
firing from the far bank—the treacherous bastards had us trapped
both sides. I put my head down and struck out for the next barge
ahead, which at least had someone steering it, and as I came

under its stern there was Moore in the water alongside, shoving for all he was worth to turn the rudder and help it from the shore. Beyond him I saw Wheeler and Vibart and a couple of others being dragged inboard, while our people blazed back at the pandies on the bank.

Moore shouted something incoherent at me, and as I seized on the rudder with him his face was within a foot of mine—and then it exploded in a shower of blood, and I literally had his brains blown all over me. I let go, shrieking, and when I had dashed the hideous mess from my eyes he was gone, the barge was surging out into the river as our people got the sweeps going, and I was just in time to grasp the gunwale and be dragged along, clinging like grim death, and bawling to be hauled aboard.

We must have gone several hundred yards before I managed to scramble up and on to the deck and get my bearings. The first thing I saw was Wheeler, dead or dying; he had a gaping wound in the neck, and the blood was pumping oozily on to his shirt. All around there were wounded men sprawled on the planks, the smouldering thatch filled the boat with acrid clouds of smoke, and at both gunwales men were firing at the banks. I clung to the gunwale, looking back—we were half a mile below Suttee Ghat by now, where most of the barges were still swinging at their moorings, under a pall of smoke; the river round them was full of people, floundering for the bank. The firing seemed to have slackened, but you could still see the sparkle of the muskets along the slope above the ghat, and the occasional blink of a heavy gun, booming dully across the water. Behind us, two of the barges seemed to have got clear, and were drifting helplessly across the river, but we were the only one under way, with half a dozen chaps each side tugging at the sweeps.

I took stock. We were clear; the shots weren't reaching us. Wheeler was dead, flopped out on the deck, and beyond him Vibart was lying against the gunwale, eyes closed, both arms soaked in blood; someone was babbling in agony, and I saw it was Turner, with one leg doubled at a hideous angle and the other lying in a bloody pool. Whiting was holding on to one of the awning supports, a gory spectre, fumbling one-handed at the lock of a carbine—there hardly seemed to be a sound man in the barge. I saw Delafosse was at one of the sweeps, Thomson at another, and Sergeant Grady, with a bandage round his brow, was in the act of loosing off a shot at the shore. And then, with a little shock of astonishment, I saw that one of the wounded men on the deck was East—and he was finished.

Why, I don't know, but I dropped down beside him and felt his pulse. He opened his eyes at that, and looked up at me, and someone at my elbow—I don't know who—says hoarsely:

"Pandy got him on the bank . . . bayonet in the back, poor devil."

East recognised me, and tried to speak, but couldn't; you could see the life ebbing out of his eyes. His lips quivered, and very faintly I heard him say:

"Flashman . . . tell the doctor . . . I . . ."

That was all, except that he gripped my hand hard, and the man beside me said something about there not being any doctor on board.

"That ain't what he meant," says I. "It's another doctor he means—a schoolmaster, but he's dead."

East gave a little ghost of a smile, and his hand tightened, and then went loose in mine—and I found I was blubbering and gasping, and thinking about Rugby, and hot murphies at Sally's shop, and a small fag limping along pathetically after the players at Big Side—because he couldn't play himself, you see, being lame. I'd hated the little bastard, too, man and boy, for his smug manly piety—but you don't see a child you've known all your life die every day. Maybe that was why I wept, maybe it was the shock and horror of what had been happening. I don't know. Whatever it was, I'm sure I felt it all the more sincerely for knowing that I was still alive myself, and no bones broken so far.[32]

*   *   *

Memory's the queerest thing. When you've been through a hellish experience—and the Cawnpore siege and surrender ranks high in that line, along with Balaclava and Kabul and Greasy Grass and Isandlhwana—the aftermath tends to be vague, until some fresh horror strikes. That barge is mercifully dim in my mind now—I know it was the only one that got away from

Cawnpore, and that of the rest, all were shot to pieces or burned with their passengers, except those which had the women and children aboard. The pandies captured those, and took the women and kids back ashore—all the world knows what happened after that. But only a few things are clear about our trip down-river—Thomson has left a pretty full account of it, if you're interested. I remember Whiting dying—or rather I remember him being dead, looking very pale and small in the bows of the boat. I remember taking a turn at the rudder, and splashing and straining in the water when we grounded on a mudbank in the dark. I remember hearing drums beating on the bank, and Vibart biting on a leather strap as they set his broken arm, and the dull splashes as we put dead bodies over the side, and the musty taste of dry mealies which was all we had to eat—but the first time that memory becomes consecutive and coherent after East died was when a fire-arrow came winging out of the dark and thudded into the deck, and we were shooting away at dim figures on the nearest bank, and fire-arrows came down in a blazing rain as we hauled on the sweeps and forced the barge back into mid-stream out of range. We rowed like fury until the fiery pinpoints of light on the bank were far behind us, and the yelling and drumming of the niggers had died away, and then we flopped down exhausted and the current carried us and landed us high and dry on another mudbank just before dawn.

This time there was no shoving off; we were wedged tight in the mud, along a deserted jungly shore, with nothing to be heard but monkeys chattering and birds screeching in the dense undergrowth. The far bank was the same, a thick mass of green, with the brown oily river sliding slowly past. At least it looked peaceful, which was a pleasant change.

Vibart reckoned we must still be a hundred miles from Allahabad, and if the behaviour of the niggers who'd showered us with fire-arrows was anything to go by, we could count on hostile country most of the way. There were two dozen of us in the boat, perhaps half of whom were fit to stand; we were low on powder and ball, and desperately short of mealies, there were no medical supplies, and it was odds half the wounded would contract gangrene unless we reached safety quickly. Not a pleasant prospect, thinks I, as I looked round the squalid barge, with its dozen wounded groaning or listless on the planks, the stench of blood and death everywhere, and even the whole men looking emaciated and fit to croak. I was in better case than most—I hadn't been through the whole siege—and it was crossing my mind that I might do worse than slip away on my own and trust to luck and judgement to get to Allahabad on foot; after all, I could always turn into a native again.

So when we held our little council, I prepared the way for decamping, in my own subtle style. The others, naturally, were all debating how we might get refloated again and press on to Allahabad; I shook them up by suddenly growling that I was in no hurry to get there.

"I agree we must get the barge refloated to take the wounded on," says I. "For the rest of us—well, for me, leastways, I'd sooner head back for Cawnpore."

They gaped at me in disbelief. "You're mad!" cries Delafosse.

"So I've been told," says I. "See here—while we had the women and children to think of, they were our first concern. That's the only reason we surrendered, isn't it? Well, now they're . . . either gone, or captives of those fiends—I don't much fancy running any longer." I looked as belligerent as I knew how. "There hasn't been much time to think things out these past hours—but now, well, I reckon I've a score to settle—and the only place I want to settle it is Cawnpore."

"But . . . but . . ." says Thomson, "we can't go back, man! It's certain death!"

"Maybe," says I, very business-like. "But I've seen my country's flag hauled down once—something I never thought to see—I've seen us betrayed, our . . . our loved ones ravished from us . . ." I managed a manly glisten about the eye. "I don't like it above half! So—I'm going back, and I'm going to get a bullet into that black bastard's heart—I don't care how! And—that's that."

"By God!" says Delafosse, taking fire, "by God—I've half a mind to come with you!"

"You'll do no such thing!" This was Vibart; he was deathly pale, with both arms useless, but he was still in command. "Our duty is to reach Allahabad—Colonel Flashman, I forbid you! I will not have your life flung away in . . . in this rash folly! You will carry out General Wheeler's orders—"

"Look, old fellow," says I. "I was never one of General Wheeler's command, you recollect? I don't ask anyone to come with me—but I left a friend dead back there—a comrade from the old Afghan days—a salt man from the hills. Well, maybe I'm more of a salt man than a parade soldier myself—anyway, I know what I must do." I gave him a quizzical little grin, and patted his foot. "Anyway, Vibart, I'm senior to you, remember?"

At this they cried out together, telling me not to be a fool, and Vibart said I couldn't desert our wounded. He wanted to send a shore-party, to try to find friendly villagers who would tow us off; I was best fitted to lead it, he said, and my first duty was to carry out Wheeler's dying wishes, and get down-river. I seemed to hesitate, and finally said I would lead the shore-party—"but you'll be going to Allahabad without me in the end," says I. "All I'll need is a rifle and a knife—and a handshake from each one of you."

So we set off, a dozen of us, to try to find a friendly village. If we found one, and the prospects of getting off for Allahabad seemed good, I'd allow myself to be persuaded, and go along with them. If we didn't—I'd slip away, and they could imagine I'd gone back to Cawnpore on my mission of vengeance. (That's one thing about having a reckless reputation: they'll believe anything of you, and shake their heads in admiration over your dare-devilry.)

We hadn't gone five minutes into the jungle before I was wishing to God I'd been able to stay in the boat. It wasn't very thick stuff, once we got away from the river, but eery and curiously quiet, with huge tall trees shadowing a forest-floor of creeper and swampy plants, like a great cathedral, and only the occasional tree-creature chirruping in the silence. We struck a little path, and followed it, and presently came on a tiny temple in a clearing, a lath-and-plaster thing that looked as though it hadn't been visited in years. Delafosse and Sergeant Grady scouted it, and reported it empty, and I was just ordering up the others when we heard it—very low and far-off in the forest: the slow boom-boom of drums.

I don't know any sound like it for shivering the soul. I've heard it in Dahomey, when the Amazons were after us, and in South American backwaters, and on a night on the Papar River in Borneo when the Iban head-hunters took the warpath—the muted rumble of doom that conjures up spectres with painted faces creeping towards you through the dark. They're usually damned real spectres, too—as they were here, for I'd barely given my order when there was a whistle and a thud, and Grady, on the edge of the clearing, was staggering with an arrow in his brow, and with a chorus of blood-chilling screams they were on us—black, half-naked figures swarming out of the trees, yelling bloody murder. I snapped off one shot—God knows where it went—and then I was haring for the temple. I made it a split second ahead of two arrows which quivered in the doorpost, and then we were tumbling inside, with Delafosse and Thomson crouched in the doorway, blazing away as hard as they could.

They came storming up to the doorway in a great rabble, and for the next five minutes it was as bloody and desperate a mêlée as ever I've been in. We were so packed in the tiny space inside the building—it wasn't more than eight feet square, and about that number of us had got inside—that only two of us could fire through the door at once. Whoever the attackers were—half-human jungle people, apparently, infected by the general Mutiny madness—they didn't appear to have fire-arms, and the foremost of them were shot down before they could get close enough to use their spears and long swords. But their arrows buzzed in like hornets, and two of our fellows went down before the attack slackened off. We were just getting our breath back, and I was helping Thomson push an arrow through and out of the fleshy part of Private Murphy's arm—and all the time we could hear our besiegers grunting and fumbling stealthily close under the temple wall—when Delafosse suddenly whoops out "Fire, fire! They've set the place alight!"

Sure enough, a gust of smoke came billowing in the doorway, setting us coughing and stumbling; a fire-arrow came zipping in to bury itself in Private Ryan's side, and the yells of the niggers redoubled triumphantly. I staggered through the reek, and Thomson was clutching my arm, shouting:

"Must break out . . . two volleys straight in front . . . run for it . . ."

It was an affair of split seconds; there wasn't time to think or argue. He and Delafosse and two of the privates stumbled to the door, Thomson yells "Fire!", they all let blast together, and then we put our heads down and went charging out of the temple, with the flames licking up behind us, and drove in a body across the clearing for the shelter of the jungle. The niggers shrieked at the sight of us, I saw the man before me tumble down with a spear in his back, I cannoned into a black figure and he fell away, and then we were haring through the trees, my musket was gone, and no thought but flight. Delafosse was in front of me; I followed him as he swerved on to the path, with the arrows whipping past us; booted feet were thumping behind me, and Thomson was shouting, "On, on—we can distance 'em!—come on, Murphy, Sullivan—to the boat!"

How we broke clear, God knows—the very suddenness with which we'd rushed from the temple must have surprised them— but we could hear their yells in the jungle behind, and they weren't giving up the hunt, either. My lungs were bursting as we ploughed through the thicker jungle near the river, tripping on snags, tearing ourselves, sobbing with exhaustion—and then we were on the bank, and Delafosse was sliding to a halt in the mud and yelling:

"It's gone! Vibart! My God, the boat's gone!"

The mudbank was empty—there was the great groove where the barge had been, but the brown stretch of water was unbroken to the wall of green on its far side; of the barge there wasn't a sign.

"It must have slid off—" Delafosse was crying, and I thought, good for you, my boy, let's stop to consider how it happened, eh, and the niggers can come up and join in. I didn't even check stride; I went into the water in the mightiest racing dive I ever performed, and I heard the cries and splashes as the others took to the river behind me. I was striking out blindly, feeling the current tugging me downstream—I didn't mind; anywhere would do so long as it was away from those black devils screeching in the forest behind. The far bank was too distant to reach, but

downstream where the river curved there were islands and sand-
banks, and we were being carried towards them far faster than
our pursuers could hope to run. I swam hard with the current,
until the yelping of the niggers had faded into the distance, and
then glanced round to see how the others were getting along.
There were four heads bobbing in the water—Delafosse, Thomson,
Murphy, and Sullivan, all swimming in my wake, and I was just
debating whether to make for the nearest sandbank or allow
myself to be carried past, when Delafosse reared up in the water,
yelling and gesturing ahead of me. I couldn't make him out, and
then the single shrieked word "Muggers!" reached me, and as I
looked where he was pointing the steamy waters of the Ganges
seemed to turn to ice.

On a mudbank a hundred yards ahead and to my right, shapes
were moving—long, brown, hideously scaly dragons waddling
down to the water at frightening speed, plashing into the shallows and then gliding out inexorably to head us off, their half-
submerged snouts rippling the surface. For an instant I was
paralysed—then I was thrashing at the water in a frenzy of
terror, trying to get out into midstream, fighting the sluggish
current. I knew it was hopeless; they must intercept us long
before we could reach the islands, but I lashed out blindly,
ploughing through the water, too terrified to look and expecting
every moment to feel the agonising stab of crocodile teeth in my
legs. I was almost done, with exhaustion and panic, and then
Sullivan was alongside, tugging at me, pointing ahead—and I saw
that the placid surface was breaking up into a long, swirling race
where the water ran down between two little scrubby mudbanks.
There was just a chance, if we could get into that broken water,
that the faster current might carry us away—muggers hate rough
water, anyway—and I went for it with the energy of despair.

One glance I spared to my right—my God, there was one of
the brutes within ten yards, swirling towards me. I had a nightmare glimpse of that hideous snout breaking surface, of the great
tapering jaws suddenly yawning in a cavern of teeth—and I regret
to say I did not notice whether the fourth tooth of the lower jaw
was overlapping or not. A naturalist chap, to whom I described
my experience a few years ago, tells me that if I'd taken note of

this, I'd have known whether I was being attacked by a true crocodile or gavial, or by some other species, which would have added immense interest to the occasion.[33] As it was, I can only say that the bloody thing looked like an Iron Maiden rushing at me through the water, and I was just letting out a last wail of despair when Sullivan seized me by the hair, the current tore at our legs, and we were swept away into the rough water between the islands, striking out any old way, going under into the choking brown, coming up again and struggling to stay afloat—and then the water had changed to clinging black ooze, and Sullivan was crying:

"Up, up, sir, for Christ's sake!" and he was half-dragging me through the slime towards the safety of a tangled mass of creeper on top of a mudbank. Delafosse was staggering out beside us, Thomson was knee-deep in the water smashing with a piece of root at the head of a mugger which lunged and snapped before swirling away with a flourish of its enormous tail: Murphy, his arm trickling blood, was already up on the top of the bank, reaching down to help us. I heaved up beside him, shuddering, and I remember thinking: that must be the end, nothing more can happen now, and if it does, I don't care, I'll just have to die, because there's nothing I can do. Sullivan was kneeling over me, and I remember I said:

"God bless you, Sullivan. You are the noblest man alive", or something equally brilliant—although I meant it, by God—and he replied: "I daresay you're right, sir; you'll have to tell my missus, for damn me if she thinks so." And then I must have swooned away, for all I can remember is Delafosse saying: "I believe they are friends—see, Thomson, they are waving to us— they mean us no harm", and myself thinking, if it's the muggers waving, don't you trust the bastards an inch, they're only pretending to be friendly . . .[34]

Luck, as I've often observed, is an agile sprite who jumps both ways in double quick time. You could say it had been evil chance that took me to Meerut and the birth of the Mutiny—but I'd escaped, only to land in the hell of Cawnpore, from which I was one of only five to get clear away after the ghat massacre. It had been the foulest luck to run into those wild men in the jungle, and the infernal muggers—but if they hadn't chased us, we mightn't have fetched up on a mudbank under the walls of one of those petty Indian rulers who stayed loyal to the Sirkar. For that was what had happened—the new niggers whom Delafosse saw waving and hallooing from the shore turned out to be the followers of one Diribijah Singh, a tough old maharaj who ruled from a fort in the jungle, and was a steadfast friend of the British. So you see, all that matters about luck is that it should run good on the last throw.

Not that the game was over, you understand; when I think back on the Mutiny, even on Cawnpore, I can say that the worst was still to come. And yet, I feel that the tide turned on that mudbank; at least, after a long nightmare, I can say that there followed a period of comparative calm, for me, in which I was able to recruit my tattered nerves, and take stock, and start planning how to get the devil out of this Indian pickle and back to England and safety.

For the moment, there was nothing to do but thank God and the loyal savages who picked us up from that shoal, with the muggers snuffling discontentedly in the wings. The natives took us ashore, to the maharaj's castle, and he was a brick—a fine old sport with white whiskers and a belly like a barrel, who swore damnation to all mutineers and promised to return us to our own folk as soon as we had recovered and it seemed safe to pass through the country round. But that wasn't for several weeks, and in the meantime the five of us could only lie and recuperate

and contain our impatience as best we might—Delafosse and
Thomson were itching to get back into the thick of things; Murphy
and Sullivan, the two privates, kept their counsel and ate like
horses; while I, making an even greater show of impatience than
my brother-officers, was secretly well content to rest at ease,
blinking in the sun and eating mangoes, to which I'm partial.

In the meantime, we later discovered, great things were
happening in the world beyond. When news of Cawnpore's fall
got out, it gave the Mutiny a tremendous fillip; revolt spread all
along the Ganges valley and in Central India, the garrisons at
Mhow and Agra and a dozen other places rebelled, and most
notable of all, Henry Lawrence got beat fighting a dam' silly battle
at Chinhat, and had to hole up in Lucknow, which went under
siege. On the credit side, my old friend the First Gravedigger
(General Havelock to you) finally got up off his Puritan rump
and struck through Allahabad at Cawnpore; he fought his way
in after a nine-day march, and recaptured the place a bare three
weeks after we'd been driven out—and I suppose all the world
knows what he found when he got there.

You remember that when we escaped the massacre at the
Suttee Ghat, the barges with the women and children were
caught by the pandies. Well, Nana took them ashore, all 200 of
them, and locked them up in a place called the Bibigarh, in such
filth and heat that thirty of them died within a week. He made
our women grind corn; then, when word came that Havelock
was fighting his way in, and slaughtering all opposition, Nana
had all the women and children butchered. They say even the
pandies wouldn't do it, so he sent in hooligans with cleavers from
the Cawnpore bazaar; they chopped them all up, even the babies,
and threw them, dead and still living, down a well. Havelock's
people found the Bibigarh ankle-deep in blood, with children's
toys and hats and bits of hair still floating in it; they had got
there two days too late.

I don't suppose any event in my lifetime—not Balaclava nor
Shiloh nor Rorke's Drift nor anywhere else I can think of—has
had such a stunning effect on people's minds as that Cawnpore
massacre of the innocents. I didn't see the full horror of it, of
course, as Havelock's folk did, but I was there a few weeks after,

and walked in the Bibigarh, and saw the bloody floor and walls, and near the well I found the skeleton bones of a baby's hand, like a little white crab in the dust. I'm a pretty cool hand, as you know, but it made me gag, and if you ask me what I think of the vengeance that old General Neill wreaked, making captured mutineers clean up the Bibigarh, flogging 'em and forcing 'em to lick up the blood with their tongues before they were hanged—well, I was all for it then, and I still am. Perhaps it's because I *knew* the corpses that went into that well—I'd seen them playing on the Cawnpore rampart, and being heard their lessons in that awful barrack, and laughing at the elephant dunging. Perhaps that baby hand I found belonged to the infant I'd seen in the arms of the woman in the torn gown. Anyway, I'd have snuffed out every life in India, and thought naught of it, in that moment when I looked at Bibigarh—and if you think that shocking, well, maybe I'm just more like Nana Sahib than you are.

Anyway, what I think don't signify. What mattered was the effect that Cawnpore had on our people. I know it turned our army crazy; they were ready to slaughter anything that even sniffed of mutiny, from that moment on. Not that they'd been dealing exactly kindly before; Havelock and Neill had been hanging right, left and centre from Allahabad north, and I daresay had disposed of quite a number of innocents—just as the pandies at Meerut and Delhi had done.[35]

What beats me is the way people take it to heart—what do they expect in war? It ain't conducted by missionaries, or chaps in Liberal clubs, snug and secure. But what amuses me most is the way fashionable views change—why, for years after Cawnpore, any vengeance wreaked on an Indian, mutineer or not, was regarded as just vengeance; nothing was too bad for 'em. Now it's t'other way round, with eminent writers crying shame, and saying nothing justified such terrible retribution as Neill took, and we were far guiltier than the niggers had been. Why? Because we were Christians, and supposed to know better?—and because England contains this great crowd of noisy know-alls that are forever defending our enemies' behaviour and crying out in pious horror against our own. Why our sins are always so much blacker, I can't fathom—as to Cawnpore, it don't seem to

me one whit worse to slay in revenge, like Neill, than out of sheer
spite and cruelty, like Nana; at least it's more understandable.

The truth is, of course, that both sides were afraid—the pandy
who'd mutinied, and feared punishment, decided he might as well
be hanged for a sheep, and let his natural bloodlust go—they're
cruel bastards at bottom. And our folk—they'd had an almighty
scare, and Cawnpore brought *their* natural bloodlust to the top in
turn; just give 'em a few well-chosen texts about vengeance and
wrath of God and they could fall to with a will—as I've already
observed about Rowbotham's Mosstroopers, there's nothing
crueller than a justified Christian. Except maybe a nigger running
loose.

So you can see it was a jolly summer in the Ganges valley, all
right, as I and my four companions discovered, when Diribijah
Singh finally convoyed us out from his fort and back to Cawnpore
after Havelock had retaken it. I hadn't seen old Blood-and-Bones
since he'd stood grumping beside my bed at Jallalabad fifteen
years before, and time hadn't improved him; he still looked like
Abe Lincoln dying of diarrhoea, with his mournful whiskers and
bloodhound eyes. When I told him my recent history he just
listened in silence, and then grabbed me by the wrist with his
great bony hand, dragged me down on to my knees beside him,
and began congratulating God on lugging Flashy out of the stew
again, through His infinite mercy.

"The shield of His truth has been before thee, Flashman," cries
he. "Has not the Hand which plucked thee from the paw of the
bear at Kabul, and the jaws of the lion at Balaclava, delivered
thee also from the Philistine at Cawnpore?"

"Absolutely, amen," says I, but when I took him into my
confidence—about Palmerston, and why I came to India in the
first place, and suggested there was no good reason why I
shouldn't head for home at once—he shook his great coffin head.

"It cannot be," says he. "That mission is over, and we need
every hand at the plough. The fate of this country is in the
balance, and I can ill spare such a seasoned soldier as yourself.
There is a work of cleansing and purging before us," he went on,
and you could see by the holy fire in his eyes that he was just
sweating to get to grips with it. "I shall take you on to my staff,

Flashman—nay, sir, never thank me; it is I shall be the gainer, rather than you."

I was ready to agree with him there, but I knew there was no point in arguing with the likes of Havelock—anyway, before I could think of anything to say he was scribbling orders for hanging a few more pandies, and dictating a crusty note to Neill, and roaring for his adjutant; he was a busy old Baptist in those days, right enough.

So there I was, and it might have been worse. I'd had no real hope of being sent home—no high command in their right mind would have dispensed with the famous Flash when there was a campaign on hand, and since I had to be here I'd rather be under Havelock's wing than anyone's. He was a good soldier, you see, and as canny as Campbell in his own way; there'd be no massacres or Last Stands round the Union Jack with the Grave-digger in charge.

So I settled in as Havelock's intelligence aide—a nice safe billet in the circumstances, but if you would learn the details of how I fared with him you must consult my official history, *Dawns and Departures of a Soldier's Life* (in three handsomely-bound morocco volumes, price two gns. each or five gns. the set, though you may have difficulty laying hands on Volume III, since it had to be called in and burned by the bailiffs after that odious little Whitechapel sharper D'Israeli egged on one of his toadies to sue me for criminal information. Suez Canal shares, eh? I'll blacken the bastard's memory yet, though, just see if I don't. Truth will out).

However, the point is that my present tale isn't truly concerned with the main course of the Mutiny henceforth—although I bore my full reluctant part in that—but still with that mad mission on which Pam had sent me out in the first place, to Jhansi and the bewitching Lakshmibai. For I wasn't done with her, whatever Havelock might think, and however little I guessed it myself; the rest of the Mutiny was just the road that led me back to her, and to that final terrible adventure of the Jhansi flight and the guns of Gwalior when—but I'll come to that presently.

In the meantime I'll tell you as briskly as I can what happened in the few months after I joined Havelock at Cawnpore. At first it was damned bad news all round: the Mutiny kept spreading, Nana had sheered off after losing Cawnpore and was raising cain farther up-country, Delhi was still held by the pandies with our people banging away at it, and Havelock at Cawnpore didn't have the men or means to relieve Lucknow, only forty miles away, where Lawrence's garrison was hemmed in. He tried hard enough, but found that the pandy forces, while they didn't make best use of their overwhelming numbers, fought better defensive actions than anyone had expected, and Havelock got a couple of black eyes before he'd gone ten miles, and had to fall back. To make matters worse, Lloyd's advance guard got cut up at Arah, and no one down in Calcutta seemed to have any notion of over-all strategy—that clown Canning was sitting like a fart in a trance, they tell me, and no proper order was taken.

I wasn't too upset, though. For one thing I was snug at the Cawnpore headquarters, making a great *bandobast** over collect-ing information from our spies and passing the gist on to Havelock (intelligence work is nuts to me, so long as I can stay close to bed, bottle and breakfast and don't have to venture out). And for another, I could sense that things were turning our way; once the first flood of pandy successes had spent itself, there could only be one end, and old Campbell, who was the best general in the business, was coming out to take command-in-chief.

In September we moved on Lucknow in style, with fresh troops under Outram, a dirty-looking little chap on a waler horse, more like a Sheeny tailor than a general. They tell me it was a hell of a march; certainly it rained buckets all the way, and there was some stern fighting at Mangalwarh and at the Alum Bagh near Lucknow town—I know, because I got reports of it in my intelli-gence *ghari* at the rear of the column, where I was properly ensconced writing reports, examining prisoners, and getting news from friendly natives—at least, they were friendly by the time my Rajput orderlies had basted 'em a bit. From time to time I poked my head out into the rain, and called cheery encouragement to the reinforcements, or sent messages to Havelock—I remember one of them was that Delhi had fallen at last, and that old

* Organisation, administration.

Johnny Nicholson had bought a bullet, poor devil. I drank a quiet brandy to him, listening to the downpour and the guns booming, and thought God help poor soldiers on a night like this.

However, having got Lucknow, Havelock and Outram didn't know what the devil to do with it, for the pandies were still thick around as fleas, and it soon became evident that far from raising the siege, our forces were nothing but a reinforcement to the garrison. So we were *all* besieged, for another seven weeks, and the deuce of a business it must have been, with bad rations and the pandies forever trying to tunnel in under our defences, and our chaps fighting 'em in the mines which were like a warren underground. I say "must have been", for I knew nothing about it; the night we entered Lucknow my bowels began to explode in all directions, and before morning I was flat on my back with cholera, for the second time in my life.

For once, it was a blessing, for it meant I was spared knowledge of a siege that was Cawnpore all over again, if not quite as bad. I gather I raved a good deal of the time, and I know I spent weeks lying on a cot in a beastly little cellar, as weak as a rat and not quite in my right mind. It was only in the last fortnight of the siege that I began to get about again, and by that time the garrison was cheery with the news that Campbell was on his way. I limped about gamely at first, looking gaunt and noble, and asking "Is the flag flying still?" and "Is there anything I can do, sir?— I'm much better than I look, I assure you." I was, too, but I took care to lean on my stick a good deal, and sit down, breathing hard. In fact, there wasn't much to do, except wait, and listen to the pandies sniping away—they didn't hit much.

In the last week, when we knew for certain that Campbell was only a few days away, with his Highlanders and naval guns and all, I was careless enough to look like a whole man again—it seemed safe enough now, for you must know that at Lucknow, unlike Cawnpore, we were defending a large area, and if one kept away from the outer works, which unemployed convalescents like me were entitled to do, one could promenade about the Residency gardens without peril. There were any number of large houses, half-ruined now, but still habitable, and we occupied them or camped out in the grounds—when I came out of my cellar I was sent to the bungalow, where Havelock was quartered with his staff people, but he packed me off to Outram's headquarters, in case I should be of some use there. Havelock himself was pretty done by this time, and not taking much part in the command; he spent most of his time in Gubbins's garden, reading some bilge by Macaulay—and was greatly intrigued to know that I'd met Lord Know-all and discussed his "Lays" with the Queen; I had to tell Havelock all about that.

For the rest, I yarned a good deal with Vincent Eyre, who'd been in the Kabul retreat with me, and was now one of the many wounded in the garrison, or chaffed with the ladies in the old Residency garden, twitting them about their fashions—for after a six-month siege everyone was dressed any old how, with scraps and curtains and even towels run up into clothes. I was hailed everywhere, of course—jovial Flash, the hero on the mend—and quizzed about my adventures from Meerut to Cawnpore. I never mind telling a modest tale, if the audience is pretty enough, so I did, and entertained them by imitating Makarram Khan, too, which attracted much notice and laughter. It was an idiot thing to do, as you'll see—it earned another man the V.C., and nearly won me a cut throat.

What happened was this. One morning, it must have been about November 9th or 10th, there was a tremendous commotion over on the southern perimeter, where someone in Anderson's Post claimed he had heard Campbell's pipers in the distance; there was huge excitement, with fellows and ladies and niggers and even children hastening through the ruined buildings, laughing and cheering—and then everything went deadly still as we stood to listen, and sure enough, above the occasional crack of firing, far, far away there was the faintest whisper on the breeze of a pig in torment, and someone sings out, "The Campbells are coming, hurrah, hurrah!" and people were embracing and shaking hands and leaping in the air, laughing and crying all together, and a few dropping to their knees to pray, for now the siege was as good as over. So there was continued jubilation throughout the garrison, and Outram sniffed and grunted and chewed his cheroot and called a staff conference.

He had been smuggling out messages by native spies all

through the siege, and now that the relief force was so close he wanted to send explicit directions to Campbell on the best route to take in fighting his way through the streets and gardens of Lucknow to the Residency. It was a great maze of a place, and our folk had had the deuce of a struggle getting in two months earlier, being cut up badly in the alleys. Outram wanted to be sure Campbell didn't have the same trouble, for he had a bare 5,000 men against 60,000 pandies, and if they strayed or were ambushed it might be the end of them—and consequently of us.

I didn't have much part in their deliberations, beyond helping Outram draft his message in the secret Greek code he employed, and making a desperate hash of it. One of the Sappers had the best route all plotted out, and while they talked about that I went into the big verandah room adjoining to rest from the noon heat, convalescent-like. I sprawled on the cot, with my boots off, and must have dozed off, for when I came to it was late afternoon, the murmur of many voices from beyond the chick screen had gone, and there were only two people talking. Outram was saying:

". . . it is a hare-brained risk, surely—a white man proposing to make his way disguised as a native through a city packed with hostiles! And if he's caught—and the message falls into their hands? What then, Napier?"

"True enough," says Napier, "but to get a guide out to Campbell—a guide who can point his way for him—is better than a thousand messages of direction. And Kavanaugh knows the streets like a *bazaar-wallah*."

"No doubt he does," mutters Outram, "but he'll no more pass for a native than my aunt's parrot. What—he's more than six feet tall, flaming red hair, blue eyes, and talks poor Hindi with a Donegal accent! Kananji may not be able to *guide* Campbell, but at least we can be sure he'll get a message to him."

"Kananji swears he won't go if Kavanaugh does. He's ready to go alone, but he says Kavanaugh's bound to be spotted."

"There you are, then!" I could hear Outram muttering and puffing on a fresh cheroot. "Confound it, Napier—he's a brave man . . . and I'll own that *if* he could reach Campbell his knowledge of the byways of Lucknow would be beyond price—but he's harder to disguise than ... damme, than any man in this garrison."

I listened with some interest to this. I knew Kavanaugh, a great freckled Irish bumpkin of a civilian who'd spent the siege playing tig with pandy besiegers in the tunnels beneath our defences—mad as a hatter. And now madder still, by the sound of it, if he proposed to try to get through the enemy lines to Campbell. I saw Outram's problem—Kavanaugh was the one man who'd be a reliable guide to Campbell, if only he could get to him. But it was Tattersall's to a tin can that the pandies would spot him, torture his message out of him, and be ready and waiting for Campbell when he advanced. Well, thank God I wasn't called on to decide ...

". . . if he can disguise himself well enough to pass muster with me, he can go," says Outram at last. "But I wish to heaven Kananji would accompany him—I don't blame him for refusing, mind . . . but if only there were someone else who could go along —some cool hand who can pass as a native without question, to do the talking if they're challenged by the pandies—for if they are, and if Kavanaugh has to open that great Paddy mouth of his . . . stop, though! Of course, Napier—the very man! Why didn't it occur ..."

I was off the cot and moving before Outram was half-way through his speech; I knew before he did himself whose name was going to pop into his mind as the ideal candidate for this latest lunacy. I paused only to scoop up my boots and was tip-toeing at speed for the verandah rail; a quick vault into the garden, and then let them try to find me before sunset if they could ... but blast it, I hadn't gone five steps when the door was flung open, and there was Outram, pointing his cheroot, looking like Sam Grant after the first couple of drinks, crying:

"Flashman! That's our man, Napier! Can you think of a better?"

Of course, Napier couldn't—who could, with the famous Flashy on hand, ripe to be plucked and hurled into the bloody soup? It's damnable, the way they pick on a fellow—and all because of my swollen reputation for derring-do and breakneck gallantry. As usual, there was nothing I could do, except stand blinking innocently in my stocking-soles while Outram repeated all that I'd

heard already, and pointed out that I was the very man to go
along on this hideous escapade to hold the great Fenian idiot's
hand for him. I heard him in mounting terror, concealed behind
a stern and thoughtful aspect, and replied that, of course, I was
at his disposal, but really, gentlemen, was it wise? Not that I
cared about the risk (Jesus, the things I've had to say), but I
earnestly doubted whether Kavanaugh could pass . . . my
convalescent condition, of course, was a trifling matter . . . even
so, one wouldn't want to fail through lack of strength . . . not
when a native could be certain of getting through . . .

"There isn't a loyal sepoy in this garrison who can come near
you for skill and shrewdness," says Outram briskly, "or who'd
stand half the chance of seeing Kavanaugh safe. Weren't you
playing your old Pathan role the other day for the ladies? As to
the toll of your illness—I've a notion your strength will always
match your spirit, whatever happens. This thing's your meat and
drink, Flashman, and you know it—and you've been fairly itching
to get into harness again. Eh?"

"I'll hazard a guess," says Napier, smiling, "that he's more
concerned for Kavanaugh than for himself—isn't that so, Flashman?"

"Well, sir, since you've said it—"

"I know," says Outram, frowning at his damned cheroot.
"Kavanaugh has a wife and family—but he has volunteered, you
see, and he's the man for Campbell, not a doubt of it. It only
remains to get him there." And the brute simply gave me a
sturdy look and shook my hand as though that were the thing
settled.

Which of course it was. What could I do, without ruining my
reputation?—although such was my fame by this time that if I'd
thrown myself on the floor weeping with fright, they'd probably
not have taken me seriously, but thought it was just one of my
jokes in doubtful taste. Give a dog a bad name—by God, it doesn't
stick half as hard as a good one.

So I spent the evening dyeing myself with soot and *ghee*,
shuddering with apprehension and cursing my folly and ill luck.
This, at the eleventh hour! I thought of having another shot at
Napier, pleading my illness, but I didn't dare; he had a hard eye,

and Outram's would be even worse if they suspected I was shirking. I near as a toucher cried off, though, when I saw Kavanaugh;
he was got up like Sinbad the Sailor, with nigger minstrel eyes,
hareem slippers, and a great sword and shield. I stopped dead in
the doorway, whispering to Napier:

"My God, man, he won't fool a child! We'll have the bloody
pandies running after us shouting, 'Penny for Guy Fawkes!'"

But he said reassuringly that it would be pretty dark, and
Outram and the other officers agreed that Kavanaugh might just
do. They were full of admiration for my get-up—which was my
usual one of bazaar-ruffler—and Kavanaugh came up to me with
absolute tears in his eyes and said I was the stoutest chap alive to
stand by him in this. I nearly spat in his eye. The others were full
of sallies about our appearance, and then Outram handed
Kavanaugh the message for Campbell, biting on his cheroot and
looking hard at us.

"I need not tell you," says he, "that it must never fall into
enemy hands. That would be disaster for us all."

Just to rub the point in, he asked if we were fully armed (so
that we could blow our brains out if necessary), and then gave us
our directions. We were to swim the river beyond the northern
rampart, recross it by the bridge west of the Residency, and cut
straight south through Lucknow city and hope to run into
Campbell's advance picquets on the other side. Kavanaugh, who
knew the streets, would choose our path, but I would lead and do
the talking.

Then Outram looked us both in the eye, and blessed us, and
everyone shook hands, looking noble, while I wondered if I'd
time to go to the privy. Kavanaugh, shaking with excitement,
cleared his throat and says:

"We know what is to be done, sorr—an' we'll give our lives
gladly in the attempt. We know the risks, ould fellow, do we
not?" he added, turning to me.

"Oh, aye," says I, "that bazaar'll be full of fleas—we'll be
lousy for weeks." Since there was no escape, I might as well give
'em another Flashy *bon mot* to remember.

It moved them, as only jocular heroism can; Outram's aide,
Hardinge, was absolutely piping his eye, and said England would

never forget us, everyone patted us on the back with restrained
emotion, and shoved us off in the direction of the rampart. I could
hear Kavanaugh breathing heavily—the brute positively panted in
Irish—and whispered to him again to remember to leave any
talking to me. "Oi will, Flashy, Oi will," says he, lumbering along
and stumbling over his ridiculous sword.

The thing was a farce from the start. By the time we had
slipped over the rampart and made our way through the pitch
dark down to the bank of the Goomtee, I had realised that I was
in company with an irresponsible lunatic, who had no real notion
of what he was doing. Even while we were stripping for our swim,
he suddenly jerked his head up, at the sound of a faint plop out
on the water.

"That's trout afther minnow," says he, and then there was
another louder plop. "An' that's otter afther trout," says he, with
satisfaction. "Are ye a fisherman, are ye?" Before I could hush
his babbling, he had suddenly seized my hand—and him standing
there bollock-naked with his togs piled on his head—and said
fervently:

"D'ye know what—we're goin' to do wan o' the deeds that
saved the Impoire, so we are! An' Oi don't moind tellin' ye somethin' else—for the first toime in me loife, Oi'm scared!"

"The first time!" squeaks I, but already he was plunging in
with a splash like the launching of the *Great Eastern*, puffing and
striking out in the dark, leaving me with the appalling realisation
that for once I was in the company of someone as terrified as
myself. It was desperate—I mean, on previous enterprises of this
kind I'd been used to relying on some gallant idiot who could
keep his head, but here I was with this buffoon who was not only
mad Irish, but was plainly drunk with the idea of playing Dick
Champion, the Saviour of the Side, and was trembling in his
boots at the same time. Furthermore, he was given to daydreaming
about trouts and otters at inappropriate moments, and had no
more idea of moving silently than a bear with a ball and chain.
But there was nothing for it now; I slid into the freezing water
and swam the half-furlong to the far bank, where he was standing
on one leg in the mud, hauling his clothes on, and making the
deuce of a row about it.

"Are ye there, Flash?" says he, in a hoarse whisper you could have heard in Delhi. "We'll have to be hellish quiet, ye know. Oi think there's pandies up the bank!"

Since we could see their picquets round the camp-fires not fifty yards away, it was a reasonable conclusion, and we hadn't stolen twenty yards along the riverside when someone hailed us. I shouted back, and our challenger remarked that it was cold, at which the oaf Kavanaugh petrified me by suddenly bawling out: "*Han, bhai, bahut tunder!*"* like some greenhorn reciting from a Hindi primer. I hustled him quickly away, took him by the neck, and hissed:

"Will you keep your damned gob shut, you great murphy?"

He apologised in a nervous whisper, and muttered something about Queen and Country; his eye was glittering feverishly. "Oi'll be more discreet, Flash," says he, and so we went on, with me answering another couple of challenges before we reached the bridge, and crossed safely over into Lucknow town.

This was the testing part, for here there was lighting in the streets, and passers-by, and Kavanaugh might easily be recognised as counterfeit. The swim hadn't done his dyed skin any good, and apart from that his outlandish rig, the European walk, the whole cut of the man, was an invitation to disaster. Well, thinks I, if he's spotted, it's into the dark for Flashy, and old O'Hooligan can take care of himself.

The worst of it was, he seemed incapable of keeping quiet, but was forever halting to mutter: "The mosque, ah, that's right, now—and then de little stone bridge—where the divil is it? D'ye see it, Flashy—it ought to be right by hereabouts?" I told him if he must chunter, to do it in Hindi, and he said absent-mindedly "Oi will, Oi will, niver fear. Oi wish to God we had a compass." He seemed to think he was in Phoenix Park.

It wasn't too bad at first, because we were moving through gardens, with few folk about, but then we came to the great Chauk Bazaar. Thank God it was ill-lit, but there were groups of pandies everywhere, folk at the stalls, idlers at every corner, and even a few *palkis* swaying through the narrow ways. I put on a bold front, keeping Kavanaugh between me and the wall, and

* "Yes, brother, very cold!"

just swaggered along, spitting. No one gave me a second glance, but by hellish luck we passed close by a group of pandies with some whores in tow, and one of the tarts plucked at Kavanaugh's sleeve and made an improper suggestion; her sepoy stared and growled resentfully, and my heart was in my mouth as I hustled Kavanaugh along, shouting over my shoulder that he'd just been married the previous day and was exhausted, at which they laughed and let us be. At least that kept him shut up for a spell, but no sooner were we clear of the bazaar than he was chattering with relief, and stopped to pick carrots in a vegetable patch, remarking at the top of his voice that they were "the swaitest little things" he'd tasted in months.

Then he lost our way. "That looks devilish like the Kaiser Bagh," says he, and fell into a monsoon ditch. I hauled him out, and he went striding off into the dark, and to my horror stopped a little old fellow and asked where we were. The man said "Jangli Ganj", and hurried off, glancing suspiciously at us. Kavanaugh stood and scratched himself and said it wasn't possible. "If this is Jangli Ganj," says he, "then where the hell is Mirza Kera, will ye tell me that? Ye know what, Flashman, that ould clown doesn't know where he's at, at all, at all." After that we blundered about in the dark, two daring and desperate men on our vital secret mission, and then Kavanaugh gave a great laugh and said it was all right, he knew where we were, after all, and that must be Moulvie Jenab's garden, so we should go left.

We did, and finished up striking matches along Haidar's Canal —at least, that's what Kavanaugh said it was, and he should have known, for he was in it twice, thrashing about in the water and cursing. When he had climbed out he was in a thundering rage, swearing the Engineers had got the map of Lucknow all wrong, but we must cross the canal anyway, and bear left until we hit the Cawnpore road. "The bloody thing's over dere somewheres!" cries he, and since he seemed sure of that, at least, I stifled my growing alarm and off we went, with Kavanaugh tripping over things and stopping every now and then to peer into the gloom wondering: "D'ye think that garden could have been the Char Bagh, now? No, no, niver—and yet agin, it moight be—what d'ye think, Flashy?"

What I thought you may guess; we must have been wandering for hours, and for all we knew we might be heading back towards the Residency. Kavanaugh's slippers had given out, and when he lost one of them we had to grope about in a melon patch until he found it; his feet were in a deplorable condition, and he'd lost his shield, but he was still convinced our plight was all the fault of the ancient he had asked the way from. He thought we might try a cast to our right, so we did, and found ourselves wandering in Dilkoosha Park, which was full of pandy artillery; even I knew we were quite out of the way, and Kavanaugh said, yes, he had made a mistake, but such mishaps were of frequent occurrence. We must bear away south, so we tried that, and I asked a peasant sitting out with his crops if he would guide us to the Alam Bagh. He said he was too old and lame, and Kavanaugh lost his temper and roared at him, at which the fellow ran off shrieking, and the dogs began to bark and we had to run for it and Kavanaugh went headlong into a thorn bush. (And this, as he'd remarked, was one of the Deeds that Saved the Empire; it's in all the books.)

There was no end to the fellow's capacity for disaster, apparently. Given a choice of paths, he headed along one which brought us full tilt into a pandy patrol, and I had to talk our way out of it by saying we were poor men going to Umroula to tell a friend the British had shot his brother. Arriving in a village, he wandered into a hut when I wasn't looking, and blundered about in the dark, seized a woman by the thigh—fortunately she was too terrified to cry out, and we got away. After that he took to crying out "That's Jafirabad, Oi'm certain sure. And that's Salehnagar, over there, yes." Pause. "Oi think." The upshot of that was that we landed in a swamp, and spent over an hour ploshing about in the mud, and Kavanaugh's language was shocking to hear. We went under half a dozen times before we managed to find dry land, and I spotted a house not far off, with a light in an upper window, and insisted that Kavanaugh must rest while I found out where we were. He agreed, blaspheming because the last of his dye had rubbed off with repeated immersions.

I went to the house, and who should be at the window but the

charmingest little brown girl, who said we were not far from
Alam Bagh, but the British had arrived there, and people were
running away. I thanked her, inwardly rejoicing, and she peeped
at me over the sill and says:

"You are very wet, big man. Why not come in and rest, while
you dry your clothes? Only five rupees."

By George, thinks I, why not? I was tired, and sick, and it had
been the deuce of a long time, what with sieges and cholera and
daft Irishmen falling in bogs; this was just the tonic I needed, so
I scrambled up, and there she was, all chubby and brown and
shiny, giggling on her charpoy and shaking her bouncers at me.
I seized hold, nearly crying at this unexpected windfall, and in a
twinkling was marching her round the room, horse artillery
fashion, while she squeaked and protested that for five rupees I
shouldn't be so impatient. I was, though, and it was just as well,
for I'd no sooner finished the business than Kavanaugh was under
the window, airing his Urdu plaintively in search of me, and
wanting to know what was the delay?

I leaned out and cadged five rupees off him, explaining it was a
bribe for an old sick man who knew the way; he passed it up, I
struggled into my wet fugs, kissed my giggling Delilah good-
night, and scrambled down, feeling fit for anything.

It took us another two hours, though, for Kavanaugh was
about done, and we had to keep dodging behind trees to avoid
parties of peasants who were making for Lucknow. I was getting
a mite alarmed, because the moon was up, and I knew that dawn
couldn't be far off; if we were caught by daylight, with
Kavanaugh looking as pale as Marley's ghost, we were done for.
I cursed myself for a fool, whoring and wasting time when we
should have been pushing on—what had I been thinking of?
D'you know, I suddenly realised that in my exasperation with
Kavanaugh, and all that aimless wandering in wrong directions,
and watching him fall in tanks and canals, I'd forgotten the
seriousness of the whole thing—perhaps I was still a trifle light-
headed from my illness, but I'd even forgotten my fears. They
came back now, though, in full force, as we staggered along; I
was about as tuckered as he was, my head was swimming, and
I must have covered the last mile in a walking dream, because the

next thing I remember is bearded faces barring our way, and
blue-tunicked troopers with white *puggarees*, and thinking,
"These are 9th Lancers."

Then there was an officer holding me by the shoulders, and to
my astonishment it was Gough, to whom I'd served brandy and
smokes on the verandah at Meerut. He didn't know me, but he
poured spirits into us, and had us borne down into the camp,
where the bugles were blowing, and the cavalry pickets were
falling in, and the flag was going up, and it all looked so brisk
and orderly and *safe* you would have wept for relief—but the
cheeriest sight of all, to me, was that crumpled, bony figure outside the headquarter tent, and the dour, wrinkled old face under
the battered helmet. I hadn't seen Campbell close to, not since
Balaclava; he was an ugly old devil, with a damned caustic tongue
and a graveyard sense of humour, but I never saw a man yet who
made me feel more secure.

He must have been a rare disappointment to Kavanaugh,
though, for at the sight of him my blundering Paddy threw off
his tiredness, and made a tremendous parade of announcing who
he was, fishing out the message, and presenting it like the last
gallant survivor stumbling in with the News; you never saw
suffering nobility like it as he explained how we'd come out of
Lucknow, but Campbell, listening and tugging at his dreary
moustache, just said "Aye", and sniffed, and added after a
moment: "That's surprising." Kavanaugh, who had probably
expected stricken admiration, looked quite deflated, and when
Campbell told him to "Away you and lie down", he obeyed
pretty huffily.

I knew Campbell, of course, so I wasn't a bit astonished at the
way he greeted me, when he realised who I was.

"It's no' you again?" says he, like a Free Kirk elder to the town
drunk. "Dearie me—ye're not looking a whit better than when I
saw ye last. I doot ye've nae discretion, Flashman." He sighed
and shook his head, but just as he was turning away to his tent
he looked back and says: "I'm glad tae see ye, mind."

I suppose there are those who'd say that there's no higher
honour than that, coming from Old Slowcoach; if that's so, I must
make the most of it, for it's all the thanks I ever got for convoying

Kavanaugh out of Lucknow. Not that I'm complaining, mind, for God knows I've had my share of undeserved credit, but it's a fact that Kavanaugh stole all the limelight when the story came out; I'm certain it was sheer lust for glory that had made him undertake the job in the first place, for when I joined him in the rest-tent after we'd left Campbell, he broke off the kneeling-and-praying which he was engaged in, looked up at me with his great freckled yokel face, and says anxiously:

"D'yez think they'll give us the Victoria Cross?"

Well, in the end they did give him the V.C. for that night's work, while all I got was a shocking case of dysentery. He was a civilian, of course, so they were bound to make a fuss of him, and there was so much V.C.-hunting going on just then that I suppose they thought recognised heroes like me could be passed over—ironic, ain't it? Anyway, I wasn't recommended at the time for any decoration at all, and he was, which seemed fairly raw, although I don't deny he was brave, you understand. Anyone who's as big a bloody fool as that, and goes gallivanting about seeking sorrow, must be called courageous. Still . . . if it hadn't been for me, finding his blasted slipper for him, and fishing him out of canals—and most important of all, getting the right direction from that little brown banger—friend Kavanaugh might still have been traipsing along Haidar's Canal asking the way. But thinking back, perhaps I got the better of the bargain—she was a lissome little wriggler, and it was Kavanaugh's five rupees, after all.[36]

If Campbell was sparing with his compliments, he was equally careful of his soldiers' lives, especially his precious 93rd Highlanders. He took a week to relieve Lucknow, feeling his way in along the route our message had suggested, battering the pandies with his artillery, and only turning his kilties and Sikhs on them when he had to. They butchered everything in sight, of course, between them, but it was a slow business, and he was much abused for it afterwards. In my opinion, he was dead right—as he and Mansfield, his staff chief, were when they wouldn't risk lives simply to pursue and punish fleeing mutineers. A general's job is to win campaigns with as little loss as may be, but of course that don't suit the critics in clubs and newspaper offices—they're at a safe distance, and they want blood, rot them, so they sneer at Old Slowcoach, and call him a stick-in-the-mud soldier.[37]

In fact, his relief of Lucknow, in the face of odds that were sometimes fifteen to one, was a model of sound sense. He got in, he took the garrison out, and he retired in good order, scratching his ear and looking glum, while ignorant asses like Kavanaugh danced with impatience. D'ye know, that Irish lunatic absolutely ran the gauntlet of pandy fire to get back *into* Lucknow, and bring out Outram and Havelock in person (with the poor old Gravedigger hardly able to hobble along) just so that they could greet Sir Colin as he covered the last few furlongs? Bloody nonsense, but it looked very gallant, and has since been commemorated in oils, with camels and niggers looking on admiringly, and the Chiefs all shaking hands. (I'm there, too, like John the Baptist on horseback, with one aimless hand up in the air, which is rot, because at the time I was squatting in the latrine working the dysentery bugs out of my system and wishing I was dead.)[38]

Poor old Gravedigger—he didn't last more than a few days

after. The dysentery bugs did for him in earnest, and we buried him under a palm tree by the Alam Bagh at the start of the retreat. I guess that suited him, and I remember the text running through my head, "And Nicanor lay dead in his harness"—it was what he'd said to me fifteen years earlier, when he'd told me of Sergeant Hudson dying at Piper's Fort. Aye, well, none of us lives forever.

Anyway, Lucknow had to be left in rebel hands, and Campbell took our army back to Cawnpore, where Tantia Tope was raging around the garrison; Campbell whipped him in quick time, and then started clearing up rebel resistance along the Ganges, while at the same time assembling a new force which would march back to Lucknow after Christmas, clear the pandies out properly, and subdue the whole of Oudh kingdom. It was fairly obvious that although mutineers were still thick as mosquitoes everywhere, and had several armies in the field, Campbell's methodical operations would have the whole business settled in a few months, if only Calcutta let him alone. I lent my gallant assistance by supervising intelligence work at Unao, just across the river from Cawnpore, where our new army was assembling; easy work, and nothing more dangerous than occasional brawls and turn-ups between the Pathan Horse and the Devil's Own,* which suited me. The only thing that ruffled my surface at all that winter was a rebuke from Higher Authority when I squired an upper-class half-caste whore to a band parade at Cawnpore,[39] which shows you better than anything how things were beginning to quieten down: when generals have nothing better to do than worry about the morals of staff colonels, you may be sure there's no great work on hand.

And indeed, we were beginning to make things so hot for the pandies along the Grand Trunk that winter that it seemed the bulk of their power was being forced farther and farther south, into the Gwalior country, where Tantia Tope had taken his army, and the rebel princelings had still to be dealt with. That was where Jhansi was: I used to see its name daily in the intelligence reports, with increasing references to Lakshmibai—"the rebel Rani" and "the traitor queen" was what they were calling her

* The Connaught Rangers (88th Foot).

now, for in the past few months she'd thrown off the pretence of loyalty which she had maintained after the Jhansi massacre, and cast in her lot with Nana and Tantia and the other mutinous princes. That had shocked me when I first heard it, and yet it wasn't so surprising really—not when I recalled her feelings towards us, and her grievances, and that lovely dark face so grimly set—"*Mera Jhansi denge nay!* I won't give up my Jhansi!"

She'd have to give it up fast enough, though, presently, with our southern armies under General Rose already advancing north to Gwalior and Bandelkand. She would be crushed along with the other monarchs and their sepoy-cum-bandit armies, and I didn't care to think about that, much. When my thoughts turned towards her—and for some reason they did increasingly in the leisure of that winter—I couldn't think of her as belonging in this world of turmoil and blood and burning and massacre: when I read about "the Jhansi Jezebel" plotting with Nana and whipping up revolt, I couldn't reconcile it with my memory of that bewitching figure swinging gently to and fro on her silken swing in that mirrored fairy palace. I found myself wondering if she was still swinging there, or playing with the monkeys and parrots in her sunny garden, or riding in the woods by the river—who with? How many new lovers had she taken since that night in the pavilion? That was enough to set the flutters going low down in my innards—and farther up, in my midriff, for it wasn't only lust. When I thought of those slanting eyes, and the grave little smile, and the smooth dusky arm along the rope of her swing, I was conscious of a strange, empty longing just for the sight of her, and the sound of her voice. It was downright irritating, for when I reflect on an old love it's usually in terms of tits and buttocks pure and simple—after all, I wasn't a green kid, and I didn't care to find myself thinking like one. What I needed to cure me, I decided, was two weeks' steady rogering at her to get these moon-calf yearnings out of my mind for good, but of course there was no chance of that now.

Or so I thought, in my complacent ignorance, as the winter wore through, and our campaign in the north approached its climax. I knew it was as good as over when Billy Russell of *The Times* showed up to join Campbell's final march on Lucknow—

it's a sure sign of victory when the correspondents gather like vultures. We marched with 30,000 men and strong artillery, myself piling up great heaps of useless paper in Mansfield's intelligence section and keeping out of harm's way. It was an inexorable, pounding business, as our gunners blew the pandy defences systematically to bits, the Highlanders and Irish slaughtered the sepoy infantry whenever it stood, the engineers demolished shrines and temples to show who was master, and everyone laid hands on as much loot as he could carry.

It was a great bloody carnival, with everyone making the most of the war: I recall one incident, in a Lucknow courtyard (I believe it may have been in the Begum's palace) in which I saw Highlanders, their gory bayonets laid aside, smashing open chests that were simply stuffed with jewels, and grinning idiot little Goorkhas breaking mirrors for sheer sport and wiping their knives on silks and fabrics worth a fortune—they didn't know any better. There were Sikh infantry dancing with gold chains and necklaces round their necks, an infantry subaltern staggering under a great enamelled pot overflowing with coins, a naval gunner bleeding to death with a huge shimmering bolt of cloth-of-gold clasped in his arms—there were dead and dying men everywhere, our own fellows as well as pandies, and desperate hand-to-hand fighting going on just over the courtyard wall; muskets banging, men shrieking, two Irishmen coming to blows over a white marble statuette smeared with blood, and Billy Russell stamping and damning his luck because he had no rupees on him to buy the treasures which private soldiers were willing to trade away for the price of a bottle of rum.

"Gi'es a hunnerd rupees, now!" one of the Micks was shouting, as he flourished a gold chain set with rubies—they were as big as gull's eggs. "Jist a hunnerd, yer honour, an' dey're yours!"

"But . . . but they're worth fifty times that!" cries Russell, torn between greed and honesty.

"Ah, the divil wid that!" cries Paddy. "Oi'm sayin' a hunnerd, an' welcome!"

All right, says Russell, but the man must come to his tent for the money that night. But at this Paddy cries out:

"Oh, God, Oi can't, sorr! How do Oi know you or me won't be

dead by then? Ready money, yer honour—say jist fifty chips, an'
yer spirit flask! Come, now?"

But Billy hadn't even fifty rupees, so the Mick shook his head
sorrowfully and swore he couldn't trade, except for cash down.
Finally he burst out:

"But Oi can't see a gintleman in yer honour's position goin'
empty-handed! Here, take dis for nuthin', an' say a prayer for
O'Halloran, Private Michael," and he thrust a diamond brooch
into Russell's hand and ran off, whooping, to join his mates.

You may wonder what I was doing there, so close to the fighting: the answer is I was keeping an eye on my two Rajput
orderlies, who were picking up gold and jewellery for me at
bargain prices, using intelligence section funds. I paid it all back,
mind, out of profits, no irregularities, and finished with the handsome surplus which built Gandamack Lodge, Leicestershire, for
my declining years. (My Rajputs bought O'Halloran's ruby chain,
by the way, for ten rupees and two ounces of baccy—say for £2
all told. I sold it to a Calcutta jeweller for £7,500, which was
about half its true value, but not a bad stroke of business, I
think.)[40]

I asked Billy later what value he would have put on all the
loot that we saw piled up and scrambled for in that one yard, and
he said curtly: "Millions of pounds, blast it!" I'd believe it, too:
there were solid gold and silver vessels and ornaments, crusted
with gems, miles of jewel-sewn brocade, gorgeous pictures and
statues that the troops just hacked and smashed, beautiful enamel
and porcelain trampled underfoot, weapons and standards set
with rubies and emeralds which were gouged and hammered from
their settings—all this among the powder-smoke and blood, with
native soldiers who'd never seen above ten rupees in their lives,
and slum-ruffians from Glasgow and Liverpool, all staggering
about drunk on plunder and killing and destruction. One thing
I'm sure of: there was twice as much treasure destroyed as carried
away, and we officers were too busy bagging our share to do anything about it. I daresay a philosopher would have made heavy
speculation about that scene, if he'd had time to spare from filling
his pockets.

I was well satisfied with my winnings, and pondered that night on how I'd employ them when I went home, which couldn't be long now: I remember thinking "This is the end of the war, Flash, old buck, or near as dammit, and well out of it you are." I was very much at ease, sitting round the mess-fire in the dusk of a Lucknow garden, smoking and swigging port and listening to the distant thump of the night guns, while I yarned idly with Russell and "Rake" Hodson (who'd fagged me at Rugby) and Macdonald the Peeler and Sam Browne and little Fred Roberts, who wasn't much more than a griff,[41] but knew enough to hang around us older hands, warming himself in the glow of our fame. Thinking of them, it strikes me how many famous men I've run across in the dawn of their careers—not that Hodson had long to go, since he was shot while looting next day, with his glory all behind him. But Roberts has gone to the very top of the tree (pity I wasn't more civil to him when he was green; I might have been higher up the ladder myself now), and I suppose Sam Browne's name is known today in every army on earth. Just because he lost an arm and invented a belt, too—get them to call some useful article of clothing after you, and your fame's assured, as witness Sam and Raglan and Cardigan. If I had my time over again I'd patent the Flashman fly-button, and go down in history.[42]

I don't remember much of what we discussed, except that Billy was full of indignation over how he'd seen some Sikhs burning a captured pandy alive, with white soldiers looking on and laughing; he and Roberts said such cruelty oughtn't to be allowed, but Hodson, who was as near a wild beast as I ever met, even among British irregular cavalry, said the viler deaths the rebels died, the better; they'd be less ready to mutiny again. I can see him yet, sitting forward glaring into the fire, pushing back his fair hair with that nervous gesture he had, and steady Sam Browne squinting at him quizzically, drawing on his cigar, saying nothing. I know we talked too of light cavalry, and Russell was teasing Hodson with the prowess of the Black Sea Cossacks, winking at me, when Destiny in the unlikely shape of General Mansfield tapped me on the shoulder and said: "Sir Colin wants you, directly."

I didn't think twice about it, but pitched my cheroot into the fire and sauntered through the lines to the Chief's tent, computing my loot in my mind and drinking in the warm night air with sleepy content. Even when Campbell's greeting to me was: "How well d'ye know the Rani of Jhansi?" I wasn't uncomfortably surprised—there'd been a dispatch in about the Jhansi campaign that very day, and Campbell already knew about my mission for Palmerston; it all seemed a long way away now.

I said I had known her very well; we had talked a great deal together.

"And her city—her fortress?" says Campbell.

"Passably, sir. I was never in her fort proper—our meetings were at the palace, and I'm not over-familiar with the city itself—"

"More familiar than Sir Hugh Rose, though, I'll be bound," says he, tapping a paper in front of him. "And that's his own opeenion—he mentions ye by name in his latest dispatch." I didn't care for that; it don't do to have generals talking about you. I didn't care for the way Campbell was looking at me, either, tapping a nail against those beautifully-kept teeth that shone so odd in his ancient face.

"This Rani," says he at length. "What's she like?"

I began to say that she was a capable ruler and nobody's fool, but he interrupted with one of his barbarous Scotch noises.

"Taghaway-wi'-ye! Is she pretty, man? Eh? How pretty?"

I admitted that she was strikingly beautiful, and he grinned and shook his grizzly head.

"Aye, aye," says he, and squinted at me. "Ye're a strange man, Flashman. I'll confess to ye, I've even-on had my doots aboot ye—don't ask me what, for I don't know. I'm frank wi' ye, d'ye see?" I'll say that for him, he always was. "This much I'm certain of," he went on, "ye always win. God kens how—and I'm glad I don't ken mysel', for I wish to think well of ye. But there—Sir Hugh needs ye at Jhansi, and I'm sending ye south."

I didn't know what to think of this—or of his curious opinion of me. I just stood and waited anxiously.

"This mutiny mischief is just aboot done—it's a question of scattering the last armies—here, in Oudh and Rohilkand, and there, in Bandelkand—and hanging Nana and Tantia and Azeemoolah higher than Haman. Jhansi is one of the last nuts tae be cracked—and it'll be a hard one, like enough. This bizzum of a Rani has ten thousand men and stout city walls. Sir Hugh will have her under siege by the time ye get there, and nae doot he'll have to take the place by storm. But that's not enough— which is why you, wi' your particular deeplomatic knowledge of the Rani and her state, are essential to Sir Hugh. Ye see, Flash- man, Lord Canning and Sir Hugh and mysel' are agreed on one thing—and your experience of this wumman may be the key to it." He looked me carefully in the eye. "Whatever else befalls, we must contrive tae capture the Rani of Jhansi alive."

If she'd been ugly as sin, or twenty years older and scrawny, it would never have happened. Jhansi would have been taken, and if a plain, elderly Rani had been bayoneted or shot in the process, no one would have given a damn. But Canning, our enlightened Governor-General, was a sentimental fool, intent on suppressing the Mutiny with the least possible bloodshed, and already alarmed at the toll of vengeance that people like Neill and Havelock had taken. He guessed that sooner or later the righteous wrath of Britons at home would die down, and that if we slaughtered too many pandies a revulsion would set in—which, of course, it did. My guess is that he also feared the death of a young and beautiful rebel princess (for her fame and likeness had spread across India by now) might just tip the balance of public conscience—he didn't want the liberal press depicting her as some Indian Joan of Arc. So, however many other niggers died, male and female, she was to be taken alive.

Mind you, I could see Canning's point, and personally I was all for it. There wasn't a life anywhere—except Elspeth's and little Havvy's—that was as precious to me then as Lakshmibai's, and I don't mind admitting it. But fair's fair; I wanted her saved without any dangerous intervention on my part, and the farther I could have kept away from Jhansi the better I'd have liked it. It wasn't a lucky place for me.

So I took as long as I decently could getting there, in the hope that it might be all over by the time I arrived. I had the excuse that the two hundred miles between Lucknow and Jhansi was damned dangerous country, with pandies and the armies of rebel chiefs all over the place; I had a strong escort of Pathan Horse, but even so we went warily, and didn't sight that fort of ill-omen on its frowning rock until the last week in March. Rose was just getting himself settled in by then, battering away at the city defences with his guns, his army circling the walls in a gigantic ring, with observation posts and cavalry pickets all prettily sited to bottle it up.

He was a good soldier, Rose, careful as Campbell but twice as quick, and one glance at the rebel defences told you that he needed to be. Jhansi lay massive and impregnable under the brazen sun, with its walls and outworks and the red rebel banner floating lazily above the fort. Outside the walls the dusty plain had been swept clear of every scrap of cover, and the rebel batteries thundered out in reply to our gunners, as though warning the besiegers what would happen if they ventured too close. And inside there were ten thousand rebels ready to fight to the finish. A tough nut, as Campbell had said.

"We'll have them out in a week, though, no fears about that," was Rose's verdict. He was another Scotsman (India was crawling with them, of course, as always), brisk and bright-eyed and spry; I knew him well from the Crimea, where he'd been liaison at the Frog headquarters, and less objectionable than most diplomat-soldiers. He was new to India, but you'd never have guessed it from his easy confidence and dandy air—to tell the truth, I have difficulty in memory separating his appearance from George Custer's, for they both had the same gimlet assurance, as well as the carefully wind-blown blond hair and artless moustaches. There the resemblance ended—if we'd had Rose at Little Big Horn, Crazy Horse and Gall could have whistled for their dinners.

"Yes, a week at most," says he, and pointed out how he had sited his left and right attacks opposite the strongest points in the rebel defences, which our gunners were pounding with red-hot shot, keeping the pandy fire-parties busy quelling the flames which you could see here and there behind the walls, flickering crazily through the heat-haze. "Frontal night assault as soon as the breaches are big enough, and then . . ." He snapped his telescope shut. "Bloody work, since the pandies are sure to fight to the last—but we'll do the business. The question is: in all that carnage, how do we preserve her ladyship? You must be our oracle on that subject, what? Would she personally surrender, d'you suppose?"

I looked about me from the knoll on which we stood, with his staff officers. Just before us were the lines of siege-guns in their earthworks, shaking the ground with their explosions, the smoke wraithing back towards us as the gunners, crawling like ants round their pieces, reloaded and fired again. Either side the pickets of the flying cavalry camps were strung out as far as the eye could see—the red jackets of the Light Dragoons, and the grey khakee of the Hyderabad troopers' coats, dusty with the new curry-powder dye. Two miles behind us, near the ruins of the old cantonment, were the endless tent-lines of the infantry brigades, waiting patiently till the guns had done their work on the massive walls of Jhansi city, behind which the jumble of distant houses stretched in the smoky haze up to the mighty crag of the fortress. She'd be up there, somewhere, perhaps in that cool durbar room, or on the terrace, playing with her pet monkeys; perhaps she was with her chiefs and soldiers, looking out at the great army that was going to swallow her up and reduce her city and fairy palace to rubble. *Mera Jhansi denge nay*, thinks I.

"Surrender?" says I. "No, I doubt if she will."

"Well, you know her." He gave me that odd, leery look that I'd got used to even in the few hours I'd been at his headquarters, whenever her name was mentioned. The popular view was that she was some gorgeous human tigress who prowled half-naked through sumptuous apartments, supervising the torture of discarded legions of lovers—oh, my pious generation had splendid imaginations, I may tell you.[43]

"We've tried proclamation, of course," says Rose, "but since we can't guarantee immunity to her followers, we might as well save our breath. On the other hand, she may not be eager to see her civilians exposed to continuous bombardment followed by the horrors of assault, what? I mean, being a woman . . . what *is* she like, by the way?"

"She's a lady," says I, "extremely lovely, uses French scent, is kind to animals, fences like a Hungarian hussar, prays for several hours each day, recreates herself on a white silk swing in a room full of mirrors, gives afternoon tea-parties for society ladies, and hangs criminals up in the sun by their thumbs. Useful horsewoman, too."

"Good God!" says Rose, staring, and behind him his staff were gaping at me round-eyed, licking their lips. "Are you serious?"

"What about lovers, hey?" says one of the staff, sweating and horny-eyed. "They say she keeps a hareem of muscular young bucks, primed with love-potions—"

"She didn't tell me," says I, "and I didn't ask her. Even you wouldn't, I fancy."

"Well," says Rose, glancing at me and then away. "We must certainly consider what's to be done about her."

That was how I employed myself for the next three days, while the guns and eight-inch mortars smashed away in fine style, opening a sizeable breach in the south wall, and burning up the rebels' repair barricades with red-hot shot. We blew most of their heavy gun posts into rubble, and by the 29th Rose was drawing up final orders for his infantry stormers—and still we had reached no firm plan for capturing Lakshmibai unharmed. For the more I thought about it, the more certain I became that she'd fight it out, in person, when our infantry fought their way hand-to-hand into her palace—it was easy, after Lucknow, to imagine bloody corpses on that quilted Chinese carpet, and the mirrors shattered by shot, and yelling looters smashing and tearing in those price-less apartments, sabring and bayoneting everything that stood in their way. God knows it was nothing new to me, and I'd lent a hand in my time, when it had been safe to do so—but these would be *her* rooms, *her* possessions, and I was sentimental enough to be sorry for that, because I'd liked them and been happy there. By George, I'd got her into my bloodstream though, hadn't I just, when I started worrying about her damned furni-ture.

And what would happen to her, in that madhouse of blood and steel? Try as I might, I could see nothing for it but to tell off a picked platoon with orders to make straight for the palace and secure her unharmed at any price—provided she didn't get in the way of a stray shot, there was no reason why they shouldn't bring her out safe. By God, though, that was one detail I'd have to avoid—no, my job would be her reception and safe-keeping when the slaughter was safely over: Flashy the stern and sorrow-ful jailer, firm but kindly, shielding her from prying eyes and lecherous staff-wallopers with dirty minds, that was the ticket. She'd have to be escorted away, perhaps even to Calcutta, where they'd decide what to do with her. A nice long journey, that, and she'd be grateful for a friendly face among her enemies— especially one for which she'd shown such a partiality in the past. I thought of that pavilion, and that gleaming bronze body un- dulating towards me, quivering voluptuously to the music—we'll have dancing every night, thinks I, in our private hackery, and if I'm not down to twelve stone by the time we reach Calcutta, it won't be for want of nocturnal exercise.

I explained my thoughts to Rose—the first part, about the special platoon, not the rest—at dinner in his tent, and he frowned and shook his head.

"Too uncertain," says he. "We need something concerted and executed before the battle has even reached her palace; we must have her snug and secure by then."

"Well, I don't for the life of me see how you're going to do that," says I. "We can't send anyone in ahead of the troops, to kidnap her or any such thing. They wouldn't get a hundred yards through the streets of Jhansi—and if they did, she has a Pathan guard hundreds strong covering every inch of the palace."

"No," says he, thoughtfully, picking at his cheroot. "Force wouldn't serve, I agree—but diplomacy, now? What d'ye think, Lyster?"

This was young Harry Lyster, Rose's galloper, and the only other person present at our talk. I'd known him any time the past ten years; he'd been a special constable with me at the Chartist farce of '48, when I took up old Morrison's truncheon and did his duty for him—me and Gladstone and Louis Napoleon holding the plebeian mob at bay, I don't think. Lyster was a smart 'un, though; given a silver spoon he'd have been a field marshal by now.

"Bribery, perhaps—if we could smuggle a proposal to some of her officers?" says he.

"Too complicated," says Rose, "and you'd probably just lose your money."

"They've eaten her salt," says I. "You couldn't buy 'em." I was far from sure of that, by the way, but I wanted to squash all this talk of intrigue and secret messages—I'd heard it too often before, and I know who finishes up sneaking through the dark with his bowels gurgling and his hair standing on end in the enemy's lair. "I'm afraid it comes down to the special platoon after all, sir. A good native officer, with intelligent *jawans*—"

"Counsel of despair, Flashman." Rose shook his head decisively. "No—we'll have to trick her out. Here's a possibility—storm the city, as we intend, but leave her a bolt-hole. If we draw off our cavalry pickets from the Orcha gate, they'll spot the weakness, and when our rebel lady sees that her city's doomed, I'll be much surprised if she don't try to make a run for it. How well do Indian women ride?"

"This one? Like a Polish lancer. It might work," says I, "if she don't suspicion what we're up to. But if she smells a rat—"

"She'll be smelling too much powder-smoke by then to notice anything else," says Rose confidently. "She'll break for the open, to try to join Tantia, or some other rebel leader—and we'll be waiting for her on the Orcha road. What d'you say, gentlemen?" says he, smiling.

Well, it suited me, although I thought he underrated her subtlety. But Lyster was nodding agreement[44] and Rose went on:

"Yes, I think we'll try that—but only as a long stop. It's still not enough. Lord Canning attaches the utmost importance to capturing the Rani unscathed; that being so, we must play every card in our hand. And we have a trump which it would be folly not to use for everything it's worth." He turned and snapped a pointing finger at me. "You, Flashman."

I choked on my glass, and covered my dismay with a shuddering cough. "I, sir?" I tried to get my breath back. "How, sir? I mean, what—?"

"We can't afford to neglect the opportunity which your knowledge of this woman—your familiarity with her—gives us. I don't suppose there's a white man living who has been on closer terms with her—isn't that so?"

"Well, now, sir, I don't know—"

"I still think we can talk her out. Public offers of surrender are useless, we agree—but a private offer, now, secretly con-

veyed, with my word of honour, and Lord Canning's, attached to
it . . . that might be a different matter. Especially if it were persuasively argued, by a British officer she could trust. You follow
me?"

All too well I followed him; I could see the abyss of ruin and
despair opening before my feet once again, as the bright-eyed
lunatic went eagerly on:

"The offer would assure her that her life would be spared, if
she gave herself up. She doesn't have to surrender Jhansi, even—
just her own person. How can she refuse? She could even keep
her credit intact with her own people—that's it!" cries he,
smacking the table. "If she accepts, all she has to do is take
advantage of the bolt-hole we're going to leave her, through the
Orcha Gate! She can pretend to her own folk that she's trying to
escape, and we'll snap her up as she emerges. No one would ever
know it was a put-up business—except her, and ourselves!" He
beamed at us in triumph.

Lyster was frowning. "Will she accept—and leave her city and
people to their fate?" He glanced at me.

"Oh, come, come!" cries Rose. "She ain't European royalty,
you know! These black rulers don't care a snuff for their subjects
—ain't that so, Flashman?"

I seized on this like a drowning man. "This one does, sir," says
I emphatically. "She wouldn't betray 'em—never." The irony of
it was, I believed it to be true.

He stared at me in disappointment. "I can't credit that," says
he. "I can't. I'm positive you're mistaken, Flashman." He shook
his head. "But we have nothing to lose by trying, at any rate."

"But if I went in, under a flag of truce, demanding private
audience with her—"

"Pshaw! Who said anything about a flag of truce? Of course,
that would blow the gaff at once—her people would know there
was something up." He tapped the table, grinning at me, bursting
with his own cleverness. "Didn't I say you were the trump card?
You not only know her well, you're one of the few men who can
get inside Jhansi, and into her presence, with no one the wiser—
as a native!" He sat back, laughing. "Haven't you done it a score
of times—? why, all the world knows about how you brought

Kavanaugh out of Lucknow! What d'ye think they're calling you down in Bombay these days—the Pall Mall Pathan!"

There are times when you know it absolutely ain't worth struggling any longer. First Palmerston, then Outram, and now Rose—and they were only the most recent in a long line of enthusiastic madmen who at one time or another had declared that I was just the chap they were looking for to undertake some ghastly adventure. I made one attempt at a feeble excuse by pointing out that I didn't have a beard any longer; Rose brushed it aside as of no importance, poured me another brandy, and began to elaborate his idiot plan.

In essence it was what I've already described—I was to convince Lakshmibai of the wisdom of giving herself up (which I reckoned she'd never agree to do), and if she accepted, I was to explain how she must make an attempt to escape through the unguarded Orcha Gate at the very height of our attack on Jhansi city—the timing, said Rose, was of the utmost importance, and the further advanced our attack was before she made her bolt, the less suspicion her people might feel. (I couldn't see that this mattered much, but Rose was one of these meticulous swine who'll leave nothing to chance.)

"And if she rejects the offer—as I know she will?" I asked him.

"Then on no account must you say anything about the Orcha Gate," says he. "Only when she has accepted the offer must you explain how her 'capture' is to be contrived. But if she *does* refuse—well, she may still be tempted to use a bolt-hole in the last resort, if we leave her one. So we shall nab her anyway," he concluded smugly.

"And I—if she refuses?"

"My guess," says he airily, puffing at his cheroot, "is that she'll try to keep you as a hostage. I hardly think she'd do more than that, what? Anyway," says he, clapping me on the arm, "I know you've never counted risk yet—I saw you at Balaclava, by George! Did you know about that, Lyster?" he went on, "charging with the Heavies wasn't enough for this beauty—he had to go in with the Lights as well!" And, do you know, he actually sat laughing at me in admiration? It would turn your stomach.

So there it was—again. Hell in front and no way out. I tried to

balance the odds in my mind, while I kept a straight face and
punished the brandy. Would Lakshmibai listen to me? Probably
not: she might try to escape when all was lost, but she'd never
give herself up and leave her city to die. What would she do
with me, then? I conjured up a picture of that dark face, smiling
up at me with parted lips when I pinned her and kissed her
against the mirrored wall; I remembered the pavilion—no, she
wouldn't do me harm, if she could help it. Unless . . . *had* she set
those Thugs after me? No, that had been Ignatieff. And yet—
there was the Jhansi massacre—how deep had she been in that?
Who knew what went on in an Indian mind, if it came to that?
Was she as cruel and treacherous as all the rest of them? I
couldn't say—but I was going to find out, by God, whether I
liked it or not. I'd know, when I came face to face with her—and
just for an instant I felt a leap of eagerness in my chest at the
thought of seeing her once more. It was only for an instant, and
then I was sweating again.

I'll say this for Hugh Rose—along with his fiendish ingenuity
for dreaming up dangers for me, he had an equally formidable
talent of organisation. It took him a good thirty seconds to think
of a fool-proof way of getting me safe inside Jhansi—I would have
the next day to prepare my disguise, with skin-dye and the rest,
and the following night he would loose a squadron of Hyderabad
Cavalry in a sudden raid on the breach in the city wall. They
would break through the flimsy barrier which the defenders had
thrown up, sabre a few sentries, create a hell of a row, and then
withdraw in good order—leaving behind among the rubble one
native *badmash* of unsavoury appearance, to wit, Colonel Flashman, late of the 17th Lancers and General Staff. I'd have no difficulty, said Rose breezily, in lying low for half an hour, and then
emerging as one of the defenders. After that, all I had to do was
tool up through the streets to the palace and knock on the door,
like Barnacle Bill.

Speaking from a safe distance, I can say it was a sound scheme.
Hearing it propounded at the time I thought it was fit to loosen
the bowels of a bronze statue—but the hellish thing is, whatever
a general suggests, you can do nothing but grin and agree. And,
I have to admit, it worked.

I don't remember the agonising day I must have spent waiting, and attiring myself in a filthy sepoy uniform, so that I could pass in my old role of 3rd Cavalry mutineer. But I'll never forget the last moment of suspense beside the siege guns, with the Hydera-badi troopers round me in the gloom, and Rose clasping my hand, and then the whispered order, and the slow, muffled advance through the cold dark, with only the snorting of the horses and the creak of leather to mark our passing towards that looming distant wall, with the dull crimson glow of the city behind it, and the broad gap of the breach where the watch-fires twinkled, and we could even see figures silhouetted as they moved to and fro.

Away to our left flank the night-batteries were firing, distant tiny jets of flame in the dark, pounding away at the flank of the city which faced the old cantonment. That was for diversion; I could smell the bazaar stink from Jhansi, and still we hadn't been spotted. Even through my genuine funk, I could feel that strange tremor of excitement that every horse-soldier knows as the squad-rons move forward silently in the gloom towards an unsuspecting enemy, slowly and ponderously, bump-bump-bump at the walk, knee to knee, one hand on the bridle, t'other on the hilt of the lamp-blacked sabre, ears straining for the first cry of alarm. How often I'd known it, and been terrified by it—in Afghanis-tan, at Cawnpore with Rowbotham, in the Punjab, under the walls of Fort Raim when I rode against the Russians with old Izzat Kutebar and the Horde of the Blue Wolves, and that lovely witch, Ko Dali's daughter, touching my hand in the dark . . .

The crack of a rifle, a distant yell, and the thunderous roar of the *rissaldar*: "Aye-hee! Squah-drahn—charge!" The dark mass either side seemed to leap forward, and then I was thundering along, flat down against my pony's flanks like an Oglala, as we tore across the last furlong towards the breach. The Hyderabadis screamed like fury as they spread out, except for the four who remained bunched ahead and either side of me, as a protective screen. Beyond them I could see the smoky glare of the fires in the breach, a rubble-strewn gap a hundred yards wide, with a crazy barricade thrown across it; pin-points of flame were twinkling in the gloom, and shots whistled overhead, and then the first riders were at the barrier, jumping it or bursting through, sabres swinging. My front-gallopers swerved in among the jumble of fallen masonry and scorched timbers, howling like dervishes; I saw one of them sabring down a pandy who thrust up at him with musket and bayonet, while another rode slap into a big, white-dhotied fellow who was springing at him with a spear. His horse stumbled and went down, and I scrambled my own beast over a pile of stones and plaster, from which a dark figure emerged, shrieking, and vanished into the gloom.

There was a fire straight ahead, and men running towards me, so I jerked my beast's head round and made for the shadows to my right. Two Hyderabadis surged up at my elbow, charging into the advancing group, and under their cover I managed to reach the lee of a ruined house, while the clash of steel, the crack of musketry, and the yells of the fighters sounded behind me. Close by the house there was a tangle of bushes—one quick glance round showed no immediate enemy making for me, and I rolled neatly out of the saddle into what seemed to be a midden, crawled frantically under the bushes, and lay there panting.

I'd dropped my sabre, but I had a stout knife in my boot and a revolver in my waist under my shirt; I snuggled back as far into cover as I could and kept mum. Feet went pounding by towards the tumult at the barricade, and for two or three minutes the pandemonium of shooting and yelling continued. Then it died down, to be replaced by a babble of insults from the defenders—presumably directed at our retreating cavalry—a few shots went after them, and then comparative peace descended on that small corner of Jhansi. So far, so good—but, as some clever lad once said, we hadn't gone very far.

I waited perhaps quarter of an hour, and then burrowed through the bushes and found myself in a narrow lane. There was no one about, but round the corner was a watch-fire, with a few pandies and bazaar-wallahs round it; I ambled past them, exchanging a greeting, and they didn't do more than give me an idle glance. Two minutes later I was in the bazaar, buying a chapatti and chili, and agreeing with the booth-wallah that if the sahib-log couldn't do better than the feeble skirmish there had just been down at the breach, then they'd never take Jhansi.

Although it was three in the morning, the narrow streets were
as busy as if it had been noon. There were troops on the move
everywhere—rebels of the 12th N.I., regulars of the Rani's
Maharatta army, Bhil soldiers-of-fortune, and every sort of armed
tribesman from the surrounding country, with spiked helmets,
long swords, round shields, and all kinds of firearm from Minies
to matchlocks. It looked to me as though Jhansi knew our main
attack was soon coming, and they were moving reserves down to
the walls.

There were ten civilian townsfolk about for every soldier, and
the booths were doing a roaring trade. Here and there were
ruined shops and houses where some of our stray shots had fallen,
but there was no sign of unease, as you'd have expected—rather a
sense of excitement and bustle, with everyone wideawake and
chattering. A party of coolies went by, dragging a cart piled with
six-pounder cartridges, and I took the opportunity to remark to
the booth-wallah:

"There go a thousand English lives, eh, brother?"

"Like enough," says he, scowling. "And every cannon-shot
means another anna in market-tax. Lives can be bought too dear
—even English ones."

"Nay, the Rani will pay it from her treasury," says I, giving
him my shrill sepoy giggle.

"Ho-ho-ho, hear him!" says he, scornfully. "You should set up
a stall, soldier, and see how fat you get. When did the Rani ever
pay—or any other prince? What are we for but to pay, while the
great ones make war?"

Just what they'd be saying in the Reform Club or the Star and
Garter, thinks I. Aloud I said:

"They say she holds a great council in the fort tonight. Is it
true?"

"She did not invite me," says he, sarcastically. "Nor, strangely
enough, did she offer me the use of the palace when she left it.
That will be three pice, soldier."

I paid him, having learned what I wanted to know, and took
the streets that led up to the fort, with my knees getting shakier
at every step. By God, this was a chancy business; I had to nerve
myself with the thought that, whatever her feelings towards my

country and army, she'd never shown anything but friendliness to me—and she'd hardly show violence to an envoy from the British general. Even so, when I found myself gazing across the little square towards that squat, frowning gateway, with the torches blazing over it, and the red-jacketed Pathan sentries of her personal guard standing either side, I had to fight down the temptation to scuttle back into the lanes and try to hide until it was all over. Only the certainty that those lanes would shortly be a bloody battleground sent me reluctantly on. I wound my *puggaree* tightly round head and chin, hiding half my face, slipped from my pocket the note which Rose and I had carefully prepared, walked firmly across to the sentry, and demanded to see the guard commander.

He came out, yawning and expectorating, and who should it be but my old acquaintance who spat on shadows. I gave him the note and said: "This is for the Rani's hand, and no other. Take it to her, and quickly."

He glowered from me to it and back. "What is this, and who may you be?"

"If she wishes you to know, belike she'll tell you," I growled, and squatted down in the archway. "But be sure, if you delay, she'll have that empty head off your shoulders."

He stood glaring, turning the note in his hands. Evidently it impressed him—with a red seal carrying young Lyster's family crest, it should have done—for after an obscene inquiry about my parentage, which I ignored, he scratched himself and then loafed off, bidding the sentries keep an eye on me.

I waited, with my heart hammering, for this was the moment when things might go badly astray. Rose and I had cudgelled our brains for wording that would mean nothing to anyone but her, in case the note fell into the wrong hands. As an added precaution, we'd written it in schoolboy French, which I knew she understood. It said, simply:

One who brought perfume and a picture is here. See him alone. Trust him.

Rose had been delighted with this—he was plainly one who

enjoyed intrigue for its own sake, and I've no doubt would have
liked to sign it with a skull and crossbones. Squatting in the doorway, I couldn't take such a light-hearted view. Assuming that
Pathan blockhead took it straight to her, she'd guess who it was
from fast enough—but suppose she didn't want to see me? Suppose she thought the best way of answering the message would
be to send me back in bits to Rose's headquarters? Suppose she
showed it to someone else, or it miscarried, or . . .

The sound of marching feet came from the gloom beyond the
archway, and I got to my feet, quivering. The *havildar* came out
of the dark, with two troopers behind him. He stopped, gave me
a long, glowering look, and then jerked his head. I went forward,
and he motioned me on into the courtyard beyond, falling in
beside me with the two troopers behind. I wanted to ask him if
he'd given the note to the Rani personally, but my tongue seemed
to have shrivelled up; I'd know soon enough. As my eyes became
accustomed to the gloom after the glare of the torches by the
gate, I saw that we were heading across the yard, with high
black walls on either side, and another torch at the far end over a
doorway, guarded by two more Pathans.

"In," growls the *havildar*, and I found myself in a small
vaulted guard-room; I blinked in the sudden glare of oil lamps,
and then my heart lurched down into my boots, for the figure
peering intently towards me from the centre of the room was the
little fat chamberlain whom I knew so well from Lakshmibai's
durbar.

The stupid bitch had told him who I was! There was no hope
of a secret offer now—Rose's fat-headed scheme had sprung a
leak, and—

"You are the officer who brought gifts from the British
Queen?" he squeaked. "The Sirkar's envoy—Colonel Flashman?"
He was squinting at me in consternation, as well he might, for I
didn't look much like the dandy staff officer he'd known. Sick and
fearful, I peeled off my *puggaree* and pushed my hair back.

"Yes," said I. "I'm Colonel Flashman. You must take me to the
Rani, at once!"

He goggled at me, his little eyes wide in that fat face, twisting
his hands nervously. And then something fluttered in the air

between us—for an instant I thought it was a moth—and fell to
the floor with a tiny puff of sparks. It was a cigarette, smoking
on the flags; a long yellow tube with a mouthpiece.

"All in good time," said Ignatieff's voice, and I believe I
actually cried out with shock, as I spun round to stare in horrified
disbelief at the doorway. He was standing there, his hand still
frozen in the act of flicking away the cigarette—Ignatieff, whom
I'd supposed a thousand miles away by now, looking at me with
his dreadful cold smile, and then inclining his tawny head.

"All in good time," he repeated in English, as he came forward.
He ground his heel on the fallen cigarette. "After we have
resumed the . . . discussion? . . . which was so unfortunately
interrupted at Balmoral."

                    *   *   *

How I've survived four-score years without heart seizure I do
not know. Perhaps I'm inured to the kind of shock I experienced
then, with my innards surging up into my throat; I couldn't
move, but stood there with my skin crawling as he came to stand
in front of me—a new Ignatieff, this, in flowered shirt and pyjamy
trousers and Persian boots, and with a little gingery beard adorn-
ing his chin. But the rat-trap mouth was still the same, and that
unwinking half-blue half-brown eye boring into me.

"I have been anticipating this meeting," says he, "ever since I
learned of your mission to India—did you know, I heard about it
before you did yourself?" He gave a chilly little smile—he could
never resist bragging, this one. "The secret deliberations of the
astute Lord Palmerston are not as secret as he supposes. And it
has been a fool's errand, has it not? But never so foolish as now.
You should have been thankful to escape me . . . twice? . . . but
you come blundering back a third time. Very well." The gotch
eye seemed to harden with a brilliant light. "You will not have
long to regret it."

With an effort I got my voice back, damned shaky though it
was.

"I've nothing to say to you!" cries I, as truculently as I could,
and turned on the little chamberlain. "My business is with the
Rani Lakshmibai—not with this . . . this renegade! I demand to
see her at once! Tell her—"

Ignatieff's hand smashed across my mouth, sending me staggering, but his voice didn't rise by a fraction. "That will not be
necessary," says he, and the little chamberlain dithered submissively. "Her highness is not to be troubled for a mere spy. I shall
deal with this jackal myself."

"In a pig's eye you will!" I blustered. "I'm an envoy from
Sir Hugh Rose, to the Rani—not to any hole-and-corner Russian
bully! You'll hinder me at your peril! Damn you, let me loose!"
I roared as the two troopers suddenly grabbed my elbows. "I'm a
staff officer! You can't touch me—I'm—"

"Staff officer! Envoy!" Ignatieff's words came out in that
raging icy whisper that took me back to the nightmare of that
verminous dungeon beneath Fort Arabat. "You crawl here in
your filthy disguise, like the spy you are, and claim to be treated
as an emissary? If that is what you are, why did you not come in
uniform, under a flag, in open day?" His face was frozen in fury,
and then the brute hit me again. "I shall tell you—because you
are a dishonoured liar, whose word no one would trust! Treachery
and deceit are your trade—or is it assassination this time?" His
hand shot out and whipped the revolver from my waist.

"It's a lie!" I shouted. "Send to Sir Hugh Rose—he'll tell
you!" I was appealing to the chamberlain. "You know me, man—
tell the Rani! I demand it!"

But he just stood gaping, waiting for Ignatieff, whose sudden
anger had died as quickly as it came.

"Since Sir Hugh Rose has not honoured us with a parley, there
is no reason why we should address him," says he softly. "We
have to deal only with a night prowler." He gestured to the
troopers. "Take him down."

"You've no authority!" I roared. "I'm not answerable to you,
you Russian swine! Let me go!" They were dragging me forward
by main strength, while I bawled to the chamberlain, pleading
with him to tell the Rani. They ran me through a doorway, and
down a flight of stone steps, with Ignatieff following, the
chamberlain twittering in front of him. I struggled in panic, for
it was plain that the brute was going to prevent the Rani hearing
of my arrival until after he'd done. . . . I nearly threw up in terror,
for the troopers were hauling me across the floor to an enormous

wheel like a cable drum, set perpendicular above ground level. There were manacles dangling from it, and fetters attached to the stone floor beneath it—Jesus! They had racked Murray to death in this very fort, Ilderim had said, and now they flung me against the hellish contraption, one grinning trooper pinning me bodily while the other clamped my hands in the manacles above my head, and then snapped the floor-chains round my ankles. I yelled and swore, the chamberlain sank down fearfully on the bottom step, and Ignatieff lit another cigarette.

"So much would not be necessary if I only sought information," says he, in that dreadful metallic whisper. "With such a coward as you, the threat is sufficient. But you are going to tell me why you are here, what treachery you intended, and for what purpose you wished to see her highness. And when I am satisfied that you have told me everything—" he stepped close up to me, that awful eye staring into mine, and concluded in Russian, for my benefit alone "—the racking will continue until you are dead." He signed to the troopers, and stepped back.

"For Christ's sake, Ignatieff!" I screamed. "You can't do this! I'm a British officer, a white man—let me go, you bastard! Please —in God's name, I'll tell you!" I felt the drum turn behind me as the troopers put their weight on the lever, drawing my arms taut above my head. "No, no! Let me go, you foul swine! I'm a gentleman, damn you—for pity's sake! We've had tea with the Queen! No, please—"

There was a clank from the huge wheel, and the chains wrenched at my wrists and ankles, sending shoots of pain through my arm and thigh muscles. I howled at the top of my voice as the wheel turned, stretching me to what seemed the limit of endurance, and Ignatieff stepped closer again.

"Why did you come?" says he.

"Let me go! You vile bloody dog, you!" Behind him I saw that the chamberlain was on his feet, white with horror. "Run!" I yelled. "Run, you stupid fat sod! Get your mistress—quickly!" But he seemed rooted to the spot, and then the drum clanked again, and an excruciating agony flamed through my biceps and shoulders, as though they were being hauled out of my body (which, of course, they were). I tried to scream again, but nothing came out, and then his devil's face was next to mine again, and I was babbling:

"Don't—don't, for Jesus' sake! I'll tell you—I'll tell you!" And even through the red mist of pain I knew that once I did, I was a dead man. But I couldn't bear it—I had to talk—and then inspiration came through the agony, and I let my head loll sideways, with a groan that died away. If only I could buy a moment's time—if only the chamberlain would run for help—if only Ignatieff would believe I'd fainted, and I could keep up the pretence with my whole body shrieking in pain. His palm slapped across my face, and I couldn't restrain a cry. His hand went up to the troopers, and I gasped:

"No—I'll tell you! Don't let them turn it again! I swear it's the truth—only don't let them do it again—oh, God, please, not again!"

"Well?" says he, and I knew I couldn't delay any longer. I couldn't bear another turn.

"General Rose—" My voice seemed to be a whisper from miles away. "I'm on his staff—he sent me—to see the Rani—please, it's the God's truth! Oh, make them let me down!"

"Go on," says that dreadful voice. "What was your message?"

"I was to ask her . . ." I was staring into his horrible eye, seeing it through a blur of tears, and then somewhere in the obscured distance behind him there was a movement, at the top of the steps, and as I blinked my vision was suddenly clear, and my voice broke into a shuddering sigh of relief, and I let my head fall back. For the door at the top of the steps was open, with my red-coated guard sergeant, that wonderful, bearded genius of a Pathan who spat on shadows, holding it back, and a white figure was stepping through, stopping abruptly, staring down at us. I had always thought she was beautiful, but at that moment Lakshmibai looked like an angel pavilioned in splendour.

I was in such anguish that it was even an effort to keep my eyes open, so I didn't, but I heard her cry of astonishment, and then the chamberlain babbling, and Ignatieff swinging round. And then, believe it or not, what she said, in a voice shrill with anger, was:

"Stop that at once! Stop it, do you hear?"

for all the world like a young school-mistress coming into class and catching little Johnny piddling in the ink-well. I'll swear she stamped as she said it, and even at the time, half-fainting with pain that I was, I thought it sounded ridiculous; and then suddenly with an agonising jerk that made me cry out, the fearful traction on my limbs was relaxed, and I was sagging against the wheel, trying to stop my tortured legs from buckling under me. But I'm proud to say I still had my wits about me.

"You won't get anything out of me!" I groaned. "You Russian hound—I'll die first!" I fluttered an eye open to see how this was received, but she was too busy choking back her fury as she confronted Ignatieff.

"This is by your order?" Lord, it was a lovely voice. "Do you know who this is?"

I'll say this for him, he faced her without so much as a blink—indeed, he even tossed his blasted cigarette aside in deference before giving his little bow to her.

"It is a spy, highness, who stole into your city in disguise—as you can see."

"It is a British officer!" She was blazing, trembling from her white head-veil all down her shapely sari-wrapped body to her little pearled sandals. "An envoy of the Sirkar, who brings a message for me. For me!" And she stamped again. "Where is it?"

Ignatieff pulled the note from his girdle, and handed it to her without a word. She read it, and then folded it deliberately, and looked him in the face.

"Sher Khan tells me he had orders to deliver it into my hands alone." She was holding in her anger still, with an effort. "But seeing him with it, you asked what it might be, and the fool gave it you. And having read it, you dared to question this man without my leave—"

"It was a suspicious message, highness," says Ignatieff, dead level. "And this man was obviously a spy—"

"You bloody liar!" croaks I. "You knew damned well what I was! Don't listen to him, Lakshmi—highness—the swine's got it in for me! He was trying to murder me, out of spite!"

She gave me one look, and then fronted Ignatieff again. "Spy or not, it is I who rule here. Sometimes I think you forget it,

Count Ignatieff." She faced him eye to eye for a long moment, and then turned away from him. She looked at me, and then away, and we all waited, in dead silence. Finally she said quietly:

"I shall see to this man, and decide what is to be done with him." She turned to Ignatieff. "You may go, Count."

He bowed, and said: "I regret if I have offended your highness. If I have done so, it was out of zeal for the cause we both serve— your highness's government—" he paused— "and my imperial master's. I would be failing in my duty to both if I did not remind you that this man is a most dangerous and notorious British agent, and that—"

"I know very well who and what he is," says she quietly, and at that the gotch-eyed son-of-a-bitch said no more, but bowed again and took himself off, with the two troopers sidling hastily after him, salaaming nervously as they passed her. They clattered up the steps behind Ignatieff, and Sher Khan closed the door after them, and that left the four of us, all cosy as ninepence— Lakshmibai standing like a glimmering white statue, the little chamberlain twitching in anxious silence, Sher Khan on the door, and H. Flashman, Esq., doing his celebrated imitation of a Protestant martyr. Damned uncomfortable, too, but something told me grateful babblement wouldn't be in order, so I said as steadily as I could:

"Thank you, your highness. Forgive me if I don't make my bow, but in the circumstances . . ."

Very gallant, you see, but the truth was that fiery pains were still shooting through my arms and legs, and it was all I could do to keep from gasping and groaning. She was standing looking at me, quite expressionless, so I added hopefully:

"If your *havildar* would release me . . ."

But she didn't move a muscle, and I felt a sudden thrill of unease under the steady gaze of those dark eyes, the whites so clear against her dusky skin. What the hell was she up to, keeping me strung up on this bloody machine, and not so much as a glimmer of a smile, or recognition even? I palpitated while she stood, watching me and thinking, and then she came up within a yard of me, and spoke, in a flat hard voice.

"What did he want to know from you?"

The tone took my breath away, but I held my head up. "He wanted to know my business with your highness."

Her glance went to the chains on my wrists, then back to my face.

"And did you tell him?"

"Of course not." I thought a brave smile mightn't be out of place, so I tried one. "I like people to ask me questions—politely."

She turned her head towards the little chamberlain.

"Is this true?"

He puffed and flapped his arms, all eagerness. "Indeed, exalted highness! Not a word did the colonel sahib say—not even under the cruel torture! He did not even cry out—much . . . oh, he is an officer sahib, of course, and—"

Poor little bastard was hoping to butter his bread on the right side, of course, but I wasn't sure he was backing a winner here; she was still looking at me as if I was some carcase on a butcher's slab. The chilling thought struck me that it probably wasn't the first time she'd contemplated some poor devil in my situation . . . God, perhaps even Murray . . . and then she turned her head and called to Sher Khan, and he came tumbling down the steps double quick, while the sweat broke out on me. Surely she wasn't going to order him to—

"Release him," says she, and I near fainted with relief. She watched impassively while he unclamped me, and I took a few staggering and damned painful steps, catching at that hellish wheel for support. Then:

"Bring him," says she curtly. "I shall question him myself," and without another word she turned and walked up the steps, out of the dungeon, with the little chamberlain bobbing nervously behind her, and Sher Khan spitting and grunting as he assisted me to follow.

"Speak well of me to her highness, *husoor*," he muttered as he gave me a shoulder. "If I blundered in giving thy *kitab* to the Ruski sahib, did I not make amends? I went for her, when I saw he meant to ill-use thee . . . I had not recognised thee, God knows—"

I reassured him—he could have had a knighthood and the town hall clock for my part—as he conducted me up through the guard-room to a little spiral stair, and then along a great stone passage of the fort, which gave way to a carpeted corridor where sentries of her guard stood in their steel caps and backs-and-breasts. I limped along, relieved to find that apart from a few painfully-pulled muscles and badly skinned wrists and ankles, I wasn't much the worse . . . yet, and then Sher Khan was ushering me through a door, and I found myself in a smaller version of the durbar-room at the palace—a long, low richly-furnished apartment, all in white, with a quilted carpet, and silk hangings on the walls, divans and cushions and glowing Persian pictures, and even a great silver cage in which tiny birds cheeped and fluttered. The air was heavy with perfume, but I still hadn't got the stink of fear out of my nostrils, and the sight of Lakshmibai waiting did nothing to cheer me up.

She was sitting on a low backless couch, listening to the little chamberlain, who was whispering fifteen to the dozen, but at sight of me she stopped him. There were two of her ladies with her, and the whole group just looked at me, the women curiously, and Lakshmibai with the same damned disinheriting stare she'd used in the dungeon.

"Set him there," says she to Sher Khan, pointing to the middle of the floor, "and tie his hands behind him." He jumped to it, wrenching the knots with no thought for my flayed wrists. "He will be safe enough so," she added to the little chamberlain. "Go, all of you—and Sher Khan will remain beyond the door within call."

Dear God, was she going to set about me herself, I wondered, as the ladies swiftly rustled out, and the chamberlain hurried by, eyeing me apprehensively. I heard Sher Khan withdraw, and the door close, leaving me standing and her sitting erect, staring at me—and then to my amazement she sprang from the seat and was flying across the room towards me, with her arms out and her face trembling, throwing herself against me, clinging to me, and sobbing:

"Oh, my darling one, my darling, my darling! You have come back—oh, I thought I should never see you again!" And her arms were round my neck, and that lovely dark face, all wet with tears was upturned to mine, and she was kissing me any old how,

on the cheeks and chin and eyes and mouth, sobbing out endearments and shuddering against me.

I'm an easy-going chap, as you know, and can take things
pretty well as they come, but I'll admit that I wondered if I was
mad or dreaming. Not much above two hours ago I'd been in
Rose's tent in the safety of British lines, gulping down a last
brandy and trying to read the advertisements in an old copy of
The Times to take my mind off the ordeal ahead, with young
Lyster humming a popular song—and since then I'd taken part
in a cavalry skirmish, and skulked through a hostile nigger city in
disguise, and been scared out of my senses by that fiend Ignatieff's
appearance, and stretched on a rack in fearful physical and even
worse mental agony, and been rescued at the last minute and
dragged and bound in the presence of a female despot—and here
she was clinging and weeping and slobbering over me as though
I were Little Willie the Collier's Dying Child. It was all a shade
more than enough for my poor bemused brain, and body, and I
just sank to my knees under the weight of it all, and she sank
with me, crying and kissing.

"Oh, my sweet, have they hurt you? I thought I should swoon
when I saw—ah, your poor flesh!" Before I knew it she was down
at my legs, soothing my scraped ankles with one hand while she
kept the other behind my head, and kissed me long and linger-
ingly on the mouth. My amazement was giving way to the most
wonderful mixture of relief and joy, and pure ecstatic pleasure in
that scented dark skin pressed against my face, her open mouth
trembling on mine. I could feel her breasts hard against me—and,
dammit, my hands were tied, and I could only strain against her
until she freed her lips and looked at me, holding my face between
her hands.

"Oh, Lucky—lucky Lakshmi!" I was babbling out of sheer
delight. "Oh, you wonderful, beautiful creature!"

"I thought you were dead," says she, cradling my head down
against her bosom—by George, that was the place to be, and I
struggled my hands desperately to try to free them. "All these
months I have mourned you—ever since that dreadful day when
they found the dead dacoits near the pavilion, and I thought . . ."
She gave a little sob and pulled up my face to kiss me again. "And

you are safe, and back again with me . . . my darling." The great eyes were brimming with tears again. "Ah, I so love you!"

Well, I'd heard it before, of course, expressed with varying degrees of passion by countless females, and it's always gratifying, but I couldn't recall a moment when it had been more welcome than now. If ever I needed a woman to be deeply affected with my manly charms, this was the moment, and being half in love with her myself it required no effort at all to play up and make the most of it. So I put my mouth on hers again, and used my weight to bear her down on the cushions—damned difficult with my hands bound, but she was all for it, and lay there drinking me in, teasing with her tongue and stroking my face gently with her fingertips until I thought I'd burst.

"Lakshmi, *chabeli*—untie my hands!" I croaked, and she disengaged herself, glancing towards the door and then smiling at me longingly.

"I cannot . . . not now. You see, no one must know . . . yet. To them, you are a prisoner—a spy sent by the British soldiers . . .'

"I can explain all that! I had to come secretly, in disguise, to bring you a message from General Rose. Lakshmi, dearest, you've got to accept it—it's an offer of life! Please, untie me and let me tell you!"

"Wait," says she. "Come, sit here." And she helped me up, pausing on the way to fondle me again and kiss me before seating me on the edge of a divan. "It is best for the moment that we leave you bound—oh, beloved, it will not be for long, I promise . . . but in case someone comes suddenly. See, I shall get you a drink—you must be parched—ah, and your poor wrists, so cruelly torn!" The tears welled up again, and then such a look of blazing hatred passed across her face that I shrank where I sat. "That beast of Russia!" says she, clenching her tiny fist. "He will pay for it—I will have him drawn apart, and make him eat that hideous eye of his! And the Tsar his master may go straight to hell, and look for him!"

Excellent sentiments, I thought, and while she filled a goblet with sherbet I thought I'd improve the shining hour.

"It was Ignatieff who set the Thugs on me that night—he's

been dogging me ever since I came to India, spying and trying to stir up rebellion . . ."

I suddenly stopped there; she, after all, was now one of the leaders of that rebellion, and obviously Ignatieff was her ally, whatever her personal feelings towards him. She put the cup to my lips, and I drank greedily—being put on the rack's the way to raise a thirst, you know—and when I'd finished she stood up, with the cup between her hands, looking down at me.

"If I had only listened to you," says she. "If there had only been more time! I did not know . . . if only I could make you understand—all the years of waiting, and trying to right injustice to . . . to me, and my son, and my Jhansi . . ."

"How is the young fella, by the way? Well, eh, and thriving— fine lad, that . . ."

". . . and waiting turns to despair and despair to hatred, and I thought you were another cold and unfeeling creature of the Sirkar—and yet . . ." she suddenly knelt down in front of me, and caught my hands, and there was a look in her great almond eyes that made even my experienced old heart skip a beat ". . . and yet, I knew that you were not like the others. You were gentle, and kind, and you seemed to understand. And then . . . that day when we fenced, in the durbar room . . . I felt something inside me that—that I had not known before. And later . . ."

"In the pavilion," says I, hoarsely. "Oh, Lakshmi, that was the most wonderful moment in my life! Really capital, don't ye know . . . beat everything . . . darling, couldn't you untie my hands a second . . . ?"

Just for an instant there was a strange, distant look in her eyes, and then she turned her head away, and her hands tightened on mine.

". . . and when you disappeared, and I thought you dead, there was such an emptiness." She was trying not to cry. "And nothing else seemed to matter—not I, or Jhansi, even. And then came news of the red wind, sweeping through the British garrisons in the north—and even here, in my own state, they killed them all, and I was helpless." She was biting her lip, staring pleadingly at me, and if she'd been before the House of Lords the old goats would have been roaring "Not guilty, on my honour!" with

three times three. "And what could I do? It seemed that the Raj—
and I hated the Raj!—was falling, and my own cousin, Nana,
was raising the standard of revolt, and to stand idle was to lose
Jhansi, to the jackals of Orcha or Gwalior, or even to the sepoys
themselves ... oh, but you are British, and you cannot understand!"

"Dearest," says I, "you don't have to excuse yourself to me, of
all people. What else could you do?" It wasn't an idle question,
either; the only treason is to pick the wrong side, which, in the
long run, she had done. "But it doesn't matter, you see—that's
why I'm here! It can all come right again—at least, you can be
saved, and that's what counts."

She looked at me and said simply: "I do not care, now that you
have come back." And she leaned forward and kissed me again,
gently, on the lips.

"You must care," says I. "See here—I've come from General
Rose, and what he says comes straight from Lord Canning in
Calcutta. They want to save you, my dear, if you'll let them."

"They want me to surrender," says she, and stood up. She
walked away to set the cup down on a table, and the sight of the
tight-wrapped sari stirring over those splendid hips set my fingers
working feverishly at the knots behind my back. She turned,
with her bosom going up like balloons, and her face was set and
sad. "They want me to give up my Jhansi."

"Darling—it's lost anyway. Any day now they'll storm the
walls, and that's the end. You know it—and so must your
advisers. Even Ignatieff—what the devil's he doing here, anyhow?"

"He has been here—and at Meerut and Delhi—everywhere,
since the beginning. Promising Russian help—making rebellion,
as you say, on his master's behalf." She made a little helpless
gesture. "I do not know ... there has been talk of a Russian army
over the Khyber—some would welcome it; myself ... I fear it—
but it does not matter, now. He remains, I suppose, as long as he
may do your government some harm ... if Jhansi falls, he will go
to Tantia or Nana." And she added, with a shrugged afterthought
that somehow prickled my spine. "Unless I have him killed, for
what he has done to you."

All in good time, thinks I, happily, and got back to the matter in hand.

"But it isn't Jhansi they want—it's you." She opened her eyes at that, and I hurried on. "They can't make terms with rebels— why, half your garrison must be pandies, with nothing to hope for; there's no pardon for them, you see. So they'll storm the city, whatever you do. But they want to save you alive—if you will give yourself up, alone, then . . . then they won't—" I couldn't meet her eye, though "—punish you."

"Why should they spare me?" For a minute the fire was back in her eye. "Who else have they spared? Why should they want to keep me alive—when they blow men away from guns, and hang them without trial, and burn whole cities? Will they spare Nana or Tantia or Azeemoolah—then why the Rani of Jhansi?"

It wasn't an easy one to answer—not truthfully, anyway. She wouldn't take it too kindly if I said it was just politics, to keep the public happy.

"Does it matter?" says I. "Whatever their reasons . . ."

"Is it because I am a woman?" She said it softly, and came to stand in front of me. "And the British do not make war on women." She looked steadily at me for several seconds. "Is it because I am beautiful? And do they wish to take me to London, as the Romans did with their captives, and show me as a spectacle to the people—"

"That ain't our style," says I, pretty sharp. "Of course, we don't make war on women . . . and, well, you see, you're—well, you're different—"

"To them? To Lord Canning? To General Rose? They do not know me. Why should they care? Why should any of you . . ." And then she stopped, and dropped to her knees again, and her lip was trembling. "You? Have you spoken—for me? You came from Lord Palmerston—have you asked them to save me?"

By George, here was an unexpected ball at my foot, with a vengeance. It hadn't crossed my mind that she'd think I was behind Rose's remarkable offer. But when the chance arises, I hope I know how to grasp it as well as the next man—carefully. So I looked at her, steady and pretty grim, and made myself go red in the face, and then looked down at the carpet, all dumb and noble and unspoken emotion. She put out a hand and lifted my chin, and she was absolutely frowning at me.

"Did you—and have you risked so much, to come here—for me? Tell me."

"You know what I think about you," says I, trying to look romantically stuffed. "I've loved you since the moment I clapped eyes on you—on that swing. More than anything else in the world."

At that moment, mind you, it wasn't all gammon. I did love her—pretty well, anyway, just then. Not as much as Elspeth, I dare say—although, mind you, put 'em together, side by side, both stripped down, and you'd think hard before putting England in to bat. Anyway, I'd no difficulty in looking sincere—not with that flimsy bodice heaving almost under my nose.

She looked at me in silence, with strange, grave eyes, and then said, almost in a whisper:

"Tonight—I did not think . . . I only knew that you were here with me again—when I had thought you lost. It did not matter to me, whether you loved me truly or not—only that you were with me again. But now . . ." she was looking at me in the strangest way, sorrowfully almost, and with a kind of perplexity ". . . now that you tell me that it was . . . for love of me, that you have done this . . ." I wondered if she was going to fling herself on me again in tears, but after a moment she just kissed me, quite gently, and then said:

"What do they wish me to do?"

"To surrender, yourself. No more than that."

"But how? If the city is to be taken, and there is no pardon for the mutineers, how can I—"

"Don't fret about that," says I. "It can all be arranged. If I tell you how—will you do it?"

"If you will stay with me—afterwards." Her eyes were fixed on mine, soft but steady. "I will do whatever they ask."

Persuasively urged, Rose had said, but I'll bet he'd never envisaged the likes of this—by George, his randy staff men wouldn't have been able to believe their eyes.

"When the city is stormed," says I, "our fellows will fight their way in to the fortress. You must be ready to make an escape—

through the Orcha Gate. We'll have drawn off our cavalry picket just there, so it can be done in safety. You must ride out on the Orcha road—and then, you will be captured. It will look as though . . . well, it will look all right."

"I see." She nodded gravely. "And the city?"

"Well, it'll be taken, of course—but there'll be no looting—" Rose had promised that, for what it was worth "—and of course, the people will be all right, provided they lie low and don't resist. The mutineers . . . well, it'll all be the same for them, anyway."

"And what will they do . . . with me? Will they . . . imprison me?"

I wasn't sure about this, and had to go careful. They'd exile her for certain, at least to a distant part of India where she could do no harm, but there was no point in telling her that. "No," says I. "They'll treat you very well, you'll see. And then—it'll all blow over, don't you know? Why, I can think of a score of nig—native chieftains and kings, who've been daggers drawn with us, but their wars have got by, and then we've been the best of friends, and so forth. No hard feelings, you see—we ain't vindictive, even the Liberals . . ."

I was smiling to reassure her, and after a while she began smiling back, and gave a great sigh, and settled against me, seemingly content, and I suggested again that it might be a capital notion to unslip my hands, just for a moment—I was most monstrously horny with her nestling up against me—but at this she shook her head, and said we had delayed already, and must not excite suspicion. She kissed me a lingering good-bye, and told me to be patient a little longer; we must bide our time according to Rose's plan, and since her people must have no inkling of it I would have to be treated as a prisoner, but she would send for me when the time was ripe.

"And then we shall go together . . . with only a trusted few?" She held my face in her hands, looking down at me. "And you will . . . protect me, and love me . . . when we come to the Sir-kar?"

Till you're blue in the face, you darling houri, thinks I—but for answer all I did was kiss her hands. Then she straightened her veil, and fussed anxiously with her mirror before seating herself on her divan, and it was the charmingest thing to see her give me a last radiant smile and then compose her face in that icy mask, while I waited suitably hang-dog, standing in the middle of the floor at a respectful distance. She struck her little gong, which brought Sher Khan in like the village fire brigade, with chamberlain and ladies behind him.

"Confine this prisoner in the north tower," says she, as if I were so much dross. "He is not to be harshly used, but keep him close—your head on it, Sher Khan."

I was bustled away forthwith—but it's my guess that Sher Khan, with that leery Pathan nose of his, guessed that all was not quite what it seemed, for he was a most solicitous jailer in the days that followed. He kept me well provisioned, bringing all my food and drink himself, seeing to it that I was comfortable as my little cell permitted, and showing me every sign of respect—mind you, in view of my Afghan reputation, that might have been natural enough.

It took me a few hours to settle down after what I had been through, but when I came to cast up the score it looked none so bad. Bar my aching joints and skinned limbs, I was well enough, and damned thankful for it. As to the future—well, I'd thought Rose's plan was just moonshine, but then I'd never dreamed that Lakshmibai was infatuated with me. Attracted, well enough—it's an odd woman that ain't, but the force of her passion had been bewildering. And yet, why not? I'd known it happen before, after all, and often as not with the same kind of woman—the high-born, pampered kind who go through their young lives surrounded by men who are forever deferring and toadying, so that when a real plunger like myself comes along, and treats 'em easy, like women and not as queens, they're taken all aback. It's something new to them to have a big likely chap who ain't abashed by their grandeur, but looks 'em over with a warm eye, perfectly respectful but daring them just the same. They resent it, and like it, too, and if you can just tempt them into bed and show them what they've been missing—why, the next thing you know they're head over heels in love with you.

That's how it had been with Duchess Irma, and that wild black bitch Ranavalona in Madagascar (though she was so stark crazy it was difficult to be sure), so why not the Rani of Jhansi? After all, her only husband had been as fishy as Dick's hatband, by all accounts, and however many young stalwarts she'd whistled up since then, they wouldn't have my style. Well, it was a damned handy stroke of luck—as well as being most flattering.

As to the surrender—well, she wasn't a fool. Here was a way out for her, with more credit and safety than she could have expected, under the wing of the adored Flashy, who she imagined would protect and cherish her happy ever after. I was all for that —for a few months, anyway, which was more than most females could expect from me. Mark you, I was famously taken with her (I still am, somehow) but I guessed I'd cool after a spell. Couldn't take her home, anyway—she'd just have to reconcile herself to waving me good-bye when the time came, like all the others.

In the meantime, I could only wait, in some excitement, for Rose to mount his assault. When a tremendous cannonading in the city broke out on the following day, with native pipes and drums squealing and thundering, I thought the attack had begun, but it was a false alarm, as Sher Khan informed me later. It seemed that Tantia Tope had suddenly hove in sight with a rebel army twenty thousand strong, to try to relieve Jhansi; Rose, cool as a trout as usual, had left his heavy artillery and cavalry to continue the siege, and had turned with the rest of his force and thrashed Tantia handsomely on the Betwa river, a few miles away. At the same time he'd ordered a diversionary attack on Jhansi to keep the defenders from sallying out to help Tantia; that had been the noise I'd heard.[45]

"So much for our stout-hearted mutineers in Jhansi," sneers Sher Khan. "If they had sallied out, your army might have been caught like a nut between two stones, but they contented themselves with howling and burning powder." He spat. "Let the Sirkar eat them, and welcome."

I reminded him he was on the rebel side, and that it would be short shrift for mutineers when Jhansi fell.

"I am no mutineer," says he, "but a paid soldier of the Rani. I have eaten her salt and fight for her like the Yusufzai I am— even as I fought for the Sirkar in the Guides. The sahibs know the difference between a rebel and a soldier who keeps faith; they will treat me with honour—if I live," he added carelessly. He was another Ilderim, in his way—shorter and uglier, with a smashed nose and pocked face, but a slap-up Pathan Khyberie, every inch.

"With any luck they will have hanged thy Ruski friend by now," he went on, grinning. "He rode out to join Tantia in the night, and has not returned. Is that good news, Iflass-man *husoor?*"

Wasn't it just, though? Of course, Ignatieff would have been daft to stay in Jhansi—we'd have hanged him high enough for the foreign spy he was. He'd be off to assist the leading rebels in the field; I felt all the better for knowing he was out of distance, but I doubted if he'd allow himself to be killed or taken—he was too downy a bird for that.

With Tantia whipped, it seemed to me Rose would lose no further time assaulting Jhansi, but another day and night passed in which I waited and fretted, and still there was nothing but the distant thump of cannon-fire to disturb my cell. It wasn't till the third night that the deuce of a bombardment broke out, in the small hours, and lasted until almost dawn, and then I heard what I'd been waiting for—the crash of volley-firing that signified British infantry, and the sound of explosions within the town itself, and even distant bugle calls.

"They are in the city," says Sher Khan, when he brought my breakfast. "The mutineers are fighting better than I thought, and it is hot work in the streets, they say." He grinned cheerfully and tapped the hilt of his Khyber knife. "Will her highness order me to cut thy throat when the last attack goes home, think ye? Eat well, *husoor,*" and the brute swaggered out, chuckling.

Plainly she hadn't confided her intentions to him. I guessed she'd wait for nightfall and then make her run; by that time our fellows would be thumping at the gates of the fort itself. So I contained myself, listened to the crackle of firing and explosion, drawing always nearer, until by nightfall it seemed to be only a few hundred yards off—I was chewing my nails by then, I may tell you. But the dark came, and still the sound of battle went on, and I could even hear what I thought were English voices shouting in the distance, among the yells and shrieks. Through the one high window of my cell the night-sky was glaring red—Jhansi was dying hard, by the look of it.

I don't know what time it was when I heard the sudden rattle of the bolt in my cell-door, and Sher Khan and two of his guardsmen came in, carrying torches. They didn't stand on ceremony, but hustled me out, and down narrow stone stairs and passages to a little courtyard. The moon wasn't up yet, but it was light enough, with the red glare above the walls, and the air was heavy with powder-smoke and the drift of burning; the crashing of musketry was close outside the fort now.

The yard seemed to be full of red-coated troopers of the Rani's guard, and over by a narrow gateway I saw a slim figure mounted on a white horse which I recognised at once as Lakshmibai. There were mounted guardsmen with her, and a couple of her ladies, also mounted, and heavily veiled; one of the mounted men had a child perched on his saddle-bow: Damodar, her stepson. I was about to call out, but to my astonishment Sher Kahn suddenly stooped beside me, there was a metallic snap, and he had a fetter clasped round my left leg. Before I could even protest, he was thrusting me towards a horse, snarling: "Up, husoor!" and I was no sooner in the saddle than he had passed a short chain from my fetter under the beast's belly, and secured my other ankle, so that I was effectively shackled to the pony.

"What the hell's this?" I cried, and he chuckled as he swung aboard a horse beside me.

"Heavy spurs, husoor!" says he. "Peace!—it is by her order, and doubtless for your own safety. Follow!" And he shook my bridle, urging me across the square; the little party by the gate were already passing out of sight, and a moment later we were riding single file down a steep alleyway, with towering walls either side, Sher Khan just ahead of me and another Pathan immediately behind.

I couldn't think what to make of this, until it dawned on me that she wouldn't have let her entourage into the whole secret— they would know she was escaping, but not that she intended to give herself up to the British. So for form's sake I must appear to be a prisoner still. I wished she'd given me the chance of a secret word beforehand, though, and let me ride with her; I didn't want us blundering into the besieging cavalry in the dark, and perhaps being mistaken.

However, there was nothing for it now but to carry on. Our little cavalcade clattered down the alleyways, twisting and turning, and then into a broader street, where a house was burning, but there wasn't a soul to be seen, and the sound of firing was receding behind us. Once we'd passed the fire it was damned dark among the rickety buildings, until there were torches and a high gateway, and more of her guardsmen in the entry-way; I saw her white horse stop as she leaned from the saddle to consult with the guard-commander, and waited with my heart in my mouth until he stepped back, saluting, and barked an order. Two of his men threw open a wicket in the main gate, and a moment later we were filing through, and I knew we were coming out on to the Orcha road.

It was blacker than hell in November under the lee of the great gateway, but half a mile ahead there was the twinkling line of our picket-fires, and flashes of gunfire as the artillery pieces joined in the bombardment of the city. Sher Khan had my bridle in his fist as we moved forward at a walk, and then at a slow trot; it was easy going on the broad road surface at first, but then the dim figures of the riders ahead seemed to be veering away to the right, and as we followed my horse stumbled on rough ground—we were leaving the road for the flat maidan, and I felt the first prickle of doubt in my mind. Why were we turning aside? The path to safety lay straight along the road, where Rose's pickets would be waiting—she knew that, even if her riders didn't. Didn't she realise we were going astray—that on this tack we would probably blunder into pickets that weren't expecting us? The time for pretence was past, anyhow—it was high time I was up with her, taking a hand, or God knew where we would land. But even as I stiffened in my saddle to shove my heels in and forge ahead, Sher Khan's hand leaped from my wrist to my bridle, there was a zeep of steel, and the Khyber knife was pricking my ribs with his voice hissing out of the dark:

"One word, Bloody Lance—one word, and you'll say the next one to Shaitan!"

The shock of it knocked my wits endways—but only for a

moment. There's nothing like eighteen inches of razor-edged steel
for turning a growing doubt into a stone-ginger certainty, and
before we'd gone another five paces I had sprung to the most
terrifying conclusion—she was escaping, right enough, but not
the way Rose and I had planned it—she was using the information
I'd given her, but in her own way! It rushed in on me in a mad
whirl of thoughts—all her protestations, her slobbering over me,
those tear-filled eyes, the lips on mine, the passionate endearments—all false? They couldn't be, in God's name! Why, she'd
been all over me, like a crazy schoolgirl . . . but now we were
pacing still faster in the wrong direction, the knife was scoring
my side, and suddenly there was a shouted challenge ahead, and
a cry, the riders were spurring forward, a musket cracked, and
Sher Khan roared in my ear:

"Ride, *feringhee*—and ride straight, or I'll split your back-
bone!"

He slashed his reins at my pony, it bounded forward, and in a
second I was flying along in the dark, willy-nilly, with him at my
elbow and the thundering shadows surging ahead. There was a
fusilade of shots, off to the left, and a ball whined overhead; as I
loosed the reins, trusting to my pony's feet, I saw the picket-fires
only a few hundred yards off. We were racing towards a gap
between one fire and the next, perhaps two furlongs across; all I
could do was career ahead, with Sher Khan and a Pathan either
side of me—I couldn't roll from the saddle, even if I'd dared,
with that infernal chain beneath my horse's belly; I daren't
swerve, or his knife would be in my back; I could only gallop,
cursing in sick bewilderment, praying to God I wouldn't stop a
blade or a bullet. Where the hell were we going—was it some
ghastly error after all? No, it was treachery, and I knew it—and
now the picket-fires were on our flanks, there were more shots, a
horse screamed ahead of us, and my pony swerved past the dim
struggling mass on the ground, with Sher Khan still knee to knee
with me as we sped on. A trumpet was sounding behind, and
faint voices yelling; ahead was the drumming of hooves and the
dim shapes of the Rani's riders, scattered now as they galloped for
their lives. We were clear through, and every stride was taking us
farther from Jhansi and Rose's army, and safety.

How long we kept up that breakneck pace I don't know, or what direction we took—I'd been through too much, my mind was just a welter of fear and bewilderment and rage and stark disbelief. I didn't know what to think—she couldn't have sold me so cruelly, surely—not after what she'd said, and the way she'd held my face and looked at me? But I knew she had—my disbelief was just sheer hurt vanity. God, did I think I was the only sincere liar in the world? And here I was, humbugged to hell and beyond, being kidnapped in the train of this deceitful rebel bitch—or was I wrong, was there some explanation after all? That's what I still wanted to believe, of course—there's nothing like infatuation for stoking false hope.

However, there's no point in recounting all the idiot arguments I had with myself on that wild ride through the night, with the miles flying by unseen, until the gloom began to lighten, the scrub-dotted plain came into misty view, and Sher Khan still clung like a bearded ghost at my elbow, his teeth bared as he crouched over his pony's mane. The riders ahead were still driving their tired beasts on at full stretch; about a hundred yards in front I could see Lakshmibai's slim figure on her white mare, with the Pathans flanking her. It was like a drunken nightmare—on and on, exhausting, over that endless plain.

There was a yell from the flank, and one of the Pathans up in his stirrups, pointing. A shot cracked, I saw a sudden flash of scarlet to our left, and there was a little cloud of horsemen bursting out of a nullah—only half our numbers, but Company cavalry, by God! They were careering in to take our leaders in the flank, pukka light cavalry style, and I tried to yell, but Sher Khan had my bridle again, wrenching me away to the right, while the Pathan guardsmen drew their sabres and wheeled to face the attackers head on. I watched them meet with a chorus of yells and a clash of steel; the dust swirled up round them as Sher Khan and his mate herded me away, but half-slewed round in my saddle I saw the sabres swinging and the beasts swerving and plunging as the Company men tried to ride through. A Pathan broke from the press, shepherding away a second rider, and I saw it was one of the Rani's ladies—and then more figures were wheeling out of the dust, and one of them was Lakshmibai, with a mounted man bearing down on her, his sabre swung aloft. I heard Sher Khan's anguished yell as her white mare seemed to stumble, but she reined it up somehow, whirling in her tracks, there was the glitter of steel in her hand, and as the Company man swept down on her she lunged over her beast's head—the sabres clashed and rang, and he was past her, wheeling away, clutching at his arm as he half-slipped from his saddle.[46]

That was all I saw before Sher Khan and the other herded me down a little nullah, where we halted and waited while the noise of the skirmish gradually died away. I knew what was happening as well as if I was seeing it—the Company riders, out-sabred, would be drawing off, and sure enough presently the Pathans came down the nullah in good order, clustered round Damodar and the Rani's women; among the last to come was Lakshmibai.

It was the first clear look at her that I'd had in all that fearful escape. She was wearing a mail jacket under her long cloak, with a mail cap over her turban, and her sabre was still in her hand, blood on its blade. She stopped a moment by the rider who carried Damodar, and spoke to the child; then she laughed and said something to one of the Pathans and handed him her sabre, while she wiped her face with a handkerchief. Then she looked towards me, and the others looked with her, in silence.

As you know, I'm a fairly useful hand on social occasions, ready with the polite phrase or gesture, but I'll confess that in that moment I couldn't think of anything appropriate to say. When you've just been betrayed by an Indian queen who has previously professed undying love for you, and she confronts you —having just sabred one of your countrymen, possibly to death— and you are in the grip of her minions, with your feet chained under your horse . . . well, the etiquette probably takes some thinking about. I suppose I'd have come out with something in a minute or two—an oath, or a squeal for mercy, or a polite inquiry, perhaps, but before I had the chance she was addressing Sher Khan.

"You will take him to Gwalior." Her voice was quiet and perfectly composed. "Hold him there until I send for you. At the last, he will be my bargain."

You may say it served me right, and I can't disagree. If I weren't such a susceptible, trusting chap where pretty women are concerned, I daresay I'd have smelled a rat on the night when Lakshmibai rescued me from Ignatieff's rack and then flung herself all over me in her perfumed lair. A less warm-blooded fellow might have thought the lady was protesting rather too much, and been on his guard when she slobbered fondly over him, vowing undying love and accepting his proposal for her escape. He might—or again, he mightn't.

For myself, I can only say I had no earthly reason to suppose her false. After all, our last previous meeting had been that monumental roll in her pavilion, which had left me with the impression that she wasn't entirely indifferent to me. Secondly, her acceptance of Rose's proposal seemed natural and sensible. Thirdly, I'll admit to being enthralled by her, and fourthly, having just finished a spell on the rack I was perhaps thinking less clearly than usual. Finally, m'lud, if you'd been confronted by Lakshmibai, with that beautiful dusky face looking pleadingly up at you, and those tits quivering under your nose, I submit that you might have been taken in yourself, and glad of it.

In any event, it didn't make a ha'porth of difference. Even if I'd suspected her then, I was in her power, and she could have wrung all the details of Rose's scheme out of me and made her escape anyway. I'd have been dragged along at her tail, and finished up in the Gwalior dungeons just the same. And mind you, I'm still not certain how far she *was* humbugging me; all I know is that if she was play-acting, she seemed to be enjoying her work.

More than I enjoyed Gwalior, at any rate. That's a fearful place, a huge, rocky fortress of a city, bigger than Jhansi, and said to be the most powerful hold in India. I can speak with authority only about its dungeons, which were a shade worse than a Mexican jail, if you can imagine that. I spent the better part of two months in them, cooped in a bottle-shaped cell with my own filth and only rats, fleas and cockroaches for company, except when Sher Khan came to have a look at me, about once a week, to make sure I hadn't up and died on him.

He and his fellow-Pathan took me there on Lakshmibai's orders, and it was one of the most punishing rides I've ever endured. I was almost unconscious in the saddle by the time we reached it, for the brutes never took my chain off once in the hundred miles we covered; I think, too, that my spirit had endured more than I could stand, for after all I'd gone through there were moments now when I no longer cared whether I lived or died—and I have to be pretty far down before that happens. When they brought me to Gwalior by night, and half-carried me into the fortress, and dropped me into that stinking, ill-lit cell, I just lay and sobbed like an infant, babbling aloud about Meerut and Cawnpore and Lucknow and Thugs and crocodiles and evil bitches—and now this. Would you believe it, the worst was yet to come?

I don't care to dwell on it, so I'll hurry along. While I was in that dungeon at Gwalior, waiting for I didn't know what, and half-believing that I'd rot there forever, or go mad first, the final innings of the Mutiny was being played out. Campbell was settling things north of the Jumnah, and Rose, having captured Jhansi, was pushing north after Tantia Tope and my ministering angel, Lakshmibai, who'd taken the field with him. He beat them at Calpee and Kanch, driving them towards Gwalior where I was enjoying the local hospitality. The odd thing was, that at the time I was incarcerated there, Gwalior's ruler, Maharaja Scindia, had remained neutral in the rebellion, and had no business to be allowing his prison to be used for the accommodation of captured British officers. In fact, of course, he (or his chief advisers) were sympathetic to the rebels all along, as was proved in the end. For after their defeat at Calpee, Tantia and Lakshmibai turned to Gwalior, and the Maharaja's army went over to them, almost without firing a shot. So there they were, the last great rebel force in India, in possession of India's greatest stronghold—and with Rose closing inexorably in on them.

I knew nothing of all this, of course; mouldering in my cell, with my beard sprouting and my hair matting, and my pandy uniform foul and stinking (for I'd never had it off since I put it on in Rose's camp), I might as well have been at the North Pole. Day followed day, and week followed week without a cheep from the outside world, for Sher Khan hardly said a word to me, although I raved and pleaded with him whenever he poked his face through the trap into my cell. That's the worst of that kind of imprisonment—not knowing, and losing count of the days, and wondering whether you've been there a month or a year, and whether there is really a world outside at all, and doubting if you ever did more than dream that you were once a boy playing in the fields at Rugby, or a man who'd walked in the Park, or ridden by Albert Gate, saluting the ladies, or played billiards, or followed hounds, or gone up the Mississippi in a side-wheeler, or watched the moon rise over Kuching River, or—you can wonder if *any* of it ever existed, or if these greasy black walls are perhaps the only world that ever was, or will be . . . that's when you start to go mad, unless you can find something to think about that you *know* is real.

I've heard of chaps who kept themselves sane in solitary confinement by singing all the hymns they knew, or proving the propositions of Euclid, or reciting poetry. Each to his taste: I'm no hand at religion, or geometry, and the only repeatable poem I can remember is an Ode of Horace which Arnold made me learn as a punishment for farting at prayers. So instead I compiled a mental list of all the women I'd had in my life, from that sweaty kitchen-maid in Leicestershire when I was fifteen, up to the half-caste piece I'd been reprimanded for at Cawnpore, and to my astonishment there were four hundred and seventy-eight of them, which seemed rather a lot, especially since I wasn't counting return engagements. It's astonishing, really, when you think how much time it must have taken up.

Perhaps because I'd been listing them I had a frightful dream one night in which I had to dance with all of them at a ball on the slave-deck of the Balliol College, with the demoniac Captain Spring conducting the music in a cocked hat and white gloves. They were all there—Lola Montez and Josette and Judy (my guvnor's mistress, she was), and the Silk One and Susie from New

Orleans and fat Baroness Pechmann and Nareeman the nautch, and all the others, and each one left her slave-fetters with me so that I must dance on loaded and clanking, crying out with exhaustion, but when I pleaded for rest Spring just rolled his eyes and made the music go faster, with the big drum booming. Elspeth and Palmerston waltzed by, and Pam gave me his false teeth and cried: "You'll need 'em for eating chapattis with your next partner, you know"—and it was Lakshmibai, naked and glitter-eyed over her veil, and she seized me and whirled me round the floor, almost dead with fatigue and the cruel weight of the chains, while the drum went boom-boom-boom faster and faster—and I was awake, gasping and clutching at my filthy straw with the sound of distant gunfire in my ears.

It went on all that day, and the next, but of course I couldn't tell what it meant or who was firing, and I was too done to care. All through the morning of the third day it continued, and then suddenly my trap was thrown open, and I was being dragged out by Sher Khan and another fellow, and I hardly knew where I was. When you're hauled out of a dead captivity like that, everything seems frighteningly loud and fast—I know there was a courtyard, full of nigger soldiers running about and shouting, and their pipes blaring, and the gunfire crashing louder than ever—but the shock of release was too much for me to make sense of it. I was half-blinded just by the light of the sky, although it was heavy with red and black monsoon clouds, and I remember thinking, it'll be capital growing weather soon.

It wasn't till they thrust me on a pony that I came to myself—instinct, I suppose, but when I felt the saddle under me, and the beast stirring, and the smell of horse in my nostrils and my feet in stirrups, I was awake again. I knew this was Gwalior fortress, with the massive gate towering in front of me, and a great gun being dragged through it by a squealing elephant, with a troop of red-coated nigger-prince's cavalry waiting to ride out, and a bedlam of men shouting orders: the din was still deafening, but as Sher Khan mounted his pony beside me I yelled:

"What's happening? Where are we going?"

"She wants you!" cries he, and grinned as he tapped his hilt. "So she shall have you. Come!"

He thrust a way for us through the crowd milling in the gateway, and I followed, still trying to drink in the sights and sounds of this madhouse that I had all but forgotten—men and carts and bullocks and dust and the clatter of arms: a *bhisti* running with his water-skin, a file of pandy infantry squatting by the roadside with their muskets between their knees, a child scrambling under a bullock's belly, a great-chested fellow in a spiked cap with a green banner on a pole over his shoulder, a spindly-legged old nigger shuffling along regardless of them all, the smell of cooking *ghee*, and through it all that muffled crash of cannon in the distance.

I stared ahead as we emerged from the gate, trying to understand what was happening. Gunfire—that meant that British troops were somewhere near, and the sight that met my eyes confirmed it. Before me there was miles of open plain, stretching to distant hills, and the plain was alive with men and animals and all the tackle of war. Perhaps a mile ahead, in the haze, there were tents, and the unmistakable ranks of infantry, and gun emplacements, and squadrons of horse on the move—a whole army stretched across a front of perhaps two miles. I steadied myself as Sher Khan urged me forward, trying to take it in—it was a rebel army, no error, for there were pandy formations moving back towards us, and native state infantry and riders in uniforms I didn't know, men in crimson robes with little shields and curved tulwars, and gun-teams with artillery pieces fantastically carved in the native fashion.

That was the first fact: the second was that they were retreating, and on the edge of rout. For the formations were moving towards us, and the road itself was choked with men and beasts and vehicles heading for Gwalior. A horse-artillery team was careering in, the gunners clinging to the limbers and their officer lashing at the beasts, a platoon of pandies was coming at the double-quick, their ranks ragged, their faces streaked with dust and sweat, and all along the road men were running or hobbling back, singly and in little groups: I'd seen the signs often enough, the gaping mouths, the wide eyes, the bloody bandages, the high-pitched voices, the half-ordered haste slipping into utter confusion, the abandoned muskets at the roadside, the exhausted men sitting or lying or crying out to those who passed by—this was

the first rush of a defeat, by gum! and Sher Khan was dragging
me into it.

"What the blazes is happening?" I asked him again, but all I
got was a snarl as he whipped my pony to a gallop, and we clattered down the roadside, he keeping just to rear of me, past the
mob of men and beasts streaming back to Gwalior. The formations
were closer now, and not all of them were retreating: we passed
artillery teams who were unlimbering and siting their guns, and
regiments of infantry waiting in the humid heat, their faces
turned towards the distant hills, their ranks stretched out in good
order across the plain. Not far in front artillery was thundering
away, with smoke wreathing up in the still air, and bodies of
cavalry, pandy and irregular, were waiting—I remember a squadron of lancers, in green coats, with lobster-tail helmets and long
ribbons trailing from their lance-heads, and a band of native
musicians, squealing and droning fit to drown the gunfire. But
less than half a mile ahead, where the dust-clouds were churning
up, and the flashes of cannon shone dully through the haze, I
knew what was happening—the army's vanguard was slowly
breaking, falling back on the main body, with the weaker vessels
absolutely flying down the road.

We crossed a deep nullah, and Sher Khan wheeled me off along
its far lip, towards a grove of palm and thorn, where tents were
pitched. A line of guns to my left was crashing away towards the
unseen enemy on the hills—enemy, by God, that was my army!—
and round the oasis of tents and trees there was a screen of horsemen. With a shock I recognised the long red coats of the Jhansi
royal guard, but for the rest they were only the ragged ghosts of
the burly Pathans I remembered, their uniforms torn and filthy,
their mounts lean and ungroomed. We passed through them, in
among the tents, to where a carpet was spread before the biggest
pavilion of all; there were guardsmen there, and a motley mob of
niggers, military and civilian, and then Sher Khan was pulling
me from the saddle, thrusting me forward, and crying out:

"He is here, highness—as you ordered."

She was in the doorway of the tent, alone—or perhaps I just
don't remember any others. She was sipping a glass of sherbet as
she turned to look at me, and believe it or not I was suddenly

conscious of the dreadful, scarecrow figure I cut, in my rags and unkempt hair. She was in her white jodhpurs, with a mail jacket over her blouse, and a white cloak; her head was covered by a cap of polished steel like a Roman soldier's, with a white scarf wound round it and under her chin. She looked damned elegant, I know, and even when you noticed the shadows on that perfect coffee-coloured face, beneath the great eyes, she was still a vision to take your breath away. She frowned at sight of me, and snapped at Sher Khan:

"What have you done to him?"

He mumbled something, but she shook her head impatiently and said it didn't matter. Then she looked at me again, thoughtfully, while I waited, wondering what the devil was coming, dimly aware that the volume of gunfire was increasing. Finally she said, simply:

"Your friends are over yonder," and indicated the hills. "You may go to them if you wish."

That was all, and for the life of me I couldn't think of anything to say. I suppose I was still bemused and in a shocked condition— otherwise I might have pointed out that there was a battle apparently raging between me and those friends of mine. But it all seemed unreal, and the word which I finally managed to croak out was: "Why?"

She frowned again at that, and then put her chin up and snapped her cloak with one hand and said quickly:

"Because it is finished, and it is the last thing I can do for you —colonel." I couldn't think when she'd last called me that. "Is that not enough? Your army will be in Gwalior by tomorrow. That is all."

It was at this moment that I heard shouting behind us, but I paid it no heed, not even when some fellow came running and calling to her, and she called something to him. I was wrestling with my memory, and it will give you some notion of how foundered I was when I tell you that I absolutely burst out:

"But you said I would be your bargain—didn't you?"

She looked puzzled, and then she smiled and said to Sher Khan: "Give the colonel sahib a horse", and was turning away, when I found my tongue.

"But . . . but you! Lakshmibai! I don't understand . . . what are you going to do?" She didn't answer, and I heard my own voice hoarse and harsh: "There's still time! I mean—if you . . . if you think it's finished—well, dammit, they ain't going to hang you, you know! I mean Lord Canning has promised . . . and-and General Rose!" Sher Khan was growling at my elbow, but I shook him off. "Look here, if I'm with you, it's sure to be all right. I'll tell 'em—"

God knows what else I said—I think I was out of my wits just then. Well, when the shot's flying I don't as a rule think of much but my own hide, and here I was absolutely arguing with the woman. Maybe the dungeon had turned my brain a trifle, for I babbled on about surrender and honourable terms while she just stood looking at me, and then she broke in:

"No—you do not understand. You did not understand when you came back to me at Jhansi. But it was for me you came—for my sake. And so I pay my debt at the end."

"Debt?" I shouted. "You're havering, woman! You said you loved me—oh, I know now you were tricking me, too, but . . . but don't it count for anything, then?"

Before she could answer there was a flurry of hooves, and some damned interfering scoundrel in an embroidered coat flung himself off his horse and started shouting at her; behind me there was a crackle of musketry, and shrieks and orders, and a faint trumpet note whispering beyond the cannon. She cried an order, and a groom hurried forward, pulling her little mare. I was roaring above the noise, at her, swearing I loved her and that she could still save herself, and she shot me a quick look as she took the mare's bridle—it was just for an instant, but it's stayed with me fifty years, and you may think me an old fool and fanciful, but I'll swear there were tears in her eyes—and then she was in the saddle, shouting, and the little mare reared and shot away, and I was left standing on the carpet.

Sher Khan had disappeared. I was staring and yelling after her, as her riders closed round her, for beyond them the gunners were racing towards us, with pandy riflemen in amongst them, turning and firing and running again. There were horsemen at the guns, and sabres flashing, and above the hellish din the trumpet was

blaring clear in the "Charge!" and over the limbers came blue
tunics and white helmets, and I couldn't believe my eyes, for they
were riders of the Light Brigade, Irish Hussars, with an officer up
in his stirrups, yelling, and the troopers swarming behind him.
They came over the battery like a wave, and the scarlet-clad
Pathan horsemen were breaking before them. And I'll tell you
what I saw next, as plain as I can.

Lakshmibai was in among the Pathans, and she had a sabre in
her hand. She seemed to be shouting to them, and then she took a
cut at a Hussar and missed him as he swept by, and for a moment
I lost her in the mêlée. There were sabres and pistols going like
be-damned, and suddenly the white mare was there, rearing up,
and she was in the saddle, but I saw her flinch and lose the reins;
for a moment I thought she was gone, but she kept her seat as the
mare turned and raced out of the fight—and my heart stopped
as I saw that she was clutching her hands to her stomach, and
her head was down. A trooper drove his horse straight into the
mare, and as it staggered he sabred at Lakshmibai back-handed—
I shrieked aloud and shut my eyes, and when I looked again she
was in the dust, and even at that distance I could see the crimson
stain on her jodhpurs.

I ran towards her—and there must have been riders charging
past me as I ran, but I don't remember them—and then I
stumbled and fell. As I scrambled up I saw she was writhing in
the dust; her scarf and helmet were gone, she was kicking and
clawing at her body, and her face was twisted and working in
agony, with her hair half across it. It was hideous, and I could
only crouch there, gazing horrified. Oh, if it were a novel I could
tell you that I ran to her, and cradled her head against me and
kissed her, while she looked up at me with a serene smile and
murmured something before she closed her eyes, as lovely in
death as she'd been in life—but that ain't how people die, not
even the Rani of Jhansi. She arched up once, still tearing at herself, and then she flopped over, face down, and I knew she was a
goner.[47]

It was only then, I believe, that I began to think straight again.
There was one hell of a skirmish in progress barely twenty
yards away, and I was unarmed and helpless, on all fours in the

dirt. Above all other considerations, I'm glad to say, one seemed paramount—to get to hell out of this before I got hurt. I was on my feet and running before the thought had consciously formed —running in no particular direction, but keeping a weather eye open for a quiet spot or a riderless horse. I dived into the nullah, barged into someone, stumbled up and raced along it, past a group of pandies in pill-box hats who were scrambling into position at the nullah's edge to open fire, leaped over a wrecked cart—and then, wondrous sight, there *was* a horse, with a wounded nigger on his knees holding the bridle. One kick and he was sprawling, I was aboard and away; I put my head down and fairly flew—a fountain of dirt rose up just ahead of me as a cannon-shot from somewhere ploughed into the nullah bank, and the last thing I remember is the horse rearing up, and something smashing into my left arm with a blinding pain; a great weight seemed to be pressing down on my head and a red smoke was drifting above me, and then I lost consciousness.

*   *   *

I told you the worst was still to come, didn't I? Well, you've read my chronicle of the Great Mutiny, and if you've any humanity you're bound to admit that I'd had my share of sorrow already, and more—even Campbell later said that I'd seen hard service, so there. But Rose himself declared that if he hadn't been told the circumstance of my awakening at Gwalior by an eye-witness, he wouldn't have believed it—it was the most terrible thing, he said, that he had ever heard of in all his experience of war, or anybody else's, either. He wondered that I hadn't lost my reason. I agreed then, and I still do. This is what happened.

I came back to life, as is often the case, with my last waking moment clear in my mind. I had been on horseback, riding hard, seeing a shot strike home in a sandy nullah—so why, I wondered irritably, was I now standing up, leaning against something hard, with what seemed to be a polished table top in front of me? There was a shocking pain in my head, and a blinding glare of light hurting my eyes, so I shut them quickly. I tried to move, but couldn't, because something was holding me; my ears were ringing, and there was a jumble of voices close by, but I couldn't make them out. Why the hell didn't they shut up, I wondered, and I tried to tell them to be quiet, but my voice wouldn't work—I wanted to move, to get away from the thing that was pressing against my chest, so I tugged, and an unspeakable pain shot through my left arm and into my chest, a stabbing, searing pain so exquisite that I screamed aloud, and again, and again, at which a voice cried in English, apparently right in my ear.

"'Ere's another as can't 'old 'is bleedin' row! Stick a gag in this bastard an' all, Andy!"

Someone grabbed my hair and pulled my head back, and I shrieked again, opening my eyes wide with the pain, to see a blinding light sky, and a red, sweating face within a few inches of mine. Before I could make another sound, a foul wet rag was stuffed brutally into my mouth, choking me, and a cloth was whipped across it and knotted tight behind my head. I couldn't utter a sound, and when I tried to reach up to haul the filthy thing away, I realised why I hadn't been able to move. My hands were lashed to the object that was pressing into my body. Stupefied, blinking against the glare, in agony with my arm and head and the gag that was suffocating me, I tried to focus my eyes; for a few seconds there was just a whirl of colours and shapes—and then I saw.

I was tied across the muzzle of a cannon, the iron rim biting into my body, with my arms securely lashed on either side of the polished brown barrel. I was staring along the top of that barrel, between the high wheels, to where two British soldiers were standing by the breech, poking at the touch-hole, and one was saying to the other:

"No, by cripes, none o' yer Woolwich models. No lanyards, Jim my boy—we'll 'ave to stick a fuse in, an' stand well clear."

"She's liable to blow 'er flamin' wheels off, though, ain't she?" says the other. "There's a four-pahnd cartridge in there, wiv a stone shot. S'pose it'll splinter, eh?"

"Ask 'im—arterwards!" says the first, gesturing at me, and they both laughed uproariously. "You'll tell us, won't yer, Sambo?"

For a moment I couldn't make it out—what the devil were they talking about? And how dared the insolent dogs address a colonel as "Sambo"—and one of 'em with a pipe stuck between his grinning teeth? Fury surged up in me, as I stared into those red yokel faces, leering at me, and I shouted "Damn your eyes, you mutinous bastards! How dare you—d'ye know who I am, you swine? I'll flog the ribs out of you . . ." but it didn't come out as a shout, only as a soundless gasp deep in my throat behind that stifling gag. Then, ever so slowly, it dawned on me where I was, and what was happening, and my brain seemed to explode with the unutterable horror of it. As Rose said afterwards, I ought to have gone mad; for an instant I believe I did.

I don't have to elaborate my sensations—anyway, I couldn't. I can only say that I was sane enough after that first spasm of dreadful realisation, because behind the fog of panic I saw in a second what had happened—saw it with blinding certainty. I had been knocked on the head, presumably by a splinter of flying debris, and picked up senseless by our gallant troops. Of course they'd taken me for a pandy—with my matted hair and beard and filthy and ragged sepoy uniform; they'd seen I wasn't dead, and decided to execute me in style, along with other prisoners. For as I flung my head round in an ecstasy of such fear as even I had never known before, I saw that mine was only one in a line of guns, six or seven of them, and across the muzzle of each was strapped a human figure. Some were ragged pandies, like me, others were just niggers; one or two were gagged, as I was, the rest were not; some had been tied face to the gun, but most had the muzzles in their backs. And shortly these brutes who loafed about the guns at their ease, spitting and smoking and chaffing to each other, would touch off the charges, and a mass of splintering stone would tear through my vitals—and there was nothing I could do to stop them! If I hadn't screamed when I regained consciousness, I wouldn't have been gagged, and three words would have been enough to show them their ghastly error —but now I couldn't utter a sound, but only watch with bulging eyes as one of the troopers, in leisurely fashion, pushed a length of fuse into the touch-hole, winked at me, and then sauntered back to rejoin his mates, who were standing or squatting in the sunlight, obviously waiting for the word to start the carnage.

"Come on, come on, where the 'ell's the captain?" says one.

"Still at mess, I'll lay. Christ, it's 'ot! I want ter get on my char-poy, I do, an' bang me bleedin' ear-'ole. 'E couldn't blow the bloody pandies away arter supper, could 'e? Oh, no, not 'im."

"Wot we blowin' 'em up for?" says one pale young trooper. "Couldn't they 'ang the pore sods—or shoot 'em? It 'ud be cheaper."

"Pore sods my arse," says the first. "You know what they done, these black scum? You shoulda bin at Delhi, see the bloody way they ripped up wimmen an' kids—fair sicken yer, wot wi' tripes an' innards all over the plice. Blowin' away's too —— good for 'em."

"Not as cruel as 'angin', neither," says a third. "They don't feel nothin'." He strolled past my gun, and to my horror he patted me on the head. "So cheer up, Sambo, you'll soon be dead. 'Ere, wot's the matter wiv 'im, Bert, d'ye reckon?"

I was writhing frenziedly in my bonds, almost fainting with the agony of my wounded arm, which was gashed and bleeding, flinging my head from side to side as I tried to spit out that horrible gag, almost bursting internally in my effort to make some sound, any sound, that would make him understand the ghastly mistake they'd made. He stood, grinning stupidly, and Bert sauntered up, knocking his pipe out on the gun.

"Matter? Wot the 'ell d'yer think's the matter, you duffer? 'E don't want 'is guts blew all the way to Calcutta—that's wot's the matter! Gawd, 'e'll kill 'isself wiv apple-plexy by the look of 'im."

"Funny, though, ain't it?" says the first. "An' look at the rest of 'em—jes' waitin' there, an' not even a squeak from 'em, as if they didn't care. Pathetic, ain't it?"

"That's their religion," pronounced Bert. "They fink they're goin' to 'eaven—they fink they're goin' to get 'arf-a-dozen rum bints apiece, an' bull 'em till Judgement Day. Fact."

"Go on! They don't look all that bleedin' pleased, then, do they?"

They turned away, and I flopped over the gun, near to suffoca-tion and with my heart ready to burst for misery and fear. Only one word—that was all I needed—Christ, if I could only get a hand free, a finger even! Blood from my wounded arm had run on to the gun, drying almost at once on the burning metal—if I

could even scrawl a message in it—or just a letter—they might
see it, and understand. I must be able to do something—think,
think, think, I screamed inside my head, fighting back the madness, straining with all my power to tear my right wrist free,
almost dislocating my neck in a futile effort to work the gag-
binding loose. My mouth was full of its filthy taste, it seemed to
be slipping farther into my gullet, choking me—God, if they
thought I was choking, would they pull it out, even for a second?
. . . that was all I needed, oh God, please, please, let them—I
couldn't die like this, like a stinking nigger pandy, after all I'd
suffered—not by such cruel, ghastly, ill-luck . . .

"Aht pipes, straighten up—orficer comin'," cries one of the
troopers, and they scrambled up hastily, adjusting their kepis,
doing up their shirt-buttons, as two officers came strolling across
from the tents a couple of hundred yards away. I gazed towards
them like a man demented, as though by staring I could attract
their attention; my right wrist was raw and bleeding with my
dragging at it, but the rope was like a band of steel round it, and
I couldn't do more than scrabble with my fingers at the hot metal.
I was crying, uncontrollably; my head was swimming—but no,
no, I mustn't faint! Anything but that—think, think, don't faint,
don't go mad! They've never got you yet—you've always slid out
somehow . . .

"All ready, sergeant?" The leading officer was glancing along
the line of guns, and my eyes nearly started from my head as I
saw it was Clem Hennidge[48]—Dandy Clem of the 8th Hussars,
whom I'd ridden with at Balaclava. He was within five yards of
me, nodding to the sergeant, glancing briefly round, while beside
him a fair young lieutenant was staring with pop-eyes at us
trussed victims, going pale and looking ready to puke. By heaven,
he wasn't the only one!

He shuddered, and I heard him mutter to Hennidge: "Christ!
I shan't be writing to mother about this, though!"

"Beastly business," says Hennidge, slapping his crop in his
palm. "Orders, though, what? Very good, sergeant—we'll touch
'em off all together, if you please. All properly shotted and
primed? Very good, then."

"Yessir! Beg pardon, sir, usual orders is to touch 'em off one arter the other, sir. Leastways, that's 'ow we done it at Calpee, sir!"

"Good God!" says Hennidge, and contained himself. "I'll be obliged if you'll fire all together, sergeant, on this occasion!" He muttered something to the lieutenant, shaking his head as in despair.

Two men ran forward to my gun, one of them pulling matches from his pocket. He glanced nervously back and called.

"Sarn't—sir! This 'un ain't got no lock, nor lanyard, please! See, sir, it's one o' them nigger guns—can't fire it 'cept with a fuse, sir!"

"What's that?" cries Hennidge, coming forward. "Oh—I see. Very well, then, light the fuse at the signal, then, and—Good God, is this fellow having a fit?"

I had made one last desperate effort to pull free, hauling like a mad thing, flinging myself as far as my lashings would allow, tossing my head, jerking to and fro, my head swimming with the pain of my arm. Hennidge and the boy were staring at me—the boy's face was green.

"'E's been carryin' on like that since we triced 'im up, sir," says one of the gunners. "Screamin', 'e was—we 'ad ter gag him, sir."

Hennidge swallowed, and then nodded curtly, and turned away, but the lieutenant seemed to be rooted with horrified fascination, as though he couldn't tear his eyes away from me.

"Ready!" bawls the sergeant, and "Light the fuse now, Bert," says the man at my gun. Through a red haze I saw the match splutter, and go out. Bert cursed, struck a second, and touched it to the fuse. A moment, and it fizzed, and the gunners retreated.

"Best stand back, sir!" cries Bert. "Gawd knows what'll happen when she goes orf—might blow wide open!"

The lieutenant shuddered, and seemed to collect himself, and then the strangest thing happened. For I absolutely heard a voice, and it seemed to be very close in my ear, and the oddest thing was, it was Rudi Starnberg, my old enemy from Jotunberg, and as clear as a bell across the years I heard him laughing: "The comedy's not finished yet! Come on, play-actor!"

No doubt it was the product of a disordered mind, as I stared at

Death in the spluttering fuse, but just for a second I realised that
if there was the ghost of a chance left, it depended on keeping
ice-cold—as Rudi would have done, of course. The lieutenant's
eyes were just on mine for an instant before he turned away, and
in that instant I raised my brows and lowered them, twice,
quickly. It stopped him, and very carefully, as he stared, I closed
one eye in an enormous wink. It must have been a grotesque
sight; his mouth dropped open, and then I opened my eye, turned
my head deliberately, and stared fixedly at my right hand. He
must look, he must! My wrist was as fast as ever, but I could just
turn my hand, palm upwards, fold the thumb and last three
fingers slowly into my palm, and beckon with my fore-finger,
once, twice, thrice—and still beckoning, I stared at him again.

For a moment he just gaped, and closed his eyes, and gaped
again, and I thought, oh Christ, the young idiot's going to stand
there until the bloody fuse has burned down! He stared at me,
licking his lips, obviously flabbergasted, turned to glance at
Hennidge, looked back at me—and then, as I tried to bore into
his brain, and crooked my finger again and again, he suddenly
yelled "Wait! Sergeant, don't fire!" and striding forward, he
yanked the burning fuse from the touch-hole. Clever boys they
had in the Light Brigade in those days.

"What the devil? John—what on earth are you doing?" cries
Hennidge. "Sergeant, hold on there!" He came striding up,
demanding to know what was up, and the lieutenant, pale and
sweating, stood by the breech pointing at me.

"I don't know! That chap—he beckoned, I tell you! And he
winked! Look, my God, he's doing it again! He's . . . he's trying to
say something!"

"Hey? What?" Hennidge was peering across at me, and I
wobbled my eyebrows as ludicrously as I could, and tried to
munch my lips at the same time. "What the deuce—I believe
you're right . . . you, there, get that gag out of his mouth—sharp,
now!"

"Arise, Sir Harry" was one of the sweetest sounds I ever heard;
so was Abe Lincoln's voice in that house at Portsmouth, Ohio,
asking "What do you want with me?" when the slave-catchers
were on my tail. I can think of many others, but so help me God,

none of them rang such peals of hope and joy in my ears as those words of Hennidge's beside the guns at Gwalior. Even as the cloth was wrenched loose, though, and the gag was torn out of my mouth, and I was gasping in air, I was thinking frantically what I must say to prevent the appalling chance of their disbelieving me—something to convince them instantly, beyond any doubt, and what I croaked out when my breath came was:

"I'm Flashman—Flashman, d'ye hear! You're Clem Hennidge! The curfew tolls the knell of parting day, God save the Queen. I'm English—English—I'm in disguise! Ask General Rose! I'm Flashman, Harry Flashman! Cut me loose, you bastards! I'm Flashman!"

You never saw such consternation in your life; for a moment they just made pop-eyed noises, and then Hennidge cries out:

"Flashman? Harry Flashman? But . . . but it's impossible—you can't be!"

Somehow I didn't start to rave, or swear, or blubber. Instead I just leered up at him and croaked:

"You give me the lie, Hennidge, and I'll call you out, d'you know? I called a man out in '39, remember? He was a cavalry captain, too. So—would you mind just cutting these damned ropes—and mind my arm, 'cos I think it's broken . . ."

"My God, you are Flashman!" cries he, as if he was looking at a ghost. Then he just stuttered and gaped, and signed to the gunners to cut me loose, which they did, lowering me gently to the ground, horror and dismay all over their faces, I was glad to see. But I'll never forget what Hennidge said next, as the lieutenant called for a water-bottle and pressed it to my lips; Hennidge stood staring down at me appalled, and then he said ever so apologetically:

"I say, Flashman—I'm most frightfully sorry!"

Mark you, what else was there to say? Oh, aye, there was something—I hadn't reasoned it, as you can imagine, but it leaped into my mind as I sat there, almost swooning with relief, not minding the pains in my head and arms, and happened to glance along the guns. I was suddenly shuddering horribly, and bowing my head in my sound hand, trying to hold back the sobs, and then I says, as best I could:

"Those niggers tied to the guns. I want them cut loose—all of 'em, directly!"

"What's that?" says he. "But they've been condem—"

"Cut 'em loose, damn you!" My voice was shaking and faint. "Every mother's son-of-a-bitch, d'you hear?" I glared up at him, as I sat there in the dust in my rags, with my back to the gun-wheel—I must have been a rare sight. "Cut 'em loose, and tell 'em to run away—away, as far as they know how—away from us, and never to get caught again! Blast you, don't stand there gawping—do as I say!"

"You're not well," says he. "You're distraught, and—"

"I'm also a bloody colonel!" I hollered. "And you're a bloody captain! I'm in my right mind, too, and I'll break you, by God, if you don't attend to me this minute. So . . . set—them—loose! Be a good chap, Clem—very well?"

So he gave the orders, and they turned them free, and the young lieutenant knelt beside me with the water-bottle, very respectful and moist-eyed.

"That was merciful," says he.

"Merciful be damned," says I. "The way things are hereabouts, one of 'em's probably Lord Canning."

There isn't much more to tell. The Great Mutiny ended there, under the walls of Gwalior, where Rose broke the last rebel army, and Tantia Tope fled away. They caught him and hanged him in the end, but they never found Nana Sahib, and for the rest, a few bands of pandies roamed about like bandits for a month or two, but were gradually dispersed.

I was back in the pavilion then, with my pads off, recovering from a broken arm and a battered head, to say nothing of a badly disarranged nervous system. I was exhausted in body and mind, but it's surprising how you pick up when you realise that it's all over, and there's nothing to do but lie back and put on weight, and you can sleep sound at nights. In the weeks of my convalescence at Gwalior I wrote my reports for Rose and Campbell, and composed another, at great length, for Palmerston, in which I detailed all my doings at Jhansi and elsewhere so far as they concerned the mission he'd given me. I told him what had happened with the Rani (the respectable bits, you understand, no romantic nonsense) and how I had been there at the end; I also warned him that Ignatieff had not been heard of again, and might still be abroad, doing mischief, though I doubted it.

(I've met the gotch-eyed bastard on two occasions since, by the way, both of 'em diplomatic bunfights, I'm happy to say. We used each other with perfect civility, and I kept my back carefully to the wall and left early.)

It was autumn before I was up and about again at Gwalior, and had received word from Campbell that I was released from my duties and might go home. I was ready for it, too, but before I left I found myself riding out on the road to Kota-ki-serai, to have a look at the spot where her people had made a little shrine to Lakshmibai, near the nullah—they thought no end of her, you know, and still do.

Well, I could understand that; I hadn't been indifferent myself,

although it all seemed far past now, somehow. They had cremated
her, in the Hindoo fashion, but there was this little painted model
temple, which I took to be her memorial, and withered flowers
and wreaths and little pots round it, and I mooched about, scuff-
ing the dust with my boots, while a few old niggers squatted
under the thorns, watching me curiously, and the bullock-carts
went by. There wasn't much sign of the skirmish where she'd died
—a few trifles of broken gear, a rusty stirrup, that sort of thing.
I wondered why she'd done it all, and in spite of what she said to
me at the last, I believe I did understand. As I'd said in my report
to Pam, she didn't give up her Jhansi. That was what had mattered to her, more than life. As to what she may have thought or
felt about me, truly—and for that matter, what I'd really felt
about her—I couldn't make up my mind.[49] It didn't matter now,
anyway, but I could always make the best of it, and remember
those eyes above the veil, and the soft lips brushing my cheek.
Aye, well. Damned good-looking girl.

I went up the Agra trunk on my way home, and down to
Cawnpore, where there were letters waiting for me, including one
from Billy Russell, congratulating me on my escape and recovery,
which he said had been the talk of Simla, where he had been
taking things easy with a game leg. He was down at Allahabad
now, following the seat of government on its peregrinations, as he
put it, and I must stop off and celebrate with him. I didn't mind
that a bit; I was ready to start enjoying life again, after all the
nonsense I'd been through, and to put me in the best fettle there
were several letters from Elspeth, in her usual rattle-pated style,
full of loving slush about her dear, darling champion whom she
was yearning to clasp again to her Loving Bosom (hear! hear!
thinks I) when he returned with his Laurels fresh upon his Brow.
She absolutely did write like this; came from reading novels, I
suspect:

> . . . the Town is full of talk of you and your Gallant Com-
> rades, especially Sir Hugh Rose and dear Sir Colin (or Lord
> Clyde as we must now call him—I own I felt a Flush of Pride
> when I thought that my Distinguished Countryman had
> chosen for his title the name of the Beauteous Stream beside

which I—humble little Me—was born, and where I spent
such Blissful Hours with my Own True Love—yourself, dear,
dear, Harry!! Do you remember?

I did—and the thought of that first splendid gallop we'd had
together in the bushes brought sentimental tears to my eyes and
set me bursting to be at her again, back in green England, away
from this bloody beastly country and its stench of death and war
and dust. Elspeth, with her golden hair and blue eyes and adoring
idiot smile and resplendent—oh, that was certainty, and happiness and jollity and be-damned!

. . . and even Lord Cardigan is civil—altho' he thinks Sir
Colin was tardy, and can have made but poor use of his
Light Cavalry, I think it was, in punishing the Rascally
Sepoys—and Lord Cardigan was very full in his attentions to
me when we met in the Row, but I gave him the Right
About, for I was certain you would wish it, and he went off
not too pleased, I thought, but perhaps he is disposed to
Toady, for he sent me a new book as a gift for you, saying
he was sure it must interest you most particularly, but I have
glanced at it and don't care for it much, since it seems to be
about rustics, and quite without that Tender Passion which I
admire in writing, and which Fills my Thoughts whenever
they turn to my Dearest of Husbands and Lovers, as they do
every minute, and my legs go quite weak. Still, I send it to
you, with his Lordship's compliments. Now then, there is the
finest scandal about Daisy Marchmont's footman . . .

I didn't care to hear about Cardigan—the mention of the name
was enough to set my jealous bile working, for it reminded me
that my darling Elspeth wasn't always the dutiful and loving
wife she pretended to be, and heaven knew how many randified
admirers had been beating our door-knocker in my absence. She'd
have no time or opportunity for dalliance when Flashy roared
back into residence, though . . . I chuckled at the thought, threw
Cardigan's present into my valise without looking at it, and

caught the train to Allahabad, where Billy Russell was at the station with a *ghari* to meet me.

He was all beams and whiskers as usual, full of fun, and demanding my news of the Jhansi and Gwalior affairs—which he knew already, of course, in their essentials, "but it's the spice and colour I'm after, old fellow, and devil a bit of those d'ye get in despatches. This business of your stealing into the Jezebel of Jhansi's fortress in disguise, now, and being carried away prisoner in the night, eh . . .?"

I parried his questions, grinning, as we bowled away towards the Fort, and then he says:

"I've got your winnings from Lucknow safe, by the by, and your prize-money. It's about all you've had out o' this campaign, ain't it—bar a few wounds an' grey hairs?"

I knew what he meant, blast him. While orders and ribbons and medals and titles had been flying about like hail among the Indian heroes, devil a nod had come my way—nor would it. You see, the irony was that while I'd seen more than my share of hell and horror in the Mutiny, I knew that in official eyes, my service must have been a pretty fair frost. I'd failed entirely in the original mission Pam had given me, and Rose had been damned stuffy that the plan to save Lakshmibai had come adrift; Lord Canning, he'd said, would be profoundly disappointed—as though it was my fault, the ungrateful bastard. But these are the things that matter, when they come to passing out the spoils, and I knew that while the likes of Rose and Campbell were having honours showered on them, and the prowess of Outram and Sam Browne and the snirp Roberts were being trumpeted round the world, poor old Flash would be lucky to get an address of welcome and a knife-and-fork supper at Ashby Town Hall.

"There's others have been well rewarded," says Billy. "Slow-coach is a lord—but ye know that. There must be about fifty Crosses flying about, and God knows how many titles . . . they might ha' done something for you. I wonder," says he, as we got out at the Fort and went along the verandah, "if a leaderette in the old Thunderer might stir 'em up, what? We can't have Horse Guards neglectin' our best men."

I liked the sound of that, rather, but as he conducted me across the hall, where Sikh sentries stood and the *punkahs** hissed, I thought it best to say I didn't mind, really—and then I found he was grinning all over his whiskers as he ushered me through a doorway, and I stopped dead in amazement.

It was a big, airy room, half office and half drawing-room, with a score of people standing at the far end, beyond the fine Afghan carpet, all looking in my direction, and it was sight of them that had checked me—for there was Campbell, with his grizzled head and wrinkled Scotch face, and Mansfield smiling, very erect, toying with his dark whiskers, and Macdonald grinning openly, and Hope Grant, stern and straight. In the middle was a slim, elegant civilian in a white morning coat with a handsome woman smiling beside him; it took me a moment to realise that they were Lord and Lady Canning.

Then Russell was pushing me forward, and Canning was smiling and shaking hands, and I was bowing to Lady Canning, wondering what the devil this was all about, and then there was silence, and Canning was clearing his throat and addressing me. I wish I could remember all of it, but I was quite taken aback to find myself thrust into this company, so unexpected . . . what was this?—"distinguished conduct on many numerous occasions, familiar to all . . . Afghanistan, Crimea, Balaclava, Central Asia . . . lately, and most exemplary, service in the insurrection of the Bengal Army . . . most gallant conduct in the defence and evacuation of Cawnpore . . . and most signally, at the direction of Sir Hugh Rose, in undertaking service of the most dangerous and difficult nature in the Gwalior campaign . . . warmest approval of Her Majesty and of her Ministers and principal advisers . . . recognition of conduct far beyond the call of duty . . ."

I listened to all this in a daze, and then Canning was passing something to Campbell, and he was coming up to me, glowering under his brows, and harrumphing.

"It is at my perr-sonal request," growls he, "that I have been purr-meeted tae bestow a disteenction that should rightly have come from Her Majesty's ain—own—gracious hands."

He reached up, and I felt a sudden keen pain in my left tit as he stuck a pin in it—I gasped and looked down, and there it was,

* Fans.

on its ribbon, the shabby-looking little bronze cross against my jacket; at first I didn't even recognise it, and then Lady Canning was leading the clapping, and Campbell was pumping my right hand and staring at me with his brows down.

"The Order o' the Victoria Cross," says he, and then he added, "Flashman . . .", but there he stopped and shook his head. "Aye," says he, and grinned at me—and God knows he didn't often grin, that one, and went on shaking his head and my hand, and the clapping and laughter rang in my ears.

I couldn't speak; I was red in the face, I knew, and almost in tears, as they clustered round me, Mansfield and Macdonald and the rest of them, and Billy slapping me on the back (and then scribbling quickly in his book and sticking it in his pocket) and I was trembling and wanted ever so much to sit down—but what I was thinking was, by God, you don't deserve it, you know, you shifty old bastard of a Flashy—not if it's courage they're after . . . but if they hand out medals for luck, and survival through sheer funk, and suffering ignobly borne . . . well, grab 'em with both hands, my boy—and then, in the august presence of the Governor-General and the Commander-in-Chief, someone started to sing, "For he's a jolly good fellow", and there were happy faces all round me, singing, until Canning led me out on to the verandah, and in the garden there seemed to be crowds of soldiers, and civilians—bearded Sikhs and ugly little Goorkhas, Devil's Own and Highlanders, artillerymen and sappers, chaps in white coats and sun-helmets, ladies in garden-party dresses, and as Canning waved to them someone shouted "Hip-hip-hip!" and the crashing "Hurrah!" sounded three times and a tiger—and I looked out at them through a mist of tears, and beyond them to the Gwalior guns and the Cawnpore barricade and the burning lines of Meerut and the battery reek of Balaclava and the bloody snow of Gandamack, and I thought, by God, how little you know, or you wouldn't be cheering me. You'd be howling for my blood, you honest, sturdy asses—and then again, maybe you wouldn't, for if you knew the truth about me, you wouldn't believe it.

"What a gratifying experience to relate to your children, colonel," says Canning, and on the other side Lady Canning smiled at me and says: "And to Lady Flashman."

I mumbled yes, indeed, so it would be; then I noticed that she was looking at me a trifle arch, and cudgelled my wits to think why—she couldn't be wanting to get off with me, not with Canning there—and then her last words sank in, my legs went weak, and I believe I absolutely said, "Hey?"

They both laughed politely at my bewilderment, Canning looking fond reproval at her. "That must be under the rose, my dear, you know," says he. "But of course we should have informed you, colonel, privately." He beamed at me. "In addition to the highest decoration for valour, which has been justly bestowed on many gallant officers in the late campaigns, Her Majesty wished to distinguish your service by some additional mark of favour. She has therefore been graciously pleased to create you a Knight of the Bath."

I suppose I was already numb with shock, for I didn't faint, or cry "Whoops!" or even stand gaping at the man in disbelief. In fact, I blew my nose, and what I was thinking as I mopped away my emotion was: by God, she's got no taste, that woman. I mean, who but little Vicky would have thought to pile a knighthood on top of the V.C., all at one go? It didn't seem scarcely decent— but, by God, wasn't it bloody famous! For over everything the words were revolving in my mind in a golden haze—"Sir Harry Flashman, V.C." It wasn't believable . . . Sir Harry . . . Sir Harry and Lady Flashman . . . Flashman, V.C. . . . my stars, it had come to this, and when least expected—oh, that astonishing little woman . . . I remembered how she'd blushed and looked bashful when she'd hung the Queen's Medal on me years before, and I'd thought, aye, cavalry whiskers catch 'em every time . . . and still did, apparently. Who'd have thought it?

"Well . . . God save the Queen," says I, reverently.

There was no taking it in properly at the time, of course, or indeed in the hours that followed; they remain just a walking dream, with "Sir Harry Flashman, V.C." blazing in front of my eyes, through all the grinning faces and back-slapping and cheering and adulation—all for the V.C., of course, for t'other thing was to remain a secret, Canning said, until I got home. There was a great dinner that evening, at the Fort, with booze galore and speeches and cheering, and chaps rolling under the table, and they poured me on to the Calcutta train that night in a shocking condition. I didn't wake up till noon the following day, with a fearful head; it took me another night to get right again, but on the next morning I had recovered, and ate a hearty breakfast, and felt in capital shape. Sir Harry Flashman, V.C.—I could still hardly credit it. They'd be all over me at home, and Elspeth would go into the wildest ecstasies at being "My lady", and be insufferable to her friends and tradesmen, and adoringly grateful to me—she might even stay faithful permanently, you never knew ... I fairly basked in my thoughts, grinning happily out at the disgusting Indian countryside in the sunrise, reflecting that with luck I'd never see or hear or smell it again, after this, and then to beguile the time I fished in my valise for something to read, and came on the book Cardigan had sent to Elspeth—what could have possessed Jim the Bear, who detested me, to send me a present?

I opened it at random, idly turning the pages ... and then my eye lit on a paragraph, and it was as though a bucket of icy water had been dashed over me as I read the words:

"But that blackguard Flashman, who never speaks to one without a kick or an oath—" "The cowardly brute," broke in East, "how I hate him! And he knows it, too; he knows that you and I think him a coward."

I stared at the page dumbfounded. Flashman? East? What the blind blue blazes was this? I turned the book over to look at the title: "Tom Brown's School Days", it said, "by an Old Boy". Who the hell was Tom Brown? I whipped quickly through the pages—rubbish about some yokels at a village fair, as Elspeth had said ... Farmer Ives, Benjy ... what the deuce? Tom trying his skill at drop-kicks ... "Rugby and Football" ... hollo, here we were again, though, and the hairs rose on my neck as I read:

"Gone to ground, eh?" roared Flashman. "Push them out then, boys; look under the beds ... Who-o-o-p!" he roared, pulling away at the leg of a small boy ... "Young howling brute. Hold your tongue, sir, or I'll kill you!"

By God, it was me! I mean, it wasn't only my style, to a "t", I even remembered doing it—years ago, at Rugby, when we flushed the fags out and tossed them in blankets for a lark . . . Yes, here it was—"Once, twice, thrice, and away" . . . "What a cursed bully you are, Flashy!" I sped through the passage, in which the horrible ogre Flashman, swearing foully, suggested they be tossed two at a time, so that they'd struggle and fall out and get hurt— it's true enough, that's the way to get the mealy little bastards pitched out on to the floor.

But who on earth could have written this? Who had dared— I tore the pages over, scanning each one for the dread name, and by God wasn't it there, though, in plenty? My eyes goggled as I read:

"Flashman, with an oath and a kick, released his prey . . ." ". . . the tyranny of Flashman . . ." ". . . Flashman was on the look-out, and sent an empty pickle-jar whizzing after them, which narrowly missed Tom's head. 'He wouldn't mind killing one, if he wasn't caught,' said East . . ." ". . . 'Was Flashman here then?'—'Yes, and a dirty little snivelling sneaking fellow he was, too . . . used to toady the bullies by offering to fag for them, and peaching against the rest of us . . .' "

I was red and roaring with rage by this time, barely able to see the pages. By God, here was infamy! Page after foul page, traducing me in the most odious terms—for there wasn't a doubt I was the villain referred to; the whole thing stank of Rugby in my time, and there was the Doctor, and East, and Brooke, and Crab Jones— and me, absolutely by name, for all the world to read about and detest! There was even a description of me as big and strong for my age—and I "played well at all games where pluck wasn't much wanted" if you please, and had "a bluff, offhand manner, which passed for heartiness, and considerable powers of being pleasant". Well, that settled it—and my reputation, too, for not a page went by but I was twisting arms, or thrashing weaklings, or swearing, or funking, or getting pissy drunk, or roasting small boys over fires—oh, aye, *that* brought back Master Brown to memory sharp enough. He was the mealy, freckled little villain who tried to steal my sweepstake ticket, damn him—a pious, crawling little toad-eater who prayed like clockwork and was forever sucking up to Arnold and Brooke—"yes, sir, please, sir, I'm a bloody Christian, sir," along with his pal East . . . and now East was dead, in the boat by Cawnpore.

Someone was alive, though—alive and libelling me most damnably. Not that it wasn't true, every vile word of it—oh, it was all too true, that was the trouble, but the devil with that, it was a foul, malicious blot on my good name . . . dear Christ, here was more!

". . . Flashman's brutality had disgusted most even of his intimate friends . . ." No, by God, there was *one* downright, shameful lie—the kind of friends I had at Rugby you *couldn't* have disgusted, not Speedicut and Rattle and that lot . . . What next? "Coward as he was, Flashman couldn't swallow such an insult . . ." and then followed a description of a fight, in which I ("in poor condition from his monstrous habit of stuffing") was soundly thrashed by a couple of fags and skulked off whining: "You shall pay for this . . ."

I believe I foamed at the mouth at this point, and yet again at the description of my drunken expulsion from Rugby, but what was even worse was the scene in which the unctuous little swabs, Brown and East, were described as praying for "poor Flashman". I hurled the book across the carriage, and set about thrashing my bearer, and only when I'd driven him howling on to the carriage-roof did I settle down and realise the full bitterness of what this vindictive biographer had done.

He'd ruined me—half England must have read the beastly thing by now. Oh, it was plain enough why Cardigan had sent it to me, the spiteful swine. How could I ever hold up my head again, after this poisonous attack?—my God, just in my moment of supreme glory, too! What would my Cross and my Knighthood be worth now, with this venom spewed on me by "an Old Boy"?, whoever the brute was . . . probably some greasy little sneak whom I'd disciplined for his own good, or knocked about in boyish fun . . . well, by heaven he'd pay for it! I'd sue the wicked, scribbling son-of-a-bitch through every court in England, I'd have every lousy penny he owned, and the shirt off his back, and see him starve in the gutter, or rot in jail for criminal slander—

"No!" I roared, shaking my fist, "I'll kill the bastard, that's

what I'll do—after I've sued him! I'll call him out, if he's a
civilian, and blow his mangy head off on Calais sands—I'll horse-
whip him publicly ..."

[At this point, with a torn page and several explosive blots, the
fifth packet of the Flashman Papers comes to an end.]

[N.B.—Flashman apparently never took action against Thomas
Hughes, the author of *Tom Brown's Schooldays*, which first
appeared in 1857 and had achieved immense success before
Flashman saw it in India. Probably he came to realise, after his
first understandable indignation had subsided, that any harm it
did to his reputation was trifling, and that the publicity of liti-
gation could only make things worse. But it is possible that he
made the threat of legal action, and demanded some retraction;
it is at least interesting that when the sequel, *Tom Brown at
Oxford*, appeared in 1861, Hughes devoted a preface to denying
any identification of himself with Tom Brown: "... neither is the
hero a portrait of myself [he wrote] *nor is there any other portrait
in either of the books*, except in the case of Dr Arnold, where the
true name is given." The italics are the editor's; the satisfaction
was presumably Flashman's.]

APPENDIX I: The Indian Mutiny

As far as it goes, and leaving aside those more personal experiences and observations which there is no confirming or denying, Flashman's account of his service in the Mutiny seems both generally accurate and fair. His descriptions of Meerut, before and during the outbreak, of Cawnpore and Lucknow and Jhansi and Gwalior, are consistent with other eye-witness accounts; at worst, he differs no more from them than they do from each other. As to causes and attitudes, he seems to give a sound reflection of what was being said and thought in India at the time.

It is still difficult to discuss certain aspects of the Mutiny without emotion creeping in; it was an atrociously bloody business, and it is not easy to appreciate entirely the immense intensity of feeling on both sides. How to explain the conduct of Nana Sahib at Cawnpore, on the one hand, or on the other, the attitude of the Christian and personally kindly John Nicholson, who wanted legislation passed for the flaying, impaling, and burning of mutineers? Flashman's observations are not without interest, but it is really superfluous to comment on them; there should not be, for intelligent people, any question of trying to cast up the atrocious accounts, or attempting to discover a greater weight of "blame" on one side or the other. Fashions in these things change, as Flashman remarks, and one should beware of fashionable judgements. Sufficient to say that fear, shock, ignorance, and racial and religious intolerance, on both sides, combined to produce a hatred akin to madness in some individuals and groups—British, Hindoo and Muslim—but by no means among all.

At the same time, it is worth remembering that the struggle which produced so much cruelty and shame was also marked by countless examples of self-sacrifice and human kindness almost beyond understanding, and by devotion and heroism which will last as long as British and Indian memory: the spirit which inspired the last stand of a handful of unnamed mutineers in Gwalior fortress was the same as that which held the wall of Wheeler's entrenchment at Cawnpore.

APPENDIX II: The Rani of Jhansi

Lakshmibai, Maharani of Jhansi, was one of the outstanding leaders of the Mutiny, and a heroine of Indian history. She has been compared, not unjustly, to Joan of Arc; on the other hand, while the evil reputation which propaganda gave her in her life-time has now been largely discounted, there remain some shadows over her memory.

The general facts about her career, as Flashman learned them from Palmerston and Skene, and as he himself describes them, are accurate—her upbringing, marriage, political attitudes, part in the Mutiny, escape, campaigning, and death. What is less clear is when and why she became actively involved in the Mutiny, for even after the Jhansi massacre (see Notes) she professed friendship for the Sirkar; it may even be that, despite her bitterness towards the British, she would have stayed clear of rebellion if she could. What is certain is that, once committed, she led her troops with great resolution and personal bravery—she was, in fact, a fine swordswoman and rider, and a good shot, as a result of her up-bringing among boys (Nana Sahib among them) at the Peshawa's court.

On a more everyday level, Flashman's impressions of Laksh-mibai and her court are borne out by contemporary accounts. He seems to have given a fair picture of her conduct of affairs and public behaviour, as well as of such details as her daily routine, her apartments, private zoo, recreations and tea-parties, and even clothing and jewellery. Other Britons who met her shared at least some of his enthusiasm for her looks ("remarkably fine figure . . . beautiful eyes . . . voluptuous . . . beautiful shape", are among the descriptions, although one added that he thought her "not pretty"). The most apparently authentic surviving portrait shows her much as Flashman first describes her. Her personality seems to have been pleasant enough, if forceful (her two most quoted remarks are "I will not give up my Jhansi", and the taunt thrown at Nana Sahib when they were children: "When I grow up I'll have ten elephants to your one!").

But her true character remains a mystery. Whether she is regarded as a pure-hearted patriot, or as a devious and cruel opportunist is a matter of choice—she may have been something of each. Her epitaph was given by her most persistent enemy, Sir Hugh Rose, speaking of the rebel leaders; he called Lakshmibai "the best and bravest".

(For biographies see *The Rebellious Rani*, by Sir John Smyth, V.C., and *The Ranee of Jhansi*, by D. V. Tahmankar. Also in Sylvester, Forrest, Kaye/Malleson.)

NOTES

1.   Lord Cardigan, who led the Charge of the Light Brigade, was a popular hero after Balaclava, but a reaction set in against him in 1856, with rumours that he had shirked his duty, and even that he had not reached the Russian guns at all. The law-suit did not take place until 1863, when Cardigan sued Colonel Calthorpe for libel on the subject; it was established that he had been at the guns, and also that he had left his brigade during the action which, although it did not reflect on his personal courage, left a large question-mark over his fitness for command.

2.   *Punch* also noted that at this dinner champagne was served at the rate of only one bottle per three guests.

3.   For once Flashman is exact with a date—it was on the 21st that Florence Nightingale had a two-hour meeting with the Queen at Balmoral. In fact, his recollections of Balmoral are so exact, even down to topics of conversation and the state of the weather on particular days, that one suspects he is indebted to the detailed diary which his wife Elspeth kept during their married life, and which forms part of The Flashman Papers. (For corroboration, see *Queen Victoria's Letters, 1827–61*, ed. Benson and Esher; *The Queen at Balmoral* by F. P. Humphrey (1893); *Life of the Prince Consort*, 5 vols., by Sir T. Martin (1875–80); *Twenty Years at Court*, by Eleanor Stanley (1916); and *A Diary of Royal Movements . . . in the life of Queen Victoria* (1883).

4.   No record can be found of a visit by Lord Palmerston to Balmoral in late September, 1856; obviously it must have been kept secret, along with the disturbing news that chapattis had appeared in an Indian regiment: most histories of the Mutiny do not mention chapattis as appearing until early in 1857.

For the rest, Flashman gives a fair picture of "Pam" as his contemporaries saw him—a popular, warm-hearted, impulsive, and (to some eyes) deplorable figure whom Disraeli described as a "painted old pantaloon". Lord Ellenborough was a former Governor-General of India, and Sir Charles Wood, although at the Admiralty when Flashman met him, had been President of the Board of Control for India from 1853–55, and was to return to the India Office from 1859–66.

5.   The missionaries were greatly displeased at a government decision in 1856–7 that education in Indian schools should be secular. The fear of Christianisation was certainly present among Indians at this time, and is considered to have been a main cause of the Mutiny. Preaching army officers were regarded as especially dangerous: Governor-General Canning, who was unjustly suspected of being an ardent proselytiser, actually said of one religiously-minded colonel that he was unfit to be trusted with his native regiment, and Lord Ellenborough delivered a strong warning in the House of Lords on June 9, 1857, against "colonels connected with missionary operations. . . . You will see the most bloody revolution which has at any time occurred in

India. The English will be expelled." This contrasts with the statement of Mr Mangles, chairman of the East India Company: "Providence has entrusted the empire of Hindoostan to England in order that the banner of Christ should wave triumphant from one end of India to the other."

6.   John Nicholson (1821–57) was one of the legendary figures of British India, and an outstanding example of the type of soldier-administrator who became known as "the desert English", possibly because many of them were Scots or Irish. Their gift, and it was rare, was of winning absolute trust and devotion from the people among whom they worked in the East; Nicholson had it to an unusual degree, and when he was only twenty-seven the religious sect of "Nikkul-seynites" was formed, worshipping him with a fervour which caused him much annoyance. As a soldier and administrator he was brilliant; as a Victorian case-study, fascinating. Since he served in the First Afghan War he would certainly have known Flashman, but it is interesting that they met as described here, since in late 1856 Nicholson should have been far away on the frontier. However, as he was about to enter on new duties at Peshawar about this time, it is conceivable that he came south first, and that they met on the Agra Trunk Road.

7.   The Guides was perhaps the most famous fighting unit in the history of British India. Raised by Henry Lawrence in 1846, and commanded by Harry Lumsden, it became legendary along the frontier as an intelligence and combat force of both infantry and cavalry (Kipling, it will be remembered, used the Guides' *mystique* in his "Ballad of East and West"). It is interesting that Flashman recognised Sher Khan as an ex-Guide by his coat, since the regiment normally wore nondescript khaki rather than a military colour.

8.   Flashman's assumption that the Rani would be much older was not unnatural. He had heard Palmerston describe her as "old when she married", which, by Indian standards, she was, being well into her teens.

9.   The General Service Enlistment Act (1856) required recruits to serve overseas if necessary. This was one of the most important grievances of the sepoys, who held that crossing the sea would break their caste.

10.   Irregular cavalry units of the British Indian armies occasionally dressed in a highly informal style, so the Afghan *rissaldar* might conceivably have been wearing an old uniform coat of Skinner's Horse ("The Yellow Boys"). But it is unlikely that he had ever served in that unit—the Guides would have been more his mark.

11.   The society of Thugs (lit. deceivers) were worshippers of the goddess Kali, and practised murder as a religious devotion which would ensure them a place in paradise. They preyed especially on travellers, whom they would join on the road with every profession of friendship before suddenly falling on them at a prearranged signal; the favourite method of killing was strangulation with a scarf. The cult numbered thousands before Sir William Sleeman stamped them out in the 1830s, but since many continued at large, and the Jhansi region was traditionally a hotbed of *thugee*, it is perfectly possible that ex-Thugs were active as Flashman says. In some cases it was possible to identify a former Thug by a tattoo on his eyelid or a brand on his back.

12.   "Pass him some of his own tobacco"—a grim joke by Ilderim's companion. "Pass the tobacco" was the traditional verbal signal of the Thugs to start killing.

13.   There was indeed a Makarram Khan, who served in the Peshawar Police, and later became a notable frontier raider at the head

of a band of mounted tribesmen, fighting against the Guides cavalry. (See *History of the Guides, 1846–1922*.)

14. The offering and touching of a sword hilt, in token of mutual respect, was traditional in the Indian Cavalry. (See *From Sepoy to Subedar*, the memoirs of Sita Ram Pande, who served in the Bengal Army for almost fifty years. They were first published a century ago, and recently edited by Major-General James Lunt.)

15. It is curious that Flashman makes no reference to dyeing his skin (as Ilderim had suggested) and indeed seems to imply that he found it unnecessary. But dark as he was, and light-skinned as many frontiersmen are, he must surely have stained his body, or he could hardly have passed for long in a sepoy barrack-room.

16. Of the sepoys whom Flashman mentions by name, only two can be definitely identified as serving in the 3rd N.C. skirmishers at this time—Pir Ali and Kudrat Ali, who were both corporals, although Flashman refers to Pir Ali as though he were an ordinary sepoy.

17. "Addiscombe tripe" refers to the officers, not the *jemadars* and n.c.o.s. Addiscombe was the military seminary which trained East India Company cadets from 1809 to 1861. Flashman's prejudice may be explained by the fact that Lord Roberts, among other famous soldiers, went there.

18. The fears and grievances which Flashman recounts probably give a fair reflection of the state of mind of many sepoys in early 1857. Rumours of polluted flour and greased cartridges, and stories like that of the Dum-Dum sweeper, reinforced the suspicion that the British were intent on interfering with their religion, breaking their caste, altering terms of enlistment, and generally changing the established order. To these were added the Oude sepoys' discontent at the recent annexation of their state, which cost them certain privileges, and resentment at the changed attitude towards them (by no means imaginary, according to some contemporary writers) of a new generation of British officers and troops, who seemed more ignorant and contemptuous than their predecessors; this unfortunately coincided with the arrival in the Bengal Army of a better class of sepoys, possibly quicker to take offence—or, according to some writers, more spoiled.

All these things combined to undermine confidence and cause unrest, and there was no lack of agitators ready to play on the sepoys' fears. The belief that the British intended to Christianise India (see Note 5) was widespread, and reinforced by such reforms as the suppression of *thugee* and *suttee* (widow-burning). The resentment which reform had created among Indian princes has been referred to; in addition, educational innovations created disquiet (see Lawrence's evidence to the Select Committee on India, July 12, 1859, E.I. Parliamentary Papers, vol. 18); so even did the development of the railway and telegraph. With all these underlying factors, it will be seen that the greased cartridge was eventually only the spark to the tinder. (See also Sita Ram, Lord Roberts's *Forty-one Years in India*, Kaye and Malleson's *History of the Sepoy War* and *History of the Indian Mutiny* (1864–80), G. W. Forrest's *History of the Indian Mutiny* (1904–12), and the same author's *Selections from the Letters, Despatches and C.S.P. . . Government of India, 1857–8*.)

19. Mrs Captain MacDowall's advice on the running of an Indian household might serve as a model for its time. (See the *Complete Indian Housekeeper*, by G. G. and F. A. S. published in 1883.)

20. The 19th N.I., who had rioted in February, were disbanded at the end of March, having refused the new cartridge. The paper which Mangal showed to Flashman was undoubtedly the March 28 issue of

Ashruf-al-Akbar, of Lucknow, which predicted a great holy war throughout India and the Middle East; however, it gave a warning against relying on Russian assistance, describing them as "enemies of the faith".

21.   Sepor Mangal Pandy (?-1857), of the 34th Native Infantry, ran amok on the parade ground at Barrackpore on March 29, apparently drugged with *bhang*, trying to rouse a religious revolt and claiming that British troops were coming against the sepoys. He attacked one of his officers, and then tried to kill himself. Pandy was subsequently hanged, along with a native officer whose offence apparently was that he did not try to stop the attack. However, this first of the Indian sepoy rebels gained an appropriate immortality: the British word for any native mutineer thereafter was "pandy".

22.   For the loading drill, see Forrest's *Selections*, and J. A. B. Palmer's *The Mutiny Outbreak in Meerut in 1857* referring to the Platoon Exercise Manual. While there is general agreement among historians on what happened at the firing parade, some differ over precise technical details; Flashman's account is sound on the whole. He states that the cartridges were not greased, but waxed, and since he does not refer to them as ball cartridges, this would seem to confirm that they were ungreased blanks. However, this would not allay the fears of the sepoys, who were apparently suspicious of any cartridge with a shiny appearance. Nor do they seem to have been impressed by the repeated assurances that it was unnecessary to bite the cartridge (which, if it were greased, would be highly polluting); as early as January, 1857, when it was announced that the sepoys could grease their own loads with non-polluting substances, it was also stated that they could tear the cartridges with their fingers (see Hansard, 3rd series 145, May 22, 1857); the response of some sepoys to this was that they might forget, and bite.

23.   The British were, in fact, more considerate and humane towards their native troops than they were to their white ones. Flogging continued in the British Army long after it had been abolished for Indian troops, whose discipline appears to have been much more lax, possibly in consequence—a point significantly noted by Subedar Sita Ram when he discusses in his memoirs the causes of the Mutiny.

24.   Lieutenant (later Lieutenant-General Sir Hugh) Gough was warned by one of the native officers of his troop on May 9 that the sepoys would rise to rescue their comrades from the jail. Carmichael-Smith and Archdale Wilson both rejected the warning.

25.   One of the first casualties of the Meerut mutiny was, in fact, a British soldier murdered in a bazaar lemonade shop.

26.   Hewitt and Archdale Wilson were extraordinarily slow in getting the British regiments on the move after the outbreak; they did not reach the sepoy lines until after the mutineers had set off for Delhi.

27.   Altogether thirty-one Europeans are known to have been murdered in the Meerut massacre, including the Dawson family, and Mrs Courtney and her three children (all mentioned by Flashman). The full list is given in the *Records of the Intelligence Department of the* N.W. *Provinces, 1857*, vol. ii, appendix. The circumstances of their deaths are horrifying enough—Surgeon Dawson was shot on his verandah, while Mrs Dawson was burned by thrown torches, and at least one pregnant woman, Mrs Captain Chambers, was murdered— but even so, greatly overstated reports of Meerut atrocities were circulated, including tales of sexual violation. It is worth quoting the statement of Sir William Muir, then head of the N.W. Intelligence

Department, in a letter to Lord Canning (Agra, December 30, 1857), that several British witnesses at Meerut were confident that no rapes took place, and they believed that the atrocities, appalling as they were, had been exaggerated. It was alleged, for example, that Riding-Master Langdale's (not Langley's, as Flashman says) little daughter was tortured to death; she had, in fact, been killed by a *tulwar* blow while sleeping on her charpoy (see the Rev. T. C. Smith's letter, dated Meerut, December 16, 1857). This tendency of many British observers to be strictly fair and impartial, even in the highly emotional atmosphere of the Mutiny and its immediate aftermath, should not be seen as playing down the atrocities; they were merely concerned to correct the wilder stories, and give an honest account.

28.   The mutiny and massacre at Jhansi took place exactly as Ilderim Khan described it. The mass murder of the 66 Britons (30 men, 16 women, and 20 children) was carried out in the Jokan Bagh on June 8, 1857; the only details which Ilderim's narrative adds to historical record are the quoted remarks of the victims and their killers. It was the second largest massacre in the entire Mutiny, and in some ways the most cruel, although it has been overshadowed in popular infamy by Cawnpore. What is by no means certain is how far Rani Lakshmibai was responsible, if at all: she protested her innocence afterwards, and there is considerable doubt about what her attitude was to Skene's three envoys before the Town Fort surrendered. (No record exists of the death of "Murray sahib" as described by Ilderim Khan, and the quotation that the Rani "had no concern with English swine", which is to be found in at least one other contemporary source, appears to rest on the evidence of a suspect Indian witness.) It is possible that Lakshmibai was powerless to prevent either the mutiny or the massacre; on the other hand, there is no evidence that she tried to, and there is no doubt that soon afterwards she was most effectively in control of Jhansi, and capable of dealing with any threat to her sovereignty.

29.   The quotation given by Flashman is the substance of the last letter which Wheeler sent out of Cawnpore after one of the most heroic defences in the history of war. Later events were to overshadow it, but it remains an epic of the Mutiny, for the conditions within the entrenchment, the figures of casualties, and even small details of the siege, were as Flashman describes them: for example, Bella Blair did die, John McKillop of the Civil Service did draw water under constant fire for a week before he was killed, and the reference to shooting horses for food, rather than riders, is authentic.

30.   Azeemoolah Khan had been sent to London in 1854 by Nana Sahib, the adopted son of the Maharatta Peshawa, to petition against the disallowance of Nana's pension and title after his father's death. The petition failed, but Azeemoolah, by his own account, had immense success in his pursuit of London society women—a boast which did not endear him to W. H. Russell of *The Times* when the two met at Missirie's Hotel, Constantinople, in 1856, and subsequently in the Crimea. Apart from being a nobleman, Azeemoolah is also believed to have worked as a teacher and as a waiter. Nana Sahib, who had joined the rebellion on the outbreak at Cawnpore, was to become the most famous of the Mutiny leaders, but Tantia Tope, whom Flashman barely noticed, was to be a far greater menace in the field.

31.   While Flashman's account of the council of war is new, it supports the known facts: Wheeler wanted to fight on, and his younger officers supported him; the older men wished to surrender for the sake of the women and children, and Wheeler finally agreed,

although he was deeply suspicious of the rebels' good faith. Nana Sahib's offer of terms, in the words which Flashman gives, was brought to the entrenchment by Mrs Jacobs, described by one contemporary as an "aged lady".

32.   Details of the massacre at Suttee Ghat are necessarily confused, but the broad facts are as narrated, and again many of Flashman's incidental memories are confirmed by other accounts. For example, Ewart was killed on the way to the ghat in a palankeen; Vibart's kit was carried and his wife escorted by rebels of his regiment; five loyal sepoys were murdered; Moore ("the real defender of Cawnpore") was killed in the water, shoving off. Some versions say that the thatch in the barges was fired before the shooting began, and one of Wheeler's servants, a nurse, said the general was killed on the shore, his head being cut off as he leaned from his stretcher; however, the probability is that he died in one of the boats. What appears to be in no doubt is the premeditated treachery of the attack; only one boat (Vibart's) escaped.

33.   The reptiles which attacked the swimmers can hardly have been gavials, which feed exclusively on fish. True crocodiles have an overlapping fourth tooth.

34.   The account of the escape down-river is true. This is independently confirmed by the narrative of Lieutenant Thomson, which describes the fire-arrows, the boat's grounding, the temple siege, escape to the shore, the boat's disappearance, crocodiles, etc. Apart from Flashman, there were four survivors—Thomson, Delafosse, Sullivan, and Murphy—who were eventually rescued by Diribijah Singh.

35.   The massacre of women and children at Cawnpore was the most notorious atrocity of the Mutiny, and provoked the most notorious reprisal by General Neill. It has been suggested that Nana was not himself responsible, and that the massacre may have been in retaliation for the indiscriminate punishment which Neill's troops had visited earlier on Allahabad and on villages during their march to Cawnpore. Without in any way condoning Neill's behaviour, which has been justly condemned by historians, it is only fair to point out that there had been no element of retaliation in previous massacres by Indians, at Meerut, Jhansi, and Delhi. What is not in dispute is the effect which Cawnpore had on British opinion, or the fury it caused in the army—a curious echo of this even lingered on into the Second World War, when tattooists in Hogg Market, Calcutta, were still offering to imprint the arms of British recruits with the legend "Cawnpore Well".

36.   Flashman does T. Henry Kavanaugh considerably less than justice. The big Irishman was undeniably eccentric—one Mutiny historian, Rice Holmes, has called him vain and self-important to the point of insanity—but his night journey to Campbell, in his ludicrous disguise, was an act of the most calculated courage. Possibly Flashman was nettled by the fact that other accounts of the exploit describe Kavanaugh's companion as an Indian; he may also have been unfavourably impressed by the somewhat immodest title of the book in which Kavanaugh described his adventure: *How I Won the V.C.* It tallies fairly closely, in general facts if not in spirit and interpretation, with Flashman's version. An excellent map of the scene of the journey is in Forrest, vol. ii.

37.   Campbell has been much criticised by some military theoreticians for his caution, and for his (and Mansfield's) reluctance to shed lives—British and mutineer; Fortescue thinks this policy may even have helped to lengthen the Mutiny. It is not a view which Flashman could be expected to share. (See Fortescue, vol. xiii.)

38.   The painting to which Flashman refers, of Havelock and
Outram greeting Campbell at Lucknow, is by a celebrated Victorian
painter of military scenes, T. J. Barker. The mounted figure shown
raising a hand in acclamation may indeed be intended to be Flashman; it bears some resemblance to the only other identifiable picture
of him as a comparatively young man—in a group of Union staff
officers with President Lincoln during the U.S. Civil War.

39.   Flashman's old friend, William Howard Russell, The Times
correspondent, makes an obvious reference to this incident in My
Diary in India (p. 188, vol. 1).

40.   Flashman's description of the looting is borne out by Russell,
who describes his attempt to buy the jewelled chain from an Irish
soldier in his Diary; their accounts are almost word for word, and
Russell even confirms that the chain subsequently fetched £7,500, as
Flashman says.

41.   Griff, or griffin—a greenhorn, a young officer. Hardly a fair
description of Roberts who, although still young, was to win his
Victoria Cross only a few weeks later. But Flashman plainly had
little liking for the legendary "Bobs", who was to become Field-
Marshal Lord Roberts of Kandahar; no doubt he was jealous of him.

42.   Roberts apart, it seems to have been a distinguished gathering
round the fire that night. William Stephen Raikes Hodson (1821–58)
was already renowned as an irregular cavalry leader and the founder
of Hodson's Horse. He was a year older than Flashman, and since
they were at Rugby together it seems quite feasible that Flashman
had been his fag. Hodson has left a mixed reputation; a brilliant
soldier, he was capable of cold-blooded cruelty, as when he murdered
the Delhi princes while they were his prisoners. He was shot at
Lucknow on March 11th, 1858, and there was a rumour (repeated by
Flashman) that he was in the act of looting at the time. Roberts
firmly denied this, with convincing evidence (see note, page 404,
Forty-one Years in India, vol. 1). Sam Browne, inventor of the belt
which bears his name, was another celebrated cavalry leader, who
became a general and won the V.C. He lost his left arm in a skirmish
some months after Lucknow. "Macdonald the Peeler" was probably
Macdonald who had been provost-marshal in the Crimea.

43.   As one of the Jhansi besiegers later put it: "The Ranee,
young, unwedded, jealous of power, sat watching the puny figures
below ... we watched and wondered what she said and did to those
best-favoured among a band of chieftains, and imagination ran wild in
the fervid heat." (See J. H. Sylvester, Cavalry Surgeon, ed. A. McKenzie
Annand, 1971.)

44.   Until the discovery of The Flashman Papers, Lyster (later
General Sir Harry Hamon Lyster, V.C.) was the only authority for the
plan to capture the Rani of Jhansi alive. No other contemporary writer
on the Mutiny mentions the scheme, and it was not until 1913, when
the Rev. H. H. Lyster Denny published a little-known work, Memorials
of an Ancient House, containing some of General Lyster's recollections,
that the story came out. According to Lyster, Rose confided the plan
to him in strict confidence, and Lyster himself did not reveal it until
many years after Rose's death. The plan was substantially as Flashman
recounts it, and involved luring the Rani into attempting an escape
by withdrawing a British picket from its position covering one of the
Jhansi gates.

45.   The battle on the Betwa (April 1, 1858) is one of the forgotten
actions, but it is a striking illustration of Rose's coolness and tactical
brilliance. Caught at an apparent disadvantage, he turned from Jhansi

and attacked the new rebel force, which outnumbered him ten to one; Rose led the cavalry charge in person, and Tantia's army was routed with the loss of 1,500 dead and 28 guns captured. (See Fortescue, *History of the British Army*, vol. xiii.)

46.   This incident took place about twenty miles from Jhansi, following the Rani's escape, when a party of British cavalry under Lieutenant Dowker caught up with her. According to popular tradition (now confirmed by Flashman's account) the rebel horseman who wounded Dowker was the Rani herself. Incidentally, Flashman is probably in error when he says the Rani left Jhansi through the Orcha Gate; other authorities specify the Bandhari Gate, and say that the Rani herself had the child Damodar on her saddle.

47.   There are differing accounts of Lakshmibai's death, but Flashman's accords with the generally accepted version. This is that she was killed in the action of Kota-ki-serai, before Gwalior, when the 8th Hussars charged the rebel camp at Phool Bagh. She was seen in the mêlée, with her horse's reins in her mouth, and was struck in the body, probably by a carbine bullet: she swayed in the saddle, crossed swords with a trooper, and was cut down. According to tradition, she was wearing the priceless necklace of Scindia, which she gave away to an attendant as she lay dying. Her tent on the battlefield was later found to contain a full-length mirror, books, pictures, and her swing.

48.   Captain Clement Heneage took part in the Charge of the Light Brigade at Balaclava, and also charged with the 8th Hussars in the action of June 17, 1858, in which the Rani of Jhansi was killed. Flashman's misspelling may have arisen through his never having seen the name written.

49.   Deplorable though Flashman's attitude to women was, there were obviously some for whom he felt a genuine attachment, and even respect—Lola Montez and the Rani of Jhansi among them. Lakshmibai obviously captivated him, but how far she returned his affection is debatable. He would turn in his grave at the suggestion, but it seems highly questionable that she spent the night with him in the Jhansi pavilion (see pages 97–9). It may be significant that he never saw her face clearly on that occasion, and his description of the encounter might seem to suggest that the lady who entertained him was a professional nautch-dancer or courtesan, rather than the Rani. It is unfortunately true that in the climate created by the Mutiny, Lakshmibai was credited with every vice ("ardent" and "licentious" were two of the adjectives employed) but there is no evidence that her private life and behaviour were not entirely respectable.

That is not to say that she would not use her feminine power (or any other weapon) for political ends; in this may be found a logical explanation of the pavilion incident. It is possible, on the basis of Flashman's account, that at that time the Rani was already deep in mutinous conspiracy, perhaps with agitators like Ignatieff, and either at their prompting or on her own initiative, decided to destroy Flashman, a potentially dangerous British agent. To lead him on, to lure him to the pavilion, and to arrange for an attack on him by professional assassins, was simple; that something of the sort actually happened is indicated by the confession which Ilderim Khan extracted from the captured Thug.

As to the Rani's display of affection for Flashman on his last visit to Jhansi, it may well have been entirely (and not partially, as he complacently assumed) prompted by her need to extract every scrap of information from him. Or—perhaps she was not entirely indifferent to him, after all; he seemed to think so, and he was not inexperienced.